THE MUTATUS PROCEDURE
(Part One)

Other novels from John David Krygelski

The Aegis Solution

Time Cursor

The Harvest

THE MUTATUS PROCEDURE
(Part One)

JOHN DAVID KRYGELSKI

STARSYS PUBLISHING COMPANY

The Mutatus Procedure

WWW.STARSYSPUBLISHING.COM

Cover art - Michael Nolan.
Art Direction - Michael Nolan - www.michaelnolanart.com
Editor - Jean Nolan Krygelski

Published by Starsys Publishing Company
WWW.STARSYSPUBLISHING.COM
526 N Alvernon Way
Tucson, Arizona 85711

ISBN 10: 0983052883
ISBN 13: 978-0-9830528-8-3
Library of Congress Control Number: 2013940769

First Edition - June 2013
Printed in the United States of America

Dedication

This book is dedicated to Jean. She is the light to my darkness. She is a balancing polarity for my soul.

Acknowledgments

Always at the top of the list is my collaborator and editor, Jean. If she directed her talents to metals rather than words, she would be the true alchemist.

I also want to thank Michael Nolan for another fantastic cover design.

Of all of my novels to date, *The Mutatus Procedure (Part One)* sent me scurrying for help the most. For tolerating my questions, patiently explaining the minutiae of their fields of expertise, and all the while actually pretending they were glad to hear from me, I would like to thank the following people:

Gerry Krautheim in Alamogordo, New Mexico, for helping to make the paintball scene at the beginning of the story more detailed and believable; SFC Bradley Bledsoe, United States Army, Wesley Chapel, Florida, for the help with some of the *tactical*; Matt Harper, Tucson, Arizona, for his invaluable assistance with the medical imaging equipment; Jim LaGuardia, M.D., VA Medical Center, Marion, Illinois, for his insights and suggestions in his field of neurology; Scott C. Forrer, M.D., Tucson Neuroscience Center, Tucson, Arizona, for our long chats about the intricacies of the mind; Scott Gumble, Tucson, Arizona, for all things computer and Internet related; Patrick Burba, M.D., VA Medical Center, Marion, Illinois, who was a wealth of information and perspectives in the complex and daunting realm of psychiatry. Patrick, your secret is safe with me. Long overdue, I would also like to thank Detective Brad Hunt, Tucson Police Department, and Officer Bobby Boone (Ret.), Tucson Police Department, for inspiring the characters of Detective Ben Hart and Officer Billy Burke in this book, as well as their first appearance in *Time Cursor*.

And, of course, all that is accurate in the respective areas of the story is to their credit; any errors are solely mine.

Chapter 1

T HE STILLNESS OF THE DESERT EVENING was broken only by the monotonous repetition of a quail's call. Whether it was a fluke of the acoustics induced by the rugged hills and arroyos surrounding the walled-in backyard, or whether the desert bird had simply, through generations of surviving in the hostile environs, developed and cultivated the talent of a ventriloquist, Judtson was unable to discern the location of the top-knotted, tedious vocalist. As he ruminated on the complexities of his environment, his mind held not a single clue as to its own impending metamorphosis, which would initiate before another day elapsed.

The constant, reassuring, and almost urgent pressure against the side of his leg, coming from Rocky, his golden retriever, caused the wondrous sense of comfort it unfailingly provided. Somewhat unconsciously, Judtson's left hand moved to the area in front of his companion's ear, his fingers probing and massaging the thick, soft fur, triggering an even more insistent sideways push from this four-legged angel. One item at a time, as if checking them off a list, Judtson evaluated the conditions. He noted the mild breeze, mentally placing this fact in the "positive" column. There was no moonlight tonight. Positive. No rain in the forecast. Positive. Completing his inventory of the evening, he relaxed, easing himself back into the nylon weave of the patio chair, and patiently watched as the back-scattered light from the sun, now well below the horizon, surrendered its dominion of the desert.

Tucson was Judtson's home. Always had been. Not the city itself. Not the potholed streets. Not the xeriscaped front yards and common areas. Not the architecture. No, it was this particular spot on Earth. This patch of desert. So rich. So full of life and surprises and danger and delight. This canvas upon which the city was painted by an assemblage of uncooperative artists. This latitude at this longitude was his home.

It did not hurt that he knew its secrets. Although the participants practiced their rituals covertly, Judtson was aware of the opportunistic night animals now emerging. The coyotes, having avoided the blistering sun by hunkering beneath the boughs of mesquites and creosotes, were standing up on legs shaky from twelve hours of inactivity and reuniting with their pack for another night of hunting. The bats, suspended inverted under bridges and culverts for the day, swarmed out and scattered, filling their needs in order of priority. First flying directly to the nearest swimming pools, of which there never seemed to be a shortage in the desert, they would swoop, circle, and swoop again, skimming the surface of the chlorinated water, gaining a mouthful on the fly, and frightening the children and many adults who were taking an evening dip. Their thirst slaked, the winged mammals would begin the methodical process of cris-crossing in the air above the yards and open landscape, using their echolocational abilities to capture insects in mid-flight.

The rabbits, both cottontail and jack, exited their temporary homes in the same manner they performed all of their actions during their brief lives, cautiously…warily…anxiously. Darting in short bursts, they sought out low-hanging branches from which they could nibble the leaves; they searched for patches of weeds upon which they could feast; and, of course, they joined in the universal hunt for water.

Judtson had always viewed the rabbits as nature's livestock. As cattle were to mankind, as krill were to the whales, these furry, meaty little creatures were born to be nothing but a meal – small, mobile machines, designed to gather desert grasses and convert this raw material into meat for the carnivores. They were fated to live a fleeting existence, evenly distributed across the plains and hills like convenience stores on four legs. It was their purpose. There could be no other explanation. The very basic concept of evolution was that organisms adapted utilizing the iterations of reproduction to improve, to hone, to develop survival skills. The more frequent the reproductive cycle, the more opportunities there were to change. This was the reason biologists meddled with fruit flies rather than tortoises.

The rabbits had the benefit of ten, twenty, thirty or more generations during the single life of one of their many predators. Yet no new traits, skills, or abilities, which might have caused them to avoid their inevitable demise, had spontaneously sprung into existence. They had not become any better at escaping from the shrill, yipping assault of a pack of coyotes. It was true that they already possessed speed superior to the coyote, as well as better maneuverability. Despite this, there was one reason the rabbits were inevitably the main course for these rangy canines. When rabbits heard the excited, intense staccato yelping from the pack in pursuit, mindless fear caused them to freeze. The only evolutionary improvement needed to avoid the vast majority of lepus fatalities would be steely nerves.

Although the creosote bush evolved to develop a foul and poisonous sap to minimize nibbling, and the boundless varieties of cacti grew sharp spines to dissuade animals from munching, the desert rabbits had never learned the circumstances to avoid, conditions to eschew, or movements to minimize which would improve their chances against their almost innumerable natural predators. Nor had they adapted to be equipped with fangs or claws so they might, at the very least, have had a fighting chance.

To Judtson's eye, the only skill acquired, as their numbers were systematically decimated, was an efficient, prolific reproductive capacity. Just as farmers and ranchers continuously tweaked their methods to satisfy the ever-growing demand for food, so did the rabbits. Nature had decided that the providing of protein for the predators outweighed any benefits of survivability for the rabbits.

Staring out into the darkening night, Judtson spoke aloud to himself and Rocky. "I wonder if they know they're the cheeseburgers of the animal kingdom."

His canine companion, not one to pass up on a *conejo* if given the opportunity, did not offer a response.

The cheeseburgers and the builders, he reflected, for the fecund rodents needed shelter, a requirement satisfied by the digging of burrows in the hard-packed desert soil, inadvertently providing daytime shelter for other Sonoran natives, the snakes, who either took advantage of the nightly attrition within the hare population to co-opt the vacated domiciles or, all too frequently, eliminated the residents preemptively.

A momentary flicker of movement caught his attention. It was an owl, soaring mere feet above the desert floor. Judtson saw owls as the superheroes of the animal kingdom. Not only possessing phenomenal night vision, owls were the beneficiaries of a truly unique evolutionary trait. Their wings, utilizing a complex and not fully understood feather pattern on the leading edge, allowed the owls to fly and rapidly descend without any telltale whooshing noise. The hapless rats received not even a moment's warning as a precursor to the claws seizing them. The feather pattern was so efficient at eliminating turbulence over the wings that NASA and several aircraft designers continued to attempt to replicate it.

The dynamic opera playing out before him masked now by darkness, Judtson was forced to manufacture the scene within his own mind, much as a stage director mentally orchestrated a play. The next cast members to join the nightly fray were the javelinas. Grunting, snorting, and emanating a foul stench, these wild boars traveled in rude packs fearlessly. With coarse fur which approached the prickliness of a porcupine, ripping fangs jutting from the front of their mouths, and a powerful musculature, these surly beasts felt free to roam through the life-and-death melee around them, almost impervious to the drama. Judtson saw them as a band of burly bikers who, while searching for the nearest strip club, stumbled onto the stage at a ballet performance, and single-mindedly and obliviously ambled across as the dancers pirouetted around them.

All of the main actors in place, the bit players arrived: the desert rats, furtively darting from bush to rock; the tarantulas, emerging from their daytime shade and beginning the slow, patient, methodical rounds in search of food and water. With an audible chuckle, Judtson recalled an evening years earlier. He and Kristen had been lounging in the pool, lazily staring at the stars above, when he noticed the furry shape of a tarantula, easily the size of his hand, its dark brown coloring making it starkly visible against the white-painted wall which surrounded their yard. At first he softly alerted his wife to its approach and watched with his usual fascination as it made its way down the wall. She, too, reacted calmly, feeling safe from her vantage, floating in the center of the pool.

With excruciating deliberateness, the creature came down the wall, reaching the textured concrete deck. Neither Judtson nor Kristen spoke, entranced by the silent, steady progress of the arachnid as it made its way toward the water. Tentatively, the tarantula extended one of its legs around the lip of the deck, testing the vertical face to ascertain the sufficiency of its grip. Then, a second leg curled, and the furry creature shifted its weight forward, the rest of the legs following.

"It's coming in!" Kristen softly exclaimed, a note of worry in her voice.

Reassuring her, Judtson answered, "They can't swim. It's just getting a drink."

As it traversed the face of the concrete lip and continued down the ceramic tile toward the surface, although the tarantula was of a size small enough to be squashed under a boot, its measured movements gave it the aura of a monster. Both Judtson and Kristen had remained motionless during the tableau, making no waves, so when the beast reached the water, the surface was smooth as glass. Rather than extending its body forward to gain a sip, the tarantula did something which startled them both. Quickly, much more rapidly than its previous movements, the giant spider stepped onto the surface of the still water and began scampering directly at them.

With frantic shrieks, Judtson and Kristen hastily abandoned their rafts and, with much thrashing and shouting, ran to the steps of the pool, as the tarantula followed. The sudden splashing and turbulence seemed not to affect the bug's ability to remain on top of the water, for, even as they were both out and standing on the deck staring, it made its way to the nearest side and climbed up the tile. Needing no further urging, the two ran to the back door of their home and entered, slamming it behind themselves before the apparently single-minded brute could chase them inside. Dripping wet, with their hearts pounding and their breathing ragged from the flood of adrenaline, they fell into each other's arms, laughing.

The wistful recollection of a more pleasant time in their marriage saddened Judtson, his reverie interrupted by a sudden, insistent vibration in his back pocket. Rocky's ears perked in reaction to the intrusion on their shared tranquility. Pulling out his phone, Judtson saw that it was a text message from Saylor, simply stating, "im here."

Tucking the phone back in his pocket, he gave a final, vigorous rub to Rocky's neck, took one more look around himself, trying to pierce the darkness, wishing he possessed the superhero vision of the owl, and spoke aloud, "Yes, this is a good night to be a freedom fighter."

Chapter 2

JUDTSON OPENED THE SIDE DOOR for Saylor. With no effusive greetings, the two silently nodded as Judtson stepped back, allowing his partner to enter the workroom and immediately pull down on the front zipper of his baggy, pea-green coveralls, revealing that he had already donned his suit.

Together, they moved to the workbench and, each opening his own locker, began strapping on belts. Noticing a difference in the routine, Saylor asked, "Why the M4 tonight? Thought you liked the AK."

With a shrug, Judtson replied, "Our last time out, the AK snagged in the shoulder strap as I swung it out the window. Thought I'd try the M4."

"It is shorter."

There was more silence between them as they finished packing the balance of their gear in zippered nylon carriers. After checking each other over, the men grabbed the carriers and weapons, and exited the workroom into the adjacent six-car garage, where they began to load up a white Camry. The nondescript sedan was chosen by Judtson based solely on its popularity. It was the most ubiquitous vehicle on the road. If word did go out on the police radios to apprehend a white late-model Camry in any one-mile-square section of town, within minutes there would be a minimum of twenty frustrated motorists standing next to the road with their feet spread and their hands on the hoods of their cars.

"Did you confirm intel?"

Saylor nodded. "Swung by on my way here. Our target is still in place."

Grunting an acknowledgment, Judtson moved around to the rear of the vehicle and opened the trunk, removing what appeared to be a clear pane of glass, edged with a one-inch-wide metal border. Squatting, he positioned the frame over the car's license plate and released his hold on it. The device slapped firmly against the plate, held by embedded magnets.

Next, using white duct tape, Judtson secured the two wires which were attached to the upper edge of the license plate cover, running a single, neat strip of tape from the plate, up the face of the plastic bumper, and into the trunk, where the wires were already attached to their points of contact. Standing up, he examined his installation and was pleased with the smoothness of his application and the color match between the tape and the bumper.

"This should be the last time we have to do that," Judtson huffed.

"Why's that?"

"Next week I'll have the plate frame permanently attached and the wires drilled through to the trunk."

"Cool."

"It'll just seem like all of the other acrylic plate covers out there."

With his comment, Judtson closed the trunk and looked at his partner. "You ready?"

Saylor indicated he was and climbed into the car, while Judtson turned off the interior light prior to opening the roll-up door. The garage remained dark as the bulb had been removed from the opener. Joining Saylor in the Camry, Judtson started the car and pulled out, careful to make certain that the garage door closed completely before they continued down the driveway to their mission.

▽

The Camry was parked at the west end of the lot in front of an old strip center on Fifth Street. The Thai restaurant attracted enough dinner customers to half-fill the lot, eliminating the possibility that the Camry would look conspicuous at this time of the evening. In contrast, Judtson and Saylor were anything but inconspicuous, wearing black suits, masks, 4+1 belts, tanks, and carrying their weapons. In deference to this fact, they lurked in the darkness, hiding behind the masonry wall which enclosed the front yard of an abandoned house just forty yards from their target.

"I'll take the back," whispered Saylor.

"Roger that."

From their vantage point, the two surveilled Fifth Street and the surroundings. Traffic was light tonight, broken into staggered bursts by the coordinated sequence of the signal lights at Swan and Craycroft. Judtson glanced down at his watch and noted that they had slightly more than thirty minutes before the target was to be moved. Tamping down the impatient tingling triggered by adrenaline, he waited through three more cycles, gaining a feel for the pattern.

With a final check of their equipment, and a last glance around to make certain none of the neighbors were out for an evening stroll with their dogs, the men slipped from behind the wall and briskly approached the target, separating from each other as it grew near.

His AK-47 up and ready, Saylor stepped around to the rear of the van and switched the selector to full automatic. Judtson, rounding the front of the vehicle, did the same. Both careful to stand slightly off to the side to ensure that neither would hit the other with an errant shot, they both pulled the triggers. Their markers made a stuttering sound, similar to the edge of a playing card dragged over corrugated cardboard, as they emptied a pod of 140 balls at a rate of twenty-five rounds per second. The paintballs exploded on contact, covering the rear and front windows of the van with an assortment of colors. Loading another pod from his belt, Saylor stepped around to the side window facing the street, and loosed another blast on the portion of the glass which was not masked.

Judtson, hearing a vehicle approaching from the west, turned to see that it was a pickup truck, gradually slowing down. He signaled to Saylor, who had also heard the arrival, and they both moved quickly away from the street as the truck actually came to a full stop parallel to the paint-splattered van. As the two men made their hasty retreat, the driver of the pickup rolled his window down and shouted to them, "YOU GUYS ARE AWESOME! WHOOOO-HOOOO!"

Now at a full run, the two made it to the perimeter of the parking lot, forcing themselves to come to a walk for the last ten yards in case any restaurant customers, filled with *pad Thai* and *tom yum goong*, were strolling to their cars. Triggered as they approached, the car alarm switched off and the doors unlocked; both men scrambled inside, slammed the doors, and Judtson started the engine immediately and drove away.

"Target One down," murmured Judtson, his voice steady.

"How can you be so calm?" Saylor's voice betrayed the residual excitement and nervousness of the moment. "All the times we've done this and you've never once even let out a whoop."

Shrugging, Judtson replied, "I don't see doing this the same way you do."

"What do you mean?"

"For you it's fun."

"It's a blast!"

"Not for me."

"Oh, come on. Not even some?"

Judtson shook his head.

"Right. It's a job." Saylor's voice dripped with sarcasm.

They reached the traffic signal at Fifth and Craycroft. The light was red. Bringing the Camry to a stop, Judtson twisted around in his seat to face his longtime friend. "Not a job…a mission."

Unable to ignore the intensity of his friend's gaze, Saylor paused, the grin departing from his face. "I know. I've got it. Same thing for me. But that doesn't mean we can't get off on it a little."

"I'll get off on it when we've accomplished something. Something long-term."

The two men stared at each other silently for a moment. The light changed to green and Judtson turned away, maneuvering the car into the southbound lane of Craycroft.

"Do you really think that'll ever happen?"

His voice even, Judtson answered, "Don't know. There are little signs we're making progress. Just not sure if it's enough. It would help if these excursions made the news tomorrow."

"They won't."

"I know. They don't want to give others the idea."

As he spoke, he steered the car into the parking lot on his right and slowly navigated across the half-filled expanse, until reaching a relatively empty section in front of Toys "Я" Us, and slipping into a space encircled by several other vacant stalls. With the engine and lights off, the cohorts awkwardly busied themselves in the tight confines of the front seat, preparing for the next assault.

Their markers cleaned and reloaded, tanks checked and situated behind the front seats rather than strapped to their bodies, Judtson got out from the driver's seat and walked around the car as Saylor vacated the passenger side. Having switched sides, Saylor asked if his friend was ready, receiving a single nod, and started the Camry. Judtson felt under the dash and flipped a toggle switch, sending electricity to the clear glass mounted magnetically over the license plate, rendering it instantly opaque. As Saylor weaved back through the parking lot toward the Craycroft exit, Judtson donned his mask and rolled down the side window.

Remaining stationary until the tail end of the signal cycle, Saylor then steered the car across all of the southbound lanes and pulled to a stop in the left-turn lane of the intersection. Now they waited, watching as the east- and westbound traffic crossed the intersection, followed by the procession of cars and trucks in the left-turn lanes of Broadway, the final two drivers tagged by the strobe flash of the traffic enforcement cameras for making their turns seconds too late. The next phase was a green light for the north- and southbound traffic on Craycroft. During this, Saylor noticed that they had accumulated three vehicles in the left-turn lane behind them. They were not police cars and did not appear to be unmarked versions, either.

"Do it!" barked Saylor, who eyed the southbound yellow.

Judtson poked his M4 out the passenger window and followed it with his upper torso, twisting around so that he was aiming the marker over the roof of the Camry and to the rear. In the center median to their left and slightly behind them stood a pole with an array of strobe lights and cameras, oriented to catch vehicles turning left from eastbound Broadway and those executing right turns from the westbound side of the intersection.

He briefly glanced at the car behind, a bright yellow Hummer, and saw a momentary look of panic on the face of the driver, a woman with flaming red hair, who immediately began rummaging on the front seat for something. The left-turn light arrived and Saylor took his foot off the brake, allowing the Camry to slowly roll forward. That was Judtson's cue and he pulled the trigger on his marker. The weapon was set for three-shot bursts, and he shifted the sights from one camera to the next on the pole with each successive burst, covering each front lens with paint.

"Go," he shouted, and Saylor gently pushed the accelerator down, moving them into the intersection more rapidly. As they proceeded through the left turn, Judtson, now sitting on the passenger side windowsill, twisted farther around and saturated the strobes. Finished with this group of targets, he looked back and saw that the woman behind them was holding up her cell phone as she followed, obviously making a video of his actions. This did not concern Judtson, as their plate was obscured and he was wearing a full mask. Before sliding back inside, he turned to face the trailing videographer and gave a thumbs-up for the camera, catching the transient smile on her face.

Dropping heavily onto his seat as Saylor completed the turn, he said, "I think we are the evening's entertainment for someone."

"What? You're kidding?" His eyes darted to the rearview mirror and he saw the woman, still following them, still holding her cell phone against the front windshield of her car.

Not waiting, Judtson clumsily climbed over the back of his seat and moved to the driver's side rear window, pressing the button and lowering it. As Saylor reached the first break in the median, he swung into the turn lane and, with no oncoming traffic, made a tight U-turn. Looking behind again, Judtson saw the woman with the cell phone, still recording.

"We're going to have to lose her soon," he shouted over the road sounds and wind allowed in by the open windows.

"Yep. Right after the next pass."

They were again approaching the same intersection, this time in the westbound lane. In preparing for this mission, they had planned the sequences to the second and now had a green light ahead. Saylor took his foot off the gas pedal and the car slowed.

"Come on...come on," he muttered impatiently, as Judtson extended his M4 out the rear window, resting his elbows on the frame.

Their speed was down to less than fifteen miles per hour and they had less than a block to go before they reached the crosswalk, when the green light changed to yellow.

"Yes!" Saylor exclaimed, and began a countdown, "14...13...12...11...10" – he paused and gulped a deep breath – "9...8...7...6...5...4...3...2...1!"

With the front bumper of the Camry mere feet from the crosswalk, the light changed to red and Saylor tapped down on the pedal, speeding up rather than stopping. He twisted the steering wheel into another left turn.

Switching the M4 from three-shot burst to full automatic, Judtson aimed to the rear and thoroughly splattered the cameras on the center median as he passed it. Not waiting to appreciate the results, he swung his aim forward as the strobes to the front and rear of them flashed, the automatic system attempting to capture the Camry in the act of running the red light. They were now through the wide intersection and Judtson again triggered the marker, this time coating not only the cameras, but the strobes, as well.

He dropped back in the seat and reloaded his marker with another pod as Saylor made a second U-turn.

"It seems we lost her," he said.

As he slid over to the passenger side, Judtson looked toward the left-turn lane they had just vacated, and saw the Hummer stopped behind the crosswalk. The driver had decided not to run the red light behind them.

"I guess she chickened out."

"Too bad," Saylor commented with a tinge of sadness.

Judtson shrugged. "This'll work. She'll be in the perfect spot for out last pass. We'll cross right in front of her."

"True."

This time, Saylor steered the Camry into the far right lane, normally reserved for buses, bicycles, and right turns, and with a glance back to make certain his partner was in position at the passenger side window, he proceeded straight instead of taking the turn.

As they passed the array placed at the corner, Judtson loosed another burst, taking out the cameras and strobes. Arriving at the north side of the intersection, he intended to do the same. The speed of the Camry was perfect. His aim was dead on. His marker was ready and the pole-mounted equipment was looming before him. Judtson ordered his trigger finger to pull. It did not. Jolted by instantaneous confusion and concern, he hurried to shift his aim as they went past the pole. No longer at an ideal angle on the target, his recalcitrant index finger responded and a largely ineffectual spray of paintballs burst out, a few striking the cameras a glancing blow, many of the others missing completely and harmlessly splattering the parking lot behind.

Visibly upset, Judtson slammed his back against the seat, tucking the M4 between his legs and violently jerking the mask from his head. He closed the side window as Saylor assumed a normal speed.

"What happened? Did your marker jam?"

Shaking his head, Judtson answered, "No! I don't know."

"What do you mean?"

As he stared straight ahead through the front windshield, his mind replayed the past few seconds. "Man, I pulled the trigger. I mean, I didn't. But I tried."

Saylor heard consternation and anxiety creep into his friend's voice. Gently, he urged, "Talk it out. Tell me what happened."

Tilting his head back against the headrest and closing his eyes, Judtson rewound the scene in his head, to the point right after his last successful volley. "I took out the cameras and strobes perfectly on the south side of the intersection. Swung the M4 around to catch the pole on the north side. I remember thinking it was too easy. Like ducks in a pond. I was comfortable. Situated. Lined up. You were driving the ideal speed. Everything was right. When we reached the sweet spot, I told my finger to pull the trigger. I TOLD it to pull the damn trigger. It just didn't."

Judtson opened his eyes and looked at his partner, seeing a small frown briefly bend the corners of his lips downward.

"What was it? What do you think happened?"

Saylor, realizing he was being observed, wiped the expression of concern from his visage and answered, "Nothing."

"Don't give me that! That has never happened to me before. What was it?"

Projecting nonchalance, Saylor repeated reassuringly, "I'm serious. It's nothing."

Frustrated, Judtson almost shouted, "Pull over. I want to talk about this."

Saylor shook his head. "Don't think that's a good idea. By now, the cops are beginning to keep an eye out for a white Camry. I really don't want to be stopped while we're still wearing these MOLLE vests and have a car full of paintball markers and gear. We can talk when we get back to your place." He reached around and flipped down the toggle switch under the dashboard, once again revealing the rear license plate. Distracted by the anxiousness from his friend, he failed to notice that the yellow Hummer was following them at a discreet distance.

Judtson forced himself to take a long, deep breath and let it out slowly, attempting to modulate his mood as Saylor continued on the northbound route, careful to observe the posted speed limit. Realizing the logic in his companion's statement, he sighed and flopped his head back again, utilizing the balance of the trip to put the twenty-second-long experience on a continuous loop in his mind.

Chapter 3

THE GETAWAY VEHICLE SAFELY PARKED inside the closed garage, the two men out of their belts and suits, gear cleaned and stowed away, Judtson and Saylor sat in semidarkness on Judtson's back porch, a few feet apart and facing each other. Neither had spoken through the arrival procedures, both lost in their own thoughts.

After taking a long sip from an iced tea, poured when they passed through the kitchen on their way to the backyard, his voice calm again, Judtson was the first to break the silence. "I know you told me it was nothing, not to dwell on it. I understand that. But I've been alive for thirty-five years, and this was the first time I've ever instructed a part of my body to do something and it just ignored me. I'm asking you to indulge me for a minute. You're the brain doc. What can cause that?"

Saylor, still holding the apple he snatched from a basket on their way out, suddenly tossed it directly at Judtson, whose hand jerked up and nabbed it in midair.

Recognizing that this act was going to be a part of his longtime friend's answer, Judtson said nothing.

"Did you consciously think about catching that?"

"No. I did it automatically."

"Right. Call it 'automatically.' Call it 'subconsciously.' Call it whatever you want. That is one level of control our mind has over the body."

Judtson, recognizing he was in for a full-blown lecture, smiled to himself as Saylor continued, "The heart doesn't pump on its own. Our brain is directing it, beat by beat – even the incremental steps of the coordinated opening and closing of the valves, the clenching of the chambers in sequence, everything. Every subtle detail of the elaborate process is being managed by the brain. It's the same thing with the 'much more complex than you think' act of breathing. Even all of the minuscule openings and closings of ducts in the lymphatic system are all orchestrated by the gray conductor in our skull.

"A lot of people think that most of those reactions are caused by chemicals. I won't bore you with the details...."

"Thank you."

"But what most people don't realize is that when a receptor within the body senses a shift in the chemicals, a shift intended to either shut down or open up some particular duct, like the glucose level in the bloodstream triggering the need for insulin, the duct isn't reacting directly to the stimuli of the chemical change; instead, it sends the data to the brain. Once the brain receives the information, it orders the duct to either open or close, releasing or stopping the release of a counterbalancing chemical."

"So, what you're saying is that the brain is involved in every process."

"Directly, inextricably, and intimately involved. Even those who are supposedly brain-dead after a drowning or some other accident, those poor souls who are in a total vegetative state, have brains which are functioning sufficiently to perform thousands, maybe millions of actions a minute. Otherwise, their bodies wouldn't be alive."

"Understood. A whole section of our brain is busy operating the machine we call 'us,' right?"

"Exactly. And nobody really knows how much of the brain is devoted to this so-called autonomic effort."

"Is that why they used to say we only use six percent of our brain? The rest is working at switching on and off my sweat glands?"

Chuckling, Saylor responded, "With *your* sweat glands, there might be as little as two percent of your brain left for you to use for other things."

Judtson threw the apple at Saylor, who caught it easily.

"That whole six-percent thing is another discussion. Let's just say, it's a bunch of bunkum."

"Bunkum? Who uses the word *bunkum* anymore?"

"Shut up."

"All right, all right, go on."

"At the very base level, we have the purely autonomic processes. The next level up would be the automatic or instinctual responses."

"Like catching the apple."

"Right. Or the eyelids blinking when there is a sudden threat to the eyes. Slapping the side of your own face when an insect lands there. Jerking your head forward when something lightly brushes the back of it. There are quite a few of them. Some are natural. Some are learned. And all of them happen before your conscious mind even has a chance to focus on the trigger stimuli."

"But I can stop them or override them. I can make myself ignore the thrown apple and let it bounce off my chest."

"You can, well, almost always, but only if you expect it beforehand. You aren't going to be able to override your reaction to a truly spontaneous event, something surprising."

"Makes sense. And after that are the conscious actions?"

"Not yet. The next level up would be internalized actions. Those are the actions we have learned and mastered so that we no longer have to focus on them consciously – typing, playing a musical instrument, driving. Have you ever noticed when you are writing that if you suddenly pay attention to the act of typing on the keyboard, you start screwing up?"

"Yeah, I have. And slowing way down."

"The reason is that when we master a process and internalize it, the conscious part of our brain actually loses the skill. We've delegated it to the shadowy area and forgotten about it, literally forgotten how to do it. When we try to take over, we're essentially novices at it. People can walk across a room with a full cup of coffee, pay no attention to it, and not spill a drop. If they suddenly look down at the cup and concentrate on what they're doing, it immediately begins to slosh over, no matter how hard they try to control it."

"That's why waitresses can dodge through a crowded restaurant all day long, like running backs carrying the ball, and not spill anything."

"Uh-huh. They've learned the skill and internalized it. The list goes on and on. It is most apparent in the performing arts, with dancers, jugglers, all musicians, et cetera. But almost everyone, in the course of a normal day, utilizes this ability."

"Never really thought about it."

"Now we are finally at the last level – the acts, motions, processes, and deeds we perform consciously. These are relatively unique, not repeated often enough to justify internalization. We are remarkably inept at performing physical acts, compared to the proficiency we are capable of during internalized actions."

"Why is that?"

Saylor sat back in his chair and took a bite from the apple. Judtson waited patiently, listening to the loud crunching, chomping sounds as his friend chewed.

"The three lower levels, especially the lowest two, have a singular advantage. They are essentially immune to distraction."

"That's good. I'd hate it if I became distracted by, I don't know, a car accident right in front of me, and my mind forgot to tell my heart to keep beating."

"Right. With the exception of some very extreme examples, the autonomic processes are never prone to distraction. There are moments during the fight-or-flight response when we can briefly forget to breathe, for example. But those are rare and we quickly recover. Again, the same is true, for the most part, with the automatic responses, just slightly less so. There are intense situations where you are so occupied with input that even a huge grasshopper could land directly on your lips and you wouldn't sputter."

"So, at that level, a bit more of the distractions creep in?"

"Yes. This pattern continues as we move up the ladder. The internalized actions – typing, playing the piano, moving in for a lay-up shot, and the like – are so much more fragile that a lot of the time we need to exert a conscious level of what we call 'concentration,' which is nothing more than building a mental barrier around the action, allowing the mind to do its work unfettered. A slip in the concentration and the person suddenly becomes aware of the incremental steps and blows it."

"That rings true. A couple of months ago I was doing a book signing and a reader handed me her copy of *The Mason's Ring*. Unless somebody asks for a specific inscription, my standard, automatic one is to write, 'I hope that you enjoy *The Mason's Ring*,' or whichever title it is. Anyway, just as I was writing that, she asked me if I'd ever read *The Shack*. Without even thinking about it, I wrote, 'I hope that you enjoy *The Shack*.' We had a bit of a chuckle about it at the time."

"Exactly. That's what I'm talking about. And your regular inscription is, or verges on being, an internalized act. Yet, at a critical moment, you were distracted. Your *hand* did something different from what you thought your brain was telling it to do. It wasn't your hand which suddenly went off the rails. It was your mind reacting to a distraction."

"We are finally getting to my question...you're saying that at the moment I was supposed to pull the trigger tonight, I was distracted."

Saylor nodded.

"I don't remember being distracted. I don't recall any other thoughts popping into my head at that moment."

"You wouldn't, necessarily. The distraction can be a micro-second long, not anywhere close to enough to register consciously. You could have been recapping what we'd done so far. You could have noticed something in the background behind that last target, which momentarily caught your attention and made you forget to pull the trigger. Could be almost anything. That's the point. That's why our brain has developed these other levels, to allow us to perform essential functions without distractions. Our conscious mind is like an ADHD person on cocaine. We are constantly bouncing from one point of focus to another; constantly shifting from being in the moment to vividly recalling a vignette from third grade; constantly registering, analyzing, and either storing or reacting to new stimuli.

"The beauty of this reality is that it is a marvelously effective survival mechanism. Let's look at our ancestors. A hunter was able to walk quietly along a trail, stalking an elk for his next meal, totally focused on sneaking up on the animal and thinking of nothing else, when a subtle sound, smell, or sight caught his attention and alerted him that *he* was being stalked by a tiger. It was that ability to instantly abandon the previous course of action and react to the new input which allowed him to survive. And it still serves us well today.

"Unfortunately, the side effect of this benefit is that we are all prone to a myriad of distractions, some of which cause us to shift gears instantly, without even knowing why."

Judtson sat back and closed his eyes, mentally replaying the disturbing event. Saylor lifted the apple to his mouth and realized that his loud bite and chomping noises would break his friend's reverie. Normally, within the context of their friendship, that would have been a perfect reason to proceed. This evening, knowing how upset Judtson was, he slowly lowered the fruit and waited.

It was a short wait. Leaning forward again and opening his eyes, Judtson recalled, "My mind *was* sort of spinning in the moments beforehand. As we crossed the intersection, I was dwelling on how perfect everything was, all of the conditions."

"That may be a part of it."

"What do you mean?"

"This observation is as just a guy, not a neurologist, but have you ever noticed how at times we do something that is the worst possible thing to do at the moment?"

"Oh, you mean like the time you dropped your new shaver into the toilet?"

Saylor laughed softly. "That's exactly what I was thinking about. You tell me if there are any parallels. I was so jazzed about that shaver, and Doni had been so excited about getting for me. I was standing in front of the toilet that morning, using it for the first time while I was...."

"I know what you were doing."

"Right. Well, anyway, I was standing there shaving, when the thought popped into my head that it would be horrible if I dropped the shaver right then."

"And then you did."

"Yep. Right into the bowl. To this day I have no idea why."

"Doni thought it was because you hated her gift."

"I know. That honestly wasn't it. If that were the case, I wouldn't have replaced it with an identical shaver. The deal is, the same way you were letting your mind wander, reflecting on how perfect the evening was for our mission, I was standing there shaving, thinking about how much I liked my present, how good my life was, how much I loved Doni. And then *bang*, or rather *splash*! There are some who believe that the mind doesn't register the negative."

"What do you mean?"

"They assert that if you are told, or if you even tell yourself, 'Whatever you do, don't spill the milkshake in the car,' the mind doesn't register 'don't.' So what you hear is 'spill the milkshake,' and that is the command you operate on."

"The difference was that you thought about not dropping the shaver; I didn't entertain any thoughts that dealt with not pulling the trigger before it happened."

"That you were consciously aware of."

"Right."

"My point is that sometimes we physically do something which is the opposite of what we intend."

"So you're saying that either I was distracted by a tiger hiding behind the camera pole, or some kind of man-against-himself psychosis decided to strike at that moment."

"Crudely put, but yes. And there's one more thing."

"Can't wait to hear *this*."

"It's called 'hypervigilance' in the parlance."

Judtson snorted softly. "I don't need a medical degree to know what that is. You think I'm a hypochondriac."

Laughing, Saylor answered, "You do have a tendency to pay a little too much attention to yourself."

"I do not!"

"You do. There have been times I thought it was because of our friendship that I went to medical school, just to be able to answer your endless stream of questions about your body."

"You're exaggerating."

"Am not. Think back. Remember the bump on your head. You were sure you had a tumor."

"It could have been," Judtson protested defensively.

"It was only a bump. Remember, you wouldn't believe the doctor until he had you feel his head so you could see he had a bump, too. And even then you weren't buying it. He had to bring in two of his office staff for you to feel their heads."

"Well, he could have had a tumor, and just not figured it out yet."

With a shake of his head, Saylor continued, "And what about the time you thought your liver felt tight?"

"Well, dammit, it did."

"How can your liver feel tight? And how do you know it's your liver, anyway? So what did that trigger? An x-ray, a CT scan, and a blood test. Oh, no, wait a minute…two blood tests because you were convinced that the nurse had switched your blood with someone else's."

"I still think she did."

"And everything came back negative."

"So? That doesn't mean there wasn't something wrong. All it means is that they haven't determined the right test yet."

"The right test for a tight liver?"

"Right."

"Judtson, that was nine years ago. Have you had any liver problems since?"

"Well, not really."

"What do you mean, 'not really'?"

"It comes and goes."

"What comes and goes? Your liver?"

"Stop it. You're starting to get me mad."

"I'm serious. See, you still don't want to let go of it."

In a soft voice, Judtson retorted, "I still get a twinge every once in a while."

Saylor reared back and laughed. "The list goes on and you know it. The vein in your leg that didn't look quite right to you, so you thought it was bulging and was going to burst."

"People have embolisms, even at my age."

Ignoring him, Saylor resumed the litany. "Or the time you decided that the color of your urine was odd. Same thing with the coating on your tongue. Or when you thought that the fluid on your eyeballs looked cloudy. And what about...?"

Judtson held up his hands. "Okay, stop!"

Leaning closer to his friend and losing the bantering tone in his voice, Saylor said, "The point is, pal, you didn't die from any of those things. You haven't developed any permanent, debilitating conditions, either. All of those trips to doctors, labs, radiologists, and specialists weren't necessary. All of the results came back negative every time."

"What about...?"

"I know. Yes, you actually did have some legitimate illnesses over the years, bona fide diseases."

Judtson started to speak but was cut off. "The difference is that those were clinically obvious. They were real. You had a measurable fever. You had a hacking cough, a sore throat. You were vomiting. You had diarrhea."

"People do occasionally get the more obscure diseases."

"You're right. They do. And when it happens, a lot of the time the doctor misses it on the initial diagnosis. But they are called 'rare' diseases for a reason."

Saylor, sensing that his friend was about to launch into his familiar arguments on the subject, hurried to keep the floor. "Let's not go down that road again. There isn't any more you can say, and I don't have anything new to add, either. You are right. At some point down the road, you may be vindicated. You may actually be fortunate enough to contract an amazingly obscure disease that, up until it attacks you, has only been observed in a small tribe of natives living along a very short stretch of the Amazon. And it will only be because of your vigilance, your incredibly intense attention to every part of your body, and your insistence that we in the medical profession bring in every possible test and expert available, that you are able to obtain an accurate diagnosis. Sadly, it won't be in time to cure you. But at least the disease, as it manifests in North America, will be named after you. In your final moments you will be able to tell all of us, 'I told you so.'"

Saylor stopped, sitting back in his chair, waiting to be told off. To his surprise, Judtson agreed, "I know. I do get a little carried away sometimes."

"A little?"

"Well, all right. A lot. Except this thing tonight...."

"Was nothing. It was the kind of incident that happens to everyone. With the distraction issue I explained, which can be compounded by fatigue, stress, a number of different factors, it was normal."

In the dim light their eyes connected. Saylor could see the familiar haunted look in Judtson's eyes.

"You're sure?"

With a heavy sigh, Saylor answered, "The problem with being a doctor is that we can never say we're sure. We're trained to remind ourselves there is always the possibility of the obscure. We're trained to remember that every time we tell a patient we are sure about anything, we've just handed some lawyer the ammunition he needs to sue us to hell and back. But yeah, pal, I'm sure."

Judtson stared down at his right hand. Saylor knew that he was focusing on the offending trigger finger, hoping that it would suddenly gain independent sentience and answer his questions directly. After nearly a minute of silence, Judtson looked back up at his friend. "All right. If you say so."

The moment Judtson's acquiescence was spoken, the muscles in Saylor's neck and back tightened. Instead of the relief he expected at having convinced his friend of the absence of a problem, a dark, foreboding chill flooded through his body, conveying an irrational, unexplainable, spontaneous conviction that he had made a monumental error tonight.

▽

Sitting in a darkened room, illuminated only by the glow of the double flat-screen monitors, the woman, utilizing video-editing software, froze the image on the screen and zoomed in. Next, she selected two separate enhancement tools from the menu bar and waited patiently as the algorithms performed their magic on the pixels. The blue progress bar reached the right-hand end of the small box, and the image crystallized. With a satisfied smile, she quickly clicked the phone icon and selected a name from the contact list. With a double-click, the connection was made, and two rings came from the speakers before a male voice answered, "Hello, boss."

"Scott, I need a favor."

Chapter 4

THE MORNING SUN, INSINUATING ITSELF through the narrow gaps in the wooden blinds, created a variegated light in the bedroom as Judtson opened his eyes. He lay motionless for a few moments, listening for the sounds of Kristen's breathing beside him. Concluding that she was either already up or simply respiring silently, he carefully turned to look at her side of the bed. The contoured, sheet-covered shape told him she was still asleep.

He uncovered himself and warily swung his legs out and down, gingerly coming to a sitting position without jostling the bed, glanced at the clock on the nightstand, and saw that it was only a few minutes after six. He retrieved his robe from the closet and tiptoed from the room. Permitting himself a sigh of relief as he reached the living room without rousing her, he proceeded directly to the kitchen and started a pot of coffee.

As it brewed, he half-walked, half-staggered in his morning wooziness, and headed to his favorite room, the library. All four of the walls were covered with bookshelves, extending to the fourteen-foot-high ceiling. The shelves were crowded with his lifelong collection of hardcovers, several signed by authors. A loop of brass pipe was mounted horizontally at the eight-foot level, circumnavigating the perimeter. An antique rolling ladder, salvaged from the former main library in Tucson before the building was repurposed, rode the rail. This was his writing haven, surrounded by the words, phrases, images, ideas, and dreams of men and women who, in his opinion, were the true masters of the craft. There was not a section on any of the shelves where Judtson's nine published works were displayed.

Dropping heavily into the leather chair, Judtson used his big toe to probe blindly under the desk until he located and tripped the switch on the surge protector strip, a necessity in monsoon season. He pressed the power buttons on the monitor and computer, listening for a moment to the hum of the hard drive spinning up, then rose and returned to the kitchen to wait for the coffee. As he picked up his mug from the drainboard, the same mug he used every single day, the one given to him by Kristen many years ago, back when..., he wondered how many times he had performed this series of actions in his life. Not just a creature of habit, he recognized that he was a slave to it, and thought it would be interesting if he could know the exact number of times he had performed this morning ritual.

As the coffee maker sputtered loudly in the final throes of ejecting the superheated water onto the grounds, he mentally calculated an estimate. Eleven years…that was how long ago he shifted his writing schedule from nights to mornings. That was also the time he had acquired his taste for coffee, abandoning the morning can of Diet Coke. Three hundred and sixty-five days times eleven was four thousand and fifteen days. Of course he would need to deduct all of the days he was not here during those years. There would have been research trips, business trips to New York to meet with Darrow, promotional junkets for television and radio interviews, as well as book signings and, of course, vacations with Kristen, until those ended.

He recognized that he did not have a sufficiently accurate recollection of all of the times he ventured out, in order to come up with a precise number to deduct from the total days, so he estimated the aggregate of them to be twenty percent. That felt about right. Deducting twenty percent left three thousand, two hundred and twelve days.

The brown stream of coffee slowed to a dribble and, holding his mug under the funnel to catch the residual drips, Judtson dumped the grounds in the trash. Then he rinsed and placed the funnel into the plastic drain basket in the left bowl of the sink. For the three thousand, two hundred and thirteenth time, he poured coffee into his mug, feeling unsatisfied with the accuracy of the final number and frustrated with himself for going through the mental exercise only to achieve a meaningless result. Adding cream and sweetener to the brew, he carried it cautiously back across his home to the library, being careful not to spill onto the carpet and remembering the discussion with Saylor about the automatic mechanism developed by waitresses for this very task.

Back in the library, coffee mug safely placed on his desk, Judtson saw that his computer had completed its boot-up process and patiently, mindlessly awaited his commands. Glancing down at the lower right-hand corner of the screen, he saw that it was just after 6:30, which meant that he had almost half an hour to kill before the Skype conference. He decided there was not enough time to immerse himself in his latest project. With his left hand, he raised the mug to his lips and took a sip, while his right moved the mouse and clicked on the icon for the game *Bricks Breaking II*. The screen was immediately taken over by a rectangular playing area filled with multicolored bricks. His eyes rapidly searched for clusters of at least three bricks in the same color, his hand manipulating the mouse to orient the pointer over the first group. His finger tapped the left button a single time, exploding the group and causing the bricks above to cascade downward.

Judtson had no interest or desire to engage in the anonymous, interactive RPG games on the Internet. Many years ago he had meticulously crafted this avatar called Judtson Kent, and was perfectly content polishing and refining the character as he went through life. Manufacturing any additional personas seemed boring and otiose to him. On the other hand, he enjoyed games which tested him in different ways. Games requiring a bit of strategy, an increasing level of dexterity, and progressive levels of pressure and challenge were his favorites, and he disdained those requiring even the most minuscule measures of luck. This taste extended back to the early, primitive video games such as *Space Invaders* and *Asteroids*. He also had no desire to compete with others on the Internet, preferring to compete with himself, always striving to better his prior high scores.

As the game gradually ticked up in tempo, adding new mixed rows of red, yellow, or blue bricks at the bottom of the rectangle, he intensely engaged in the play, losing all sense of time until a soft *beep* alerted him that the other members of the conference were calling his computer for a connection. The distraction caused him to miss an obvious combination of bricks, and the ascending mass rapidly reached the top, ending the game.

With a soft sigh, he closed the window and clicked on the blinking icon in the task bar, opening the conference software. Within moments, he was watching a split screen containing two faces; the illusion created was that they were looking at him. On the left was the visage of his agent, Mitch Murray. Judtson took in the details of the image bemusedly, noting that Mitch had arranged his laptop and webcam such that the other participants could not help but see that he was sitting on his balcony in Malibu with the clear blue ocean breaking on the sands behind him. On the right was the facsimile of Darrow Shugrew, Judtson's publisher. Judtson was aware from previous visits to Darrow's office that his media people had created the web conference backdrop to maximize the aura of solid respectability they wanted to project. Judtson knew that captured within his own video image was a six-foot-tall, green, stuffed Gumby, which appeared to be casually lounging in the background against the bookshelves. He also knew that his backdrop was no less consciously contrived than the others.

"Judtson, good morning." The slightly out-of-synch movement of Darrow's mouth during the greeting was distracting.

"Morning, Judtson!" Mitch's words were overly jovial, prompting Judtson to wonder for the thousandth time whether his agent had missed his calling and should have been either a game show host or a telemarketer.

Judtson responded to both, and the three engaged in the mindless pleasantries required as a preamble to the true purpose of the meeting, until Murray finally broached the main topic. "Have you given any thought to what we discussed three days ago?"

Leaning forward in his chair, moving his face closer to the webcam, Judtson replied in a matter-of-fact manner, "If you are asking if I've thought about it, the answer is *yes*. If you are asking if I've changed my mind, my decision is *no*."

Completely uninterested in Mitch's reaction, he stared at the two-dimensional face of his publisher, watching as Darrow's eyes focused on the bottom of his screen for Judtson's response. Due to some disease or accident, Judtson had never known the details, Darrow was completely deaf and had been his entire adult life. There was no doubt, in Judtson's opinion, why the man had chosen the literary field, dealing exclusively with the written word as his life's work. In person, he was quite adept at reading lips, as long as the participant in the discussion spoke slowly and clearly and did nothing to block his mouth. With the advent of video conferencing and the tendency of the Internet to jump jerkily from image to image in the portion of the screen which was in motion, lipreading was essentially impossible. The Internet geeks, of course, had a solution for this problem. Darrow's video-conferencing software contained a speech-to-text module, which generated the equivalent of closed captioning across the bottom of his monitor.

"A division of snow?"

The unfortunate side effect of the software was the inevitable mistranslation of speech, resulting, at times, in some truly humorous interpretations. Fighting off an amused grin, Judtson slowly restated, "No, Darrow. What I said was that I have not changed my mind."

Again, there was a slight pause as Shugrew read the caption. Judtson had realized, shortly after the advent of the Internet conferencing technology, that the short span of time, between the act of finishing his comment and then being able to focus on Darrow's face as he read the text, gave him an unfair advantage. Not only was Darrow's reaction not lost in the mental clutter of a quickly evolving verbal exchange, but the elapsed seconds gave Judtson the opportunity to prepare his next remark.

As he read Judtson's words, Darrow's face stiffened. It was not clear if this was a manifestation of frustration or anger. "Judtson, you are making a monumental mistake. You are throwing away so much of what we...you...have built over the years."

"I don't think so. I think my readers are intelligent enough and open-minded enough to follow me on this."

Murray interrupted with a harsh laugh. "Judtson, you are wrong. Your books, the whole body of your work, which we shouldn't forget has sold more than two hundred million copies worldwide, speaks to, hell, panders to the sizable segment of the population we fondly call skeptics. They see you as the rational antidote for the Zecharia Sitchins, David Ickes, and Alex Joneses of the world."

"I know that, Mitch."

"I know you do. But I don't think you are focusing on the true nature, the hard-wired personalities of your readers."

"What do you mean?"

"They are not a kind and gentle lot. I've seen it in the past. You don't build up any credibility with these folks and then ease them into a different mind-set. You are a purely utilitarian object to them. As long as you are fulfilling your role as a harsh and brutal debunker, you remain their hero. They will gush over you, send you flattering letters and emails, quote you, watch your guest appearances on cable, post links to your videos on their Facebook pages, tune in to your show and, most important, buy your books. But the minute, hell, the instant they sense you are willing to even consider an idea they believe to be fringe, they will turn on you the same way the survivors in an epidemic movie turn on a member of their group when he starts to show the first symptom of the disease. And you will be amazed at how vociferous these formerly fawning fans can become. If public stoning were still in vogue, at that point you would be a bloody corpse on the town square."

Judtson hesitated, not that he was swayed by Murray's words; rather, he was at a momentary loss for precisely how to respond. Darrow, having caught up with the conversation, added, "He's right, Judtson. They will not follow you. You are going to essentially flush your entire audience down the toilet."

"I don't care."

"You don't care!" The loud exclamation from Mitch crackled the speakers.

"No, I don't. The theme and direction of all of my books did not result from a cold and calculating desire to exploit some lucrative niche identified by focus groups. I have always written what I believed. What I believed just happened to have an audience."

"A damn big one."

"You're right, Mitch. It has been a damn big one. And I am thankful for the benefits I've received from that audience."

"Don't you think you owe them?"

"Of course I owe them. That's the point. I have always believed that I owe them two things — the best writing I can produce and the truth."

His agent barked a rude laugh. "Judtson, what do you think? That this is some movie and you're the heroic, crusading star? You say something like…'and the truth,' and the sound track will suddenly blast out a dramatic 'DA-DAAAA'? This is real life and *you* need to get real."

Before Judtson could snap back, Darrow, fulfilling his role in the good cop / bad cop routine they had obviously planned, asked in a conciliatory voice, "Do you actually believe that the content in your current draft is true?"

Judtson stared directly into the small lens of the webcam in a futile attempt to make eye contact with his publisher, and said, "I know it is."

The three men fell silent for a moment. Judtson knew that they would have also planned and rehearsed the next turn in the conversation, if it reached this point. He waited, curious as to how they would play it. His curiosity was unequivocally satisfied as Darrow, in an emotionless tone, stated, "Contractually, we are under no obligation to publish it."

Although he had expected this to be a game of hardball, the flat, bald-faced statement surprised him. He turned to look at his agent and saw that his expression was impassive.

"Mitch, you work for me. You are *my* agent, not Darrow's employee. Don't you have anything to say about that?"

Murray shrugged. "He's right. They don't have to publish any book they don't like."

Feeling his back muscles tightening and the early surges of adrenaline spurting into his body, Judtson leaned forward. "Then I'll take it to another house."

"You can't."

"What do you mean, I can't?"

"Darrow has the exclusive rights to your work."

His temperature rising, Judtson asked, "So he can decide never to publish me again and I have no options? That's ridiculous."

"No. It's not that you can never publish again. There is a term to your contract. When it expires, you can simply decide not to renew it. Then you can go elsewhere. Until then, he owns all of your work product."

"And when does the contract expire?"

"About two and a half years from now."

"Wait a minute. I just remembered something from that contract. It says that if they don't publish me, they've broken the contract. Isn't that in there?"

With a rueful smile, Darrow answered, "You are right, Judtson. There is a clause to that effect. If you submit a manuscript to us and we do not publish it, we would be in default and you can terminate the contract."

"Well, there you go. Either publish it or I'm walking."

"Judtson, you may, of course, pursue that avenue. However, I think you'll discover that the steps, the time frame involved, would not be to your liking."

Suddenly suspicious, Judtson asked, "How long?"

"Each increment of the process has contractual time limitations. As of now you have only submitted a version which you yourself have described as a draft. The delivery of what is merely a draft does not even start the clock ticking."

"Okay, I'll call it the final manuscript."

"I expected that you would say that. We would begin the editing of the manuscript. We are allowed six months to perform this and provide you with the edited version. Included in the edited version would be multiple requests for you make specific changes. You would more than likely refuse to make those changes. Contractually, upon receipt of your refusal, we are then allowed to hire an outside writer to make the changes."

"But I have final say on the book. I *know* that's in the contract."

Shugrew nodded an acknowledgment. "You do. That's true. So after we've given you the contractually required three months to make the changes, which you will refuse to make, then we have six months from that point in time to obtain a rewrite from a third party of our choosing. After the rewrite is completed and we submit the revised content to you for approval, which you, of course, will refuse, we then have another six months to perform another rewrite...."

"All right. I get the picture. What's the bottom line? How long can you drag it out?"

Darrow sat back in his chair, a smug smile across his face. "If all of the contractually allowed maximum time periods are utilized, it can take more than three years. At that point, if we have not been successful in producing a *mutually* acceptable manuscript, you would be free to go elsewhere. Obviously, by then your contract with us would have expired anyway."

Judtson spent a moment taking this all in. He had never been one to blindly sign any contract in his life and did recall, in general terms, the sequence Darrow had described. He also knew that there would be no logical reason for his publisher to bluff, as it would be a certainty that Judtson would talk with his attorney shortly after this conference ended.

"Mitch, is there anything you can do to help me?"

Shaking his head, the agent responded, "Not really, Judtson."

"Then I can't see any reason for you to remain in this conversation." With this comment, Judtson clicked on the conference icon and brought up the active screen, terminating the connection to Malibu. Instantly, the left rectangle disappeared from the screen, leaving only Darrow.

Judtson took a deep breath in an attempt to steady himself. "Darrow, I *do* recall those clauses. You are right. I can't force you to publish my book. Nor can I sell my book to anyone else."

He watched Darrow read the captioning, and was actually able to discern the conscious effort the man made not to break into a triumphant grin after he absorbed Judtson's words. It was child's play to follow the thought processes of his publisher, as he watched him put a friendly and propitiative expression on his face.

"Judtson, I'm glad you understand. I was truly hoping that this wouldn't...."

Holding his hand up to catch Darrow's attention, Judtson interrupted, "I said I couldn't *sell* my book, Darrow. What I *can* do is give it away."

Shugrew's eyes flared widely as he read Judtson's words, the features of his face freezing in mid-transition.

"Judtson, please. You are making a monstrous mistake."

"Will you please stop beginning every sentence with my name."

"Ju..." – he paused, took a breath, and continued – "I know you don't regard me as a friend, especially at this moment."

"True."

"But, as someone who has known you and worked with you for years, please don't go in this direction."

"Why not, Darrow? What's the big deal? If I trash my following, I can build a new one."

There was an earnestness in the publisher's voice that nearly reached Judtson.

"That isn't the point. It isn't the following. It isn't the money."

"Then what is it?"

A long pause met Judtson's query. It was as if Shugrew had been wrestling with a decision, when he finally cleared his throat and said, "Only that it is a serious mistake. You are running headlong toward a cliff, and I'm merely trying to divert you before it is too late."

Judtson felt certain that the words his publisher had spoken were not what he actually wanted to say. "I don't understand. What do you mean, I'm running off a cliff?"

Almost wistfully, Darrow answered, "I'm afraid there's nothing more to say."

"Then I guess there is no point in continuing this discussion. You have made your position crystal clear. And I believe I have, as well. Have a good day."

With another click of the mouse, the right rectangle vanished, and in the sudden silence, Judtson heard a noise from behind. Startled, he turned to see who or what had caused it. Yet he did not. His shoulders had not swiveled to the side. His head remained oriented as it had been, despite his wish to the contrary. His eyes still stared straight ahead at the monitor.

Chapter 5

Kᴇʟsᴇʏ ʙᴀᴛᴍᴀɴ ꜰᴇᴅ ᴛᴡᴇɴᴛʏ-ᴅᴏʟʟᴀʀ ʙɪʟʟs into the reader, one after another, watching the total balance due decrease with each insertion. As the sum moved into the negative, she stopped and waited. The singsong female voice programmed into the system instructed her to take her change from the cash slot, to remove the receipt from the printer, and to not forget her items.

"Are you going to tell me to look both ways before I cross the street and remember to wash my hands after going to the toilet?"

She scooped up her change, tore off the receipt, and grabbed her three bags of groceries. Leaving the cart in front of the self-service counter, she marched toward the exit. As she approached the white plastic columns positioned just inside the doors, a group of liberally pierced and tattooed teenaged girls loudly entered the store. At a glance, it seemed to Kelsey that all of the girls were on their phones, talking to people other than the friends who were with them. Or perhaps, she thought, they were so addicted to the devices that they were actually all talking to each other.

As she passed the shrill group, the red lights on top of the columns began to flash, accompanied by a discordant electronic chime and an authoritative prerecorded voice:

"Apparently, we neglected to remove a security device from one of your items. Please return to the nearest cashier immediately!"

"Buzz off!" she grumbled and continued to walk forward, as a male employee, wearing a red vest and pretending to be the greeter when he was, in fact, the loss-prevention person for the store, briskly stepped between her and the exit and said, "Excuse me. I'll need to check your bags."

Kelsey stopped and forced a smile. "Couple of things. First off, I was walking out as that gaggle of girls walked in. All of them were on cell phones. Most of them were carrying Coach purses they probably just shoplifted from the mall. But instead of considering that, you stopped me."

"Ma'am, I...."

Holding up a hand to stop him from speaking, she continued, "I know, I know. They were coming in and I was leaving. You'll have your chance at them on their way out. That's not the point. Second, what I would like is for you to call your manager over."

"Why would I need to do that?"

"Why would you need to do that? Because a customer – yes, that's right, I am a customer, not a suspect – a customer has requested the presence of the manager. Do you have an issue with that?"

The LP employee, plainly displaying his irritation with Kelsey for not acknowledging his authority, pulled a small cordless phone from his belt, pressed a button, and paged the manager. Finishing, he returned his attention to her. "Now, while we're waiting, I need to check your packages."

Maintaining the plastic smile, she retorted, "Actually, since I am showing no inclination to leave your store, you don't. We'll wait."

Moments later, a middle-aged, balding man, also wearing a red vest, approached. Before he could speak, the LP employee stepped toward him and, leaning close to his ear, whispered something. The store manager's face remained impassive as he heard the brief narrative from his staffer. Careful to maintain a friendly expression on his face, he turned to Kelsey. "My name is Randy Cranston. I'm the store manager. Is there something I can help you with?"

"Hi, I'm Kelsey," she said, reaching out to shake his hand. "How long have you been at this store, Mr. Cranston?"

"Almost five years."

Her forced smile broadening, she responded, "Five years! That's surprising."

The manager's professional friendliness slipped a bit. "How so?"

"Well, Mr. Cranston, this has been the most convenient store for me to use for the past thirteen years. For the great majority of that period, I have done basically all of my shopping here. In fact, I began shopping here at this store the day of its grand opening. I'm not one of those organized people who make lists and manage to buy everything they need in one trip a week. Actually, I'm so disorganized that I probably come here three, four, sometimes five times in a week, sometimes twice in a day. With this hair, I'm pretty distinctive. So, what surprises me, Mr. Cranston, is how a person can come in that often to a business establishment since the first day it opened, and spend plenty of money in it for that long, and the manager, who's been at the store for five of those years, doesn't even recognize her, much less know her by name."

"Miss…ahh, Kelsey, I apologize. I…."

She stopped him with a hasty wave of her hand. "That's not really the point, Mr. Cranston. It's just an interesting sidebar to the issue."

"I see. Your point, then?"

"My point is that life is a series of choices. We all make them every day, hundreds of them. What some people understand, down to the very core of their being, is that choices have consequences. You, Mr. Cranston, are now faced with a simple choice. Either you can instruct your security guy to examine the contents of my bags, or you can instruct him to thank me for shopping here and wish me a good day. But I thought that you should know, in advance, the consequences of your two choices. It's kind of a multi-step process. If you choose the former, I *will* cooperate. I will allow him to rummage through my items and compare them carefully to my receipt, making me feel like a common thief. At that point, there are two possible outcomes. One is that he will find that I have hidden in one of these bags, I don't know, a curling iron with a still-active RFID tag, an item not on my receipt. You'll call the cops, I'll be arrested for shoplifting, and you will have saved your employer the $9.38 cost of the curling iron. The other possibility is that he will check it all out and everything will be in order. I'll receive an insincere 'Sorry for the inconvenience,' and be allowed to leave."

Cranston listened patiently as she continued.

"If you do choose the former, Mr. Cranston, regardless of whether I leave here in handcuffs or bristling from the faux apology, you will have lost a good customer for the rest of my life. And not just from this store – from any store in your chain. The net result of this decision will be to cost your employer the profits from my purchases averaging more than $100 a week for the next forty years of my life. That's well over $200,000. If your profit margin, conservatively speaking, is only two percent, that is $4,000 net – quite a bit more than the $9.38 the fictitious curling iron cost.

"If, on the other hand, this guy" – she jerked her thumb in the direction of the LP employee – "*assumes* I am a good customer and an honest lady, thanks me for my patronage, and wishes me well, you have kept a customer. By the way, either decision is perfectly fine with me. So, what's your pleasure?"

Cranston took only a few seconds to mull over her words, the formerly counterfeit smile gradually replaced with one substantially more real. He turned to the employee, who had been audibly sighing and rolling his eyes through Kelsey's comments. "Joe, I suggest that you express to our longtime customer your appreciation for her continued business and wish her an excellent day."

Joe stared at his boss intently, the muscles in his jaw visibly flexing.

"Joe, our customer is waiting. As am I."

Turning to face her, and through gritted teeth, he muttered, "Thank you for your business, ma'am. Have a good day."

Smiling broadly, she answered, "Why, thank you, Joe. And, Mr. Cranston, it was a pleasure to finally make your acquaintance."

She whirled and stepped through the automatic doors, leaving the two behind. Crossing the parking lot swiftly, while softly whistling a formless melody, she arrived at her yellow Hummer, keyed the alarm which unlocked the doors, and climbed in quickly.

Her radio, tuned as always on a news/talk station, filled the cabin with the agitated voices of a panel arguing the pros and cons of the newest in a string of executive orders from the White House, this one granting substantially broader powers to the Department of Homeland Security.

With her curiosity piqued and the incident at the supermarket forgotten, Kelsey turned up the volume as one of the guests, Samuel Beckleman, a longtime bureaucrat and the current Secretary of Homeland Security, was defending the order: "Our country is currently facing many threats, not all of them from outside our borders...."

"Isn't that the truth!" Kelsey commented sarcastically.

The man continued, "If we are going to be able to ensure the safety of our citizens, it is critical for law enforcement to have the tools it needs. This newest weapon in our arsenal can make a profound difference. Now that we have the unfettered ability to receive a broader search warrant from the courts, obtained by using a more reasonable definition of probable cause, domestic terrorists in the midst of stockpiling assault rifles, explosives, or chemical weapons for use against us can be interdicted before they commit the crime."

"WHAT? ARE YOU KIDDING ME?" screamed Kelsey, so furious at what she was hearing she almost did not notice the bicyclist driving well outside his lane. She swerved at the last possible second and laid on the horn. The blast of sound startled the rider, causing him to overcompensate and ram his slender, fragile front wheel into the curb.

As she drove by, Kelsey twisted in her seat and flipped him off, yelling, "Stay in your lane, moron!"

The bicyclist jumped free of his vehicle and angrily scooped up a handful of rocks, throwing them at the receding rear of the Hummer.

▽

What's going on? Turn, dammit. TURN! This is like that trigger finger thing. I knew it. There is something wrong with me. Somebody is behind me. I know it. And I can't look to see who the hell it is! TURN! LOOK! NOW! Oh, wait, here we go. My eyes are leaving the screen, and my head is rotating! Oh, for Pete's sake, I'm finally turning around.

"Judtson, what's wrong?" It was Kristen, standing in the doorway behind him, wearing her white nightgown, her shoulder-length blond hair tousled from sleep. "You look…you look freaked out or something."

Judtson stared at her, his eyes stretched wide, his breathing ragged. Despite the panic and anxiety he felt at the moment, he was still able to take in and analyze his wife's face, her expression. He was able to distinguish the absence of any concern whatsoever. Only curiosity displayed as she took in what must have been a truly bizarre sight, for he was certain that he surely resembled someone who only moments before had transformed back to his human form after a long night of prowling and howling in his wolfman alter ego.

Rather than rushing to his side to hold and comfort him, she remained where she was, further illustrating and reinforcing her uncaring attitude. "I said, what's wrong?"

Gradually calming his frenzied breathing, Judtson fought down the residual panic triggered by the lack of responsiveness of his body, and was able to respond. "Just a very frustrating conversation with Mitch and Darrow. I guess I somewhat lost it."

Her eyes bored into his. "I heard the tail end of it. What was that about releasing your next book for free?"

Ignoring the syntax of her question and not wanting to once again point out that the word *free* should never be preceded by the word *for*, he answered, "Yep. That's the plan."

"Why on Earth would you want to do that?"

"Because Darrow made it clear he won't release it. And, contractually, I can't sell it to anyone else. It's the only option remaining."

She sighed, her frustration apparent. "Why can't you drop this whole ridiculous thing?"

With a shake of his head, fleetingly grateful for the fact that he was able to effectuate the movement, Judtson replied, "Not going to happen. You know that. We've been down this path a thousand times already."

Kristen's mouth twisted into an expression of disgust and, without another comment, she abruptly turned and walked away.

Switching off the computer and toeing the power strip off, Judtson left the library. Thankfully, Kristen had not returned to their bedroom and he was able to hastily dress without further discussion, going through the motions absentmindedly, preoccupied to the point of obsession with the latest fracture in the linkage between his mind and his body.

He slipped out the front door of their home, snatching his mirrored sunglasses on his way out and feeling relieved not to have encountered Kristen during his departure. Although still early in the day, the desert seemed to amplify and rebroadcast the sun's radiant heat back upward, so as Judtson walked, he felt as if he were a slice of bread between two glowing heat strips in a toaster. He traversed the one-hundred-yard distance briskly, wary of rattlesnakes, who would just be ending their day and returning to cooler shelters. The terrain abruptly changed from native to pseudo-native as he neared the adjacent home. The tan, hard-packed soil and randomly sized and scattered chunks of granite which littered the surface, detritus from age-old fracturing and revealed by tempestuous monsoonal rains, were replaced with homogenized, unicolored, and uniformly sized stones imported from the old quarry at Dragoon. The expanse was artfully broken up by saguaros, barrel cacti, ocotillos, creosotes, palo verdes, and mesquites, deliberately positioned to appear as though they were naturally occurring.

It took two rings of the doorbell until Saylor swung open the hand-carved, imported Mexican door. Before he could say a word, Judtson blurted, "It happened again!"

▽

The ceramic plate made a loud clunk on the glass tabletop as Doni left an assortment of bagels and veggie cream cheese for the two of them, returning in a moment to drop off two cups of coffee.

"I'd love to stay here and chat with both of you, but I've got plenty to do and I appear to be on my own this morning."

"Thanks, babe," Saylor said with an affectionate grin, ignoring his wife's playful sarcasm.

"I'm sorry, Doni. I didn't mean to barge in like this. I...."

She paused to gently place her hand on Judtson's. "I'm teasing, Squirrel. You seem pretty frazzled. Talk to the boss. I'll catch up on the melodrama later."

Judtson smiled at her. "Thanks."

She turned back to Saylor. "Don't forget, we have a date night." She kissed him lightly on the top of his head and went back inside, leaving the two men alone on the patio.

The contrast between Saylor's life and his own was stark, as Judtson noted with envy the obvious level of affection and respect the two had for each other.

"You are so lucky."

Saylor, who had been watching the retreat of his wife into the house, turned back toward his best friend. "Don't start that again. It makes me feel crummy."

"Why? It's true."

The corner of Saylor's mouth curled up sardonically. "We both know how crappy things are with you and Kristen. Sometimes I feel as though I'm eating a feast in front of a starving man. It's uncomfortable."

"Gee, I'm sorry I'm making *you* uncomfortable. It must be an irritating distraction from your otherwise idyllic existence."

"You want to drink that coffee or wear it?"

Finally forcing a weak smile, Judtson picked up a garlic bagel and began smearing it with veggie spread.

"So what happened this morning?"

As Judtson finished his bagel prep, he briefed Saylor on the conversation with Mitch and Darrow. Anger instantly spread across his friend's face when he described the final moments of the conference.

"After all the money you've made for Shugrew...hell, for both of them. I can't believe they would just cut you off like this."

"To be honest, I was surprised, too."

"It doesn't make sense. Whether you stick with the old formula or do this new thing, people are going to buy your books."

"That's what I thought. They were acting as if I were their golden goose and about to commit *hara-kiri*."

With a shrug, Saylor said, "That's not why you came dashing over here. You said *it* happened again. What happened?"

Resisting the urge to rebut the use of the word *dashing*, Judtson went on to describe his inability to turn around to face Kristen.

"I know I'm probably exaggerating. I'm sure I am. But it felt as though I couldn't turn around for three or four minutes."

"Right. I'm certain your perceptions were a bit skewed at that point. It was more than likely only a few seconds."

"I know. Even so, what in the hell could be causing this? It has happened twice now in as many days."

Judtson looked down and realized that he was still holding the bagel, unbitten, and had been throughout the entire recapping of the events this morning. For a brief moment, this fact began to panic him, until he recognized the utter normalcy of it and took a bite.

"The two incidents have a common factor. Last night you were smack-dab in the middle of breaking the law. This morning you were torpedoed by your publisher and betrayed by your agent. In both of them, you were under stress – a lot of it. In both situations, your adrenaline was through the roof. And all of this is exacerbated by the, uh, tense situation between you and Kristen."

"I've been under stress a number of times in my life. Nothing like this has ever happened."

"I know. I understand, and I don't have any clinical reason to hang my hat on when I suggest that stress is causing this. You do have a tendency, pal, to come up with maladies no one in my profession has heard of before. Stress, and all of the attendant chemicals it triggers in your body, can have some very poorly understood consequences. It seems to be a likely culprit, especially since it is a common element in both events. Does that make any sense?"

"I guess so. I don't know."

Saylor studied his friend's face and his body language. He had no doubt that Judtson was worried, deeply so. And although his friend had a history of obsessing on hundreds of imagined ailments over the years, this situation, this case, as he was beginning to view it, felt different.

"Look, I'm shooting in the dark here. Let me do a little research when I go to the office today. Let me see if I can find any similar cases in the literature."

His words had the desired impact. Judtson's eyes brightened slightly. His posture stiffened a bit.

"That would be great. Thanks."

Saylor shrugged. "No big deal. If there is some new, weird physiological phenomenon cropping up, I ought to know about it, anyway."

"I know this is a dumb question, since you have no idea why I'm occasionally disconnecting from my body, but is there anything you think I should be doing?"

With a smile, Saylor responded, "Chill out. Get calm. Stay calm. Try some yoga, maybe meditation. You need to lower the stress levels. As a matter of fact, there is something we can check which might tell us if we are on the right track."

"What?"

"Swing by the office today. We'll take some blood and send it to the lab. If you are having over-the-top stress issues, it should show up in your cortisol levels."

"Cortisol?"

"That's the chemical the body produces to modulate stress. It is relatively slow to dissipate. People who are in extremely stressful jobs for long periods, like soldiers or air traffic controllers, will occasionally have levels off the charts. It will definitely give us a feel for the severity of the problem."

"Okay. I can come by later this morning."

The spoken course of action had the desired effect. Saylor could see his friend visibly relaxing with the knowledge that something was being done.

$$\nabla$$

Pulling the bright red '68 Oldsmobile 4-4-2 convertible into the driveway of his office building, a sixty-year-old house on Pima that Judtson had converted, he reached up to punch the button on the garage door opener, paused, and changed his mind. He was not planning on staying long enough to need the shelter from the merciless sun, so he parked beside the intensely yellow Smart car. The diminutive mode of transportation was yet another manifestation of the quirkiness of his only employee.

The irony in his parking lot was not lost on Judtson: his gas-guzzling Detroit iron, with cylinders large enough to accommodate a man's fist, juxtaposed with the energy-efficient, environmentally friendly, rolling office chair driven by his assistant. The building itself was unmarked other than the street number. The exigencies of Judtson's fame dictated that the facade display no signage or any other indication that he officed here. He quickly covered the few paces from the driveway to the front door, rushing to enter the air conditioning.

What had once been the living room of the old ranch-style house was now an open, multipurpose work space. Predominantly a reception area, it also served as the mail room, copy room, and work station for Judtson's office mate.

"Morning, boss."

"Good morning. Ricky, I have to ask, how can you live with yourself?"

After six years, accustomed to his boss's idiosyncracies and sense of humor, the young, blond, and almost painfully slender assistant rolled his eyes and asked, "Why is that, Judtson?"

"Well, get real…your extravagance, your willful disregard for the planet."

Ricky did not respond, patiently smiling and waiting.

"I mean, you must have burned two or three thimbles-full of fossil fuel coming to work today. It's just disgraceful. Don't you care what you're doing to the environment?"

Pursing his lips for a moment, biting back the first three sarcastic comebacks which popped into his mind, Ricky finally said, "You're right, sir. I probably should donate my car to a worthy charity and start walking to work."

Deadpan, Judtson snapped back, "Don't be ridiculous. Walking in Tucson! You'll get a melanoma. No, ride a bike. That's the ticket."

With a slight grin, Ricky played along. "A bike. I hadn't thought of that."

"Well, you should. Besides, I think you'd look great in spandex. Think about it. Your slender, muscular buttocks flexing back and forth over the tiny little seat of the ten-speed, right at eye level for all of the passing ecologically insensitive drivers to see."

Unable to choke back a snort, Ricky asked, "Have I fulfilled my subordinate's obligation and humored you long enough yet? If so, I have some actual work-related items to bring to your attention."

Judtson walked to the front edge of Ricky's desk. "Yes. Your performance this morning was barely adequate but singularly unsatisfying. I guess we can move on now. What do you have?"

They spent the next few minutes going over requests for interviews, book signings, and other appearances. Judtson did not need to prioritize them for his assistant, as Ricky had been a quick learner and knew his boss's preferences.

"Voice mail awaits you on your computer, as do your culled and flagged emails. Your snail mail is on your desk. I didn't know what time you were coming in today, so I shut off your computer."

"Thanks."

As Judtson turned to enter his office, Ricky's voice stopped him. "There is one thing on the pile I wanted to mention."

"What's that?"

"The padded manila envelope on top. The one with 'Personal and Confidential' scrawled all over it on both sides."

"Yes?"

"It wasn't in the PO Box. It was leaning against our front door this morning."

There was a subtle undercurrent of concern in Ricky's voice, a reaction Judtson did not share. Although their building was anonymous, it was not all that difficult to determine property ownership in this privacy-stripping age of the Internet.

"I'm sure it's only another manuscript some local author wants me to read."

Ricky shook his head a bit too emphatically. "Too small. Not bulky enough."

"Doesn't matter. Instead of paper, it's a disc, flash drive, whatever."

"I guess. I just don't like anyone knowing we're here."

Judtson laughed, trying to lessen his assistant's tension level. "You've been watching too many fan-stalker movies on Lifetime."

"It's true! I have," he agreed emphatically. "And you know what I've noticed in every single one of them?"

"No, but I'm sure you're about to tell me."

"That the hardworking and loyal assistant is always killed by the obsessed fan in the first fifteen minutes of the movie."

Judtson turned back toward his office and gibed over his shoulder, "In that case, you're definitely safe."

Right as he passed through his doorway, a wadded piece of paper bounced off Judtson's back. Chuckling to himself, he turned on his computer and, while waiting for it to boot up, glanced at the foot-high stack of mail from today, pinned beneath a lead sphere which had been sent to Judtson years ago. The sender had included a message that the ball of lead was "proof" that the Earth had been created as a result of the planet Tiamet fracturing due to the passage of Nibiru through our orbit. Judtson had decided at the time that it would make an excellent paperweight. As Ricky said, the manila envelope rested atop the pile. No address was written, only Judtson's name. There was also no return address. He noted that Ricky's description of the "Personal and Confidential" notation being *scrawled all over* the envelope was a bit florid, as it was only written once on the face in rather small print and down at the lower right-hand corner. Picking it up and turning it over, he saw that the same note appeared only once on the back, as well.

As the envelope came lined with plastic bubble wrapping, he could not determine the contents by feel and was about the open it, when his cell phone suddenly played a snippet from the theme song of *The Avengers*, the ringtone he had selected for incoming text messages from Saylor. The message on the small screen was brief: "check your emails now."

His computer had finished its sequence. A click on Outlook opened incoming emails. Judtson selected the private account, known only to a few people, and Saylor's was at the top of the short list. The message had a single line of text, "You'd better check this out," and a link, which he clicked.

The link took him instantly to YouTube, where he found a video box with the heading "Paintball Heroes." Feeling an involuntary tightening in his abdomen, he selected the play button and watched as his and Saylor's adventure from the previous night was jerkily enacted on the screen. This was obviously the video shot by the woman in the yellow Hummer, and he stared at it raptly.

The picture quality was surprisingly good, considering that she shot the sequence at night and through her windshield. He was impressed with her ability to keep the white Camry in the frame as she followed them through the intersection and through the U-turn. The sound track was sprinkled with an occasional "Oh, wow!" or "This is so cool!" and each paintball assault was punctuated with a very adolescent-sounding giggle.

Judtson leaned forward to stare closely at the screen, watching himself as he was captured in the picture leaning out the passenger window while they passed in front of her and approached the final target, and hoping that there would be some clue in the video explaining why he was unable to pull the trigger. There was, of course, nothing helpful, and he leaned back after watching the late-firing marker almost completely miss the target with its volley.

The video showed them driving away, and Judtson expected the clip to end. To his surprise, the woman executed an illegal right turn from the far left lane and followed them, continuing to chronicle their getaway. His mind replayed the anxious discussion between himself and Saylor, which he remembered vividly as happening right then, recalling that he had asked Saylor to pull over so they could talk, followed by Saylor's refusal and insistence that they get back to Judtson's house and out of sight.

He suddenly bolted straight up in his chair, his eyes glued to the gently bouncing image of the white Camry driving north on Craycroft, knowing that at any moment the opaque screen over the license plate was about to become clear, switched off by Saylor. He could not remember the exact moment, but knew that it had been turned off before they reached Speedway. Seconds ticked by. The Camry was registered to Judtson. Even if the video was too blurry for the YouTube viewers to read, the police would enhance the image and discern the letters and numbers.

He felt beads of perspiration popping up on his scalp and neck as he watched the video. The Camry drove through Fifth Street and continued its journey north. In the distance, the traffic signal for Speedway was visible in the frame, and when he was certain that their denouement was at hand, the image froze for a second before the playbox was filled with suggested related videos.

A loud exhalation of relief burst from Judtson, and he realized he had been holding his breath for the past twenty to thirty seconds. Twisting in his desk chair, he punched a button on the phone and speed-dialed Saylor's office, knowing that his friend's cell phone would be turned off during office hours.

The overly perky voice of the receptionist, Melanie, burst loudly out of the speaker. "It's a *great* morning at Desert Neurology. May I help you?"

"Melanie, Judtson. Is Saylor with a patient?"

"Oh, *hello*, Judtson! Dr. Costello told me you'd be calling. Yes, he is. Do you want me to interrupt him?"

"No," Judtson replied, refraining from asking Melanie why he was "Judtson" but Saylor was "Dr. Costello." "That won't be necessary. Just have him call me when he's free."

"Absolutely! I will let him know the *minute* he's out!"

Momentarily distracted by a mental image of Melanie maintaining the same effusive personality in her personal life, and then deciding that this could not possibly be the case or by now he would have read about her being bludgeoned by her husband or even an appliance repairman, Judtson responded, "Thank you, Melanie. And you have a *great* day!"

"Oh, thank *you*, Judtson. And you have an *even greater* day!"

He could not break the connection quickly enough, yet continued to stare blankly at the telephone on his desk for a full minute, concluding that even the briefest interaction with Melanie had the same effect on his mind that pulling up the film on an Etch A Sketch had on the drawing.

Consciously rebuilding his morning and finally remembering what he planned to do next, he turned back to the monitor and re-queued the video. He saw that the screen name of the person who posted it was "anarchy_groupie." Just as he selected the option to play it in full-screen mode, he noticed that it already had more than three million hits.

This time it no longer held his interest. He returned his attention to the stack of mail, again picking up the mysterious manila envelope, rapidly tearing it open, and dumping out the contents on his desk. There was a single sheet of paper and a SIM card. The handwriting on the note inside was the same as on the envelope. The message was short and unsigned:

"You guys are awesome. And don't worry – your secret's safe with me. Here is the SIM card from my phone with the original video. I only kept the 'edited' version."

His direct line rang. Judtson checked the caller ID and picked up the handset rather than using the speakerphone.

"I saw it."

Saylor's voice was subdued. Obviously, he did not want to be overheard as he said, "That thing is all over the 'net."

"Yeah, it has already had three million hits."

"Check it again. It's approaching four."

Judtson tapped the F5 key on his keyboard and the screen refreshed. "Good God! How did you find out about it?"

"Facebook. A bunch of my friends have posted it on their pages, and now everyone is re-posting it. We're stars, man."

Judtson snorted. "Anonymous stars."

"Well, yeah. Isn't this what you wanted?"

"I did. I do. But it was a close call. If that video had been shot by an unfriendly sort, we'd have been busted."

"Oh, I know. I damn near wet my scrubs this morning waiting for our license plate to pop up at the end of the video. It stops seconds before I turned off the opaque cover."

"Speaking of which…." Judtson went on to tell his friend about the manila envelope Ricky found leaning against his office door, and its contents.

After he finished his recap with a reading of the note, Saylor whistled. "So she knows who you are?"

"No kidding."

"No, I'm amazed." Saylor sounded almost breathless. "That's fast. Think about it. We did that last night. She got the license plate number and was able to run it down until she found out it was yours, posted an edited video on YouTube, and dropped off the envelope at your office, all before Ricky got there."

"True. And my office address doesn't come up in any normal directories. She also would have had to do a property search on Pima County Maps to find it."

"Some smart gal."

"A smart gal with connections. The only people who can turn a license plate into a name are law enforcement."

"Well, look at the bright side. At least the note wasn't a blackmail demand."

Judtson laughed. "I hadn't thought about that: 'Give me twenty grand or I'll turn the full video over to the cops.'"

"I think she likes you." There was a teasing tone to Saylor's voice.

"Right."

"No, really! She's probably a fan."

"Maybe," Judtson conceded reluctantly.

Saylor changed the subject. "Hey, when are you coming by?"

Judtson eyed the stack of mail, opened his phone slips on the computer, and looked at the total. There were more than fifty messages. Finally, he checked Outlook for incoming emails on his private business-related address, finding at least eighty which might or might not require his immediate attention.

"I'll be right there."

Chapter 6

CIRCLING THE LOT THREE TIMES IN SEARCH OF SOME SHADE where he could park his car, Judtson was finally able to pull into a just vacated space beneath the boughs of a large sycamore, a tree foreign to the desert because of its broad water-aspirating leaves. He hastily crossed the asphalt and entered the lobby of the four-story office building, his mind reanalyzing the morning's events. Sliding his sunglasses up to perch on the top of his head, he reached the elevator and pushed the call button.

▽

The distinctive red convertible, entering the parking lot below, caught Saylor's eye as he sat at his desk, dictating notes for a patient's chart.

▽

Wondering about the mysterious video chronicler from the night before and whether the two of them would ever meet, Judtson realized the elevator had not yet arrived.

He saw that the floor indicator for the car was on the number one, the lobby, but the doors had not opened. Perplexed, he realized that the call button was not lit. The now familiar sensations of incipient panic rattled him as he tried to remember whether his arm had risen, whether his finger had actually touched the button. He was not sure.

A harsh grunt of frustration burst from Judtson as he reached up to punch the button, or at least had set into motion what he believed to be the appropriate thoughts to initiate the action. Yet his right arm dangled unresponsively at his side. With his breathing suddenly accelerating and sweat prickling from all over his body, Judtson could feel a full-blown anxiety attack triggering within him.

Button! Arm! Hand! Come on. Get up and punch the button!

As he internally shouted at his oblivious appendage, he knew that this was not the normal method of directing his body's actions, but realized that he had no idea what the actual mechanism was. Desperately struggling to calm himself, Judtson shifted his mental attention to his left arm and hand, willing them to carry out the task deemed distasteful by the opposing extremity. This other arm was equally insubordinate, obviously having decided to join in the mutiny against him.

What's happening to me? What is going wrong? I'm becoming unwired. Rotten connections between my brain and the rest of me. What am I going to do? I can't just stand here. Well, I guess I can since that's what I'm doing. I can't call anyone. Why am I still staring at the elevator button? I want to be looking at my left arm. Now my eyes won't even move! Oh, my God, no. Help me, please.

Through the fog of his roiling terror, at the fringe of his peripheral vision, Judtson saw the elevator doors open.

They're opening! Maybe I did actually press the button. Yes, that's it. Maybe I did. Maybe I'm just going crazy. That would be better than this. Whatever this is.

"Judtson?"
Recognizing Saylor's voice, he tried to turn. Tried to speak. Nothing.

My voice isn't working, either! I can't speak!

"JUDTSON!" He heard his name shouted into his ear, grateful his hearing remained functional. The vague image moved beyond the outermost boundary of his viewing area, and he felt a firm, almost insistent grip on his shoulder. His name was being repeated and repeated again, each iteration more urgent than the last. He felt a second hand on his other shoulder.

Saylor was mortified by what he saw. His best friend was before him, standing rigidly and facing the blank wall beside the elevator doors. Judtson's face was an intense, worrisome red, his breathing shallow and rapid, his shirt soaked with perspiration.

Firmly grasping both shoulders, Saylor torqued his friend's body around toward his. He expected Judtson to move his feet in an acquiescence to the pressure, to participate in the process and shuffle around to face him. Instead, the two feet remained planted, and Saylor's efforts were only rewarded with a corkscrewing of Judtson's body.

Barking out Judtson's name over and over, Saylor had twisted him around to the point where he could see his face full on. His eyes met Judtson's blue eyes which had been so familiar to him since the two men were children. What he saw caused him to become irrationally terrified. In the midst of a countenance completely engulfed by panic, anxiety, and fear, the eyes, still fixed in the downward cast formerly oriented to view the call button, were calm, serene, steady…and completely foreign. The horrifying incongruity, between what was the rest of his friend and these windows to his soul, caused Saylor to involuntarily jerk his hands away from Judtson's shoulders. The sudden release allowed the muscles, still calibrated for an orientation toward the wall, to swivel the torso back to its former position, as would a rubber mannequin which had been unnaturally twisted by pranksters.

"Oh, my God." None of his years of training and study had prepared Saylor for what he was seeing.

Saylor, help me! Please help me! Do something!

Forcing a deep breath and consciously summoning the discipline inculcated within him by years of experience in the ER, Saylor pulled out his cell phone and speed-dialed his office, noticing without acknowledging that his hand was shaking badly.

He cut off Melanie's greeting, shouting, "We have an emergency. I need Liz down in the lobby with my bag. Call 9-1-1 for an ambulance and paramedics. Urgent! Melanie, repeat my instructions."

She did, accurately, with all traces of the bubbly effusiveness completely vanished from her voice. He flipped the phone closed and moved to interpose himself between Judtson and the wall. The eyes were locked in the same spooky orientation but, for the moment, they were not Saylor's main concern. His mind ticked off the possible ramifications of what he was observing: hyperventilation, the initial stages of shock, the possibility that a heart attack could occur at any moment. Without his BP cuff, he had no idea how elevated the vital readings would be. As he seized Judtson's left wrist, his finger sought and found the artery almost immediately. He checked the second hand on his watch and began counting the pulse, the rapid beats making it difficult to keep up. Giving it a full thirty seconds, he doubled the count and was stunned that the number was nearly 200 beats per minute.

Across the lobby from where he stood, the steel door to the stairwell flew open, crashing loudly against the masonry wall, and his nurse, Liz Genz, rushed out. He was relieved to see that she had dashed down the three flights of stairs rather than waiting for the elevator.

"What do we have?" she asked breathlessly, pulling open the old-fashioned doctor's bag, gasping when she recognized the patient. "Oh, my God, it's Judtson."

"I have no idea. First, let's get him down on the floor. Then, check vitals."

She nodded and Saylor, sandwiched between Judtson and the wall, slid against the rough brick face, moving to the opposite side of his friend; and the two of them, supporting Judtson's torso and neck, tilted him back. Fleetingly, Saylor's mind visualized a wooden figure being removed from the window of a cigar store. He shifted one of his hands to cradle the back of Judtson's head, just before bringing it to rest on the floor. The surreal juxtaposition of the static body and the visible manifestations of a full-blown panic attack bewildered him as he snatched the penlight from his bag and flashed the pupils. Their dilation response was perfectly normal. Liz already had the cuff on Judtson's arm, her stethoscope earpieces in place, and was pumping the rubber ball, inflating the cuff.

"Is he having a seizure?"

"I don't think so. I don't know. Dammit, I don't know!"

Despite not having the benefit of hearing the arterial reaction to the diminishing pressure as it transitioned through the systolic to the diastolic via the stethoscope, Saylor stared at the gauge, hoping to deduce a reading. With a quiet hiss, the remaining air in the cuff was released, and Liz looked up. "Pressure is 192 over 120."

"Not good at all." The high readings elevated his level of concern. "Liz, check his pockets for receipts. We need to find out where he might have stopped for a meal. This could be caused by something he ingested."

She began digging through Judtson's pockets immediately.

The familiar pattern of checking Judtson over had a composing effect on Saylor. The shrill wail of a siren penetrated into the lobby and reached his ears. He hoped it was the ambulance.

Kneeling beside his friend, Saylor leaned forward and positioned his face directly in the line of sight of the oddly fixed eyes. "Judtson, I don't know if you can hear me. If this is…if this is what we talked about this morning, then you are in there. I know you are. And you're panicking, freaking out. I don't blame you, but you need to listen to me. Please. Whatever is going on with you, we'll find it. We'll fix it. I promise. For now, if you don't calm down, if you don't get your anxiety under control, you are gonna stroke out, buddy. You are going to burst a blood vessel in your brain. You're going to have a heart attack. Something bad. Something I might not be able to fix is going to happen. You need to help me. You need to help me right now…and then, I promise, I will help you. I *will* figure this thing out."

There was no outward indication of understanding or acknowledgment in Judtson's eyes. They might as well have been perfect glass reproductions. However, after he spoke, Saylor detected a subtle reduction in the rate of Judtson's breathing. The ragged panting from his open mouth ameliorated ever so slightly and continued to diminish, followed by a slight and yet discernible decrease in the intense reddish hue of his complexion.

Saylor was about to ask Liz to recheck blood pressure, when he saw that she had anticipated this and was again rapidly inflating the cuff wrapped around Judtson's arm. Saylor stroked the side of his friend's face. "That's it, pal. Bring it all down. Calm down. You're doing it. You are still in control."

"It's 170 over 105."

Saylor allowed himself to relax slightly. The main problem, the bizarre phenomenon from which Judtson was suffering, remained a mystery, an enigma. In any case, it appeared that the immediate crisis was lessening.

As he watched over his friend, he noticed that a fly landed on Judtson's rubicund and perspiring temple. Instinctively, Saylor started to brush it away and suddenly stopped himself, watching with clinical curiosity as the insect scurried up the temple to the crease adjacent to Judtson's eyelid, pausing only a moment before scampering across the surface of the eyeball itself, and coming to a stop directly on the pupil.

Hearing a gasp from Liz as she was, no doubt, observing the same thing, Saylor detected absolutely no attempt on Judtson's part to react to these invasive stimuli. The eyelids did not reflexively jerk closed. The eye did not even move within its socket. This small, extemporaneous experiment spoke volumes to Saylor, as he heard the lobby doors opening and the rattle and bustle of the paramedics arriving with their equipment.

▽

"I don't understand, Saylor. What happened?"

Saylor and Kristen stood together in the hallway outside Judtson's room at St. Joseph's Hospital, both facing the glass separating them from the now sleeping figure.

It was the nature of Saylor's chosen field of neurology that he all too frequently had the dreadful task of informing spouses, parents, children, and other loved ones about life-altering or, in many cases, life-ending conditions. For better or for worse, a certain skill level was acquired. What he had discovered years earlier was that this was frequently a moment of unintended revelation for the family members. A former patient, a homicide detective, had told him years ago that figuring out which suspect was the perpetrator was the easy part of his job. When Saylor asked why, he explained that the average person who suddenly became a killer had absolutely no experience with talking to a detective in that situation. After years of investigating murders and questioning hundreds of people, both guilty and innocent, seasoned detectives gradually developed a profile of each in their minds. Having never been an innocent suspect before, the guilty ones needed to consciously construct what an "innocent" person would say. Consequently, everything about them was a little off. When innocent people were first confronted with the news of the murder and then later questioned about their involvement, their reactions were fluid, natural, and real. According to the detective, the perpetrators' mode of consciously reacting almost always stuck out like a sore thumb.

The initial determination was certainly not foolproof, the detective explained. There were pathological liars who could appear quite natural and real in their interviews, probably because they were capable of believing they had not committed the crime, and therefore could allow themselves to respond automatically. There were also some who were at the mercy of their own thoughts. They might have hated the victim. They might have, in fact, wished the victim dead, even plotted it in their minds. And despite the fact that they had never acted upon these daydreams, they experienced a nearly overwhelming guilt for what they had felt and thought. That guilt caused them not to trust their natural reactions during an interrogation. But other than the complications caused by those two particular groups, the rest of the time the evaluation was quite dependable.

As his field was primarily a specialty of the mind, Saylor was fascinated with this insight and immediately noticed a parallel in his practice. Although not as rare as participating in an interrogation, the discussion of dreadful medical news about loved ones also had the elements of repetition and familiarity on the part of the doctor, and either substantial or complete inexperience at receiving this sort of news on the part of the family members. The spouses, parents, or children who wholeheartedly loved the patient were predictable in their reactions. The flow of emotion – panic, anger, fear and, eventually, curiosity and resolve – was a pattern he had seen hundreds of times and recognized instantly.

The other group, those who did not care or those who might actually despise the patient, recognized that they were in a situation where society had expectations of them, and therefore instantly took conscious control of their reactions. Again, because it was a foreign situation for most, they had to wing it, make it up as they went along. Saylor had learned that the homicide detective was right; the consciously controlled responses were almost painfully obvious. Judtson's wife, Kristen, fell into this latter category.

"I don't yet, Kristen. I'm sorry."

"Is he in some kind of a coma?"

"That's a possibility. We need to run a few tests first before I can narrow anything down or rule anything out."

He watched her as she stared through the glass at her husband. The word which popped into his mind to best describe her expression was *impassive*.

"There wasn't any warning of this, was there?"

As she asked the question, she turned to Saylor. Her eyes seemed to bore into him, making him feel slightly uncomfortable. Without consciously going through any sort of decision process, he opted to lie. "No. Nothing he mentioned to me prior to the incident."

Her stare lingered, and he was certain he detected a flicker of disbelief before she turned back to look at Judtson's unconscious figure. "What tests are you planning?" Her voice was flat, emotionless.

"As of now, MRI, CT scan, EEG, EMG, full blood work-up. I haven't decided what other tests are appropriate yet. I'm going to be consulting with a couple of other specialists later today to get their input."

"What's an EMG?"

"An electromyogram. It's used to detect abnormal electrical activity of muscles, such as might pop up in conditions like muscular dystrophy, peripheral nerve damage, Lou Gehrig's, myasthenia gravis, and others."

"Is he okay now?"

Her question struck him as a non sequitur. "Considering that he is in a totally dissociative state and heavily sedated, yeah, he's great." He instantly regretted the tone of his answer.

She turned to face him, her brow furrowed. "Saylor, I didn't mean it like that. I'm just…I'm not thinking all that clearly."

Forcing a grin, he reassured her. "It's all right. I didn't intend to sound harsh or abrupt. It has been a rough day for me, too."

She leaned toward him and kissed him lightly on the cheek. "I know. I know how much he means to you. And I'm sure you are going to do everything you can."

Saylor only nodded, saying nothing.

Taking his hand, she said, "You'll let me know if…?"

"Of course."

"Thank you, Saylor."

She turned and walked away. He could not help but think that any other wife would have stayed, insisting upon accommodations within her husband's room.

▽

Saylor stood beside the hospital bed, where he had stayed except for brief departures to tend to urgent issues. He was looking down at his friend of almost thirty years, relieved that the sedative he had ordered upon their arrival in the ER had worked. His apparent motive to the paramedics who had rolled Judtson in, as well as for the benefit of the attending physician and nurses, was to stabilize the patient…to further bring down the respiration rate, pulse, blood pressure, and all of the other outward signs of hyperanxiety. His unspoken, secret, and desperate need was to see if the powerful dose had any effect on those eyes.

He was unable to think of them as Judtson's. He knew Judtson's eyes better than he knew anyone's, even Doni's. And those two blue orbs belonged to someone else, someone he had never met before, someone he did not care to know. His fear, as he watched the RN perform the injection, was that those eyes – which had remained open, static, and eerily calm throughout the process of shifting Judtson to the gurney and into the ambulance, and throughout the short, frenzied trip to St. Joseph's – would simply continue to stare, to persist in maintaining the slightly downcast, disimpassioned gaze.

During transport, he had even brushed Judtson's eyelids down with the edge of his hand, partially to test the reaction but mostly to block them from his view. The lids instantly sprang open, back to their former state, in much the same way that Judtson had swiveled back to face the elevator button when Saylor released the grip on his shoulders. This small, normally insignificant reaction of the muscles and nerves irrationally frightened Saylor, so he felt a flood of relief when the injected single milligram of lorazepam quickly took hold, and the contrarious eyelids began to droop, finally closing completely.

The last thing I remember being able to see is the ceiling of the emergency room – the hanging examination light, the curtain tracks, the acoustic tiles, the flush-mounted speakers spaced evenly throughout my line of sight. Those were the items dominating the fixed boundaries of my vision. There was an occasional face of a stranger, obviously a nurse, who would fleetingly enter the frame. And yet, not once did I see Saylor. I knew he was right there with me, because I could hear his voice giving orders to the people around me, though he never made an on-screen appearance. Wow. That's really what it was like, like watching a movie.

I could only see what the director wanted me to see, not what I wished to look at.

Right now, for example, I can only see a dark, slightly reddish nothingness. Maybe I'm dead. No, that's stupid. I can hear noises. Voices in the background. The whoosh of the air conditioning. Other miscellaneous clunks and clatters of activity.

Am I in a darkened room? Could be, I guess. But that doesn't make any sense. I know I went to the hospital. I watched the whole thing. I should still be there. It sounds as though I am. And hospital rooms are never dark, not this dark. Doctors, nurses, they all need to see when they come in to check on you. I bet I know. My eyes are closed. Oh, crap! My eyes are closed! And I don't know if I can order them to open anymore!

Saylor heard the steady *beep-beep-beep* of the pulse monitor abruptly step up in frequency. He leaned over his friend and gently placed his hand on the side of Judtson's face.

"Judtson? Are you awake?"

Nothing. No reaction. No acknowledgment. Suddenly, he had an inspiration. "Jud? Jud?"

Judtson's eyelids instantly snapped open.

"Don't *ever* call me that!"

The tension evaporated from Saylor's body, unnoticed until it had been alleviated. Not only had Judtson answered, his eyes were open. And, best of all, they were again Judtson's eyes.

"Please get your hand off my face. You know I hate my face being touched."

Saylor withdrew his hand and laughed a little too loudly. "You're back."

Judtson started to sit up in the bed, making it halfway before the wooziness from the sedative arrested his progress, causing him to flop heavily back down.

He shifted his gaze to look at Saylor almost unbelievingly, grateful for this simple act, the ability to direct his own line of vision, and could see the residue of worry and concern etched into his friend's features, visibly competing with the current influx of relief and elation.

"*Now* do you believe me?"

Saylor's face creased in a wide smile. "Man, that scared the hell out of me."

"Scared you? I'm the one in here. How do you think I felt?"

His exhilaration over the reunion giving way to curiosity, Saylor asked, "How *does* it feel? What is it like? I mean, from the inside."

Judtson took a moment to collect his thoughts and memories. "It's terrifying. I'm not even sure I can describe it. It could be what hell is like. You're in there. You're still thinking. You're still *you*. But you are just a damn helpless passenger along for the ride."

Saylor tried to visualize the experience. "That is hard to really wrap my head around."

"I know. I couldn't have imagined it before this started happening. Now that you've seen it with your own eyes, maybe you can tell me what in the blazes is happening to me."

There was a swivel stool on wheels in the corner of the room. Saylor rolled it to the side of the bed and perched on it. "Wish I knew."

"Oh, that's just stupendous. I finally managed to convince you and you're stumped."

Holding up his hands defensively, Saylor explained, "Right now, your symptoms are all I've got to go on. We need to run some tests."

"Like what?"

Saylor ran through the same list he had given to Kristen earlier.

"Do you at least know what you're looking for? Has anyone else in the world ever had these symptoms?"

Saylor paused, torn between telling Judtson the truth which would frighten him, and lying to keep him calm. He chose the latter. "Oh, yeah. Not a lot of cases, but a few."

Judtson's eyes narrowed. "I know you well enough to know when you are feeding me a load of crap. This is one of those times."

"Well, maybe not your exact symptoms, though there are a few cases with similarities. Once we run the tests, we can eliminate certain things and maybe narrow it down."

"Eliminate what things?"

More comfortably, Saylor answered, "What happened to you could be some kind of a seizure. Could even be PTSD."

"Post-traumatic stress disorder! I haven't been in combat."

"Wouldn't be necessary. PTSD can manifest in people as a result of an array of stressors – abuse, a car accident, a mugging, a job loss, even a divorce."

Saylor added a slight emphasis to the last word.

"I know things are bad with Kristen. Really bad. But I haven't gone over the edge about it."

"We need a psychiatrist to address the PTSD aspect. I don't even know if that's the right avenue. I'm just telling you what can cause the type of episode you had."

"A shrink, huh? You think I might be going nuts?"

They had been friends far too long for Saylor to pull a punch. "Haven't you considered it?"

Judtson fell silent, gazing down at the front of the hospital gown.

Saylor hurried to continue. "Before we even get to that point, we need to make sure that all the wiring is good and that all of the gizmos in you are performing per the manufacturer's specs. That's why we need the tests."

More subdued than a minute earlier, Judtson looked back up at Saylor. "Okay. No garbage. Tell me again...what are you trying to eliminate with the tests?"

Taking a large breath and exhaling slowly, Saylor reluctantly gave him the list. "Brain tumor. Neuronal misfirings resulting in basically an electrical storm in your head. A blood clot in the brain. Evidence of a mini-stroke. Multiple sclerosis. There are more."

"And any of those could be causing what happened?"

Saylor shrugged. "Possibly. Or even a rare combination of any two. It's hard to say."

"Anything you're not telling me?"

"Other than the fact that you have a huge red pimple on your forehead, no."

After a full minute of silence, Judtson smiled. "All right. Let's get this show on the road."

"Thanks." Saylor hopped up from the stool, sending it rolling across the room and banging into the wall under the window.

"One thing first."

Freezing in mid-stride, he eyed Judtson suspiciously. "What's that?"

"Get me the hell out of here."

"We will. As soon as the tests...."

"Now! And stop saying 'we' as if there were two of you."

"Come on, Judtson. The equipment is here. The technicians are here. You are here. Just stick it out until we...I run them all."

"No! I am not staying in this place. More people die in hospitals than anywhere else."

Saylor tried to argue but was cut off. "I don't need to pick up a case of MRSA while I'm waiting for the radiologists downstairs to find time for me in their schedule. There are radiology labs and all of the other labs scattered across town. I'll do the tests, only I'll do them as an outpatient."

"I don't think you should be driving. What if you...what if you have another episode while you're behind the wheel?"

Grinning mischievously, Judtson retorted, "Good thing I have a best friend who is willing to drop everything and shuttle me around."

As much as Saylor wanted to snap back, the dissolution of the conviction from only a short time ago, the fear that he had forever lost this personality so dear to him, brought an involuntary smile to his face. Without a word, he crossed the room to the closet, retrieved Judtson's clothes, and tossed them at his friend.

"Do you think you can get your own sorry ass dressed, or do I need to send a grumpy old nurse in here, with cold hands and a bad attitude, to do it for you?"

▽

As Judtson dressed, Saylor took care of the release paperwork and called his office, instructing Liz to schedule the various tests as soon as possible and to send an email to his phone with the times. He spoke with Melanie and told her to reschedule any patients who had not yet arrived, putting them off for a few days if possible, and then to pick up the two of them at St. Joseph's. Saylor paused for a second and asked her to put Vance Abbott, his partner in the practice, on the phone.

Vance came on the line. "Saylor, what the heck happened? Liz filled me in on some of the details prior to transport. Is Judtson okay?"

"Don't know yet, Vance. He responded to the sedative. Now that he has regained consciousness, he seems to be his old cantankerous self. But I'm going to run a few tests."

"What was it? Some sort of seizure?"

"As I said, I don't know yet."

"If there's anything I can do to help, let me know."

"Well, would you mind seeing my patients for a few days, at least the ones who can't be rescheduled?"

"Of course not. I've already taken in the ones you left sitting out front when you went downstairs to meet Judtson."

"Thanks. Oh, and if you wouldn't mind poking around a little, I could use the help on some research."

"Other patients presenting the same symptoms?"

"Exactly."

"I'll see what I can find. You'll keep me posted."

"I will, Vance. Thank you, again."

"Not a problem."

Judtson emerged from his room and unsteadily crossed the hallway to stand beside Saylor, grabbing the edge of the nurses' station for support.

"I promised Kristen I'd let her know if anything changed. You want to call her?"

Judtson shook his head, clamping his mouth tightly to hold back the wave of nausea the movement triggered.

After issuing a brief instruction to the nurse seated at the station, Saylor dialed his phone while an orderly hurriedly brought a wheelchair, positioning it behind Judtson. Kristen answered on the second ring and, fudging the facts slightly, he told her that Judtson was just now coming out from the sedation and appeared to be back to normal. He once again noticed the lack of an appropriate emotive response as she calmly took the news and expressed the suitable sentiment of relief.

During his conversation with Kristen, he watched as the orderly and a nurse were slowly easing Judtson down into the wheelchair, and noticed that his friend was accepting the ride without his typical protests. When Kristen mentioned her intention to come to the hospital later, he told her that it was not necessary, that he would be checking Judtson out and bringing him home soon. She also absorbed this fact flatly, and he broke the connection.

Judtson was staring at him. "I imagine that she was barely able to contain herself at the good news."

Saylor bit back all of the comments he was contemplating, not wanting to engage in this discussion while surrounded by several of the hospital staff, and answered neutrally. "Yeah, she was glad to hear you're okay."

"I'll bet."

"Come on, let's go." Moving around behind the wheelchair, he grasped the handles and quickly pushed Judtson toward the elevator.

▽

Melanie was parked outside the automatic doors, waiting. Before Saylor could lock the wheels on the chair and lend assistance, Judtson was already up and out of it, grabbing the door handle.

"Shotgun!"

Climbing in the back, Saylor remarked, "You must be feeling better."

Instead of answering, Judtson turned to Melanie, who was looking at him with concern. "You lied to me."

She was caught off-guard by his remark. "What...what do you mean, Judtson?"

"You told me it was a great morning at Desert Neurology. Didn't feel so great to me."

Melanie glanced back at her boss, who was shaking his head bemusedly and, smiling broadly, she retorted, "It *was* a great morning, at least until you arrived."

Saylor chuckled from behind as Judtson harrumphed, dropping his head back against the headrest without saying another word until they arrived at the office.

Not wanting to leave a restored classic in the parking lot for the rest of the day, Judtson insisted that they take his car. After a token protest, Saylor partially relented, agreeing to leave his car under the covered parking until he and Doni could pick it up later, but stated emphatically that he would do the driving. Once again his intentions were thwarted; before he could get behind the wheel, Judtson had already climbed in and turned the ignition. The full-throated roar of the 390 horsepower W-46 package drowned out any muttered comments.

Judtson expertly manipulated the Hurst Dual/Gate shifter, and they surged backward out of the parking space and laid a double strip of rubber in first gear. Saylor felt the vibration from his phone and checked to find an email message from his office, informing him that Judtson was scheduled for an MRI in less than two hours at an independent radiology lab nearby. The muscle car squealed out of the lot and onto Wilmot Road, heading south. They encountered a red light within seconds and, after they were safely to a stop, Saylor sighed. "We need to be at the MRI lab in about an hour and a half."

"Where is it?"

"Fifth and Wilmot."

"That's close. Cool. Hungry? Oh, wait. Is it okay to have an MRI on a full stomach?"

"They're going to zap your head, not your abdomen."

"So it's all right?"

"YES! You're the one who was nauseous from the sedative. What do you feel like eating?"

"Probably shouldn't have Mexican."

"Probably not."

"Chinese?"

"No!"

"Sandwich?"

"Sure."

"Eegee's?"

"That's fine."

The light changed to green and the cars in front of them moved forward. As soon as there was a clear path, Judtson punched the accelerator, whipping a squealing right on Speedway. They drove the half mile to the restaurant, with Saylor closely watching for any sign of a recurrence, ready to grab the steering wheel should Judtson suddenly go inert. Arriving without incident, the two men entered the comfort of the air conditioning, and ordered meatball subs, potato salads, and mango eegees. The bill was a little more than twenty dollars, and Judtson dropped two twenties on the counter. One at a time, the clerk picked up the two bills and held them above his head, staring intently at each in the light. Seeing this, Saylor groaned quietly, knowing what was to come. Satisfied that his customers were not counterfeiters, the young man pulled three fives, three singles, and some coins from the cash drawer and counted them out. Judtson dropped the coins in his pocket, laid the bills on the counter side by side and, one by one, picked up each five and held it above his head, mimicking the clerk as he carefully examined each bill.

As he went through this procedure, the young man stared at him with mild disbelief. When Judtson finished studying the third five-dollar note, he handed it back to the clerk. "I need a different bill. This one's no good."

"What?"

"It's no good. Do you have another? If not, I'll take five ones."

The young clerk picked up the five and stared at it. "I don't see anything wrong with it."

Judtson shrugged. "I'm sure you haven't taken the class on fives. They've only taught you what to check on twenties or higher. Believe me, it's no good and I'm rejecting it."

The clerk opened the cash drawer and pulled out another five. Saylor noticed that the "rejected" five had been placed off to the side, and he laughed to himself, visualizing the discussions to occur later as the young man and the manager tried to find the flaw. Judtson made a show of thoroughly checking the new bill before jamming it into his pocket.

It was far too late for there still to be any lunch customers and a little too early for a dinner crowd, so the dining room was empty. After getting their food, they chose a booth farthest from the counter, seeking as much privacy as possible from the employees.

"Well, at least the line wasn't as long as the last time you did that."

Shrugging, Judtson said, "It's rude. And they need to know what it's like to be on the receiving end."

"They already know, when they are customers someplace else."

"That doesn't reach them. They're zombies. They just accept it. When someone does it to them at some convenience store, they aren't bothered, because *their* bosses make them do it, too. We are at the point where nobody reacts to any indignities anymore…whether it's a TSA pat-down at the airport or some seventeen-year-old punk acting like a Treasury agent, while I stand there docilely hoping I pass his test so I can have a sandwich. We all just accept everything, no matter how outrageous it is."

"I know. I know. We've had this talk a thousand times."

"I keep hoping that people, like the guy at the counter, get it. You know, understand what I'm doing and start doing it themselves. We need to quit being sheep. We need to take back everything that we've lost."

"One thing is certain."

"What's that?"

"You are definitely back from wherever you went for a while."

Judtson paused as he thought back to earlier in the day. "I know I've already asked you this, but what do you think is happening? And don't answer me with the usual doctor's evasiveness, man. Tell me what you really think."

Saylor tried to suck the mango-flavored ice up the straw, popped one of his ears, and gave up, scooping out a mound with a spoon. "I really *don't* know. I was going to talk to some other docs today. I was going to do some research. I asked Vance to get that started. Until I can find other cases, I don't have a clue."

"You think it's bad wiring in my head?"

"No, I don't. That's just my area of expertise, so I'm comfortable there. If I were an ID guy...."

"A what?"

"An internist specializing in infectious diseases. Then, I'd be looking for all of the obscure parasites, viruses, amoebas, bacteria, and prions that only affect left-handed, short people living on west slope of the Andes. And that might make sense considering that you recently got back from Peru. If I were a psychologist, I'd be dusting off every old textbook I have on dissociative disorders. If I were an endocrinologist...."

"I get the picture."

"The point is, Judtson, one of those disciplines has the answer. Or it could be another one I haven't even thought of yet."

"Like a proctologist?"

Saylor barked a short laugh. "That hadn't occurred to me. It does make sense, though, now that you mention it. Seriously, I need to do enough tests to eliminate anything in my field."

"Then you can pass me off, right? So I'm not your problem anymore."

"Jerk! It's my starting point. A psychiatrist won't even want to talk to you until I've eliminated all possible physiological causes."

"Back to the shrink again. Great!"

With a sigh of exasperation Saylor explained, "Come on. You felt it. It happened for a longer period this time, long enough for you to actually study what was going on, from the inside. You have to admit that there might be some kind of psychological explanation."

His usual animation dampening, Judtson shrugged. "I guess. Seriously though, is it really possible to be completely cut off from your own body like that, and have it simply be something you're doing to yourself? I mean, it just doesn't feel plausible to me."

"I'm not the expert. From what I've read and from the few patients I've referred to those guys, yes, it is. I brought up PTSD earlier only because I've had a few cases come in. In the extreme, when they are in the midst of a full-blown flashback, they can be sitting at a dining room table at their parents' home having Thanksgiving dinner, and the sound of a car backfiring outside triggers an event. Suddenly, they don't even see the turkey, the parents, the room, anything that is actually, physically around them. Instead they are seeing, smelling, hearing, feeling, and even tasting an event that happened to them in Iraq. It's totally real to them. They are *there*, completely immersed. And there *isn't* any physical cause – no bad wiring, no tumor, no stroke, no aneurysm. They are, as you put it, doing it to themselves. But phrasing it that way is a terrible injustice to them because there is nothing they can do to control it at the time."

"I'm definitely not having any sort of flashback when it happens. I'm still in the moment. I'm engaged. I'm observing."

"I know. It isn't the same thing; it just serves to illustrate how full and complete the illusion can be, how real it can feel to the person."

"*Full and complete*? You've ridden way too many rides at Disneyland. 'Please wait for the ride to come to a full and complete stop before exiting,' they say in their redundant way."

"You're a jerk."

"I believe you've mentioned that."

"So what I'm trying to tell you is that what you went through is different from a flashback, but don't be fooled by the fact that it seemed real. The mind can do that."

Taking a bite from the sandwich, unknowingly dripping marinara sauce onto his shirt, Judtson absorbed Saylor's words throughout the process of chewing, swallowing, and taking a mouthful of mango slush. "It's making me view this whole idea of consciousness, and even reality, differently."

"It should."

"What do you mean?"

"Look, with the exception of psychiatry and psychology, my field is really the only one where we have essentially no true understanding of cause and effect. An orthopod can x-ray, CT scan, or MRI a knee, identify the fact that there is a tear in the cartilage, and go in and surgically repair it. A nose picker can...."

"Nose picker?"

"Ear, nose, and throat specialist."

"Okay."

"Anyway, he can look at a perforated eardrum, surgically steal a slice of tissue from the mastoid, and build a new membrane. The list goes on. Practically every other area deals, for the most part, in a clear, identifiable, understandable realm where they can see what's broken and fix it. Yet, when we get to the mind, it suddenly becomes mysterious. A patient can have a minor stroke and a small segment of the brain is starved of oxygen. Afterward, that patient is perfectly fine except that he or she can no longer remember the names of anything in the produce section of the grocery store."

"Is that true?"

"Yeah. There are lots of examples like that. And the very concept of consciousness has never been satisfactorily defined, at least in a way everyone can agree upon. Hell, there are times when I come to the conclusion that consciousness shouldn't even be possible, considering the mechanisms available for the creation of it. And then I start thinking about the concept of reality and I really lose it."

"I never knew you were so deep."

Saylor made an expressive hand gesture at his friend and continued, "We travel through life compiling data from the five senses. That's what we do. We're like probes sent to a foreign land with the purpose of gathering information. The brain takes this input and forms an opinion as to what reality is. But that opinion is based upon interpretation, slanted and colored by personal history and experiences, political agenda, phobias, et cetera. Two different people experience the same so-called reality and come away with two very different images or recollections of it. Which version is the true reality? And does that make it any less *real* for either of them?"

Judtson did not respond, taking in all that Saylor was saying.

"There have been tons of experiments that illustrate the subjectiveness of what we experience, like the one where they took a group of people and fitted them with glasses which couldn't be removed by the subjects. The glasses turned everything around so that the subjects were seeing a mirror image of the world around them. Within days, their minds adapted. They soon saw everything normally, at least what was normal for them. Then the experimenters removed the glasses, allowing the subjects to again see the world as they had previously. Guess what? For a few days, everyone saw the world in mirror image."

"They had retrained themselves while the glasses were on, and had to lose the training."

"Exactly. The stated reason for the experiment was to demonstrate the flexibility of the mind. But the conclusion I drew from it was that we are all free to interpret our world however we want. We are under absolutely no obligation to remain true to reality, because reality is subjective. Change the paradigm, and we'll change along with it, without batting an eye."

"No pun intended."

"None."

"Changing the subject, what totally freaked me out during the last episode was discovering that I have no idea how to actually do something as simple as lifting my finger."

As Judtson spoke, he rested his hand on the table and stared at it for a moment, until his index finger slowly rose. "See, it just happens. For some reason, I am unable to follow the path, the mechanism of nerves and muscles, which causes it to happen."

"It's autonomic."

"Yeah, but what does that really mean? Are we, 'we' being our conscious minds...are we locked out of the process? I feel like the captain of a ship, shouting into one of those tubes, ordering 'Full speed ahead,' except that I'm a captain who has never been below deck. I've never even seen the engine room, never had a chance to talk to one of the men down there. I have no idea what processes need to occur before the propeller starts spinning faster. I just yell into the tube and it happens."

"Good analogy."

"Thanks. Guess I'd make a good writer. I didn't want a compliment from you, dammit; I wanted some insights...some explanation as to exactly how it works."

"Not going to get it from me."

"Then who can tell me, if not a hotshot neurologist?"

Saylor shrugged. "Beats me. Maybe a shaman. Maybe one of the metaphysical weirdos you debunk on your show."

"Thanks again."

Swallowing another spoonful of mango, Saylor leaned forward. "That's what I'm trying to tell you. I don't know. We don't know. No one in any of the fields of medicine or science knows, although Vance has an interesting theory."

"What is it?"

"Well, he is quite a bit more religious than I. He believes that our consciousness is not a part of the brain, not even a part of the body."

"What does he think it is?"

"He thinks that our consciousness, the active participant in this conversation right now, the entity that, in our own opinion defines who we are...."

"Will you just tell me? What do you want, a drum roll?"

"He thinks it's our soul."

"He thinks that our consciousness is our soul?"

"He does. And he believes that our mind is essentially an organic hard drive, that it's the soul which does all of the thinking and all of the ordering, like the captain yelling into that tube down to the engine room."

Judtson pondered Saylor's words for a minute before speaking. "You know, if he's right, if that really is how it works, then what happened to me makes sense."

"Why?"

"If the 'me' you are talking to now is the soul, some conscious entity living inside this body, and the separate brain and body simply choose to ignore me...Saylor, that's exactly how it felt."

Chapter 7

LOOKING OVER THE SHOULDER OF THE RADIOLOGIST, Saylor studied the digital images from the MRI of Judtson's head, uttering a soft "Okay" as he finished examining each one, letting his colleague know when he could move on to the next. After the series finished, he waited, anxious to hear the opinion of the specialist. Prior to the MRI, the technician had administered gadolinium to Judtson; the substance was used to accentuate any abnormal blood flow through the brain and highlight any clusters of veins which might cause a problem in cognitive function.

"Everything appears normal."

Saylor agreed, inwardly wishing that there had been some small, treatable anomaly visible on one of the images. He thanked him and walked out to the waiting area, where Judtson was pacing. As soon as his friend saw his entrance, he stopped and stared expectantly. Saylor shook his head as he reached him.

"I don't know whether to be happy that my brain is fine, or disappointed."

"I know what you mean."

"While I was waiting, I remembered that horrible show on TV. I think it was an old *Twilight Zone*, the one where the bad guy put an earwig in the other guy's ear, and the bug ate its way through the brain."

"Yeah, I remember that one." Saylor shuddered. "Gave me the creeps. Nope. No earwig. Nothing."

They both turned and began walking toward the exit. "Well, what's next?"

"The rest of the tests are scheduled for tomorrow. I suggest a low-key evening and a good night's rest, just in case whatever is happening to you is stress related."

As they approached the red convertible, Saylor checked his shirt pocket. "I don't have my script pad with me. Let me call Liz."

"What for?"

"I want to get some Valium for you."

"Valium. You know how I am about that kind of stuff."

"Tough. What do you prefer...feeling a little out of control or going on another trip back into hell?"

"Get in. We'll go to the CVS down the street."

Along the way, Saylor connected with Liz and gave her the dosage information, asking her to call it in for him. His words must have had an effect on Judtson, Saylor thought, as he noticed that his friend's driving verged on being sedate, rather than a typical white-knuckle trip.

The pharmacy drive-thru had a line of three cars. Neither man spoke during the wait. Finally, it was their turn at the window, and Judtson looked over. "Do you have a prescription for Kent?"

The young girl on the other side of the glass, cradling the intercom phone against the side of her head with her shoulder, replied, "I'm sorry, I couldn't hear you. Could you repeat that, please?"

"KENT! A prescription for KENT."

"Tent?"

"If you would hold that phone up to your ear, instead of halfway down your cheek, you might be able to hear me. It's Kent. K...E...N...T!"

Saylor leaned closer and said, "How's that 'controlling your stress level' working for you?"

"Oh, Kent! Is that your first or last name?"

Hearing her question, Saylor began to laugh.

"Miss...." Judtson leaned out his window and shouted into the microphone, "How many people in the course of your day come in and ask for their prescriptions by their first names?"

"Pardon me?"

Saylor gently placed his hand on Judtson's arm, hoping to short-circuit the coming tirade. For once, his friend acquiesced and took a deep breath. Continuing in a calm voice, he said, "Never mind. Kent is my last name. My first name is Judtson. Do you have a prescription ready for me?"

Smiling sappily at him, she typed for a moment on the suspended keyboard. "Yes, Mr. Kent, we do. Oh, I see that the prescription you are picking up is a controlled substance. I'm afraid you'll have to come inside to get it."

Before Judtson could work himself into another frenzy, Saylor leaned toward the driver's side window. "Thank you. We'll be right in."

Glaring at the tech, Judtson slammed the shifter into first gear and peeled away, drove around the building to the front, and parked. Still fighting his temper as they walked inside, he said, "Maybe Valium is a good idea, after all."

Saylor laughed again, and they walked the depth of the store back to the pharmacy counter and picked up the prescription, Judtson compliantly showing his identification without a verbal treatise on the subject of a business recognizing its customers.

At Saylor's urging, they found a drinking fountain and Judtson took one of the pills. As they returned to the car, Saylor blocked the driver's side door, his hand outstretched. "Keys."

Starting to put up an argument, Judtson reconsidered and dug out the key ring, tossing it to his friend. "Don't burn out the clutch."

Judtson wanted to return to his office, and as they neared it, they both saw the ostentatious yellow Hummer, the same intense shade as Ricky's car, parked in the driveway. The Smart car, which would have looked like a recently birthed offspring to the hefty SUV, was gone, and Judtson fleetingly entertained the image of the General Motors behemoth gobbling it for a snack.

Saylor slowed their approach as he saw it. "Is that the same one...?"

"From last night? Definitely seems like it."

"What should we do, keep going?"

"Why? Go ahead and pull in."

"I don't know."

"Hey, you're the one who said she was probably a fan."

"It's just…."

"Pull in! It's fine."

There was not enough room for the Oldsmobile on the driveway beside the Hummer, so Saylor parked behind it, blocking her exit, assuming it was she. He killed the engine, and as the silence began to envelop them, they both heard a female voice come from the corner of the garage that was obscured by the visiting Hummer.

"Hi, guys!"

Being the nearer of the two, Judtson answered as he climbed out of his car. "I'm sorry. Do we know you?"

She stepped into his view. In the sunlight, her hair appeared to be even more red than it had the night before in his rearview mirror, her eyes and most of her face obscured by oversized sunglasses. She wore a T-shirt with the question "Where am I going, and why am I in this handbasket?" printed on the front.

"You should. I'm the one who turned you two into Internet stars. Have you seen how many hits that video has had? I just checked it on my phone, and it's more than six million so far."

Saylor walked between the two vehicles and joined Judtson. The woman spun to face him. All of her movements were quick, jerky, almost aggressive. Pointing a thumb at Judtson, she said, "I know who he is. Who are you?"

"Saylor."

Her hand suddenly shot up to cover her mouth. "Oh, crap. I don't even know…. Were you the other guy last night? Oh, my God, I might have really…."

"It's okay," Judtson answered, entertained by her animated demeanor. "He was my partner last night."

Saylor started to protest and abruptly stopped himself, understanding that it was already too late.

"Thank God. I really could have put my foot in my mouth. Last night you had masks. It's just that there are two of you and there were two last night, and I just assumed…. Are you going to invite me in, or do we have to stand here and sweat?"

His amusement escalating in reaction to her rapid-fire delivery, Judtson gestured toward the front door. "Of course. Let's go in, but not until you at least tell us who you are."

A brief smile lit up her face. "Sorry. Yes. You're right. That would be the polite thing to do. I'm Kelsey. Kelsey Batman."

"Batman!" Saylor's disbelieving outburst induced an indignant glare from her.

"Yes. Batman."

"Is there any lineage to that name?" he asked. "Or were your parents big fans?"

"Real name. Traced it back five generations. Are we going to go inside, or do I need an umbrella? My complexion doesn't get along that well with the sun, even this late in the day."

"Oh, that's right," Judtson chimed in. "Redheads are more sensitive to sunlight."

Her eyes flickered back to him. "I said my name was real, not my hair color. I may prefer my hair red, but I like my skin pale."

Leading the way to the front door, Judtson pulled out his keys and asked over his shoulder, "I can't believe that Ricky left while you were hanging out here. Or did you arrive after he was gone?"

"No. He is such a nice…ummmm, assistant, secretary, aide, office manager, whatever he is. Anyway, no, I arrived here while he was inside. God, it must have been an hour ago. I just marched in and told him I wanted to see you. I'm afraid he was a little flustered at first."

"I can believe that."

She continued without reacting to Judtson's comment. "He said you weren't here and he didn't know when you'd be back, or even if you would. I bet that's what he's supposed to say, right?"

They were inside, and Judtson gestured to one of the lobby chairs for her to sit. "No. Not really. It was actually the truth."

"Sure it was. Anyway, I told him I'd wait. That kind of flipped him out at first. He kept telling me I couldn't stay, he hadn't heard from you, you were probably not going to return, and I should leave."

Judtson visualized the interaction, laughing inwardly at the image of poor Ricky attempting to deal with this whirlwind.

"Then we started talking, and he calmed down some. We have a lot in common, me and Ricky. I mean, Ricky and I. You're the writer, so which is it?"

"Ricky and I."

"Right. By the way, is he gay?"

"Yes. He is."

"He's a cool guy. We had a nice talk."

"About what?" Judtson asked suspiciously.

"Not you! He was a good boy. He wouldn't say a word about his boss. No, we talked about all kinds of stuff, like the militia guy who just disappeared."

"Whoa!" exclaimed Saylor, struggling to keep up with her thread of consciousness. "What militia guy?"

A derisive laugh burst from her. "Don't you two listen to the news? The head of one of those militia groups in Kingman just disappeared. Vanished! Nobody knows what happened or where he is. His wife and son were on TV talking about it."

"I hadn't heard about that."

Kelsey huffed in frustration at their ignorance and continued, "And after we talked about that, he told me I really did have to go. Right then! He said he was going home for the day and I couldn't stay. I tried to tell him that I would wait out front, but he insisted. He wouldn't leave until I was gone."

"But you're here," Saylor blurted out, trying to jump into the fast-moving conversation.

She flashed a smile in his direction. "I left. He left. I drove around the block and came back. Here I am."

With her last comment, she spread her arms outward.

"I guess we owe you a 'thank you,'" Judtson remarked, changing the subject.

"For what? Oh, that's right. My editing of the video. Yep, I did catch the license plate. Quite clearly, actually. Your butts would have been toast."

"Thank you."

Her shoulders rose in an emphatic shrug. "No big deal. I thought what you did was cool. Why would I bust you?"

"I thought you were probably a fan of his," suggested Saylor.

"A fan. Are you kidding? No way. His books stink! I hate them. As a matter of fact, when my friend looked up the license for me and told me whose car it was, I almost left your plate in the video."

"Why do you hate my books?"

"Why? You're joking, right?"

"No, I'm not."

"Okay, okay, *The Mason's Ring*, for example. As far as you're concerned, those guys are just a bunch of harmless buffoons riding around on tricycles and wearing fezzes."

"They're not?"

"Of course they aren't, and *you* know it. They're the front organization for the Knights Templar. They've got that huge fortune the Templars left behind that nobody ever found. They've got the Holy Grail. Probably the Arc of the Covenant, which means they control the spooky power from that thing. Everybody knows they call the shots, pull the strings, pick both candidates for President so it doesn't matter who's elected."

"Everybody knows?"

She huffed at him impatiently. "Everyone they haven't gotten to or brainwashed. And your other books! You might as well be the paid publicist for the Illuminati, like the book you did on them. Or maybe I should say, *for* them. What was it called? *Shedding Some Light*?"

"*Shining the Light.*"

"Whatever, and what about UFOs? I suppose that the ten million people who've actually seen them are all crackpots or suffering from simultaneous mass hysteria! You're just a flack for them!"

"Them?"

"Yes, them! The bad guys. The aliens. The Bilderberg Group. The Trilateral Commission. Skull and Bones. The Club of Rome. You are such a shill that they've probably got a statue of you next to the giant owl at Bohemian Grove."

She finally stopped to gulp a breath. Both Judtson and Saylor were struggling mightily to hold back their laughter. Able to choke it back enough to speak, Judtson managed to ask, "Then why didn't you turn me in? It sounds as though you would be doing yourself and your fellow conspiracy buffs a favor."

She took the large sunglasses off and fixed Judtson with a steady stare. "Like I said, I almost did. Not that it would matter. One phone call from you to one of your Rockefeller or Rothschild buddies and you'd be out again. And then I realized, hold on, now you owe me."

He stopped laughing. "So this is some kind of blackmail? Isn't that a little risky? If I'm so well connected with the Illuminati, aren't you taking a chance that the black helicopters are going to show up for you?"

The accusation of a felony did not intimidate her in the least. "No, I'm not worried about the 'copters. I've got my own way of dealing with those creeps. And, yep, guess you could call it blackmail. I prefer to think of it as just being persuasive."

Curious, Judtson leaned forward in his chair. "And what do you want to persuade me to do?"

"It's simple, Bozo. Start telling the truth."

"Bozo? The truth about what?"

"Don't play games with me. You know. The truth about all of it. All of the stuff you've been covering up for them."

Judtson had no idea how to respond, when Saylor chose the moment to speak up. "You're too late. He has already swung over to your side."

Her eyes sprang wide as she turned to face him. "My side? Swung over? What do you mean?"

"Go ahead, ask him. Ask him what his next book is about."

Shooting a quick, meaningful glare at Saylor, Judtson said, "It's about Puma Punku."

She slid excitedly to the edge of her seat, her eyes flashing with excitement. "Puma Punku? The port built overnight by the giants hundreds of thousands of years ago? Wow!" Her eyes suddenly narrowed suspiciously. "Wait a minute. You're going to do another one of your hatchet-job, cover-up books on it, aren't you?"

Saylor jumped in and, with a broad smile on his face, offered, "No. He has seen the light. He's a believer now."

Rapidly looking back and forth between the two of them, Kelsey was clearly attempting to determine if she was being toyed with. "I don't know whether to believe you or not."

"Believe it. He's in hot water over it, with his publisher, his agent, practically everyone."

"Saylor! Knock it off."

Judtson turned back to her. "I met an archaeologist for my show. His name is Carlos Cabrillo Villarreal."

"I know him. I mean, I know who he is. He's the illegitimate grandson of that Austrian guy."

"*Claims* to be," Judtson clarified.

"I know a person can be an illegitimate son, or at least that used to be the case in the days prior to political correctness. But can someone be an illegitimate grandson?" The question came from Saylor, and both of them turned to stare at him blankly for a moment, before continuing their conversation as if he had not spoken.

"I read his blog about his dig down there."

"Then you know what I know."

"He convinced you."

Judtson appeared uncomfortable. "I guess you could say that."

"And your next book is going to be about what he found?"

"Uh, yes. Substantially."

Her earlier suspicion returned instantly. "What do you mean, 'substantially'?"

"Well, he showed me something, something which is not on his blog yet."

"*Really*?" Her voice was nearly a squeal. "Tell me. Tell me. What did he show you?" As she begged, she was actually bouncing on the edge of her seat.

Judtson let his breath out slowly. Her enthusiasm was infectious and he was trying to maintain a modicum of calm. She was such an overwhelming force of nature that even the Valium was not a match for the tidal wave that was her personality. "Kelsey, I just met you. You seem very nice and all that, but I don't think I want to start talking about the contents of my next book with a perfect stranger."

She made a rude sound with her lips. "That's ridiculous! What's the big deal?"

With a shake of his head, he explained, "Because I don't need a repeat of the video from last night. Except this time it'll be a sneak peek at Judtson Kent's next book going viral all over the Internet."

"What's wrong with that? It'll sell books."

"She has a point," Saylor interjected, still grinning.

"Saylor, butt out. Kelsey, I have PR people. I don't need any help in that area."

"You mean you used to have PR people."

"Saylor!"

"I'm just saying...."

She paused for a moment. It was the first time she was at a loss for words. Judtson watched her mind work as she thought about what he had said, and searched for a rebuttal. The precise moment it occurred to her was obvious. "Well, Judtson Kent, there is that little matter of the video with your license plate."

"Back to the blackmail, huh? I thought your note said that I had the only copy of it."

"I lied."

"You know what I think? I think you're lying now. I think you did give the only unedited copy to me."

She glared at him and bit her bottom lip for a second. "Damn you! All right. It's true. I did. Since I was nice enough to do that, don't you feel that you owe me a little? Can't you at least give me a hint? Something?"

Judtson sank back into the overstuffed chair and studied Kelsey silently. She was sitting so far forward on the seat that Judtson was afraid it would flip out from beneath her, her muscles taut as a bowstring, her face rapt, her eyes staring unblinkingly at him. Next, he glanced at Saylor. The residue of a grin was still on his friend's face. As they locked eyes, Judtson was able to discern an almost imperceptible nod.

Looking back at her, he said, "All I can say is that for the first time, someone has finally found something which will blow away all of the skeptics – something so solid, so real, so specific that it's indisputable."

Chapter 8

THE TWO MEN WERE SITTING AT THE BAR in Saylor and Doni's kitchen, munching tortilla chips and salsa as Doni made dinner. Saylor took a sip of iced tea.

"Doni, I'm sorry I'm screwing up your date night with Saylor."

When he and Saylor had arrived from their day together, she met them at the door, clearly expecting only Saylor and obviously ready for an evening out. Despite this, Judtson was not able to detect even the slightest hint of irritation as she saw him.

She cocked her head slightly and grinned. "No big deal. He's no fun anymore, anyway."

"You guys really don't need to babysit me. I can go home. I'm sure that I'm fine."

Doni reached past Saylor and placed her hand on Judtson's. "Knock it off, Squirrel. From what I've heard so far, you could check out at any moment. And it's not as if you could run over here or even call us when it happens. Besides, sitting around here all evening and staring at you while we wait for you to make your next trip to zombieland sounds a lot more exciting than the evening we had in mind."

Judtson could not help but grin. "I don't know whether to say 'thank you' or 'go to hell.'"

"Either's fine."

As Doni worked on dinner, he called Kristen, telling her that he was next door and that Saylor wanted to keep an eye on him this evening. She made an almost sincere-sounding comment about being glad he was okay, and said she would wait up for him. He told her that would not be necessary. In fact, he might stay over and sleep on their couch tonight so Saylor could check on him. The conversation ended without any expressions of affection from either end of the line.

As he broke the connection, Judtson turned to his friends. "Okay, now you two can stop pretending you weren't listening."

"Judtson, we...."

He held up his hand to stop Saylor in mid-sentence. Before Judtson could speak, Doni remarked, "So, is she throwing on some clothes and dashing over here to see you?"

"No. I think she has to shampoo her hair or something."

"Bitch!"

"Donatella!"

"What, Saylor? What has Squirrel done to deserve this kind of crap?"

"I'm not saying he has done anything," he answered defensively. "It's just none of our business."

"Come on, guys. Don't argue about me right in front of me. I'm supposed to remain calm, remember?"

He and Saylor described the entire day to Doni as she stood at the stove frying enchiladas, and filled in the details she had not yet heard. She took it all in without comment, waiting patiently for them to finish. Their narrative continued as she turned off the burner under the hot oil, set plates with four sizzling enchiladas, smothered in a dark red sauce, in front of each of them, and then slid onto the middle stool with her own plate in hand. Ignoring the bizarre aspects of Judtson's freakish episode, her first comment was about Kelsey's name.

"I can't believe that name," Doni said between bites. "Kelsey Batman. That has to be made up."

"She swore it was her real name. She said she traced it back five generations."

"Sorry, I still don't believe it." She took another bite of food, catching the dripping cheese with her fork and tucking it into her mouth. Chewing and swallowing the mouthful, she turned to her husband. "So, Mr. Brain, what's happening to our pal here?"

"I'm getting tired of saying this, but I wish I knew."

"Great. The rest of the tests are tomorrow?"

"Yes, and we should get back some of the blood results by that time, too."

"So we're in a holding pattern till then?"

"I'd say so. Vance said he'd do a little research for me. Maybe we can find similar cases somewhere. I'm also consulting with a few other docs tomorrow."

"Okay. Now that I've satisfied my social obligation to our friend here by asking all of the proper and solicitous questions, tell me, what did Kelsey Batman look like?"

Saylor provided the standard husbandly response that their unexpected chronicler was "average" and "kind of plain."

"I don't know, Saylor. I thought she was pretty hot stuff," Judtson embellished puckishly. "I noticed that you couldn't take your eyes off that tight T-shirt she had spray-painted on."

Forcing a mock smile, Doni swung around to her husband while brandishing her fork. "You didn't mention a T-shirt, *honey*."

"Thanks a lot, Judtson. Baby, he's pulling your chain. I didn't notice her shirt."

"Uh-huh," she grunted skeptically.

"It was sort of a funny shirt, Doni." Judtson smiled. "It said, 'I see your lips moving, but all I hear is blah, blah, blah.'"

"That wasn't it. It said…." Saylor stopped quickly, but not quickly enough.

"Go ahead, *baby*. Tell me what the tight little T-shirt you didn't even notice said."

Judtson laughed at his friend's discomfort as Saylor glared at him.

The conversation continued through dinner and dessert, all three avoiding any negative or tension-inducing topics. Judtson felt comfortable and safe, wrapped in the familiar environment with his two friends. At some point in the evening, they had moved from the bar to the living room. Doni made a pot of green tea, and they sipped and chatted until Saylor noticed that Judtson had fallen asleep in his chair.

They decided to let him sleep as he was, rather than waking him only to move to the couch, and they tiptoed to their bedroom for the night. Saylor's sleep was fitful. He awoke several times to check on his friend, suspecting that he would not be able to tell if the transition had occurred as Judtson slept, and fearful each time he sneaked into the living room that he would be confronted by Judtson, sitting bolt upright in the chair, with both hands tightly gripping the armrests, and those terrifying eyes boring straight into his soul.

Judtson awoke in the morning with a crashing neck pain from his overnight position. The moment he opened his eyes, he saw Saylor sitting across the room and watching him.

"All right, this is creepy. Have you been sitting there staring at me all night?"

He could see that his utterly normal, completely Judtson-like comment triggered a visible display of relief on Saylor's face.

"Yeah. All night, man. Just sat here and watched you sleep."

"He did not!" Doni's voice came from the kitchen. "We both got up about fifteen minutes ago. Get in here! Breakfast is almost ready."

Saylor smirked at his friend and stood up. "We'd better go. Last time I was late for her scrambled eggs, I ended up with them in my shirt pocket."

"You've got that right," she shouted.

With a chuckle, Judtson stood, his back and neck popping loudly as he unwound from the contorted slump in which he had slept, and then followed Saylor into the kitchen. After breakfast, he went to his own home to shower and change clothes, promising that he would be back in no more than forty-five minutes. Rocky was waiting for him at the front door with his tail wagging furiously, as he always did, somehow knowing when his master was arriving. Judtson was thankful that Kristen had already departed, and although he had no idea where she would have gone, he realized that he did not care. He dropped to his knees and hugged his loyal best friend, reveling in the softness of the golden fur.

Performing the routine tasks of shaving, showering, and brushing his teeth, with Rocky never more than a foot or two from him, Judtson went through the familiar procedures with a conscious feeling of gratitude for each motion, every action that he felt he controlled. Although the exercise seemed fruitless, his mind remained focused on the successive increments of the acts, trying to identify and understand the underlying steps in the neuronal and muscular process, hoping to gain a working knowledge which might come in handy the next time. The next time. Maybe, he thought, maybe there would not be a next time. Maybe the elevator incident yesterday was it. The last one. Maybe he was fine.

He did not believe this line of thought for a moment and rushed through the last steps of his routine, finally sliding into a long-sleeved shirt, a comfortable pair of blue jeans, socks, and New Balance sneakers. As usual, he had a difficult time tying the laces as Rocky, seeing his hands come down to dog level, repeatedly interposed himself between Judtson and his shoes. Next on the agenda was making a quick trip to the kitchen to ensure that Rocky was left with enough water for the day. There was no such thing as leaving a bowl of food for him; he gobbled it all the moment his bowl was filled. With a final affectionate squeeze for his chum, Judtson dashed out the front door and hurriedly crossed the patch of desert back to what he now viewed as something of a refuge.

Saylor's nurse had scheduled a full day of tests, and the two friends made the rounds. One by one the tests were completed, with Judtson under or in front of millions of dollars worth of machinery, and Saylor standing with the technicians and overseeing the process. In some cases, because of Saylor's presence, the physicians who specialized in interpreting the results stood with him, ready to provide immediate analysis out of courtesy for their colleague. As they watched, Saylor gave them a brief overview of Judtson's symptoms, hoping that one of them might have heard or read about a similar case. None had, until the final test of the day when a neurologist, overseeing the technician as she administered the electromyogram, thought he recalled reading a preliminary paper with a similar description of symptoms.

Saylor prompted him for details, but the young doctor was unable to recall any. "It was so unusual that I printed it out. It's in my office somewhere, in one of my stacks. I'll find it later today and email it to you."

"Do you remember if there was a diagnosis?"

"No. Sorry, I don't."

Saylor had to tamp down the urge to insist upon accompanying the doctor back to his office right at that second to search for the paper. "You'll look for it today, then?"

"I will, and I'll email it as soon as possible. Should I send it to your office?"

"No. Send it to my personal email; that will come straight to my phone."

Saylor gave his address. The technician administering the EMG signaled that she was done, and the two doctors reviewed the results together.

Entering the waiting area, Saylor found Judtson sitting in a chair, thumbing through a copy of *Us Weekly* magazine. He thought to himself that this was quite different from yesterday when Judtson had been almost frantically pacing, and he mentally thanked the inventor of Valium.

Dropping into the adjoining chair, Saylor uttered a single word to sum up the results, "Zip."

"So we're batting zero today."

"We are, except for one thing."

"What's that?"

Saylor told him about the neurologist who *thought* he *might* have read a preliminary paper about a patient with similar symptoms. As he spoke, he saw his friend's mood elevate.

"That means I might not be the only one."

"True. You might not. And that's always the case. Even rare diseases and conditions are shared by others. I've never heard of anyone developing a malady that, as the Brits say, is a 'one off.' A lot of times there is a lag. In the pre-Internet days, doctors had to rely solely upon the published journals to let them know about something new. It was a tedious, long process. Sometimes it took months, even years until the doc or researcher wrote a paper, followed by peer review. It took so long that too many times other patients with the same condition suffered or even died while their doctors waited through all that time, to eventually find out somebody else had found a treatment or cure."

"There's a delay now, isn't there? I've heard that the paper is still subject to peer review before it's published."

"True. But in the past few years, there has been such an outcry about viable treatments being withheld during the process that the journals have relaxed their rules prohibiting the release of data, so long as the paper is properly identified as being preliminary and not peer-reviewed."

"Did he give you the paper?"

"He's going to look for it. He's sure he printed it out."

Judtson accepted the answer with equanimity. "Okay, we wait. Where to now?"

"Well, we're done with tests. That was the last one."

"Then I suggest we split up. I have a ton of things to do and I think you have a medical practice to run."

"I don't know," Saylor responded doubtfully.

"What are we going to do? Hang out together from now on? Come on, Saylor. The incidents were happening fairly rapidly. The first one was in the evening, and the second and third both happened the next morning. There hasn't been one since. I don't know if it's the Valium or the therapeutic power of your mere presence, but there hasn't been an episode in almost thirty hours now. Maybe whatever was wrong with me has spontaneously fixed itself."

"That doesn't usually happen."

"How do you know it didn't happen with this thing? You've never even heard of the symptoms, so you have no idea what the normal course would be. It might have just been, I don't know, a little blood clot stuck somewhere in my head, and now it has broken free and everything is fine. Isn't that possible?"

"It's possible, I suppose," he conceded skeptically.

Judtson twisted around in his seat to face him. "I know you're worried about me. I appreciate that. I know that you want to be standing right in front of me the next time it happens. In all actuality, if it does, what are you going to do about it, anyway?"

"We could...."

"We could what? Check me back into the hospital? I hate those places and you know it."

"It helped yesterday," protested Saylor.

"What it helped yesterday was that I was freaked out. That's what you treated. That's what you brought under control, not the other thing."

"You don't know that. The lorazepam might have done something to break the cycle, get you out of the seizure or whatever it was."

Judtson shrugged. "It might have. The point is, it hasn't happened in well over a day now. We don't know whether it's going to happen again. If it does, I'm not going to flip out this time. I'm ready for it. I have the Valium in me, and I'm mentally prepared. There wasn't anything life-threatening about the episodes themselves. The only risk was my emotional reaction."

Saylor started to make a comment as Judtson continued, "And the other possibility is that it won't happen again. If that's the case, we can't keep going through our lives joined at the hip. You have your practice. You have Doni. You have a life."

"Doni is worried about you, too."

"I know she is, but eventually she's going to get tired of having two husbands in the house."

Obviously not yet comfortable, Saylor said, "I don't know. I don't feel right cutting you loose today."

"I have an idea. I know you're concerned that when I go into one of those seizures or trances or whatever they are, I can't get my body to respond to even let you know."

"True."

"I will carry my cell all the time, every minute. I'll take it with me to the bathroom. It'll be right outside the shower. It'll be on the nightstand while I sleep. Call me whenever you want. Hell, call me every hour. Send me a text message and I'll send a one-letter or one-number response. That way you'll know I haven't caught a train to the Twilight Zone."

"Every hour?"

"Yep."

"You'll answer me right away?"

"Promise."

"If you don't, you know I'll be sending the paramedics."

"I know."

"Even if you're in the...?"

"Saylor! I said I'd answer you, no matter where I am. Okay?"

Not at all happy, Saylor begrudgingly agreed, "All right. I guess."

▽

His office empty, Saylor sat at his desk answering calls from patients, ordering prescriptions, and reviewing various lab results from the past few days. Liz had placed the LabTech results for Judtson's blood tests at the top of the pile, knowing he would want to see those first. His eyes went directly to the summary of abnormal readings at the top. Nothing was flagged as out of range.

"Another dead end," he muttered, setting the paper aside. The next sheet on the pile was the test specifically for cortisol. As he expected, the reading was above the normal range, although not drastically high.

He punched the speed dial on his desk phone and called his partner. After the third ring, Vance answered, speaking loudly into the phone over the noise of a crowd. "Saylor. How's Judtson?"

"He seems to be fine at the moment."

"What? I can't hear you. I'm at my son's game."

"HE'S OKAY RIGHT NOW," Saylor shouted. "I'LL LET YOU GET BACK TO THE GAME."

"Okay, but wait. I did some preliminary research. Found a couple of cases that come close."

His interest piqued, Saylor asked, "EITHER HAVE A DIAGNOSIS?"

"No. They put them in circulation because they're stumped, as well. I left them on your desk."

His eyes sweeping the cluttered surface, at the far corner Saylor saw a folder marked "Judtson" in Vance's handwriting. He snatched it up and looked inside. "FOUND IT. I'LL LET YOU GET BACK TO THE GAME. THANKS."

"No problem. You're coming in tomorrow?"

"YES. I'LL BE IN."

"See you then."

"OKAY. THANKS AGAIN."

"No problem."

Saylor broke the connection and began reading the case notes. Vance was right; in the two other cases, the attending physicians were as clueless as he was. Posting the cases was a shot in the dark for both of them, as they obviously had run out of options and were down to hope, the hope that someone, somewhere, would see the strange set of symptoms online and offer some helpful direction.

He jotted down the phone numbers and email addresses of both doctors, noting that one was in New York City and the other in Washington, D.C., both in a time zone substantially later than Saylor's and well past anyone's office hours. Next, he composed a single email, planning to address it separately to the physicians, describing Judtson's case and asking if they had made any progress with their patients.

As he typed, a small pop-up box appeared in the lower corner of his screen, alerting him that there was a new email arriving and that it was routed to his personal address. A moment later, his cell phone vibrated, emitting a single chime, telling him that it had also received the message. He clicked on the box and the incoming message displayed. It was from the neurologist he had met during Judtson's EMG. Apparently, he had found the preliminary paper. Selecting the link to display the PDF, Saylor was mildly surprised that it was written by one of the two doctors he was in the midst of writing, the neurologist in New York.

The patient described in the paper had a progression of symptoms nearly identical to the ordeal suffered by Judtson. Saylor's level of concern worsened as he read the narrative describing the patient's experience as escalating, the episodes becoming more intense and each time lengthening in duration.

The New York neurologist was thorough. He had run all of the same tests as Saylor. He had consulted with all of the same specialists Saylor was planning to speak with. He had tried an array of medications, including Valium. None had any lasting efficacy. None delayed the progression. Saylor's mood darkened with each sentence he read, seeing nothing, no avenue, no method, no technique untried by his unknown colleague on the East Coast.

Reaching the final paragraph, Saylor was startled. The neurologist, making only a halfhearted attempt to conceal his elation, stated that his patient had spontaneously gone into remission. The episodes suddenly ceased. There had been no warning, no traceable reaction to any treatment at the time. The patient simply stopped experiencing the episodes.

At the time the paper was written, the patient had gone almost a month without an incident. Saylor glanced at the top of the page and saw that the paper was dated over a month ago. He finished the email to the other physician located in Washington, D.C., adding a question as to whether he had also witnessed the sudden remission observed by the New York doctor. He then composed an email to the New Yorker, describing Judtson's symptoms and asking whether his patient was still in remission. He took a moment to proofread both emails before dispatching them through the electronic ether.

A quick look at his desk clock told him that he was late checking on Judtson. Instead of a text message, he decided to call him, telling him what he had found.

Judtson answered on the first ring. "This isn't a text message."

"Found a couple of cases like yours."

"You did? You're not serious. What...how are they?"

"Haven't heard the outcome of one of them yet, but the other patient suddenly got better. The episodes, the 'breaks' as the doctor called them, stopped all on their own."

Saylor listened to a moment of silence as Judtson digested the fact. "How long did it take? Have the things come back at all? Any residual effects?"

"Whoa, partner. I read a preliminary paper. It was the same one the neurologist told me about. I have an email out to the doc in New York but probably won't connect with him until tomorrow. So, what I told you is all I know right now."

"Just stopped, huh?"

"Yes. By the way, how are you?"

"I'm good. Nothing has happened. I'm doing some writing right now."

"Okay. I'll let you get back to it."

"Saylor?"

"Yeah?"

"Thanks."

"You bet."

They ended the call.

▽

Her hand poised on the mouse, her eyes flitting back and forth across the screen, Kelsey read the posting on the website. Finishing her second reading of the paragraph, she shouted, "Those rats!"

Chapter 9

J UDTSON WAS IN A SAWMILL. It was bitterly cold and he was lying flat on his back, being carried forward on the rubber conveyor belt. He tried to get up but could not. He was able to raise his head enough to glimpse his body, expecting to see restraints holding him down, but saw none. He tried to sit up again, but failed. He tried to roll off the moving belt, but was frozen in place. All he could do was move his head and his eyes.

He heard a shout from above, piercing the raucous din of the mill. It was someone calling his name. He turned toward the sound and saw Saylor and Doni on a catwalk high above him, faces panicked. They were both shouting and pointing in the direction of his travel as they ran along the walkway. He lifted his head and looked the way they were pointing. Less than thirty feet away, he saw the massive spinning blade at the end of the conveyor.

With renewed urgency, he tried again to get himself off the conveyor, to no avail. He desperately looked up at his friends, who were madly scrambling to reach a ladder at the far end of the catwalk. In a somewhat detached manner, his mind calculated their speed and the distance they needed to travel, compared it to the rate he was moving forward, and knew they would never make it in time. The screaming whine of the blade was rising to a crescendo as it drew nearer. He stole another glance in its direction, when he spotted something which made his blood run even colder. Just above and to the side of the spinning blur of a blade, there was a small glass enclosure, obviously the operator's booth. Inside the booth, her hand firmly gripping the control handle of the conveyor belt and a wicked smile twisting her face, was Kristen.

He shouted to her, having no idea if his voice could be heard inside the glass booth. He begged her to stop the belt. He frantically beseeched her to halt the spinning blade. His words must have been audible to his wife, because her reaction to them was to cock her head back and laugh, pulling back harder on the handle. Judtson felt the speed of the belt increase under him.

Now mere yards from the front edge of the blade, he could smell the ozone from the electric motor which spun it. He could feel the draft created by the jagged teeth of the blade hungrily ripping through the air at several thousand revolutions per minute. His mind was still attempting to force his body to respond, to roll off the belt before it was too late. But the only response to his mental pleadings was a wild thrashing of his head. As he traveled feetfirst toward his death, his legs were spread and he was now so close to the blade that it was almost between the heels of his shoes. His mouth opening wide to scream, he looked again at the glass booth…at Kristen. She was leaning forward, her forehead nearly pressed against the glass, her eyes wide in horrid anticipation.

Judtson started to avert his eyes, not wanting the evil glee on her face to be the last image he saw as he died, when he perceived a blur of movement behind her. Kristen was so engrossed in the anticipation of witnessing his painful, imminent rending that she did not notice the door to the booth open. She did not hear the person rush her from behind. She did not see the flash of red hair or the 2x4 raised high above her head. She never knew what hit her, as she let go of the lever and crumpled to the floor unconscious. The moment the lever was released, the conveyor shuddered to an abrupt stop, the furiously whirling blade only inches from Judtson's groin.

At last, Judtson's body was responding. He pulled his legs up and rolled off the conveyor belt onto his bedroom floor. Completely disoriented from the dream, it took him a minute to recognize the insistent buzzing coming from his nightstand as his cell phone vibrated rhythmically. Grabbing it in the darkness, he touched his thumb to the screen, bringing it to life, and saw the text message from Saylor. "Checking in. How are you?"

His body calming as the perception of his current reality supplanted the previous images of the sawmill, he twisted around on the floor, sitting up with his back braced against the side of the bed, and typed in an answer. Rocky, realizing his buddy was out of bed, rose from his corner cushion and trotted to him in the darkness, laying his head on Judtson's lap.

"At least you could have saved me from the sawmill."

He sent his message and waited, grinning in the darkness.

It was less than a minute before Saylor responded, "I did."

"No, you didn't. Not this time."

"Who did? Doni?"

"Kelsey Batman."

"Ur kidding?"

"Nope."

"Weird. Later."

"Later."

Judtson put his phone back on the nightstand and idly rubbed Rocky's nestled head for a minute, making a small withdrawal from the reservoir of serenity banked by his furry angel. He made a mental note to tell Saylor tomorrow that one other change in the dream was that there were no longer any restraints holding him down on the conveyor belt. Twisting around, he looked across the bed at the mound that was Kristen. He knew she must be awake. The sawmill dream, in the past, had elicited shouts and moans from him, as he thrashed and on some occasions eventually fell to the floor, a spectacle surely impossible to ignore, much less sleep through with ease. But rather than acknowledge her sentience which would necessitate an interaction with him, she was choosing to feign unconsciousness. And that was probably for the better, he thought, especially since this was the first iteration of the recurring nightmare which featured her in the lead role of villain.

▽

As Judtson pulled into his office driveway, he saw that the Hummer was parked beside Ricky's car, blocking his own access to the garage. Somehow Kelsey's presence did not surprise him, and he was thankful the driveway was long enough for him to fit the Olds behind the Smart car, without the rear bumper extending out into the street. As he strode to the front door, he noticed the quickness of his step and realized that he was looking forward to seeing his eccentric new acquaintance.

Kelsey was standing next to Ricky at his desk, and the instant Judtson entered, both jerked their heads around to face him and both began speaking at once.

"Boss, I tried to tell her that she can't just keep loitering here, waiting for you."

"Judtson, I'm so glad you came in this morning. You are not going to believe what they did."

Closing the door behind himself, he held up his hands in a defensive gesture. "Ricky, it's okay. Kelsey, who are they, and what did they do?"

Ricky's mouth crinkled in a comic-book configuration of chagrin at the fact that his staked-out position was not being backed up by Judtson. Kelsey began speaking in her typical staccato style.

"I was on the Internet last night. I checked the website for the cable channel your show is on. I wanted to see if they had a teaser or preview or something about the program you taped with Villarreal."

"And?"

"It's gone!"

"What's gone, the cable channel?"

"NO!" Her voice stepped up an octave. "The show. There isn't even any mention of it."

Judtson hesitated, trying to grasp what she was saying. "That's normal. It wasn't supposed to air for another month or so. There wouldn't be anything on the website yet."

He could see the muscles in her jaw clench in frustration for a brief moment. "I'm telling you, it was there and they pulled it. I don't think it's going to air."

"How do you know?"

"You can tell…. Hey, can I use Ricky's computer? Let me show you."

Judtson glanced at his assistant and was amused by the proprietary panic on his face.

"Let's go in my office. You can show me there."

Relieved, Ricky almost gushed, "Your computer is on. I did have a chance to do that before…before Miss Batman arrived."

Laughing, Judtson held his arm out to his side, gesturing toward the door to his office. She hurried in and, without invitation, dropped into his chair behind the desk and seized the mouse, working it hastily. He removed his cell phone from his pocket and placed it on the desk, taking a spot behind her and watching as she expertly navigated to the cable website, clicked on the link to his show, and immediately found the link to the page listing upcoming programming.

"Okay, now look. There are your shows, just the way it all appeared last night."

"Right. As I told you, they probably haven't put it up yet."

She twisted around in the chair and faced him impatiently, her eyes flashing. "When was the airdate?"

Judtson thought for a moment. "I don't remember exactly, but I know it was in the latter part of August or early September."

"You're sure?"

"Yes, I'm sure."

Using the wheel on the mouse, she scrolled down the listings of programs. Beside each title was a brief synopsis and the airdate. "Look, here are all the shows for August." She scrolled down farther. "And here are all the September shows, all the way through the end of the month. Do you see it?"

His eyes scanned the screen. "No. I don't. That doesn't necessarily mean anything, though. They might have decided to run it later."

She shook her head vehemently, her shoulder-length red hair whipping back and forth from the motion. "I don't think so. Check this out."

Scrolling even farther down the page, she reached the end of the listings. "Look, here's the comment section. Good grief! There are more than the last time I checked, a bunch more."

He began reading the comments.

"Hey! What happened to the Villarreal program? I was looking forward to that one."

"You had the show about Puma Punku on the schedule for September, and now it's gone. What gives?"

"Okay, guys. I know I'm not going nuts. Where's the show about the spaceport in Peru? It was on the schedule. I know it was."

"Glad to see some sanity exists within your organization! Whoever jerked that stupid show, where Judtson was going to interview that nutcase Carlos Cabrillo Villarreal, deserves a promotion."

As he read, Judtson could feel his neck tightening. Reaching around Kelsey, he took control of the mouse and scrolled down. There were at least a hundred comments from people who had seen the show on the schedule and were anywhere from mildly curious to suspicious of a conspiracy to supportive of the decision.

"See what I mean? It was obviously there. They pulled it. You didn't know?"

"No. I hadn't heard anything about pulling it from the schedule."

"Let me show you something else."

She grabbed for the mouse, inadvertently placing her hand on top of his. There was an awkward moment before she lifted it, allowing him to relinquish the device. Closing the window to his program, she typed a string into the search engine and clicked the button to the right of the box. Within .04 of a second, there were displayed tens of thousands of listings containing his name and the name of Villarreal. Taking only a few seconds to scan the list, Kelsey clicked on the one she was attempting to find, and a new window opened.

She pointed at the screen as she spoke. "Here. This is the one I found earlier. Some guy, one of your fans I guess, took a screen shot of your upcoming schedule so he could record your shows. Look!"

Judtson studied the framed box. It was the September schedule for his shows, and the first program of the month was on the topic of Puma Punku and featured Carlos Cabrillo Villarreal. Under the screen shot was a comment by the man who had posted it: "Here's a screen shot of Kent's schedule that I took three days ago. The show on Puma Punku is now gone from the schedule. I sent a query to the network about this, but they haven't answered yet. Anybody know what's going on?"

"She's right, boss."

Judtson turned to see that Ricky was standing in his doorway.

"When I checked your emails this morning, the volume was up about four hundred percent, and everyone was asking about that show."

Whether it was due to the contagiousness of Kelsey's suspicion or the ominous nature of Darrow's comment at the end of their call, outlandish conspiratorial ideas and theories began popping up all over the landscape of Judtson's mind. Like the arcade game, he knocked each one of them back down into its hole with a metaphorical mallet, consciously focusing on some of the more mundane explanations.

"Ricky, get Emily on the phone."

As Ricky hastily returned to his desk, Kelsey asked, "Who's Emily?"

"My producer for the show."

She nodded and sprang up, moving around to the other side of the desk and plopping into one of the visitor chairs, as Judtson took his seat behind the desk.

Without bothering to use the intercom, Ricky shouted through the open doorway, "She's on line one."

Not trusting Kelsey to remain quiet if he used the speakerphone, Judtson snatched up the handset. "Good morning, Emily."

"Judtson, how are you?"

He could not help but be aware of Kelsey as she squirmed in her seat. The T-shirt she was wearing today read, "Who's your daddy? Aleister Crowley?"

"Been better, Emily. Hey, what happened to the Villarreal episode? I noticed it wasn't on the schedule."

There was a longer pause on the line than Judtson thought would be appropriate if there had been a routine answer for his question. Finally, she spoke. "Oh, it has just been rescheduled."

"That's what I assumed. What's the new airdate?"

There was another pause. "It's...it isn't set yet."

"Emily, what's the deal?"

"What do you mean, Judtson?"

"Well, this hasn't ever happened before. I've never had a show pulled off the schedule and postponed indefinitely. And there has never been a change in the schedule where I haven't been consulted. Besides, you are sounding a little weird."

His last comment was met with a nervous giggle. "Judtson, I'm sorry. I don't mean to sound...how did you put it...weird? It's just that I've got three people standing in front of me right now, waiting for answers on things. Sorry."

"What about the rest of it? Why was it pulled, and why wasn't I contacted, Emily?"

"Actually, Judtson, I don't know. I found out about it yesterday. I was trying to get some answers so I could call you."

"Okay. Who pulled it? Who made the decision?"

"Uh...well, it was my mother."

"Your mother?" he barked harshly into the phone. "Why would the network VP be involved? This is a production issue, not finance."

"I...Judtson...I really don't know," she stammered.

"Sorry, Emily. I didn't mean to shout at you. Could you get her on the phone for me?"

"It's all right, Judtson. Sure, I can try. Hold on."

Listening to the music while he was on hold, Judtson covered the mouthpiece with the palm of his hand. As he spoke to Kelsey, he noticed that Ricky had returned to his doorway, obviously curious, as well. "She says that she didn't even know about it."

"She said her mother pulled it from the schedule?" The question came from Ricky.

"Yeah. Without explanation, apparently."

"Her mother?" Kelsey snorted. "Is this a cable network or a work-at-home scheme?"

Judtson's gaze swung back to her. "Her mother is the number-two person at the network. But she's the head of finance, vice-president, and chief financial officer. Nothing to do with programming."

Shaking her head in disgust, Kelsey muttered, "Gotta love nepotism."

He heard a click, abruptly ending the music in mid-song. "Judtson, she's not in the building."

"She has a cell phone, doesn't she?"

"I tried it. It went straight to voice mail. I left her a message there and I left a message with her secretary. I told her that you really wanted to talk to her."

"Okay. By the way, what's the status of that show? Is production finished with it?"

Relieved that the subject had changed, Emily answered, her voice brighter. "I think so. I believe the final edit was a few days ago. I can check."

"Would you?"

"Sure. I'll call you back."

"No need. Just send me an email."

"Will do."

"Thanks, Emily."

They broke the connection and he replaced the handset on its base, turning to face Kelsey.

"She left a message on her mother's phone."

"And you believe that?"

"What do you mean?"

"Do you honestly think that a mother would see a call coming in from her own daughter and let it go to voice mail?"

"She might have been in a meeting and had the phone turned off or in her purse."

"Right." It was clear Kelsey did not accept his supposition. "I would have thought that a big-time operator like you would have rated a real producer for your cable show, not some ditzy daughter of the boss. I mean, come on, how good is she? And what is she, nineteen, twenty years old? I could barely hear her voice coming out of the earpiece, but she sounded like Minnie Mouse. Why do you put up with that? Judtson? Judtson?"

Kelsey leaned forward in her chair and practically yelled, "Judtson!"

Ricky, still in the office doorway, took a step into the room.

"Ricky, what's wrong? Is he having some kind of fugue state or something?"

"I don't...." Ricky hurried forward, coming around the desk to where Judtson was sitting immobile, his hand gripping the telephone, his eyes fixed rigidly on Kelsey.

Oh, no! It's happening again! Not again! At least I'm not alone. Thank God, I'm not alone. I need to stay calm, not freak out this time. This is the same deal. I lived through the last one. I'll live through this. It'll go away. It will go away. It has to go away.

"Boss! BOSS!" Ricky was shouting almost directly into Judtson's ear, his hand on the unmoving shoulder, shaking him.

"Ricky, what's going on? What is this?"

"I don't know. I...it has never happened before."

"Should I call 9-1-1?"

"Maybe. Yes, I think we should." He continued jostling the rigid form of Judtson as Kelsey instinctively reached for the desk phone. She had to pry Judtson's fingers from around the handset, and forcibly pushed his hand aside to gain access. The stiffness of his muscles, and the tendency of his hand and arm to revert to their former position, spooked her as she slipped the phone out from under his persistent grasp.

Before Kelsey could dial the number, she was startled by the sudden notes from Judtson's phone, still lying on the desk.

"That's Saylor! I know his ringtone," Ricky shouted. He grabbed the cell phone and read the text message.

"He's asking Judtson if he's okay."

"You'd better tell him he's not."

Rather than answer with a text message, Ricky dialed Saylor's number.

Chapter 10

===

KELSEY PACED NERVOUSLY IN THE PRIVATE CONSULTATION ROOM Saylor had arranged for them to use, just off the lobby at St. Joseph's Hospital. Ricky sat at the small desk, drumming his fingers loudly on the laminated top.

"You said that it had never happened before?"

"Kelsey, you heard what Saylor told us. I guess it *has* been happening lately, but I didn't know anything about it."

Ricky stared at the stranger who had suddenly enmeshed herself into their lives, and was again baffled by how she was able to accomplish the feat. After all, she had only appeared, unannounced, at Judtson's office yesterday. And here she was, having been involved in private conversations between Judtson and his cable show producer, then prodding Saylor and Ricky himself about his boss's privileged medical conditions, and now waiting here in the consultation room as though she were a family member. The social norm was that she would have parted ways with them when the paramedics were loading Judtson into the ambulance. Instead, she insisted upon riding in the back, with Judtson, the short distance to the hospital. What was truly strange was that both Ricky and Saylor had reacted to this as if it were perfectly normal.

There was no doubt she had a powerful personality...nearly overwhelming, he decided. Her effortless hubris, in virtually all he had witnessed her do since they first met, was phenomenal. She had a way of merely assuming that all of them would go along with whatever she wanted...no, demanded...from them. And they all did, he thought, even Judtson! Of all the people Ricky had ever met, his boss was the most resistant to being led, manipulated, coerced, or trapped. He was never intimidated. He never cowed. The slightest hint that someone was attempting to steer him caused Judtson to dig in immediately, to rebel. According to Saylor, he had always been that way, since he was a child. Saylor said that the psychologists referred to this trait as an "ascendant personality." When, in his early twenties, Judtson had taken the Minnesota Multiphasic Personality Inventory, this trait was more pronounced still. And yet, he allowed this woman to steamroll right over him.

Ricky did not think it was attractiveness which held them all in thrall. She was pretty enough, he guessed – flashy red hair, high cheekbones, intense blue eyes, a trim and fit figure which she displayed unabashedly with those tight T-shirts and even tighter blue jeans. Ricky had been Judtson's assistant for years and knew him very well. Because of the tenure of the relationship, he felt that he also knew Saylor fairly well. Neither of them was prone to fall head over heels for some flashy tart. Yes, he thought, Judtson's relationship with Kristen was pretty rocky right now, but he never noticed any tendency in his boss to begin indulging in extracurricular activities with the nearly countless female fans who practically threw themselves at him. He also knew that Saylor adored Doni and would never even entertain the thought. Of course, that left him. And her attractiveness, he concluded, would have zero effect on him.

Then what could it be? He had to admit there was something about her, something hard to describe. It was almost as if everyone had felt more alive around her, as if everything were more intense…as if she were some kind of a drug. No, he realized, that was not quite it. It was more like a hit of pure oxygen.

His thoughts were interrupted by the opening of the door and the entrance of Saylor.

"How is he?" Kelsey asked before Ricky could manage a word.

"Still the same," Saylor answered flatly. "We're running an electroencephalogram now."

Speaking quickly to get his question in ahead of Kelsey, Ricky asked, "What does that tell you?"

"An EEG measures the brain's electrical activity. We did one yesterday when he was normal, not in his current state. I want to see if there is any difference now."

"Like what?"

Saylor moved to the nearest chair and dropped into it heavily. "All of Judtson's readings were fine yesterday. There are some cognitive disorders, such as associated with seizures, where the test will show what is basically an electrical storm inside his head."

Kelsey gasped loudly. "Do you think he's having seizures? Is that what's happened?"

Shrugging, Saylor answered, "No. I don't know. But I think it would be a good idea to eliminate the possibility."

From the overhead speakers came a coded message. "That's for me," Saylor said and reached for the desk phone. After connecting with the operator, he spoke briefly and hung up. "Kristen has arrived. I told them to send her here."

"Who's Kristen?"

"Judtson's wife," Ricky answered, a shade of testiness inadvertently creeping into his voice.

"His wife!" Kelsey made no show of reacting to Ricky's tone. "I didn't know he was married."

The door opened and Kristen stepped in. "Saylor, how is he?"

"It happened again."

"Oh, no. Do you know yet what's causing it?"

"No. I'm trying, Kristen. But I haven't been able to figure it out."

She averted her eyes from Saylor and saw the others. "Ricky, how are you?"

He stepped forward, intending to comfort her, when something in her demeanor stopped him short. "I…I'm fine. Worried about the boss."

She next focused on Kelsey. "And you are?"

Kelsey moved toward her, extending her hand. "I'm Kelsey. I'm a friend of Judtson's."

Kristen looked down at the extended hand and did not reciprocate. "A friend of Judtson's? I don't recall that he ever mentioned you." Her voice was chilly.

"Oh, we just met. Just a couple of days ago. I just happened to be at his office today when this occurred."

Saylor and Ricky both stood nervously, watching the scene play out and knowing that there was nothing either of them could say to affect the outcome.

Kristen forced a plastic smile. "Perhaps you could excuse us now. I'd like to talk with my husband's doctor."

Before Kelsey could respond, Ricky said, "I'll be going, too."

Kristen turned to him. "No, Ricky. That's fine. You're welcome to stay."

He glanced at Kelsey, noticing that her face was flushed, and suddenly felt a tinge of sympathy for her as she spoke. "You're right, of course. I have no business being here. I'll be going."

Her eyes cast downward, she wiped the palms of her hands on her jeans and hurried to the door, pulling it open. As she was about to step out, she turned back to Saylor. "Will you let me know…?"

"I'm sure that you can check with Ricky on my husband's status in a few days," Kristen interjected before Saylor could say a word. "It was a pleasure meeting you. Kelsey, was it?"

Kelsey's eyes darted from Saylor's to Ricky's for a moment. She then mumbled something about it being a pleasure as well and departed, closing the door with a loud *thunk*.

Whirling back to face Saylor, Kristen snapped, "Saylor, who in the hell is that?"

"We both just met her. She's a fan of Judtson's," he lied convincingly.

"It's true," Ricky chimed in. "She popped into the office for the first time yesterday and came back today."

"Ricky, how did she get here?"

"She followed us. When Judtson went into his state, she was at the office and decided to tag along."

"Why was she *here*, Saylor, in this room? If she's only a fan, it seems as though you would have had her wait in the lobby."

Saylor allowed a trace of irritation into his voice. "Kristen, I had other things on my mind at the time, like taking care of Judtson."

She stared intently at him for a moment before shifting her gaze to Ricky, trying to gauge their veracity by reading their eyes. Giving up, she sighed. "I'm sorry. I was probably a bit bitchy. It's only that this whole thing happening with Judtson has me on edge. And then, walking in here and seeing her hanging out with you two like some longtime friend…*or something*…got to me."

Saylor put his hand on her shoulder. "There is no 'or something' and you should know it. She's a fan, albeit a rather intense one, and that's it."

They were interrupted by a knock on the door. After stepping away to open it, Saylor spoke with someone outside for a few minutes and returned to tell them, "The EEG was completely normal."

▽

Saylor sat at the courtesy desk provided for visiting physicians and checked his emails. Judtson was once again sedated to unconsciousness. Ricky had returned to their office to take care of any unfinished business and lock it up for the day. Kristen had looked in on her husband before making a vague comment about needing to go home for a while.

Saylor's eyes scanned the list and spotted an email from the neurologist in New York. Double-clicking on it, he saw that his East Coast colleague had acknowledged his email and, rather than answering his questions, had provided his cell phone number, with a comment that Saylor could call until 10:00 p.m. Eastern time. Saylor grabbed the desk phone and tapped in the number.

"This is Dr. McWhorter."

"Dr. McWhorter, this is Saylor Costello in Tucson."

"Yes, Saylor. You're the one with the case in Arizona. How is the desert this time of year? And by the way, I'm David."

"Hot."

"Ahhh, yes. I remember that well from my internship at UMC. But it's a dry heat."

"Not this time of the summer. It's monsoon season."

There was a chuckle on the line. "I recall those days, as well. You'd come back from grabbing a bite to eat at lunchtime and the sky would be clear. You'd step outside two or three hours later and there was so much rain, thunder, and lightning it would seem like the end of the world."

"When were you here?"

"1989."

"The afternoon storms have become much less clock-like since then."

"That's curious. Well, so much for the pleasant excursion into the past. You inquired about my patient with the breaks."

Saylor explained, in more detail than he had provided in his email, the course of Judtson's condition, including the most recent event.

"It sounds very consistent with my case."

"And your patient had a spontaneous remission or cessation?"

"She did."

"Are you still in contact with her?"

"I am. And obviously, you're wondering whether she remains free of the breaks."

"Yes."

"She does. Not a single incident. Not even a recurrence of the initial minor breaks."

"Why do you call them 'breaks'?"

"What would you call them?"

He thought for a moment. "We've been referring to them as episodes, incidents, even seizures."

"I've never found any evidence that they're seizures, have you?"

"No, I haven't. As I mentioned, he's in the middle of an episode as we speak. I ordered an EEG, and all activity was normal. 'Breaks' they are, then. Anything else you think I should know?"

"As a matter of fact, there is. Since I first disseminated the case study, I've heard from others with similar, you could even say identical, cases."

"I saw the preliminary paper on the one in D.C."

"Yes, that is one of them. But there are others, as well."

Saylor's interest was piqued. "How many?"

"I've heard from a total of seven. Eight, counting yours."

"All of them now in remission?"

"Four, at the moment. The most recent remission was only declared yesterday."

"This is amazing. It sounds as though we might have something new."

"Indeed it does. Since it appears that I have 'patient zero,' I've taken the liberty of contacting the CDC. They are looking at all of the cases. Epidemiological studies have already begun. If you don't mind, I'll inform them of yours."

The first thought which came into Saylor's mind was how Judtson would react if he knew that every aspect of his life was being scrutinized by the Center for Disease Control. "I'd better talk to my patient first."

"Right. The Feds do tend to get a little invasive."

"That's an understatement."

McWhorter laughed. "I'll let them know that there is an unidentified 'patient eight' and leave it at that for now."

"Thank you. I do have one more question, David. Based upon your experience with your patient and the information you've received from the other docs, can you hazard a guess as to how close to remission my patient might be?"

There was a brief silence on the line as the New York doctor thought. "You said that he is in the midst of his second full-blown break, correct?"

"Yes. Well, there have been two major ones of lengthy duration, preceded by a full break which lasted only minutes or possibly seconds. Prior to that, he noticed minor unresponsiveness from his body."

There was another pause. "Four remissions are not many to go on. But if I were to hazard a guess, I'd say he's fairly close. The other cases where remission hasn't occurred are all in roughly the same stage as yours. Remember, this isn't a condition in which the symptom is ongoing and its cessation, like a fever breaking, is clinically obvious. It's up to each attending physician to decide when his or her patient has gone long enough without suffering from a break, in order to call it a remission. Even so, all of the cases, from first symptom to cessation, progress fairly rapidly."

Before terminating the call, Saylor thanked him and they exchanged pleasantries and commitments to remain in touch.

▽

This is strange. I'm not sure, but I think that I'm asleep. I was sedated again. Or at least the "I" who is out there in the world is asleep. Yet I'm not. I'm in here wide awake…thinking, wondering, trying to regain control. I'm definitely not unconscious. I'm not dreaming. Or maybe I am. Maybe I'm dreaming that I'm not dreaming. How can I tell? In a way, it almost feels as though I'm plopped in a very dark room, a room with no doors, no windows. I can't get out. But no one can get in, either. And that's sort of oddly comforting.

The input I'm receiving from the eyes…huh, I notice that I don't refer to them as my eyes…anyway, the input I'm getting from them is the same darkness which I now recognize as being covered by the eyelids, but without the reddish hue. I've figured out that it means the room is dark, so there isn't any light filtering through the closed lids and being tinted red from the blood in the veins. My ears pick up the more muted sounds of the hospital during the middle of the night as the staff outside the door to my room go through their routines. Every once in a while…I have no real sense of time…someone comes in – I suppose it's a nurse – and checks on me, checks my blood pressure, checks my pulse.

I can also hear the rhythmic sound of my own breathing. I can feel the bed I'm lying in. I can smell the antiseptic smell.

Saylor told me that these episodes are going to simply end. I wish he knew when. I have to admit that I'm getting used to them. Let's just say, I'm not panicking the way I was at first.

▽

Kelsey was still wide awake, her eyes burning from strain and fatigue as she stared at the monitor in her darkened bedroom. Yes, she was objectively curious about the phenomenon happening to Judtson. It was unusual enough, strange enough to catch her attention. But she also had to admit that she cared about Judtson Kent. She had never expected to even like him, and she could not really say that she did. All of the books he had written over the years had infuriated her. Not only did they debunk practically everything she believed in, they conveyed a tone of contempt and ridicule toward those who dared to cling to the various ideologies. She had been planning on despising him. Yet, there was something different within him, something she recognized, something which resonated with her.

The text on the screen was now updating and scrolling every few seconds, new comments pushing previous postings down. She had started a new thread on her blog: a thread describing, without mentioning him by name, the ordeal Judtson was experiencing. The time was well after midnight, and she had attracted more than twenty participants to the discussion. Some of them were familiar to her. It was not that they were people she had ever met, or even people whose real names were known to her; they were the "regulars" in countless chats on countless topics.

Kelsey thought that some of them were "pretty cool." On the whole, their comments, insights, observations, and opinions had frequently been valuable. She regarded this anonymous assemblage as her posse, her think tank, her monster squad. The initial thread had kick-started their conversation. She only jumped in when the direction was getting too far afield, too esoteric, and she had to rein them back in, to keep them on point, a role she had to fulfill often.

So far, the discussion had covered the possibility of the government putting something in the air or the water, some chemical or gas which was causing Judtson to have these blackouts. Although Kelsey had very little faith in the integrity or trustworthiness of the government, this explanation did not quite ring true for her, so she nudged the group off the topic. The participants tossed out for consideration the possibility of cosmic rays being the culprit, cosmic rays either from the sun or generated by spacecraft orbiting the Earth. She nudged again.

One of the posse, screen name "Gaiya," put forth the thought that Judtson was more sensitive to ambient heat and that he was the first victim in what would become a widespread epidemic triggered by global warming. Nudge.

A new participant, screen name "Alchemist," joined the discussion, and Kelsey bolted upright from the tired slouch she had sunken into earlier. Alchemist, whoever he or she was, was her favorite chat buddy. Despite the fact that she had no idea as to Alchemist's gender, she found that she always thought of the writer as male. He was always insightful, always able to inject a profound and original thought or suggestion when everyone else was caught up in an endless loop of clichéd blathering. She often wondered if Alchemist might be a librarian or some sort of curator at the American Museum of Natural History in New York, because he had an astounding bank of knowledge from which he drew. It was almost spooky. She had never once fact-checked anything he mentioned and caught him in an error. Alchemist's terse comment – "Sounds like mind control to me" – sent a powerful shiver up her spine.

▽

Switching off the computer and monitor, Saylor stood up. The sudden flood of dizziness, exacerbated by fatigue and the rapid change in blood pressure, caused him to grab the edge of the desk for support.

"Saylor, are you all right?"

He turned to see Patrick Worden approaching, a concerned expression on his face.

"Just a little tired. I'm okay."

He released his grip on the desk and stood straight, as if to demonstrate that fact.

With a sardonic grin, Worden said, "No one ever wants to admit to me that anything's wrong."

"Do you blame us?" Saylor retorted with a chuckle. "One poorly chosen phrase and you've got us locked up in a padded room for observation."

Hitching up one pant leg, Worden perched on the edge of the desk next to Saylor. "What none of you realize is that the exhibiting of denial is the most damning symptom of all. I heard that you were looking for me."

"I was. I have a case in need of your input."

"I have the time right now if you want to talk about it. Do you want to sit back down?"

Saylor shook his head. "No, I think I do better staying upright."

He went on to describe Judtson's progression of symptoms, up to and including his current state. As he talked, Saylor anticipated more of a reaction from the psychiatrist. He finished by commenting, "I would have expected a look of surprise, or at least curiosity. Is this a syndrome or disorder familiar to you?"

"Familiar in that I recognize it, yes. In the sense that it is common, no."

"I've never come across anything like this. As a matter of fact, my research on the web yielded some other neurologists around the country with similar cases. None of them mentioned a psychiatric explanation."

Worden shrugged. "You know how patients can be. Most people avoid us like the plague. It's as if they think that coming to a psychiatrist would be either admitting defeat or surrendering themselves to a shaman or witch doctor."

"There is some truth to that. Well, what do you think it is?"

"Generically, it falls into the category of a dissociative disorder. Specifically, it sounds like depersonalization disorder."

"Which is?"

"Most commonly a symptom of an underlying anxiety issue, although not always. The classic definition of DPD is that the patients suffer from persistent or recurring feelings of being detached from their own bodies. This includes a feeling of detachment from their own mental processes, a sense of automation, a feeling that they are in a movie. We even include the so-called out-of-body experience in this diagnosis."

"Does it usually show up in this way? With the patient going into a kind of catatonia or trance?"

"As I mentioned, this isn't a disorder I've had much personal experience with, Saylor. The few patients I've seen remained essentially functional. They only described what they perceived at the time. I've never had a case present in this extreme."

"It sounds to me as if patients who suffer from this DPD could be normal other than the fact that they *perceive* themselves to be detached, as opposed to an actual physiological separation."

"Perception is what we deal with in my field most of the time. But I wouldn't separate the two as if they were black and white."

Saylor thought for a moment. "I did forget to mention a detail which might be significant, in that it doesn't fit with the possibility that we're dealing with a perceptual issue rather than a physiological one. When my patient had the break – as a doctor in New York calls it – in the elevator lobby, I laid him down on the floor. I've already described how rigid his body was and how his eyes remained fixed in the orientation they had before I moved him."

"Yes."

"What I didn't tell you was. . .as he was lying there, a fly landed on his temple and walked onto his open eye, pausing directly upon the pupil."

"Really? That is odd."

"That's an understatement. The corneal reflex is the only reflexive connection in the body which bypasses the brain completely. Must have been a hard-wired mechanism from the early evolution of the delicate eye. It can't be consciously overridden, because it doesn't even go through the brain. Patients who are in a coma will blink if you puff air at their eyes. Patients who are flatlined on the EEG will blink. Someone in a full vegetative state, with absolutely no cognitive functions and on life support, will blink."

The psychiatrist leaned forward, intrigued. "There truly is no method for short-circuiting the mechanism?"

"Only one. The surface of the eye can be anesthetized. Eye surgeons do it so they can operate without the corneal reflex interfering."

"Then the eye doesn't feel the invasion, so it doesn't react."

"Right. But my patient's eye was not anesthetized."

"Clearly not."

"So you can see why I'm having trouble fitting a psychiatric disorder onto all the symptoms."

"I wouldn't rule it out completely. Conversion disorders, also anxiety related, can cause very real physical symptoms, such as blindness, without the presence of any physical cause. This could somehow be an extreme manifestation of that. I would like to see your patient."

"He's sedated and unconscious at the moment. The last time this happened he reverted back to normal when he regained consciousness. Needless to say, there isn't any guarantee that it will be the case this time."

"Assuming he does return, I would definitely like to speak with him."

"That will be up to him."

"Of course."

Worden paused a moment, staring intently at Saylor's face. "You don't have an ethical conflict with this patient, do you?"

Startled, Saylor blurted, "What do you mean?"

"He's obviously a friend. You know that isn't a good idea, ever."

"I know. I know the ethics involved. Yes, he is a friend. Not only that, he's my best friend. And I am his. That's part of the problem. He won't deal with anyone *but* me. If I weren't treating him, I would be concerned that he might go untreated."

"Be careful, Saylor. You know the pitfalls."

"I do. Oh, there was one more detail I forgot to mention."

"If you are going to tell me that when he returns from these breaks, he reports conversations with dead people, I'm not sure I want to hear it."

Saylor laughed. "No. Nothing like that. The neurologist in New York told me that he is aware of eight cases similar to Judtson's, including four which have gone into spontaneous remission. He's predicting the same outcome for Judtson."

The psychiatrist tilted his head slightly, intrigued. "Sounds as if it could be a flight into health."

"I've thought the same thing…that the symptoms were the manifestations of a psychological struggle or conflict of some sort and that the sudden remission was the brain rebelling against the condition and running headlong back into wellness."

"Exactly."

"But don't you find it strange that there have been absolutely no previous cases like these in the medical literature, and now there are suddenly a total of nine instances around the country?"

"There are some possible explanations for that, such as misdiagnosis in the past, or failure to report on the part of the patient. The tendency of patients not to discuss with a doctor something which might cause them to be considered insane is a powerful influence."

"That may be true. But it feels like something new, maybe something environmental – a new chemical contained in some product and recently introduced into society, a new aerosol or food additive, something. Dr. McWhorter in New York thinks that he has 'patient zero' and has reported it to the CDC. They've already begun the epidemiological evaluations."

"Well, if your patient recovers, I'd still like to chat with him. It never hurts to approach something new from all directions."

Saylor shrugged. "It couldn't hurt."

"I take it you've eliminated all of the possible physiological causes?"

Saylor ran down the list of tests, including the repeat EEG he ordered while Judtson was in his current state. "I think we've covered the bases, and there's no indication of a physical issue involved so far. We are waiting on the results of some of the blood tests."

"Toxicology?"

"Right. Toxicology, heavy metals. We're checking everything we can think of. The results do take a while."

The two doctors parted company, with Saylor promising to keep Worden apprised of Judtson's condition and progress. The corridors of the hospital were as quiet this time of night as they ever got. As Saylor walked, his mind continued to sift through all of the information he had gathered. "Leave it to Judtson," he complained to himself. "He would come up with something no one has heard of before."

The door was open and he walked quietly into the dimly lit room. Out of professional habit, his eyes first trained on the saline IV hanging from the rack beside the bed, and then on the monitor displaying the heart rate and blood pressure, with the sound of the device's beeping muted in deference to the resting patient. Everything appeared normal...everything except the fact that the man tied in to all of the paraphernalia, the one he was trained to only think of as the patient, was the one person in the world he was closest to, other than Doni. And that person, that friend, was lying perfectly still on the bed.

"I'm here, Judtson." He spoke softly. "Been here almost all night. In between checking on you, I've been doing some research. I've talked to some other doctors. You already know that there was one other patient who had this...whatever it is, and has spontaneously come out of it. I found out tonight that there are actually a total of eight others with the same symptoms. And four of them have come out of it so far. It looks as though you should, too. I just wish I knew when, pal."

He stared at Judtson's face in the shadowy light. It was peaceful, tranquil.

"I know that you hate having the cannula in your nose. It's one of those things we do here. When you wake up and you're back from wherever you go, you can jerk it out and throw it on the floor."

With a single chuckle, he continued, "That's why I okayed it. I thought maybe it might make you come back sooner."

Judtson's left hand, the one with the oximeter connected to his finger, was on top of the covers, and Saylor took it and squeezed gently. "I'm bushed, man. I can't think anymore and I can barely walk. I'm going to go home for a while and get some sleep. I'll be back soon. If you wake up before I come back, they know to call me. Next time I see you, be Judtson, okay?"

Go get some sleep, Popeye. You're worthless to me when you get this tired. And stop worrying about me. I'll be fine. Especially now that I know there are four others who've beat it. But when I do wake up and come back, I'm going to get even with you for this cannula thing in my nose.

Chapter 11

"Honey, wake up. Saylor, honey, come on. The hospital called. Judtson's awake."

Saylor awoke with a start, his eyes jerking open to the sight of Doni leaning over him, gently shaking his shoulder.

"He's awake?" he mumbled, slurring his words.

"Yes, he is. They just called."

"Is he…?"

"Back? Yes. They said he removed his own IV, got out of bed, and threw the cannula in the toilet."

Saylor laughed. "Yep, he's back. What time is it?"

"A little after seven. You got a good four-hour power sleep."

As he forced himself to sit up, he noticed that she reached for something on the nightstand. Surprised, he was pleased to see that it was a welcome mug of coffee, and she handed it to him with a smile when he had finished moving.

He took it gratefully. "Wow, coffee in bed. You never let me have it here."

"That's 'cause you spill." She kissed him gently on the forehead and stood up from her perch on the edge of the mattress. "Now get up. The Squirrel-man is waiting. And if you don't get there soon, he'll have half the staff on that floor in tears and ready to quit."

"Where are you going?"

"Oh, I don't know. I think maybe I'll get dressed, have breakfast, do the laundry, drop off your dry cleaning, pick up some groceries. And then after that, I'll head over to La Paloma for my facial and mud bath, followed by my tennis lesson from Lars, with whom, by the way, I am having a passionate affair."

"Okay, baby. Have a good day."

She paused at the door to their bedroom and glowered back at Saylor. "I knew you weren't listening. Your mind is already at the hospital with Judtson."

He looked up at her innocently. "Not true. Heard every word. I hope Lars is better in the affair department than he is as your tennis coach. Your backhand stinks."

She stuck out her tongue and blew a raspberry at him before turning to leave, muttering, "This life as a doctor's wife is great!"

Laughing, he climbed out of bed, only spilling a few drops of the coffee on the Designers Guild sheet.

▽

When Saylor arrived, he found that Judtson was out of the hospital gown, dressed and sitting in the visitor chair, instead of lying in bed where he had left him a few hours earlier. He also saw that a nurse, whom he knew only as Angela, was still in the room, taking down the IV bottle and straightening out the tangle of tubes and wires Judtson had made in his hasty self-extrication.

As soon as Judtson espied Saylor's approach through the open door, he sprang up. "About time, man."

"I suppose you want to get out of here."

Angela glanced over at Saylor with a look intended to convey that she could not agree more. He winked at her and turned to his friend. "Let's go. I'll sign you out."

Saylor suspected that the entire staff was eager for the departure, as the paperwork was already prepared, on a clipboard, and ready for his signature at the nurses' station.

As they left, he turned to Judtson. "It seems you made your usual impression."

"Are you joking? They liked me there."

"Of course they did."

"No, really. They came in every few minutes this morning, two...three of them at a time, to visit with me and check on me."

Saylor laughed. "Pal, that wasn't because they liked you. They simply wanted all the hospital personnel to see you with their own eyes. They knew no one would believe their stories otherwise."

Judtson came to an abrupt halt as they approached the automatic doors at the exit. "That's not true! Is it? Am I that bad?"

Saylor looked into his friend's eyes and saw that he was serious. "That bad? No. I wouldn't call it 'bad.' Doni and I love you. Ricky's nuts about you. It's just that you take some getting used to."

He started to take a step forward, but Judtson showed no sign of wanting to move, a cloud of vulnerability across his face that Saylor had not seen since they were in seventh grade. "That's really it, isn't it?"

"What do you mean?"

"Only the three of you. I guess Kristen used to love me. Now she doesn't even like me. So that's all I have, three friends in the whole world. Four, counting Rocky."

"You've got millions of friends. People love you."

"Saylor, those are fans, not friends."

He could think of nothing to say in response.

"Those people read my books. They like what they read. But that isn't 'me,' any more than a handmade chair *is* the guy who made it. You can love somebody's work but hate him as a person."

"They don't hate you."

"You're right. They don't. Because they don't know me."

"Judtson, that's bulls...!"

"No, it isn't!"

Judtson turned on his heel and walked through the automatic door. Saylor followed, and they crossed the visitor lot into the area reserved for physician parking, neither saying a word. The two climbed into Saylor's pickup truck, and he started the engine, quickly setting the air conditioner to full power.

Before he could drop the shifter into reverse, Judtson turned in the seat and faced him. "Sometimes I'm not even sure about you."

"Judtson! That's nuts. You're my...."

Holding up his hand to stop Saylor, Judtson said in a soft voice, "I know I'm a pain. I'm a jerk. I'm needy. I'm embarrassing. Crazy. I drag you into stuff that, if you get caught, could ruin your career and your reputation. I think that you just hang with me because you feel as though you have to, because you feel sorry for me or something."

Saylor's voice took on a stern tone. "Listen to me. You are my friend and you are the best friend I could ever imagine having. We have been friends since elementary school."

"You can't possibly enjoy what I put you through. And what I put you and Doni through. We're not kids anymore, Saylor. You have a job, a profession. You have a wife. But I'm still acting the way I did when I talked you into nailing Mrs. Temple's shoes to the floor."

"That was *not* your idea. It was mine. And who was the one who brought the hammer and nails to school that day?"

"You."

"Right. I know because I brought the nails in my pocket, and one of them went into my thigh when I sat down. I had to get a tetanus shot."

Despite himself, Judtson felt the corners of his mouth curling up. "Yeah. I remember."

"I'm sure you do. And I bet you remember scaring the devil out of me when I showed you how infected the wound was. You convinced me that they were going to have to amputate and that I'd have to get a peg leg."

"It would have been perfect." Judtson was laughing as he recalled the time. "You know, *Saylor*, *Popeye*, *peg leg*. It all fit."

"Thanks. I had nightmares about that for months. And whose idea was it to scare Doni out of her wits that night she was babysitting?"

"That was classic. All three of us had seen *Scream* together. She should have known we'd try to re-create that opening scene. Okay. You're right again. That was your idea, even though you've made me take credit for it ever since that night."

"Well, yeah! She was furious. I did want to marry her someday."

"Yeah! Well, so did I."

Judtson's comment made Saylor stop cold. "You did?"

The joviality had suddenly evaporated from the conversation. "I loved her, too. You know that."

Saylor stared hard at his friend. The fragile vulnerability had returned to his face; and yet, this time it was different.

"I was always terrified that you would decide to go after her. I was sure she'd drop me in a second to be with you."

Shaking his head, Judtson reassured, "No way. I saw how she looked at you when we would walk into the room together. I never had a chance and I knew it."

"I don't know about that. You should have heard how she would talk about you when we were alone – 'Judtson this' and 'Judtson that' and 'Isn't Judtson a riot!' I used to get jealous."

"She might have talked about me. But it was probably the same way the zoologist who first observed the duck-billed platypus would have talked incessantly about his new, freakish discovery. Besides, even if she did like me, I wouldn't have done that to you. I couldn't have."

Saylor fell silent. As did Judtson. After two or three minutes passed, Saylor put the truck in reverse and backed out of the space.

▽

At Judtson's request, they drove to his office. Along the way, they talked, careful to keep the subject on Judtson's condition. When they arrived, both of them were surprised not to see the Hummer in the driveway.

"Judtson!" Ricky exclaimed as they entered; he immediately jumped up from behind the desk to greet his boss.

"You're not going to hug me, are you?"

"Are you all right?"

"As all right as I ever get."

"You had me so worried."

"I had myself worried, too. But I'm fine."

"Thank goodness. I had no idea what you've been going through, until Saylor told me while you were…."

"In la-la land."

"I was going to say, while you were in the hospital."

"Thanks for calling Saylor so quickly."

Ricky shrugged off the comment. "What is it like? How do you feel when it happens?"

"It feels as though I'm having an out-of-body experience without being out of my body."

"What do you mean?"

"I'm completely disconnected from my body, in that I'm not controlling anything. I'm still receiving the input from all five senses. I'm still conscious, still there. But it's all only one-way. I'm cut off."

Ricky shivered. "That's terrible. It sounds like a recurring dream I had when I was a kid. I used to think that when we died, only our bodies died, not our minds…and that through the whole course of events, through the death, the funeral, and then" – he shuddered again – "being buried forever, I would still be conscious and just lying there in a dark coffin for all time, aware of every minute of it, especially the worms…."

"Enough! I get the picture."

He was instantly apologetic. "I'm so sorry. That was a horribly stupid thing to tell you after what you just went through."

"You're right. It was very creepy and nasty of you."

A sudden pinched expression on his face, Ricky snapped, "Actually, I'm not sorry at all. I see that your episode hasn't dampened your more boorish tendencies."

Judtson could not help laughing. "Maybe we could cover some business while I'm still with you. After all, you never know when I'm going to have my next *episode*."

"That's true. I have no idea how I'm going to keep my day organized if you're going to keep randomly flaking out on me. I put all your calls on phone slips, in case I needed to bring them to you at the hospital."

He stepped back to his desk and picked up the stack of slips and began thumbing through them, handing them to Judtson after reading each one. "Emily called. As did her mother, Dorothy Benson. Dr. Villarreal called for you. Mitch Murray. Miss Batman called. Four times. And the rest are the usual assortment of fans, talk radio producers who want to book you on a show, and independent bookstores wanting you for a signing, including that pest Henry Thompson from Blake's Books."

"I thought you had a publicist to handle your scheduled events," Saylor interjected.

"We do," Ricky answered. "And I direct all of the callers to her, but sometimes they insist on trying to speak with Judtson personally."

"Why?"

"Because the publicist turns them down. They think if they talk directly to Judtson, he'll take them off the list."

"List? I haven't heard about a list."

Ricky smiled. "It was created by the boss before my time with him. Apparently, when he was first starting up and hoping to get his name out there, he was quite aggressive in contacting talk shows and bookstores, trying to set up appearances."

"I remember those days."

"The names on the list are the people who were either rude or condescending, or who never returned his calls."

"They're jerks," Judtson added.

"And now that you're a big-time author…."

"It's payback time."

"Got it. Makes sense to me. Well, I'm going to let you get to your work. Do you want me to pick you up later?"

"Yes."

"I can give you a ride home," offered Ricky.

"And ride as a passenger in that motorized roller skate of yours? Yes, Saylor, please, please pick me up. If you get busy and can't make it, I'll walk."

"That's four miles from here, and it's over a hundred degrees today," Ricky protested.

"Does that tell you anything, Ricky?"

Laughing, Saylor said good-bye to them and left.

"I have no idea why I felt so bad when you were in your *episode*. After coming back here and working alone for the rest of the day, I went home yesterday in one of the best moods I've had in years."

"I'll do my utmost to check out again as soon as possible."

"Would you, please?"

With a theatrical huff, Ricky spun and walked back to his desk as Judtson went to his office, clutching the phone slips. Returning to the same seat in which he had slipped away yesterday, he dialed the number for Dorothy Benson. She answered on the second ring. "This is Mrs. Benson."

"Hello, Dorothy."

There was only the slightest pause as she stifled her reaction to his using her first name. "*Mister* Kent, Emily told me that you wished to speak with me."

"I presume your daughter told you why."

Another slight pause. "She did. You are curious as to the status of your program with Carlos Cabrillo Villarreal."

"I am."

"We have taken it out of the schedule for the foreseeable future."

He kept his voice even. "And why is that?"

"We've decided that the direction of that particular program was not consistent with either your format or the overall format of the network."

A harsh bray of laughter burst from Judtson. "You're kidding, right? Not consistent with your overall format."

"No, I am quite serious."

"So, let me get this straight. I understand that the name of your network is The World of Science. But which of your shows do you think the Villarreal program most conflicts with, *The Swamp Pigs of Louisiana* or *The Kings of Dumpster Diving*?"

She did not rise to the bait. "The decision is made. I assure you that there will be no effect on your compensation or any impact on your personal schedule. We will pick up the slack created by its absence with a premature rerun, until you've had an opportunity to record another show."

"Dorothy, you're assuming I'm inclined to make another show with you. However, that aside for a moment, could you please explain why the chief financial officer of the network is even involved in a programming decision?"

"This was not a decision made by myself."

"You just used a reflexive pronoun in the objective case without a nominative referent. If you were to state it properly, accommodating your supererogatory and redundant style, you would have said 'This was not a decision *I* made by myself.' So who made the decision, Dorothy?"

This was one of the times Judtson wished he had been using Skype, as he could only rely upon her vocal inflections as he tried to deduce her irritation. "The matter was decided jointly by the various department heads. It was not taken lightly."

"I'm so relieved by that, Dorothy. It is a pity that none of the participants, in the midst of their thoughtful deliberation, felt it appropriate to include me in the discussion."

"That was, possibly, an error on our part. But I'm afraid the decision is made."

"Understood. And as I've said many times in my life, decisions have consequences."

"Is that some sort of a threat, Mr. Kent?"

"Some sort of a threat? I suppose it is. I'll leave it up to you to ferret out which sort it might be. Good day, Dot."

Terminating the call, Judtson speed-dialed Emily.

"Hello, Judtson."

"Emily. You called?"

"Yes, I did. Did you hear from my mother?"

"Yes. We had a very pleasant chat. What's the status of the show? Is the editor finished with it?"

"He is. Why do you want to know, if it isn't going to run?"

"I'd like you to burn a copy of it for me."

There was a long pause. "I don't know, Judtson."

"Emily, I'm working on a book on the same topic as that show. I'd just like to have it as a reference."

"I guess it would be okay."

"Thanks. When can you get it for me?"

"Probably right after lunch. I'll email a link. You can download it from there."

"Perfect. Thanks."

"No problem, Judtson. Talk to you soon."

He hung up and glanced at the balance of the phone messages, picked up the one from Mitch, crumpled it, and tossed it into the wastebasket. Judtson wanted to phone Kelsey next, but decided he should probably return the call from Carlos. After seven rings, Villarreal's voice-mail announcement came on, so he left a message.

When he phoned Kelsey, she answered on the first ring. "Judtson! How are you?"

"I'm fine, Kelsey."

"Oh, thank goodness. That really freaked me out yesterday! What happened?"

He gave her the background, starting with the first incident during his paintball escapade. When he finished, she immediately asked, "Does Saylor know what's causing it?"

"No. No one does."

"Really?" The tone of her voice conveyed a healthy level of suspicion.

"What? What are you thinking?"

"I don't know. Maybe it's nothing. Maybe it's just crackpot stuff."

"You? Crackpot? Come on, now."

He heard a nervous giggle over the phone line. "After your wife arrived…. I didn't know you had a wife."

"I do."

"Anyway, after she arrived at the hospital and kicked me out…."

"She kicked you out?"

"Oh, nobody told you? I went to the hospital with you."

"I know."

"They did tell you?"

"No. I remember."

"I don't understand. You were out of it."

"When I'm in one of those things, I can still see, hear, all of it. What I can't do is react."

"Oh wow, that's weird! Okay. So you know I went to the hospital. We were waiting in a lounge Saylor put us in, when Kristen…is that her name?"

"Yes."

"Kristen showed up and basically told me to get out of there so the legitimate people could talk."

"I'm sorry about that. She's…."

"No, it's okay. I didn't blame her. I would probably react the same way if I had a husband and he was in the hospital and I came in and some redheaded floozie was there."

"You're a floozie? I haven't heard that word in years."

"No! I'm not! But I probably look like one. Hey, this isn't the point."

"Sorry. What is the point, Kelsey?"

"The point is, I went home and got on my blog and started a new thread describing what happened to you."

"You didn't…?"

"No, I didn't put your name on it. I was just trying to find out if anyone in the world had heard about something like this."

"What did you find?"

"There's this guy. I think he's a guy. All I know is his screen name. It's 'Alchemist.' And he is real cool. Whenever I'm knee-deep in some chat about a real intense, deep subject and he comes online, his comments are always the best. He's just like real smart, you know. Or something. But he can just distill what everyone else is saying and make sense of it all. He also seems to really know a lot of things – science things, history things, lots of things."

"What did he say, Kelsey?" Judtson was too entertained by the way her mind worked to be frustrated by the time it took her to get to the point.

"He thinks it's mind control."

"Mind control? By whom?"

"Well, he really wouldn't know, would he?"

"Does he have a theory?"

"Sort of. He thinks it might be an experimental program by the government. They haven't gotten the bugs out of it yet. That's why you keep popping in and out."

"Why me?"

"Maybe you have the ideal brain profile for the test?"

"What?"

"I don't know. He doesn't know. I'm guessing."

"So the two of you think I'm part of a test group?"

"Group? There are others?"

"I thought you knew. Saylor told me that there are a total of eight other people with the same symptoms, and that four of them simply got better all of a sudden."

"That is bizarre. Maybe you *are* part of the test group."

"Maybe. Saylor tends to think that there might be something new in the environment causing it."

"Like some new ingredient in soda pop?"

"Or a new additive in a cleaning product, a new preservative in food, even a new chemical in clothing."

"The Chinese! We're getting all our clothes from them now, and who knows what they are putting in the material. This could be a test of a new weapon against us."

"Whoa, Kelsey. I'm not saying that's what it is. The CDC is studying the other patients with the symptoms."

"Oh, the CDC. I feel much better now. And four or five years from today, when they finally find the cause, we'll all be...I don't know what to call it...'zombie people' by then. By the way, did you ever hear back from Emily's mommy?"

"I did."

"Well, was I right?"

"You were. It's indefinitely off the schedule."

"Did Mommy say why?"

"She said that the content didn't fit in with the format of the network."

"Right! What else are they going to say?"

"They?"

"They! The ones behind all of the things happening to you."

"Kelsey, you don't really think that the same people who decided not to run the Villarreal show are behind my episodes or breaks or whatever they are?"

"Of course not, Pollyanna. It's all just a massive coincidence."

"How could they be doing it? Saylor has run all sorts of tests, including an MRI. If there was...I don't know...some kind of implant in my head, he would have found it."

She made a sound with her lips which, over the phone, sounded like tearing paper. "You don't think they are good enough to get past that?"

Judtson had to laugh at her persistence. "Okay. I suppose if there were some massive, invisible conspiracy controlling everything, they could pull it off."

"Of course they could," she responded as if his comment had been free of sarcasm. "Remember, they've been at it for hundreds, even thousands of years."

Chapter 12

CHECKING HIS EMAILS, JUDTSON FOUND THE LINK from Emily and began the download. The file was huge. Sitting idly and watching the progress bar creep upward imperceptibly did not appeal to him, so he left it unattended and walked to the outer office where Ricky was typing.

"Hungry?"

Ricky stopped and looked up. "I brought lunch. Did you want something?"

"Does Eegee's deliver?"

"No, but I can make a run. What do you want?"

"Meatball sub and a...."

"Mango eegee."

"Right."

"No problem. Be right back."

Ricky departed, and Judtson returned to his desk to finish checking his emails. Mixed in with the long list were three from Carlos. He selected the oldest of the three.

> "Judtson, I noticed that the program on which I appeared has been removed from the schedule. Do you know why? Are you even aware that it has? I hope there is no problem. Please let me know the status and the new date for airing. Thank you. Your friend, Carlos"

Before replying, Judtson thought he would first read the other two. He clicked on the second one.

> "Judtson, I have not heard back from you yet and wanted to inform you that I called your network. They told me that the show was not going to be put on! Ever! Is something wrong? Did you uncover something which made you change your mind about what I told you and showed you? As you know, it was my intent to release my findings on your show. If it is not going to be broadcast, I have no

choice other than to place the information elsewhere. I have also made a call to your office. Please let me know what is happening. Regards, Carlos"

He moved on to the third, which had arrived only two hours ago.

"Please call me. I must speak with you. Something is happening. Something I cannot explain. Carlos"

Judtson, concerned by the tone of the final email, decided to phone Carlos again. He once more heard the voice-mail announcement and left another message, this time telling Carlos that he had read the three emails and that he, too, was flummoxed by the network's decision, was looking into it, and would get back to him as soon as he found out anything. He left his personal cell phone number in the message, hung up, and then replied to the third email, restating the message he had left on voice mail.

Intending to peruse the rest of his emails, Judtson found that he was unable to concentrate on the others, as his mind was fixated on the final message from Carlos. What was the inexplicable event that was happening? He closed his email program and checked on the download status of the show. Seeing that it was finished, he clicked on the file and the video viewer opened, displaying the introduction.

"What the heck?"

It was not the program with Carlos, but an earlier episode on the topic of crop circles. Unbidden, Kelsey's comments and opinions about what was happening to him came into his mind.

▽

Ricky hurried to the front door, gripping the paper bag which held the foot-long sandwich. Tucking the ice-cold drink between his forearm and his body, he reached for the knob, startled to find it locked. The frozen drink already chilling his rib cage, he knocked on the door and waited. There was no shouted answer from Judtson; most likely it was masked by the traffic noise. He knocked again.

Ricky could understand why he might fail to hear an answer. What he could not understand was why Judtson had not yet come to open the door. The sun was baking him and he knew that the mango ice was rapidly turning into a gooey liquid. Exasperated and acting on pure impulse, he reached awkwardly around his body with his free hand to a side pocket to dig out the keys to the door. They were, unfortunately, on the same side where he precariously clutched both the bag and drink. The motion of twisting caused his arm to squeeze a bit too hard on the eegee. Everything that happened next occurred within a matter of seconds, but Ricky viewed it in an exaggerated and inexorable slow motion. The lid popped off and the Styrofoam cup collapsed against him, violently ejecting its contents. The icy slush instantly saturating his shirt triggered an involuntary release of the paper bag, plopping it onto the sidewalk. The weight of the foot-long meatball sub exceeded the strength of the bag, which ripped open, unleashing the ill-fated lunch. Coincidentally, the cylindrical sandwich struck the sidewalk perpendicular to the angle of the slope and quickly began rolling resolutely toward the street.

"OH, NO!" Ricky shouted as he turned to catch his boss's sandwich on its route to the curb. But he only made it one step before his shoe landed squarely on the mound of frozen slush from the drink. As his foot flew out from under him, Ricky flailed forward like a wide receiver diving into the end zone, arms outstretched, trying to intercept the intended repast even as he fell face-first onto the sidewalk. His fingers missed the bulk of the sandwich, and succeeded only in snagging the flapping edge of the butcher paper as it rolled away from him, which was all that was needed for the hapless meal to roll out of its wrapping, as it continued on an inevitable descent toward the street. He watched helplessly as the naked sub spun forward, expelling its load of meatballs as it went. Unencumbered by the mass of meat, the sub roll came to an abrupt stop; but the three marinara-coated balls tumbled to the gutter, leaving red trails in their wake to delineate a most ignominious fate.

Groaning, Ricky slowly stood up, careful to avoid the now fully melted mango syrup, and irritably took stock of the situation. He saw that both his shirt and slacks were soaked and stained, and even if he could get the stain out, one knee of his pants had torn in the fall. As he inventoried the casualties of the incident, his anger grew. Turning abruptly, he pulled the keys out of his pocket, stomped toward the building, and opened the office door, tossing it wide until it slammed into the wall.

"Judtson!" he called out.

The office was silent. He could feel the wet slime creeping downward from his abdomen and bypassing the waistband of his briefs.

"Judtson, this is going to be a very costly lunch for you when I turn in my next expense report."

There was no answer as he walked in, closing the door behind himself.

"Judtson?"

Everything looked exactly as it did when he left. His computer was still on. The door to Judtson's office was still opened. Ricky peered in, but the room was empty. His anger was dissipating, rapidly replaced by worry. He moved to the restroom door, which was closed. He knocked. "Judtson, are you in here?"

Again, there was no answer. He tried the knob and it was not locked. Cautiously, he opened the door. The restroom was also empty. With a new urgency, he swiftly checked the rest of the building, almost dashing from room to room. Judtson was obviously gone.

His hands were shaking as he dialed Saylor's phone number.

▽

Saylor arrived to find Ricky on the phone. He heard him saying, "Okay, Kristen. I just wanted to check and see if he was with you."

. . . .

"No, I'm sure it's nothing. He probably either walked somewhere or called a cab."

. . . .

"Of course, I'll call you as soon as I find him."

As Ricky hung up the phone, Saylor lifted one eyebrow and asked, "What happened to you? You're a mess."

Speaking rapidly, Ricky described the sandwich incident outside the front door.

"And when you came in, he was gone?"

"Yes. I've checked everywhere, including outside. He's not here."

"Have you tried his cell phone?"

Ricky retrieved something from his desk and held it up. It was a phone. "I did. Then I heard it ringing in his office. He left it here. Saylor, I'm worried. Could this have anything to do with his episodes?" Ricky's voice conveyed his growing concern.

"I don't know for sure. I really can't see how. When they've happened in the past, he simply went still. You saw it."

"I know. But I wasn't sure if he might just like, I don't know, wander away."

"I have no idea."

Saylor skirted Ricky's work area and went into Judtson's office, sitting down at his desk. The computer was still turned on, and he checked to see what Judtson might have been working on or looking at before he disappeared. There were no open programs, only the main screen filled with shortcut icons. Next, he picked up the pile of phone slips and thumbed through them. Finishing the stack, he went to the top and examined them again. He turned to Ricky, who was standing beside him.

"When I was here earlier and you gave these to him, you mentioned that Carlos Villarreal had called."

"Yes, he did."

"Wasn't there a phone slip for that call?"

"Yes. Why?"

"It's not here."

"What do you mean? Can I see them?"

Saylor handed the stack to Ricky, who speedily riffled through them. "You're right. It isn't. You think he took that one with him?"

"I don't know. It's odd, that's all."

"I'm sure it was there. I read them all to him."

"I know."

Saylor turned to the computer and opened Judtson's email program. His eyes went straight to the inbox where he read the list.

"You preview his emails, don't you?"

"Yes."

"Were there any emails from Villarreal?"

"Yes, there were three."

Saylor pointed at the list on the screen. "They're gone."

"What?"

Ricky leaned forward and read the list himself.

"I *know* they were there."

"Did you read them?"

"Yes. I always do."

"What were they about?"

"It was a little weird. The first two were about finding out that the show had been canceled. He wanted to know if Judtson knew, and why it happened. The third one was the strange one. It was shorter...abrupt...and all it said was that something was happening, something he couldn't explain. He urgently wanted Judtson to call him."

"That was it? No details about what was happening?"

"None. But the first two had a salutation at the beginning and a formal closing at the end. The last one had neither of those. It was terse."

Saylor leaned back in Judtson's chair and tried to make sense of the details he was gathering. Nothing was fitting together. "Why would he delete the emails?"

"Are they in the trash folder?"

With a click of the mouse, Saylor checked. "No."

"Then he not only deleted them, he purged them from there, too. Just a second. I'm going to check something."

Ricky left and Saylor could hear him shuffle papers in the outer office for a minute. He returned even more unsettled. "My copy of the Villarreal phone message is gone."

"What?"

Ricky handed the spiral-bound phone slip pad to Saylor. "Look, the second yellow sheet down from the top is missing. The phone messages before that page are there, and so are the ones after it. Judtson took out the entire page which had that message on it."

Saylor spread out the blue phone slips on Judtson's desk, putting them in chronological order. All of the messages had backup copies in the book, except for a total of four – the Villarreal message, as well as the message from Mitch, Judtson's agent, and two others from radio stations.

"There's a phone slip in the trash can!" Ricky exclaimed, bending over to retrieve it. He unwadded the paper and, disappointed, said, "It's the message from Mitch."

"I wonder if he talked to Villarreal? Did you hear him make a call by the time you left?"

Ricky shook his head. "He made some calls. I can't hear him from out there, but I do have a way to check."

He left again and this time Saylor followed him back to his desk. As Ricky worked the mouse, he explained, "We have a call-manager feature on our phone service. It tracks all incoming and outgoing calls, call duration, everything."

"It doesn't record the conversations, does it?"

Ricky smirked at Saylor. "No. Okay, here we go…here's the…oh, my God!"

"What's wrong?"

"It has been purged. It's gone."

"The call from Villarreal?"

"No! Everything! Every incoming call. Every outgoing call. Gone. Zapped!"

"Only today's?"

"No, the whole thing. The entire log is wiped clean from today back to the time we started the service."

"I know I'm sounding a little redundant, but why would he do that?"

"That's the thing, Saylor – he can't. Those folders can only be purged by the administrator. Judtson never wanted to be bothered with things like that, so I'm the only one with the password to do it."

Everything Saylor was hearing still did not fit together into any sort of coherent answer, yet the direction of all the clues sent a shiver up his spine. "I think we'd better call the police."

▽

Doni arrived at Judtson's office to find the driveway filled with two police cruisers, Saylor's truck, and Ricky's car. She parked on the street, hurriedly climbed out, and trotted to the open front door to discover three uniformed officers and one man, who appeared to be a detective, talking to Saylor and Ricky.

Saylor looked over the shoulder of the detective and saw her. "Doni, you're here!"

He stepped around the man and met her halfway, wrapping his arms around her.

"Saylor, honey, I came as soon as I got your text. What happened? Where's Judtson?"

"I don't know. He sent Ricky to get him some lunch. When Ricky got back, Judtson was gone."

"Why the cops?" she asked in a soft voice only Saylor could hear. "He might have just gone somewhere. You know Judtson."

"I don't think so, baby." He proceeded to tell her the odd things he and Ricky had found.

After he detailed them all, she reached up and touched the side of his face gently. "It could still be nothing. Even if he didn't have a car here, someone could have picked him up. It could have been some spur-of-the-moment thing."

"I don't know. It's possible, I guess. But his phone is here. With the episodes he has been having, he promised me he'd keep it with him all the time."

"And he is always so reliable."

Saylor smirked at her. "You're right. He does get a little flaky sometimes. But who would come get him?"

Without hesitation, she answered, "Kelsey Batman?"

Saylor's eyes widened for an instant. "I didn't think of her. It's worth checking."

He turned to Ricky, who was standing across the room and answering questions from one of the police officers. "Ricky."

"Yes, Saylor."

"Do you have Kelsey's phone number handy?"

He nodded and excused himself, went to his desk, and jotted down her number from the open pad of phone slips. As he handed her number to Saylor, the detective, who had followed his steps, asked, "Who is this Kelsey person?"

"Detective Garrett, this is my wife, Donatella."

Garrett shook Doni's hand and mumbled that it was a pleasure to meet her.

"Kelsey Batman," Saylor explained, "is a friend of ours and Judtson's. My wife suggested that Kelsey might have come by while Ricky was gone and picked Judtson up."

Saylor noted the tightening of the muscles around Doni's mouth and was thankful that she resisted the urge to comment on his statement that Kelsey was a friend of *theirs*.

"So I thought I'd give her a call."

Garrett nodded and Saylor stepped a few feet away, tapping the numbers into his phone.

"Hello."

"Kelsey, this is Saylor."

"Saylor! Why are *you* calling me? Is everything all right? Is Judtson okay?" Her quick-fire questions were saturated with concern and made obvious the answer to the question he was planning to ask.

"So he isn't with you."

"With me? No! You don't know where he is?"

Saylor brought her up to date on Judtson's disappearance, noticing that Doni had moved closer to him so she could listen to his side of the conversation.

When he finished, Kelsey told him, "He called about an hour and a half ago. He sounded fine."

"He didn't mention anything about going somewhere?"

"No. Not at all."

"What was the conversation about?"

"Well, he told me that I was right about the cable show on Villarreal being canceled. Then he told me about the other people with his symptoms and how four of them have recovered. Then I told him my blogging friend's theory."

"What was that?"

"Well...uh...it's a little far out, Saylor. It's just some guy on my blog. I don't even know who he is. His name is Alchemist."

"Alchemist?"

As Saylor repeated the name, the detective, Ricky, and Doni all suddenly glanced at him with curiosity. He shook his head in an attempt to convey that it was nothing.

"Yeah, that's his screen name. Like I told Judtson, I don't even know if it's a *he*."

"What's his theory?"

She took a deep breath before answering. "He thinks it might be mind control."

Saylor fought the urge to repeat what she said, mindful of his audience.

"I see."

"Anyway, so he's just gone?"

"Yes. We have no idea where he went."

"I'll come over. Maybe I can help search or something."

"No, Kelsey, that's all right. The police are here."

"Police! Whoop-de-do. Now I feel much better."

He ignored her sarcasm and continued, "I think they have things under control. I wanted to check and make sure you hadn't picked him up."

"No. He's not with me."

"I'd better go now."

"Okay. Saylor, please keep me posted. I'm worried."

"So am I. And, yes, we'll let you know."

He ended the call and turned to Garrett. "She has no idea where he may be. He's not with her."

His brow slightly furrowed, the detective asked, "Exactly who is she again?"

"As I said, a friend. Judtson and I have only known her for a few days."

"Do you think there is a possibility that there is some sort of relationship between them?"

"Oh, absolutely not."

"It's possible you wouldn't know."

"Not a chance. There is nothing in his life I don't know about. We've been best friends since grade school. We even live next door to each other."

"That's true," Doni added. "Saylor wishes he didn't know quite as much as Judtson tells him sometimes."

Still suspicious, Garrett asked, "Like what?"

She shook her head dismissively. "That was merely a figurative phrase, Detective. There are no deep, dark secrets in Judtson Kent's life."

"Detective Garrett?" The voice came from one of the uniformed officers standing in the doorway to Judtson's office. "You may want to come and see this."

Garrett accompanied him into the office, followed by Saylor, Doni, and Ricky. Saylor immediately noticed a flash drive stuck into the front USB port on Judtson's computer; it had not been there when he checked the computer earlier. On the screen, still in the paused mode, was the video taken by Kelsey of their paintball escapade. As soon as they were assembled, the uniformed officer clicked the mouse and the video commenced, showing the entire event. As it neared the end, Saylor held his breath. The video did not stop at the point prior to revealing the license plate, as it had on the version he had seen on YouTube.

"I called in the plate," the officer stated. "The Camry is registered to Judtson Kent."

Wishing he were suddenly invisible, Saylor remained silent as Garrett started to turn toward him. The detective was about to speak, when the officer added, "And I found this on the desk." As he handed the sheet of paper to Garrett, Saylor was able to read the first few words – "You guys are awesome" – before the paper was turned away from his line of sight.

When he finished reading the note, Garrett, his face even more stern and serious than it had been, turned to Saylor. "You said you're his best friend?"

Struggling for a moment to find his voice, Saylor finally answered, "Yes, sir."

"And there isn't anything in his life you don't know about?"

"Well, pretty much anything."

Garrett stared intently at Saylor, allowing the tension to build for a full minute; then he asked, "So, Dr. Costello, is that you in the Camry with your *best friend*?"

Saylor glanced at his wife who was looking at him sadly, blinking back a single tear and biting her lower lip.

Returning his gaze to the detective, his voice flat and emotionless, he said, "Yes, it is."

▽

Doni and Ricky squirmed uncomfortably on the plastic and metal chairs in the front lobby of the downtown police headquarters.

"Ricky, I don't understand why the police officers and a detective were there. I know Saylor called them. But they usually don't even respond until someone has been missing for...what, twenty-four hours? And why a detective, for Pete's sake?"

"I know. I wondered the same thing. When he called, Saylor told them that Judtson was suffering from a medical condition which resulted in unpredictable breaks. I guess, in a situation like that, they show up right away. As for the detective, I'm not sure. Maybe it's because Judtson is a celebrity."

They both fell silent again. Unable to sit still, Doni stood and walked to the display commemorating the capture of John Dillinger by the Tucson Police. For the third time today, she read the narratives detailing the event and examined the artifacts, weapons, and pictures. Ricky joined her and whispered, "I guess they haven't done anything worth mentioning since the thirties."

Despite her mood, Doni giggled at his comment. The secure door separating the lobby from the rest of the building swung open and Dennis Rosen came out, followed by a rumpled and shuffling Saylor.

Doni ran to her husband and hugged him. He returned the embrace, tucking his face into the crook of her neck as she sobbed with relief.

"That didn't take long," Ricky commented to the attorney.

Rosen shrugged. "It's what I do. Actually, it was easy. Saylor's a physician with ties to the community, blah, blah, blah. He'll need to appear for a hearing, but that date hasn't been set."

The four walked outside. The relentless sunshine of earlier had given way to the beginning stages of an afternoon monsoon. The dark gray clouds were rapidly tumbling in from the southeast, and the leading edge was directly overhead. Intense lightning bolts stabbed at the city every few seconds, followed by almost earsplitting claps of thunder. The wind was gusting, carrying dust and debris in its thrall as it whipped around the building.

Rosen shouted over the wailing cacophony, "I need to get back to my office before this hits."

Doni nodded and Saylor yelled to be heard above the wind, "Thanks, Dennis."

With a brief wave, the lawyer trotted to his car. Ricky had ridden with Doni in Saylor's truck, which was parked across the street from police headquarters. As they approached, Ricky saw the wind tear something loose from under the wiper blade and he chased it down the street, trying twice to bend over and snatch it up, only to have the gusts toss it a few feet farther away each time. He finally stepped on it and bent down to grab the yellow paper. "A parking ticket!" he shouted back at Doni and Saylor.

Before they could respond, the sky abruptly opened and torrents of water crashed down, instantly drenching the three of them as Doni dug into her purse for the keys to the truck. She managed to extract them and pressed the button on the alarm, disarming it and opening the doors.

She slid in first from the driver's side, with Saylor following to position himself behind the wheel as Ricky hastily clambered into the passenger side.

The three were jammed together on the truck's seat, soaking wet and filling the crowded cab with an odd pungent odor. The downpour savagely pounded on the metal roof, creating a low-frequency roar inside. Their exhalations were already beginning to fog the windows.

"Well, at least I've finally gotten most of that sticky mango syrup off me."

Saylor started to laugh, joined by his wife and Ricky; it built up to a point where the three were near hysteria. With the tension of the past hours partially released, the laughter slowly subsided.

Catching her breath, Doni twisted in the seat. "Saylor, honey, are you all right?"

He nodded. "Actually the process was sort of interesting. Would have been more so if it hadn't been happening to me."

"What are they charging you with?"

"Destruction of public property. They're trying to make it a felony, and they want to include all of the earlier forays. Dennis said all they can really hang on me is the last one. He's fairly sure he'll be able to get it down to a misdemeanor, but he is pretty ticked off that I admitted to it."

"What about Judtson? Are they trying to find him?"

"Detective Garrett said they were canvassing the neighborhood around his office. Since he isn't driving one of his cars, they can't put out a BOLO."

Ricky untucked his shirt and wrung it out onto the floor of the truck. "What's a BOLO?"

"Hey, I don't want that sugar stuff on my floor mats!"

"Sorry." He let go of the crumpled wad of fabric.

"I think it stands for 'Be on the lookout.'"

"Isn't that what they used to call an APB or 'all points bulletin'?"

"I guess. Have you been watching fifties cop shows on TV Land?"

Ricky's face twisted in a show of disgust. "Of course not! I don't watch television. It's in all of my old detective novels."

Doni giggled loudly. "You read detective novels?"

"Yes!" he answered defiantly, his voice breaking and ruining the effect. "What's wrong with that?"

"Nothing, nothing." She held up her hands defensively. "I was a little surprised, that's all."

"What did you think I read, romance novels?"

Saylor laughed. "Guys, come on. Enough. We need to be thinking about where Judtson might be."

"You're right," Doni promptly assented, happy to change the subject.

Ricky made a show of flopping heavily back into the cushion of his seat, the motion accompanied by a loud sigh.

Doni leaned forward and stared through the sheet of water on the windshield. "I hope he isn't out walking in this."

"Right," Saylor agreed.

"Do you really think he walked out of there on his own?"

"What do you mean, Ricky?"

"You saw all of it, Saylor." As Ricky spoke, he counted off the items on his fingers. "The missing phone message, the torn-out page in the book of phone slips, the purging of the call log, the double-deleted emails from Villarreal."

"What do *you* think happened?" Doni asked him when he had finished, a trace of worry creeping into her voice.

"I think he was taken."

▽

Saylor reached the end of the street and turned left, cruising at just over ten miles an hour, his eyes darting to the left and right as he continued his search. The three of them agreed that they would be more effective if they split up. Doni was checking all of the places they had thought of where Judtson might have gone. Ricky was methodically working his way through the residential streets north of Pima, as Saylor searched to the south. They were both trying to cover the distance Judtson reasonably could have walked from his office.

The rain had stopped as quickly as it started, and the streets were already drying. The arroyos were nearly empty, having rapidly conveyed their loads of storm water to the Pantano and Tanque Verde Washes and the Rillito River, which branched through the city, serving as collectors for the eventual delivery to the Santa Cruz River on the west side of Tucson. The watershed system had once again fulfilled its function of efficiently removing the water from the city, save for the numerous, scattered man-made retention/detention basins constructed by land developers at the behest of local codes. These ad hoc reservoirs were dribbling their stored water into the natural system in a metered flow, intended to mimic the volume produced by a monsoon prior to the advent of water-impervious parking lots, rooftops, and streets.

Saylor slowly passed a young boy who was carrying his sneakers and walking barefoot in the slender stream channeled by the gutter of his street. His eyes cast downward, the child was watching the progress of a small plastic sailboat, which was already scraping its shallow bottom on the asphalt, canting wildly in its jerky progress. Saylor's own mind wandered back to his childhood, and he recalled the many times that he and Judtson would dash out after a deluge, toy boats in hand, and meet at the arroyo behind their homes.

When the storm had been sufficiently intense, the normally bone-dry and sandy wash would be flowing to the top of its banks, the water sluicing so rapidly that the surface was heavily rippled with turbulence. To begin the race, they would cast their boats onto the roiling surface, occasionally having to sprint alongside the channel to keep up with the flow. Carrying long sticks, they would intervene when their crafts became entangled in the branches of a creosote growing along the boundaries of the waterway. In the aftermath of a particularly brutal monsoon, the impromptu regatta could lead them as far as a mile away from home.

As he had countless times before, Saylor recalled the day he fell in. His catamaran had become so ensnared in the brambles of a still-rooted tumbleweed that his long pole was ineffectual at extricating it. Judtson's cabin cruiser was gaining a substantial lead as Saylor cautiously dug one foot into the soft side of the bank and leaned out over the edge of the water, trying to reach his boat. The saturated soil under his shoe collapsed, and he plunged into the torrent. To this day he vividly recalled how cold the water felt as he went under. The force of the flow was overwhelming, and he was instantly disoriented. He tried to open his eyes, but they were stung by the grit and mud in the water. Carried along with the current, Saylor had no idea which direction was up and found himself battered as he was dragged, scraped, and tumbled against the rocky banks.

Panic pushed out any possibility of rational thought and he began to flail, desperate for his head to somehow pop up above the surface, giving him an opportunity to gulp a much-needed breath. The sensation of being carried along with the rampaging water was much like being inside a turning cement mixer, and he was slammed repeatedly against the sides and bottom of the wash. Each impact forced him to lose a bit more of his precious oxygen, yet he fought the urge to open his slammed-shut lips, knowing that inhaling the filthy water would be the end.

Indistinguishable from the other buffeting he was suffering, there was an abrupt collision with something directly in his path. His limbs writhing, he fought to push away from it, when he suddenly felt an arm fiercely wrap around him. Saylor managed to stop thrashing and felt himself jerked upward until his head broke the surface of the water. Gratefully, he opened his mouth and hungrily gulped the air. Only after satisfying his urgent need for oxygen was he able to focus on how he had been saved. He was clinging for dear life to Judtson, who still had one arm wrapped around his chest, just under his armpits. Judtson's other arm, his right arm, was taut and extending straight upward. Saylor looked up and saw that lashed tightly around Judtson's wrist was his leather belt. Looking farther upward, he saw that the other end of the belt was looped around a slender gas pipeline, which spanned the arroyo barely a couple of feet above the waterline before diving back below ground.

Saylor opened his mouth to speak, only to have it fill with water. Spitting and sputtering, twisting his head around so his face was away from the direction of flow, Saylor shouted, "Thanks!"

"Shut up!" Judtson answered.

There was nothing they could do but hold on to each other until the water subsided. They remained dangling for approximately twenty minutes, the coursing water swinging them on the belt like a tetherball in a windstorm. They took turns eyeing the surface of the water upstream for any sign of a large branch or other object which might be careering toward them. No floating projectile appeared, and the flow gradually diminished until they were finally hanging straight down. When the water level dropped to Saylor's waist, he released his bear hug on Judtson. His muscles resisting the command to relax for a moment, Saylor dropped down the foot or so to the sandy bottom. Whether from the abuse his body had taken during his wild tumble, or merely caused by the subsidence of adrenaline in his system, he came close to losing his balance, and staggered a few steps to remain upright.

Turning back to his friend, he saw that Judtson's right hand, dangling above the cinched belt that was tied to his wrist, was a dark blue hue, verging on purple. Judtson's eyes were fixed upon Saylor's; however, his face was strangely inanimate, almost as if he were unconscious.

"Judtson!" he called out, as he pushed through the nearly chest-high water back to the hanging figure. There was no audible response. He could see Judtson's mouth open and move; even though he was trying to speak, no sound was emerging.

As Judtson twisted in the weaker current, Saylor bent his knees, dipping his head below the waterline, and wrapped his arms around Judtson's thighs. Holding on tightly, he stood straight up, hoping to relieve the pressure on his friend's wrist.

"Move your hand!" he shouted. "Wiggle your fingers!"

From his position he could not tell if Judtson was able to follow his orders, or if he had even heard them.

"Judtson! Come on, buddy. Answer me. Can you move your hand?"

There was no longer any wind, and the reduced velocity of the water through the arroyo made its progress virtually silent. Had it not been for the quieter conditions, he would not have heard his friend's muted response. "Popeye, get your face out of my butt."

Unable to hold back, Saylor burst out laughing. Judtson joined him, and the two, locked in their absurd pose, shuddered with hysterical spasms. Catching his breath, Saylor asked, "Can you get the belt off your wrist?"

"I already tried. It's too tight."

Saylor thought for a moment. "I can get you down, but I'll have to let you go for a minute or two."

"Okay. But make it fast. I don't have any feeling in my hand."

"I'm going to let you go now. Here goes."

As slowly as he could, Saylor lowered his friend until he was once again suspended by the belt. He hurried to the bank of the wash and started to climb up the side, only to twice slip back down into the now waist-high water.

"Hurry up, Popeye. I think my hand's gonna break off."

Digging his fingers into the muddy soil, Saylor successfully scrambled up the side and ran to the spot where the gas pipe exited the ground next to the arroyo. He threw one leg over the pipe and, leaning forward, slid across the top until he reached the center point where Judtson had looped the belt around its circumference. Digging into the pocket of his soaked blue jeans, he pulled out the cheap switchblade he had surreptitiously purchased during a trip to Nogales, Sonora with his parents.

As he pressed the shiny button on the side, the blade snapped out and open. He then lay down on the top of the pipe, hooking his ankles and wrapping one arm around it so he would not fall back into the muddy water. With his free hand, he began sawing on the wide leather belt. Judtson silently stared up at him.

It took less than thirty seconds of frantic cutting until the blade sliced through enough of the leather for Judtson's weight to finish the job. The belt separated, and two things happened at once: Judtson fell down to the floor of the wash, and the portion of the belt above the cut snapped upward, slapping Saylor directly across his face.

The sting from the belt was the last thing on Saylor's mind, and he allowed himself to swing around to the bottom of the horizontal pipe. He uncoupled his ankles and his lower body dropped first. Then he released his arm lock on the pipe and dropped into the ditch next to Judtson, who was already clawing at the tightened knot on his wrist.

"I can't budge it," he panted, a subtle note of desperation in his voice.

Saylor still clutched his knife. "Let me cut it."

He expected Judtson to put up a fight about having the blade so close to his wrist, but was taken aback when he extended the hand to him instantly. The discoloration of the skin had worsened.

Surprised by the steadiness of his own hand, he carefully worked the tip of the blade into the middle of the knot and slowly began cutting.

"Hurry, Popeye!"

Rather than arguing, Saylor intensified his strokes, and soon the soaked leather split open, the knot unraveling. Judtson immediately began to massage his hand, kneading it like dough, when he suddenly yelped in pain.

"What's wrong?"

"God, this hurts."

"Oh, that's normal."

"What do you mean, 'that's normal'?"

"It's just the blood rushing back into your hand."

Judtson looked at his friend dubiously. "You sure?"

"Course I'm sure."

Biting his lower lip to fight off the pain, Judtson resumed rubbing. The two stayed in the arroyo as the water level continued to drop and until the first traces of healthy coloration reappeared in Judtson's hand.

Chapter 13

THE THREE SEARCHERS HAD CONVENED at a neighborhood coffee shop, sitting at an outside table and staring into the surrounding darkness, each lost in a separate reverie. The silence was eventually broken by Doni. "As well as we know him, it's hard to believe we can't think of somewhere else we should be checking."

"That's why I'm sure there are no other places to check. We know Judtson well enough to know that he doesn't have any hangouts," Saylor answered.

"He really doesn't have any friends except for us, does he?" The question came from Ricky, who was sipping from the third cappuccino he had purchased since their arrival.

"Not really. Just Doni, you, and I."

Doni's eyes were directed into the distance, as if she might see her friend ambling down the street in the darkness. Wistfully, she commented, "If he were here, he would correct you right now."

"Why? For what?"

"Just Doni, you, and me...not you and I."

The pathos of her comment silenced them again, as they sat grimly, virtually oblivious to the sounds of the traffic noise and the occasional customer at an adjacent table talking too loudly into a cell phone. Their desperate contemplation was suddenly broken by the ringtone from Saylor's cell. Snatching it up from the tabletop, he glanced at the screen. "It's Judtson's home number."

He immediately pressed the button, answering the phone and setting it to speaker. "Judtson?"

"Hi, Saylor, it's Kristen."

"Oh, hello, Kristen." He felt the rush of excitement drain away.

Her voice casual, she said, "I thought I'd let you know that Judtson's home."

"What? He's home? When...?"

"He just arrived, I don't know, maybe twenty minutes ago."

"Is he all right?"

"Yes, he's fine."

"How did he get home? Where had he been?"

"He said that he wanted to think. He walked home."

Saylor could feel the muscles in his neck tightening. "Can I talk to him, Kristen?"

"He's asleep right now. After he got here, he went straight to bed."

Staring blankly at the phone and at a loss for something to say, Saylor repeatedly flexed and relaxed his jaw muscles.

"Saylor, are you still there?"

"Kristen, it's Doni. Did you let the police know?"

"Hi, Doni. Of course I did. They want to talk to him, you know, about the other thing, but they agreed to wait until tomorrow."

Doni glanced at her husband to see if he wanted to say anything else. His face was rigid, a mask. She continued, "Well, thanks for letting us know."

"No problem. I knew you were worried."

"You'll ask Judtson to call us when he wakes up?"

"I will. I'd better go now. Good night, Doni. Good night, Saylor."

Doni answered, "Good night, Kristen."

It was clear that Saylor was not going to respond, so Doni reached out and tapped the phone to break the connection.

"What is *wrong* with her?" Saylor's comment was so emphatic that nearby customers turned to stare at him curiously. He ignored them and continued, "Twenty minutes! She *knew* we were all out searching for him! How dare she treat me like that! Like some casual acquaintance!"

Doni put her hand on his. "Honey, that's Kristen. She has been that way for a long time now. What I don't understand is why Judtson didn't call us."

"I know! I can't believe he would just leave his office and wander around all afternoon, then walk home and go to bed without letting me know."

"He has been under a lot of stress lately," Ricky offered softly.

Saylor turned to look at him as if he had forgotten his presence at the table. "Maybe, I guess. It doesn't feel right."

▽

Saylor had a wretched night. He and Doni took Ricky back to his car, and then headed home. After parking his truck in the garage, Saylor walked directly to Judtson's house and rang the doorbell. Kristen answered and stood in the doorway as they spoke, not inviting him inside, and telling him that Judtson was sound asleep and that she did not want him awakened. Saylor resisted the urge to push her aside and march into the bedroom to see his friend for himself. Instead, he thanked her, elicited another promise to call him the moment Judtson woke up, then turned and trudged back to his own home. Doni was waiting for him at the front door.

He described the brief conversation, and the two of them went out to their patio where they sat together in silence. The outside air was thick with post-thunderstorm humidity and the temperature was still in the upper nineties, despite the fact that it was late in the evening. He switched on the ceiling fan, wandered back into the kitchen, and poured a tall iced tea for himself and one for Doni.

Returning to the patio, he finally felt a need to talk. The majority of the conversation centered on the mundane. Neither of them wanted to speak about Judtson, nor did either actually have anything new to say on the subject. The mindless chat continued until it lapsed once again into longer and longer periods of silence. Following a particularly extended interval, Doni suggested they go to bed and Saylor reluctantly consented.

His sleep was fitful, alternating between a consciousness dominated by concern and worry, and an unconsciousness plagued by nightmares. The pattern continued until the first rays of sunlight rudely entered the bedroom. Saylor rolled out of bed, snatched his cell phone from the nightstand where he had left it, and went to the kitchen to make coffee, checking the phone to make certain he had not inadvertently missed any calls during the night.

Before the coffee maker could complete its sibilant, sputtering routine, Doni staggered into the kitchen. Her eyes were slightly bloodshot and underscored with bags, indicating that she, too, had not slept well.

"You look like hell," she muttered to Saylor as she pulled a mug down from the shelf.

Saylor was leaning against the counter waiting. "You, on the other hand, look like heaven."

The corner of her mouth fought against the deep crease in her cheek, embedded by a night of lying facedown on a fold, and managed to curl slightly upward. "You're sweet. Blind as a bat, but sweet."

With a final loud gurgle and hissing sigh, the coffee maker finished its task. They both poured cups, doctored them with cream and sugar, and adjourned to the patio once again.

After a few minutes, Doni turned to him purposefully. "I've been thinking, honey."

"That's excellent. It's good to try new things."

She reached over and slapped him on the arm.

"I'm serious. What are we really worried about?"

"What do you mean?"

"I know we were all freaked out. Think about it, though. Apparently, the only thing that happened yesterday was that Judtson took a long walk."

"I guess that's true."

"What I'm saying is, he's fine. He's home. Nothing actually went wrong."

Saylor consciously forced his mind to view the circumstances of the previous day from a different perspective. "Except it was all so strange – Judtson's disappearing like that and not calling me, then the whole thing with the missing phone slip, the calls zapped from the log, and the deleted emails."

"You're right. It was a little weird, but not *that* weird. You have to admit, Judtson is not always the most predictable person in the world. He probably has some explanation."

"It still doesn't feel right."

Doni leaned forward and gently placed her hand on Saylor's arm. "Don't get mad at me for saying this, but I think your concern really boils down to one thing. You can't stand being left out of Judtson's life, even for a minute. What's driving you nuts is that he wandered around all afternoon and evening, decided to go home, talked to his wife, went to bed, and not once, during all that, did it occur to him to call his buddy Saylor. That's the crux of the problem."

"Well, yes, there is that."

"Of course there is. You two have always been joined at the hip. It has been that way for as long as I've known you. I've spent most of my marriage believing that if Judtson and I were both in a life-and-death situation and you only had enough time to save one of us, you'd save him."

"Doni, that's not true! At least I'm glad you finally realized that."

"I didn't say I did. What I finally realized is that it *is* true."

Saylor twisted around to face her full-on, the steel feet on his chair sliding on the concrete and causing a loud, screeching noise. "Doni, baby, that isn't true! It isn't! Not even close."

She stared into his eyes for a moment. "I knew you would say that."

"I mean it."

She sighed. "I'm just glad that I was never the type of wife who forced you to make a choice.

I think I would have lost."

He took both of her hands in his and held them firmly. "I *love* you."

"You love him, too."

"I do. But it's not the same thing. Please, baby, don't feel like this. I can't stand it if you do. You are first. Then it's Judtson. I swear it."

She examined him dubiously. "Are you sure?"

"Yes! I'm sure!"

She again stared at him. A full minute passed before she broke the silence. "Okay. I suppose I believe you."

He kissed her. It was a long, intense kiss. When they separated, he leaned back in his chair while retaining his grip on her hands. "I guess this is my week for unpleasant revelations."

"How so?"

"This morning you hit me with this, and yesterday Judtson told me a couple of things that blew me away."

"What things?"

"First, he told me that he really doesn't think I like him."

"You're joking?"

"No. I'm not. And *he* wasn't, either. He thinks I only hang out with him because I feel I have to, or because I feel sorry for him."

"That is amazing."

"I know. Well, he's having a bit of a crisis of confidence. He honestly doesn't think *anyone* likes him. He sees himself as an immature, irresponsible, obnoxious jerk, and can't understand why anyone would want to be his friend."

"Good God. What was the other revelation?"

"I'm not sure I should tell you this."

"Listen, mister, you'd better...."

Saylor held up his hands in surrender. "I'm kidding. I'm kidding. He told me that when we were growing up, he always wanted to marry you."

"Oh, I knew that."

"You did?"

"I would have been blind not to notice that – the way he would stare at me with those big cow's eyes."

"Cows don't have blue eyes."

"Whatever."

"When did you know?"

"From about seventh grade."

"You could tell in seventh grade that he wanted to marry you, just by the way he looked at you?"

"No. Not just the way he looked at me. The big tip-off was when he kissed me."

"Wait a minute! He kissed you?"

"Yeah. So?"

"You kissed Judtson?"

"That's how it works."

"You never told me about that."

She smiled innocently. "And when could I have told you?"

"What do you mean, when? Right away."

"Oh, sure! That would have been a good idea. Okay, here's how it was. I liked you. I liked

Judtson. I knew you two were more than just best friends. If I had told you in seventh grade, there could have been only two possible outcomes. Either you would have decided to beat up Judtson, your friendship would have ended, and I would have had to pick between the two of you right then. After all, I couldn't have stayed friends with both of you if you weren't speaking to each other. Or that pseudo-noble guy thing would have kicked in, and you would have decided that I was his girl and you had to back off. Either way, I would have lost."

He thought about her words for a moment. "I guess that makes sense. But you certainly could have told me later."

"Nope. Once you don't tell a secret immediately, it becomes bigger and bigger. It becomes more dangerous, more hurtful simply because you've withheld it. I couldn't have told you at any time while we were dating, for the same reasons I already explained. I couldn't have told you when we were engaged. Judtson was going to be your best man at the wedding. I was afraid you'd change that, and it would have been sad. And then, after we were married, I don't know, there never really seemed to be a good time to tell you."

"Till now?"

"Till now."

"Did you like it?"

"Like what?"

"Kissing Judtson. Did you enjoy it?"

Her eyes widened. "Saylor, don't go there. It was seventh grade."

"Did you?"

"Saylor!"

"Did you?"

The doorbell rang. He could not help but notice the expression of relief on her face as she jumped up. "I'll get it."

"Hey! Answer my question first."

"Later, honey. It's probably Judtson at the door."

He stood at once and followed her. "Just a *yes* or a *no*. Did you like it?"

Her pace accelerated and she reached the front door, opening it. "Judtson!"

Saylor arrived a moment later and saw his friend standing on the porch. "Hey, come in. How are you?"

Judtson smiled at them. "I'm fine, but I don't have the time to come in right now."

"Oh, you can come in for a second," Doni said eagerly. "I'll get you a cup of coffee."

"No, really, I can't. Thanks. Kristen told me that you wanted to see me, so I decided to come over for a quick stop before I head out."

Saylor stepped onto the porch with Judtson. "Well, tell me what happened yesterday. Why did you just disappear like that? You had us all freaked out."

Judtson had taken a step back to accommodate Saylor's presence. "I am truly sorry about that. I needed some time. There is so much happening now, so many things hitting me all at once. Between the issues with Kristen, and the problems with my publisher, the cable show, everything…it was all beginning to pile up. I wanted to be alone and think."

Saylor looked back at Doni and noticed that her brow had furrowed slightly. She came out and stood beside him. "Judtson, are you sure you're okay?"

"Yes. I'm fine. I did get soaked in that rain yesterday. When I got home, Kristen got me into dry clothes and made some soup. After that, I went straight to sleep. I must have slept almost eleven hours."

"No more episodes?" she asked.

"None. I think they might be over."

"That would be great."

"Judtson," Saylor pressed him, "we noticed that you had wiped out all of the calls and emails from Villarreal. What was the deal with that?"

"Oh, those. That was part of the decision I've made."

Saylor, wishing that he could read his friend's eyes through the reflective sunglasses, pursued the line of questions. "What decision?"

"I have no idea why, but I've been charging headlong in the wrong direction for some time now, Saylor. I saw that clearly yesterday. Villarreal was a part of it. He might even have been the trigger for my change now. I'm not sure. I just realized that I need to get back on track."

"Track? What track are you talking about, Squirrel?"

"I've been out of control, Doni. Doing incredibly foolish things. Immature, selfish things. Flushing my whole career, my whole following, over a silly story I wanted to write. Deliberately alienating my agent and my publisher. And, especially, treating Kristen the way I have been. Worst of all, now I'm responsible for getting Saylor in trouble with the law. Kristen told me about that this morning. I think it's time for me to grow up."

Saylor and Doni connected with a furtive glance. He could see that she was as concerned or, at the very least, as curious as he. Returning his gaze to Judtson, Saylor noticed that a wasp had landed on his friend's face.

"Judtson, there's a wasp on your cheek!"

He pointed at the insect and Judtson swiped his hand in that direction, simultaneously shooing away the wasp and accidentally knocking off his sunglasses.

"I'll get them," Doni offered, quickly bending over.

She handed the glasses back to Judtson, who immediately slid them back on and said, "I should be going. I have an appointment this morning with the detective about our little paintball fiasco."

Doni leaned forward and gave him a brief kiss on his cheek. "Okay, Squirrel. Be careful."

He turned and walked away, following the well-worn path across the front yard back to his home. Doni turned to her husband. "You didn't say good-b…. Saylor, what's wrong?"

Saylor was staring across the yard at the retreating figure.

"Honey? Saylor?"

After Judtson disappeared from his view, he turned to Doni. "Did you see his eyes?"

Chapter 14

Ricky was checking voice mails, when the door opened and Judtson arrived.

"Boss! Saylor called and told me you made it home last night. Are you all right?"

He came around the end of his desk to meet Judtson.

"I'm fine, Ricky. Thanks for asking."

Hesitating in mid-step, Ricky continued, "We were worried sick. I must have driven up and down a hundred streets yesterday looking for you."

"I'm very sorry," Judtson apologized, his tone formal. "It was not my intent to put all of you through any trouble."

Staring at his superior curiously, Ricky ventured again, "With the episodes you've been going through, I was afraid you were sitting in some culvert somewhere, unable to move."

Judtson shook his head and repeated, "I'm fine. I just needed to walk. I needed some time to think. Are all of my messages ready?"

"Uh, sure, boss. They're all on your computer."

"Thanks, Ricky."

Judtson turned and walked into his office, as his assistant stared after him. A vague sense of unease nibbled at the edges of Ricky's mind.

At his desk, Judtson tapped the speed-dial button for his agent, who answered on the third ring.

"This is Mitch."

"Mitch, Judtson."

A trace of wariness crept into Murray's voice. "Hello, Judtson. Thank you for returning my call."

"Actually, I'm not purely returning yours, Mitch. I wanted to speak with you. I need to apologize."

The surprise was evident as the agent responded, "Apologize? Apologize for what?"

"I've treated you shabbily lately, and I wanted to let you know that I appreciate all of the work you put into representing me. I know I haven't been an easy client."

A forced chuckle came out of the speaker. "You have your moments, Judtson, but nothing I haven't been able to handle. Remember, I deal with authors twenty-four/seven. They are not exactly a bunch known for their people skills. If they did possess those skills, they probably wouldn't spend years of their lives sequestered in a room writing, while everyone else is socially engaged, as it were."

"That's kind of you to say, Mitch, although it doesn't excuse my behavior. I'm truly sorry."

"Think nothing of it, Judtson."

"That wasn't the only reason for my call."

"What else, pal?"

"I wanted to let you know that I've dropped the Villarreal project."

There were a few seconds of silence before Murray, his voice neutral, asked, "Dropped the Villarreal project? What do you mean?"

"It's dead. I've lost interest. I'm not going to proceed with it in any fashion whatsoever."

"That's great, Judtson!" the agent exclaimed enthusiastically. "It really is. I hope you don't mind my telling you that I think you've made the right decision."

"As do I. Would you be kind enough to inform Darrow? And also, let him know that I'm starting on my next book immediately."

"What will be the focus of the new book, if you don't mind my asking?"

"I don't mind at all. I'm planning on delving into the subject of the pyramids."

"The pyramids? What's the slant?"

"There's a fairly large fringe group actually of the belief that the pyramids are tens, if not hundreds, of thousands of years older than the accepted science. I think it's time to clear the air on the subject."

"Excellent. That should be a fabulous book. There will be a huge audience on the topic. I'll most certainly brief him. I think it's safe to say that he'll be ecstatic."

Ricky was standing off to the side, directly outside Judtson's door, as his boss disconnected from Mitch and tapped in another number. Over the next few minutes, he listened as Judtson, still utilizing the speakerphone, called Dorothy Benson and apologized for his attitude during their previous conversation. He then called Emily and told her he would be at her disposal for the taping of a replacement episode to fill the hole in the schedule left by the cancellation of the Villarreal show.

When he heard Judtson phone Kristen, picking up the handset instead of using the speaker, to schedule a lunch date with her, he was unable to bear it another minute and hurried outside, entering Saylor's cell number as he stepped into the heat.

Not even waiting for Saylor to finish his greeting, Ricky blurted, "That's not Judtson!"

"You noticed it, too?"

"Noticed it? You can't be serious! Why didn't you tell me?"

"I didn't want to prejudice you. My interaction with him this morning was pretty brief and I wanted to make sure I wasn't the only one to see it."

"It is most definitely *not* only you. I don't know who that is, but it is not Judtson Kent!"

As he talked to Saylor, Ricky had moved farther from the front door, to the end of the garage. Rounding the corner, he exclaimed, "Whoa! What's this?"

"What's what?"

"Saylor, is there anything wrong with Judtson's car?"

"Not that I'm aware of. Why?"

"Because he came here in a car I've never seen before."

"A white Camry?"

"How did you know?"

Trying to sound casual, Saylor answered, "It's just another car he owns. So tell me, what is he doing?"

Ricky described the phone conversations, finishing by relaying the initial moments of the call to Kristen. "And it wasn't only that. The moment he walked in, he was different. This is the first time *ever* that he hasn't teased me or joked with me about something. What happened? Why is he acting this way?"

"I don't know, Ricky. I suppose it could be a normal change. Recently, he broached the subject that he thought he was being immature and irresponsible. He might have had some kind of an epiphany."

"Is that possible? To this extreme, I mean."

"I don't know."

"Uh-oh."

"What's wrong?"

"Kelsey's pulling in."

"This should be interesting."

"I'll call you back."

"Please do, and Ricky...?"

"Yes?"

"Don't tell her anything before she sees him."

"Okay."

Kelsey parked the Hummer and jumped out, wearing pea-green cargo pants and another of her trademark T-shirts. "Ricky, thanks again for letting me know Judtson's okay. Is he inside?"

"He is. But he was making phone...."

She had already brushed past him and was barreling through the front door. All he could do was follow her. Making a beeline straight for Judtson's office, she paused in the doorway when she saw that he was still on the phone. Judtson saw her and held up one finger, indicating that he would be only a minute or so. She spun around and bumped into Ricky, who had come up directly behind her.

She whispered, "Has he said anything to you about his disappearance yesterday?"

"No. Not a word, other than saying he needed some time to think."

They heard Judtson end his call to Kristen with the comment, "Sweetheart, I love you, too. See you at lunch."

He hung up the phone. "Hello, Kelsey."

She breezed in and sat in one of the guest chairs across from him.

"So where did you go yesterday? And why did you just leave like that, without telling anyone? You must have done it right after we talked on the phone. Why didn't you tell me that you were going to go play hide-and-seek?"

A neutral smile was fixed upon his face as he answered. "I appreciate your concern, Kelsey, and I'd love to chat. Unfortunately, I'm quite behind on my work at the moment. Would you mind making an appointment? I'm positive that Ricky can fit you in within the next couple of days."

She stared at him dumbstruck, her jaw dropping open.

"Kelsey, is there a problem?"

"Uh...no...not at all. *I'm* fine. Uh...sure. I'll...get with Ricky. Sorry to disturb you."

"Not a problem. Always happy to see you. I appreciate your understanding."

He turned abruptly away from her and gave his attention to the computer screen. Kelsey continued to sit and stare at his profile for a full minute before she slowly stood and walked out of his office, without once garnering even a glance from Judtson.

She and Ricky walked together to the front door and opened it. He was about to step outside with her, when Judtson shouted, "Ricky! I need my notes on Egypt!"

"One second, boss!"

He trotted back to his desk as Judtson added, "And while you're at it, could you find the phone number for Henry Thompson at Blake's?"

"Sure thing!"

An anxious expression on his face, Ricky looked back at Kelsey, who was standing in the open doorway waiting.

"I would like Thompson's number right away!"

"Okay, boss."

Ricky snatched up a note pad and a pen, scribbled something on it, and hurried back to Kelsey, handing her the folded note. Silently, he mouthed, "Bye," and trotted back to his desk.

"Ricky?" Judtson called.

"Coming."

Kelsey gave him a quick wave and left. After she was sitting in the Hummer, she opened the note and saw that Ricky had written "Call Saylor." Under the scrawled message was a phone number. She sat quietly in the driver's seat for a full two minutes, the stifling heat inside the confined space triggering an eruption of sweat on every inch of her body. Oblivious to her own discomfort, she did not turn the key to start the engine and air conditioner; instead, she stared intently at the front of Judtson's office, motionless.

▽

Throughout the morning, Saylor made repeated attempts to contact Patrick Worden. Every time he called the psychiatrist's office, Worden would be in with a patient. When Worden returned the calls, Saylor would be occupied seeing patients of his own. They were finally able to connect during lunchtime. Saylor succinctly briefed his colleague on the most recent events, at the conclusion asking, "Patrick, what do you make of this?"

Worden paused for a while, assimilating the described changes in Judtson, before he answered. "I know that we ended our last conversation about Mr. Kent with a caveat from me pertaining to the hazards of a physician treating his own friend. In one sense, this illustrates the pitfalls; in another, it demonstrates that I was wrong."

"How so?"

"It's obvious, Saylor. If you did not have a shared history with Mr. Kent, then from what you've described, his current condition would appear to you, as a *detached* observer, to be one of health and normalcy, at least normalcy within the confines of our medical definitions."

"True."

"His noticeable change in personality only amplifies the need for him to visit a competent psychiatrist. I am very hesitant to provide any sort of diagnosis without an opportunity to see him."

"I understand, Patrick. I really do. And I will do my best to get him in to see you. But I would appreciate some guidance."

There was an audible sigh from Worden. "Very well. However, I am making it clear that we are having a discussion in the purely hypothetical."

"Of course." Saylor struggled to curb his frustration and waited.

"Assuming, for the purpose of this conversation, that the details you presented are perfectly accurate and unbiased, two possible diagnoses come to mind. The first relates to something we already discussed."

"The flight into health?"

"Exactly. From my perspective, it is possible that Mr. Kent has finally completed an arduous journey from the person he was into the person he wishes to be. This possibility is supported by his recent comments to you, in which he was consciously reevaluating his lifestyle, demeanor, and personality...not only reevaluating those things, but finding them to be wanting."

"Does that sort of thing actually happen? Where a major shift in basic personality occurs?"

"It does. An obvious example is the case of an addictive personality, a trait which tends to pervade almost every aspect of a person's life. The popular cliché is alcoholism or the abuse of illegal or prescription drugs; however, it can manifest in other ways – sexual promiscuity, obsessive exercise or bicycle riding, gambling, gluttony. The list goes on. In many cases, the person suffering from this will abruptly make a radical change in personality, a change which eliminates, or in some cases substitutes, the object of the addiction. This generally occurs after the person has hit bottom, so to speak."

"I see."

"Mr. Kent has confessed to you that he believes he has no friends in the world, implying that it is his own repugnant persona which is responsible for that condition. Couple that with the turmoil in his professional life and the rapidly deteriorating state of his marriage, as you have described it, and he very well may have hit the proverbial bottom, triggering a sort of epiphany."

Saylor chuckled to himself, remembering that he had used that exact word earlier with Ricky.

Worden continued, "Mr. Kent sounds like an intelligent and complex person. He would see the mosaic of his personality traits as an elaborate construct, and recognize the interrelated qualities of each component. It would take that degree of sophistication to make the kind of shift you've described."

"Patrick, if what you've just described is indeed the case, is this a permanent change in Judtson?"

"That's hard to say. Again, returning to the example of alcoholics, the highest percentage of them relapse into their former lifestyle. They attempt the change after they've made a mess of their lives, but as soon as they are able to stabilize the various elements of their environment, they return to the comfort of the bottle. So, Mr. Kent may dabble in his new reality for a time and decide that his previous reality was more exciting, satisfying, and rewarding. On the other hand, he may be quite pleased with his new life and cling to it ferociously."

"You mentioned two possibilities?"

"I did. And it is the second possibility which I am most uncomfortable discussing without the benefit of seeing Mr. Kent."

"Patrick...."

"I didn't say I wouldn't, Saylor, only that it is a much more extreme possible diagnosis and one which certainly shouldn't be tossed about lightly."

"You're referring to schizophrenia, aren't you?"

"I am. Or at least that is one of the two avenues I would consider when attempting a differential diagnosis. The other would be dissociative identity disorder."

"Multiple personality disorder."

"That is the popular phrase for the condition."

"Patrick, I must confess that I don't know the distinctions between schizophrenia and dissociative identity disorder."

"Don't feel too bad, Saylor. Many don't. Schizophrenia is a 'formal thought disorder.' Symptoms frequently include hallucinations, delusions, or disruptive thoughts. It is believed to have a biological basis. In fact, research labs utilizing PET scans have identified aspects within the brains of diagnosed schizophrenics which vary from what is considered the norm. Since it is a biologically based syndrome, it tends to react to treatment which is chemically oriented."

"Medications."

"Exactly. On the other hand, DID is considered to be a 'neurotic disorder.' It is more experiential than biological. If the eventual diagnosis is DID, the treatment is typically long-term therapy."

"Is either of these a likely possibility?"

"Saylor, there is no way I can ascribe any sort of likelihood without some sessions. What I am saying is that both are disorders which could conceivably explain what has occurred with your patient. Schizophrenia aside, there is a possibility that the Judtson you are now seeing is a personality which has been the dormant, suppressed, or submissive personality throughout his life. For some reason, possibly triggered by the upheavals in his current life, this new personality has been let out of the cage, so to speak, to deal with his ongoing crises."

"Is it possible that I would not once have had a glimpse of this alternate Judtson in three decades?"

"Very possible. It might not have *ever* emerged until now. Or it could be a personality which would manifest only at times you, specifically, were not present. And Mr. Kent is at the age when DID frequently strikes."

"Of the three, which is most likely to have caused the breaks Judtson was experiencing?"

Another pause preceded Worden's answer. "Among the three, I suppose the most likely culprit would be DID."

"Why is that?"

"I'm fairly far out in left field here, but the trancelike states you observed might have been the first tentative appearances of the current personality. And, for some reason, due to either a struggle between the two Judtsons, or an almost pathological shyness, the new personality froze upon its initial emergences. You did mention that after the breaks were over, Mr. Kent had full recollection of everything which had transpired. Although in most cases of DID, there is a clean transition from one personality to the other, or others, with no shared memories, there are rare manifestations where both are present. I imagine that the conflict between the two could possibly be immobilizing."

"And the absence of the corneal reflex?"

"Ah, yes. The fly. I cannot incorporate that phenomenon into any of the probable diagnoses, at least not at this time, and not without personally examining the patient."

"You mentioned a PET scan earlier. To be honest, it hadn't occurred to me to order one on Judtson. Are you recommending that I do?"

"MRIs and CT scans tell us quite a bit about structure, not chemistry. The PET scan might uncover a chemical abnormality the other tests wouldn't show. One never knows."

"I'll do it. Or at least I'll try. I'm not sure I'll have the same influence with him that I had before. If it is DID, what is the prognosis?"

"Except for the extreme cases, we've had good success with a coordinated regimen of therapy and medication."

"I thought you said that DID was not physiological. Why would meds help?"

"I said that it was not a biologically based disorder; however, I also mentioned that the emergence of alternate personalities can be triggered by stress. We frequently utilize tranquilizers or anti-depressants as an aid during the therapy process. If, on the other hand, my first hypothesis is correct and Mr. Kent has made a contemplative, deliberate, and conscious alteration to his personality, you must decide, Saylor, whether an overt attempt to return him to the Judtson Kent whom you personally prefer is in his best interest as a patient."

"You're telling me not to be selfish."

"Exactly. And I'm reminding you of your responsibility as a physician."

"I understand. As I said, I will do my best to get him to come in to see you."

"I appreciate that. Not only do I hope I can help him, but I must admit I am very curious, as well."

▽

Kristen Kent sat at the table waiting, sipping from a glass of white wine and feeling bewildered by the difference in her life that the last eighteen hours had made. She realized that she was sitting alone and grinning. Almost the moment Judtson had walked through their front door last evening, there had been a dramatic change, a change for the better, a change she had never dreamed was even possible. It was as if the past several years had been erased and he was, once again, the man she had thought she married.

In retrospect, she was amazed by how profound the transformation was. She had been sitting in the activity room, absent-mindedly watching television and feeling vaguely guilty. She knew that Saylor, Doni, and Ricky were all out looking for her husband, and yet she was passively idle at her house, rationalizing the decision by telling herself that she should be there in case he came home. Rocky was lying quietly in a corner of the foyer, on the cool ceramic tile floor near the front door, his usual location when Judtson was absent. And, as was typical, the golden was anything but relaxed as he waited for his master's return.

It was odd, she decided as she now recalled the moment, that the dog had not anticipated Judtson's arrival. Rocky was still lying in his spot, not standing with his nose pressed to the door, not wagging his tail, when the front door suddenly swung open and Judtson stepped inside, soaked from the earlier thunderstorm. She had jumped up and immediately hurried to the bathroom for a towel. As she replayed the scene, she shook her head in a mixture of shame and amusement. This initial action was so indicative of the eroded state of their relationship. Certainly she was glad to see Judtson; nonetheless, her first thought was only that he was dripping on their floor.

As she returned to the foyer, towel in hand, he said something to her which caused her to stop in her tracks. It was a simple enough statement, she knew, but one she had not heard from his lips in years. Smiling broadly, with his hair plastered down from the rain, he uttered, "Hello, sweetheart." Her breath caught in her throat. She hesitated for only a moment, afraid this was just another cruel tactic. Her fear instantly allayed by the look in his eyes, she dropped the towel, forgotten, on the floor and ran to him, embracing him with an intensity that had been absent for a very long time, oblivious to the fact that her clothes were rapidly getting saturated.

The passion of the moment escalated and they kissed, a deep and searching kiss, followed by another and then another. Her long-sublimated primal desires flared and she clawed at his clothes, tearing them. His actions mirrored hers, and they made love on the floor in the foyer.

In the aftermath, they talked. Now dry and both wearing terry-cloth robes, they sat beside one another on the couch, neither able to refrain from maintaining physical contact as they spoke. Judtson had poured out his heart to her, recalling and reliving all of the hurtful moments of the past few years and begging for her forgiveness. She, too, recited her own transgressions and asked the same. They answered each other with a tender kiss and a promise to put it all behind.

It was then that Judtson mentioned how Saylor and Doni were probably worried about him. She had tensed, expecting him to say that he was going to get dressed and walk next door to let them know he was fine. To her surprise, he asked her to call Saylor and tell him that he was home but had gone to sleep. This request, so out of character for Judtson, was another powerful indication that her husband had changed. She happily made the call.

Deeply immersed in her reverie, she did not notice Judtson enter the restaurant until he slid into the booth beside her and kissed her.

"You looked as if you were somewhere else," he commented.

She smiled at him. "I was replaying last night."

"I've done that a few times today myself. Thinking about last night *and* this morning."

They were both grinning at each other when the waiter appeared. "Good afternoon. I'm Kyle. I'll be serving you today."

As Judtson turned to answer him, Kristen held her breath, waiting for her husband's usual response of "Good afternoon, Kyle. I'm Judtson and I'll be your customer." She was pleasantly surprised when he merely ordered a glass of wine.

"Thank you."

He turned back to her. "For what?"

"For not embarrassing me with the line you always say."

He chuckled. "Oh, the 'I'm Judtson and I'll be your customer' line?"

"Yes, that's it."

"You won't be hearing that one again. It's just a bit too childish."

She feigned glancing around the room. "All right. Where's the pod? Where's the real Judtson?"

He kissed her lightly on the cheek. "You prefer the other Judtson?"

"Oh, God, no! Please, no! I want this Judtson."

"Okay, then. Don't look a gift horse in the mouth."

▽

After leaving Judtson's office, Kelsey drove straight back to her home. During the trip, she called Saylor and described the brief and unsettling visit. Saylor told her that he was concerned, but was not particularly forthcoming with details. They ended the call, both agreeing to speak later.

She briskly maneuvered the Hummer through the winding driveway to her house, and parked it under the porte cochere. Hopping out, she hurried inside, went directly to her study, and sat at the computer. With a few clicks of the mouse, she was on the home page of her blog, where she hastily typed, "Alchemist. Are you there? I need to talk to you."

Her muscles taut as a spring, she teetered on the front few inches of the leather chair and waited, staring silently at the blinking cursor, her left leg bouncing nervously. After a few minutes, she repeated the message. Again, no response.

"Damn, I wish I had his email address!" she muttered.

Ninety minutes elapsed with no response from the mysterious stranger. After numerous attempts to elicit a reply to no avail, her frustration boiling over, she typed, "Alchemist!!!! Please answer me!!!! I need to talk to you about Judtson!!!!! Something has happened to him!!!!!"

The moment she hit the enter key, she regretted using Judtson's name on the blog. Quickly, she seized the mouse and moved the pointer to the small x beside her last post to remove the message, when a comment appeared right below it.

"I'm here."

It was from Alchemist.

Her intention to delete the post forgotten, she typed, "Can we talk somewhere other than this blog? Email? IM? Anywhere a little more private."

She waited impatiently for an answer. In less than a minute it came. "Of course. Meet me at the link below. Open an account. As soon as I see you are online, I'll *ping* you for an IM chat."

Below the message was a blue link. Kelsey typed a hasty "Thanks," logged off, and followed the link, hurriedly creating a new account, using the same screen name as she used on her blog, "Batgirl." Within moments, the query arrived, inviting her to a chat.

After the connection was made, she filled Alchemist in on the latest bizarre details of her newfound acquaintance's ordeal, and ended the narrative with a question, "You still think this is mind control?"

"Don't you?" he answered almost immediately.

"Not sure. What's your opinion?"

"I have no doubt."

"Why?"

"I've seen it elsewhere. This is not the first."

"Where? When?"

"All over the planet, from the distant past until today."

"How is it being done?"

"The method is a quite ancient practice. It is called the 'Mutatus Procedure.'"

Chapter 15

===

SAYLOR FINISHED HIS DAY AT THE OFFICE by reading an email from McWhorter, the doctor in New York. The neurologist informed him that three more of the patients were now considered by their attending physicians to be in remission; he then inquired as to the current status of Saylor's patient.

Saylor typed his reply. "It has only been a little more than a day since the last break. I am not sure how long I should wait without the advent of another before I declare him in remission, although I'm certain this is too soon."

Pausing, his fingers poised over the keyboard, he debated whether to share with the stranger his concern about the change in Judtson's personality. Deciding to hold off on that particular facet until he had gathered more information, he ended the message by promising to keep McWhorter updated, and sent it.

He shut down his computer, turned off the lights in his office, and walked down the hallway, hoping to find Vance. His partner's office was dark and empty, as was the rest of the suite. Apparently, his office mates had already wrapped up their work for the day and departed.

Locking the front door to his suite, he made his way out of the building and to the parking lot. Lost in his own thoughts, he did not even recall the act of driving home, not focusing on his surroundings until he was parked in his garage. There was a moment of indecision as he was torn between walking next door to see Judtson and entering his own house. He activated the closer and went inside where Doni was waiting for him.

"Hi, Saylor-man."

"Hello, babe," he answered, his voice flat.

She cocked her head slightly, her long black hair partially covering her right cheek and most of her chin. "How well did you handle your first-ever Judtson-free day?"

Despite himself, Saylor felt a vague anger. "What kind of question is that?" he asked testily.

"Oh, dear. Not well, I see. Follow me, baby. I have a nice dinner all ready for you – spaghetti, huge meatballs, slices of buttery garlic toast, and a hand-tossed salad with your favorite homemade dressing."

"I'm not...."

"You're not what? Hungry? I've been working on this for hours. You are going to eat it."

"Doni...."

She reached out and took both of his hands in hers. "Saylor, honey. I know you're stressed. I know you're worried about Squirrel. I am, too. Okay? But I'm not the enemy, so don't turn on me. Even if something bad is happening to our pal, we still need to eat. After that...after our systems are overwhelmed by carbs and fat, we will focus our attention on the situation together."

He looked into her eyes and saw the combination of love, concern, and a touch of frustration. Leaning forward, he kissed her on the forehead and whispered, "Okay. Let's eat."

She released her grip on his hands, and he walked toward the kitchen.

"Huh-uh. Not the kitchen bar tonight."

He stopped, a quizzical expression on his face.

She pointed to the alcove beside them, smiling. "Dining room."

"The dining room? Honestly?"

With an insouciant shrug, she caught up to him and took his hand. "Thought it would be nice."

He allowed himself to be led into the rarely used room and saw that she had created a beautiful setting on their expansive teak table. "Wow! Candles and everything."

"Of course. Sit down. I'll get dinner."

"I'll help."

"Sit down, I said. This is my night to serve the 'master' of the house."

Allowing himself an ironic chuckle, he obeyed, pulled out a chair, and sat, picking up the linen napkin, which she had folded to resemble a peacock. As she disappeared into the kitchen, he shook out her work of origami and laid it across his lap. Using the silver tongs, he absentmindedly filled both of their salad bowls. Doni returned a minute later with a chafing dish, filled with bubbling sauce and meatballs.

"That smells wonderful."

"Thanks. Be right back."

On her next trip, she delivered the platter of garlic toast, fresh from the oven, its aroma instantly filling the room.

She returned again with the spaghetti and set it down, taking the chair next to him and scooting it closer to his. As they ate, he told her about his day, intuitively avoiding even the slightest mention of Judtson until they had finished the meal. Both feeling overly full, they finally leaned back in the dining room chairs. Doni wiped a trace of frosting from the corner of her mouth, removing the remnant of a three-chocolate layer cake she had baked for dessert, and turned to face him. "Okay. We made it through my fabulous meal without mentioning the subject once. And I thank you for that. I know it wasn't easy. Now, tell me what's new with Judtson."

Saylor took a sip of coffee and brought her up to speed on the day's developments. He shared Ricky's comments about how Judtson, in one day, had virtually reversed every single one of his long-standing and passionately held positions on multiple issues. He described the cold and aloof meeting between Judtson and Kelsey. Then, Saylor finished the narrative by recapping his conversation with Patrick Worden.

"So Worden thinks that Judtson either is clinically nuts or has simply hit bottom and finally grown up?"

"Basically. What do you think?"

She shrugged again. "Beats me. He has always been a little crazy, in an endearing sort of way. You have to admit he became more extreme after college. Maybe we are both too close to view this objectively. You said that Worden wants to see him?"

"Yes, he does."

"Good luck with that."

"I know."

"What's a PET scan?"

"Positron emission tomography. Essentially, an x-ray, an MRI, or a CT scan looks at the structure of the brain, density and things of that nature. A PET scan gives us some information about what is happening in the brain chemically…whether all of the chemical processes which are supposed to be occurring actually are, and whether there is something happening chemically which is out of place."

"Sounds like a good idea."

"I'm sure it is. It's just the thought of convincing him that's the problem."

Doni stood up. "Well, no time like the present. Let's go next door and talk to him. Maybe together we can do it."

"What about the dishes?"

"Leave them. We'll clean up later."

▽

Judtson and Kristen were sitting close together on the sofa. Doni and Saylor, in chairs across the room from them, glanced at each other meaningfully. Neither could recall a recent time when the Kents had actually cuddled.

"So you think I should have a session with this Dr. Worden?"

"I don't see what it could hurt, Judtson," Saylor answered, working to keep his voice casual. "It hasn't been much more than a day since the last break. We have no idea whether they've stopped or not. I think it's the prudent thing to do."

"You're still worried that Judtson will have another episode?" The question came from Kristen, who was pressed tightly against the side of her husband, holding his hand.

"I don't know if *worried* is the right word, Kristen. But we certainly can't rule out another one. And the problem is that we can't predict when it will happen. It could even be while Judtson's driving."

"And that would be disastrous," Doni emphasized, shaking her head.

"Oh, my God," Kristen gasped, putting her free hand to her mouth. "I hadn't thought about that."

Judtson smiled reassuringly at his wife. "I think they've stopped. I don't think I'm going to have more breaks."

"We all hope that's the case, Judtson," Saylor interjected firmly. "But, as I said, it hasn't been all that long yet. It's way too early to decide they're over."

"Saylor might be right, sweetheart."

In response, Judtson shifted his gaze from Kristen to Doni and finally to Saylor, before he spoke. "Okay. I don't see any harm. I'll do it. Go ahead and set it up."

Kristen immediately turned to face Saylor squarely. "I have a question. This psychiatrist only wants to see Judtson about the episodes or breaks or whatever they are?"

Applying his best sincere expression, Saylor answered her. "That's it. Why?"

Her eyes bored into his for a moment. "I was wondering, that's all. I don't see a reason for him to start poking around in Judtson's head, going back to whether he was bottle-fed as an infant and all that."

Saylor forced a casual laugh. "No. Nothing like that, Kristen. Just the episodes."

"You're sure?"

"I'm sure."

"All right."

Relieved, Saylor stood. "That's great. It's a good decision."

"I think so, too," Doni added, standing.

Kristen and Judtson walked them to the front door.

"Judtson, I'll check with Ricky in the morning to find out when you're free, and then I'll schedule a time with Dr. Worden."

"Thanks."

They wished Judtson and Kristen a good night and left. As they cautiously made their way through the dark desert back to their own home and were safely out of earshot, Doni nudged her husband's arm. "I never realized what a good liar you are."

Saylor laughed. "You, too."

"Getting him to see Worden was a lot easier than I thought it would be."

"I know," he agreed. "Did you notice anything weird?"

"You mean other than the two of them hanging on to each other like teenagers, for the first time in years, no. Why? What did you notice?"

Arriving at their front porch, he unlocked the door and they entered. The two walked directly to the dining room and began to gather the dirty dishes from the dinner table. "Doni, in all of the times we've been there...all of the countless visits we've had at Judtson's, there has been one absolutely unchangeable constant."

She paused in the act of picking up the serving plates. "Enough of the dramatic build-up. What did you see?"

"Where was Rocky while we were there?"

Doni stared up at the ceiling as she tried to recall. "I think...yes, he was...he was lying in the foyer. What's the big...? Oh, you're right. That pooch is *never* more than two inches away from Judtson."

"That's right. Never. He was just stationed in the foyer in the same spot where he always is...when he's waiting for Judtson to come home."

▽

First thing the following morning, Saylor contacted Ricky and told him that Judtson had agreed to a session with the psychiatrist. Excited by the news, Ricky gave him several options in Judtson's schedule. Next, Saylor called Worden's office. They had a cancellation in the schedule for the next day, and he told the receptionist to plug Judtson into the slot.

When he called Ricky to let him know the time of the appointment, Judtson's assistant abruptly asked, "Are you free for lunch today?"

Glancing at his own schedule, Saylor answered, "Yes, sure. Why?"

"Kelsey called. She wants to talk to both of us."

"I can make it. Did she say why?"

Ricky sighed with mock exasperation. "You know her, so secretive."

"Okay. Send a text with the location and I'll be there."

"See you later. I'd better go. Judtson just pulled in."

Saylor said good-bye and hung up the phone. His mind wandered back to the previous evening. There was no doubt that the suddenly revived relationship between Judtson and Kristen was odd.

Yet he could not honestly find fault with this particular turn of events. If it had been the only change in Judtson, he decided that he would probably enthusiastically support the shift. He then thought about the change of mind Judtson had apparently undergone on the topic of Villarreal's research. Again, standing alone, this was not especially damning. After all, there had recently been a lot of pressure to abandon this project. One by one Saylor ticked off the other changes as had been reported to him by Ricky. It was inescapable that, individually, they were all quite reasonable.

"So why do I feel as though something horrible has happened?" he asked himself aloud. As his mind sorted through all of the facts, all of the variables, he found that he returned, time and time again, to one thing. One issue. One image he could not merely dismiss as a reasonable, normal, understandable change. In the moments he had spent with Judtson since his return from the disappearance, every time Saylor looked at his old friend, he knew, beyond a shadow of a doubt, that the two blue eyes looking back at him belonged to someone else, someone he had never met.

▽

Saylor stood outside the massive oak doors in front of Kelsey's home. Before ringing the bell, he took in his surroundings. Her place was a mansion surrounded by acres of land. Not the usual Southern Arizona native landscape, the grounds were walled-in and cleared of the saguaros, prickly pears, chollas, creosotes, and all of the other indigenous flora. Although the palace was built in the Catalina Foothills, all of the rolling topography of the zone had been bulldozed flat and masked with a crushed, quarried rock of a predominantly salmon hue. And, to his surprise, it remained completely barren; not a single desert broom or ambrosia poked through the imported ground cover.

Turning his attention to the house itself, he saw that the exterior walls, rather than being coated with the ubiquitous stucco of the region, were made of cast-in-place concrete. The small cone-shaped depressions left by the snap ties, which had secured the vertical forms, were symmetrical and evenly spaced across the surface, creating an almost industrial appearance. Judging by the reveals on the entry doors and the nearby windows, the walls appeared to be approximately one foot thick.

This structure was built either by someone who really hated termites, he thought to himself, or by someone who wanted a fortress. He rang the doorbell, or assumed that it rang since he could not hear any sound from inside. Within seconds, the door swung open and Kelsey greeted him.

"Saylor! Thanks for coming. Ricky's already here."

"I know. I saw his car."

She giggled and looked past him at the bright yellow Smart car parked beside Saylor's truck. "Of course you did. A little hard to miss. Anyway, come in. I made lunch."

She whirled and walked away energetically, leaving him to close the door and follow her. The contrast between the stark, austere exterior of the home and the interior was dramatic. In the foyer, which was larger than Saylor's living room, the floor was covered with an Italian marble and accented by a massive and apparently authentic Persian rug. The intricate hand-woven piece was at least twenty feet long. Overhead dangled an elaborate chandelier, composed of thousands of sparkling faceted crystals, in the aggregate weighing hundreds of pounds.

Stepping briskly to keep up, Saylor followed her through what he guessed to be the living room, dominated by a black-lacquered grand piano. Several paintings of the classic style competed for space on the walls with hundreds of objects. Although no common denominator was apparent to Saylor among the countless types of collectibles or their origins, the one consistent theme was that each piece, as much he was able to focus upon the individual items as he walked, was breathtakingly beautiful. Ornate, glittery silk fans which were adjacent to jeweled tiaras ensconced upon custom gold-leaf shelves, and then juxtaposed with delicate shadow boxes, containing miniature ceramics and pressed florals, all fleetingly caught his attention. The furniture in the room was Victorian in style, the prevalent motif an intense burgundy velour with cream-colored fringe.

The combined effect was overwhelming. He knew that had he not seen it with his own eyes and only had it described to him, he would have been certain that the only possible outcome for such a decorating technique would be a hopeless, cluttered jumble. Yet that could not have been further from the truth. He almost delighted in letting his eyes flit from point to point, finding one visual feast after another.

"Kelsey," he called to her, realizing he had unconsciously slowed to appreciate the view. "Your home is amazing."

She did not slow down or look his way, but merely tossed out, "Thanks," and turned the corner. Saylor quickened his pace and caught up with her at the end of a short hallway, just as she was entering the kitchen.

"Saylor!" The shout came from Ricky, who was sitting at a hand-carved mahogany table, large enough to seat twenty.

The transition in style from the living room to the kitchen again startled Saylor. While the first room was delicate, classic in its execution, this room captured the essence of a working kitchen in a royal castle. Dark variegated brickwork covered the walls. The floor was hardwood, but not highly polished, more closely resembling the well-utilized surface of a butcher block. The appliances were all of a commercial brand and pewter in color.

"Kelsey, this setup could feed two hundred easily," Saylor remarked, his eyes dancing around, darting from the suspended copper cookware to the soot-coated hearth of a fireplace, complete with a hanging cast-iron kettle.

"Isn't it cool?" Ricky practically gushed.

Accepting the comments with a smile, Kelsey sat beside Ricky at the table. Saylor noticed a stack of papers and a laptop in front of her.

"Come and sit down," she said, patting the chair next to her. "I want to show you both a couple of things before lunch is ready."

Obediently, Saylor took the seat.

With her characteristic rapid-fire pace, she began, "I connected with Alchemist last night. I told him what's happening to Judtson."

"Do you know who this Alchemist is yet?" Saylor asked.

"No. I don't. I haven't asked him. I probably should. Maybe next time we talk. Anyway, I told him all about what is happening. I expected him to be stumped or surprised or something. But he told me that what I described isn't unique."

"I already know that. I've spoken with a doctor in New York. Apparently, there are eight other cases like Judtson's."

Her head jerked in Saylor's direction. "The personality change has happened eight times?"

"No. I guess I wasn't clear. I was talking about the fugue states, breaks, episodes, whatever we want to call them."

"Already know that. Judtson told me in the phone call before he was taken."

"Taken?"

"Yes! Taken. You don't think he just wandered off for a long walk and went home a different person, do you?"

"I've spoken with a psychiatrist. He seems to think it is possible."

A rush of breath burst from Kelsey's mouth, her shoulders dropping to accentuate the frustration she was feeling. "Of course he would say that."

With a wry grin, Saylor asked, "You don't believe him?"

She slapped the palms of her hands on top of the pile of papers and swiveled her head back and forth between Ricky and Saylor. "Maybe you should listen to what I have to say. Then you can decide."

Saylor stared at her. He could not deny her sincerity or the intensity of her passion at the moment. "Ricky, are you buying into the possibility that Judtson is the victim of some conspiracy?"

Ricky, leaning forward so that he could look around Kelsey, answered, "I don't know, Saylor. There were some weird aspects to his disappearance. You know that."

"I do. You don't think they could all be explained by his change of heart?"

Kelsey jerked her head back and forth to face them as they spoke, her red hair tossing violently with each twist, but she remained silent.

"Saylor, maybe Judtson did go for a long walk. Maybe he had some traumatic change of heart and decided to mend fences with Kristen, Mitch, Dorothy, Darrow, and the rest. I suppose that's all possible. Maybe he did decide to drop the whole Villarreal thing and go back to writing the kind of books he has always written. That's possible, too. And God knows I can understand his parking that gas-guzzling muscle car and switching to the Camry. I suppose he could view them all as decisions consistent with finally growing up."

"Exactly. So what's the problem?"

Ricky leaned farther forward, resting his forearms on the table. "Think about it, Saylor. Before I left him alone, he was still the old Judtson. He talked to Kelsey after I took off to get lunch. According to her, that conversation lasted four or five minutes. When he talked to her, he was *still* the old Judtson. Are we supposed to believe that from the moment they hung up until I returned with the sandwich, there would really have been enough time for him to do a complete reevaluation of his life, conclude that he was on the wrong track and needed to make all of those fundamental changes, dispose of the Villarreal phone slip, tear out the page from my book of slips, delete Villarreal's emails and scrub them from the trash bin on his computer, go into the phone-manager program and, without the benefit of knowing my password, purge all the phone records from our system, and then casually amble out the front door for a stroll? I guess what I'm saying is that he *could* have gone through some gigantic revelation during the long walk. I can see that. What I am not buying is that he was able to pull off a comprehensive retrospective of his life and then take care of all the other things in the space of what…about fifteen or twenty minutes?"

Saylor mulled over Ricky's comments. "It's a tight squeeze, I agree. But the whole self-analysis which led him to the change was already a work in progress. It had been going on for a couple of days. Maybe it finally gelled at that moment, right after talking to Kelsey. That would leave enough time to do the other things and go out the door before you came back."

Ricky emphatically shook his head. "It doesn't make sense…."

Kelsey interrupted, "There's one more thing. I had just started discussing this with Ricky when you got here."

"What's that?"

"Ricky told me that when the cops arrived, there was a flash drive in the USB port. And that's what had my video on it, the video that got you busted."

"Yes. That's true. Why is that significant?"

"I didn't put the video on a flash drive when I dropped it off at Judtson's. I gave him the SIM card out of my phone."

"He could have copied the video off the Internet."

"No. The version on the Internet...."

"That's right. It didn't have the license plate."

"Bingo!"

"Well, he could have copied it from the SIM card."

"That's what I thought. But Ricky told me that Judtson's phone is different from mine – different brand, model, everything. My SIM card wouldn't work in his. And the only other way to copy a SIM card is with some fancy equipment that you guys don't own and would never need."

Saylor thought about what she said. "So, you're saying that not only did a person or persons unknown come in and kidnap Judtson...obviously without a fight or there would have been some damage at the office...but they were also the ones who eradicated all of the Villarreal things, and deliberately left the flash drive for the police to find."

"Uh-huh. That's what I'm saying."

"That's pretty outlandish."

"That's what they count on."

"*What's* what *who* count on?"

"They...and I don't know yet who they are...count on their actions being dismissed as outrageous and ludicrous. That's how they get away with what they do."

Filled with a conflicting array of emotions, Saylor begrudgingly admitted, "I've been suspicious, too."

Eagerly, Kelsey asked, "About what?"

He told her about his visit the previous evening and the uncharacteristic behavior of Judtson's golden retriever, also sharing the unsettling feeling he had whenever he looked into his friend's eyes.

"Dogs know. Everybody knows that," Kelsey declared in a matter-of-fact voice.

Saylor glanced down at the stack of papers in front of his hostess. "What do you have there?"

Smiling as if she had won a victory, Kelsey began, "Alchemist told me that what has happened to Judtson has happened several times throughout history. There have been leaders, clerics, scientists, generals and, in recent times, journalists who seemed to be heading in one direction, who all seemed to be on the verge of finding out something they shouldn't, when all of a sudden they abruptly just lost interest. They suddenly dropped whatever avenue they were pursuing, even though in some cases they had been obsessed with the topic, and then simply dismissed it as some absurd, childish fantasy."

"Is this true?" Ricky asked.

"I've done the research." She tapped the pile with her fingertip. "There's a lot here, although I'm sure not all of it. In case after case, story after story, what I described has happened. And it goes back centuries."

"And Alchemist thinks there is a single group behind it?"

"Yes, Saylor, he does."

"How do they do it? You mentioned mind control to me on the phone yesterday."

"That's just it...it isn't exactly mind control."

"What is it?"

"Alchemist told me they call it the 'Mutatus Procedure.'"

"The Mutatus Procedure? Do you know what that means?"

She nodded, relishing the moment of suspense, before she answered. "*Mutatus* is Latin. It literally translates to 'he has been changed.'"

Chapter 16

T HE WHITE VAN WAS PARKED NEAR THE GATE of Kelsey's property, its markings indicating that the vehicle was a delivery van for a local dry cleaner; yet, the owner of that business would have been surprised to discover the existence of this additional truck in his fleet. The driver made a show of getting out from behind the wheel and stretching his legs, lighting a cigarette, and spreading out a map on the truncated hood. Depending on the amount of time the passengers in the rear required, he would finish the smoke and climb into the cab, open a lunch pail, and spread out a sandwich, a bag of chips, and a pack of donuts on the dashboard so that anyone passing close to him would think he had merely stopped on his route for a meal.

Inside the back of the van, two men sat silently at consoles. With a keystroke command from one of them, a small parabolic dish on the roof of the truck elevated slightly to clear the wall and obtain a line of sight on the nearest window of Kelsey's house. Once the dish was positioned, the technician inside tweaked the controls while staring at the monitor. Receiving nothing in passive mode, the man typed in a command and activated a laser.

$$\nabla$$

"This seems pretty bizar…," Saylor was saying to Kelsey, when he was interrupted by a piercing, repeating tone.

"What is that?" he asked, but she was already in motion, jumping up from the chair and running to the wall abutting the fireplace. She slammed the heel of her hand onto the face of a cream-colored panel, flush with the wall, and it sprang open, revealing a flat-screen monitor and a recessed keyboard. The monitor was displaying the area outside the front doors, and Saylor, following her, could see his pickup truck and Ricky's car on the screen.

"What's going on?" Ricky asked, also hurrying to stand behind Kelsey.

"Somebody is up to something," she answered cryptically, her finger repeatedly tapping the space bar of the keyboard, rapidly changing the exterior views. Each successive image clearly originated from one of the multiple cameras built into the outside wall of the house, and displayed the enclosed grounds. After completing the circle, she tapped another key and the view switched to outside the perimeter wall. Again, she quickly moved through the views until she shouted, "Gotcha!" The screen showed the white van and the driver, visibly hunched over a map.

"Kelsey, that's a dry cleaner. He seems to be lost."

She tore her eyes away from the monitor just long enough to give Saylor a look of disdain. "You think so, huh?" She reached up and tapped a part of the picture. "Why would a dry cleaner have a parabolic listening dish mounted on the roof of its delivery van?"

Saylor looked at the screen. "How do you know that's a listening device? It could be some satellite link back to the main office...you know, so they can tell the driver to pick up items from a call-in order."

Shaking her head emphatically, she explained, "Satellite dishes point up, Saylor. At satellites. Not horizontally at people's houses. Besides, innocent dry cleaner's vans, with innocent dishes on the roof, don't generate a laser beam."

"What?" Ricky yelped.

"That's what triggered the alarm. They shine a laser beam at a window. Windows normally vibrate from noise inside, like conversation. The laser can measure distance so accurately that it can measure those vibrations, and a computer can translate them back into speech."

"You're kidding me."

"No. I'm not, Ricky."

"So anybody can drive down the street and shine a laser at my windows and record the conversations inside?"

"Right."

Saylor interrupted, "And they are listening to us right now?"

She turned to face him, a proud grin spreading across her face. "Nope. Not my windows. They are double-dampened and have a film lattice on the surface which senses a laser and triggers the alarm. Our visitors are listening to total silence right now. I wanted to rig up something which would amplify the laser and bounce it back to the source. You know, fry the receiver. But my guys are still working on that."

"Your guys?"

She ignored him and continued, "So, in the meantime, we have to settle for something almost as good."

She turned back to the keyboard and typed in a command. With a flourish, she tapped the enter key and then dashed away, leaving the two in the kitchen.

Following at a run, Saylor shouted, "What did you do?"

He chased her through the living room and foyer, where she came to a halt at a window beside the front doors. As Saylor came to a skidding stop on the tile floor, he felt as much as heard a low-pitched rumble.

Not in the least bit breathless, Kelsey explained, "Since I can't bounce back the laser, I do the next best thing. I rigged up the windows so the exterior panes work like the diaphragm on a speaker. One keystroke, and those folks are getting a lot more than they bargained for."

"I don't understand," Ricky said between panting breaths.

"The laser is tuned to pick up vibrations from the window which are very subtle and faint. The little surprise I just sent was anything but subtle."

$\triangledown$

Inside the van, the technician who had been monitoring the laser was screaming in pain, jerking the headphones from his head and throwing them to the floor. The other technician, realizing that they had been discovered, pounded loudly on the wall. The driver, hearing the signal, dashed to the open door of the cab, completely forgetting about the map on the hood. He had left the engine running, so he hastily dropped the vehicle into gear and sped off, leaving behind a plume of dust.

$$\triangledown$$

Since their only view from the window was the parabolic dish scooting away, the three returned to the kitchen and checked the monitor, which was only displaying the remnants of the dust cloud left by the hastily departing van. Kelsey retrieved the video capture from the hard drive and replayed the rapid retreat. After the three watched the soundless tableau, Kelsey turned to them and said, "I think lunch is ready."

Saylor and Ricky were both subdued as she casually opened the door to the oven and, using a wooden peel, removed six calzones from the oven.

"Go on, sit down," she ordered, sliding the toasted stuffed dough onto a serving dish.

They compliantly returned to their seats, neither saying a word as she took a salad out of the refrigerator and placed it on the table. "Papaya and pomegranate juice okay?"

She interpreted their silence as an answer in the affirmative and brought a glass pitcher filled with a reddish juice, positioning it beside three tall glasses on a silver platter. With the efficiency of an experienced waitress, she scooped a calzone onto each of three plates, filled three salad bowls to almost overflowing, and then poured the juice before sitting down.

"I would give those a couple of minutes to cool off or you'll burn yourselves," she cautioned, taking a sip of juice. "I'm sorry I didn't ask earlier. I hope neither of you is vegetarian or lactose intolerant. Those are filled with sausage, pepperoni, spinach, and cheese. By the way, Saylor, do you still think this is all some normal, innocent, run-of-the-mill change of heart by Judtson?"

Saylor, who had yet to touch any of the food, was staring at her. Several more seconds passed before he found his voice. "How can you be so calm? Serving us lunch as though nothing happened?"

Stabbing at the salad with her fork until it was fully loaded, she shrugged. "What's the big deal? They were listening to us. Or trying to." She filled her mouth with the forkful of greens and chewed vigorously, then continued, "All it tells me is that we are on the right track."

He glanced at Ricky, who was sitting motionless and also staring at Kelsey with his mouth agape. Frustrated, Saylor reacted a little more loudly, "Right track? They? Kelsey, who in the hell are you?"

The corners of her mouth curling upward, she was clearly enjoying his discomfort. "Already told you. Kelsey Batman."

"You know what I mean. Why do you live in this fortress? Why do you have the cameras and laser sensors? Why do you know about all of these things?" By the end of his string of questions, Saylor's voice had risen in pitch.

She took another slow sip of the juice and deliberately placed the glass down, appearing to come to a decision. "Okay. If we are going to be working together, you should know."

"Working together? Wait a…."

She held up her hands to stop him. Her voice was softer, her cadence more deliberate and calm. "Call it whatever you want. You, Ricky, probably your wife, and I are in this thing now whether we want to be or not. I'm guessing by what we saw a few minutes ago that it has gone too far. It's now past the point where we can all go back to our regular lives and just forget about it."

Clearing his throat, Ricky finally joined the conversation. "Kelsey, *what* has gone too far?"

"You two need to understand that what happened to Judtson is just one trick in their bag, maybe their newest one. For a very long time they have utilized a lot of different methods to neutralize anyone who discovers something that he or she, or the rest of the population, isn't supposed to know. If they can merely discredit someone so that the person is simply viewed as a crackpot, they will. But if the person has too high a profile or too much credibility, they have to take it a step further."

"Like Judtson," Ricky murmured.

"Exactly. He has built up a huge following. He has established himself over the years as a reasonable, intelligent person, an authority. If he were to spill the beans, his words would have more weight with the general public. They can't afford that."

"And what if the technique, what did you call it. . .?"

She answered Ricky, "The Mutatus Procedure."

"What if the Mutatus Procedure doesn't solve the problem for them?"

She broke eye contact and looked into the distance, her voice flat. "Then people have single-car accidents on deserted roads, or they are in plane crashes, things like that."

The three were quiet for some time as her words sank in. Saylor finally broke the silence. "You still haven't told us who you are, Kelsey, and why you are so deeply into all of this."

Her eyes returned to fix upon his. "Are you familiar with 'the cloud'?"

"The cloud?"

"Yeah, the cloud. The Internet. . .the cloud."

"Not really. I guess I've heard about it. It has been mentioned in ads, although I don't have any idea what it is."

"Well, I won't bore you with the details. Basically, 'the cloud' is a term for off-site storage and computer services which, among other things, replace computers and servers at homes and businesses."

"I see," Saylor said, making it clear that he did not.

"The benefits of it are amazing. Before the cloud, there were two classes in computing: the haves and have-nots. There were government institutions, universities, and major corporations who owned expensive, massive computing systems, and there were small businesses and individuals who owned relatively small systems. The cloud allows those smaller entities access to the benefits of the monster systems. It also provides essentially unlimited storage capacity for files, and mind-blowing computing power. It eliminates the need for businesses to make enormous investments on equipment, because they can satisfy all their needs in the cloud. Heck, the cloud is even being sold to businesses to replace their phone systems."

"I'm not entirely certain I understand."

"Look, it isn't important that you do. What's important to understand is that before the cloud, we had all of our stuff and did all of our work essentially on our own computers. And we could protect what we wrote and what we did and what we said, with varying degrees of success, through firewalls and, in a worst-case scenario, by simply unplugging. Once we move our data to the cloud, it's all out there. It's no longer something we can wrap our arms around and protect. And it's no longer something we can unplug from, in order to segregate our stuff" – she gestured at the terminal near the kitchen – "because our stuff isn't in here anymore. It's out there. It's in the cloud. And once it's in the cloud, anyone can get at it. As is the case with so many new technologies, the benefits are great, and the potential for abuse is also great.

"In a way, it's like banking. Either you can hold your assets in your own possession, as paper currency, gold or silver, bonds, et cetera. You can have a safe at home, keep them with you, protect them. Get the idea?"

Saylor nodded.

"Or you can keep your money in the bank. You can have your paychecks deposited directly, pay your bills electronically, use debit cards for purchases. Most of the financial institutions, when you buy gold from them, hold on to *your* gold. They send you a piece of paper showing how much gold you own. But *you* don't have it. *They* do."

"Okay."

"Same thing with information. If you have all of your computer equipment on your premises, and everything you do – all of your work product, all of your transactions, all of your emails, everything – is kept on your equipment, they have to get into your equipment to get at it. It's not impossible to do. Hackers are darn good at it. But it is still yours, if you know what I'm saying. But once it is all done in the cloud, it isn't anymore. Like the banking I described."

Ricky, who had not touched his calzone, leaned forward. "I'm not sure I get it yet, Kelsey."

"All right. Let me ask you a question. If you did all of your banking electronically, and I mean all of it, including all of your bill paying…and all of your investments, too, so that you didn't even receive the actual, physical stock certificate…what would happen to your money and assets if the banking industry shut down? If you went to the bank, and the doors were just locked? If you went online to your bank's website, and all you got was the 'unable to connect' screen? If you called them, and it just rang and no one answered?"

Ricky shivered. "I don't even want to think about that."

"Exactly. It would be a nightmare. Well, the cloud is being used by some businesses and individuals for almost everything – health records, personal information, human resource and employment records, payroll, billions of personal photographs. The list goes on forever."

"What does all of this have to do with…?"

"I'm getting there. The one flaw with the cloud…the inherent problem which has caused the government, the military, and a few others to shun it…has been security. Since all of our data is basically lumped together with everyone else's data, the way our money is lumped together with everyone else's money at the banks, the massive server farms out in the middle of nowhere, which make up the cloud, have taken the position that security is the problem of the user."

"Is that hard to do?" asked Saylor.

Kelsey laughed. "Yes, it is hard to do! It's like trying to protect your personal drop of water once it has been added to the ocean. People have tried. Major software companies have busted their buns trying to come up with a bulletproof, secure system. Once rock-solid security can be promised and delivered, the final obstacle standing in the way of absolutely everyone using the cloud just goes away. The creator of the ultimate security system becomes unbelievably wealthy. Most of the holdouts jump into the cloud. Everybody's happy."

Saylor took in his surroundings. "You created it, didn't you?"

Kelsey answered with a subtle nod. "My father and I did it."

"That's a good thing, right?"

"I thought so. All I could see was a world where everyone had access to the biggest and the best, while keeping digital pictures of Grandma safe." Kelsey's voice softened. "My father didn't agree. Even before we finished it, he was talking about the dangers of putting our software out there."

"Why?" Saylor asked, a little confusion in his voice. "It sounds like a great idea."

"That's what I thought. But the problem with a security system, any security system, is the people behind it."

"Okay. Go on."

"Let's say that you have a security system in your home."

"I do."

"And let's say that you pay a company to monitor the system so that if something happens, they can dispatch the police or fire department."

"I do that, too."

"As long as the monitoring company and all of its employees are legit and honest, it's great. But what if they aren't? What if the company…or what if just one key person at the company is a bad guy? At that point, what you've done is hire the wolf to guard the henhouse. He can let his accomplices know when you are gone for the evening or when you've left for vacation. And then, when his partners enter your home, he can make sure no alarm is sounded, no police are dispatched. Nothing."

"I haven't thought about that."

She shrugged. "Most people don't. Believe it or not, it happens quite a bit around the country. The point is, prior to the advent of monitored security systems, we spent money on strong locks, maybe bars on the windows, even guard dogs. And we would conscientiously stop the delivery of newspapers and mail while we were out of town so that crooks couldn't tell by driving past the house that we weren't home."

"True."

"Now that home security is offered, we willingly give all of that information to total strangers, *assuming* they won't abuse it. In the scenario where we have an evil security-monitoring company, we are now much more vulnerable than before. Same thing with our data. We kept it on our own computers. We encrypted it. We put it behind a firewall. We developed good habits, like not opening attachments on strange emails. We bought good software to protect us from attacks and updated it daily. And all of this was fairly effective at protecting our precious data."

Ricky, who had been listening raptly, said, "I think I see what your father's concerns were, but how does this translate to the cloud?"

Kelsey tilted her head back and stared at the ceiling. "We took a route entirely different from the industry norm of ordinary user-accounts and encryption. We stole a very old idea, safe-deposit boxes. Each user puts his or her data into a virtual box in the cloud. Just like a friendly neighborhood banker recognizes a customer, this virtual box can tell whether the user trying to open it is the owner of the data or not."

"You and your father invented the Safe-Deposit e-Box?" Ricky sounded impressed. "Almost everyone I know uses it, including me."

Kelsey nodded and continued, "But people lose keys. When that happens at a bank, they physically drill the lock to get in. In the amorphous world of electronic data, there isn't an analogue to that. So the only option was that we, the creators of the box, could also open it, if the customer requested that."

"That's where your comparison to residential security monitoring comes in, isn't it?" Saylor asked.

"Right. Thousands, millions of trusting customers, each with a safe-deposit box, each filling it with precious data and believing it is safe, and one person…one entity can open all of the boxes at any time."

Ricky leaned forward. "You wouldn't ever do that, would you?"

Turning back to her lunch guests, she answered wistfully, "No. I wouldn't. Neither would my father."

"Then what's the problem?"

She stared at them, lingering for a moment on each of their faces. "Eighteen months ago my father was returning from a few days at his cabin. It was the middle of the day. The sky was clear. His truck was less than six months old and in perfect condition. He had no history of any health issues and never drank alcohol or did any drugs. The road conditions were perfect and there was no other traffic when he drove through a guard rail and plunged eight hundred and twenty-nine feet into a canyon."

"Oh, my God," Saylor murmured.

Kelsey's voice was flat as she continued, "The truck exploded into flames, making it impossible to perform an autopsy on his body or do any meaningful forensic analysis of the truck itself."

Both men were silent as they absorbed what she had said.

"There was an investigation, if you could call it that. The official conclusion was that he had committed suicide."

Saylor looked at Kelsey questioningly, saying nothing.

"No. He wasn't in the least bit suicidal."

She picked up the nearly room-temperature calzone on her plate and took a bite, chewing it slowly. Neither Ricky nor Saylor spoke, waiting for her to resume.

"Shortly after his death, I was approached by some quasi-governmental agency. They wanted to buy the company. They wanted to control the key. I told them to pound salt. Then, two weeks after I refused, they tried to kill me."

"What?" Ricky blurted.

Her head jerked a slight nod. "I was asleep when two men came into my house in the middle of the night. I guess it was supposed to seem like a robbery or home invasion or whatever, but they didn't try to take anything. Nope, they passed right by thousands of dollars worth of stuff and came straight to my bedroom. Obviously, their only goal was to kill me."

"But...."

"I know. Why am I alive? Completely unbeknownst to me, my father had left behind security. He knew, or suspected, something would happen. He also knew I wouldn't take it seriously. The bad guys made it as far as the hallway leading to my bedroom door, when my father's man, who had followed the two into the house, stopped them."

"Stopped them?" The question came from Saylor.

Fixing her eyes upon his, a slight upward curl at one corner of her mouth, she answered, "Blew them away. Both of them." Her audience was, again, speechless as she resumed. "The cops, of course, were worthless. They didn't care that this happened right after my father was killed. They didn't care that the two intruders ignored all my valuables and were making a beeline straight for my bedroom on the second floor. They didn't care that the two supposed 'common street thugs' were sophisticated enough to disable my alarm system, and were both carrying silenced 9-millimeter pistols. All they cared about was quickly declaring it a burglary gone bad and closing the file."

"Incredible," Ricky declared, shaking his head.

"Sit tight. I'll be right back." Kelsey stood abruptly and walked out of the room. When she returned a minute later, she was holding a sheet of paper in her hand.

"That night...the night of the break-in, my guardian gave me something."

She laid the paper flat on the table for both to read.

To my dearest daughter –

I know that you have always believed the best about people. Although I've known how misguided this belief was, I have never been able to bring myself to shatter the illusion. I feared that your perspective on mankind was the cornerstone of your ability to enjoy life so intensely, so delightfully. That joy, which I have experienced vicariously, was a quality I could not make myself destroy. But if you are reading this letter, something has happened and I am no longer with you, which means that you are in grave danger.

Kelsey, there are bad people in the world – nasty, vile, repugnant, and evil people. I am sure that even you know that. What you do not know, what you have never once allowed yourself to grasp, is that they are not merely a scattered, ineffectual, and random sprinkling of despicable individuals. They are a cohesive, organized, and determined brotherhood. This force, this band of abhorrent men and women have been operating for hundreds, perhaps thousands of years. They have meddled, tampered, influenced, and controlled people and governments for centuries.

Despite years of effort, I have never been successful in identifying who they are or what they truly desire. Yet, you must understand that, due to your misfortune of being my only offspring, and in light of the fact that I am now deceased, you are certainly their next target.

Trust no one except the man I have left behind to protect you. I wish that I could have discovered more about the cabal of shadows, if only to help you through the balance of your life. I am sorry for the situation I have created and cast you into. I am even more saddened by the thought that the optimistic, joyful soul of my beloved daughter must now surely have darkened and turned toward the path of cynicism. Be safe, my beautiful daughter.

Your father

"The next day I moved out of my place and into this one. This was my father's home. Right after his death, I couldn't even make myself come here. Too many memories. Too much pain. But following the incident at my house, I realized that he had designed and built this place as a fortress for a reason, and that I'd better take advantage of it."

Saylor, the first to finish reading the letter, turned to look at Kelsey. "I am truly sorry about your father."

She said nothing. Her eyes were focused on some faraway object, visible only to her. When Ricky finished reading and sat back, Kelsey finally spoke. "I guess it's about time you met my guardian angel."

She twisted around in her chair and, in a loud voice, called, "Romeo!"

A moment later, stepping into the kitchen from an adjacent hallway, came a mountain of a man. Wearing camouflage pants with a green T-shirt stretched tightly across his muscled chest, well over six feet tall, black, his head shaved and gleaming, the man joined them at the table.

"Saylor, Ricky, I'd like you to meet Romeo Jones."

Chapter 17

Rᴏʙʏɴ ʀᴇᴇᴅʏ ᴡᴀs sɪᴛᴛɪɴɢ ᴀᴛ ʜᴇʀ ᴅᴇsᴋ, reviewing the upcoming schedule, when a knock at the door interrupted her. She glanced up to see one of her assistants standing with a man in a gray jumpsuit.

"Yes, Nadia. What is it?"

"Sorry to interrupt, Ms. Reedy. The technician from RadTech is here to work on the PET/CT."

Robyn looked past Nadia and addressed the man. "Is there something wrong with the equipment? I hadn't heard anything about it."

He stepped forward. "No, ma'am. Well, not exactly. The system isn't off line or anything like that. During our last routine diagnostics, we noticed some anomalies in the dedicated UPS and decided it should be replaced soon. The new one arrived yesterday, and I'm here to hook it up."

Her eyes efficiently swept the schedule. "It seems that you picked a good day. We only had one scan scheduled for today and it cancelled. How long should it take?"

"No more than an hour."

She nodded. "Go for it."

▽

Patrick Worden sat behind his desk, performing a familiar mental routine. Over the years he had become quite adept at clearing his mind. In this case, it was the information about Judtson Kent previously provided to him by Saylor Costello that he wished to remove. It was critical for him to remain as objective as possible. He did not want to begin the session with preconceived notions based on any facts he had been told about Kent. His exercise, honed to near perfection, consisted of visualizing each of those facts as a distinct symbolic physical object. He would then pack each piece away in a box. As each box was filled, his mind closed the flaps, and he would seal the carton with strong tape.

The preparation complete, he stood and walked out to the waiting room where Kent was seated. After introductions, Worden brought Judtson into his office, pulled closed the outer door, then latched the inner one, and indicated that his patient should sit in the wing-back chair beside a small round table which held only a delicate Tiffany lamp.

Judtson sat, and Worden took the other seat across from him. Picking up his notepad and pen, the doctor smiled reassuringly. "I don't know if you've ever had the pleasure of a session with a psychiatrist in the past, Judtson. The format is quite simple. We chat."

Kent returned the smile. "Chat away."

"What is your main concern that brings you to see me today?"

"I'm not sure that I have one. I don't know how much Saylor told you...."

"Let's just assume he told me nothing. I'd like to hear it from you."

"Okay. A few days ago I started noticing that my body wasn't doing what I told...." He went on to describe all of the events leading up to the visit, finishing the narrative by emphasizing that he was now convinced the episodes had stopped.

"Why do you believe the episodes, as you call them, will not resume?"

"I don't know. No real reason, I suppose. It's only a feeling."

Worden made a note on his pad and then continued. "Let's talk about you, rather than the episodes. Have you noticed a change in yourself in the period of time prior to the first event until today?"

He watched carefully as Kent thought about the question for a moment before answering. "I am different. But I don't think one has anything to do with the other."

"Different in what way?"

"I think I've finally grown up." Judtson chuckled at his own comment. "Funny thought. Growing up in my thirties."

"What have others told you about your recent behavior?"

Judtson smiled to himself. "Depends on the person you ask. My wife thinks it's great. She had been putting up with me for a long time, to the point where it had essentially destroyed our marriage. Now, she's ecstatic. As for my friends, they haven't really come right out and mentioned anything; even so, I can tell that they think I've pulled a Dr. Jekyll and Mr. Hyde. By the looks on their faces, I don't think they are quite as happy with the change as Kristen is."

"Do you agree with them?"

"Agree with whom, Kristen or the others?"

"All of them."

"I'm happy with the person I am now, so I guess I would agree with Kristen that I've changed for the better. Saylor, Doni, and Ricky are just going to have to live with it."

"Now I'm going to ask you about the period of time including the first episode all the way through to today. Have you had periods of time for which you have no memory?"

"No. Not that I recall." Realizing the humor in his own answer, Judtson laughed.

"I know that you've already described the episodes to me; however, I'd like to ask if you have felt detached from your own body or your environment other than during the actual events?"

"Not at all."

"What has your mood been like lately?"

"It has been great since I came to my senses. I actually haven't been this happy in a long time."

"In the period of time leading up to the first event, what stresses, problems, or adverse events had affected you recently?"

Judtson described the friction between himself and both his publisher and his agent, the frustration he initially felt when he discovered that the show on Villarreal had been cancelled, and the tense and unpleasant relationship with Kristen. "I figured out that each of those things, every one of them, was because of me. Because I was being an ass, a jerk."

"How are the relationships in your life now?"

Judtson shrugged casually. "Some have improved, like with Kristen, Mitch, Darrow, and the people associated with my cable show. The jury is out on Saylor, Doni, and Ricky. Either they are going to be happy with the new Judtson, or they aren't."

"Have you had any auditory or visual hallucinations?"

"No."

"Have you used mind-altering drugs?"

"None."

"Any physical symptoms you cannot explain?"

"Since the episodes stopped, no."

"Have you felt that others meant to harm you, were watching you, or that someone else was controlling you?"

YES! Yeeeeeeeessssss!!

Worden saw Judtson take in a breath to answer, but then noticed a sudden pause. For an instant there was a subtle change in his patient's eyes before his prior nonchalant demeanor returned.

"No. Not at all."

"Have you been feeling guilt or remorse for any reason?"

Kent shook his head. "Not anymore. Well, yes, actually. I feel horrible for the way I've treated Kristen during the past few years."

Worden jotted another note. "Have you felt as if you wanted to run away from your present life and start over with a new identity?"

"That's funny because that is exactly what I've done, without running away. I feel as if I have started over."

The session continued with more questions from Worden, who frequently went back to some of Judtson's previous answers or referred to his own notes to obtain more detail, until the fifty minutes had elapsed.

As they stood and shook hands, Worden said, "There are two more things. I noticed when I reviewed the notes from Dr. Costello that you have had several tests, including an MRI and a CT scan. What was missing, in my opinion, was a PET scan. I would like to schedule you for one."

Judtson, his tone neutral, asked, "Why?"

"A PET scan gives us a look at your brain chemistry. With the breaks, or episodes, you had, I think it should eliminate some possible organic causes. It would, from my perspective, round out the analysis and allow us to move on."

Shrugging, Judtson acquiesced, "Sure. Why not? You mentioned two things?"

"Yes. The other is a Minnesota Multiphasic Personality Inventory. I believe you have taken one in the past."

"I have."

"If you have the time, I'd appreciate it if you could take one now."

Judtson glanced at his watch. "Sure. I have the time."

"Excellent." Worden followed him out into the lobby and asked the receptionist to get Judtson situated in the consultation room with the test and to make the appointment for the scan. They said their good-byes and the doctor returned to his office, leaving Judtson in the lobby.

As he walked to his desk, Worden paused in mid-stride, reflecting on the end of the session for a moment before sitting down. Opening the file, he found Saylor's number, called him, and left a message.

▽

The technician was in the middle of packing his tools, when Robyn Reedy entered the PET/CT room. "I hope you're finished. I just found out that the scheduling desk gave the afternoon cancellation to another patient."

She noticed the man had a sheepish expression as he straightened to face her.

"Is something wrong?"

"Not really, I guess. I pulled the old UPS off and started to connect the new one, but I realized they had sent me the wrong one."

Her mouth tightened in a grimace. "So we're off line? I'll have to reschedule the appointment?"

"It isn't off line. I connected it directly without the UPS."

"What does that mean? I thought the backup power supply was necessary."

"Normally, it is. But this facility has surge protection and generator power as a backup on the main system. The UPS was redundant, anyway."

She eyed him dubiously. "Are you certain? The last thing I want to do is pump a patient full of radioactive FDG and not be able to complete the procedure. Redoing a PET is never a good idea. Shouldn't you at least reconnect the old one?"

"I checked with my office. They checked with the main office. Everyone at both places is sure it will be fine. Since the UPS I disconnected was giving us some bad readings, they all decided it was better to remove it."

"I'm going to need a letter from your office before you leave."

"No problem."

▽

Saylor finished with his last patient of the morning and briskly walked to his office, anxious to speak with Worden. His staff told him earlier that the psychiatrist had phoned, and he had exerted a conscious effort to keep his attention on the two patients he needed to see before he could return the call. It had been enough of a struggle to keep himself focused on the details of his routine ever since his bizarre interlude at Kelsey's, and now his curiosity about Worden's preliminary diagnosis was another powerful distraction.

Closing his office door too quickly, he unintentionally slammed it as he hurried to his desk. Snatching up the phone, he entered Worden's number, hoping to catch him between patients. He knew he did not have the patience for another long ordeal of phone tag. The receptionist told Saylor she could put him through immediately.

"Hello, Saylor."

"Patrick, how did it go?"

"To be honest, a differential diagnosis is not something we can complete in a single session. . . ."

"I understand that, Patrick. What was your first impression?"

Worden hesitated for a moment, finally answering, "If I were to give you a snap judgment at this point, I'd say that the first scenario we discussed, the flight into health, is the most likely explanation for what is happening with Mr. Kent."

"You think that all of this – the breaks, the personality change, all of it – could simply be Judtson's decision that he wasn't happy with who he was?"

"Again, it is far too early to tell. And attributing the breaks to a flight into health is a stretch, I admit. But I did not hear anything in our conversation to directly support a diagnosis of either schizophrenia or DID. Although, at this point, I cannot rule either of them out. He does appear to be quite happy and comfortable with his new persona."

Saylor stared out his window at the Catalina Mountains to the north. His silence prompted Worden to ask, "Saylor, are you still there?"

"Sorry. I'm just taking it in."

"Are you unhappy with my conclusion? Would you have preferred that your friend was suffering from a dissociative disorder?"

"No. Not at all," he answered defensively.

"Mr. Kent is very pleased with the change in his relationship with his wife and his business associates. With regard to his friendship with you and two others...."

"My wife, Doni, and his assistant, Ricky."

"Yes. His attitude is that he hopes the three of you can accept his transformation. All of you have a choice. Either you can react to his change by resisting it, or you can support him. Obviously, the latter would be my recommendation."

"Of course. And we certainly will."

"Excellent. As you requested, I was successful in persuading Mr. Kent to submit to a PET scan."

"You are good."

"Not really. I merely suggested it and he agreed."

Saylor let out a short laugh. "It *is* going to take some time for me to get accustomed to the new Judtson Kent. When is he scheduled for the scan?"

"Actually, we were able to get him in late this afternoon. I believe it was set at four forty-five."

"That was fast."

"We were fortunate that there was a cancellation."

"Will you be seeing Judtson again?"

"Yes. He scheduled an appointment for next week. One more thing. Before he departed, he took the MMPI. You mentioned in our previous conversations that he had taken one in the past. Would you have access to the prior scoring? Considering that we are keeping all of our options open with Mr. Kent, I'd like to compare the two outcomes."

"I don't have the old test results, but I'm sure Judtson does. He keeps everything. Do you want me to get them for you?"

"You certainly can. Or I can ask him myself."

"I'll see if I can pick them up tonight."

"That would be fine."

Saylor thanked Worden and terminated the call, immediately punching the numbers for Ricky's cell phone.

"Hello, Saylor."

"Ricky, I have a strange request."

"With all that has happened lately, I doubt it. What do you need?"

"I know that Judtson keeps a lot of his personal papers at the office."

"Yes, he does. Why?"

"Years ago he took a personality test called the MMPI. Do you happen to know if a copy of his results might be filed with those papers?"

"Not off the top of my head. But if so, I know where it would be."

Saylor gave Worden's email address to him and asked that he send the results to the psychiatrist if he found them.

"I'm on my way back there now. I'll check first thing."

"Thanks."

His next call was to Melanie at the front desk, and he found that his last appointment of the day was at three-thirty.

"Good," he said aloud. "Plenty of time to meet Judtson at the radiology lab."

▽

Ricky pulled open the filing drawer in Judtson's office and found the thick accordion file he remembered. On it, scrawled in Judtson's handwriting with a felt-tip marker, was the label "College."

He carried it to his own desk and unwound the binding string. After a few minutes, he exclaimed, "There it is!"

The copy of the test results was identified with a cover sheet and totaled five pages. Ricky dropped them into the scanner, creating a PDF. When the process completed, he sent the digitized sheets to the address Saylor had given him for Dr. Worden, along with a brief note.

▽

I feel so alone! Since this happened, I've seen Saylor and, of course, Kristen, and Doni, Ricky...even Kelsey. Or, more accurately, I've seen the glimpses of them this guy has allowed me to see. He, whoever he is, steers the eyes. So I can be in the same room with Saylor, and yet the guy is making me look at Kristen constantly. Even if I do see them, I can't interact with them. I tried, at first. I screamed at the top of my...what?...mind to get their attention. But all they see is this other guy, the one who is now running me. When they talk to Judtson, they are talking to him, not me.

I think Saylor suspects something. I'm almost convinced he does. I know Kelsey does, simply by the way she reacted to how the guy treated her. I keep wishing Saylor would grab me by the shoulders and look me right in the eye and talk to me. Not him. Me. My fear now...my terror night and day...is that Saylor is going to give up. Give up on me. Just leave me in here alone forever. I have no idea what he can do. But one thing is definitely as sure as hell...I hope he tries...and keeps on trying until I'm out of here again.

I'm in my living room now. By myself. Kristen has gone to the store. The guy is reading some notes on the pyramids. What's weird is that I can't even synchronize myself to his eyes when he's reading. I don't know why, but I can't capture the words as his eyes fly over them. The difference, I suppose, is the process of control. I must only be able to comprehend if I am the one controlling the eye movements.

The guy is taking a break. He's letting his eyes wander around the room. His view pauses on Rocky, who's curled up in the foyer. That's where he has been ever since this happened to me, except for trips outside. He's waiting for me to come home. At least, my buddy knows the difference. He hasn't given this guy the time of day.

I guess, for some reason, Rocky has caught his attention, because the guy has stopped his eyes on him. Rocky is looking back disinterestedly.

HEY! ROCKY!

I'm trying the mental screams again.

RRRRROOOOOOOOCCCCKKKKKKYYYYY!

What? Wait a second. I'll be damned. Those big floppy ears perked up. He's cocking his head quizzically.

ROCKY...ROCKY...ROCKY!

He hears me! He's scrambling to his feet. He's trotting across the room. He's standing right in front of us, smiling, wagging his tail. He's looking at me! At me, dammit!

Thankfully, this guy is still looking at him. I hear his voice.

"What's wrong, Rocky? What's the matter?"

I continue my mental shouts, and my four-legged pal seems to be ignoring the guy's words and staring through him. At me! The guy reaches out to pet him, and Rocky takes a step back. He doesn't want to be touched by the guy, and yet he's staring at our eyes. His tail is still wagging. I hear the guy grunt with frustration and mutter something nasty, but I'm yelling my brain out.

Following the irritated comment, the guy's eyes look away from my first connection to the outside world, and he stands up. The second our eye contact is broken...I mean the instant that the guy breaks my connection with Rocky...I hear, through the guy's ears, a sudden growl. The view quickly flickers back to my pal, who is staring up at the now standing guy and snarling, his teeth bared. He shouts at Rocky to back off and skirts him, heading down the hallway to the library. As we walk away, I can hear Rocky barking at us.

The guy slams the door behind himself, obviously preventing my buddy from following us in.

▽

The one-mile drive from Saylor's office to the radiology lab took approximately twenty minutes. Yet another storm was slamming the city, and the winds were approaching fifty miles per hour, the dust reducing the visibility to less than a hundred yards. Rain had not yet begun to fall as he parked outside the lab. Bracing himself, Saylor opened the door against the vicious winds, which instantly whipped into the cab of the truck. Quickly, he got out and slammed the door. With his head bowed, he ran across the parking lot to the building entrance, startled by the nearby flash of lightning and the almost instantaneous earsplitting thunder which followed.

He found Judtson in the waiting room, calmly reading an old issue of *People* magazine, and was again struck by the difference in his friend. The old Judtson would have been pacing, punctuating his circuit around the room with snippy comments to the receptionist, updating her regularly on how many minutes past his appointment time he had waited.

Prior to joining Judtson, Saylor informed the front desk that he was a physician attending the test and would appreciate it if they would inform the technician. He dropped into the chrome and leather chair beside Judtson, who finished reading a paragraph before greeting him.

"Hi, Saylor. I appreciate your coming, but I think I can handle a simple test on my own."

"I know. Worden told me it was scheduled for this afternoon and the rest of my day was free, so I thought I'd come by. I am curious, you know. Did they already give you the injection?"

"Yes. About an hour ago." Judtson looked back down at the magazine and began reading once more.

Saylor stared at him for a minute. "Judtson, are we okay?"

Again, there was a brief hesitation before he took his eyes away from the article. "Sure. Why?"

"You're different."

"Yes, I am. You already know that."

Fighting back a vague frustration, Saylor retorted, "I do. I know that you felt as if you were going in the wrong direction previously, and you decided to make a change. I understand that. And if you are happy, truly happy, then of course I support it. It just seems that I'm one of the casualties of this change. Ever since your disappearance, I don't get the impression that you are even happy to see me."

There was no time for a response. The door next to the front desk opened and a white-coated lab assistant, holding a digital tablet, announced, "Mr. Kent."

Judtson stood and turned back to Saylor. "We can talk about this later, can't we?"

"Of course." Tamping down his emotions, Saylor rose to follow him through the open doorway.

▽

The technician who was to administer the PET/CT scan was in her forties, with sandy-colored hair pulled back in a tight ponytail.

"I'm Robyn Reedy," she said with a friendly, practiced smile, clearly intended to put the patient at ease. Saylor extended his hand. "I'm Dr. Costello, Mr. Kent's neurologist. And this is Judtson Kent."

She turned her attention to Judtson. "Pleasure to meet you, Jud."

Saylor involuntarily stiffened, prepared for the inevitable chastising from Judtson which always followed this shortening of his name. Instead, he shook the technician's hand and smiled back. "Good to meet you, Dr. Reedy."

With a shake of her head, she corrected him. "I'm not a doctor, merely the technician who will be administering your scan. And Robyn is fine."

She motioned to one of her assistants, who led Judtson into the adjoining room where the table and the white doughnut-shaped scanner were located. Saylor followed the technician to the console and took an empty seat beside her. They watched through the glass as Judtson was situated on the table.

The preparation was minimal, and within two minutes Robyn, using the intercom, talked Judtson through what he should expect and told him that all he needed to do was relax. Watching with his normal curiosity, Saylor noticed her eyes sweep the console in what he assumed was a last-minute check, before she keyed the microphone again and told Judtson they were starting.

The process was fully computerized, so all she needed to do was click on a large icon in the center of the monitor, which was instantly replaced by the ubiquitous question box, asking if she was sure. She selected the affirmative and sat back. Saylor had never attended a PET/CT scan in the past and had no idea what to expect. From all appearances, it was the same as a normal CT scan.

▽

Outside, the monsoon was rapidly intensifying. Ferocious winds ripped tree limbs and palm fronds loose, hurling them hundreds of yards. Large, widely spaced raindrops, accompanied by quarter-sized hail, began pelting the buildings, vehicles, and landscape. Lightning struck repeatedly, each strike followed moments later by a thunderous crash. The intervals between the discharges shortened progressively until the spacing was mere seconds.

A private security guard, posted in the parking lot outside the radiology lab, watched in fascination as the several-mile-high thunderstorm cell, with its ominous greenish-black facade, bore down on him menacingly. He jumped, startled, as a lightning bolt struck one of the grounded pole lights in the lot, the instantaneous crash of thunder momentarily deafening him.

From his vantage point under the front canopy at the entrance, he could see the leading edge of the storm just to the south of him as it moved closer, an opaque gray palisade no more than half a mile away. Although the vicious winds were out of the north, sucked under the storm cell by the intense convection activity of the system, coming over the rooftop of the building he guarded and keeping him dry for the moment, he was beginning to feel that his position was tenuous. With his eyes glued to the tableau before him, he back-stepped toward the entrance until he felt his shoulders touch the doors. Turning, he gripped the handle on the aluminum storefront entrance just as a massive lightning bolt struck the building.

The flash from the strike was fleetingly blinding; the explosion of thunder, coetaneous. And, as the current was conveyed through the conductive elements of the building, the guard felt the powerful jolt of electricity come from the metal handle of the door, pass through his body, and exit through his wet shoes, seeking a ground in the saturated concrete sidewalk. A second later, he released his grip and dropped to the ground, unconscious.

▽

Saylor and Robyn noticed the momentary flash of brightness from the overhead lighting, followed by a brief flicker. Reedy's eyes immediately scanned the computer monitor in front of her.

"What was that?"

Chewing on her bottom lip, she answered, "Not sure, Dr. Costello. Looks like some kind of power surge."

Saylor's concern was obvious. "Is Judtson...Mr. Kent all right?"

She raised her hand and with her index finger tapped the screen. "He should be. The system has real-time diagnostics, and they are showing that everything is nominal." As she spoke, her thoughts returned to earlier in the day when the technician had removed the UPS and left the system directly connected to the building power.

As if hearing her unspoken words, he asked, "Isn't there surge protection on this machine?"

"Specifically on the PET/CT, no. Our electrical system is segregated into two separate subsystems, one for general usage and the other for our equipment. The equipment circuits have a master surge protection built in, and we also have a generator for power backup. There is a second generator for all nonessential circuits. It must have kicked in. That's what caused the lights to flicker."

Saylor leaned forward, moving his face closer to the glass, and stared at the unmoving figure of his friend. "So both systems switched to generator?"

"Yes. That's what my status screen is telling me."

"The scan is still running?"

She glanced again at the monitor. "Yes, it is. And I'm not getting any alerts or error messages." Her voice was steady and even.

He sat back in the chair, keeping his eyes on Judtson. Reedy relaxed slightly and thought to herself that it was just her luck that this was the first electrical anomaly she ever had during a test; that it would happen on a day she allowed the UPS, which had built-in surge protection in addition to a battery backup, to be removed; and that the anomaly happened while the procedure was being observed by a patient's physician.

▽

The humming stopped. The test must be finished. A white-coated technician did something I couldn't see, and the brace holding my head motionless is releasing me. I hear a sound from across the room, and I guess the guy wants to see what is causing it, because the eyes look that way. I can see Saylor and that Robyn Reedy coming in. Saylor seems to be worried and he is hurrying over to me. The technician holds my arm as I sit up, and Saylor, standing right in front of me, asks me if I'm all right.

That's a joke, I think. If you consider being a prisoner inside my own head all right, I guess I am.

Saylor studied his friend's face. "Judtson, are you all right?" As their eyes connected, he was suddenly slammed with a jolt of adrenaline.

"If you consider being a prisoner inside my own head all right, I guess I am."

Chapter 18

"JUDTSON?" SAYLOR ALMOST SHOUTED. "Judtson? Is that...is that you?"

A rapid-fire gamut of emotions, including confusion, fear, and surprise, showed on Kent's face. His eyes darted around the room, glancing at Robyn Reedy, the other technician, the door to the room, and finally back to Saylor. He then looked down at his own hand and clenched it in a fist, relaxed it, and repeated the process.

Still staring down at his fist, he gasped in wonderment, "I'm working."

More loudly, disbelief and joy coloring his inflection, he repeated, "I'm working! I'm out!"

Saylor, now gripping Judtson's shoulders, watched the progression. When his friend's eyes returned to connect with his, he was relieved to see that they, once again, were Judtson's.

This time staring directly at Saylor, Judtson allowed a tentative smile to creep across his face. "I seem to be back." His voice was shaky.

"Is something wrong?"

The question came from Reedy, who was standing next to the two of them, an intensely concerned tone evident in her words.

Without releasing his hold on Judtson, Saylor turned to answer her. "No. Not at all, Robyn. Everything is just fine."

She did not seem convinced, but clearly had no idea what her next question should be. Pressing Saylor to see if he was sure did not seem like the correct approach to take with the attending physician of the patient.

He turned back to Judtson, while struggling to appear calm and in control. "We'd better go."

Judtson, his eyes darting from object to person to object around the room, nodded compliantly and slid off the table, standing unsteadily. Saylor, fighting off the urge to begin whooping like a drunken college student at a basketball game, thanked Reedy and her assistant and, holding on to support Judtson, walked him from the room. As they traveled the hallway route to the lobby, Judtson began to speak. Saylor quickly hushed him, preferring to wait until they were out of anyone's earshot.

They reached the lobby, and Saylor looked across the room and through the front windows.

He could see there was a full-blown monsoon storm outside, and had a moment of indecisiveness, weighing whether they should sit down in the crowded lobby or brave the torrent. Judtson, reading his thoughts, supplied the answer. "Out! I need to get out of here. I don't care about the storm."

Saylor took two strides toward the exit, when he suddenly froze.

"What's wrong?" Judtson asked worriedly.

"We have no idea what caused you to go away for a while. Hell, we don't even know what brought you back. But I just remembered that your departure happened as you were out walking in a storm."

A trace of his old confidence restored, Judtson explained, "It wasn't the storm, Popeye. Listen, we need to get out of here, into your truck or someplace where we can talk, and I'll tell you what happened."

"You remember?"

Judtson nodded emphatically. "Every single minute."

Saylor cocked his head for a moment as he looked at Judtson, who could not help but compare the motion to his golden retriever's recent reaction. "Okay, come on."

"You can let go of my arm now."

Smiling, Saylor released his grip. "You're feeling steady enough?"

"Yes. Now can we please get the hell out of this joint?"

The two turned and pushed through the double doors. As they exited, they noticed the paramedics kneeling beside a man who was wearing a security guard uniform and sitting on the concrete, his back against the wall of the building. The guard was laughing and telling his story about getting hit by lightning. They rushed past this scene and, arriving at the end of the canopy, broke into a full run through the gale-force wind and pelting rain. Judtson followed Saylor to his truck. Reaching it, they scrambled in, drenched and panting heavily. The din from the deluge sounded as if the entire drum line from a high-school marching band were practicing their triplets by hand on the roof and hood.

Too impatient to wait until he had caught his breath, Saylor, between gasps for air, asked, "What…happened?"

Judtson twisted around on the seat to face his friend. "Before I start, I need to say two things to you."

"What?"

"First, thanks."

"For what? I didn't actually do anything. Well, maybe I did. Maybe it was the PET…."

"Saylor! Shut up, will you?"

"Okay."

Judtson grinned. "I don't know what happened to bring me back. I'm not sure if it was connected with you or the PET scan, or whether it was going to happen on its own. That's not the point. The point is, you didn't give up on me. And I just wanted to say thanks."

"You're welcome. What's the second thing?"

The smile left Judtson's face. His tone became serious. "Please don't let it happen again."

"How can I promise that? I don't even know…."

"If you'll shut up a minute, I'll tell you."

"Okay. Tell me."

Twisting around so that his back was against the seat, Judtson leaned his head against the padded rest and closed his eyes. His voice was soft, almost flat in inflection. Saylor had to lean closer to hear him clearly over the pounding rain.

"I was at my desk. Ricky hadn't been gone for longer than a minute or two when I heard the front door open. I thought it was he, coming back for some reason, so I got up and walked out to the lobby. The second I made it through the doorway of my office, two men grabbed me."

"Grabbed you? Who were they?"

"I don't know. I didn't recognize them and, as of this minute, have no idea who they were. Anyway, there was a third man and he rolled Ricky's desk chair over to where they were holding me. They sat me down in the chair. I was trying to fight them but, man, they were strong. As they held me, the third man walked behind me. Before he moved out of my range of sight, I saw him pull something from his valise. Something with straps and wires. I didn't recognize it. Don't know what it was. I was screaming, thrashing, trying to kick somebody, when I felt this thing...I guess it was the strap-and-wire thing I had seen...slip onto my head from behind.

"Whatever it was...whatever that device was...it worked fast, because it was only a few seconds later that I thought I was still fighting them, but realized I wasn't. I was sitting. Docile, like a cow. The two men had released their holds on me. I figured out right away that I no longer controlled where my eyes looked, exactly the same as the other episodes. I no longer controlled anything."

Judtson opened his eyes and turned to face Saylor. His face, dripping from the run through the downpour, conveyed an intensity, a furor mingled with a fear Saylor had never seen from his friend at any point in their lives. "It was like the earlier episodes, but different. I was cut off...a passenger. I was in there. Every minute. Every second. Yet I had absolutely no contact with my body. Nothing!"

"Go on."

"I went kinda nuts at first. I was...I don't know how else to describe it...I was screaming and ranting, panicked inside my own head. Remember when you saw me in your elevator lobby during that episode? You thought I was going to have a heart attack or a stroke or something."

"I'll never forget that."

"Well, they must have worked the bugs out of it, because this time my panic, my emotional reaction to what was happening, didn't reach the exterior. Not a bit. The severing of 'me' from 'me' was complete and absolute."

"The three guys...what did they look like?"

Allowing himself a brief chuckle, Judtson answered, "You aren't going to believe this, but they all looked like Jake and Elwood."

"The Blues Brothers?"

"Uh-huh. White shirts, black suits, black fedoras, and black sunglasses."

"The 'men in black'!"

"Right."

"You're kidding."

Judtson's response was to simply stare at him.

"All right. You aren't kidding. That's just too weird."

"That's what I thought."

"So, what happened next?"

"They left me sitting in the chair while they went to work. From the spot where I was, I couldn't see much, and they didn't say a word to each other during the whole thing. I could hear that they were going through papers and gathering stuff. I think one of them was in my office."

Saylor told Judtson about all of the strange things he and Ricky had discovered, as well as the flash drive with the incriminating video.

"Judtson, you hadn't somehow created that flash drive from Kelsey's SIM card, had you?"

He shook his head. "They must have brought it with them. That doesn't make sense, either. I don't know. I guess it must be a part of their plan to tie us up with the cops."

"What about after that? Where did you go, and why were you gone for so long?"

Staring out the front windshield, Judtson noticed that the intensity of the storm was lessening somewhat. "You know that little park, the one close to Fifth and Alvernon?"

"Yeah."

"They took me there. I'm thinking that they wanted to make sure the transition stuck and I wasn't going to revert or something. I don't know because they never did say a word to me. They took me to the park, and we sat together at one of those concrete picnic benches for a long time. The 'real me' was going berserk the whole time. But the 'external me' just sat there with them. They kept watching me. As I said, I think they were waiting for the 'real me' to somehow get back out again. Even when it started to pour, the four of us sat like fools in the rain."

"That's strange."

"Seriously, man. After quite a while, and I don't know how long because I couldn't even make myself glance down at my watch, the four of us stood up and got into their truck. They drove me to my house, dropping me off a few doors down."

"What did they drive?"

Judtson rolled his eyes. "Guess."

Saylor, befuddled for a moment, mentally made the connection. "A black SUV?"

Nodding, Judtson added, "With heavily tinted windows."

"Did you happen to see the plates?"

"Nope. The other guy's eyes never looked at them."

The rain outside was diminishing, and they were able to see to a distance of approximately thirty feet around the truck. Materializing through the grayness, a black Escalade became visible, parking directly across from them, and backing into its space, with its front windshield facing toward them.

"What the...!" exclaimed Judtson.

"We should go."

As he spoke, Saylor started the truck, flipped on the wipers, and shifted into gear.

"Even with the wipers on, I can't see inside that thing," Judtson muttered, bending forward close to the glass in a vain attempt to improve his view.

"Its front windshield is probably tinted, too."

"Let's go."

Saylor tapped the gas pedal and cranked the steering wheel to the left, pulling out of the space. As they left the lot, Judtson turned in his seat and watched the SUV. It remained motionless.

The young man in the Escalade, oblivious to their departure, chuckled aloud as he read the text message on his phone and immediately began typing his response.

As Saylor steered north, driving cautiously in the rainstorm, Judtson commented, "I still can't believe I'm back. I thought I never would make it."

Saylor kept his eyes on the road. "We need to make sure you stay back."

"Do you know what the strangest thing was about it all? I didn't sleep."

"What do mean? Kristen said you did."

"No. That's what's strange. He slept, but I didn't. While he was unconscious, I was awake the entire time. Thinking."

Saylor was silent as he attempted to absorb this fact. The detail, like so much of what was happening to his friend, did not fit in with anything he thought he knew about how the human mind worked. His analysis was interrupted by Judtson.

"There was one incident which made me feel a little connected."

"What was that?"

"Last night or early this morning…I had no way of telling…I was in there, thinking. And I was trying to determine some way to get out, to get control of 'me' again. During this whole thing, I really lost it a few times and my thoughts would go all over the place."

"That's understandable."

"So I was imagining that I was trapped in a wooden cell and that I had a crowbar. I was imagining using the bar to rip out the planks in the walls, in the floor, even in the ceiling. It made symbolic sense that if I could get through the walls and out of that room, I could control 'me' at that point."

"Okay."

"Obviously, it didn't work. The more planks I ripped out, the more layers of planks there were. I finally gave up."

"So where was the connection?"

"Later, when he woke up and was having breakfast with Kristen, he told her about his dream and basically described exactly what I had been visualizing, that he had been trapped in a room and was trying to escape by using a crowbar on the walls."

Saylor risked looking away from the road for a moment to glance at Judtson. "That is strange. What you were thinking, what you were visualizing, became his dream."

"Exactly."

Neither spoke for a moment as Saylor struggled to fit this new piece of the puzzle in with the rest of what he knew. The silence was broken again by Judtson. "What do you think brought me back?"

Saylor took a deep breath and let it out slowly before answering. "I haven't really had a chance to focus on that yet."

"Could it have been the scan? How does it work?"

"That's when it happened, so it is the logical starting point. The PET/CT is a combination of a PET scan and a CT scan. I think you already know what a CT is."

"Basically a 3-D x-ray."

"Right. The x-ray emitter and the receiver rotate around your head in that doughnut-shaped ring, taking a series of pictures until a three-dimensional image of the brain is built."

"What is a PET scan?"

"The PET scan is passive, at least passive in the sense that it isn't bombarding your skull with anything during the test. You are injected with a radioactive isotope an hour prior to the test. The tissues in your head absorb the isotope at varying levels, based upon their chemical composition. The PET scan sensors in the doughnut ring pick up the radioactive decay from the isotope and map it."

"Why are they done together? That seems a little extreme."

"The image made by the PET scan looks like a Doppler image of a thunderstorm…you know, the yellow, green, and red blob they show us during a weather forecast."

"Yes."

"Imagine if they showed us the Doppler without the map underneath it. We wouldn't have any idea where the storm was, what cities it was affecting, or anything. It would be a meaningless blob."

"I understand."

"The PET scan gives us the image and the CT scan gives us the map of the brain so that the image makes sense. If the PET scan shows a bright red spot…an anomaly…the CT would show that the problem is in a very specific spot in the prefrontal cortex, for example."

"So, let me get this straight. While I was having this test, my brain was pumped full of a radioactive isotope, and it was being blasted with x-rays coming at it from every direction."

"Right."

Judtson laughed. "You say 'right' as if it were a normal thing."

Chuckling, Saylor answered, "Hey! It brought you back, didn't it?"

"We don't know yet, do we? What other factors could there have been?"

Thinking back to the power surge, Saylor answered, "Apparently, right in the middle of your test, the building was struck by lightning."

"What! Oh, yeah, I remember seeing that security guard with the two paramedics as we were leaving. He was talking about being struck."

"Something happened. I don't know for a fact whether it actually hit the building or something close by. All I know is that there was a power surge, the lights flickered, and the backup generator came on."

"I thought this was like a bad movie before. Now it's sounding as though I'm Frankenstein."

"But, hey, that was a good movie."

"Which version? Boris Karloff?"

"Gene Wilder."

"Thanks. By the way, where are you going?"

"Nowhere in particular. Where do you want to go?"

"Home."

Saylor glanced at him. "Home? Are you sure?"

Judtson nodded. "Yes. I'm sure. I need to get out of these clothes and...I should talk to Kristen."

A loud sigh came from Saylor. "She's not going to be happy that *you* are back."

"I'm certain that's right. But I should talk to her, anyway."

As they drove, Saylor filled Judtson in on the strange lunch meeting at Kelsey's. When he finished, Judtson shook his head and said, "Between what happened to me at my office involving the guys in black, and the stakeout van at her place, it's obvious we're in the middle of something."

"I can't see any reasonable explanation."

"We need to figure out what it is."

"That we do."

"And we need to do it quickly, before they come back and strap that thing on my head again. I have a feeling that on the next visit, they'll be bringing one your size."

The two drove the rest of the route in silence. By the time Saylor pulled his truck into Judtson's driveway, the rain had stopped and rivulets of water were flowing across the concrete.

"Good luck with Kristen."

"What do you mean? You're coming in with me."

Saylor held up his hands defensively. "I don't think that would be a good idea."

"Why not?"

"It was evident when you were the bogus Judtson that she was suspicious of me. She was convinced I was trying to turn you back into this Judtson. And Kristen was pretty damn happy with the other one."

"Well, you *were* trying to turn me back into this guy. Besides, if there is some gigantic conspiracy going on, how do we know she isn't in on it? The minute I walk in, she might be waiting with that strap-on gizmo. No, I'm not going in alone."

Saylor thought through what his friend was saying. He did not relish the idea of dealing with Kristen; yet, he also knew that he did not want to lose Judtson again.

"All right."

He turned off the engine, and both men climbed out. As they walked toward the front door, Judtson said, "I'll go in first."

"I'll cover you."

With a short laugh, Judtson reached into his pocket for his keys.

▽

Kristen was sitting in the living room, curled up with a book, and heard the key in the lock. She dropped the novel on the floor beside the chair, not caring that she had lost her place in the story, and sprang up at once. As she hurried to greet Judtson, she noticed that Rocky had also leapt to his feet and run to the entrance, ramming his nose against the gap between the door and the jamb, his tail wagging furiously.

She hesitated, feeling an unbidden fluttering in her chest. Forcing herself, shaking off the negative feelings and murmuring aloud that it was probably nothing, she walked forward, more slowly than before. Her despair deepened as the door swung open and the golden retriever, not waiting for Judtson to fully enter, jumped up, planting his front paws on his master's shoulders, and began frantically licking his face. Looking over Judtson's shoulder, she could see Saylor behind him. Her gut tightened further.

"Whoa! Easy," Judtson exclaimed, overwhelmed by the enthusiasm of his furry pal's greeting. He wrapped his arms around Rocky's torso and hugged him, the embrace forcing the canine to shift his exuberant licking to Judtson's ear and the side of his head.

In the midst of the barrage of affection, Judtson made eye contact with Kristen. She saw, despite the spontaneous grin triggered by the effusive greeting from Rocky, an immediate expression of sorrow in her husband's eyes as they connected with hers. The message clear, her heart instantly sank.

"Down, boy! Time to get down!" As he spoke, he gently placed his hands on the golden's shoulders and pressed him toward the floor. Rocky seemed to understand and, stealing a final lick across Judtson's face, dropped down to all fours. He planted himself in front of his master, smiling broadly and wagging his tail. Judtson stepped around him and walked forward. Kristen's comprehension of what had happened was plainly written across her face. Now closer, he could see a single tear trailing down her cheek. The sight of it made his heart sink, as well.

"Hello…sweetheart." His voice was tentative, wavering.

Hearing his greeting, a lone sob burst from her as she whirled and ran to the bedroom, slamming the door behind herself. Judtson turned to Saylor, who was standing in the doorway, clearly uncomfortable.

"Stay out here. I won't be long."

Saylor nodded, dropping to one knee and petting Rocky. Judtson followed her, grateful that the bedroom door was not locked. As he entered, he saw that she was lying facedown on the bed, crying. Sitting beside her, he gingerly placed his hand on her shoulder. Reacting to his touch, she squirmed farther away, covering her head with a pillow.

"Kristen." His voice was soft. "Kristen, please."

The volume of her sobs diminished slightly. Still, she made no sign of turning over.

He squeezed her shoulder. "Kristen, I'm sorry."

She tensed at the sound of his apology, then rolled even farther away from him on the bed so that he could see her face.

"You're sorry?" Her voice broke. The tears had dissolved her eye makeup, and black smears surrounded her eyes and smudged her cheeks. Dragging the sleeve on her arm across her face, oblivious to the mess she made of the blouse, she sat up, keeping the width of the king-sized bed between them. "This is cruel."

"Cruel?"

"Yes, dammit! Cruel. I had you back! For a little while. I was sucked in and I believed."

Judtson reached across the bed for her hand, but she pulled it away. "Kristen, something was wrong. Something was wrong with me. I was messed up. There was a problem in my head."

A ragged chuff came from her. "Problem in your head? But now you're all fine?"

He nodded.

Her tone was rough, aggressive. "So the sweet, kind, loving Judtson who cares about me and acts like a civilized human being is some sort of illness? The man who can go out in public with his wife and not humiliate her every time anyone speaks to him has some sort of disorder? The writer who actually gets along with his publisher, agent, and producer is the sicko? But the rude, pompous, overbearing, supercilious, obnoxious, self-centered, and childish Judtson is the healthy one?"

He absorbed her words as he would have taken physical punches, passively...knowing that, from her perspective, a perspective he had become sensitized to in recent days, he deserved the assault. Softly, gently, he answered, "You know that I've always been a pompous, overbearing, supercilious ass from the day you met me."

She shook her head violently, her hair swirling in saturated clumps. "No! You weren't. You don't even remember, do you? Not to me. When we first met, when we dated, when we got married, you were the Judtson I had up until a few hours ago."

He thought back. "I was still that way in public, like the time we went to the movies and...."

"Don't! Don't start bringing up the damn stories of the Judtson-jerk."

"The Judtson-jerk?"

"That's what I've called you in my head each time you've acted that way. You're right. You were like that in public. But you were different with me. I thought you would grow out of the other stuff. I was sure of it. Instead, the other stuff became who you were inside our home."

He stood and walked around the bed, wanting to sit closer to her.

"Don't! I don't want to be touched."

He paused, standing at the foot of the bed, shifting his weight from one foot to the other repetitively.

"You're right, I guess."

"You guess? See, you can't even admit it without some wriggle room."

"You're right." He had to stop himself from adding "I suppose" at the end of his statement.

"So what? Who cares if I'm right? What does that change? As you walked in the front door, soaking wet, and smiled at me and called me 'sweetheart,' I recognized you. It wasn't some pathological manifestation. It was the old Judtson. The one I fell in love with. The one I married. You came back for a little while. You teased me. Now you're gone again. And you and your damn Siamese twin Saylor are going to make certain that I never see that Judtson again."

"This isn't Saylor's fault."

"Oh, no? He sets up the appointment with the psychiatrist. The psychiatrist, no doubt his friend, talks you into the brain scan today. You come back from the scan and...this. But, no, it isn't your old buddy Saylor's fault. Not at all. Nothing could ever be Saylor's fault. Well, *he* should be happy now. He has his playmate back."

"Kristen, please," he pleaded, "just listen to me for a minute. I was there…this Judtson, the one you hate…inside my head the whole time. I was conscious, trapped, panicked, and terrified. I couldn't get out. I couldn't speak. I don't know how to explain it. The whole time you were with the other guy, whoever he was, having lunch, making love, I was right behind these eyeballs, trying to get your attention. Trying to get you to help me!"

His description reached her for a moment. She said nothing, staring intently at him. When she finally spoke, her words stunned him. "So now the other Judtson…the one I love…the one who loves me…is trapped in there. Now *he's* probably trying to get my attention, trying to get out."

Judtson had no idea what to say. The image she created sent a shiver up his spine and conveyed beyond a doubt exactly how irretrievable their relationship was.

Motivated by guilt and sadness, he offered, "I do love you. I can try to change."

"No, you can't." The statement was absolute. Her voice, no longer trembled by emotion, was flat, cold.

"I'm not saying that I can become a different person. I know I can't. But give me a chance to change how I treat you. Please."

Kristen continued looking at him, her eyes boring into his. After a moment, she spoke, her voice soft, fragile, vulnerable. "I don't know, Judtson. I don't think so."

"What can it hurt? Just a chance. If I don't change, you can leave me, hit me over the head with a baseball bat, whatever. All I'm asking for is a chance."

She stood up next to the bed and took a deep breath, slowly exhaling to steady herself, walked to him, and placed her hands on his shoulders, keeping her arms rigid to not invite any more contact. "I need some time right now. I need to get away, somewhere by myself. I need time to think."

Judtson nodded silently.

Chapter 19

T HE VIOLENT SUMMER STORM HAD PASSED. Saylor drove Judtson back to the radiology lab to pick up his car. He could tell that his friend needed some time after the encounter with Kristen, and said nothing during the drive. Both men kept the silence until they parked next to the Camry, when Judtson opened his door, slowly got out, looked back, and asked quietly, "Meet me at my office?"

"I will."

Judtson started his car and drove away, with Saylor right behind. Neither of them noticed the black SUV, maintaining a discreet distance as it followed them out of the parking lot.

▽

As it was late in the day, Ricky had already departed. Settling in at Judtson's office, Saylor called Doni and was describing the outlandish events of the afternoon, while Judtson phoned Ricky.

The first to complete his conversation, Judtson waited for Saylor to disconnect, then asked, "What did she say?"

With a lopsided smirk, Saylor answered, "She said all the right things and asked all the right questions, but I'm pretty certain the moment we hung up, she called the guys in white coats to come pick me up."

Judtson laughed. "I can't say that I blame her."

Saylor's mind traveled back to the incident at Kelsey's. "We should probably give our redheaded friend a call."

"Ricky is. He was going to right after we hung up."

The two rehashed the details of the PET/CT scan and the lightning storm, in an attempt to understand what had actually happened to restore Judtson. They decided that they would contact the technicians at the radiology lab the next morning to try to gather more facts, when they heard the front door of the building open.

"I locked the door," Saylor said in a hushed voice.

"It must be Ricky," Judtson surmised, before shouting, "Ricky, is that you?"

His query was met with silence, and they both rose to investigate just as a man appeared at Judtson's doorway. He was tall, wearing a black suit, a black hat, and sunglasses, and he was brandishing a gun.

Saylor was the first to react. "What the hell is...?"

"Sit down," the man ordered, his voice firm.

Hesitantly, they returned to their seats as the intruder entered the office, followed by a second, shorter man who was dressed like the first and also carried a pistol.

"Who are you?" Judtson asked, the steadiness of his own voice surprising him.

"That doesn't matter," the tall one answered, his voice devoid of expression. He stepped closer to Judtson, and a third, heavyset man entered the room, carrying a valise connected to the plastic-strap head device Judtson had earlier described to Saylor. Recognizing the contraption, Judtson shouted something unintelligible and started to spring from his chair, when the first man grabbed his shoulders and forcefully slammed him back down, hard. Quickly positioning himself behind the chair, the man wrapped his arms around both it and Judtson's chest and arms, pinning him in.

Saylor frantically scanned his surroundings, hoping to spot something he could use for a weapon. They were obviously here to reprogram Judtson, or whatever the procedure was called; and Saylor was certain they would have no use for him afterward. His eyes landed on the lead paperweight. There was no way he could reach it and do anything with it before taking a bullet.

Helplessly, he watched as the third man began to slide the mechanism onto his friend's head. Saylor madly tried to think of something he could do to disrupt their actions. Despite his desperation, he was coming up blank. Judtson, visualizing a return to the mental purgatory from which he had only recently been liberated, was thrashing wildly in his chair. Still, the man behind him was too strong, his grip too secure. The heavyset stranger was attempting to place the device, but Judtson's violent shaking and twisting was making it difficult. The man patiently matched Judtson's panicked movements and the horizontal, circular band was halfway down his forehead, when they all heard a shout from the doorway.

"FREEZE, JERKBALLS!"

The man closest to Saylor reacted, spinning toward the voice. Seeing the momentary distraction he needed, Saylor lunged forward and snatched up the lead sphere from the desk. Pivoting, he swung, cleanly connecting with the side of the man's head. The impact from the dense, heavy ball was so powerful that it knocked the stranger's black fedora across the room. The man crumbled to the floor a moment later, unconscious before he landed, blood already gushing from the head wound.

Turning to confront the intruder who had been restraining his friend, Saylor saw that he had released his bear hug and was raising his pistol to aim at the doorway. From the corner of his eye he saw the muzzle flash coming from Ricky's pistol, and then another as Judtson's assistant fired a second time. The tall stranger staggered and collapsed against the wall behind him, sliding slowly downward and leaving a trail of blood smears on the surface.

Judtson, the instant he was turned loose, sprang out of the chair and turned to face the man with the programming device. The man had already dropped it and was reaching inside his coat for a weapon. Without a thought, Judtson bent forward and seized the arms of the chair from which he had just escaped. With all his weight behind it, he pushed forward. The wheeled chair rammed into the heavyset man, knocking him backward, where he tripped on his supine companion and went down.

Even as he fell, he managed to pull his gun clear of his jacket and was bringing it to bear on Judtson, as Saylor, who had come around the desk, gripping the heavy lead paperweight with both hands, raised it high above his head and brought it down hard, smashing it into the forehead of the remaining assailant. The impact had its desired effect. The man's arm and hand went limp and the pistol dropped to the floor beside him. Saylor snapped it up immediately.

Ricky approached slowly, still holding his gun with both hands and pointing it at the man on the floor.

"I think you can put that away," Saylor said, dropping to one knee and feeling for a pulse at the carotid. Finding none, he moved to the other two men and checked them, finally standing to face his friends. "They're dead."

"All of them?" Ricky asked, his voice shaking from the residual flood of adrenaline. He flipped the safety on and tucked the pistol into a concealed holster inside his pants.

Saylor nodded. "Yep."

Judtson turned to look at his assistant. "*Freeze, jerkballs*? Jerkballs!" A slight smile curved his lips upward.

Ricky's face flushed. "I wasn't...I had no...."

"I've heard of dirtballs, scumbags, assholes...but 'Freeze, jerkballs'?"

Saylor, releasing his pent-up tension with laughter, came to Ricky's rescue. "Hey, give him a break. He saved my life and saved you from a trip back to wherever you were before."

"Really!" Ricky agreed indignantly. "It's not as though I had a chance to plan it. It was the first thing that popped into my head."

Unwilling to drop the issue, Judtson argued, "With all of the detective novels you read, it seems as if you could have come up with a more fitting phrase. I'm surprised our three bad guys didn't just burst out laughing when they heard it."

Ricky, his face bright red from the exhilaration of the last few minutes, stared at Judtson for a moment before saying, "It's good to have you back, boss."

He took a step forward, and Judtson raised both of his hands in front of himself. "You're not thinking about hugging me again, are you?"

Ricky stopped short. "Jerkball!"

Laughing from the exchange, Saylor asked, "Are we going to call the cops?"

"Why not?" Judtson asked. "This was obviously self-defense."

"I'll tell you why not," Ricky retorted. "They are probably in on it."

"In on it? I don't know."

"Saylor," Ricky chided, "get real. Of course they are. If we call them, they're going to take all of us in. Then they'll split us up. God knows what will happen to you and me, but as soon as Judtson is out of our sight, he's going away again."

"Do you actually think so?" Saylor appeared unconvinced. "Judtson, what do you think?"

Before he could answer, they heard the front door open. Instantly, Ricky pulled out his gun and moved to the office door, pressing tightly against the jamb. Saylor, still holding the pistol he had retrieved from the dead man, came up behind him.

"Judtson! Saylor! Ricky!"

"It's Kelsey," Judtson exclaimed, relieved, and stepped past his two friends into the lobby, where he was confronted by a mountainous man pointing the barrel of an AK-47 directly at him, the weapon resembling a toy in his hands.

Judtson froze and automatically raised his hands above his head. Simultaneously, he heard Saylor, who had followed him out of the office, and Kelsey, who was standing behind the armed man, begin to speak.

"Judtson, it's okay. That's Romeo," Saylor reassured.

"Hey, it's only the two of us," came from Kelsey.

He then saw Kelsey, carrying some sort of small machine pistol, step out from behind the stranger. Judtson put his hands down, and the man, who was apparently called Romeo, lowered his weapon.

"What's going on? There's a black Tahoe out front. I thought…."

Smiling, Judtson told her, "You were right. Just a minute or two late."

He stepped back and gestured for her to check inside his office. Hurrying to the doorway, followed by Romeo, she stopped abruptly as she saw the bodies. A small gasp rushed through her lips, and Romeo silently stepped past her into the room, moving from one supine figure to the next and satisfying himself that they were not a threat. She turned to face the three. "What happened?"

Saylor hastily filled her in on the incursion. When he finished the narrative, Romeo was the first to speak. "We need to move out. Quickly."

Judtson stepped closer to Romeo and looked him up and down, while asking Kelsey, "This is awesome. How did you manage to find a colossal guy with a voice like Darth Vader to be your sidekick?"

A short giggle preceded her answer. "He found me. But he's right. We'd better get out of here. There'll be others."

"Others?" The nervous question came from Ricky.

"Shouldn't we call the police?" Saylor had obviously not yet given up on the idea.

Kelsey shook her head violently. "Absolutely not. We can't trust them."

"See," Ricky exclaimed. "I told you."

"I don't know."

Kelsey faced Saylor, her words coming out rapidly. "Look, maybe they're fine. Maybe the cops *are* good guys and it would all be cool. But we can't take the chance. These guys have backup. Probably a lot of backup. And if they don't report in, that team will be on their way. They'll probably get here before the cops. If that happens, we're dead meat. Let's get to my place where we can hunker down and defend ourselves. We'll figure it out from there."

Saylor continued to appear skeptical.

"I'm in," Ricky responded immediately.

Kelsey turned to Judtson, who nodded. "Makes sense to me. We'll follow you."

"Huh-uh. If you had your old muscle car, that would work, but your Camry, Saylor's truck, and Ricky's…little slot car…all of them have modules with GPS. They can track you."

"Slot car!"

"Doesn't your Hummer?"

She ignored Ricky's protest. "It has been, uh, modified, Judtson. Come on, we need to roll."

Romeo motioned at the pistol still held by Saylor. "Where did you get that?"

"From one of them."

"Leave it. It might be chipped."

"Chipped?"

"Tracking chip."

Saylor studied the pistol. "Really?"

The big man shrugged, the casual move straining the fabric of his T-shirt. "Maybe, maybe not. But it's never a good idea to bring anything from the other side with you."

Saylor started to lay the gun on the edge of Ricky's desk, when Romeo said, "Let me have it. Maybe we can do some quick damage control."

When Saylor handed the gun to him, Romeo leaned his rifle against the wall, pulled out a pair of blue nitrile gloves, and stretched them over his massive hands. Methodically, he extracted a white handkerchief from his pocket and thoroughly wiped down the butt. He asked Saylor to again describe exactly what had happened. After hearing the scenario, Romeo turned to Ricky and pointed at his gun. "Is that registered?"

"No. I bought it from a friend who got it off Craigslist."

"I need it."

"What?" Ricky clutched his pistol possessively.

"I need it now!"

With no further argument, Ricky handed over his pistol and watched as Romeo wiped it down and placed it into the hand of one of the dead men, firmly pressing the fingertips onto the areas where there should be prints. He then found the lead ball, which Saylor had dropped on the floor after killing the third assailant, and wiped it before imbuing the surface with prints from the stranger who had died from Ricky's shots. He stepped back and surveyed the scene for a moment. "Guess it will have to do. Let's clear out."

Kelsey looked at Judtson. "Anything from here you need?"

Thinking for a moment, Judtson nodded. "Yes. Just one thing."

He returned to his office and, careful to step over the bodies, walked to the bookcase on the far wall. In the center of the shelves, at eye level, was a collection of wildlife and nature books, taller than the others and buttressed by bookends. Sandwiching the collection between his palms, he lifted them from the shelf and placed them on his desk. Revealed was a small wall safe. A few rapid spins of the dial and the safe door opened. Judtson reached in with both hands and unplugged two wires from a slender black box, grabbed it, and pulled it out. He closed the safe, spun the dial, and replaced the books.

With the metal case in hand, he turned to the others who were watching from the office doorway. "I'm ready. Let's go."

"What's that?" Saylor asked.

"External backup for my computer."

"I didn't even know you had a safe there."

Judtson grinned at his friend. "Now you know my one and only secret."

"Guys! Come on. We gotta get going!" Kelsey urged, motioning to them.

"Wait, I thought of something," Saylor barked. He dashed to the chair where Judtson had been restrained and picked up the valise and headset dropped by the stranger.

He glanced at Judtson, as he hurried from the office. "I thought we might need this if we're going to determine what they're doing and how they do it."

▽

Kelsey drove the Hummer, and Romeo amply filled the front passenger seat. The others sat in back. Ricky was silently staring out the side window as Saylor put his hand on the younger man's arm. "Are you all right?"

Without turning, Ricky, his voice subdued, answered, "It's just sinking in. I killed someone."

"You didn't have a...."

"I know all that. I've been telling myself over and over again that I didn't have a choice. But that doesn't make it any easier to deal with."

Judtson, listening in on the conversation, said, "I didn't even know you carried a gun."

Ricky looked at his boss. "I started right after I began working for you."

"What? Why?"

"All the crackpots. All the nuts who wrote the crazy stuff to you. We talked about it. You know I was always worried about some wacko bursting into the office."

Judtson only nodded.

"Well, I'm glad you had it," Saylor told him, "and I'm pretty sure Judtson feels the same way. If it had not been for you coming in and doing…what you did, he'd be back in la-la land and I'd probably be dead."

Unable to think of anything else to say to make Ricky feel better, Saylor pulled out his phone. Romeo, seeing his actions, twisted in the front seat to face him. "That wouldn't be a good idea."

Saylor paused. "What's that?"

"Using the phone."

"Why?"

"GPS," Judtson answered.

"They can be tracked. You should turn it off and pull out the battery. All of you." As Romeo spoke, he reached into the zippered duffle on the floorboard between his feet and pulled out a large plastic bag. It was filled with cell phones. As the three men in the backseat removed the batteries from their own phones, he pulled out three and handed them around. "These are charged up. The GPS is disabled and they have a couple of other features, as well."

He looked at Saylor and asked, "Who were you going to call?"

"My wife."

"Do you know where she is right now?"

"She should be at home."

"Is there a landline? Not a home cell phone but an actual hard-wired phone."

"There is. Why?"

Before Romeo could respond, Kelsey answered, talking over her shoulder as she drove. "These days, the money, personnel, and attention are all spent monitoring cellular transmissions. Nobody wastes any time listening to the old system."

"Who's listening?"

"If you're asking me their names or their outfit, I couldn't tell you. But I'm sure it's the same group those three guys on Judtson's office floor work for."

"Why is it okay to use one of these?" As Saylor asked, he held up the new phone.

"The transmission is scrambled. No matter what number you call, it's routed to the same number, where it's unscrambled, and then the connection is made from that point to the landline you dialed. It isn't foolproof, so we still need to practice good habits on the phone, be careful about what we say."

"I was going to tell her to meet us at your place. I guess I shouldn't do that."

"Why not?"

"That would tell them where we're going, right?"

Kelsey shrugged. "If they don't already know that, they'll figure it out soon enough. Be careful not to mention anything at all about what happened back there. And don't say your name, hers, Ricky's, Judtson's, or mine."

"Why not?"

She sighed, obviously becoming slightly frustrated at having to explain something everyone should know. As she paused, Romeo interceded, "Thousands of cell phone calls are made at any given moment. They can't possibly listen to all of them, so they use computers to monitor the conversations. The computers utilize algorithms. Every call is scanned in real time for keywords,

keywords they've selected to flag a call for recording. That's the point where an actual person will listen to it."

"And you can bet that all of our names are now on their list," Kelsey added.

Turning to Judtson, who had been silently listening to the exchange, Saylor commented, "You're unusually quiet. Are you buying all of this?"

With no animation or inflection to his voice, Judtson answered, "I just spent some time as a prisoner in my own head. I was brought back by a lightning bolt. Three men in black came into my office and held us at gunpoint while they tried to strap some contraption on me which would have sent me back into mental oblivion. Yeah, I guess you could say I'm buying this."

Saylor looked back and forth between Judtson and Kelsey. "This is weird."

"What is?" she asked.

"I can't decide if I've suddenly been dropped into some Ludlum story or a late-night science fiction movie."

She shrugged again. "A little of both."

▽

Upon their arrival and after the Hummer was safely locked inside the garage, Judtson asked Kelsey if she had a computer he could use. As Saylor and Ricky followed Romeo to another part of the house, Kelsey led Judtson down a hallway.

"What are you going to do?" she asked as they walked.

He was still holding the hard drive he had retrieved from the safe. "All of this started after I interviewed Villarreal. Everything I had about what he told me is on this."

She led Judtson into a large room, which, although completely out of place in the middle of a residence, would have been perfectly normal in the IT department of a major corporation. Two rows of three-sided cubicles filled the center of the room, each cube with its own work station, all of them empty. The floor was covered with resilient tile to reduce static electricity. At the far end, sitting on a raised platform, was a man in his thirties, wearing black pants, a black T-shirt, and black combat boots; he was surrounded by a circle of six computer monitors.

"Hi, Scott," Kelsey shouted. "Anything?"

As the two reached him, Scott looked away from one of the flat screens and answered her, disregarding Judtson completely. "Not yet."

"Scott, this is Judtson. Judtson, Scott Gumble."

The man shifted his attention to Judtson. "Hello."

Judtson began to extend his hand, when he caught a subtle shake of Kelsey's head. He dropped his hand back down to his side and said, "Pleasure to meet you."

"Scott, Judtson needs to use one of the stations. He has an external he wants to connect."

"I'll have to scan it first."

"No problem," Judtson replied and handed the drive to him. He made no move to take it, and Judtson, after an awkward few seconds, set it down on the table.

The moment Judtson was no longer in contact with the piece of hardware, Scott, who was wearing fabric gloves and had a ground strap fastened to his wrist, snatched it up. In quick, fluid motions, he picked up a screwdriver and opened the case, revealing the actual hard drive inside. Extricating it, he selected a dock from the assortment of devices on his table and slipped in the drive.

"Let's give him a minute or two," Kelsey murmured and stepped away. Judtson followed until they were standing several feet from the platform.

"Don't you think it might be time to share what Villarreal told you?"

Judtson nodded, pulled a rolling chair out from one of the work stations, and sat down. Kelsey perched on the edge of the desk, waiting.

"How familiar are you with Puma Punku?"

"Well, I know that it is a lot older than the mainstream archaeologists claim. Maybe tens of thousands of years older. I've heard it was a spaceport. The lore is that it was built in one day by the aliens. It's at an elevation of something like 13,000 feet. There are incredibly large H-shaped stones which were carved and crafted to an amazing tolerance, considering the tools that the indigenous people of the time would have possessed during either epoch. It's close to Tiahuanaco, which has its own interesting history, and it is also right by Lake Titicaca, where tons of UFOs have been sighted."

Judtson chuckled. "Not bad. As you probably know, the site is littered with the massive stones, carved in very elaborate and precise geometric shapes, several configurations in addition to the H shape."

"Right."

"And, as you said, most of the mainstream archaeologists argue that it was built around 1,500 years ago by the ancestors of the Inca."

"But it's a lot older, isn't it?"

Judtson shrugged. "Figuring out the age of the stones isn't that easy."

"Because radiocarbon dating doesn't work on rock."

"They've dated it by analyzing the organic material in the soil buried beneath the rock."

"That wouldn't be foolproof, would it?"

"Normally, up until a few weeks ago, I would have said that it was."

"But now?"

"Not so sure."

"What changed your mind?"

Judtson stared at her a moment before he spoke. "You know that Villarreal had spent a lot of time studying Puma Punku, right?"

"Yes."

"Did you know that, prior to his work at that site, he worked at Baalbek?"

Her eyes widened. "Baalbek? The ancient city in Lebanon?"

"One and the same."

"I don't know much about it."

Scott approached the two. "It's clean and connected. You can use this station. It's drive M." He turned and walked away.

"Thank you, Scott," Kelsey said to his retreating back.

Judtson swiveled in the chair and turned on the terminal. As he waited for it to boot up, he continued, "In Greco-Roman times, it was named Heliopolis, and the Romans built some fairly massive structures, such as the Temple of Jupiter, on top of the tell, or mound. In doing this, they repeated the same habit or tradition practiced everywhere. They built on top of older structures. Some controversy existed at first as to whether anything was beneath the Roman structures. When that discovery was made, the archaeologists found the lower building to be made from cut stones which were unbelievably massive. The most amazing were the stones in the trilithon on the western side – three gigantic rectangular blocks estimated to weigh around eight hundred tons each. They found a larger stone remaining attached in a nearby quarry, almost as if the project had been interrupted. That one has been estimated to weigh one thousand tons or more."

"Wow!"

Judtson grinned. "It gets better. The first determination by the archaeologists was that these gigantic, milled stones were the foundation of a previous structure. I guess they were able to stretch their imaginations far enough to surmise that a primitive people, using enormous work contingents and brute force, dragged these stones into place."

"Yeah, right!" she interjected sarcastically.

"The more they explored, the bigger the surprise. Recent excavations have found that the eight-hundred-ton rectangular blocks were not a foundation at all. They were the top course of a buried structure. They have excavated four additional layers of immense stones, many weighing one hundred to two hundred tons, and some even larger, estimated at up to four hundred and fifty tons each."

"The massive stones were placed on top? How do the mainstream guys explain that?"

"They can't really. Not in any satisfactory way. They are clinging to the concept that the people built earthen ramps adjacent to the walls and dragged the stones up the ramps where they could slide them onto the top of the other layers, and then removed the ramps."

"That's ridiculous."

"Uh-huh. But that isn't the real surprise."

"What do you mean?"

"Villarreal located his dig adjacent to the buried building. Believe it or not, he was actually the first to do so. What he discovered was even more amazing."

"Which was?"

"It would seem that the people who built the megaliths beneath the Roman structures had followed the same practice of building on top of something already built."

Kelsey let out a small gasp, covering her mouth with her hand. "There was another building beneath?"

"Exactly."

"How old was that one?" As she asked, Judtson grabbed the mouse and opened his imported drive.

"He was still trying to figure that out precisely, but he suspected from his preliminary work that it was at least forty thousand years old."

As Judtson spoke, he found the sub-folder he was searching for and opened it. Watching over his shoulder, Kelsey could see that the folder was filled with jpeg files.

"But, Judtson, how does this tie in to Puma Punku? Or does it?"

He turned back to face her. "Oh, it does. You no doubt know that Puma Punku is a mess. If you visit the site, which I have, it looks like the floor of a kindergarten after playtime, except the preschoolers would have to be giants. Blocks of all shapes and sizes are strewn everywhere. You find a sizable platform, one or two vertical stone structures, lower remnants of walls. The rest is just pieces, albeit very elaborately carved and milled pieces, with inverted recesses and drilled holes. It was the specific, well-defined configuration of some of the pieces which drew Villarreal back to Puma Punku."

"Why?"

"When his dig reached the lower, much older stone structure at Baalbek, he saw something which looked familiar to him."

"Dammit, Judtson, what was it?"

He grinned at her. "I'm a writer, remember. I have to take my time getting to the point."

She forced a rapid exhale from her lips, directing it upward so that it fluttered her red bangs.

"Villarreal returned to the Andes and, with great difficulty, arranged for the transport of one of the massive carved stones to Lebanon. It's funny to think about crediting the ancient people with moving these things, because of the incredible logistics he encountered moving one."

"Spare me the details."

"Okay. He had to book space on a cargo ship to get it there. Once in port...."

"I asked you to skip the details!"

"All right, all right." He turned back to the monitor and seized the mouse as he spoke. "Villarreal had left a team behind to prep the site...or rather, prep a specific spot on the dig. The older wall he had found was constructed of interlocking blocks. Near the top of that wall, there was a fractured piece. He guessed that it might have been damaged at the time the next layer of work, thousands of years later, occurred. Anyway, Villarreal's team cleaned out the broken section. After the H-piece arrived from Puma Punku, by using a heavy-duty crane, they were able to position the imported piece in front of the hole."

"It matched, didn't it?"

Instead of answering, he clicked on one of the files and a picture instantly appeared on the screen. It showed the substantial H-shaped block, suspended by steel cables, slid part way into a matching opening in a stone wall. In the photo was a man working on the rigging team. He was standing on a scaffold adjacent to the block, holding a nylon strap.

"Notice the man on the scaffold?"

"Yes."

"He gives you a sense of the size of the stone."

"Unreal!"

"Kelsey, not only did a stone this large slide into the hole, it fit perfectly. And when I say perfectly, I'm talking about a tolerance of approximately a millimeter all the way around, including all of the inside corners."

He closed the picture and opened another. The cables were gone and the imported stone was fully into the wall, its surface perfectly flush with the others.

She stared at the photograph on the screen silently. Judtson could almost perceive her mind attempting to grasp the ramifications of what he had told her, recalling his own mental struggle when he first saw it.

Before she could gather her thoughts to speak, Judtson continued. "The milled stones at Puma Punku are from a quarry several miles from the site. They are made up of andesite, which is a very tough stone to carve and is native to the Andes. That's why it was named andesite. There aren't any known andesite quarries or deposits anywhere in Lebanon and, even if there were, that would not explain something else Villarreal discovered."

She tore her eyes away from the picture and looked at him. "What was that?"

"All rocks everywhere have a specific signature. Whether they are granite, quartz, or andesite, none of them are purely that substance. They will have a distinct mixture of other, local elements. Chemists, geologists, and metallurgists are quite good at analyzing a rock and determining which region or even which specific quarry it came from."

"Got it."

"Obviously, the imported stone came from the quarry near Lake Titicaca. But Villarreal took samples from several of the other stones in the long-buried wall in Lebanon and had them all tested."

As Kelsey grasped the direction Judtson was heading, she came close to slipping off the edge of the desk. "You're not saying...?"

"I am. From what he could tell, the wall in Lebanon, maybe tens of thousands of years old or even much older, half a world away from Bolivia and separated by two oceans, was built with blocks quarried at Lake Titicaca."

Chapter 20

As JUDTSON AND KELSEY RETURNED TO THE GROUP, he saw that Doni had arrived and Saylor was in the middle of describing the latest turn of events. Looking away from Saylor, Doni glanced for a moment at Judtson before her eyes traveled to Kelsey.

Saylor, standing up, performed the introduction. "Doni, this is Kelsey Batman. Kelsey, this is my wife, Doni."

Walking briskly, Kelsey crossed the remaining distance and extended her hand. "Doni? Is that a nickname?"

They shook hands. Doni took in the bright red hair, and the T-shirt, bearing the sentence "Humpty Dumpty was pushed!" and answered, "It's short for Donatella."

"Your parents were Renaissance aficionados?"

Not waiting for Doni to answer, Judtson interjected, "Fans of *Teenage Mutant Ninja Turtles*."

Without taking her eyes off Kelsey, Doni chuckled. "Pay no attention to Squirrel. It was my grandmother's name."

Kelsey turned to Judtson. "*Squirrel?*"

"Nickname," was all Judtson offered as an explanation.

"I figured that out. Why 'Squirrel'?"

"Don't you have a nickname?"

There was a momentary hesitation before she answered, "No."

Giving a nasty look to Doni, Judtson changed the subject. "Maybe some other time. Right now we have a lot to talk about."

"That's an understatement," Saylor agreed. "What's our next move?"

They all arranged their seats in a circle as Judtson asked, "Where's Romeo?"

"Romeo? *That's* the name of the guy who met me when I arrived?"

"Romeo Jones," Saylor explained to his wife. "He decided to station himself outside. I guess he's expecting company."

Kelsey nodded. "I'd say that's a safe bet."

For the benefit of the group, Judtson noted, "I briefed Kelsey on the Villarreal discovery. Which reminds me, I need to get in touch with him. At this point, I think he needs to be warned."

"Don't you think it's too late?" The question came from Ricky, who seemed to have recovered somewhat from the emotional fugue state following the shooting.

"What are you saying?"

"Think about it, Judtson. That last message from him was strange. There was something wrong, something happening. And then the messages stopped."

"Maybe they took him out." Kelsey voiced the opinion without any inflection.

Judtson whirled around in his seat to face her. "Killed him?"

"We don't know. But I wouldn't put it past them. Haven't you tried to reach him?"

"I did. I left a voice mail. I sent an email."

"Has he responded?"

A cloud of dread filled Judtson as he replied, "No. Nothing."

Kelsey stood up. "I'll ask Scott to see if he can track him down. In the meantime, all of you need to think about others who might be in danger."

Ricky appeared surprised by her comment. "What others?"

"Spouses, children, people close to any of you who could be nabbed and used against you."

She left the room. Judtson noticed that Doni was staring at her as she left. There was a long lull in the conversation as the group absorbed the grim reality of their situation.

Judtson broke the quiet. "I should call Kristen and make sure she goes somewhere safe."

"Good idea, Squirrel," Doni agreed.

Kelsey was already returning and sat back down, this time choosing a spot on the couch beside Judtson. "I don't think this place is going to be all that secure for us in the long term. And we're going to need to be mobile."

"Any suggestions?" Saylor asked, clearly worried.

Kelsey thought for a minute. "I have a spot. It might work."

"Where?"

"I own one of the old Titan missile silos south of Tucson."

"You bought a missile silo?" Ricky sounded incredulous.

"Yeah. A few of them were put up for auction a while back. Thought at the time one of them might come in handy. We've stocked it with food and water. I've got one guy there, kind of a combination guard and caretaker."

"Is it safe?"

Kelsey turned to answer Doni. "It was built to withstand a nuclear blast. It was also designed to be impenetrable from a land attack. When the blast door is closed and the steel entrance is secured, it's a fortress."

Changing the subject, Judtson asked, "Ricky, do you have anyone to call?"

Ricky shook his head. "No. No one. If they might move as fast as Kelsey says, you'd better warn Kristen."

"You're right." He stood up and walked to the far end of the room.

His voice timid, Ricky asked, "Kelsey, do you have any idea who these people are?"

Frustration showing on her face, she answered, "No. The Internet is full of wild speculation about all kinds of secret organizations and societies, ranging from shadow governments to shape-shifting reptilian aliens from another planet. There is obviously something going on...someone behind this, with some pretty amazing resources and technologies...but I have no idea who it might be."

"What do we do next? Just hide for the rest of our lives?"

She sighed expressively. "Whoever it is, whatever it is, is probably the same group who killed my father and tried to kill me. I think that the reason this is happening now is that Judtson was getting close to something. We need to find out what that was."

Ricky looked uncomfortable. "If they are as powerful and ruthless as you say, don't you think we might be biting off more than we can chew?"

"We might be. But, as you said, if we don't do something, we will spend the rest of our lives hiding like rabbits until they do find us, which they eventually will."

When Judtson returned, Ricky met his eyes at once and asked, "How did that go?"

"Okay, I guess. She thought I was nuts, at first. I tried to talk her into going out to the silo with us; she wouldn't hear of it. I think I convinced her to stay with an out-of-town friend." He let out a heavy sigh. "Kelsey, do you think she really is in danger?"

"Hard to say. Saylor told me a little about how your relationship was with her before the conversion...."

"Not that good."

"So he said. Since they came to do it again, they are obviously aware that you are back to the old Judtson. As far as they know, she despised the old Judtson and the old Judtson despised her. Hopefully, that means they might not see her as a valuable hostage."

"I wouldn't want anything to happen to her because of me."

The guilt and vulnerability in his voice touched Kelsey. She reached out and placed her hand on his. "I know. But if she won't go to a safe place, we can't exactly kidnap her and force her to go."

"Maybe she'll change her mind."

"In the meantime," Kelsey began, her voice stronger and more assertive, "we need to figure out what the secret was you were about to discover. The sooner we get to the bottom of this, the better for all of us. Let's check with Scott. Maybe he found something about Villarreal."

She stood and Judtson followed her into the computer lab. Scott was already leaving his area as they arrived.

"He's alive."

Judtson stepped forward. "How do you know?"

"Well, he's generating emails, making phone calls, charging on his credit cards, and there's even a video of him doing a lecture on YouTube put up by one of his students. That post was dated today. He has also been active on Facebook and Twitter."

"I'd like to see the lecture."

"Sure," Scott answered softly and returned to his desk. After a few rapid keystrokes, the video filled one of the flat-screen monitors. It was evidently taken using a cell phone situated several rows back; the quality was not exceptional, but it was clear enough for Judtson to recognize the scientist.

"Could you turn up the sound a little?"

Scott complied and Villarreal's voice, mixed with background shuffling and other noises, jumped out of the speakers. The lecture was on the topic of Puma Punku, and it quickly became obvious that Villarreal was teaching his students the standard scientific dogma of the day regarding the site, rather than his recent findings. He was, in fact, castigating those "fringe" scientists who stubbornly clung to the myths and lore of the area as truth.

Kelsey, who had moved next to Judtson to watch the lecture, decided she had heard enough. "This doesn't look good."

Judtson shook his head. "No, it doesn't."

"Last time I saw them, his personal website and blog were filled with his field work and theories on Puma Punku." She turned to Scott. "Why don't we check those?"

Working the mouse, Scott opened Villarreal's website, displaying it on an adjacent monitor, leaving the lecture video running on the other.

"That's strange," Kelsey said quietly.

Instead of the home page for his site, they were viewing a blank screen with a message written in English and Spanish: "Site under construction. Will be online soon." Not only was his site not there, his blog was no longer online.

Judtson stared at the screen. "We need to get down there. I need to see him."

$$\nabla$$

The Gulfstream IV carried only three passengers on its flight to La Paz. It had been hastily decided that Ricky, Saylor, and Doni should stay at the silo for the time being. Kelsey and Judtson sat at a small table near the front of the cabin. Romeo positioned himself at the rear.

"I've made arrangements for a car when we arrive. El Alto is about an hour's drive from Villarreal's office on campus. According to Scott, he should be there."

Nodding in acknowledgment, Judtson commented, "I know I wanted to come down to see him, but now that we're almost there, I haven't decided what I'm going to say."

With an impish grin, Kelsey teased, "You're good, Squirrel. I'm sure you'll think of something."

Judtson glared at her. "Will you please stop that?" He stood and walked to the rear of the cabin.

Laughing to herself, Kelsey let her mind travel back to a day more than twenty years ago when she and her father were watching her favorite sitcom, *Frasier*. The episode was about the ugly chair Frasier's dad, Martin, insisted upon keeping. It had provoked a conversation between her and her father that she had never forgotten:

"See, Dad, you're as bad as Martin."

"What do you mean?"

"Well, he's got that hideous green recliner right in the middle of Frasier's gorgeous living room, and he won't get rid of it."

Innocently, her father asked, "What's your point?"

"You know! You've got that crummy-looking chair you've had forever, and you won't throw it away, either."

"Why should I? I love this chair."

She stood up excitedly and gestured at the rest of the room. "Dad! Look at all of our stuff. That *thing* doesn't go with any of it."

Her father stared at her for a minute, a slight twinkle appearing in his eyes. "Maybe you're right. Maybe I am like Martin. But you know what? You're just like Frasier."

"I am not."

"Yes, you are. You're obsessive, fussy, anal, and pushy."

"Dad!"

"Oh! And I just remembered that his real name is Kelsey, too."

Her eyes narrowed suspiciously. "So?"

A broad smile filled his face. "That's it. I think from now on, I'm going to call you 'Frasier.'"

"FRASIER! That's a boy's name."

"It doesn't matter. It fits you to a *T*. You've always wanted a nickname. You didn't like 'Katydid,' which I thought was perfect for you because the katydid won't let go once it bites into something."

"It's gross! It's a bug!"

"And after you were in that play in school, I wanted to call you 'Bumblebee.' You were cute in that yellow and black costume."

"I hated that costume. I hated my part. I hated that name."

Shrugging, he turned his attention back on the television, adding nonchalantly, "Frasier, it is."

Listening to the steady hum of the engines, Kelsey giggled softly, warmed by the memory. And over the years, she had never dissuaded him from calling her "Frasier." The best she could do was obtain a promise that he would never use it in front of anyone else.

▽

Villarreal was in the middle of a lecture when they arrived. The two stepped into the large hall and quietly took seats in the last row, leaving Romeo outside. The professor was a lean, athletic-looking man in his early thirties, and his lecturing style was not to remain at a podium, but to be in constant, energetic motion.

Kelsey leaned toward Judtson so her whisper could be heard. "Do you speak Spanish?"

"No," he whispered back. "Do you?"

"No. What I don't understand is that the lecture we found on YouTube was in English."

"As I recall, he does classes in each language."

She nodded and they sat back in their seats and waited for the class to finish, comprehending nothing of what was being said.

At one point in the lecture, Judtson caught Kelsey's attention. "Watch! He must be talking about Puma Punku."

Villarreal had switched on a digital projector, and a picture of the carved stones flashed upon the screen behind him. They both noticed that as he gestured toward the picture, he made a comment which brought the entire class to laughter.

After the lecture was completed, most of the students filed out of the hall, followed by Kelsey. The few remaining walked to the front of the room to speak with Villarreal. Judtson followed the latter group, standing at the fringe.

As the professor was speaking to one of the young students, there was a momentary break in the wall of bodies around him and he made eye contact with Judtson, who had no idea what reaction to expect. However, to his surprise, a smile spread immediately over the man's face as he raised his hand in a small wave of greeting. Relieved that his recent friend did not bolt for the door, Judtson waited patiently until all of the students had their face time and left the hall.

The moment he finished with the last one, Villarreal, who had been sitting behind a desk, sprang up and walked to Judtson, his hand outstretched. "Judtson, *mi amigo*, an unexpected pleasure."

"Carlos, it is good to see you, my friend."

"What brings you back to Bolivia? Not that I am not happy you came here."

"I am back to see you. Your string of emails, particularly the final one, concerned me. And when I answered, you didn't respond. I thought something might be wrong."

Villarreal spread his arms wide, as if showing off a new outfit. "I am sorry to be the cause for such a long journey for nothing. As you can see, I am fine. Nothing is wrong. Nothing at all. I am afraid you have traveled all this way for nothing. And I also apologize for not responding. That was quite inconsiderate of me."

Judtson noticed that, although the words seemed appropriate, there was something missing. He pressed him. "Carlos, your two emails prior to the last, and your phone call, all pertained to the show...the program the network was to air."

Villarreal interrupted, "Yes, yes, that was the subject of my call and emails. But that is no longer a matter of concern."

"Don't you still wish for the show to air?"

"No. Not especially. In fact, I would prefer that it did not."

"Why? You were excited about getting the word out. I don't understand."

With a dismissive shrug, he answered, "I was, perhaps. But I am no longer. I fear that I was carried away with youthful, reckless exuberance."

Judtson stared hard at his friend's face. This was most certainly Villarreal. There could not be any doubt about that. And yet, the man standing before him did not *seem* like the same man. As he watched, he could feel the muscles in his neck tighten.

"Carlos, what are you saying? Are you telling me that the things you discovered, the facts you shared with me, are not true?"

The constant smile slipped from his face as he replied, "That, I am embarrassed to admit, is precisely what I am saying."

"How can that be? The stone fit perfectly at Baalbek. And the rest of the wall in Lebanon was made of andesite. You had it tested."

The slightest hint of irritation at being pressured began to manifest on the professor's face. "Judtson, I am afraid we were both the victims of a cruel hoax."

"A hoax? That's not possible."

Villarreal turned to his desk and opened a leather valise, pulling out a bound report. Turning back to face Judtson, he handed it to him. "At the request of my department head, I had the samples we extracted from Baalbek retested at a different metallurgy lab. There is no andesite contained in that wall, only native Lebanon rock quarried from an adjacent site."

Judtson held the report without looking at it. "What about the fit? The way that H-shaped stone fit perfectly into the wall on the other side of the world. That can't possibly be a coincidence."

The irritation on his face gave way to outright anger as he huffed, "That was an abominable practical joke."

"A joke?"

Carlos nodded curtly. "Several of the students who work with me on the digs are all members of the same fraternity. When we first uncovered the buried wall in Baalbek, they spotted the coincidental, interlocking shape of the blocks...."

"Coincidental? You're joking, aren't you?"

"No, I am not." Villarreal's answer was terse. All traces of the former friendliness were evaporating. "I, too, was struck by the incredible unlikelihood of two cultures, separated by oceans and continents, coming up with the same building-block configuration. That conclusion was born from ignorance. Once I moved past my naive excitement and actually consulted with others, including specialists in structural issues, I discovered that the H-shape is an inherently stable building block. Any culture, moving beyond the elemental stage of stacking square or rectangular stones, would discover the benefits of the shape, quite on their own."

Judtson was dubious about what he was hearing but wanted Villarreal to continue. "Okay."

"As I was saying, when the students who were working on the dig at Baalbek saw the similar stone configuration, they, behind my back, made precise measurements of the opening that had the fractured stone. As we remained together in Lebanon, other members of their fraternity, using modern stone-carving tools, modified an existing block at Puma Punku so that it would fit."

"Wouldn't that work be obvious on the stone?"

"There are ways to chemically weather a stone to conceal such trickery."

"So, when you returned to Puma Punku, you were basically led to the stone?"

"It was handed to me like a gift, Judtson. I had, of course, assigned the task of measuring stones to my students. They found, or rather pretended to find, the one which was taken to Baalbek."

"What about the first results, from the other metallurgy lab? Am I supposed to accept that they were in on the joke?"

Villarreal stared off in the distance, disgust visible on his countenance. "I supervised the extraction of the samples from the Baalbek wall, of course. Then I delegated the actual transmission of the material to one of the students. He simply sent pieces they had obtained from the milling work they had done on the Puma Punku stone. Of course the lab found it to be matching andesite; it was from the piece we had transported, not the wall in Lebanon."

"This is all very hard to fathom, Carlos."

"Believe what you would, Judtson. After I discovered the sham, the students were confronted. They admitted their prank and have been suspended. So you see, I am actually quite happy that your program will not be shown. It would have been the end of my career. And I apologize for coming to you with my inaccurate and incorrect findings. I am certain that you, as well, would have suffered substantial shame when the hoax was eventually revealed."

They spent several more minutes discussing the details of the incident, before Judtson thanked Villarreal and promised to be in touch with him soon. He left the professor in the lecture hall and began looking for Kelsey. His search was not a long one. He found her standing in a corridor outside Villarreal's office, talking to someone he did not recognize.

As she spotted him, she held up a finger to indicate she would be done soon, so he waited several yards away. He was too far away to be able to discern details from the conversation, but was able to tell by tone and body language that Kelsey was finishing her chat. She turned and hurried to Judtson, thanking the woman from over her shoulder as she left, and the two began walking to the rental car.

"What did Villarreal say?"

Judtson described the details of the professor's explanation, interrupted repeatedly by loud snorts of skepticism and exclamations of "Yeah, right!" from Kelsey.

When he finished, she asked, "Do you buy any of that?"

Judtson hesitated for a moment before answering, and she verbally leapt upon him. "Judtson! No way! You don't seriously buy that story, do you?"

"I suppose it's possible."

She huffed at him and increased her pace. Judtson rushed to keep up.

"Well, maybe you won't be so willing to dive headfirst into his barrel of crap after I tell you what I found out. That lady I was talking to as you walked up...."

"Yes. Who is she?"

"She is Villarreal's secretary. You've never met her in your past dealings with him?"

"I've spoken with her a few times on the phone, but I always met Carlos in the States or at his digs. What's her name?"

"Lydia."

"That's right. I remember now. What did she tell you?"

Kelsey came to an abrupt stop. It took Judtson two paces to react, and he turned back to face her.

"It seems that Carlos Villarreal went down the same rabbit hole as someone named Judtson Kent."

He stared at her dumbly. "What are you talking about?"

"Let's get in the car before we talk any more about this."

"Okay. By the way, where's Romeo?"

Rolling her eyes with amusement, she remarked, "You're not very observant, are you?" She jerked her thumb to point behind them and to the left. When he looked, he saw the big man pacing them from approximately thirty yards away. They reached the rental car, and Judtson and Kelsey sat in the backseat while Romeo drove.

"Now, talk. Tell me what she said."

Although Judtson had buckled in, Kelsey ignored the restraints and twisted around on the seat to face him, tucking her leg beneath and sitting on her ankle. "I am so glad, by the way, that she spoke English. Otherwise, it would have been a very short conversation. Talking to her reminded me of talking to Ricky and Saylor when you went off to la-la land."

"You mean...?"

"Exactly! On about the same timetable as you, her boss started complaining that he felt a little off. I guess it was subtle stuff he was noticing."

"Boy, I remember that."

"He asked her to made an appointment with his regular doctor. Then a neurologist. Then a psychiatrist. Finally, he had her schedule an MRI."

"Yep, sounds familiar."

"No kidding. And then, *bang*! Out of the blue he came into the office and he was different. She had no idea exactly what was different about him, but since she has been with him for years, she knew something was off. He told her that he was fine. Then the first thing he did was have her shred all of his notes on Puma Punku and Baalbek. Everything! Files, field notes, everything. And he deleted it all from his computer. Obviously, whatever head trick they pulled on you, they used on him, too."

Judtson dropped his head back and closed his eyes, going through the process of assimilating and organizing all that he was learning. Kelsey instinctively recognized what he was doing and remained silent. When he opened his eyes, he realized that he was still holding the metallurgy report Villarreal had handed to him. He glanced down at the binder, prompting Kelsey to ask, "What's that?"

He flipped it open and riffled through the pages. "This is the second report from the lab."

"The one which says that the samples from Baalbek are not andesite?"

"Right."

"Obviously bogus. Do you think the lab is in the bad guy's pocket?"

"No need. All they would have had to do was send the lab some other samples, some from indigenous rocks in Lebanon."

Romeo partially turned in the front seat. "Where are we going?"

Kelsey looked questioningly at Judtson, who shrugged. "Let's just drive for now," she answered. The big man nodded.

"Judtson, do you think that it's possible to bring Villarreal back? You know, the way Saylor did with you."

Judtson stared out the window of the car for a moment, finally saying, "I don't think he has any idea how it happened."

"It wasn't just the PET scan?"

"We don't know with any certainty, only I would guess that the other side wouldn't do something to people which could be undone by a routine procedure. No, there was that lightning strike during my scan. A power surge. Something."

She faced forward and flopped back in the seat. "We need to figure it out. Not just to rescue Villarreal, but in case we have to do it to you again."

"You're right. I'll call Saylor and get him working on it."

Kelsey leaned forward. "Romeo, we need a landline. Find a pay phone."

▽

Saylor sat alone in Robyn Reedy's office. It had not taken much to concern her that a lawsuit was possible from Judtson. Acting as if he were on their side and would also be named in the coming court action, Saylor had convinced her that they needed to determine exactly what had happened during the procedure.

She returned with a man Saylor had not met in his previous visit.

"Dr. Costello, this is Matt Wheeler. He's the tech rep from RadTech, the manufacturer of the equipment involved." The two men shook hands.

Wheeler, who appeared to be in his middle forties, although it was difficult to judge due to the fact that his head was shaved, took the seat next to Saylor. "Ms. Reedy has explained your concerns and asked me to help. What can I do?"

"She told you about the...event during Mr. Kent's PET scan?"

The man nodded and said nothing.

"I'm afraid that whatever happened either caused or was coincidental with a mental change in Mr. Kent. He is now blaming the scan. I've been attempting to dissuade him, but my guess is that he is only days away from retaining counsel, and at that point I am certain that this lab, your company, and I myself will be named in the suit. We need to ascertain precisely what occurred, and we need to do it quickly if I have any hope of being able to talk him out of taking such a drastic step."

"I understand."

Wheeler began tapping the screen of the iPad he had brought in with him, until he opened the file he was attempting to locate. He read over his notes for a moment before speaking. "All of the equipment the lab leases from my company, including the combination PET/CT scan, is equipped with real-time diagnostics and monitoring. A second-by-second record of the scan was stored."

Inwardly, Saylor gave a sigh of relief, surprised by their good luck.

"First off, there was a lightning strike. Unfortunately, it was a direct hit to the facility and resulted in a major power surge. The surge was of a degree far beyond the anticipated levels for such an occurrence. The equipment involved was connected to a segregated power source with integrated surge protection. Despite this protection, the equipment appears to have been affected."

The man glanced meaningfully at Reedy and paused.

Saylor decided to fish. "So far this sounds like an 'act of God.' No doubt the question will be asked in court, so I'd better know now...was there anything different or unusual about the configuration of the PET/CT equipment when the incident happened?"

Out of the corner of his eye, Saylor noticed that Reedy was fidgeting, absentmindedly tearing a Post-it note into small pieces.

"I'm not sure what you mean," Wheeler hedged.

"In reality, I don't even know what I'm asking. You're the experts here. All I want to know is if there was anything different prior to the lightning strike. Anything at all."

The rep looked at Reedy, who nodded at him almost imperceptibly.

"Well, there was something. This particular piece of equipment normally has a UPS attached."

"An uninterruptible power supply?"

"Exactly. The UPS also has a surge protection circuit built in."

"You said 'normally'?"

"We had disconnected it in the morning. It was to be replaced at that time, but the new UPS was not the correct unit for the equipment. A different UPS, the proper one, was ordered and the equipment was put on line without it."

Saylor began to speak, when he was interrupted by Reedy. "The UPS was considered to be redundant. The electrical system which feeds the PET/CT is an isolated, grounded system with generator backup and very heavy-duty surge protection. The manufacturer specs do not even require the UPS."

Saylor held up his hands. "I understand. I do. It's only that we all know how lawyers can make something as innocuous and legitimate as this sound to a jury." He turned back to Wheeler. "Please go on."

Glancing back down at his pad, the tech cleared his throat and continued. "As you probably know, the PET scan itself is a passive machine. The lab injects a radioactive isotope, FDG, into the patient an hour beforehand, and the PET scan is an array of sensors which pick up the emitted radioactive decay from the brain and map it. Since different parts of the brain absorb varying levels of the isotope, the map provides the radiologist with information on the condition of the brain tissue and any chemical changes which may be taking place.

"The problem with a PET scan is that it produces an amorphous, unmapped image. It would be useless unless the image could be precisely overlaid on a map of the brain. That's where the CT scan comes in. Now *that* is an active scan. It is, in simple terms, a rotating x-ray emitter and receiver which takes picture after picture of the brain, creating a 3-D image at the same time the PET scan is gathering its data. Merge the two and you have the PET scan data superimposed upon an accurate map, showing where the data apply inside the patient's brain."

"As a neurologist, I only deal with the end result. I want to make sure I understand the process. During a PET/CT, the patient's brain is saturated with a radioactive isotope, while at the same time being bombarded with x-rays from all directions?" As he spoke, Saylor smiled inwardly as he remembered Judtson's earlier summation of the process.

"Crudely put, Doctor, but yes. That is what is happening during the test."

"Do we know how the lightning strike affected the equipment?"

"We do. As I mentioned, we have a detailed, moment-by-moment record of the test. X-rays are a part of the electromagnetic spectrum which includes radio waves, light, cellular phone transmissions. They each have unique properties due to their particular frequency. Under normal circumstances, the x-ray emissions of a CT scan are at a carefully calibrated frequency. It seems that the power surge attributed to the lightning strike caused the x-ray emitter to briefly shift to another frequency. What happened next is an almost unbelievable coincidence."

Saylor shifted forward to the edge of his seat, his curiosity mounting.

"The anomalistic frequency transmitted into Mr. Kent was precisely the same frequency with which the radioactive isotope that was in his head resonates."

Wheeler sat back as if he had finished with his explanation. Saylor stared at him blankly. "I don't understand. What is the significance of that?"

"I'm an engineer, Doctor, not a neurologist. If you are asking me what effect it would have had on his brain, I'm afraid I can't answer that. The resonance would have caused the isotopes, already deeply absorbed into his brain tissue, to become excited and vibrate at the same frequency as the x-rays. Our lab at the home office is still testing this, yet it would appear that not only would they vibrate, but the excitation of the isotopes would cause a measurable increase in the radiation output from each molecule."

Trying to visualize what the technician described, Saylor paused for a moment before he said, "This is a lot of information for you to have put together on short notice. I only called Ms. Reedy to set up this meeting an hour ago."

Jumping in, Reedy explained, "When Mr. Kent's test was completed, I was concerned. The fact that there was some sort of power anomaly was apparent at the time. As you recall, his immediate reaction after the scan was odd."

Saylor nodded. "To say the least."

"I was already aware of the fact that we had taken the UPS off line prior to his test. When I saw his post-test behavior and, to be candid, yours as well, I became concerned that the power fluctuation might have caused a problem. That's when I called Mr. Wheeler. He and his people have been working feverishly on it since."

"I'm very glad you did. This has been most helpful."

Saylor hesitated for a moment, trying to think of a way to ask his next question without raising their suspicions. "Mr. Wheeler, would it be possible to get a copy of your results, including the details of the frequency shift, intensity, duration, and the like?"

Wheeler looked to Reedy, who answered for him. "I'm afraid not. My superiors, and Mr. Wheeler's, are all concerned about the possible litigation. Since you are Mr. Kent's attending physician and you were present at the test, it was decided to share our findings with you. However, turning over the data is beyond the scope of what we've been instructed to do."

Feigning irritation, Saylor retorted, "Forgive my bluntness, but this is exactly how lawsuits happen, and exactly why we so often are not victorious. Let's not lose sight of the fact that I *am* Mr. Kent's physician. I am also a neurologist. If I have any opportunity to be successful in treating him, I cannot do that without *all* of the available data. And I do mean all. Despite a fear of litigation, we can't forget that my first responsibility is to my patient, not the damn lawyers. I should remind you, Ms. Reedy, so is yours."

Her face tight and pinched through the course of his tirade, she visibly swallowed before responding. "Dr. Costello, I fully understand what you are saying. And I know you understand my position. It is not my decision to make."

She cut Saylor off, not giving him an opportunity for a rebuttal. "However, I do agree with you. If you wouldn't mind, I'd appreciate it if you could give Mr. Wheeler and me a few minutes to call our respective bosses."

Forcing a polite smile onto his face, Saylor stood. "Of course."

▽

Saylor was lost in thought as he crossed the pavement to Kelsey's Hummer, which he had borrowed for the trip, the two flash drives provided by Reedy and Wheeler safely tucked in his pocket. Nothing in his training or experience was helpful to him in understanding the process which had occurred in Judtson's head during the scan. He was so intent on solving the puzzle that he did not notice the black Tahoe enter the parking lot as he pulled out.

He called his office and had Melanie give him Dr. McWhorter's phone number in New York. He went on to tell her that he had to leave town for a few days, and ended the conversation before she could ask him why.

Next, he tapped in McWhorter's number, glancing at his watch and adding the time change. It was going to be close; he was not certain of the New York neurologist's office hours. A voice answered on the third ring. Saylor identified himself and asked for the doctor. The receptionist told him that McWhorter had not been in the office all day. Saylor's gut tightened as an unnamed fear suddenly crowded its way into his mind.

Dreading the answer, he asked, "Have you spoken with him today?"

"Oh, yes. Twice. In between trips to the bathroom. I guess he has a pretty bad case of food poisoning." She was chuckling at her boss's discomfort. Relieved, Saylor left a message for McWhorter to call him, and broke the connection.

▽

Saylor pulled into the access drive from the two-lane road south of Tucson; the tires shuddered twice as he crossed a cattle guard. The first entrance to the silo compound was not gated. The tall chain-link fencing with loops of concertina wire at the top stopped on both sides of the narrow pavement, and the only apparent barrier was a substantial speed bump. Thirty feet ahead of the hump was a call box, mounted on a diagonal pipe. Saylor stopped at the box and pressed the button. Moments later a male voice Saylor knew to belong to Luis, the caretaker/guard, came out of the speaker.

"Who is there?"

"Saylor." He smiled for the array of mounted cameras observing him at the moment.

"Doctor, come on in."

"Thank you."

Saylor lightly touched the gas pedal, and the Hummer crawled over the speed hump and safely traversed the narrow metal grate concealed behind it. When they had first arrived at the silo, Luis showed him that unless he stopped and identified himself, there would be a problem. The now innocuous-looking grate held retractable, angled steel spikes, similar to those used at exits from paid parking garages, which were intended to shred tires. Once a person was cleared by the guard, the spikes were lowered, allowing safe entrance.

After passing the grate, Saylor watched in his rearview mirror and saw the row of teeth rise up and lock into position. He drove for almost a quarter of a mile on the hilly, twisting lane, the final two hundred yards becoming an extreme serpentine course, terminating at the second barrier. This entrance was a solid metal gate built into a tall masonry wall. There was another call box and Saylor stopped a second time. After he identified himself once again, the gate swung open and he passed through, making his way to the small concrete shack. The only feature breaking the smooth concrete surface of the shack was a single steel door.

He parked and entered the diminutive building, hearing the locking bolts snap back into place and secure the door behind him. Inside the musty-smelling hut was the top of a metal staircase descending down into the lower level. The stairs were enclosed on both sides with cast-in-place concrete walls, and his footsteps on the treads echoed loudly as he descended through the multiple landings and switchbacks. He finally reached the bottom, where he caught sight of Luis. The man was short and stocky with the physique of a bodybuilder. He was seated at a work station equipped with a bank of monitors and, without taking his eyes off the screens, welcomed Saylor.

"Hello, Doctor. Safe trip?"

"It was. Quiet here?"

Luis quickly glanced at him, laughing. "Quiet is an understatement in this hole."

He returned his gaze to the monitors and remarked, "It looks like you weren't followed."

"That's good. Any word from Kelsey and Judtson yet?"

"*Nada. Nada* damn thing."

Saylor chuckled. He stepped through the open vault door which separated the stairwell from the secure area and immediately began searching for the others. At the end of the first corridor, in a room set up as a lounge, he found Doni. She was reclined on a sofa, reading a book. Hearing him, she looked up.

"Hey, Saylor-man."

"Hi, honey."

"Did you get what you needed?"

"I think so." He proceeded to tell her what he had learned at the radiology lab.

When he finished, she whistled. "Wow. It sounds as if Judtson really got zapped."

"Yes, it does. I'm going to call him and let him know what I found out."

He left her in the lounge and, after taking a few wrong turns, managed to find his quarters. The cell phones were useless down in the silo, so he used the landline, calling the hotel where Judtson and Kelsey were supposed to be staying. After having the front desk ring Judtson's room and getting no answer, he had them try Kelsey's.

"Hello."

"Kel...I mean, hi." Breaking the habit of using names on a phone call was not going to be easy.

"Hey, how'd it go?"

"Very well, I think."

"Let me get Squirrel for you."

"Okay." Saylor smiled, noting that Kelsey had already adopted Judtson's nickname.

A moment later he heard his friend's voice. "What's up?"

Keeping the details vague, Saylor told Judtson what he had learned at the radiology lab.

"Do you think we can...?"

"We should be able to, although we're going to need some rather expensive stuff."

"Or access to theirs."

"True, but I'm not sure how receptive they'd be to that. By the way, after I left the lab, I had a thought. We need to get the names of the eight others who had your symptoms."

"Great idea. Hadn't thought of that. Can you get them?"

"They are supposed to be kept confidential."

"Who has them?" It was Kelsey's voice. She had obviously picked up an extension.

"The CDC."

There was a moment of silence as she thought. "I might just have a way."

Chapter 21

SAYLOR WAS AGAIN BEHIND THE WHEEL OF THE YELLOW HUMMER, and was parked in front of the corporate terminal at Tucson International Airport. As he waited, he read for the third time the list of names Scott had handed him shortly before he left the silo. Kelsey's computer whiz had not told him how he had obtained the list, and Saylor had not inquired, assuming that he was better off not knowing.

On the list was McWhorter's patient in New York, as well as the Washington, D.C. patient they had discussed in general terms. The other names and locations were not familiar to him, except, of course, for the second to the last name, Carlos Cabrillo Villarreal.

He jumped, startled, as a loud thump shook the Hummer. Dropping the list, he looked up to see Judtson grinning at him playfully, the palm of his hand hovering inches above the hood. Romeo, shaking his head disapprovingly, was already circling the vehicle, approaching the driver's door. Saylor hurriedly retrieved the dropped paper from the floorboard and climbed out, knowing the big man preferred to do the driving. As he opened the door to the rear seat, he noticed Kelsey's T-shirt and laughed. "I see it didn't take long for you to capitalize on Judtson's nickname."

The shirt was white, and written across the front in black letters was "I have reason to believe the squirrels are mocking me."

She sat in the front passenger seat and twisted around to face him. "He won't tell me why he's called that."

As Judtson slid into the Hummer beside him, Saylor answered, "That is totally up to him. You aren't going to get it from me. But how did you manage to get that shirt so quickly?"

She winked. "That's *my* secret."

"Enough about me," Judtson groused. "Let me see the list."

Saylor handed it over as Romeo pulled away from the curb.

"I almost expected to see the three of you return with Villarreal handcuffed and gagged."

"I suggested it," Kelsey said half seriously. "Squirrel here talked me out of it."

Judtson lowered the list and glared at her briefly. "Will you stop calling me that? Saylor, do you recognize any of these names?"

"Other than Villarreal's, no. Do you?"

Judtson read the list again. "Three or four of them are familiar, but I can't quite make the connections."

"Can I see it?"

He handed the sheet to Kelsey who was still hanging over the back of her seat, facing them. Scanning the names, she exclaimed, "I know this one! Dean Copeland. He wrote *Secret Agenda*."

"You're right! Now I remember him."

"Who is he?" Saylor asked. "What was *Secret Agenda* about?"

"He's a retired NASA scientist," Kelsey explained. "His book, *Secret Agenda*, was a tell-all about how NASA was covering up proof of extraterrestrials on the Moon and Mars."

"Really? Any of the others ring a bell?"

She finished looking over the sheet and shook her head. "No."

Saylor took back the list and added, "All Scott included were names and addresses. He's working on a more complete profile of each of them now. Maybe that'll jog your memories."

"Maybe," Judtson acknowledged. "Any progress on being able to repeat the procedure?"

"I've got a call in to Robyn Reedy and Matt Wheeler at the lab. They haven't called back yet."

"That's odd," Kelsey commented. "Don't these people all jump every time a doctor calls?"

"Your estimation is a bit inflated, though you're right. They usually do get back to us fairly quickly."

"Saylor, give up the 'us' routine. There is only one of you," Judtson teased. "I have an idea. They should be there now. Why don't we stop and pay them a visit? I can play the angry patient ready to sue."

Saylor thought about it for only a minute. "Sure. Why not?"

▽

"I'm sorry, Dr. Costello, Ms. Reedy isn't at work today," the receptionist informed him with an insincere smile.

"Really? Is she ill?"

"Well, yes. She did call in sick."

"How about Matt Wheeler? May I see him?"

Her brow furrowed, a display of confusion Saylor suspected was a frequent visitor to her face. "I don't know anyone here by that name. Oh, wait. He's the guy from the equipment company, isn't he?"

Trying hard to remain courteous, Saylor answered, "Yes, that's right. He's that *guy*."

"He doesn't work here. I mean, he works here because a lot of the equipment here is from his company. But he doesn't actually work here."

"I think you're trying to tell me that his office is somewhere else?"

She smiled brightly. "Yes. That's right."

"Could we get his address?"

She took a minute to find his contact information on her computer, then clicked the mouse and turned to stare blankly at the laser printer beside her, becoming completely immobile.

Judtson cleared his throat to get her attention. "Miss, maybe you could just write down the address. You know, with a pen and some paper."

She tore her eyes away from the still-idle printer and looked at him blankly for a moment before blurting out, "Why, yes. I could."

She fumbled for a pen and hastily wrote the address on a yellow Post-it, handing it to Saylor.

They thanked her and walked away, hearing the printer finally begin to hum as they made their departure.

▽

The two men returned to the Hummer and headed to Wheeler's office. They again left Kelsey and Romeo outside and tried to see the tech rep, but were informed that he was out on an appointment. Rejoining the others in the Hummer, they decided to wait in the parking lot. The next forty-five minutes were filled with discussions about what they should do next, focusing primarily on how they would get Villarreal back to the states for the reversal. In the midst of their brainstorming, they saw a white Altima pull into a reserved space; Wheeler, distinctive due to his shaved head which shone in the bright sunlight, got out of the car.

Judtson and Saylor hastily exited the Hummer and approached him.

"Mr. Wheeler," Saylor called out as they moved to intercept him on the sidewalk in front of the building.

He turned and instantly recognized Saylor. His expression conveyed that he was not happy to see him.

Stopping, he said, "Dr. Costello?"

First introducing Judtson, Saylor asked, "Would you have a few minutes to speak with us?"

The man's eyes darted back and forth between the two. "I'm afraid not. I'm running late for another appointment at the moment."

Before Saylor could say anything, Judtson responded. "We asked your secretary earlier. She told us that you were returning from your last appointment of the day."

After a moment's hesitation, Wheeler demurred, "I'd really rather not, if you don't mind."

"We do mind," Judtson pushed. "This is really rather important."

Oddly, Wheeler looked around the parking lot for several seconds, at last turning back to them. "Okay. Let's go inside. It's too hot out here."

They followed him, and he asked the receptionist if the meeting room was free. She told him it was, so he led them down a short hallway to a small room with a round table and four chairs. After they were seated, Wheeler spoke. "I honestly have nothing further to say."

Saylor sensed a worrisome shift in Wheeler's demeanor since their last meeting. "Matt, is something wrong? The last time we spoke, you were very interested in helping."

There was, once again, a hesitation before answering. "Wrong? No. Not at all. I'm only concerned about discussing the incident in front of the patient, at least without our corporate attorney present."

Judtson decided to be direct. "Mr. Wheeler, I'm not going to sue you, the lab, or your employer. In fact, since it was your equipment involved, I would actually like to thank you. And if you would care to have that in writing, I'd be happy to sign anything."

Wheeler did not appear to be moved by Judtson's comment.

Saylor leaned closer. "There's more to this, isn't there?"

He could tell by the subtle flicker of worry on the man's face that he was right. "Matt, I'm going to be candid with you. We need your help. Something is happening, something we don't fully understand and can't completely explain. What I can tell you is that the freak event during Judtson's procedure didn't harm him in any way. In fact, it helped him. It somehow reversed something inside his head, something someone else had done to him, and brought him back from a very spooky place."

Wheeler stared intently at Saylor. When he replied, his voice was subdued. "I don't understand what you're telling me. And I'm not even certain I want to. But how does what you're saying tie in with the fact that, right after you left from our meeting, two Homeland Security agents appeared at the lab?"

"What?" The nearly shouted question came from Judtson.

"What did they want?" Saylor asked in a calmer voice. "What did they say?"

They waited through another long pause as Wheeler came to a decision.

"They told us, Robyn and me, that you and Mr. Kent were the primary subjects of an ongoing investigation. They refused to tell us the nature of the investigation, yet demanded that we turn over to them all the information we provided to you."

Saylor turned to look at Judtson. "They must be trying to figure out how you were reversed." He then addressed Wheeler. "Did you?"

"I initially refused. I asked them to provide a court order. That's when they informed me that they could take us both into custody and hold us indefinitely without charges or bail. They said that they could do this without even informing our families as to our whereabouts."

"Oh, my God," Judtson sighed.

"So you gave it to them?"

Saylor saw the man's back stiffen in response to his question. This time as he spoke, his voice was stronger. "No. I didn't. I don't particularly care for bullies and tyrants, and this is still America, even if just barely."

"But you're not locked up somewhere. Were they bluffing?"

Wheeler shrugged, a slight smile showing on his face. "I have no idea if they were or not. I did give them things – several files, all of my maintenance notes on the equipment. I even gave them the diagnostics result from the PET/CT machine. Only not the right one."

Saylor chuckled as Judtson asked, "What do you mean? What did you give them?"

"When Robyn first called me and alerted me to the issue, I pulled the diagnostics data from your scan. That's what I gave to Dr. Costello. I also put the equipment through a test run to ensure it was operating properly and to establish a baseline. I gave the two men that data."

"So it showed nothing."

"Right. All of the readings were nominal."

"Out of curiosity," Judtson asked, "what did the two men look like?"

Wheeler snorted dismissively. "They looked like Agents J and K, at least in how they dressed."

"From the movie *Men in Black*?"

"Exactly. In fact, they didn't remove their dark glasses through the entire meeting, or I guess you could call it an interrogation. At first it was tough to take them seriously. It felt like being in the middle of a bad joke. But there was something in their demeanor, their attitude, that...I hate to admit this...they scared me."

"What you did...what you decided to give them, instead of the real stuff, took guts. Trust me, I know what these people are capable of doing."

"Judtson's right. These are not nice people. What did Ms. Reedy tell them? She knew the truth."

Leaning back in his chair, Wheeler explained, "They kept us together the whole time. I've probably watched too many cop shows, so I assumed they would split us up. They never did. She picked up on my cue and told them that we were still investigating the incident."

Recalling something, Judtson said, "Were you aware that she called in sick today?"

"No. I wasn't. You don't think...?"

Judtson shrugged. "It could be nothing. It is a strange coincidence, though."

"Especially if they didn't buy your story," Saylor added.

Wheeler snapped forward in his chair and pulled out his cell phone.

Before he could use it, Judtson stopped him by placing a hand on his wrist. "If you're going to call her, please use my phone instead of yours."

He looked confused. "Why?"

"We may be overly paranoid, but if we're not, they are monitoring your phone. This one is safe."

His mouth twisted in doubt. "This is getting a little 'out there.'"

"Maybe so. But what's the harm?"

"I need to use mine to get her number."

"I guess that would be fine."

Wheeler tapped the screen on his phone twice and then slid the heel of his thumb over it repeatedly until he found Reedy's name. He took the phone Judtson offered and entered the number.

"Are you calling her at home?" asked Saylor.

"Does anyone call anyone at home anymore? I have her cell number."

He activated the speakerphone and laid it, face up, on the table.

On the second ring, a female voice answered, "This is Lucy."

"Uh, hi, Lucy. This is Matt Wheeler. I'm a friend of Robyn's. Is she there?"

"Oh, hello, Mr. Wheeler. Mom has mentioned you. I'm her daughter. You called me at our house. She's not home, but she left her phone here today. You should try her at work."

"I already...." As the words began, Judtson held one finger to his lips, stopping him with a shake of his head.

Understanding, Wheeler said, "I will, Lucy. Thank you."

He broke the connection.

"This isn't good," Saylor muttered.

"Are you two positive you're not blowing this beyond all proportion?"

Saylor made eye contact with Judtson for a moment and saw his friend give him an almost imperceptible nod.

"I think it might be a good idea to tell you about our last experience with this group." Saylor described the incident at Judtson's office, leaving no details out of the narrative. When he finished, he studied Wheeler's face as the man processed the information. The course of the internal struggle was clear by the gamut of emotions exhibited. Saylor remained silent, waiting for Wheeler to speak.

As he finally did, his voice was soft and subdued. "You know, after those two guys left, I called Homeland Security. According to the person I spoke with, they do not have any agents with those names."

"That actually makes me feel a little better," Judtson commented.

"Why is that?"

"Well, wouldn't it be worse if our government was in on this, or even behind it?"

"That doesn't prove they aren't," Saylor rebutted. "All five of them, the three at your office and the two Matt met, could be from some unnamed agency and just use Homeland Security or any other convenient public agency to serve their purposes."

"That's true, I suppose."

Wheeler, listening to this, sighed loudly, apparently coming to a decision. "Maybe you are both nuts. But I guess I am, too. I hope I don't regret this. What do you need from me?"

Saylor grinned at him. "Thanks."

"Don't thank me yet. One hint, one tiny little clue, one indication that you both should be locked up in padded rooms, and I will run away so fast all you'll see is the trail of dust behind me, like in a Road Runner cartoon."

"Understood. Actually, what we need might be relatively simple. We need to be able to replicate what happened to Judtson during the scan."

Wheeler's eyes widened. "Replicate it? Why?"

"Two reasons," Judtson interjected. "The first one should be fairly obvious in light of the attack at my office. They are trying to turn me back into the other Judtson. If, somehow, they succeed, I want Saylor to have a way to undo it."

"Makes sense."

"The second reason is that we've found others we believe have also been converted."

"Others? How many?"

"At this point, one, for sure. There may be as many as eight."

"Eight?"

Saylor shared the information regarding the other CDC cases around the country.

"And all of the others are presumably happy with the way they are now?"

"More than likely."

Wheeler glanced away for a minute, his eyes focusing on some unseen point in the distance. Suddenly, a partial smile curled his lips. "So, let me get this straight. The two of you want me to set up a lab with modified equipment so that you can bring these others to me, bound and gagged, in the middle of the night. I can see it now. I'll be wearing a white lab coat and cackling wildly as you strap the unwilling subjects to the table, and the lightning is flashing crazily as I flip the switch."

The man's colorful description elicited a laugh from Judtson. "Yep. That's about it."

Wheeler looked at Judtson first, then Saylor. "I'm in."

▽

"Saylor, this is strange."

Judtson and Saylor were back at the silo, alone in the dining room. Judtson was reviewing the biographical information Scott was able to gather from the Internet on each of the eight names on the list.

"What is?"

"We have Villarreal, of course. By the way, how did Villarreal make it on a CDC list since he lives in La Paz?"

"The CDC shares information with the World Health Organization. Nasty new diseases come from all over, and Americans travel so much."

"That makes sense. Anyway, in addition to Carlos, an archaeologist, we also have an immunologist, a geologist, a former astronaut, a chemist, Copeland, another author, and a TV producer."

"That's kind of an unusual mix, but what's strange?"

Judtson leaned back in his chair. "I have no idea why the immunologist and geologist are on the list. The former astronaut is widely ridiculed by his fellow space cowboys for having gone 'round the bend. He has done several interviews where he swears he has seen UFOs. The chemist, a researcher, recently lost his funding because he wouldn't drop his avenue of study...the possible uses for something called monoatomic gold. Copeland, of course, wrote the book exposing his former employer for concealing the true nature of the missions to the Moon and Mars. The author on the list was his co-writer. And the TV producer works for *The Jack Bailey Show*."

"How does he tie in to this?"

"She. What Scott found on the web was that she had invited Copeland and his co-writer to be on the show. She was planning on devoting an entire hour to their book. According to the blogs, the offer was withdrawn at the last possible moment, literally hours prior to the appearance."

Thinking over what Judtson had said, Saylor asked, "What about the connection to the chemist? I've never heard of monoatomic gold."

"Nor have I."

"It's a critical element for the Annunaki," said a voice from the doorway behind them. They turned to see who had spoken.

"Doni?" exclaimed Saylor.

Judtson stared at her blankly.

Enjoying her husband's surprised expression, she walked into the break room and took one of the empty seats at the table. "What, Saylor-man? For all those long hours while you've been at work, what do you think I've been doing, perfecting my meatball recipe?"

He cocked his head to the side. "Element for the...what did you call them?"

"The Annunaki."

"Right. Who are they?"

"According to Zecharia Sitchin, the...."

"Whoa! Who is that?"

Doni sighed and, in a voice normally reserved for explaining the complex process of tying one's shoes to a seven-year-old, she said, "A scholar and writer. He was one of the few people who could actually read the Sumerian tablets. He said in his books that the Earth was settled by aliens from another planet, Nibiru. They were called the Annunaki and they came here for our gold."

Saylor rolled his eyes in disbelief. "Right!"

She flashed a look of irritation at him. Before she could comment on his skepticism, they were interrupted by a blurred flurry of motion from the doorway, bounding into the room and running straight for Judtson.

"Rocky!" he shouted as the excited golden retriever jumped up, planting his front paws on Judtson's chest.

Saylor turned to see Ricky standing in the doorway, a broad smile across his face as he enjoyed watching the reunion.

"That was a good idea."

"Thought so, too. Especially since Judtson told me that Kristen was going to leave town. Who was going to feed him and give him water?"

Judtson looked up at Ricky and, as his retriever energetically licked his neck, was able to utter a heartfelt "Thank you."

Reaching into his pocket, Ricky told him, "That isn't all I brought." He tossed an object across the room, and Judtson was able to extricate a hand quickly enough to catch it.

Seeing the set of keys, his face brightened. "You brought the Olds!"

"Since Kelsey mentioned earlier that the old beast didn't have any gizmos built in which allowed it to be tracked, I thought you might want it. I need to tell you something that happened as I was driving it down here."

Judtson instantly became alarmed. "You didn't have an accident, did you? If you dented...."

Ricky held up a hand to stop him. "Just so you don't embarrass us both with your outpouring of concern for my well-being, that's not what I meant. About halfway here, cruising down the highway with the top down, in over a ton of steel, with an engine under that long hood slamming me back into the seat every time I even touched the gas pedal, I suddenly realized that I could never in a million years get behind the wheel of my car again."

The four of them laughed as Judtson declared, "Been trying to tell you that for as long as I've known you."

"Well, you were right. When this situation is over, I'm going to get one of those for myself."

Ricky pulled a chair over to the group and sat, as Rocky slipped down from Judtson's lap and took his normal position at his master's side.

His voice now serious, Saylor asked Judtson,"What's our next move?"

"I think we need to bring Villarreal back."

"Back here, to Tucson?"

"No, well, maybe. I was referring to bringing him back from mental exile."

"Do we know, for sure, that he has been zapped?" The question came from Ricky.

Judtson described the details of his trip to La Paz, emphasizing what Kelsey had learned from Villarreal's secretary. "Ricky, you spoke with him enough times before all of this happened. You know how committed he was to his research and his findings."

"True. Committed is probably an understatement. More like obsessed. But how can we be one-hundred-percent certain that he hasn't had a change of heart?"

There was a brief period of silence as everyone considered Ricky's doubts, the reflection broken by Saylor. "We aren't planning on hurting him. As far as I know, the PET/CT, even modified to cause the frequency shift, shouldn't do any damage."

"In other words," Judtson added to Saylor's statement, "if he hasn't been zapped, as you put it, then nothing will happen to him when we try to zap him back. He'll remain who he is. Except he'll probably be more than a little furious at us."

"I'd say that's a safe bet," Ricky concurred. "Even if the procedure does nothing, we'd still be guilty of kidnapping."

"On the other hand, if he is trapped inside his own head, living in that same hell I was, we need to set him free. And we need to do it soon."

Chapter 22

═══════════════════════════════════════

J UDTSON, WITH ROCKY TROTTING ALONGSIDE, followed the short corridor, looking for Scott.
During the tense days of the 1960s and 1970s, when the facility was loaded with a single Titan
missile and staffed with serious and intense young men who were charged with the responsibility
of launching the deadly projectile on a moment's notice, there was always someone stationed in the
communications room, ready to receive fateful orders – orders which never came.

An unusual holdover among those who served in this capacity was a tendency, for the balance
of their lives, to snatch up a ringing telephone before it could complete its first ring. Others in the
room, even those much closer to the phone, never had a chance to answer it.

The relatively small room, essentially a cubicle, had been commandeered by Scott. Equipment
racks had been bolted to the bare concrete walls, and his desk was rigged with five large flat-screen
monitors. As Judtson entered with Rocky, Scott was staring intently at one of the screens and typing
so speedily that his fingers were nearly a blur.

There were no other chairs in the confined space, so Judtson stood, waiting patiently until he
was noticed.

"Hey, Judtson."

"Scott, how are you?"

"Okay."

Judtson had to strain to hear the man's voice, as he had a habit of speaking at a barely audible
level. Pointing at the desk, Judtson said, "With all this high-tech stuff, what is that doing here?"

The object of interest was an old-fashioned yellow telephone. The desk phone had a dial rather
than the touch-tone buttons of later models.

With a slight grin, Scott explained, "That is the original phone for this room."

Staring at the antique device for a moment, Judtson remarked, "You mean *the* phone?"

His grin broadened. "Yep. That's the one the launch order would have come in on."

"No kidding. Does it still work?"

"Oh, yeah! Western Electric made good stuff. The bell is loud. I mean loud, even when I turn
it all the way down."

Judtson chuckled. "I guess they wanted to make certain it was heard."

"It would have been heard, all right. What's up?"

"I recorded a cable show with Carlos Villarreal. The network dropped it from the schedule. I tried to get my producer to upload a copy to me, but the program she sent was a different show. I was wondering if there might be any way to get the right one."

"I assume it's digital."

"Yes."

"So they should be storing it on their server."

"I guess so."

"What network?"

"The World of Science."

"Oh, that paragon of scientific inquiry." More than a tinge of sarcasm colored his voice.

"That's the one."

Turning back to face his keyboard, Scott found their website within seconds. As he clicked to the site map, he said over his shoulder, "I'll find a way in. Just give me a little time."

"I hope they didn't delete it."

"They probably wouldn't. Even if they did, I might still be able to find it."

"I'll let you get to it. Thanks."

Already lost in the details of his new quest, Scott did not bother to answer. Stepping out of the room, Judtson bumped into Kelsey.

"Hey, Squirrel. What are you up to?"

"Stop with the 'Squirrel' thing, will you?"

"Why? It's your nickname, isn't it?" She smirked at him as she asked the question.

"Never mind. I asked Scott if he could somehow download the Villarreal program from the network."

Her eyes brightened. "Great idea! Are we going to put it on the Internet?"

He began walking, and she followed as he answered. "Not sure. I thought it might come in handy."

"Either way, it'll be good to have. Are you hungry?"

"No. I wouldn't mind something to drink. Rocky's probably ready for some water, too." The golden's ears perked at the mention of his name.

They found the dining room empty, and Judtson filled a bowl with water and bent over to set it down. Rocky began thirstily lapping from it before it was halfway to the floor. After standing for a while and smiling as his friend eagerly drank his fill, Judtson turned to the refrigerator to take out a can of soft drink for himself and watched Kelsey as she found a frozen meal and stuck it into the microwave.

"What was it like?" she asked, punching the buttons on the control panel and starting the machine humming.

"What was what like?"

"You know, being trapped in there. In your head."

"Horrible."

"I got that. I mean the details. What was it *like*? You're the writer. Describe it."

Judtson was once again intrigued by Kelsey's persona. There was, of course, her usual intensity. He was not yet fully accustomed to that, although it was becoming familiar. As they waited for her food to cook, the two were standing at the counter and she was closer to him than he would normally tolerate. The distance between them, while not even a foot, failed to elicit his usual discomfort. She stared up at him expectantly, her eyes wide. Unconsciously, he shifted his gaze downward and focused on her lips and saw that they were slightly parted. She became aware of the focus of his attention and moved slightly closer still.

The shrill tone burst from the microwave, startling them both. He turned and walked to the table as she opened the appliance door and removed her meal.

When they were both seated, he spoke, watching her rip the plastic film from the top of her food. "At first, it was terrifying. You saw me the time it happened at my office. I had already learned to handle it somewhat by then. But during that first major break, in Saylor's lobby, I completely freaked out. I lost it. He was certain I was going to have a heart attack or something."

"Maybe that's why they do it that way."

"What do you mean?"

"Kind of slip you in and out of it a couple of times at first. You know, to get you used to it. Otherwise, if they zapped you once and you stayed zapped, you might just drop dead."

Judtson thought about it. "I don't know. Maybe. The first times it happened, though, there were no guys in black with strap-on devices. It only involved me."

"That's true."

"I think there's something in me...inside my head...something that's supposed to take me where they want me to go. And they can control it remotely. Or, at least, they are supposed to. I think it might be defective. They kept trying, but I kept coming back. That would explain the previous incidents. It would also explain why they had to come get me while Ricky was gone. They probably had to strap on that thing to make whatever is inside me work right."

He could see her mind assimilate what he had said. "That makes sense. If that's true, we may see you checking out on us from time to time."

A panic struck him as he absorbed her words. "I didn't think about that. If they can't nab me and do it with the helmet or whatever it is, they probably *will* go back to activating it remotely."

"Remember, there was a difference between what happened before and your total transformation. In the earlier incidents, you basically locked up, went catatonic on us. After they grabbed you, you were Judtson 2.0."

He shrugged. "True. Plus, during the first incidents, my emotions had an external effect on my body. I had extreme panic attacks, and that caused my blood pressure and heart rate to shoot up. Later, when they transformed me, I was completely losing it, but on the outside I was tranquil. The truth is, I don't really know what happened or how it worked."

"We'd better figure it out. In the meantime, you were starting to tell me what it was like in there."

"Kelsey, it was scary. That's not nearly strong enough. Terrifying would be a more accurate description. When I had the second major episode, the one that happened in front of you, what helped me to stay calm was believing that I would come back again. After the bad guys did what they did to me, I determined rather quickly that I wasn't going to return. I was completely berserk – mentally screaming and railing, trying to regain control, trying to communicate with someone on the outside. When you came to my office after it happened and he, the other guy, basically dismissed you...the whole time I was screaming to you at the top of my...mind."

She thought back to that visit. "I'm so sorry, Judtson. I didn't pick up on it."

"Not your fault. No one did. While he talked with Saylor, Ricky, Doni, any of you, I was bouncing off the inside of my skull, trying to reach out. It never worked. The only one I made some kind of connection with was my furry friend here."

Kelsey squirmed in her chair, tucking one leg underneath herself. "I heard about that."

Smiling at the recollection, Judtson described the brief event in the living room and how Rocky had responded to him. "Other than those few seconds, I was completely cut off from everyone."

"My God. I can't even imagine what that would have been like."

"Kelsey, the thing is...I was in there...." He tapped the side of his head. "Everything I can feel now, and taste and see and hear and smell, I was able to experience then. Except it was all a one-way proposition. I was receiving all of it, but I could control none of it. All of the aspects of living, all of the minute details of being a functioning person, the things we take for granted were gone. Like right now, as we are talking, my eyes are constantly in motion. I am choosing to look at your left eye, or your right one. I can decide to glance over your shoulder or look out at the hallway if I hear a sound. I can reach down and scratch Rocky's ear. When I was trapped inside, I couldn't do anything *I* wanted to do. The 'me' you are talking to now, this Judtson, this consciousness, could only see what the other Judtson wanted to look at. I could only touch what he directed his hand to contact."

"That's spooky!"

"That's an understatement. I was a helpless passenger. Two of the senses, hearing and smell, were basically passive. If there was a sound in my proximity, I heard it. I wasn't dependent upon him to listen to it. If there was an odor, I smelled it. And, of course, I tasted everything he put in his mouth. But I couldn't decide what he put in there."

"In a way, it sounds like a demonic possession."

"Yes and no. It depends on which entity or consciousness you're talking about."

"What do you mean?"

"In the books and movies where the character is going through his or her normal life when all of a sudden the devil possesses the person, the devil at that point is in control of the person's body. However, in most of the plots, the possessed consciousness inside can be called out, summoned, brought to the foreground. There is an implied struggle for control of that individual. In my case, there was no struggle, no contest at all. I was effectively cut off from my body, from my life. Well, almost totally."

"Almost? The Rocky thing?"

"There was that. But there was something else, too. What I haven't mentioned yet was that after the transformation, I never fell asleep."

"What? You were awake the whole time?"

"I was. Every minute. Even as he slept, I was awake, thinking."

"I'm surprised you didn't go nuts."

Judtson winked at her. "How do you know I didn't? Seriously, there were several times I *was* afraid I was losing it. Anyway, I did link with the other guy, in a manner of speaking. While he slept and I was wide awake, I conjured a mental image of escaping."

He went on to tell her the scene he had described to Saylor about the room with the wooden planks.

"When he woke up the next morning, he told Kristen about a dream he had and described the room, the crowbar, the entire thing."

Kelsey gasped. "You made his dream?"

Judtson nodded. "I did."

"That is bizarre. So there *was* a kind of a connection between you."

"Yes. There was. And I took a bit of gleeful satisfaction from that discovery."

She burst out laughing. "You were going to make his nights miserable from then on, weren't you?"

"Oh, yeah! After I heard about his dream, I decided that every night when he went to sleep, I would create images of what I would do to him if I could."

"I'll bet you were planning some fairly colorful scenarios."

"Let's say that they were going to include saws, ice picks, axes, and wood chippers."

She giggled as she visualized what he had planned, the amusement lasting only a few moments; then the mirth left her face. Kelsey leaned forward and, in a muted voice, said, "I just thought of something. If you are out here with me, is he in there trying to get out right now?"

Remembering Kristen's comment along those lines, he felt the same disquieting feeling. Before he could respond, Scott suddenly appeared in the doorway. "Got it."

Judtson looked at Kelsey. "He's fast."

Her meal still untouched, she stood and glanced back at him. "You have no idea."

▽

"Judtson, you cannot be serious. I was misled and incorrect in my statements on that show. You cannot release it. I forbid it!"

Judtson, utilizing a speakerphone for his call to Villarreal, winked at Saylor and answered, "Forbid it all you want, Carlos. I'm posting it on the Internet."

"You cannot! You must not, please. I will call my lawyer. I will obtain an injunction." The scientist's voice was verging on shrill.

Pausing for a moment, intending to convey that he was mulling over the request, Judtson finally spoke. "Carlos, tell you what, I'll compromise."

"Compromise? How?"

"Come up here. Come back into the studio with me and we can record another interview."

"You will run the new interview rather than the first?"

"No. I won't do that. But I will add your new comments to the end of the old one. That way, you'll have a chance to explain your position."

This time it was Villarreal's turn to pause. Without waiting for his decision, Judtson added, "It's not as if you had a choice. I'm going to release it either way. It runs either with or without the additional interview."

They heard a loud sigh of exasperation from the speaker. "Very well. I can be there tomorrow."

"Excellent. I'll book the studio time."

"Judtson, you promise me that you will not release the other until I arrive?"

"You have my word."

They broke the connection, and Judtson looked at Kelsey and Saylor. "At least we won't have to commit kidnapping in a foreign country now."

Saylor nodded. "It does make it easier. I'd better check with Wheeler and see if he's ready."

▽

With the Hummer parked in the passenger pick-up zone at Tucson International Airport, Judtson was standing on the sidewalk beside Romeo, waiting for Saylor to end his phone call. Nervous that Villarreal would arrive before they had a clear plan of action, he looked at his watch twice, glaring at Saylor between the time checks. Saylor feigned obliviousness and continued talking to Wheeler, his hand cupped in front of his mouth to prevent others from overhearing the details.

Terminating the call, he turned to Judtson. "He has it ready. Or rather, he hopes it's ready."

"What does that mean?" Irritation was clear in the question.

"How can he tell if it's going to work or not? He has modified a scanner to replicate the frequency shift that his diagnostics data gave him, but that doesn't necessarily guarantee it is going to work. What caused you to come back could've been something else, something which didn't even show up on the data."

Shrugging, Judtson admitted, "That's true. All right, we'll know when we try it on Carlos. And I still think your plan to tell him that we're taking him to the production studio and then just drive him to the lab is dumb. As soon as he sees where we've taken him, he's going to bolt."

Saylor stepped closer in an attempt to keep their conversation private on the busy walkway. "It's better than your ridiculous idea."

"What's wrong with mine? We tell him we need to make a brief stop at the lab on our way...."

"And then what? Remember, we need to inject him with the isotope. How are we going...?"

They were interrupted by Villarreal exiting the automatic doors. He was carrying a single small bag. After the greetings and introductions were over, the four men climbed into the Hummer, and Romeo navigated the serpentine lane out of the airport area.

As they drove north, Carlos and Judtson immediately engaged in a discussion which quickly became heated, with Villarreal continuing to attempt to dissuade him from releasing the video. As the two argued, Saylor, who sat in front, surreptitiously opened the small hinged case containing the hypodermic with the isotope. The debate in the rear seat continued until they reached the parking lot of the lab. It was now late in the day and there were no cars present.

Villarreal, noticing that they had parked, took in his surroundings and said, "Where are we? This is not the place where we did the other interview."

He then read the sign on the front of the building. "Radiology lab? Judtson, what is going on here?"

As Judtson fumbled with an explanation, Romeo slipped the gear shifter into park, unbuckled his shoulder harness, and twisted around in the seat. While Judtson was still talking, Jones, using his left arm, swung at Villarreal, catching him cleanly on the chin.

"Romeo, what the hell are you...?" Judtson started to protest.

"He's out," the big man said flatly. Turning back in his seat, he told Saylor, "Give him the shot. It needs to be in him an hour, right?"

"Uh, yeah," Saylor stammered, stunned by the sudden act.

"Then you'd better stick him."

Not certain whether Romeo would take his next swing at him, Saylor scrambled out of the passenger seat and exchanged places with Judtson, who was staring at Romeo in disbelief. In less than a minute, Saylor checked the unconscious Villarreal for a pulse, to make sure that the punch had not killed the man, and then injected the isotope. As he finished, Jones got out from the driver's side and opened the door beside the slack figure. Sliding one massive arm under Villarreal's legs and the other behind his back, he lifted the inert professor out of the Hummer, as a mother would pick up an infant.

"We need to get inside."

Both Judtson and Saylor reacted instantly, with Judtson slamming the door to the Hummer and following Jones toward the front doors of the lab. Saylor speed-dialed Wheeler's number as he hurried to keep up with the others. His call was answered on the second ring and he told Wheeler they were there. By the time the trio arrived at the entrance, their new accomplice was already unlocking the doors, his eyes widening when he saw Romeo toting the limp Villarreal.

"What the hell?"

Jones brushed past the sputtering Wheeler as Saylor explained, "We didn't have any choice.

He's just unconscious."

"I don't know about this," he muttered as he locked the doors behind the group.

Stopping to face him, Saylor spoke directly. "Matt, what did you expect? Did you think that we were going to be able to bring in these people and have them voluntarily climb up on your table? They've been altered. They're going to put up a fight."

"I know. I mean, I guess I knew that." His eyes darted to Romeo, who was patiently standing and holding Villarreal, whose head was lolling back like a rag doll's. "It's just...."

"I understand," Judtson said, forcing a calming tone into his voice. "It's a bit of a shock. But when we bring this man back from the purgatory he has been in, the last thing in the world he's going to want to do is complain or press charges. If anything, he's going to think you are a hero."

The technician, showing no sign of moving, stared at the unconscious professor and said nothing, his contemplation interrupted by Jones. "Where can I put him down?"

The matter-of-fact tone of the question ended his reverie, and Wheeler sprang forward. "Follow me."

They crossed the large waiting area and passed through a set of double doors. Wheeler led them down two corridors until they entered the same room where Judtson had received his scan.

"Lay him down on that table," he instructed, gesturing at the platform with the doughnut-shaped ring at one end. "How long has it been since the injection?"

"Only about ten minutes," Saylor answered, checking his watch as Romeo gently placed Villarreal on the table.

Taking a deep breath and letting it out slowly, Wheeler said, "Then we wait."

Judtson eyed the still figure. "What if he wakes up before we're ready?"

"I'll handle it," Romeo assured him in a barely audible voice.

Shaking his head hastily, Wheeler blurted, "No need for that."

He reached down and opened a compartment built into the side of the table, revealing stored straps. "We occasionally need these to restrain a patient for the scan. The rest of the time we keep them out of view. You know, for psychological reasons. They should hold him."

With a soft grunt, Romeo bent down and pulled out the straps, passing them over Villarreal's body, clicking them into the recessed receptacles on the other side, and pulling them snug.

"I think he's disappointed," joked Judtson in a whisper directed at Saylor.

▽

Wheeler, Judtson, and Saylor were behind the shielded glass, sitting at the same console where Saylor had observed Judtson's procedure with Robyn Reedy. Jones remained beside Villarreal, who had awakened to find himself strapped to the table. He, at first, protested loudly, but soon acquiesced to Romeo's persuasive presence and now lay quiet and still.

"Matt, has anyone heard from Robyn yet?"

"No," he answered Saylor, his face a mask of concern. "The police have been notified. She seems to have simply disappeared."

"Not sure what help they'll be," Judtson commented dryly.

Wheeler turned to him. "Do you think the bogus Homeland Security men killed her?"

"I wouldn't put it past them. Either that or they have her. They're holding her."

"Maybe converting her," Saylor suggested.

"Oh, my God!"

"I know," Judtson empathized. He looked down at his watch. "It has been almost an hour. I'm going to go out there and talk with Carlos for a minute before we do this."

"What good will that do?" asked Saylor.

"I don't mean *that* Carlos, the one on the table. I mean the one inside. I think I should let him know what we're about to do."

"We don't even know if this is going to work."

"That's true. But, believe me, the Carlos inside will be happy to know we're trying."

Judtson stood and left the room. As he approached the table, he could see an expression of pure hatred on the face of the supine man. Leaning forward directly over him, he stared into Villarreal's eyes.

"Carlos, I'm aware that you can hear me. I just wanted you to know that what they've done to you, they also did to me. I was locked up inside exactly like you."

The man on the table screamed up at him, "You're crazy! What are you talking about? You are all going to pay for...!"

Judtson gave a curt, meaningful look to Romeo, who stepped to the head of the table and placed his large hand over Villarreal's mouth. Bending down, the big man whispered into his ear. "One more word and you'll regret it. Shut up and let the man talk."

Heeding the warning, he stopped. Judtson continued, "We're only a few minutes away from trying to replicate the procedure which set me free."

The eyes of the man on the table conveyed panic and fear; however, he remained silent.

Reaching down to where the professor's hand was strapped to the table, Judtson placed his own hand on top of Villarreal's and squeezed it reassuringly. "This may or may not work. I hope it does. It should. But I wanted to let you know that we know. We know you are in there. And we won't give up until we can get you out."

For a moment he was certain that there had been a brief flicker of understanding...of relief; that, somehow, Carlos had managed to communicate that he understood what Judtson was saying.

Wheeler's voice came over the speaker. "We're ready. The two of you need to come in here."

Judtson looked down at the eyes one more time. "Here goes, Carlos. See you in a few minutes."

Releasing the man's hand, he and Romeo walked away, leaving Villarreal alone. When they joined the others, Wheeler had already commenced the preprogrammed scan. Tapping a final keystroke, he explained, "I decided that whatever it was that happened to Judtson had nothing to do with the PET sensors or the CT receivers."

"That makes sense," Saylor agreed. "They're passive."

"Right. We don't need either of them unless we want images of his brain. The only possibility was that whatever brought Judtson back was somehow a combination of the isotope and the modulated frequency of the x-ray emitter. To be thorough, I programmed the machine to start out at the correct, or normal, frequency and then to change to the other frequency at precisely the same point in the scan and for the same duration."

"Good idea. We don't know for sure which part of Judtson's scan actually did the trick."

"Exactly. It very well might have been the reaction of the isotope to the normal frequency and no one else they've converted has ever had a PET/CT before. It isn't that routine a test."

Wheeler leaned forward slightly and peered through the glass, as if trying to observe the invisible processes as they occurred. "It's a shame that we can't experiment with each step of the procedure to see which actually does the trick."

"Not this time. Maybe the next one."

Wheeler turned to Judtson. "I still can't believe I'm here doing this. I must be nuts. Well, for now let's hope this works. Then I'll think about the others."

No one had anything else to say, so they waited in silence until the computer beeped a single time and a box appeared on the screen, informing them that the programmed sequence had been completed.

Judtson, who had been watching the progress, dashed for the door before Wheeler could say a word. As he neared Villarreal, his pace slowed and his mind instantly filled with a jumble of doubts. *What if I'm insane? Delusional?* he thought to himself. *What if everything is explainable by that?*

He shook off the incertitude and quickened his pace once more, arriving at the table in seconds. Immediately stepping to the end of the platform where the cream-colored ring surrounded Villarreal's head, he looked down. Judtson's heart leapt when he saw his friend smiling up at him.

"Carlos?"

The man's grin broadened. "Thank you, *mi amigo*! *Gracias*."

Chapter 23

"**Y**OU KILLED THEM?" THE QUESTION ERUPTED FROM VILLARREAL as he listened to Judtson's description of the incident at his office.

"We did," Judtson answered cautiously, not knowing the man well enough to be able to predict his reaction to the violence.

"That is wonderful! From your description of them, they could very well be the same men who dispatched me to my personal hell. In my days of mental confinement, I have imagined countless deaths for those devils."

Judtson chuckled. "I understand, believe me."

After Villarreal's procedure, they had returned to the silo and the two of them were alone in the lounge.

"I have a thousand questions…."

"As do I. Please, go ahead, Carlos."

"How did you ever manage to recruit that man at the lab? What is his name?"

"Matt Wheeler."

"Yes, Mr. Wheeler. What is happening to us is macabre in the extreme. Even though I have gone through it myself, it is nearly impossible for me to believe. Convincing a stranger, a person in his position, must have been difficult."

Judtson thought back to the meeting he and Saylor had with the technician. "I don't think we would have been successful persuading him if he hadn't been on the receiving end of a visit from our friends in black."

"What do you mean?"

"From what I can tell, Matt is not the sort of man who cares to be pushed around. I think their heavy-handedness, not to mention the sudden disappearance of his colleague immediately after their visit, got his back up, so to speak."

Carlos nodded to indicate his understanding. "It is ironic, then, that we have them to thank for their assistance in recruiting the man."

"That it is."

In her typical bustle of color and motion, Kelsey burst through the doorway.

"Dr. Villarreal? I'm so glad you could join us."

"In more ways than one," Judtson added, provoking laughter from the others.

With an abruptness which seemed as though it would have hurt her, Kelsey dropped heavily into the chair opposite Carlos. At that same moment Villarreal rose from his to meet her, almost as if she were sitting at the other end of a teeterboard upon which he rested. Seeing his gentlemanly gesture, Kelsey sprang back to her feet just as he sat back down, continuing the playground illusion. He then rose again, this time synchronizing with her, and extended his hand, which she reached out to grasp.

Amused by the comical aerobic display and slightly out of breath, he said, "I understand that you are our gracious host. It is a pleasure to meet you, Miss...."

"Batman. Kelsey Batman."

"Miss Batman, of course."

Judtson concluded that Carlos either had never heard of the Caped Crusader or was a master of his expressions and inflections, as there was no hint of disbelief or amusement at the introduction. They were both finally seated.

Villarreal asked, "Am I correct to understand that there are others?"

Kelsey and Judtson briefed him the on the group of seven, including the names, as well as their respective fields of work or research. When they finished, Judtson commented, "I'm certain there is something that connects all of us."

Villarreal paused, pondering the information. "It would appear so."

"Obviously, everybody on the list knows something that the bad guys don't want to get out," Kelsey stated definitively.

The archaeologist sat back in the overstuffed wing-back chair, deep in thought. As he did, Judtson studied him, not for the first time fascinated by the differences between the two of them. Where he was tall, two inches above six feet, Carlos was no more than five-seven. His own hair was brown, fine, and unruly with a tendency to stick straight out from his head. Villarreal's was thick, black, neatly trimmed, and perfectly in place. His taste in attire gravitated toward blue jeans and sweatshirts; whereas, the archaeologist, when not immersed in the environment of a dig, seemed to prefer conservative tailored suits with vests, white shirts, and flawlessly knotted ties. Every time Judtson had seen him, Carlos had been cleanly shaved, even in the field; he himself was perpetually overdue for a beard and moustache trim. The only apparent commonalities between them were their age, both in their thirties, and their passion, verging on obsession, for uncovering the hidden truths in the world.

Kelsey interrupted the reverie. "Dr. Villarreal...."

"Carlos, please."

"Okay, Carlos, call me Kelsey. I want to make sure I understand everything. While you were 'fooks' Carlos...."

"*Fooks* Carlos?" interrupted Judtson.

With a smile, she explained, "I was having some work done at my place. Painting, mostly. And I had an idea that I got from a picture in a magazine. The title of the article was 'The Art of Faux Painting.' I showed it to the man I hired, who wasn't exactly the sharpest knife in the drawer, and he said, 'Oh, you want that wall fooks painted?' It was all I could do not to laugh out loud right in front of him, but it stuck in my head. Been using it ever since."

"Fooks, it is," Judtson acknowledged, chuckling.

"Anyway, Carlos, while you were fooks Carlos, you were telling the world that you had been the victim of a prank, that the Puma Punku stone didn't actually match the gap in the wall at Baalbek, and that the wall at Baalbek wasn't actually quarried andesite."

"That is correct. That was what my alter ego was propagating."

"Is any of that true? *Were* you deceived by your students?"

Villarreal's answer to her question was accompanied by a dismissive shake of his head. "Absolutely not."

She leaned even farther forward in her chair. "Please don't get me wrong, but how can that be? It seems like your students would have come forward when you began putting out this load of...propagation, both to protect their own reputations and because they would have known the truth."

"You are quite correct, Miss Batman. I am sorry, Kelsey. They did speak up. However, they all approached me, or I should say my alter ego, rather than daring to publicly oppose what I was saying. They were understandably upset at my public position."

"How did you handle that?"

"I told them the same thing I told everyone else, that there were cheats among them, and that we had all been deceived."

"Didn't they demand to know the identity of the so-called pranksters?"

Villarreal smiled. "My students do not *demand* from me. They are far too respectful. Of course, they did inquire. I merely told them that the investigation was ongoing and I could not disclose the names. Between the Puma Punku site and the Baalbek site, there had been a very large number of students involved, and many had rotated through the projects on one-month schedules. There was a large-enough pool of suspects that none of the students could successfully deduce anything."

"Makes sense. My other question is more on point to our current issue. I know that you had proved the stones used to build the lowest level of Baalbek were actually quarried and carved in Puma Punku, half a world away. I know that Judtson was going to spill the beans on this discovery."

"Very true."

"Well, no offense. That is a really cool fact and everything, but is keeping it a secret actually worth all of this?"

"No offense taken. That is the exact question I have been contemplating. And, no, I am not convinced that it is. As much as we all prefer to believe that our work is earthshaking in magnitude, the release of my findings would have caused quite a stir. Of that there is no doubt. Yet, it would hardly have been world changing."

Judtson spoke up. "Not on its own. If it were a piece of a puzzle...a very important piece...then it would justify the extreme measures the other side is taking."

"So, what's the rest of the puzzle? And who is the other side?"

"I don't know the answer to either question, Kelsey."

"Nor do I," offered Villarreal.

"But I do think we know where the other seven pieces are to be found."

Kelsey looked at him. "Obviously, you mean the other people on the list."

Judtson nodded that he did.

"So, it would appear," Villarreal said softly, "that our next order of business is to gather up the others and return them to our realm. At that point, hopefully, we would hold enough of the pieces to fit the puzzle together."

"I agree, Carlos. I don't see any other way to find out."

Kelsey swung her gaze back and forth between the two men before speaking. "I still can't believe we were able to get you here and turned back into the real deal without interference from the bad guys."

"I think you might have surprised them, Kelsey," Judtson speculated. "You are probably the wild card."

"Me? I don't get it."

"I'm sure they were keeping an eye on Saylor and me. I just don't think they expected us to have an ally with millions of dollars, untraceable vehicles, burn phones, and a missile silo."

Kelsey's grin was cut short as Judtson added, "But, now that we have Carlos and we've turned him back into the real Carlos, I don't think we can count on the other side being quite so passive from this point forward."

▽

The shop was eerily quiet this time of night, Wheeler thought. He sat perched on a tall stool at one of the work benches in the normally bustling testing and repair facility of RadTech, in the island of light produced by the motion-activated, lay-in fluorescent fixture above. His mind was still reeling from the dramatic recovery of Carlos Villarreal earlier in the evening.

"What have I gotten myself into?" he asked himself, his voice unnaturally loud in the deserted workshop.

Shaking off the self-induced jitters, he focused on the monitor, which was displaying, in parallel windows, two sets of diagnostics data: the first from the original event, the recovery of Judtson Kent; and the second from tonight's event, the restoration of Dr. Villarreal. He studied the synchronized stream of numbers and lines, satisfying himself that his programming had flawlessly replicated the first set.

Once he was certain he had created a valid baseline for future applications, Wheeler slid off the stool and moved to the lead-lined testing chamber, triggering successive overhead lights to flicker on as he walked across the room. He opened the shielded door and entered. Resting on the work bench in the center of the small chamber was a device which appeared to have been assembled by the science club at a high school. With perforated flat straps made from a heavy nylon hybrid, he had fashioned an adjustable half-dome, upon which he had mounted two black boxes and an array of sensors. Wiring sprouted from each of the components, which was what gave the device its Rube Goldberg appearance.

He double-checked all of the connections and placed the device upon the Styrofoam mannequin head. With a final visual once-over, he backed out of the chamber and closed the door, returning to his work bench. Using the mouse, he minimized the data display and opened the control interface.

"Here goes!"

With an exaggerated flourish, he tapped a key and watched as the program actuated his device. The feedback from the sensors began instantaneously; however, until he could run the software comparing it to the baseline, he would have no idea if his impromptu invention was functioning properly.

As he waited, the cell phone Romeo had given him began to vibrate in his pocket, causing him to jump. Fumbling, he pulled it out and answered, "Yes," proud of himself for remembering not to use his own name the way he normally answered calls.

"Yo, it's J.K."

Wheeler chuckled at the silliness of the amateurish subterfuge. "How's our friend?"

"Awesome."

"That's great. What's up?"

"Oh, you weren't sleeping, were you?"

Wheeler laughed into the phone. "After the evening I had, no way."

"Well, we were talking and realized that things are probably going to escalate at this point."

"What does that mean?"

"We've decided that we've been fairly lucky so far. In terms of visits from our friends. But now our luck is sure to change."

A chill traveled up Wheeler's spine as he heard the clumsy warning. He reached out and manipulated the mouse, minimizing the current window and clicking through the menu until he found the icon for the building's security cameras. "What do you think is going to happen?"

As he asked the question, the monitor filled with a tiled mosaic of video feeds from multiple cameras inside and outside the building.

"Don't know. Just to be safe, maybe you should move in with us."

His eyes scanned the small thumbnails. "I don't...wait a sec."

He shifted the mouse quickly and clicked on one of the outside views, which expanded to fill the screen. The exterior building-mounted cameras were capable of low-light images. What he saw startled him.

"What's happening?"

Rolling his finger on the mouse wheel, he zoomed in on one particular view of the parking lot.

"Jud...I mean, J.K., I think they're here."

"WHAT?" Judtson's shouted reaction was so loud, it stung Matt's ear.

"I'm looking at a video feed from the parking lot, and a black SUV is sitting there, on the opposite side of the lot from where my car is parked."

"You're not home?"

"No. I came back to work. I'm working on...." He stopped himself, not wanting to broadcast his efforts through the airwaves. "Never mind that. I had some work to do."

He heard Judtson move the phone away from his mouth and bark something unintelligible to another person, followed by a muted answer from the other voice before Judtson came back to the conversation. "Okay, we have people on their way. Are you locked in?"

"Oh, yeah. Locked in, and I've got cameras displaying both entrances and the hallway between me and the outside."

The tension in Judtson's voice was palpable over the phone. "They're all clear?"

Wheeler switched back to the multiple-view screen, and his eyes raced to scan all of the images. "I don't see anyone. Just the SUV. They must be waiting inside the truck for me to come out."

"As I said, we have people on their way. Same address where we met?"

"Right."

"You might want to grab what you need from there and get ready to hit the road. I've never asked you this before...do you have a wife or kids?"

"Nope. Just me."

"Good."

"I never thought so until now."

"Put the phone on speaker mode and stick it in your pocket. Start gathering whatever you want to take. Unfortunately, we're not very close to you, but at this time of night we should make good time. And keep an eye on those cameras."

"Got it."

Wheeler kept the video feeds on the main monitor and moved the test he was running to a second screen. The program was complete, and he saved the data to a flash drive on his key ring and shut down the prototype. Hurrying, he crossed the room and reentered the chamber. He efficiently disconnected the power and data feeds from his creation and snatched it up from the bench, leaving it mounted on the foam head. Cradling it against his chest, he dashed across the shop, weaving around the numerous work benches which were loaded with miscellaneous electronics in various stages of disassembly, and activating one ceiling light after another.

He reached the equipment closet and found a large metal Pelican case. Kneeling, he placed the case on the floor and opened it awkwardly with his free hand. Designed for the transporting of sensitive gear, the Pelican was lined with soft foam, sculpted in the pattern of the bottom of an egg carton. He laid the head, with his device still mounted, on its side and tentatively lowered the lid to determine if it would close. It did. Stretching up to the shelf, he pulled down a bin filled with an assortment of soft foam pieces, and padded the open space around the head, then slowly closed the lid again, this time latching it, and grabbed the handle.

Standing, he left the closet and returned to his work bench. With a quick check of the cameras, he saw that nothing had changed, and set about gathering the balance of what he thought he might need.

▽

Romeo parked the black Hummer, his own vehicle, a block away from the address Judtson had given him. The sound system was loudly playing *Carmina Burana* by the New York Philharmonic. He switched it off and turned to face Luis.

"Straightforward approach. You take the passenger side, and I'll take the driver's."

Luis chuckled. "Are we polite tonight? Do we knock?"

Grinning broadly, Romeo felt between the bucket seats and retrieved two steel bars, handing one to Luis.

"Sure. We knock. With these."

The men exited the truck, not concerned about being visible from the interior light as it had been disabled earlier. Romeo slipped his cell phone out of his pocket and called Kelsey.

"Yes," she answered brusquely, expecting his call.

"Are we in contact with our man inside?"

Kelsey, sitting next to Judtson, answered, "We are."

"Everything still cool?"

"As a cucumber. No change. No movement."

"Let him know we're here."

"Roger that," she answered, relishing the opportunity to use military lingo.

▽

"Hey," Judtson shouted into his mouthpiece to get Wheeler's attention.

"No need to shout. Had the phone right by my ear."

"You ready?"

"Yep. Got everything I might need."

"Okay. They are there. Be ready to move. Or, if it goes the wrong way, be ready to run."

"Goes the wrong…?"

"Don't worry. It won't. But be ready."

"All right," Wheeler answered, not at all calmed by Judtson reassurances.

He zoomed in on the view of the SUV and initially saw nothing other than the vehicle. He was about to ask Judtson if his people had the right address, when suddenly, from the left edge of the screen, he saw first one figure and then a second slowly approaching the black truck from the rear. It was nearly impossible to see them; they were wearing dark clothing and had some sort of black covering over their faces. The two more accurately resembled shadows as they closed the distance to their target.

"I hope the folks in that SUV aren't just a couple of teenagers who decided to use my parking lot for a make-out session."

"That makes two of us," Judtson answered.

Wheeler watched with fascination, amazed that, despite the grainy image, poor lighting, and absence of a dramatic soundtrack, the reality of what was happening was much more powerful than any suspense movie he had ever seen. He guessed that one of the two men was probably the huge specimen who had brought Villarreal into the lab earlier in the day, or yesterday at this point as he looked at the time display on the screen. He had no idea who the second shadow was, but watched as they separated behind the SUV and, crouching down, duck-walked forward until they were beside the rear seat doors.

From the angle of the camera and the orientation of the parked vehicle, Matt was able to see both sides of the truck as the two men sprang into violent action.

▽

Romeo made a soft clicking sound with his tongue when he was in position. Waiting until he heard an acknowledgment from his partner, he rose up, the steel bar already in position behind his head. With a single swing, the window on the door to the backseat exploded. Through the interior, he could see that Luis had timed his swing almost perfectly. Having had the same concern as Wheeler, Romeo was relieved to see that the front seat was occupied not by teenagers, but by two grown men who, both startled at the force of the sudden crashes, were twisting in their seats to face the rear.

Romeo did not wait to see if they were drawing weapons. Dropping the bar on the pavement, he reached inside the compartment and shoved the muzzle of his pistol against the driver's cheek, aware from his peripheral vision that Luis had done the same to the man in the passenger seat.

"Don't move," he growled. "Put your hands up where we can see them. Now!"

The two men slowly raised their hands. Luis saw that the man on the passenger side had managed to grab his own gun in the split seconds after the glass had shattered, and was still holding it in his right hand.

"Reach back and hand me that gun," he instructed. "Keep it pointed at your own head the whole time and do it slowly."

Despite their circumstances, the driver decided to speak. "You two have no idea what you're dealing with."

Romeo shifted his gun away from direct contact with the man, to prevent any temptation he had to go for it, and leaned farther into the cab. His deep voice, coming just inches from the stranger's ear, murmured, "Neither do you."

The man on the passenger side, reacting in slow motion and keeping the barrel of his gun pointed at his own head throughout the process, moved the pistol to the space beside the headrest, where Luis, using his free hand, grabbed it and shoved it into one of the pockets on his vest.

"Now," Luis barked at his man, "put your hands on top of your head and bend forward so that your face is pressed against the dashboard."

The stranger complied, and Luis stretched his arm over the seat, pushing the button on the inside of the front door, opening all of the door locks.

"Watch him," Luis grunted at Romeo, then backed out of the rear window and roughly pulled open the front door.

"Out and down. Now!"

The man climbed from the truck, keeping his hands on top of his head, and took a single step toward Luis.

"I said *down*! On the pavement. Face first."

Keeping his gun trained on the stranger, Luis grabbed a nylon zip cuff from one of his vest pockets as the man clumsily dropped to his knees. Pretending to lose his balance and fall forward, the stranger suddenly pulled a knife out from a sheath concealed under his back collar and thrust it forward and upward at Luis, ramming it into his chest.

The sudden movement and the sharp shout of surprise from Luis provided the distraction the driver had been waiting for. Unable to see Romeo from his position, the man assumed that he would be looking at his partner at that moment. He jerked the handle on his door, flinging himself out as his hand dived under his coat for his 9mm, and hoping that Romeo, whose large frame was still jammed into the rear window, would be unable to react quickly, leaving him vulnerable.

The driver tumbled from the tall SUV, twisting as he fell to the asphalt, landing heavily on his right shoulder, and rolling onto his back. Ignoring the flash of pain from the impact, he saw that Romeo had backed out of the window opening and was turning to face him. He pulled the trigger hastily and his shot ricocheted off the rear door next to the big man. He swung the barrel to the right and again pulled the trigger, but this time his shot was matched with a muzzle flash from the gun in Romeo's hand. The .45 caliber slug slammed into the stranger's chest like a piledriver, shredding his arteries and lung, and continuing on its path until it struck the solid pavement behind. Its kinetic energy unspent, the now-deformed lead projectile bounced upward and severed the man's spine, before lodging in his heart and bringing it to an abrupt halt.

Romeo, staggered by the intense pain in his chest from the man's second shot, rushed around the front bumper to the passenger side of the truck, where he found the other stranger lying on his back in the parking lot, his face bloodied, and Luis leaning against the side of the SUV, staring down at him.

"You okay?" Romeo asked his partner.

Luis looked up and grinned. "Glad we wore these," he answered, pointing at the partially exposed MTV under his sliced shirt.

He saw Romeo grimace and grab the side of his chest. "What about you?"

The Army Ranger leaned against the fender of the truck and rubbed the area where the bullet had struck him. "Same thing. Except mine stopped a bullet instead of a knife. Man, a 9-millimeter shot from three feet away hurts like hell! Your guy alive?"

Luis stepped closer to the supine figure. "Pretty sure he is. All I did was kick him in the face."

Romeo glanced down at the steel-toe boots on his partner's feet. "Oh, that's all? You'd better check for a pulse."

"Will do. Cover me in case he's faking."

Romeo still held his gun and brought it to bear on the man. "I don't think he's faking, but you're covered."

As Luis, careful to remain out of the line of fire, bent over and felt the stranger's neck, Romeo pulled out his phone with his free hand and speed-dialed Kelsey's number. She answered on the first ring.

"You guys are awesome!"

Allowing himself a smile, Romeo answered, "That's right…we're on camera." He turned and waved at the security camera mounted at the corner of the building.

"Hello," Kelsey said into the phone. "Just as you guys arrived, Wheeler streamed the feed to us. We've been watching from here."

"Great! Now I can't make up a story about why I didn't bring these two in unharmed the way you wanted."

"Hey, I saw the whole thing. You're cool! But you should have taken out the driver sooner."

"Almost did. When he was bolting out the door, I could've put a round in him through the seat back. Except that I thought I could grab him while he was breathing."

"You shouldn't have cut it so close. He just about got you."

"Naw. I had the vest on."

"Romeo, dammit, he was on the ground…shooting up at you. He could've shot you…lower…below the vest. Next time, play it safer."

He grinned and shook his head. "Okay, boss."

Then he glanced at Luis, who nodded silently.

"It seems that the other one is still with us."

"Bring him in, but zipper him up first."

"Will do. It's time to tell our friend inside to grab whatever he wants to take with him and meet me in the lot outside the front door."

Kelsey spoke with Judtson for a moment before she came back. "He just killed the video feed. He's on his way."

▽

Judtson and Kelsey were waiting outside the entrance shack when the black Hummer pulled in after the incident. Romeo parked close to the door and was the first to hop out of the vehicle. As Kelsey headed to his side, Judtson, seeing Wheeler climb down from the passenger seat, moved to meet him.

"Welcome to our base, Matt."

Wheeler was opening the rear door and grabbing a metal case and a large duffel bag. He turned back to face Judtson, eyeing the tiny concrete structure with the single door.

"We're all going to fit in there?"

Laughing, Judtson answered, "Looks are deceiving. Here, let me help you with that stuff," and extended his hand toward the metal case.

Matt swung it out of his reach and handed him the carryall. "You can carry this if you'd like. Thanks."

As he took the duffel from Wheeler, Judtson noticed that Luis and Romeo were pulling a stiff vinyl bag from the open rear hatch.

Jerking his head in that direction, he asked Wheeler, "I assume that's our hostage?"

"Yep. My two escorts weren't much on answering questions on the way here. What's with the bag?"

Judtson turned and moved toward the shack, replying as he walked, "I asked Kelsey the same thing. It's shielded in case the man has any kind of tracking device on him."

"Smart."

Judtson glanced back at the others. "She didn't tell me how he could breathe in that thing."

"There's a breathing tube through it. I saw them tape a mouthpiece on him before they closed it up."

He shook his head in response. "Good way to keep him quiet, too."

They reached the inside of the shack just as Kelsey caught up with them. Judtson performed the introductions. "Matt Wheeler, Kelsey Batman."

Kelsey extended her hand. "It's a pleasure to meet you, Matt. We owe you quite a bit for bringing back Judtson and Carlos."

Shifting the steel case to his left hand, he shook hands with her. Eyeing the descending staircase caused him to break into a grin. "Okay. I get it. This is the Batcave."

She tilted her head back and laughed, the sound reverberating inside the concrete and steel structure. "I hadn't thought of that."

"Must have been the subconscious motive for buying it," offered Judtson.

Before she could answer, Romeo came to the doorway, the plastic-encased figure casually slung over his shoulder, and saw that the three of them were blocking his access to the stairs. "Maybe we could move this little chat down below."

▽

With their hostage secured in an alcove at the bottom of the actual missile silo in the complex and his injury treated, the group, except for Romeo and Luis, gathered in the lounge and were joined by Saylor. After he was brought up to date by the others, he noticed the metal case.

"What did you bring us, Matt?"

Wheeler, who still had the residual traces of bewilderment in his eyes from the night's series of events, clicked open the latches on the case and lifted the lid as he spoke. "After our procedure with Carlos, I started thinking about the logistics of doing it that way seven more times on people who were all over the country."

With a mischievous smirk, Kelsey said, "You mean the thought of us flying around kidnapping people and bringing them to your lab bothered you?"

"A little. I thought it might be easier if we could make the actual working guts of the thing portable."

He pulled out the mannequin head with the jumble of boxes and wires attached, and placed it on the table.

"It's not pretty. If RadTech were going to sell it, we'd have a lot of work to do on the case or helmet or whatever we'd call it, but it has the x-ray emitters…capable of the identical output as the big machine."

"That's amazing," Judtson murmured. "How were you able to make it so compact?"

"Couple of reasons. The first one is presentation. It's a trick my company learned years ago from the people who made and sold electronics like stereos, VCRs and, later, DVRs to the general public. Ever open one of those up? The case is quite a bit bigger than needed to house the actual components inside."

"Why?" asked Kelsey.

"If you are trying to get a person to shell out a few hundred dollars for your machine, it has to *look* as if it's worth the money. Same thing in the field of medical equipment, except the numbers are quite a bit larger. If you are asking a radiology lab or a hospital to pony up half a million bucks for a CT scan, it'd better look like a machine out of an episode of *Star Trek*."

Judtson chuckled. "I guess that makes sense."

"Anyway, that's only one of the reasons I could make it so small. The other one is that the PET/CT has several components we don't need. The big doughnut-shaped ring, which surrounds you as you're lying on the table, has these x-ray emitters inside, but it also has the sensors which pick up the radiation from the isotope absorbed in your brain cells. We don't have a need for that. Additionally, it has the x-ray receiver. That is mounted on the precise opposite point of the ring to catch the x-rays as they exit. And last, the whole setup, x-ray emitter and receiver, rotates with the ring, shooting pictures as it goes. That's how we get the 3-D finished product."

"And none of that is needed either."

"Right," he acknowledged Judtson. "All we need are these little black boxes." As he spoke, he pointed at the two rectangular cases mounted to the straps. "However, there is one issue with portability."

"Shielding the personnel?" offered Saylor.

"Exactly. When we do the CT scan, the tech is on the other side of a lead-shielded wall."

"I've always wondered about that. Why are they hiding behind a lead wall while I'm lying on the table being blasted by x-rays?"

"A lot of people do wonder about it, Kelsey. It all comes down to dosage. When you get a normal x-ray or even a CT scan which, at the heart of it, is still an x-ray, you are being exposed to about the same amount of radiation as you get on a cross-country flight at 30,000 feet. That's considered to be a safe level of exposure. The tech, on the other hand, is performing several tests a day, day in and day out. That exposure is much greater."

"Isn't there damage to you every time you get an x-ray?"

He smiled at her. "Yes, there is. Cells, and even DNA, have self-repairing mechanisms. It is believed that the level of damage which occurs from a single x-ray is minimal enough that the body can repair it. Unfortunately, the genetic and cellular damage done by x-rays is cumulative. If we didn't shield the technicians, their bodies would never be able to keep up with the damage."

"Matt, can't we wrap this thing with a shield?" asked Saylor.

Wheeler, using both hands, lifted the mannequin head and handed it to him, explaining, "There's a weight issue."

Hefting it, Saylor commented, "You're not kidding. What is this, about twenty pounds?"

"Not quite. Sixteen. And I should be able to get that down some. I'm just not sure we can add sufficient shielding to this and not make it so heavy that it's unwieldy."

Saylor set it down on the table. "What's the alternative? As we travel around and do this to the rest of the people on the list, do we simply plan on seven or eight exposures and hope for the best?"

"No. You've all seen the heavy lead vests they put on patients at dental offices."

Saylor and the others nodded.

"The key with x-rays is that they travel in a straight line. I haven't installed this component on the device yet, but I was planning on mounting small laser pointers, aimed outward in the directions of travel of the x-rays as they exit the patient's head."

"So we either stay out of the line of fire or make sure we have the lead vests on to protect us?"

"Right. It's not one-hundred-percent perfect. For only seven procedures, it should be fine."

"Don't x-rays go right through walls?" Kelsey asked. "What about other people nearby?"

Saylor answered her. "As he said earlier, each one is comparable to a cross-country commercial flight. Someone casually exposed won't be getting any more harmful a dose than our subject."

"And distance is a factor," Matt added. "The farther the x-rays travel, the more diffuse the beam, the weaker the dosage."

Kelsey nodded. "We probably shouldn't strap this thing on one of our targets in the middle of a crowded room."

"That's probably a good idea," Judtson laughed. "If only from a PR perspective."

Chapter 24

JUDTSON TOOK A SIP FROM HIS COFFEE, watched the late-morning pedestrians as they hurried past the sidewalk café where he was waiting for Kelsey, and thought over the two days since Matt Wheeler had arrived at the silo. The engineer had huddled up with Scott, who helped him put the finishing touches on the headset. They had managed to obtain more equipment and were able to fabricate two additional devices. Unfortunately, they had no way to test Wheeler's invention and would not know if it worked until it was tried on their first subject.

With a final strategy meeting in the lounge, they had broken up into groups, each outfitted with two lead vests, a headset, a laptop, and three syringes filled with FDG, the spares in case of a problem. Saylor, paired with Villarreal, was traveling to California to meet with, and hopefully convert, the former astronaut on the list. Ricky, Matt, and Romeo were already situated in New York and were planning how they would approach the television producer. Judtson and Kelsey had checked into a hotel in Washington, D.C. last night, which, according to Scott, was the same hotel where the author from the list was currently staying.

"It's not even nine yet and it's already horribly humid! I hate this place."

Judtson looked up to see Kelsey arriving, and smiled at her. "A little different from Tucson."

"Different? This is vile. By the time I got dressed after my shower, I felt like I needed another one. How can people live here?"

She took the other chair at his small table and continued, "I think this is why our politicians are so screwed up…their brains are rotting from the dampness."

Judtson laughed. "Or they are so miserable here that they take it out on us."

He glanced down at her T-shirt, which was plastered against her skin. The printed message for this morning was "I know the voices in my head aren't real…but they sure have some great ideas!"

"Where do you get these shirts? How many do you have?"

"The shirt-of-the-month club. So what's the plan for today?"

Judtson reached into his pocket and pulled out a small envelope. "Clarkson is an author. I'm an author. I casually bump into him, invite him to the bar for a drink, and slip him this. He passes out, and we take him up to my room."

"You sound pretty confident. Is this your usual dating technique?"

He ignored her and resumed, "And once we get him up there, we give him a shot of FDG, wait an hour, and zap him. I do have a question, though. I know he was on the CDC list, but what do we know about him? How do we know he has been converted?"

"That sounded like two questions," she quipped, and leaned closer to speak in a softer voice. "Scott did some more digging. He was able to access the file on Clarkson from the CDC. It wasn't much help. But the guy had a blog and that was the tip-off. As we already knew, he was the author who collaborated on *Secret Agenda*."

"The Copeland book."

"Right. Their book was already released, so it didn't have anything to do with their conversions. But I guess that several times in interviews and on his blog, Clarkson and Copeland both talked about their follow-up book, which was really supposed to blow the lid off things."

"Okay."

"Right after Clarkson started to complain to his doctor about the same symptoms you had...you know, his body not paying any attention to him...all of a sudden he announced on his blog that he wasn't going to release the next book. Said it was all rubbish and that he and Copeland had dropped the whole thing."

"Sounds familiar."

"Yes, it does. Enough to be convincing?"

"I think so. I hope so. If we're wrong...if we slip this man a roofie, take him up to my room, pump him full of a radioactive isotope, bombard his skull with x-rays...and nothing happens, we are going to have one ticked-off author who is going to go straight to the police and file kidnapping charges against us."

"I never dreamed," she said, smiling, "when I followed you that night during your paintball prank, that I would be getting into such an exciting adventure."

He returned the smile. "It's probably a little early to describe all of this as an exciting adventure. It might turn out to be something fairly horrible before it's over. Especially if we end up in a federal prison somewhere."

Judtson noticed as he finished his comment that the lighthearted amusement on her face changed subtly, nearly imperceptibly, into something else. She reached across the small table and very slowly and deliberately placed her hand on top of his. Her eyes, normally flitting rapidly from one point to another, fixed intently upon his. "Maybe. Either way, it has been worth it."

The direction of the sudden shift in the tone of the conversation was unmistakable. Setting down his cup of coffee, he put his other hand on hers. "I thought you said you hated me."

He expected to elicit a laugh. Instead, her eyes widened slightly as she leaned even closer to him. "I did." Her voice was deeper, throaty. "Maybe I still do. But there's always a fine line." He felt her hand gently squeeze his.

"Between love and hate?"

The grin returned, its message much different from the last. "Love? Who said anything about love?"

The intensity of her directness was disconcerting. "Now I know how the mouse feels."

She arched one eyebrow. "What mouse?"

"The one trapped in a corner by a cat who has decided to play with it for a while."

"I wouldn't mind playing a little."

Unbidden, the image of Kristen, standing before him and crying, painted itself on the canvas of his mind. Taking in a deep breath and releasing it slowly, Judtson spoke, his tone conveying the message more clearly than his words. "Not now, Kelsey."

He expected an angry reaction or, at the minimum, irritation at being rebuffed. What she did surprised him as she rose from her seat and leaned over the table, kissing him lightly on the forehead. As she lowered herself back into the chair, Kelsey delicately extricated her hand from his and said, "I understand."

▽

Hearing the timid tapping on the door of his suite, Romeo set aside his well-worn copy of Jack London's *White Fang* and crossed the room. Peering through the peephole, he saw that it was Ricky in the hallway, glancing furtively from left to right. Grinning to himself, he abruptly jerked open the door, causing his team member to skittishly jump back.

Deadpan, he asked, "Nervous, Ricky?"

Taking a tentative step forward, his face slightly flushed, Ricky answered, "Of course I'm nervous."

Moving to the side, Romeo gestured for his visitor to enter. "Come on in."

Ricky brushed past so swiftly that Romeo felt a swirl of air wash over him. He closed the door and followed.

"You'd better sit down."

Pacing briskly, his heavy combat boots thumping loudly on the floor, Ricky said, "I don't think I can." The slender bundle of pent-up energy glanced down at the table beside the chair and saw the opened book. "You've been *reading*? How can you *do* that?"

Romeo dropped back into the seat. "It's a skill I learned early. I think it was first, maybe second grade. I don't remember."

"I mean *now*?" Ricky was executing a tight circuit back and forth in front of the big man, causing Romeo's head to swivel to follow him. "With what's going on and what we are planning to do, how can you calmly sit and read a book?"

"Ricky, if you don't sit down right now, I'm going to break one of your legs."

The words froze him in place. "You're joking! You are joking? Right?"

Romeo did not answer, his face a mask of impassivity.

Jerkily, Ricky's head twisted around in a rapid survey of his immediate surroundings, his eyes alighting upon a straight-back chair at the table. "I'll get that chair."

He nearly dashed to it and dragged it close to where Romeo was sitting, turning it to face the man and sitting down, barely touching the cushion.

"Move back a little, Ricky. That's too close."

"Oh, sure!"

Jumping up, he adjusted the chair a few inches and sat again.

"That's an improvement. Now, take ten very slow, very deep breaths, blowing each one out through tightly pursed lips even more slowly."

Ricky was only halfway through the first inhale when Romeo, the volume of his voice a notch up, ordered, "I said slowly!"

Gulping the air already in his mouth and exhaling quickly, Ricky began again, this time more compliantly. As he performed the exercise, the big man softly counted each breath aloud until the desired number had been reached.

"Feel better now?"

Blinking, Ricky seemed to take an internal inventory before answering. "Somewhat."

"Excellent. By the way, what's with the combat boots? Last time I saw you, you were wearing regular slip-ons."

Ricky glanced down at his feet. "I got them from Scott. He told me they'd be better for what I was going to be doing in the field."

A slight smile curved Romeo's lips. "From Scott, huh?"

"Will you answer my question now?"

"Which was?"

"How can you be so calm? We're about to commit kidnapping."

"No, we're not."

"Of course we are! We're going to nab a female television producer against her will, shoot her full of some radioactive chemical, and strap an x-ray machine on her head. That's kidnapping and God knows what other offenses."

Romeo shook his head in disagreement. "Ricky, it isn't kidnapping. It's a rescue mission."

"What...?"

Holding up his hand to silence his companion, Romeo asked, "Do you think Dr. Villarreal wants to press charges against us?"

"Well, no. He actually stopped me in the hallway at the silo and thanked me...and I had nothing to do with his...conversion."

"Rescue. It wasn't a conversion. It wasn't a procedure. It wasn't a kidnapping. It was a rescue. The bad guys took him and locked him up, albeit inside his own head, but they locked him up nonetheless. We busted him out. Now we're going to do the same thing for this poor woman. Think about it, Ricky. Remember what Judtson said – how he was a passenger inside his own skull, frantically trying to figure a way out. Dr. Villarreal described the same thing. And this woman we're here to rescue, although she might seem normal on the outside, is going berserk right now, feeling as if she's trapped in there forever."

The steady cadence of his words had a slight calming effect. "I understand that, I guess. No, I do. It doesn't guarantee that until we convert her back, she isn't going to resist. And then there are the others."

"What others? The bad guys?"

"Oh! Nuts! I didn't even think about them. No. I meant other people. We might not be able to get to her alone. There might be someone nearby who decides to be a hero or something. Then what?"

"By the time we make our move, all of those concerns will have been addressed. That's why it is critical that we put together a good plan."

"And why me? I can understand why you're here. This is what you do. And having Matt with us makes sense. It's his machine. Why did Judtson and Kelsey send *me* on this...mission?"

One corner of Romeo's mouth curled up in a sly smile. "They didn't. I requested you."

"What? You requested me? Why me? I'm no commando or mercenary or whatever the right term is."

"I heard what you did before I arrived at Judtson's office. You were the one who saved him. You were the one who put the round on the target when it needed to be done. That's why."

"But that was different. It just happened. I didn't plan it."

"I know. And that's exactly the kind of person I need on my team...someone, when the stuff hits the fan, whose first instinct is to take care of business, not panic or run away."

Ricky stared at the big man for a minute, in an attempt to read him, to determine the sincerity of his words. "You really did request me? Why not Luis?"

Romeo nodded. "We need him to remain at the silo with the others and with our prisoner. I wanted someone back there with experience, just in case."

▽

Despite all of the time Luis had spent at the missile installation, standing at the bottom of the silo itself provoked a disquieting feeling in him. His mind knew that he was surrounded by steel plating and massively thick concrete walls. He was aware of the fact that the top of the cylinder was covered and sealed with the horizontal track-mounted blast door. He was, in fact, hiding within one of the best-fortified locations in the world. Yet, when he emerged from the connecting passageway and stepped onto the steel platform, descending the wall-mounted stairs to the bottom, his treads reverberating with each step, he felt irrationally vulnerable.

Intellectually, he surmised that it was a primitive reaction to being at the bottom of a hole; that the vast open tube created the illusion in his subconscious mind of being trapped in a well, easy prey to anything above. However, this analysis did not ameliorate his mild case of jitters as he approached their hostage, who was handcuffed, tied, and taped to the side of a perforated structural-steel column. Shaking off his unsettled feeling, he circled around the man to face him, sidestepping to avoid the tripod-mounted video camera.

Silently, he studied the stranger as if hoping to garner a clue about the man, his mission, or his superiors, purely from his appearance. When he and Romeo had brought their captive guest here, they had stripped him down to his underwear before binding him to the column. Every aspect of the stranger was noteworthy only in that it fit within societal and biological norms. He was only slightly more than average height. His build, while fit and trim, was not overly muscular; his brown hair, trimmed so as not to be conspicuously short or long; his face, clean-shaven. His eye color was brown, as well, and the two normally revealing windows to the psyche were calm, steady, and placid. He bore no tattoos or other markings. As Luis stood in front of him, the stranger displayed no interest in his captor whatsoever.

Luis was yet again surprised by the demeanor of their unwilling guest. The man was trussed up tightly, kept vertical, deprived of any food or water, and wearing around his neck a modified dog-training collar which had been designed to keep him awake by providing an electrical shock each time his head sagged down from fatigue or the onset of sleep. Still, the expression on his face was utterly quotidian, as though he were standing on a subway platform waiting for his train.

"Hi, Bob."

Luis, having no idea what the stranger's name actually was, as there had been no identification on his person, adopted one for conversational purposes.

"Brought you some tea. Thirsty?"

The stranger's eyes did not deign to meet his as Luis spoke.

"I imagine that you are. Here you go."

Reaching into a large pouch slung around his waist, Luis pulled out a plastic bottle filled with a brown liquid. He approached the man from the side while unscrewing the lid. Careful to keep his hands and arms out of biting range, he held the container up to the prisoner's lips, but the man did not open them. There was no noticeable resistance or hostility from the stranger, no tightening of the lip muscles to keep out the mouth of the bottle. His face was as passive during the act of defiance as that of an infant who was simply not thirsty at the moment the nipple of a bottle was put to his mouth.

Luis allowed himself to feel a small bit of professional admiration for the stranger, knowing that the man must certainly be very thirsty at this point in his captivity.

"Come on, open up," he urged gently.

The hostage did not respond. Adding slight pressure, Luis insinuated the tip of the bottle between the man's lips and tilted the bottom slowly upward, allowing some of the liquid to flow into the stranger's mouth. There was no show of machismo to spit it out, no overt rebelliousness. The man's mouth was simply relaxed, allowing the tea to run out the sides and dribble down the front of his body.

Lowering the bottle, Luis shrugged. "Okay. Thought we'd do it the easy way. Guess not."

He tossed the bottle casually to the side and it skittered across the concrete floor, slipping its contents as it rolled and leaving a dark stain in its path. Overlapping echoes created the aural illusion of a multitude of tumbling containers. Reaching back into his pouch, Luis first removed a full-face breathing mask, sliding it over the top of his own head but leaving it up, resting upon his forehead. He then extracted a pair of nitrile gloves and pulled them on, giving each a final snap for dramatic effect.

"Bob, have you ever heard of Devil's Breath?"

As he spoke, he closely watched his prisoner's eyes for a reaction. There was none.

"Nasty drug. It's getting pretty popular on the streets. It's a natural variant of scopolamine. I know that you know what that is, the old so-called truth serum. Well, the punks in the neighborhoods have really latched onto this stuff. You can put it in a drink. You can add it to a cigarette. And once somebody ingests it, that person is your slave. There was a kid in New York who was offered a cigarette at a bar. Next thing he knew, he was sitting on the floor of his apartment the next day. His place was completely emptied of everything – his computer, his TV, his furniture, his clothes, all of it. The place was stripped bare. He went downstairs and asked the doorman if he had seen anyone toting out his stuff, and the doorman said that he had, that four men loaded it all on an unmarked moving truck. When the kid asked why he didn't stop them or call the cops, the doorman told him because he…the kid…had been one of the four.

"And the kid didn't remember any of it. Not a bit. You can use Devil's Breath to get someone else to commit a crime for you. They think that you can even get a person who's on the stuff to murder somebody for you."

Luis pulled out what appeared to be a respirator with an attached neoprene bag, and resumed his narrative in a conversational tone.

"It was in the tea. You could have just had a drink. But no, you wanted to do it this way. So here goes. The Devil's Breath is in the squeeze bag here. I'm going to hold the respirator on your face. You can refuse a drink. And you can hold your breath for a while, maybe quite a while. But eventually you're going to have to take a breath. And the longer you hold out, the deeper that first breath will be. I'll be waiting."

He pulled the face mask down over his own nose and mouth to protect himself from any of the chemical which the man might exhale. He then pressed the respirator onto the stranger's face and stood patiently, his free hand poised on the bag, waiting for the man's first inhale.

Predictably, the stranger held his breath. Luis silently counted, knowing that professional divers were capable of not inhaling for as long as three minutes. When his mental count approximated two and a half minutes, he saw the telltale signs indicating that the hostage was about to gasp for air. Luis was ready and his squeeze on the bag was timed perfectly.

Removing the respirator from the man's face, Luis waited patiently, carefully setting the device on a nearby stool, in the event he might need it for a second dose. The stranger's detached stoicism gradually gave way to a glazed, dull expression. Removing the gloves and his own mask, Luis, standing off to the side of the prisoner, spoke. "Who do you work for?"

It was the same question he had asked countless times with no answer; now, under the influence of the Devil's Breath, the man immediately began to speak. As he did, Luis was gripped with confusion and an eerie tightening of his back muscles. Once the stranger was talking, he could not stop. And the more he spoke, the more uneasy Luis felt.

▽

A native of the Sonoran desert, Saylor, in his prior trips to the West Coast, was normally unable to keep his eyes off the vista of the Pacific Ocean. This time, however, as Carlos drove north on the always crowded I-5 corridor between San Diego and Los Angeles, Saylor concentrated on the printout, punched and inserted into a three-ring binder by Scott prior to their departure from Tucson. It was a compilation of interviews, website posts, and blogs from the former astronaut who was the target of their journey.

"Carlos, I don't know what to believe in this."

The archaeologist, not glancing away from the road, answered, "Why?"

Sticking a Post-it to mark his spot, Saylor closed the binder. "According to Meade, back in the fifties a UFO landed on the dry lake bed inside Edwards Air Force Base. He was stationed there at the time and was on patrol with another airman when it happened."

"He witnessed it?"

"According to him, he did a lot more than see it. After it landed, he and his partner drove their Jeep right up to it and radioed in the contact. While they waited, Meade walked all the way around it and took pictures of the ship or craft or whatever it was. He shot one full roll of film, twenty-four exposures, then changed out the roll for a fresh one and shot some more."

"This actually occurred?"

"He says it did. As he was halfway through the second roll, his captain arrived and saw what he was doing. The officer asked Meade if he had shot any more pictures, other than the ones in the camera. Meade lied and told him *no*. The officer confiscated the camera and ordered both Meade and his partner back to their post."

"So Meade kept the first roll?"

"Yes. The rest of the story is hearsay, but according to Meade, the captain had a group of men construct a tent around the ship and guard it. One of Meade's best friends on base was detailed to pick someone up at the airfield. He delivered the VIP to the ship, and the man went inside the tent, and presumably the ship, for more than four hours. When he emerged, Meade's buddy drove him back to the airfield."

"Amazing!"

"You haven't heard the best part yet. As the airman was driving, his passenger asked him if he was curious about what had happened inside. Naturally, Meade's friend said that he was. The VIP told him to pull over for a minute so they could both have a cigarette. That's when the visitor proceeded to tell the airman that he had met for the four hours with aliens from another planet."

"You are joking!"

Saylor shrugged. "I'm only telling you what's in all his interviews. Anyway, according to the VIP, the aliens were there to prepare us for entry into a family of planets."

"Like the Federation on *Star Trek*."

"Exactly. But there was one condition. *This* federation never accepted a new planet into the group as long as that planet was divided and ruled by several governments."

Villarreal risked looking away from the jumble of traffic for a moment. "I do not like where this is going."

"I know. Apparently, they told our envoy they would return when all of our borders were dissolved and there was only a single ruling entity for them to deal with."

"One-world government."

"Right. And from what Meade says his friend told him, they, the aliens, promised to solve all of our problems at that point – food, energy, everything."

"This sounds like the plot of at least a hundred movies."

"I know. And to prove that they meant what they said, as a teaser, they gave us a sampling of their technologies."

"Which ones?"

"I haven't read that part yet."

"I do not know if I believe any of this."

"I'm not sure I do either, Carlos."

"Why would this unnamed VIP tell all of this to a lowly airman?"

"I guess he said that no one would believe him anyway, so why not? And the VIP wasn't unnamed. I was saving that."

"Who was it?"

Saylor paused, waiting until Villarreal glanced away from the road for a moment. "According to Meade, the man who met with the aliens was President Dwight Eisenhower."

$$\triangledown$$

Judtson sat at the hotel bar, sipping his ginger ale. He chanced a fleeting look over his right shoulder and winked at Kelsey, who was alone at a small table. It was evening and the lounge was beginning to fill with patrons. She had changed out of her usual attire of T-shirt and jeans, and was wearing a strapless dress and stiletto heels. The silky fabric of her outfit was red and almost matched the intense color of her hair, which she had spent an hour in the hotel salon getting coiffed into a classic upswept style. He had to admit that she made a striking figure. He was not alone in that assessment; during the forty-five minutes since they had come down to the bar, a steady procession of men had approached and then rapidly departed her table. He had no idea what she had said to prompt such hasty retreats and found himself wishing he had been close enough to overhear the rebuffs.

The two of them were not waiting in the lounge merely out of blind hopefulness that their target would happen to wander in for a drink. Earlier in the day, Judtson had mentioned to the hotel manager that he had heard Clarkson was staying at the hotel, and that he would not mind meeting him. The manager, trained to protect the privacy of his guests, normally would have neither confirmed that the author was staying there nor provided any other information. However, he was fully aware that he was speaking to *the* Judtson Kent and offered to call the man's room and arrange a meeting.

Judtson feigned discomfort. "That would be awkward. I admire his work and would like to pass that on to him, but if you arrange a formal meeting…well, let's just say that it would become a bit more than what I intend."

The manager, accustomed to the egos and foibles of his more prominent guests, agreeably said, "Of course. I understand completely." With a conspiratorial smile, he continued, "I can tell you that Mr. Clarkson seems to have made a habit of indulging in a drink or two in the lounge every evening when he returns to our hotel."

As Judtson reran the conversation in his mind, he glanced at his watch and noted that it was after seven. A few minutes later, he spotted Clarkson entering the room. Recognizing him from his photographs, Judtson was struck by the owlish, scholarly persona of the man. To ensure that the author was entering with the intention of staying, he swiveled back to face the bar and watched in the mirror as their target slid onto a bar stool several seats away and ordered a drink. Anxious to proceed with their plan, Judtson turned and stood, giving a fleeting smile to Kelsey as he walked along the bar. Approximating the purposeful walk of someone going to the restroom, he made a show of abruptly stopping when he reached Clarkson.

"Excuse me. Aren't you Alfred Clarkson?"

The expression on the man's face was neutral as he turned. Authors, even those as popular as Judtson Kent, did not share the burden of public recognition enjoyed or despised by movie or rock stars.

"I am, sir," he responded politely. His eyes focused on Judtson's face, and it was obvious that there was some recognition but not sufficient to attach a name.

Judtson extended his hand. "Judtson Kent. I'm a fan of yours."

The man's eyes widened substantially as the name sank in. He quickly took the offered hand and shook it enthusiastically. "My God! Judtson Kent! A fan of *mine*? Please, sit down."

He sat upon the adjacent stool just as Clarkson's drink arrived. Ignoring it, the man continued, "I must say I am quite flattered, Mr. Kent. Your books occupy a prominent location on my library shelves."

"Why, thank you. And please, my name is Judtson."

"And mine is Al. Can I get a drink for you?"

Judtson gestured vaguely in the direction of his former seat at the bar. "I have one back there. I'm not intruding, am I? Are you expecting anyone?"

"No. Not at all. I just finished a very long and tedious day of video conferencing with my editor, and was about to unwind."

Inwardly relieved that no one was coming to meet Clarkson, Judtson chuckled knowingly. "Been there, done that. Let me guess. Your publisher is using you to break in a new, young, and very promising editor."

Clarkson laughed. "New, yes. She has been with them for all of three months, arriving fresh from an internship at Doubleday. Young, absolutely. She graduated from Columbia this year. Promising? Of that I am not at all certain. I spent almost two hours this afternoon explaining the concept of pacing to her."

"And she probably still didn't grasp it."

"I'm sure not. The one thing that she seemed to grasp was her hair, which she twirled constantly."

Judtson joined the man in his amusement. "You haven't mentioned gum chewing. That's a blessing."

"So it is, but only due to the fact that I insisted, during our first session three days past, that she remove the offending wad of cud."

Shaking his head in commiseration, Judtson commented, "I don't envy you."

With a wry grin, Clarkson confessed, "I crave the day when I have approached your stature in the industry, Judtson. I am convinced your publisher would not dare to saddle you with a tattooed twit for an editor."

"I admit that those days are behind me. Would you excuse me for a moment while I fetch my drink?"

"Of course."

He walked to his earlier seat and picked up the half-empty glass of ginger ale, giving Kelsey a slight nod as he did. Returning to Clarkson, he remarked, "Before I recognized you, Al, I was on my way to the restroom. I should probably...."

"Oh, please do. I'll keep watch over your drink."

"Thanks."

As Judtson turned the corner, he allowed himself a brief look back and saw that Kelsey was moving from her table toward the bar. He entered the restroom and found an empty stall. Immediately, he retrieved the small waxed-paper envelope from his wallet, tore a corner from it, folded it over, and stuffed it in his shirt pocket.

When he came back to his seat, Kelsey was occupying the stool on the opposite side of Clarkson, who smiled at him and said, "Judtson, it appears that you have an admirer. She joined me and asked if I could introduce her to you."

Leaning forward slightly to face her, he asked, "To what do I owe the honor?"

Kelsey reached across the front of Clarkson, offering her hand. "Oh, Mr. Kent. I'm such a huge fan."

As he shook her hand, he noticed that the very natural gesture gave her an excuse to position her torso against Clarkson's right arm. The man was smiling broadly and staring intently at her face, which was only inches from his.

"A pleasure to meet you, Miss...?"

"Teel. Shelby Teel."

"Quite a lovely name." He released his grip on her hand and noticed that she maintained her stance snugly pressed against Clarkson, who did not seem to mind.

"Thank you, Mr. Kent," she gushed. "I have adored your books since the very first one came out. I have every one of them. In hardcover, of course."

Judtson was enjoying her performance. "I appreciate that, Miss Teel. Were you aware that Mr. Clarkson is an author, as well?"

Her reaction flawless, Kelsey's eyes twinkled with excitement as she turned to look at him directly, keeping her face in close proximity. "You *are*? What have you written?"

Stammering, he answered, "Well, for the most part I've only been the co-writer on several works."

She disregarded the self-deprecating tone in his answer. "That's fascinating. Which authors have you worked with? What are your titles?"

As she spoke, she backed slightly away from him and straightened to an upright position on the seat. As if she were a powerful magnet and he, iron, Clarkson followed her motion, swiveling his stool to face her and edging forward on his seat in an unconscious attempt to recapture the nearness he had been enjoying moments before.

"Probably my best-known book was one that I wrote with a retired NASA scientist."

"You wrote *Secret Agenda*?" She practically squealed with delight.

"That's the one," he answered, his ego drawing him irretrievably into her emotional display, which Kelsey encouraged by placing her hands on his knees.

"I've read that! I can't believe my good fortune at meeting you! This is amazing! I have so many questions about it...."

Comfortable that nothing short of an explosion would distract their target from his rapt attention to Kelsey, Judtson surreptitiously removed the tiny envelope from his shirt pocket and bent open the folded corner. With his other hand, he casually grabbed Clarkson's untended drink from the bar and lowered it below the counter height, using his own body to carefully shield his actions from the sight of other lounge patrons. It only took a second to empty the powder into the drink. Dropping the envelope to the floor, he quickly stirred the mixture and replaced the glass on the bar.

With a final look, determining that no powder was visible on the glass or in the liquid, Judtson interrupted the animated conversation between Kelsey and Clarkson. "I'd like to propose a toast."

Clarkson turned back. It was obvious that he had completely forgotten about Judtson.

Judtson picked up his ginger ale and lifted it. "To readers. May they never fade away."

Clarkson raised his own drink. "I will second that."

Kelsey joined the toast. "And to writers. May you never run out of ideas."

The three drank. Judtson happily observed that Clarkson drained over half of his cocktail.

▽

Lisa Trippiano finished the last sip from her latte and was tossing the cardboard cup into the trash can beside her desk, when the insistent buzzing from her phone vibrating caused her to miss the easy shot. Ignoring the cup as it rolled across the aisle, she began shuffling the scattered papers on her desk, searching for the buried device. She found it and tapped the screen. "This is Lisa."

"Lisa, Brandon. Got a minute?"

"For you, boss? Sure. Be right there."

Tucking the phone into the back pocket of her slacks, she grabbed a notepad and hurried to the elevator, feeling guilty about using it instead of taking the stairs up the two flights to her assignment editor's office. Upon arriving, Lisa saw that her supervisor had a guest sitting at his desk, and she could not help but notice that the stranger appeared nervous.

"Lisa," Brandon said as she walked in, "this is Ricky Ingram. Lisa is one of our associate producers."

She shook hands with the man, not expecting the firmness of his grip.

Turning to Brandon, she asked, "What do we have, boss?"

Her editor was just under thirty years old, young for someone in his position. Lisa knew it did not hurt that he was the son of the star of their show.

"Mr. Ingram is the personal assistant to Judtson Kent."

"Really?" she said, her curiosity piqued.

Nodding, he continued, "Apparently, Kent has been acting very strangely lately. Mr. Ingram, as well as several others who are close to Kent, are concerned that he may be having some…mental issues."

She glanced at Ricky, who was sitting quietly, and then looked back at her boss. "Acting strangely how?"

"I guess, among other things, he has become convinced that UFOs are real, that little green men are all over the place. The usual stuff."

Startled, she exclaimed, "Judtson Kent? You're kidding. There is no bigger skeptic anywhere! He has made a career out of it."

"I know. That's what makes this a good story."

As she addressed her supervisor, Lisa's eyes flitted in Ricky's direction meaningfully. "Boss, could we talk for a minute?"

With a broad smile, he answered, "I know what you're thinking, Lisa – that Mr. Ingram is a disgruntled employee seeking some sort of revenge against his boss. We've already discussed that and he has been quite candid with me."

Ricky finally spoke. "I've brought proof. Some of his recent writing. A video."

"A video. Of what? Kent having a chat with an invisible alien?"

Before Ricky could answer, Brandon cut in. "No, Lisa. The story goes beyond that aspect. It seems that Kent is totally losing it. He was recently arrested by the police in his hometown."

This surprised her. "Arrested? For what?"

"Vandalism and destruction of public property," Ricky answered, going on to describe the paintball episode and the video made by Kelsey.

Her eyebrows lifted. "I think you may be right. This is sounding like a good story, especially with video."

"There's more," Brandon added. "He's also having some marital difficulties."

A red flag suddenly rose in her mind. "Please don't take this wrong, but I'm not so sure about taking Mr. Ingram's word for that."

"Oh, you don't have to," Ricky assured her. "Kristen Kent has accompanied me here."

Looking around the room, Lisa asked, "Where is she?"

"Back at the hotel."

"And she's prepared to talk to us? About her personal issues?"

Ricky nodded. "I think so."

Addressing her boss, Lisa said, "I'll grab a crew. We can go over there and do the interview right in her room."

"Ma'am, I don't think showing up with a camera and sound crew would be a good idea."

Lisa turned back to face Ricky, her tone suspicious. "Why not? I thought you said she wanted to talk to us."

"I said I *think* she does. I'm pretty sure she does. She wouldn't have come to New York if she didn't. I just think it would be better if you come first, let her get to know you a little, make her comfortable with you before you show up with cameras."

Mulling it over for a moment, she shrugged. "Okay. I guess that makes sense. Shall we set up a time?"

"She's waiting right now," Ricky offered.

"Now? I've got a ton of stuff to...."

"Lisa," Brandon interrupted. "This could be a good piece. I think your other work can wait."

Lisa stopped, turning to look first at Ricky, then at her boss, and finally agreeing. "Ahh, why not?"

▽

Although he and Romeo had previously decided that it would be fine for Mrs. Costello to briefly man the security console from time to time so that he could have breaks, Luis was nervous about leaving his station. Rather than indulging in a leisurely hot shower, he rushed through the process anxiously. Toweling off, he donned clean underwear and reached into his closet for a fresh shirt. In his haste, he accidentally dislodged his tactical vest from the wall hook where he kept it at the ready, and it fell to the floor with a loud *thunk*.

Perplexed, he bent over and picked it up. Luis knew his gear well and realized immediately that it was heavier than it should be. The first pocket he checked held the answer, a 9mm Glock. Staring at the gun blankly for a moment, Luis remembered that he had taken it from Bob, their hostage, back at Matt Wheeler's parking lot and had not left it behind or sequestered it in a shielded bag as they returned.

"Damn!" he uttered in anger. Trotting to the bed, he sat and quickly broke the piece down. It took him under a minute to find what he was afraid might be there. Tucked into a modified space in the butt grip of the Glock was a tiny electronic device, powered by a button-cell battery.

"How could I be so stupid?" he shouted to the empty room. Although the small device would be ineffectual inside the underground complex, he ripped the battery away from the transmitter and hastily finished getting dressed. At a full run, he arrived at Scott's work area in under two minutes. Not waiting to be acknowledged, he barked, "We need to send a message to Romeo. Right away."

"What's the message?"

His face in a contortion of frustration and anger, Luis spit out, "Tell him his idiot partner brought a tracker back to the silo."

Scott's eyes widened. "So they know where we are?"

"Damn right they do!"

▽

Saylor stood at the back of the small crowd, composed mostly of grade-school children, and listened to Meade who was addressing the gathering at the Discovery Science Center in Santa Ana. As he feigned interest, his thoughts were focused on their plan. He was grateful for their good luck providing them with this opportunity of a public event.

Meade, now in his seventies, had been one of the last to visit the Moon and was talking to the group about his career. As he watched the children on a field trip to hear this man, Saylor was saddened by their reactions to his words. There were no rapt expressions, no wide-eyed look of wonder on the countenance of a single child in the audience. In fact, without exception, boredom was the rule as they endured the experiences of this person who had actually walked upon the Moon.

Perhaps, Saylor thought, it was the absence of a dynamic computer-generated visual representation of the events Meade described – the de rigueur marketing ploy for this jaded generation who were seemingly incapable of engaging their own atrophied imaginations, and required spoon-fed imagery – which caused these children to indulge in eye-darting connections with their peers, punctuated by the attendant knowing smirks and soft giggles. Whatever the explanation for their discourtesy, he found himself slowly beginning to despise this assemblage for their displayed attitudes and the resultant impartation of contempt to this hero who had accomplished a feat none of them would ever equal in their lifetimes. Focusing, instead, on Meade, Saylor saw that the man was unaffected by the lack of communication with his audience. Perhaps long accustomed to an apathetic response, he seemed to be addressing the air above their heads.

Completing his presentation, he asked for questions. Not a single one of the schoolchildren raised a hand. Off to the side of the group was a young woman who, Saylor decided, was of college age. Too young to be a teacher, she could perhaps have been a chaperone. He was not sure whether she was part of the field trip or someone directly interested in Meade. Without bothering to raise her own hand, taking advantage of the disinterest of the children, she said, "Captain Meade, I've followed your interviews and remarks over the past few years and was fascinated by your description of the alien landing at Edwards Air Force Base."

As she spoke, Saylor noticed the fleeting look of distaste on Meade's face.

"I can't help but wonder," the young woman continued, "why you have just recently changed your story on these events."

Meade took two steps in her direction. As he answered, the timbre of his voice dropped slightly, conveying a more commanding tone than he had used with the children. "Young lady, I have not changed my story, as you put it. I have denied it. The incident described never occurred."

Unintimidated by his authoritative shift in demeanor, the woman persisted, "Are you saying that you made it all up? That it was all simply a lie?"

With a single dismissive nod, Meade responded, "That is exactly what I am saying."

Skepticism and outright disbelief defined her features as she pursued the line of questions.

"Why would you say these things? Why would you make up a story like that?"

"I am ashamed to admit, young lady, that I missed the attention. I craved the spotlight I had enjoyed through much of my earlier life. That ridiculous story of little green men, landing at a United States military installation and having an afternoon tea with our President, was my shabby and pathetic attempt to return to the public eye. Nothing more."

The woman appeared unconvinced as she chewed on her lower lip for a moment, brushing her long hair back from her face to rest behind her shoulder. "Captain Meade," she finally said, "I'm afraid that I just don't...."

"This is not the time or the place for this discussion, Miss," Meade interrupted, turning back to address the schoolchildren. He thanked them for coming, invited them to spend the rest of their day studying the exhibits at the center, and urged them to consider careers in science. Rather than spreading out into the hallways and alcoves as he suggested, the children remained where they stood, all of them instantly retrieving phones from their pockets or backpacks so that they could check for and respond to text messages they had missed during the program. Not a single student approached Meade to thank him or ask a question. To this group, he had already ceased to exist.

Saylor, remaining in his spot by the door, watched as Meade pivoted toward him and briskly walked forward. As he was nearing Saylor, the astronaut was intercepted by the assiduous young woman. "Captain Meade, I'd...."

Before she could finish her sentence, he whirled to face her. "Miss, as I said a moment ago, this is neither the time nor the place. Now if you will excuse me."

He resumed walking in the direction of the exit without waiting for a response. The woman watched him depart, a perplexed expression on her face. Saylor fell into pace alongside Meade.

"Captain Meade, my name is Dr. Saylor Costello."

Without breaking his stride, Meade asked, "A doctor? Would that be a real doctor, or are you one of those crackpot, so-called doctors of UFOlogy?"

Allowing himself a chuckle, Saylor reassured him, "Medical doctor, sir. Neurologist."

The two men cleared the exit and came to a stop on the sidewalk outside the building. Saylor was relieved to see that the curious woman had not followed.

"M.D., huh? What can I do for you, young fellah?"

Saylor glanced back toward the interior. "I imagine you get a lot of that?"

Meade shook his head in obvious disgust. "More than you could believe. They come out of the woodwork."

"I sympathize."

The man's eyes, probably at one time a deep blue, now aged to a steely gray, strayed for a moment back toward the entrance before returning to look at Saylor. "It's what I deserve, I suppose."

"How so?" As Saylor asked, he found himself staring deeply into those eyes, trying to detect the same unsettling phenomena which had been so obvious in Judtson's, and concluding that without the benefit of knowing Meade prior to the change, it was pointless.

"Young man, you really aren't someone who spends his evenings glued to the plethora of *space alien* programs on cable, are you?"

"Not much of a television watcher, sir."

"Well, if you don't already know what a fool I've made of myself, I should probably treasure you as one of the few and not spoil it by telling the story."

"That's fine with me, sir."

"I thank you for that. Now, did you come here today to shake the hand of an old astronaut or was there something else?"

Saylor chuckled at the man's directness. "Both, actually. I am a member of a research team studying Parkinson's disease."

Meade's eyes narrowed. "And you're thinking after my recent stunt that I must have a few screws loose?"

Saylor emphatically shook his head. "Not at all, sir. Quite the opposite. The epidemiologists on the team have found an interesting anomaly. It would appear that among the relatively sizable group of men who have been in space, not a single astronaut has acquired the disease. Statistically, this would be almost impossible unless there was some causal connection."

"That's interesting. Now that you mention it, I can't think of anyone in our group who has it. Go on."

"The romantics among us immediately leapt upon the commonality that all of you have been in space, and that there was something in the experience which conferred the apparent immunity."

"We also went through the same training...received the same batch of inoculations. A lot of guys went through the whole program with us but never went up. Couldn't it have been something they did to all of us on the ground?"

When Saylor had concocted this ruse, he had anticipated the question. "That's the thing I found most interesting. Again, according to empirical data, there were three men in the program for every one who went up. As you know, back then it was only men. The incidence of Parkinson's among the others, those who never went into space, is essentially identical to the normal population. The only common variable among those who haven't fallen victim to the disease is spaceflight."

"Well, I'll be damned. That *is* interesting. What do you need from me?"

Surprised at how easily the plan was working, Saylor consciously fought down his excitement and, with forced nonchalance, replied, "Nothing too invasive. Blood test, tissue samples."

"I'm not a doctor, but there doesn't seem to be much you can tell from those things."

With a smile on his face, Saylor answered, "You're correct, sir. There isn't. This is a long-term study, and right now we are basically building the database, eliminating as many possibilities and accomplishing as much as we are able while the subjects remain...alive. The rest of what we'll need has to come later, which means that the other request I have for you today is that you sign a consent form allowing us to take a sample of brain tissue."

"Postmortem, I hope."

Saylor laughed. "Yes, sir."

"That's good because I don't think I can spare any at the moment. Well, I've spent most of my earlier life getting poked, scoped, scraped, prodded, and sampled by NASA, so I don't see the harm in one more go-around, especially for a good cause."

"Excellent, sir."

"Where's your clinic? Do I need to set up an appointment?"

"Actually, sir, our clinic is back in Arizona. I've traveled here with a nurse, who is back at our hotel. We're staying at the Doubletree right around the corner. If you wouldn't mind coming there, we can do everything in five minutes."

Meade stiffened. "I don't know. Maybe...."

Putting on his most reassuring smile, Saylor interrupted, "Of course, I understand. I'm a complete stranger who approached you at a speech and I've asked you to come back to my room so I can take some of your blood. I'd be suspicious, too."

Pulling out his wallet, Saylor removed a business card. "Tell you what, here's my number and email. Please check us out and let me know what works for you. The only reason I'm here today with the nurse is that we've already contacted one of your colleagues, Eugene Cernan. He has agreed to meet us later today and give us what we need. I found out you were making this appearance and I guess I was trying to be too efficient and save myself another trip. But I can certainly come back when it's convenient for you, or we can make arrangements at one of the local hospitals."

Saylor was tense. This was the riskiest part of the wholly fictitious gambit. He hoped that Meade did not have his fellow astronaut's cell phone number in his speed dial. After studying the card for a moment, Meade pulled out his cell phone and tapped in a number. Saylor could feel nervous sweat popping out all over his back.

Saylor listened to Meade's side of the conversation.

"Good afternoon. Is Dr. Costello in?"

- - - - - - - - - -

"I've been referred to him and I'd like to schedule a consultation."

- - - - - - - - - -

"So, he is out of town at the moment?"

- - - - - - - - - -

"Thank you very much. I'll call back next week."

Meade ended the call and looked up. "You're going to jab Gene, huh? What the heck. I've got nothing to do this afternoon, anyway."

▽

Judtson finished his third reading of the printed instructions provided by Matt, and glanced at Clarkson who was unconscious and bound to a chair.

"Is our friend still asleep?" asked Kelsey as she came through the open doorway from the adjoining room. He noticed that she had changed out of her red dress and was back in her normal outfit.

"He is. I rather liked your other look."

She snorted. "Tough. I'm a lot more comfortable in this. Heard from the others?"

Judtson nodded. "Saylor just called. They have Meade knocked out. Ricky sent me a text. Trippiano is in the same shape. They're both waiting for us."

It had been decided that it would be prudent, since this was going to be the first attempt with Wheeler's modified machine, for the other two groups to hold off injecting the FDG until they heard from Judtson and Kelsey that the procedure worked.

With a quick glance at her watch, Kelsey said, "It has been about an hour. Are we ready to give this thing a try?"

Judtson put the heavy lead vest over his head and draped it across his torso, then stood and walked to the small table they had set beside Clarkson's chair, checking that the power cord was plugged into the wall outlet and that the red LED on the transformer was still lit.

"Sure. Let's do it."

"Judtson?" Kelsey's face hinted at an unfamiliar emotion.

"Yes?"

"What if we're wrong? What if we're completely nuts?"

"Then we are going to have one mad-as-hell author on our hands."

He carefully placed the improvised helmet on the unconscious figure's head and opened the control window on the laptop as Kelsey squatted in front of the chair, her vest already in place, ready to spring into action if Clarkson suddenly awakened. Turning on the dual laser pointers, Judtson ensured that neither he nor Kelsey was in the direct path of the x-rays. He dragged his finger on the touchpad and, bringing the arrow to hover over the initiating button, softly said, "Here goes," and tapped the pad.

The device was silent and Judtson had to check the laptop screen to be certain he had started the process. Neither spoke, waiting anxiously as the time ticked off on the screen. When the display showed only sixteen seconds remaining, Clarkson's eyes suddenly flew open and darted frenetically, taking in his surroundings.

"AARRGGGHHH!" he shouted, igniting a panic in both of them that they were somehow causing him pain. Hastily, Judtson moved the pointer to abort the procedure and grabbed the helmet, pulling it off Clarkson's head. As he set the device on the table, Kelsey sprang up and firmly gripped their subject's arms. "Al! Al Clarkson! Are you okay?"

Clearly agitated, he jerked his head spasmodically, his eyes cycling repeatedly back and forth between Kelsey and Judtson. His breathing was rapid and ragged, his face flushed. With a visible attempt to regain self-control, Clarkson sucked in a lung-filling breath. Rearing back his head, with his mouth wide open, he unabashedly shouted, "OH, MY GOD! I'M OUT! I'M OUT!"

Chapter 25

JUDTSON, KELSEY, AND LUIS WERE GATHERED in a semicircle behind Scott, their attention riveted to the video displaying on one of the monitors. On the screen, the hostage Luis referred to as Bob was speaking so quickly and steadily that it seemed as if he did not even pause momentarily for a breath. His voice was clear and loud on the recording, and yet none of them could understand what he was saying.

Embedded on the upper-right corner of the image was a time/date stamp. Judtson had noted the time when the drug given to Bob had taken effect. "He has been going nonstop for eleven minutes now."

"What's he saying?" Kelsey asked, the excited and agitated monologue continuing in the background. "Does anyone understand him?"

"I certainly don't. Anybody recognize the language?"

Luis answered Judtson. "I don't. I've listened to it at least ten times now, and there isn't a word in what he says that I understand."

"Scott?" The query came from Kelsey.

The technician turned away from the monitor and shook his head. "Nope. It's not anything I've ever heard. I've downloaded every voice recognition software and translation program I could lay my hands on. Nothing recognizes it. Nothing converts it."

"Any ideas?"

"Sure. I'm just not convinced they're *good* ideas."

Kelsey looked at her tech quizzically. "What are they?"

"One option is to take some random samples of the speech and email them to linguists and universities around the world. Or I could even put parts of it up on blogs and social media, asking people if they recognize it."

"Why haven't you done any of that?"

"Paranoid, I guess. We don't know what he's saying. What if the passage I happen to put out there is Bob telling the world that he is being held a prisoner and describing where he's being kept? Someone who does understand the language would…."

"Call the cops," she finished.

"Or worse," Judtson added. "We could accidentally be putting ourselves into the hands of the bad guys."

"Too late," Luis interjected. "I've already done that."

Judtson centered his attention on the incoherent monologue and, as he listened, noticed that there was something inherent in the words, the tone, or the cadence which was triggering a faint, prickling tingle of unease.

▽

The television producer, Lisa Trippiano, was sitting in a corner of the lounge, talking excitedly to Clarkson, the two comparing their experiences in mental exile. Judtson and Kelsey stood across the room, keeping an eye on them as they talked.

Kelsey nudged Judtson with her elbow. "It looks like there's a little more than a casual friendship between those two."

Judtson studied the interaction between the author and the producer for a minute. "If there is, it's only a one-way thing."

"How so?"

"He might as well be a puppy the way he's staring at her, but she doesn't appear to notice."

Turning his attention away from the reunion, Judtson said, "I just got a text from Saylor. He and Villarreal are on their way back with Meade."

"Went smoothly?"

He nodded. "Without a hitch. I guess Meade started talking constantly the minute the sedative wore off."

"Anything good?"

"Oh, yeah! I guess he still has a batch of pictures he took in the fifties that he has never released. Saylor didn't say in the text what it's all about, but they made a stop to pick them up."

Kelsey snickered at him. "For all the research you've done for your books, Squirrel, you sure aren't up on your UFO lore. He shot pictures of an alien ship after it landed at Edwards Air Force Base back when he was stationed there."

"I *have* heard of that." Changing the subject, Judtson gestured in the direction of their two new guests. "It appears that Wheeler's gizmo works like a charm."

"Uh-huh. It absolutely does. This is a lot better than grabbing these people and dragging them back here to the lab against their will."

"By the way, I didn't mention it in D.C., but you were great back there."

"It was fun. I really got into the role."

"Role? A literary groupie?"

"I was thinking more along the lines of high-priced call girl." Her gaze pierced him as she spoke.

Feeling a blush coloring his cheeks, Judtson added, "And you looked fabulous in that red dress."

A modest smile crept onto Kelsey's face as she nearly whispered, "Thank you. Glad you noticed."

Breaking the tension of the moment, he cleared his throat and looked back at their recent arrivals. "Has Scott made any progress on figuring out the headpiece we took from the dead guys?"

Kelsey shook her head. "Not yet. We've been keeping him pretty busy, and I think he's waiting for Wheeler to help him."

"Makes sense." Judtson paused, an absorbed expression on his face.

"What are you thinking?"

He shifted his gaze back to her. When he answered, his voice was lower and serious. "I was wondering how much time we have."

Sensing his concern, Kelsey's brow furrowed. "What do you mean?"

"I'm still trying to wrap my mind around some kind of theory about the bad guys...who they are, how big the organization actually is, how powerful. We don't have enough facts yet to nail any of that down. From what we've seen, the group must be fairly large and potent, and they've now lost Villarreal, Clarkson, Trippiano, and Meade...."

"And you."

"True. It almost seems as though they have been underestimating us, staying a step behind us, playing catch-up. But now, with our newest converts, that will change. I think they will have to step it up, become more overt, more direct."

As she contemplated his words, Judtson saw Kelsey's mask of brash bravado slip for a moment, allowing him a glimpse of an emotion he had not yet seen from her...fear. The change lasted only a moment before she returned to her typical self-confident state. "You're probably right. I say, let the games begin."

▽

"I did a brief stint in one of these installations in the sixties, during the Cuban Crisis," Meade said as they approached the first pole-mounted speaker at the entrance to the silo.

"No kidding," responded Saylor as he lowered the window and brought the Hummer to a stop.

"Man, I'm telling you those were tense times. All we could think about was that phone ringing, the order arriving to turn the keys. We couldn't sleep. We couldn't eat. I think everyone on the crew lost...."

Saylor only half-listened to the Cold War story as he leaned out the window to press the button on the intercom. Seeing that he had slightly overshot his mark, he slipped the Hummer into reverse and started rolling back to where his finger could touch the button, when two things happened simultaneously: Romeo's voice came from the speaker, asking Saylor to identify himself; and the front windshield of the truck exploded outward, blanketing the hood of the truck with a shower of glass pebbles.

"GET DOWN!" Saylor shouted as his foot instinctively mashed the gas pedal to the floor.

▽

Romeo, watching the camera view of the entrance, slammed the heel of his palm down on the red alarm button of the console, leapt up from his chair, and grabbed his AK-47 on the run, dashing up the staircase to the surface as the motorized vault door to the complex swung closed behind him.

▽

Immediately realizing that the Hummer was still in reverse and was careening backward on the narrow lane, Saylor slammed on the brakes and dropped the truck into drive as he hunkered lower in the seat to minimize his profile. Now in forward gear, the powerful engine of the Hummer roared as his foot stabbed the pedal, propelling them toward the entrance and clipping the steel post of the intercom as they rocketed past. Instantly, he heard one of the rear side windows shatter, and shouted over the din, "Are you both all right?"

Meade, who was in the front seat beside Saylor and bent forward so that his head was below the sill of the window, boomed out, "I'm fine. What the hell's going on?"

Saylor ignored his question. "Carlos!" he yelled.

From the backseat came a muffled answer he was unable to hear clearly over the screaming engine and the roar of wind coming in through the absent windshield. Satisfied that Villarreal was at least able to respond, he focused on the road ahead, jerking the steering wheel slightly to the right and barely clearing the fence post installed at the edge of the pavement. Saylor suddenly flew upward into his seat belt as the Hummer climbed the speed hump.

An ugly smacking sound reached his ears and he guessed that whoever was shooting at them had hit the steel body with his third shot. A second later, two almost coinciding explosions came from the front and Saylor knew that Romeo must not have lowered the steel teeth at the barrier. He was proved right a moment later when the front end of the truck dropped down precipitously at the same moment the rear wheels hit the teeth.

His ears were filled with the screeching sound of rims digging into the asphalt road as they quickly shed the wildly flapping remnants of the tires. The momentum of the heavy truck kept them moving forward, but Saylor could feel that they were rapidly decelerating. With his foot still jamming down the gas pedal, the rear wheels, also rims to pavement, spun uselessly, throwing off dual rooster tails of sparks in their wake.

▽

Romeo burst through the ground-level door at a full run, reaching his black Hummer in seconds. The engine was started and he was already rolling before he bothered to slam the door, cranking the steering wheel hard and fighting a spin as the truck burned rubber tracks onto the lane. Leaning forward as he drove, as if this would give the truck more speed, he manhandled the large vehicle through the serpentine route, several times grazing the high curbs lining the roadway on his approach to the steel gate. Taking his eyes off the road for only a moment, Romeo pressed a button on the dashboard, activating the gate opener, and had to momentarily tap the brakes to avoid hitting the barrier as he careered through, nearly succeeding as the passenger side rearview mirror was sheared off by the gate's edge.

His eyes hastily sweeping the area, he shouted, "Where are they?" expecting Saylor to have made a run for it all the way to the gate by now.

The tires on the Hummer squealed and smoked as he pushed the truck through the dips, hills, and curves of the lane. As he crested the fourth rise, he saw the yellow Hummer and understood why they had made so little progress. "Dammit, I forgot to drop the teeth," he rebuked himself angrily.

Despite the distance, he could see that Saylor's vehicle was only moving forward slightly faster than a crawl, sparks shooting out from the rear wheels, and was barely about fifty yards past the first entrance. What he saw next made his blood run cold, as two men, dressed in black full-body suits, were running through the entrance and steadily gaining on the crippled Hummer. He ground his foot even harder against the already floored pedal.

▽

"Come on, move!" Saylor shouted at their truck to urge it forward, looking in his rearview mirror and seeing the two attackers running through the opening in the fence. Out of the corner of his eye, he caught sight of the black Hummer approaching at breakneck speed from the silo, and knew that it was going to be close. Too close.

"I need a gun," he barked loudly in frustration.

"A gun?" The question came from Meade, who was still crouched down beside him. "Why the hell didn't you say so?" He rose up and faced the rear of the vehicle, seeing the two armed men closing in at a dead run.

"Keep rolling!" he ordered and shoved his hand beneath his coat, pulling out a military issue M9. Shifting to a kneeling position on the seat cushion, he leaned against the seat back and extended both arms, pointing the pistol toward the rear. As he lined himself up, he glanced at Villarreal, who was lying on his back on the floorboard, staring at him.

With a wink at his supine companion, Meade instructed, "Stay down," flipped the safety off, and pulled the trigger once, shattering the back window. Instantly, he shot three more rounds, rapid-fire. None connected with the two men but had the desired result of causing them to dive onto the dirt at the side of the road.

The yellow Hummer had slowed to less than ten miles per hour, making their escape excruciating despite the fact that the attackers had momentarily stopped. One of the strangers, obviously the sniper, unslung his rifle from his back and was shifting it into position for another attempt. Meade saw this, yelled, "He's setting up for a shot!" and steadied his pistol as well as he could in the bouncing truck, emptying the clip in the shooter's direction and hoping for a lucky hit.

Meade could see the man steady the long barrel of his rifle and knew that the next shot was imminent. Yet before there was a muzzle flash from the rifle, he saw the sniper suddenly swing the barrel to his left and, at the same time, noticed a black blur race past the driver's side of their truck.

$$\triangledown$$

As Romeo neared the melee, his mind spun through the limited options he had. The Hummer carrying Saylor and the others was limping forward. The two men could easily outrun it on foot. And he was still too far away to intervene. From his vantage, Romeo could not see that Meade had opened fire on the attackers and had no idea why they suddenly dived to the ground. However, this sudden change in the tactical situation made Romeo's next move obvious. A snarl twisting his mouth, he wrenched the steering wheel to his right and bounced the Hummer over the concrete curb onto the hard-packed desert soil. The wide-track vehicle, finding less traction on the dirt, only wanted to fishtail for a moment before it straightened out under his competent steering and settled into a straight path, like a torpedo in calm water.

Romeo lowered his bulk as much as possible as he saw the sniper point the barrel of the rifle directly at him. Focused on the shooter, he was vaguely aware that the second attacker was desperately rolling off to the side, attempting to put more distance between himself and his partner. Making a slight adjustment in his trajectory, Romeo then dropped his upper torso to his right, lowering himself even farther just as the sniper's bullet hit the windshield, exploding it inward, but missing Romeo and ricocheting off the inside of the roof somewhere behind him.

One shot was all the sniper was able to get off before the huge front tire of the Hummer caught him. In a split second, the broad tire slammed the barrel of the rifle into the dirt, pinning the shooter's right hand beneath it. Traveling forward, the wheel followed the man's hand and arm and chewed its way over the length of his body. The effect on the sniper was similar to a boot stepping on a packet of ketchup. The second stranger was not much luckier. Even though he was able to avoid the other front wheel on the passenger side, the man's shoulder was snagged by the frame as the Hummer thundered over him. Dragging him beneath, it bounced over the curb and returned to the lane just in time to traverse the protruding steel teeth and rocket over the speed hump.

Romeo slammed on the brakes, bringing the truck to a twisting stop. He jumped out, AK-47 in hand, and peered under the Hummer. One glance at what remained of the man told him that there was no threat. Stepping quickly around the vehicle, he checked the area behind, spotting the sniper, and was again satisfied with his work. As he circled the Hummer, his eyes scanned the surrounding desert, searching for any other members of the team who might have held back.

The yellow truck had come to a stop and the three men had climbed out, walking back to him. One of the three, an older man, was holding a pistol, and Romeo immediately figured out what must have caused the two assailants to take cover.

As he walked, Saylor looked down at what had been the sniper. "Good God!"

Villarreal also made the mistake of looking, and instantly felt spasms in the muscles of his neck, as he staggered and grabbed onto Saylor's shoulder for support.

Romeo noticed the older man casually take in the view of the body and continue walking with no visible change of expression on his face. Arriving where Romeo stood and extending his hand, he said, "Good driving there, young fellah. I'm Jimmy Meade."

Instinctively, as he always did with women and old men, Romeo took the offered hand gently, only to be startled by an iron grip in return. Stepping up the intensity of his own grip, Romeo smiled. "Romeo Jones, sir. And aren't you the astronaut?"

The man grinned back. "Astronaut was less than one percent of my time in service. I was United States Air Force for more than forty years. And you?"

"Army Ranger, sir. Captain, it's a pleasure to meet you."

"Knock off the 'captain' crap. That's only for snot-nosed kids and pretty young ladies. It's Jimmy." He eyed Romeo up and down, and added, "Man, they're making Rangers a lot bigger than *I* remember them."

▽

"Are they okay?" The worried question came from Doni, who was pressed against Kelsey's back and staring anxiously at the security monitor.

The group, including Ricky, Luis, Judtson, Wheeler, Clarkson, and Trippiano, had dashed to the security station behind the now-closed vault door when the alarm had sounded. They were all clustered at the console, except for Luis, who was holding an M-16 at the ready and was stationed by the vault door.

"It looks like it," Kelsey answered, manipulating the mouse and ordering the camera near the entrance to zoom in on the four men standing beside the black Hummer.

"Oh, thank God!" gushed Doni, relieved.

Kelsey, using the speakerphone on the desk, called Romeo. She could see him on the monitor as he pulled the phone out of his pocket.

"R.J.," he answered tersely.

"Everyone all right?"

He turned and faced the camera, knowing he was on screen. "Hello, boss. We're in a lot better shape than the other guys."

She could not help but giggle at his comment. "I saw that. Is it okay to drop the tire barrier and open the gate and door?"

She watched as he slowly turned a full 360-degree rotation.

"It looks clear from here. Anything on the perimeter cameras?"

She quickly scanned the views from all cameras. "Looks good."

"Open them up."

The group was above ground, waiting as the black truck pulled up, the occupants all clearly visible through the front opening where the windshield had been. Doni ran to the front passenger door, met Saylor as he dropped to his feet, and clinched him in an embrace. Judtson walked over and stood behind her as the rest of the men disembarked.

Kelsey met Romeo and took him off to the side. "This is so strange. Just a couple of hours ago, Judtson and I were talking about the possibility that they were going to escalate."

"I think that's a safe bet," the big man answered, his eyes constantly in motion, surveying their surroundings for a possible threat. "If this is a taste of things to come, I'm not so sure about using this place for a base camp."

Confusion coloring her features, Kelsey asked, "Why? This silo is a fortress."

"It is. And it's a great place to have if the plan is to crawl inside, lock the doors, and fight off an attack."

"Then what's the problem?"

"The problem is that we need mobility, and the ingress and egress from here is much too vulnerable. We're out in the middle of nowhere. The terrain is hilly…just enough topo to provide cover for snipers, like our friend out there. As we come and go, we are going to be sitting ducks for another ambush."

"Is there any way to address that?"

Romeo shrugged. "Sure. But we can't do it from the ground. You've only got two trained men…Luis and me. We can't patrol twenty-four/seven. And even if we could, it's too big an area. Bad guys could move into position while we're patrolling and take us out on our next round. The only viable option is from the air. Continuous helicopter patrols. Maybe stationary aerial platforms…blimps with cameras, motion sensors, and night vision. Drones would work. Another option is installing motion-sensitive cameras and infrared detectors extending way past the outside perimeter. We'd probably need to have the grid all the way out to the highway."

"I don't care what it costs."

"I know that. But implementing would take time. Even if you threw a ton of dough at the problem, it would take days, if not weeks, to get it done. And when it was done, considering what we're up against, how could we be certain that the whole system wasn't actually installed by the bad guys, leaving themselves a back door to get through?"

Chewing her bottom lip, Kelsey mulled over his words for a moment. She glanced in the direction where Judtson was standing and talking to Saylor. Catching his eye, she motioned for him to join them. "I hadn't thought about that. What do you have in mind?"

Judtson walked to them as Romeo answered, "We split up. One body stays here. That would be the converts, Scott, Matt, Ricky, Saylor, and Mrs. Costello, guarded by Luis. There's no reason anyone in that group would need to leave for the time being."

Hearing what Romeo was saying, Judtson asked, "What's going on?"

Kelsey and Romeo explained their concerns to him.

"Makes sense. That leaves the three of us."

Romeo nodded. "We'd be the mobile detachment, small and fast moving. We'd handle the rest of the conversions. We'd keep on the go and do whatever else needed to be done out in the world."

"That might work," Kelsey acknowledged. "If we're going to avoid the silo, what do we do with the new converts?"

"Bring them here. Maybe one at a time. Maybe save them all up for a single drop. I haven't thought that through yet. If we drive them in, we'll come in at night. Snipers and night vision goggles aren't a good combination. Our other option is to fly them in on a 'copter. Whichever way we go, we do it only once each. I have a feeling that if we repeat anything, they'll be ready for us."

Curious, Judtson pressed him, "How can they be ready for either of those techniques?"

"If it were up to me, what I'd do if I saw that my target was only coming and going at night would be to either plant IEDs in the road…."

"IEDs?"

"That's what they call them in Iraq and Afghanistan. Improvised explosive devices."

"Mines?"

"Basically. Or my second choice might be an RPG."

"That one I do know. Rocket-propelled grenade."

"Exactly. You don't need to have a clean daylight view to hit the side of a truck with one of those."

"What about using the helicopter?"

Romeo grinned at Judtson. "I know you've heard of shoulder-launched SAMs."

"I have. Surface-to-air missiles."

"They're readily available. The Russians sell them on the black market. Peasants in third-world countries all over the place have them strapped to their donkeys or camels. I'm sure our friends could obtain one."

Kelsey spoke up. "We don't even know if these guys are part of our government. They did show Homeland Security IDs to Matt. If they are, they would have access to all of this stuff."

"True," Judtson agreed.

▽

"Why can't I go?" The question came from Saylor, immediately following Judtson's explanation of their plan.

"You're whining!"

"Having a fourth person won't matter, and I'm going to go stir-crazy in this hole."

The two of them were alone in the kitchen, sitting at one of the dinettes.

"Look, Popeye, you need to be here with Doni. Besides, I want you to continue debriefing the converts we have, as well as the others when we bring them in."

Saylor thought about what Judtson said for a moment. "That doesn't wash. The best person to debrief them and put together what they have to say is you."

"So you think I should stay here and *you* should go off alone with Kelsey?"

"Sure. Why not?"

"Oh, I don't know. I think Doni might not like that."

"Oh!" Judtson's comment stopped Saylor. "Well, maybe…."

"No. No 'maybes.' Here's how it works. Romeo is the pivotal person, so we start with him. He's the one who can safeguard whoever goes out. And since he's Kelsey's employee, bodyguard, whatever you want to call him, he insists that she stay with him. Now, either just the two of them go out, or there's a spot for one more, but only one because that's the maximum Romeo feels he can protect. It would make no sense to send out any of the converts, and Luis needs to stay here and hold down the fort. Scott needs to be near his equipment, and Matt needs to figure out the strap-on gizmo."

"True."

"So that leaves you, me, Ricky, or Doni."

"Okay."

"Doni is out. You would never let her go."

"True."

"And she won't let you go."

"Also true."

"That leaves either me or Ricky. I talked to him. He doesn't want any part of it. He'd much rather stay here in the silo."

"All right," Saylor sighed. "I guess that leaves you. At least I'll drive the three of you to the airport."

"No. As much as I'd rather have you drive my car back, we're taking Luis."

"Why? I thought he needs to stay with us."

"Romeo decided that it would be best, in case there might be some trouble coming back in."

▽

"You wanted to see me," Judtson said as he entered the IT room.

Turning in his swivel chair to face Judtson, Scott replied, "Something just popped up. Thought you might want to know about it."

"What's that?"

"You asked me to saturate the Internet with your Villarreal cable program, which I did. I used a nasty little robo-malware, and the show is now embedded on thousands of servers all over the world."

"Cool."

"But that isn't why I called you. What did you say your producer's name was? The lady you asked to upload the program to you?"

"Emily Benson. Why?"

Rather than answering him, Scott turned and clicked on a minimized button at the bottom of his screen. Instantly, a news story from the *Los Angeles Times* filled the screen. The headline for the story was "Cable television producer killed in fire."

Judtson stepped closer to read the text as Scott spoke. "There was a fire in her relatively new condo in Brentwood. It started in the middle of the night while she was sleeping. They're guessing that she must have awakened at some point and tried to crawl out, because they found her body halfway across the living room floor."

Scanning the article, Judtson asked, "Do they know what caused it?"

"Nope. 'Undetermined cause' is all they're saying. They're speculating that it might have been an electrical problem, but they don't know."

"Do you think the two are related?"

"You mean the release of the video and her death? Maybe."

"Why would they blame her?"

Scott looked sheepish as he answered, "Remember you told me that she had uploaded the wrong episode for you?"

"Yes."

"When I hacked in and swiped the right one, I was trying to make sure that I didn't leave a trail. I changed the server's log to reflect that she had actually uploaded the real program instead of the bogus one."

The man's normally soft voice became even more subdued. "I think I might be responsible for her death."

Seeing the tragic expression on the technician's face, Judtson attempted to assuage his anxiety. "You can't blame yourself, Scott."

"Who else? I dummied up the trail which led them straight to her. The fire happened less than twenty hours after I released the video."

"We don't even know that it wasn't an accident. And even if it wasn't, how could you know they would react that way? None of us would have guessed that."

The man looked down, obviously avoiding eye contact. "There's no way around it. If I hadn't done what I did, she'd still be alive."

"Listen, we're learning as we go here. These people are clearly willing to take things further than we ever would have thought."

He then remained silent, allowing the man time to think. After a few minutes, with a visible effort, Scott lifted his gaze to Judtson and stood up. "Don't worry about me. I'll be fine. It'll take a while, that's all."

▽

Judtson finished packing his suitcase and squatted to give Rocky, who had been waiting expectantly through the process, some attention. His canine companion, reading the clues, knew that his master was leaving again and pressed to his side. There was a knock at the door and Judtson shouted, "Come in!"

The door opened and it took him a moment to recognize the woman standing there.

"Kelsey, what did you do to your hair?"

She reached up and casually flipped it. "Dyed it. This is actually pretty close to my natural color."

"Your normal color is black?"

She stopped in mid-stride. "You don't like it?" He could not tell if she was feigning or was actually hurt.

"No! I do. I think it's great. It just surprised me."

She walked in the rest of the way and knelt beside him, enthusiastically rubbing Rocky's belly. "I thought, since we're going to be traveling on commercial instead of the Gulfstream, I'd change my look a little."

"Okay," he said, conveying a lack of understanding.

"Oh, for Pete's sake, you know they have cameras at all the airports, facial recognition software and all that. And you know they're going to be watching for us. You need to change your appearance, too."

"Oh, sure. On the way to the airport, we can stop at a party store and I can wear a fake nose and glasses."

Slightly frustrated, she snapped, "When are you going to take all of this as seriously as you should?"

He grinned in an effort to defuse some of her intensity. "I'm getting there. I really am. It's a big leap from the things I always believed."

"Well, I've told you before and I'll say it again...you were full of prunes then."

"Thanks."

"You're welcome. Now, come on, let's go. We have a plane to catch."

They both stood. "Kelsey, you never explained why we aren't using your plane."

"It's unguarded at the hangar. Romeo's afraid they've already hidden a tracker somewhere on it or in it."

Judtson suddenly blurted out, "That reminds me." He opened a dresser drawer and removed a compact plastic case, opened his suitcase, and tucked it in.

"What's that?"

"You'll see," he answered nonchalantly. "Well, at least we're flying first class." He caught the look on her face. "We *are* flying first class, aren't we?"

"No. Romeo thinks that would be too high-profile, especially out of a small airport like Tucson's."

Judtson suddenly burst out laughing.

"What's so funny?"

"I was visualizing Romeo shoehorning his body into a coach seat. Never mind. I'm fine. Coach is going to be worth it, just to see that."

▽

After Judtson, Kelsey, and Romeo departed, Saylor went to his room hoping to find Doni. She was not there and he remembered that she was going to work out in the gym. The prospect of sweating on an elliptical or working the free weights did not appeal to him, so he dropped into a chair and turned on the television, flipping rapidly through the hundreds of channels fed down into the silo by an above-ground dish. Nothing capturing his attention, he moved to the desk and checked his emails. Scanning the accumulated list, he spotted one from Patrick Worden. The subject line referenced Judtson's MMPI test.

He opened the email and read it. Worden wasted no time getting to the point.

> "I have compared the two MMPI tests administered to Mr. Kent. To be honest, I am perplexed. The test taken while he was in college had fairly extreme results on some of the scales. He scored high on the Pd, or Psychopathic Deviate scale, a measure of conflict, struggle, anger, and respect, or lack thereof, for societal rules. He also scored somewhat high on the Paranoia scale, which is a measure of level of trust, suspiciousness, and sensitivity. Mr. Kent was above the norm on the Hypomania (level of excitability) scale and the Social Introversion scale, as well.

> "I'm not intending to convey that Mr. Kent was burdened with a severe disorder. He apparently was able to remain quite functional through that period, although he would certainly have been regarded as eccentric and something of a misfit."

Saylor chuckled at this comment, thinking about Judtson's personality over the years. He resumed reading the email.

> "What has perplexed me are the results of the recent test taken in my office. All of the above abnormalities were completely absent. In fact, in all of my years of practice, I have never come across a patient whose scores were as normal across the board as Mr. Kent's. That's not to say the normal scores are, in themselves, abnormal. I'm certain that my own experience is slanted due to the fact that people who have come in to me as patients have a problem to begin with or they wouldn't have come.

> "As you may or may not know, the MMPI is also heavily dosed with questions which allow us to determine if the patient is deliberately manipulating the test results. It is possible to fool the test; one person in seven does. Even serial killers have been known to take the MMPI and provide perfectly normal results in all of the scales without raising the red flags for faking or defensiveness. But

"Oh, cool! They have bubble-gum flavor!" Her excitement was infectious, and they both pulled the large-sized cups from the dispenser, snapped on the domed lids, and filled them to the top. Jamming the spoon-straw through the hole, Kelsey licked the overflow from the plastic as Judtson approached the counter.

The clerk, in a flat monotone, asked, "Did you find everything you needed?"

As Judtson opened his mouth to speak, Kelsey smiled broadly at the clerk and said, "Actually, no. We were looking for a linguistic expert who could help us decipher a language we've never heard before."

The young girl behind the counter went slack-faced, having no clue what the appropriate response might be. Rebooting her brain, she addressed Judtson, who was still chuckling under his breath at Kelsey's comment. "Will this be all for you?"

"Yes. Thank you."

The clerk scanned a plastic laminated sheet on the counter, which contained UPC bar codes, and told Judtson the amount due. As he pulled out cash, she asked, "Would you like to donate to the United Way?"

He placed a five-dollar bill on the counter and asked, "Would *you* like to donate to the Salvation Army?"

She was reaching for his money as he asked the question, his words stimulating a spontaneous giggle from Kelsey. The clerk's hand stopped in midair, inches from the bill, but the pause was only for a second. Picking up the five, she stared at Judtson and said, "That's rude."

With a look of innocence on his face, he responded, "Actually, here's the deal. I am your customer. I came in here because we are thirsty, not because I was driving down the street and felt a sudden urge to make a charitable contribution. It was you who chose to attempt to embarrass me in front of my friend by putting me on the spot. I would say that you are the one who is rude."

"We do it because the United Way is a worthy cause. It helps a lot of people."

From the corner of his eye, Judtson could see that Kelsey was struggling to maintain her composure during the dialogue. "Miss, I'm not going to get into the percentage of donated money given to the United Way which actually makes its way into the hands of people who need it; I'll let you do that research. But I do resent companies like yours putting customers in a position where they feel humiliated if they don't give money to *your* charity, especially if there is a line of strangers waiting behind them as they're asked."

The clerk huffed and performed an exaggerated eye-rolling before she scoffed, "Whatever."

Angrily tapping the screen on her computer, she entered the amount tendered, and in her haste omitted the decimal point. As the drawer opened and she read the amount of change due, she once again locked up, her hand hovering over the cash drawer.

"Miss, that's $1.39 you owe me, not $496.39."

He could see her jaw muscles clenching repeatedly for a moment as she struggled to do the math in her head. Giving up, with another loud huff, she pulled two dollar bills from the drawer and slapped them on the counter.

Judtson picked up the bills, and as they walked out, Kelsey looked back at the clerk and, in a cheery voice, added, "Have a good day!"

The storefront door was barely closed behind them as they both burst into loud laughter. Judtson cut in front of Kelsey and veered toward the passenger door, intending to open it for her, when she said, "No. Wait. Don't open it. I've always wanted to do something."

He moved his hand away from the door handle and stepped back as she grasped the top of the passenger door and vaulted over it and into the Olds. Her attempt to execute the maneuver failed miserably as her foot snagged on the frame of the vent window. Instead of landing neatly on the seat, Kelsey rotated as she descended, so that her final position was on her back, sideways across the passenger seat, with both feet hanging outside the car, her head resting on the driver's side, and her back arched over the gear shifter.

Laughing even harder, Judtson extended his hand to help her. "That was smooth!"

Now nearly hysterical, Kelsey took his hand, pulling herself upright and drawing her feet inside the car. Even Luis and Romeo were fighting back their laughter. "How did Tom Selleck do that into that tiny sports car?" she managed to ask between loud hiccuping guffaws.

"And his legs are a lot longer than yours," Judtson rejoined, circling around the car and getting in by the conventional method. "I think he probably used a stunt double."

"Hey, look!" she exclaimed, holding up the cup still filled with bubble-gum-flavored ice. "Didn't spill a drop."

Reaching over to straighten her sunglasses, which were slightly askew, he smiled at her. "You're fun."

Kelsey's free hand came up and lightly touched his. "So are you."

Romeo leaned forward toward the front seats, interposing his face between them. "Can we go to the airport now?"

▽

Villarreal, Clarkson, Meade, and Trippiano were gathered in the lounge with Saylor and Doni. The discussion for the previous hour had jumped from one possible scenario to another, as all of the participants added their perspectives.

"I don't know if we're getting any closer or not," Saylor commented. He had been certain that these people would provide the answers and was feeling a mild frustration beginning to build.

"I'm not sure," Doni remarked. "We're certainly getting a clear picture that there is a widespread conspiracy. We already knew what Carlos had uncovered and was about to make public. Al is convinced that he was brainwashed or mentally sidetracked, or whatever we want to call it, so that he would cancel his plans to release the second book he had been working on with Copeland, the one which was going to blow the lid off the secrets NASA has been keeping from us about the Moon and Mars. And that ties into Lisa's story. At first she was all ready to go with a program on the topic, having Copeland and Al as featured guests, but she was suddenly told by her boss to drop it. The abrupt change in him made her suspicious and she refused to abandon the story. That's when she got her visit from the Blues Brothers. And, of course, Captain Meade. . . ."

"I told you, young lady, it's Jimmy," interrupted the astronaut, eavesdropping on the recap.

She smiled. "Sorry. *Jimmy* has the photos of the alien craft from the fifties."

"I know all of that," Saylor said. "I still don't see the connection."

"You should. The discovery Carlos made basically proves beyond a shadow of a doubt that we were visited by aliens a long time ago. Who else could have transported those stone building blocks around the world? Al's next book was on the topic of man-made structures, or I should say structures impossible for nature to create, on the Moon and Mars. Jimmy's incident and pictures support a key part of it. And Lisa was about to present a lot of the information to the public, blowing the cover-up wide open."

He shook his head, amused at his wife's summation. "So you think we're looking for little green men?"

"Grey men. And no, I don't. I do think it's obvious that the government has been trying to cover this up for quite a while. What we don't know. . .yet. . .is why."

Scott entered the lounge carrying a handful of papers. In his usual manner, he skipped any greeting and plunged directly into his purpose for coming. "I've been driving myself crazy working on the gibberish from the hostage. I found a program which literally transcribes speech phonetically, rather than trying to interpret it. Here are some copies of the transcription."

He dropped the stapled sets on the table as Saylor asked, "Does it make more sense in print?"

With a shrug, Scott answered, "Not to me. After I did it, I created a little program which randomly selected small chunks from it, not enough to give anything away if someone understood it, and did a Google search."

"Find anything?"

"Not really. Well, maybe a clue. From several of the samples, Google kept suggesting alternate spellings…."

"I hate when it does that!" Doni commented.

"This time it might have been helpful. I don't know. The majority of the suggested spellings were in Hungarian. And right under that, Egyptian and Aramaic."

Villarreal bolted upright in his seat. "What did you just say?"

"I was talking about the suggested spellings…."

"No, I heard all of that. Which three languages came up the most when you ran the phonetic transcriptions?"

"Hungarian, Egyptian, and Aramaic."

Reaching across the table, Villarreal grabbed one of the stapled printouts and began scanning the text.

"What's the significance, Carlos?" Saylor asked, caught up in the man's excitement.

Quickly looking over the rows of text, Villarreal answered without glancing up. "Many of the dead languages, such as Phoenician, Etruscan, and Macedonian, left their marks on modern language. The Phoenician language morphed into Punic, a North African Semitic language which later influenced Maltese, as it is spoken today, although there is some disagreement on that. Several of the words, names, and phrases in ancient Etruscan survive in modern Italian. The same is true with Macedonian. Hardy bits of that long-deceased tongue are still spoken in Greece and certain Slavic regions. However, the oldest written language on Earth was thought to have completely died out long ago. It was not until recently that a number of scholars came to believe they had found linguistic roots tracing back to it in three very distinct and disparate languages."

"Hungarian, Egyptian, and Aramaic," offered Doni.

"Precisely."

"Those are three cultures I never would have connected."

"True. Most would not. But the more time passes, the more languages disseminate. That gives you a sense for exactly how ancient the original language was. This first written language predates all of those cultures. In fact, essentially all cultures."

She edged forward on her seat. "My God, you're talking about Sumer, aren't you?"

Villarreal nodded. "I have no idea, at this juncture, whether this is the case. Before we jump to any conclusions, I would like to get both the audio and this phonetic transcript to a linguist I know. He is a man who has made the study of the Sumerians his life's work. If he confirms what I suspect, our hostage is speaking in a tongue which man's ears have not heard for approximately four thousand years."

▽

Judtson adjusted his seat back and reclined, eliciting indignant, muttered comments from the pinched-faced woman behind him, upset because his movement caused her glass of Chablis to slosh some of its contents onto her knees. Since this was the same woman who had berated the flight attendant earlier for not knowing if the salad was organic, he ignored the remarks and closed his eyes, thinking back over their circuitous journey. So far they had traveled to Houston, St. Louis, and Seattle and were now en route to their final stop in San Diego before returning to Tucson.

In the seat beside him was Dean Copeland, the retired NASA engineer and physicist, fully converted back from his mental purgatory and currently napping. Across the aisle, Kelsey was softly conversing with the geologist, Bal Singh, whom they had located and converted at a conference in St. Louis. In the row in front of Kelsey sat Romeo, spreading out into the extra seat she had paid for, and his companion, Dylan Falt, the immunologist they had tracked down at his home in the Northwest.

They had been lucky. All three of the hastily concocted plans to draw the men into secluded locations for the conversion had gone well. And all the men, their alter egos returned to the forefront, were enormously grateful for the rescue and more than happy to join them in their quest.

Judtson recalled a conversation with Kelsey, just after their second round of successful conversions. He had expressed surprise that they had not yet encountered any opposition to their efforts. After having essentially stolen Villarreal and the others away, he had expected that they, whoever they were, would be keeping an eye on the remaining members of the list. Her answer was not one he expected.

She told him that their group of eight was probably only the tip of the iceberg; that all over the world, the consciousness-converted victims might number into the hundreds, even the thousands; and that their CDC list was a fluke unanticipated by the bad guys. And, she concluded, if all of that were the case, how would the other side have known which of their flock to guard?

He had to admit that her theory made sense. It was probably the only logical explanation for why they had not encountered a "Jake and Elwood" at each subject's location. The ramifications of her theory gave Judtson a very disquieting feeling in the pit of his stomach. He had been certain that once they gathered up all of the people on the list and converted them, they would know everything. If what she said turned out to be the case, their efforts were only going to result in obtaining a handful of pieces to a very large, very complex jigsaw puzzle. He hoped that the eight would be enough to reveal the picture.

▽

Ricky, stir-crazy from the confining space of his quarters in the silo, decided to move around a little. Hopping up from his bunk, he left the room and walked unhurriedly down the steel-lined hallway toward the lounge. As he approached, the sound of laughter from several people spilled into the hallway. Quickening his step, he reached the doorway and saw Saylor, Doni, Jimmy Meade, and Lisa Trippiano around one of the tables. All four were near hysteria. The moment he turned the corner and entered, Lisa was the first to notice his arrival and gulped back her laughter, slamming her lips tightly shut. The others, noticing this, turned to see the cause, and all of them stifled their guffaws as one.

Leery, Ricky asked, "What? What's so funny?"

Her face red, Doni managed to answer, "Oh, nothing."

Ricky's suspicion heightened. "Right! Nothing! Come on, what is it?"

Catching his breath, Saylor did his best to adopt a sincere expression. "Really, Ricky. Nothing."

Ricky glowered at the four and stomped to the kitchenette area, where he poured a cup of coffee. The group behind him were silent as he did this, until he opened the refrigerator door for the creamer, when he suddenly heard Lisa yell, "FREEZE, JERKBALL!"

Her bellow was instantly followed by all of them again bursting into frenetic peals of laughter.

Whirling around, Ricky glared at Saylor and shouted over the din, "YOU TOLD THEM!"

"Why suspect me?" he responded, trying to look innocent. "I think it has become an urban legend by now!"

$$\triangledown$$

The final person on their list, Chris Ashby, the chemist, worked as a professor at UC San Diego and, according to Scott's research, lived in La Jolla. After they had secured hotel rooms for their entourage, Judtson and Kelsey, leaving Romeo at the hotel to protect their converts, drove to the campus in the rental they had obtained with bogus identification.

"Should one of us go in and make sure he's there today?" Kelsey asked. "I can drop in and audit his class."

Judtson was studying the class schedule provided by Scott. "He's not lecturing right now; it's a lab and appears to be upper division, so there's probably only a small group of students. If you and I go in, he'll spot us. We can't take the chance that he'll remember us when the time comes to make our move."

"If we're going forward with our current plan, it might actually help if I went in."

"How so?"

"If I'm going to come on to him later, wouldn't it make sense that I've been almost stalking him?"

Judtson turned his attention away from the schedule and chuckled. "You are actually getting into this whole Mata Hari seductress thing, aren't you?"

"Hey, it's fun. So what do you think?"

Staring out the windshield at the grassy campus for a moment, Judtson shrugged. "Okay. Why not?"

Before he could change his mind, Kelsey hopped out of the rental and was crossing the lawn to the front of the chemistry building. Judtson watched her as she hurried away and, not for the first time, was amazed at how entangled in his life she had become. As he replayed the many scenes from their brief friendship, his mind stumbled over consciously unperceived fears, worries that he had ignored or avoided to this point, as the hull of a boat would scrape and shudder encountering hidden boulders in shallow water.

Forcing himself to put aside his positive prejudice toward Kelsey, Judtson reexamined the objective facts of how she had suddenly sprung into his predicament, appearing at pivotal moments, and essentially taking charge of his life, as well as Saylor's and now all of the others' lives. He realized he had to admit the possibility that she was some sort of agent who had infiltrated... *infiltrated what?* he asked himself. The group back at the silo would certainly not have been set free from their mental exile and brought together were it not for Kelsey and her people and resources. He, Ricky, Doni, and Saylor would not or could not have done it, even if it had occurred to them to try.

Conceding the suspicious nature of her interjection into his dilemma, Judtson decided, as he had each previous time this concern intruded into his thoughts, to trust his instincts. And his instincts told him that Kelsey was exactly as she appeared... another victim of the bad guys; a vital, alive, and energetic woman who dived headfirst into every situation she encountered.

Satisfied with his working conclusion, he sat back in the driver's seat, dismissing the line of thought, or at least that was his intent. Yet, despite the typical pleasantness of the San Diego day and the almost elysian tranquility of the lushly landscaped grounds surrounding him, a vague worry niggled at the edges of his thoughts.

▽

Using the layout emailed to them by Scott, Kelsey found the chemistry lab, opened the door, and entered, making a point of appearing as casual as possible. The room was filled with parallel work benches and tall stools, mostly occupied by students. Kelsey's expectation, of finding the students clad in white lab coats and tinkering with bubbling beakers and vials suspended above Bunsen burners, was totally shattered. The young males and females, wearing everyday street clothes, were, without exception, bent over their laptops and tablets. There was not a bubbling beaker in sight.

As she had entered the lab, Kelsey spotted Ashby, whom she recognized from a picture, standing at one of the benches and talking to a young man. He noticed her enter and excused himself, stepping away from the bench and walking up to her. As he approached, Kelsey assumed a broad smile.

"Hello, Miss. Can I help you?"

"Are you Professor Ashby?"

"I am." His answer was polite and even.

Kelsey stuck out her hand. "Very cool. I've heard wonderful things about your classes and I was thinking about signing up for one."

He accepted her handshake. Planning to set the stage for later, she held her grip on his hand longer than normal and stepped slightly closer. He was tall, a little more than six feet in height, and slender. With blond hair and blue eyes, she had to admit that he was quite handsome and surmised that he was probably quite popular with the female students on campus.

"That would be great, Miss...?"

"Teel. Shelby Teel," she answered, staying with the fictitious name she had created for Clarkson.

"Miss Teel. Are you currently a student here?"

As he asked the question, Ashby relaxed his grip on her hand. Not wanting to create an awkward moment, she released his and replied, "Not yet. I just moved to San Diego from Tucson and haven't had a chance to do anything yet."

"Tucson? Were you attending the University of Arizona?"

"I was. Go Cats!"

"I have a friend who teaches there. Perhaps he was one of your professors. His name is Blaylock."

To avoid getting cornered, Kelsey dodged the question and changed the subject clumsily.

"It's a big school. I didn't know him. I should be going. I only wanted to peek in for a minute." She stepped back a pace.

"And I should be getting back to my students. Thank you for dropping in, Miss Teel."

Kelsey thanked him and hurried out the door.

▽

"How late is he going to work?" The impatient complaint came from Kelsey, who was squirming in her seat beside Judtson. "Are we sure that's his car?"

Amused by her fidgeting, he answered in an overly calm voice, "According to Scott, it is. We're in the faculty lot, and that's the correct license plate, make, and model."

It was almost dark and Ashby's Prius was the only vehicle remaining in the parking area.

"Well, based on his schedule, his office hours ended an hour ago. What's he doing in there?"

Instantly, there was a knock on the side window, causing both of them to jump. Jerking his head around, Judtson saw that it was Romeo outside their car.

As the big man climbed into the backseat, Kelsey asked, "What are you doing here? I thought you were going to stay with the converts."

"You two were gone a long time and hadn't bothered to call me, so I thought I'd see if there was a problem."

"What did you do with the group?" asked Judtson.

"They should be okay. I left all three of them in one room. They're locked in. I left a gun with Copeland since he said he was a marksman. What's going on here?"

Kelsey sighed, conveying her impatience. "I was going to make my move as he walked to his car. But we've been waiting for *hours*!"

Romeo twisted around to look at the chemistry building. "Which window is his? Is the light on?"

"Hey! Good idea," Kelsey exclaimed, pulling out the building layout and grasping for the switch of the vehicle's interior light.

Romeo reached over and grabbed her wrist before she could turn the light on. "That's too obvious. Use this."

He handed her a penlight from his pocket. As she began to switch it on, Judtson interrupted, "Never mind. Here he comes."

They could see, approximately a hundred yards across the lawn, that the front door to the building was open and a figure resembling Ashby had come out.

"You're on."

Judtson's green light to Kelsey was unnecessary as she had already opened her door and sprung out, moving quickly to position herself near his car.

As the two men watched her, Romeo shook his head. "I don't like this."

"What's wrong?"

"Probably nothing. But it's dark and too wide-open here. You stay in the car. I'm going to back her up."

Before Judtson could respond, Romeo was out and made a circuitous path, concealing himself relatively close to Kelsey's position. Judtson locked the doors and sat back.

▽

Kelsey waited until Ashby, who had been talking on his cell phone as he walked, noticed her standing by his car. She heard him tell the person on the phone that he needed to go, breaking the connection. With a slightly disconcerted expression, he said, "Hello, Miss...Teel, was it?" He stopped a few feet from her.

Stepping forward to partially close the distance, Kelsey smiled broadly. "Hello, Professor Ashby. I know this looks a little strange, but I was wondering if you'd like to have a drink?"

He pursed his lips, clearly not quite comfortable with the situation. "If you don't mind my asking, Miss Teel, how long have you been waiting by my car? Since you left my lab?"

Allowing herself a nervous giggle, Kelsey gushed, "Oh, no. That would be *too* weird. That was, what...four hours ago? No, I've spent most of the afternoon checking out the campus, grabbing a bite, kind of soaking up the ambiance of the place. I was just heading back to my apartment, when I saw your car and thought I'd hang out for a little while. You know, just to see if you'd like a drink...or something." As she finished her rambling explanation, Kelsey took another step forward, moving closer to him.

To her chagrin, she saw him take a compensating step backward. "How did you know this was my car?" The suspicion in his voice was unmistakable, and she realized that he was not as much a slave to his libido as she had assumed the typical college professor would be.

Working to keep her voice light, she went on, "I look like a stalker, don't I? It's not that bad, really! I had the whole day set aside just to get the feel of things. I've been here since this morning." She paused momentarily. When Kelsey resumed, her voice had a softer, more suggestive tone. "I confess, I saw you arrive earlier. I guess I liked what I saw. I followed you inside the chemistry building and found out who you were. That's why I popped into your lab today." She stopped talking and presented her best vulnerable look as she waited for him to take the bait, hoping he could appreciate it in the darkness and counting on the male ego's tendency to overrule logical thought.

She was relieved to see the suspicion diminish on his face, replaced by a wry smile. "Miss Teel, I'm flattered. I truly am. Unfortunately, I'm afraid you've wasted your time."

Kelsey started to speak; however, the professor held up his hand to stop her and continued, "I am running quite late. That was my date for the evening on the phone as I walked up. He is impatiently waiting for me so that we can have dinner."

Her hand flew up her mouth. "Oh" was all she could think to say.

"So if you will excuse me, I really must be going."

"Of...of course," Kelsey stammered, taking three steps back toward the rear of his car. "I'm very sorry."

Ashby stepped forward and pushed the button on his key chain. The car alarm chirped once and the doors unlocked. "No, please. No reason to apologize."

As he spoke, he opened the car door and turned to face her.

"As I said, I truly am quite flattered. You are a very lovely...."

In the middle of his sentence, his head suddenly jerked forward and the professor went limp, collapsing. Before his body could impact the asphalt, Kelsey saw a beefy arm snake around his chest, stopping his descent.

"Romeo?"

Her bodyguard stepped forward, still clutching the unconscious man. "Yeah?"

"What did you do?"

Illuminated by the interior car light, she could see him smile. "I executed Plan B."

Chapter 27

LEADING THE PROCESSION, Kelsey and Judtson arrived at the airport security checkpoint first, getting into the short line. Romeo, directly behind them, spoke softly to Kelsey. "I still think we should have driven."

Winking at Judtson, Kelsey teased, "You're just mad because the plane was fully booked and you couldn't get an empty seat next to you."

"No. That isn't it. Well, maybe a part of it. But it's only a six-hour drive from here. We could have rented a van, and then Luis wouldn't need to leave the base to pick us up."

"We can rent something when we get there," she answered.

The last of the passengers in front of them moved through the metal detector. Judtson emptied his pockets into the plastic container and set his bag on the x-ray conveyor, walking through the sensor and triggering the flashing red light and the alarm.

"Please step back through," the TSA employee, a reed-thin man in his mid-fifties with a mustard stain on his shirt, ordered.

Kelsey and the others waited as Judtson returned.

"Raise your arms," the man told him brusquely.

"Wouldn't that be 'Raise your arms, please'?" Judtson asked and was ignored. Kelsey noticed, as the surly man began tracing an outline around Judtson's body with a wand, a slight grin creep onto her companion's face.

"Oh, this should be good," she murmured.

Hearing her, Romeo asked, "What's wrong?"

"I know that look."

The beeper on the wand sounded as the agent swung the metal detector between Judtson's legs. Returning the wand to his work station, the man said, "Turn around and stand with your feet apart."

Judtson did not move, and a moment later the man spat out, "Please!"

"Much better."

Kelsey watched with anticipation as Judtson, his hands still resting on his head, turned his back on the agent and spread his stance. Beginning at the ankles, the man began patting him down, working his way upward. When he reached the inside of his mid-thigh, an earsplitting alarm blared, startling the TSA screener and causing him to spasmodically jerk upward, slamming one of his hands into Judtson's groin, evoking a shout of pain. At the same time, the second agent, who had been handling the other aisle of passengers entering the concourse, ran over, obviously flustered.

A third TSA employee, sitting on a stool at the x-ray screen, jumped up and grabbed Judtson's carryon, which seemed to be the source of the shrieking alarm. As she zipped it open, two uniformed police officers arrived at a full run, their hands on their holsters, their eyes darting as they tried to figure out what was occurring.

In the midst of the commotion, Kelsey glanced at Judtson and saw he was laughing at the antics of the uniformed people around him.

The woman standing at Judtson's bag was holding up the black plastic case Kelsey had seen him drop into his suitcase before they left the silo.

"HOW DO YOU SHUT THIS OFF?" she yelled over the alarm.

Calmly dropping his hands to his side, Judtson walked through the metal detector and took the case from her. He thumbed a concealed button on the side, and the device abruptly went silent.

The first agent, the thin man who had been frisking him, angrily walked toward him, stopping inches from Judtson's chest.

"What do you think you're doing?" the man shouted, compensating for the loud ringing still in his ears.

Looking innocent, Judtson answered, "Doing? Nothing."

The two police officers joined them, one taking the plastic case away and examining it. The TSA agent turned to the cops and demanded, "Arrest him."

"For what?" asked Judtson. "Creating a loud noise? I didn't turn it on; you did."

The skinny man appeared ready to explode. "What do you mean, I did?"

Shrugging nonchalantly, Judtson, his expression deadpan, explained, "I'm a public figure. I have security concerns and always travel with a bodyguard." He paused and tilted his head in Romeo's direction. "Everywhere I go, I always wear a transmitter on my thigh. That plastic case is the receiver and the alarm. I guess when you were feeling me up a moment ago, you were a bit too, uhhh, into your work and you set it off."

One of the two police officers, the man holding the case, handed it to Judtson. "I recognize you. You're Judtson Kent. My wife reads all of your books."

"Thanks."

The TSA agent, his face now a bright red, wheeled on the cop. "Aren't you going to arrest him?"

The officer glanced at his partner for a moment before he answered, "For what?"

"I don't care! Interfering with a federal agent in the prosecution of his duties!"

"Like the man said, you were the one who set off the alarm, not him."

"He didn't warn me that it was there!"

"Did you ask?" The question came from Judtson.

Becoming even more agitated, the man barked, "No! I don't have to ask!"

Judtson, directing his gaze at the cop, smiled. "Officer, to the best of my knowledge, I am under no obligation to inform strangers that I am wired with a security device. Am I correct?"

"Stranger? I'm a TSA officer!"

The policeman, grinning back at Judtson, said, "As far as I know, Mr. Kent, you are correct." Turning to the agent, he continued, "I don't see any laws broken here."

The skinny man's eyes bulged, but he choked back further comments, and the two officers walked away.

Whirling back around, the agent pointed at Kelsey and Romeo. "So they are with you?"

Judtson nodded. "They are."

A gloating smirk replacing the apoplectic anger on his face, the little man rushed back through the metal detector, motioned for the female agent to follow, and confronted Kelsey, grabbing her arm. "Miss, come with me. We need you to submit to a *random* full search."

The instant the man's hand touched Kelsey, Romeo's shot out and gripped the agent's slender wrist, squeezing hard. "Not today, pal."

▽

"Well, Romeo, seems you got your way," Judtson joked as he maneuvered the rented full-sized passenger van onto the freeway, heading east.

He heard a soft snort from the big man sitting behind him. "That wasn't exactly what I'd call keeping a low profile."

Kelsey laughed. "I loved it. Did you see the look on the pip-squeak's face when Judtson's alarm went off? I thought he was going to wet his pants!"

"Yeah, that was really funny," Judtson commented sourly. "You weren't the one who got punched in the.... It still hurts."

Kelsey laughed harder. "Hey, you brought it on yourself. You could have put that button somewhere else, like your armpit."

Judtson adjusted the rearview mirror, checking to see if there were any black SUVs following them, and realized that with all of the seats filled with their guests, the inside mirror was not much help. He scanned the two outboard mirrors at the heavy San Diego traffic behind them.

"I think it's a California thing, but there must be at least four big black SUVs in back of us."

Romeo twisted around in his seat. With a grunt, he said, "We'll be able to tell when we get over the hill and the traffic thins out. If they are bad guys, they won't make their move in this traffic, anyway."

Raising his voice slightly, Judtson called out, "Professor Ashby?"

Ashby, sitting in the farthest row back, turned his attention away from Falt, the immunologist, with whom he had been talking. "Yes, sir?"

"We haven't had that much time to chat since you joined us. I'm curious as to why they zapped you. You had already lost the funding for your research. Weren't you basically shut down at that point, or was it something else altogether?"

The professor leaned forward, unspooling the shoulder restraint to its limit, and rested his arms on the back of the seat in front of him. "It's true that I lost the government grant for my work. But I was only shut down, as you put it, for a matter of weeks before I was approached by a private source who offered to provide funding, actually substantially more funding than my prior grant. I was zapped, as you put it, just days after I received that offer."

Judtson glanced at Kelsey, who was staring quizzically at him. "That's interesting."

She nodded. "Maybe we have an ally out there."

Addressing Ashby, Judtson asked, "Who made the offer?"

"I wish I knew. The source of the initial offer was vague. I was only told that it was a foundation."

"Didn't that make you a little suspicious?"

"Of course. I'm always very careful about the people I associate with. They assured me that they would fully disclose the source when papers were to be signed. If I wasn't comfortable with the entity then, I'd be allowed to withdraw."

"Damn!" Kelsey muttered softly.

▽

"Keep moving," Romeo instructed Judtson as the van approached the entrance to the silo. "Don't stop for anything."

Romeo called Luis and had him drop the tire barrier and open the gate, clearing their path. Twisting around in his seat, Romeo, squinting to see in the darkness, watched the rear and saw the steel teeth snap into the upright position after they passed. Waiting until they were through the second entrance, he made certain the gates closed behind them.

As Judtson parked near the surface entrance, he saw that Meade was waiting for them, casually holding an AK-47 as if it were a nine iron. Luis emerged from the shack, also armed, and trotted to a spot approximately one hundred yards behind them, his back to the van.

"Everybody stay inside until I signal," Romeo ordered as he climbed out. He flashed a quick smile at Meade. "It appears that you've been recruited, Captain."

"What did I tell you about that 'captain' crap? And no, I wasn't recruited. I broke a lifelong rule."

Romeo's smile broadened. "You volunteered?"

"Yep."

"You must have broken that rule at least one other time."

"Why's that?"

"I always thought the only way into the astronaut program was to volunteer."

The gray-haired man shrugged. "That doesn't count. I was drunk."

Romeo laughed, his eyes surveying the area around them to the extent that it was illuminated by the lights from the van. Seeing nothing of concern, he whistled a single note to Luis, who, without looking back, pulled a remote control from his vest and pressed a button. Instantly, high-intensity floodlights, which were mounted in an array around the shack, flared on, blanketing the grounds with light out to the perimeter wall. At the same time, he motioned to the passengers in the van, shouting, "Hustle! Hustle!"

The doors opened and Judtson, Kelsey, and the four others piled out and began to jog for the entrance. Romeo whistled again and Luis, who now glanced back to make sure everyone was in motion, began backing up, his rifle at the ready. When all the civilians were inside, Romeo instructed Meade to follow them, then Luis, as he brought up the rear and closed the steel door, locking and barring it.

As he turned to follow the others down the stairs, he saw that Judtson had held back.

"Romeo, why the floodlights? I thought we wanted to come and go in the dark?"

As Romeo descended the metal treads, he answered Judtson, who followed. "NVGs."

"What?"

"Night vision goggles. If they're out there watching, they're going to be using NVGs to be able to see us. Staring through NVGs, which amplify ambient light, is painful as hell if you're suddenly hit with a bright light. In addition to the pain and shock, your pupils slam shut in reaction."

"I understand. So at the moment you were moving us from the van to the entrance, when we were the most vulnerable, you hit them with the lights. They briefly go blind, have to pull off the goggles, and need a minute or two to adjust."

"And by then we're all inside."

The two reached the bottom of the stairs and crossed through the vault door. "Romeo, you're smarter than you look."

The big man paused, a subtle smile giving him away. "You know what? Ricky was right about you. You are a soup sandwich, aren't you?"

Judtson broke into a wide grin. "Yep, a real waste of skin."

Chapter 28

T HE LOUNGE, ORIGINALLY DESIGNED to accommodate the launch crews stationed in the silo, was crowded. With the exception of Romeo and Luis, the entire group congregated in the room. All of the available seating was filled by those first to arrive, and several others were perched on the counter top of the cabinets, which lined one wall. Judtson, Saylor, and Kelsey were standing near the doorway. The noise level was especially high due to the multiple conversations between the members of the recently converted group.

"This is it," Judtson commented softly to the two. "If the answer isn't in this room, I'm not sure what our next move would be."

As he talked, he watched as Copeland and Clarkson talked to each other in animated tones. "Those two are certainly happy to be reunited."

"I still can't imagine what it's like to be locked away inside your own head." The remark came from Saylor. "Or what it's like to suddenly be out again."

"Hope you never find out, pal. So Villarreal thinks our guest is speaking Sumerian?"

"He's not certain. He does know a man who's an expert on the language, so he and Scott just sent some samples to him."

"Doesn't seem as if it would be that hard to figure out."

"Carlos explained it to me. I think I understand. What it comes down to is that no one in modern history has ever heard it spoken. There are tons of tablets – hundreds, maybe even thousands, I don't know – with text. But it's all pictographic."

Judtson chuckled. "They weren't nice enough to include any pronunciation guides?"

"No. Well, I guess there actually are some clues. The Sumerians were the oldest civilization with a written language. Somewhat later, the Akkadians came about. They were neighbors and interacted, but their languages were different. On a few of the later Sumerian tablets, they referenced some Akkadian words. Since they didn't know how to write them, they basically spelled them phonetically. Linguists supposedly have a better feel for the Akkadian language, so by working backward, they've made assumptions on how Sumerian speech sounded."

"That's pretty iffy," Kelsey interjected. "If the Akkadians were later than the Sumerians, I don't see how that would work."

"Carlos said it is fairly shaky. We're basically dealing with wild guesses. Hopefully, his friend can make some sense of it."

"So we wait and see?" asked Judtson.

"That's all we can do."

Looking over the group in the lounge, Judtson shrugged at Saylor and Kelsey. "Okay, let's get started."

Clearing his throat in the socially automatic gesture of a speaker vying for attention, he began, "Everybody!"

The myriad of conversations quickly died, and the group turned to face him. "For some of you it has been a rather long day and I know you're getting tired."

Copeland, the NASA scientist, spoke up. "I'm so happy to be out of my head that I don't think I'll sleep for a week."

Several in the room laughed. "If you're worried about somehow slipping back into Neverland, I can tell you that it hasn't happened to me," Judtson assured him.

"Yet!"

Judtson chuckled at Copeland's comment. "That's true. Yet. Let's hope we don't ever return there. In the meantime, now that we're finally all together, I think it's critical that we figure out exactly what's going on and who is behind it."

Many heads nodded and Judtson continued, "I'm going to go around and ask questions. But please, if anyone hears an answer that triggers something for you, speak up. Carlos, we've had the most time to talk. For the sake of the group, please describe what you were working on before you were...sent away."

Ever formal, Villarreal stood to address the assemblage and told them about his discoveries in Puma Punku and at Baalbek, finishing the recitation with the geological confirmation of the source of the building blocks found in Lebanon. The final revelation had a predictable result as the room was immediately filled with overlapping conversations and questions.

"I know that what Carlos said is astounding. It blew me away the first time I heard it. What I want to do at this point is keep moving forward. If something he said prompted a new fact or idea, share it. If all you want is to ask questions, let's hold those until everyone has spoken."

The jumble of voices died down. Judtson resumed, "Jimmy, if you wouldn't mind, I'd like you to go next."

Meade stayed seated and told the group about his encounter with the flying saucer, as he called it, and the visit from Eisenhower, as related by his friend. He finished his narrative by saying, "On my way here, after these youngsters pulled my bacon from the fire, I dug out the pictures I took of the ship. Scotty was nice enough to print some extra copies."

He opened a manila folder and handed out several stacks of eight-by-ten, black-and-white prints, walking one set to Judtson, who had not yet seen them.

The first picture was taken perhaps fifty yards back from the craft. "That looks like the spaceship from *The Day the Earth Stood Still*," remarked Kelsey, who was craning to see the photographs.

"It does. The original, not the remake," added Saylor.

Judtson passed that photo to Kelsey and examined the next, which was a similar view, only closer. The ship was obviously circular and came to a sharp edge around the circumference, widening rapidly toward the center and abruptly bulging to create a dome-shaped structure on the top. It was resting upon the dry powder of the lake bed on four extended struts. He passed the second picture to Kelsey, who had handed off the first to Saylor, and they worked their way through the remainder of the shots. The perfect symmetry of the craft resulted in all of the views appearing identical; however, by the background it was obvious that Meade had walked all the way around, snapping pictures as he went. Meade's partner had posed with the ship in several of the photos.

As the three pored over the prints, Meade distributed the remaining stacks among the group, speaking as he did. "The problem I've always had with these pictures is that they are hokey as hell. As the young lady said, they look like something out of a 1950s movie. I never believed they were going to convince anyone."

"That's their plan," Copeland stated authoritatively.

Judtson instantly took his eyes away from the pictures to focus on the NASA scientist. "What do you mean?"

Meade moved off to the side and leaned his lanky frame against the wall as Copeland stood up. "It's clever if you think about it...put the true design of their spaceship in a hundred cheap movies, have their agents dress up in those goofy black suits and sunglasses. I don't know if you have seen them yet, but the black helicopters they actually use have been turned into a cliché, a bad joke...a buzz phrase...to make anyone who reports seeing them an automatic candidate for the loony bin. Let me ask all of you in this room a question. Before all this happened...before each of you stumbled upon your piece of the puzzle and started to believe there was something going on...how did you react if you happened upon an interview or a story on the Internet, where the witness to some bizarre event mentioned a flying saucer, men dressed in black, or the black helicopters? From my own experience, I already know the answer. It didn't matter to you if the eyewitness was a police officer, a military or civilian pilot, or from any of a hundred other fields which would, under normal circumstances, confer substantial credibility; you just unceremoniously dismissed all of them and everything they said."

Copeland paused and turned slowly, checking the reactions from the group. The majority were nodding their heads in agreement.

"I don't think this is an accident or a coincidence. I'm confident that this is a deliberate strategy. Too many people have seen far too many things. They...the other side...can't possibly cover it all up. So the next best thing...an ingenious strategy, actually...is to saturate the public with dribs and drabs of truth, and then to add plenty of patently absurd wackos who are deliberately put forward as believers and proponents of the truth, in order to make the entire subject taboo for someone who wants to be considered normal and sane. You should know this, Mr. Kent. You were their biggest ally, their prominent propagator of misinformation. I cannot think of anyone else who has done as effective a job of savaging those who attempted to get out the word."

Judtson started to respond, when Copeland held up his hand to stop him and continued, "That wasn't an attack, trust me. You are simply blessed with a talent for writing...a gift which allowed you to make a fortune and disseminate the accepted wisdom to the masses. You might have been a useful pawn to them, but I've come to believe you were an unwilling one."

Taking a moment to allow his words to sink in, Judtson acquiesced, "Fair enough. That rings true when I think about the reactions from my agent, publisher, and cable network as I was changing direction."

Copeland laughed. "I'm sure their response was swift, heavy-handed and, from your perspective, drastically out of proportion to your acts."

"That about sums it up, yes."

"I know. I experienced similar treatment with the release of *Secret Agenda*. My superiors and co-workers at NASA, my colleagues in my field of science, and many of my friends turned on me, viciously in some cases. Even my wife of twenty-eight years told me she'd leave me if I didn't drop this tomfoolery and get back to, as she phrased it, *real science*."

His mind flashing back to Kristen, Judtson uttered, "Yes."

"So I lost my wife. My children think I've gone over the edge, are embarrassed by me, and won't have anything to do with me. I have a four-year-old granddaughter I've never seen. Of course I lost my position. I lost my friends. Hell, even the IRS began auditing me yearly."

Saylor, who had been listening quietly, asked, "Why would they...and we still don't know if *they* did...need to do all of that if they can simply strap their device on your head and turn you into a compliant sycophant?"

Copeland paused before answering. "I don't know. I was wondering about that myself as we traveled here."

"Maybe," Matt Wheeler suggested, "they didn't have it prior to this. It's possible their conversion device is a new invention or technique for them."

"That could be," acknowledged Saylor. "When the first signs happened to Judtson, I did quite a bit of research in an attempt to find other cases. The precursor symptoms of the conversion were not in any of the existing medical literature. All of your cases were the first reported, all at about the same time. This does bring up something I've been curious about. Kelsey, Matt, Romeo, Luis, Scott, Doni, and I are buying into this. So we obviously aren't somehow incapable of accepting the facts."

Judtson faced his friend. "Yes, that's true. What's your question?"

"Why? Why are we immune to the brainwashing? Why didn't they try to zap all of us?"

"I think I can answer that," Meade responded. "Ever since I began talking about my little experience in the dry lake bed, for the last fifteen years or so, most people react in the same way Mr. Copeland here describes – derisive, rude, dismissive, even angry. But there have always been some folks...granted, a relatively small group of them...who believe me, who buy it. I don't know what makes these people different, immune from the mind-set of the mainstream, but there have always been some."

"That's true," Kelsey added. "All you have to do is check the Internet. There are plenty of people who really embrace these things, are even obsessed with them. There are organized groups. They have meetings. They're out there. So I don't think we're that rare, Saylor."

"I have a feeling the segment of the population who are open-minded...receptive...about it," Judtson commented thoughtfully, "are probably tolerated by them, as long as we don't become the majority."

"Or begin to attract people who are too influential," added Kelsey.

Villarreal spoke up. "Saylor, I think the *ability* to grasp the facts, to be open-minded, must be the norm in the general population. Perhaps the vast majority can be convinced. If it were not possible to change their minds, why would our foes even bother with their orchestrated campaign of character assassination and disinformation?"

"If the majority have it," Meade snorted, "it must be dormant."

There was a lull in the conversation, which Judtson utilized. "All food for thought, definitely. We still have quite a bit of ground to cover. If you all don't mind, I'd like Mr. Copeland to share his discoveries."

No one objected, so the scientist began, "It's Dean, by the way. I don't know how many of you have read my book...."

Kelsey raised a hand, as did Matt. Saylor raised his copy of the book. "I've started it."

"Three out of a group this size isn't bad, I guess. Well, a portion of my mission at NASA was photo analysis. With my training, I was tasked with mapping geological formations and locating potential sites for future landings, with special emphasis on identifying possible ice or water deposits underground. This gave me access to one hundred percent of the images from the Moon and, later, from Mars. I guess they were comfortable that I was with the program, because they didn't bother to censor, filter, or in any way prevent me from seeing some things, things that changed my whole view of our world."

The anticipation in the gathering was palpable as he continued, "I'll begin with our Moon. As far as the world is concerned, Neil Armstrong was the first living, breathing being to set foot on that dusty satellite. During that first mission, there were some bizarre details, like the communion or Masonic ceremony when they landed, which I'm not going to get into right now. There has been ample speculation about those things on the Internet. I'll just stick with my specialty. He and Buzz Aldrin snapped hundreds of pictures while they were on the surface. As it circled the Moon, the lunar orbiter also continuously snapped pictures of the terrain. This was the protocol for all of the missions that followed. All told, there were tens of thousands of photographs taken. In the course of my analysis, I began finding anomalies, photographic evidence of features and objects which should not have been present on a heavenly body never visited by anyone before."

"Like the Data head," Kelsey interrupted.

"Yes," Copeland acknowledged. "That and many more."

"The Data head?" The question came from Lisa Trippiano.

With a half smile, he explained, "There was an episode years ago on the TV series *Star Trek: The Next Generation*, where the crew of the Enterprise found the head of their robot officer, Data, lying among some artifacts from the 1800s. I believe the title of that program was 'Time's Arrow.' One of the photographs I examined of the Moon showed an object that resembled the head from a robot, lying on the surface of the lunar dust. The name caught on."

Saylor quickly riffled through his copy of Copeland's book until he found the page. "Here it is." He handed the opened book to Trippiano, who did an almost comical double-take at the page and then passed the book down the row.

"We've all had our fill of skeptics," Chris Ashby said as he examined the picture. "But couldn't that simply be a rock which, in that particular light, looks like a head?"

Copeland nodded curtly. "Of course it could. If that photo were the only oddity from the batch, I would not be standing here. It was what I began to find in many, many other pictures that put me on this path. In the interest of brevity, I'll summarize that I found literally hundreds of objects, features, structures, and lights which, in my opinion and the opinions of other experts, could not have been present without the intervention of an intelligent life."

At this point, Judtson interrupted, "You're saying that someone had been to the Moon prior to that first landing?"

"According to the photographic evidence, not only had someone visited our Moon, but bases had been built there."

"Who was it?" blurted Kelsey.

Copeland responded to her with a shrug. "I have no way of answering that."

"Did NASA know?"

"I have my own opinions as to what they knew and when they knew it. However, I'll stick with the facts at this point. While I was at NASA, I worked quite closely with Harold Billings, the head photo archivist. He was responsible for the tracking and safekeeping of the photographic and film inventory, and he was the man I went to every morning to check out the materials I needed for the day, turning them back in to him every evening.

"When I first began to notice the anomalies, I naturally assumed that my employer was genuinely interested in truth and knowledge. Not wanting to be regarded as a crackpot myself, I took my time and put together a fairly persuasive collection of pictures before I went to my supervisor. I made an appointment with him and presented my evidence. To be honest, I was surprised at the time by his impassivity. I had expected a stronger reaction. After all, I was showing him what I considered to be proof of the existence of extraterrestrial intelligence and proof that they had been to our Moon! Instead, he thanked me for my diligence and promised to get back to me. He did not even ask me to leave my photos.

"That evening I turned my package back in to Harold. I guess he could tell I was troubled and asked me what was wrong, so I told him and showed him what I had found. We talked for more than three hours, sitting at a table and poring over the pictures together. Harold's reaction to the evidence was what I had expected and not received from my supervisor. By the end he was exhausted, as was I. We finished up and he put everything back in the bonded vault for the night. I went home and got drunk.

"The next day I came in late, and Harold was waiting for me. He told me that what I had shown him had affected him profoundly. He hadn't slept much and came to work early, anxious to share my findings with a friend who worked in the photo lab. When he arrived at the lab, what he saw infuriated him. There were four techs already at work, busily airbrushing negatives... *negatives*... the only original copies of photographs in the days prior to digitization. Maintaining his cool, he chatted with one of the techs he knew, and the man told him they had all been brought in the previous evening to do this work. Standing beside the tech, Harold could see that the negative he was airbrushing was one of the pictures I had shown him. The man was airbrushing out a tower structure in the picture."

"Oh, my God!" gasped Ricky.

"Concerned, Harold rushed back to the vault and checked on the prints. Here's where I need to take a moment to explain the normal procedures for photo archiving. When negatives arrive, four sets of prints are made of the stills and four sets of film are made from the film negatives. All the sets are stored together in the vault. When Harold specifically checked the vault file for the prints of the pictures I had presented to my supervisor and to him the day before, they were removed... gone. He checked the log and no one had signed them out."

"So they were lost forever." The comment was from Meade.

Copeland turned to answer the astronaut, a slight smile on his face. "Sometimes I think God watches over me. If I hadn't decided to share my findings with Harold... if we hadn't stayed there so late... he wouldn't have been so tired and eager to get home that he put my stack in his desk drawer inside the vault, instead of with the others. No, we saved those original prints."

"Didn't they notice that the set was missing?" Ricky asked.

"Guess not. After this, Harold and I decided to keep a low profile. We knew that if we pushed the issue we'd be out on our ears and would never have access to the materials again. I went to my office and resumed my normal duties. Harold did his job at the vault, pretending that nothing had happened. The next morning, as soon as he came to work, he checked and found that the missing prints had been replaced overnight with new prints, made from the airbrushed negatives."

"I'll be damned," Meade muttered. "Doesn't surprise me a bit."

"After all of the Apollo missions were completed and the program was discontinued, I left NASA as a full-time employee, but continued to work for them as a paid consultant. This was my role during the subsequent unmanned missions to Mars. You can imagine my reaction as I examined photographs and video from those expeditions and found what appeared to be structures on our neighboring planet. It was not until I found astounding photographic evidence relating to Mars that

I decided to publish *Secret Agenda*."

"And all hell broke loose, I'll bet!" Meade remarked.

"Yes. It was at that time my wife left me. I became estranged from my children. My peers shunned me. And, generally, I became an object of ridicule. One of the coinciding events at the time was that NASA ordered Billings, who was still the senior archivist of all photographs and film, to destroy every single print and negative from all of our lunar missions."

"What?" The animated question came from Lisa Trippiano. "They ordered the eradication of all of the photographic evidence of man's only venture to the Moon?"

"They did. Fortunately, Harold and I had copied and hidden *some* of the materials which we felt to be the strongest evidence. When he received the order to destroy everything, he argued. He fought them hard. It became clear that they were not going to back down, so he spirited out one of the four complete sets of prints, destroying everything else."

Lisa dropping heavily back into her seat. "Unbelievable. Does he still have them?"

"I don't know. We remained in contact for quite a while, and during all of our conversations, he frequently referenced the photos, so I thought he did. Yet recently, just weeks ago, as Al and I were working on our second book, I contacted Harold."

Copeland paused; an expression of sadness appeared on his face. "I'm not sure if you are interested in going out and rescuing any more people, but if you're looking for potential candidates, I suggest Harold Billings."

Judtson perked up. "He was changed?"

"You could say so. He wasn't overly rude to me or anything like that. He was pleasant, polite, and not the least bit interested in cooperating with us on the next book. I asked him if anything was wrong, and his only answer was that he had decided the whole issue was silly. *Silly!* For God's sake! Of course I asked him if I could have the complete stash of pictures, and he told me that he had given them all back to NASA."

The room was silent until Judtson, in a muted voice, said, "I'll bet you're right. It sounds as if he has been converted."

Copeland went on to detail some of his findings on Mars, which included numerous pictures of angular, symmetrical structures, as well as the famous face.

"One of the differences," Copeland explained, "between the lunar landings and the Mars expeditions was that we had real-time video and photographs being transmitted back to Earth from the landers and robotic rovers. Al and I set up the equipment to record all of the images we could directly off broadcast channels. Prior to the release of *Secret Agenda*, NASA, on their website, posted much of the video and still photography. If we hadn't recorded the live images, we never would have had the ability to compare the two. The photos which had been broadcast live showed much of the extremely persuasive evidence from Mars, but the exact same pictures or videos posted on the NASA site did not show the features."

"Photoshopped!" Ricky sneered derisively.

"Exactly."

Copeland kept the floor for another half an hour, answering questions from the group. When he finished, Judtson asked Al Clarkson if he had anything to add. The owlish writer stood up. "As you know, I was the co-writer of *Secret Agenda*. Although both Dean and I were subjected to mind-boggling pressure and unrelenting ridicule for releasing the book, one of the positive benefits of bringing it out was that we became the Woodward and Bernstein for the segment of the population who believed what we had said in the book. The end result of this notoriety was an avalanche of information, artifacts, and photographic evidence at our doorsteps.

"It seemed that all of the people who knew things or had seen things, yet never had the courage to come forward on their own, felt perfectly comfortable coming to us with their stories and bringing us whatever evidence they had."

Copeland nodded as his partner spoke.

"To be sure, ninety percent of what was brought to us was bogus, in one way or another. As for the remaining ten percent, most of the information or materials provided lacked sufficient substance or verifiability to be useful. However, just like finding a diamond in a ton of ore, there were certain nuggets, certain revelatory pieces of the puzzle, which prompted us to plan a follow-up book. That book was in progress at the time Dean was converted. It is my opinion that they believed his conversion would bring the project to a halt. At that point, nothing had happened to me. It wasn't until after the radio interview in which I announced my plans to proceed with the second book, even if I was doing so without Dean, that the precursor symptoms, as Saylor called them, and then the full conversion befell me."

Kelsey had been listening raptly. "I had heard that you were planning the second book and that it was going to present irrefutable evidence. What was in it?"

"*Secret Agenda* dealt with the Moon and Mars, revealing the cover-ups and hinting at the true mission of NASA. The second book was to be a bit closer to home. I found that an interesting phenomenon occurs in people as they age. The ambition which causes most of us to be obsessed with careers, the ego which prevents us from performing public acts that will result in ridicule, and even the desire to keep our families safe and free from harassment all fade in importance or necessity when we reach the seventh decade of life.

"Men who were directly involved in incidents from the middle of the previous century...men who had maintained their silence or, in fact, actively supported the official story...came to us, in many cases bringing proof. One who contacted us was Captain Meade's old friend, the driver who ferried President Eisenhower to and from the saucer."

"Well I'll be...," the captain remarked.

"Others were retired Air Force men who had been involved in the initial response to Roswell or the gathering of materials...and bodies...from that site, for transport to the installation now known as Wright-Patterson."

"Bodies!" exclaimed Kelsey. "We really do have the bodies of the greys?"

Clarkson nodded.

"So that alien autopsy film was legit?"

A smile creased the author's face. "No. It actually was not." Before she could ask her next question, he continued, "The film was a fake, created with the help of some special-effects people. What might surprise you is that it was created by the Department of Defense and deliberately circulated on the Internet."

"Why would they do that?"

"They would do it, Kelsey, to divert us and distract us from the truth."

"Which was?"

"That an understanding of the workings of those so-called bodies recovered from the Roswell crash site would not require the skills of a pathologist, but rather the talents of electrical and mechanical engineers."

"They were robots?" The question was nearly shouted by Judtson.

"Robots, androids, call them what you will. They were essentially bionic, a marriage of organic and mechanical, but primarily servos, circuits, and the like."

Among the stunned gathering, Matt Wheeler was the first to find his voice. "That makes sense.

An android would be much better suited than a biological being for the ordeal of long-distance space travel."

The other members all began speaking at once, filling the room with an indecipherable din.

Giving the group a few minutes to digest Clarkson's revelation, Judtson held up his hand for attention.

"Again, I want to remind everyone that we will have ample opportunity to delve into the details later. To move on, I'd like to go to Lisa. I have a general idea of what happened with you. I guess you were going to air a program with Dean and Al about *Secret Agenda* and the upcoming book."

"I was, except I don't think that was why they mentally neutered me."

"Oh? What was it, then?"

"You see, the project was effectively dead. In the days and weeks leading up to the moment my boss told me to drop the story, not only was he behind it one hundred and ten percent, so was his boss. They were both persuaded by the facts and evidence, and were totally into getting Dean and Al's story on the air. After my supervisor abruptly instructed me to drop it, I pushed back. I went over his head. His boss also wanted it to disappear. They expected me to be a good little producer and obey, but I wouldn't let it go until it suddenly became apparent to me that I was onto an even bigger story."

"Bigger story?"

"You're kidding, right? Two hard-charging members of the upper management of a broadcast network suddenly turning into a couple of...nebbishes, I guess. It wasn't as if they were walking slowly around the offices glassy-eyed and speaking in a dull monotone. Nothing like that. They were essentially the same people, personality-wise, only without the highs and lows, without the intensity. But, and this is hard to explain, it was almost as if you had spent years with your best friend and knew she was a die-hard political liberal. I mean hard-core, to the bone...poster of Che Guevara on her wall...liberal. And then one day you went to visit her and found her listening to Glenn Beck and quoting Rush Limbaugh."

Meade, still leaning against the wall, barked a short laugh. "Maybe she just wised up!"

"That's not my point. My point is that people don't simply change that way. My two superiors went from black to white overnight, no gray area, no transition, and I couldn't even get them to talk to me about it or even acknowledge the change. That's when I started digging. I began interviewing their friends and relatives. I was finding out that those people had, for the most part, also noticed the change. Right as I was getting close, getting a clear picture of what had happened, they converted *me*."

"I don't understand," Ricky remarked, a befuddled expression on his face. "Al and Dean had done other shows. I had heard them talking about their upcoming book on a nationwide radio program. Why did the bad guys zero in on you and your bosses?"

"I think I can answer that," Judtson offered. "Probably the other shows all pandered to the so-called fringe. A segment on *Secret Agenda* and the next book would more than likely have been sandwiched between an interview with a person who went camping with Bigfoot and an exposé revealing that the President was actually guarded by invisible Secret Service agents. As long as Copeland and Clarkson remained on that circuit, they weren't a threat. As a matter of fact, doing so played into the bad guys' hands; the two of them diminished their own credibility without any outside help. On the other hand, Jack Bailey has always had a reputation for being a straight-up newsperson. His show, on which Lisa is one of the producers, has won all kinds of journalism awards. His past guests have included heads of state and Nobel Prize winners."

"That's true, boss. Jack Bailey is basically the television version of you."

"In some ways, yes. He isn't specifically categorized as a debunker, as I am...or was, but he's probably comparable in terms of credibility. And it looks as though that's the threshold, the trigger for our foes. Anyway, we have a lot to cover tonight, so I'd like to move on again if it's all right with everyone."

Judtson paused and no one objected.

"Bal Singh, if you wouldn't mind."

The geologist stood to address the group, speaking with only a hint of an accent from his home country of India. "I must admit, especially after listening to the other speakers, I am flummoxed as to why I was chosen to be converted."

"What were you working on in the weeks and months before it happened?" prodded Judtson.

The slightly built man shrugged almost imperceptibly. "Nothing which has not been the focus of my efforts for several years. I am a specialist in tectonics, devoting all of my efforts to understanding the plate movements and the resulting geological formations along the Pacific Ring of Fire. The only connection I can see between my work and what I have heard tonight is that I was on the verge of allocating much of my time to an examination of the Andes in South America. The Andes range, of course, is where Doctor Villarreal's subjects, Puma Punku and Lake Titicaca, are located."

"With the others," Judtson offered, "the conversion seems to have happened just as they were on the brink of either a breakthrough of some sort, or going public. Was your work coming close to a significant fruition? Or were you planning on the release of a paper in the near future?"

"Both, actually. Or at least I thought so. My field has an especially shallow and narrow understanding of the actual forces at work when major plate shifts occur. We know the results can be very dramatic, producing enormous mountain ranges such as the Himalayas, the Rockies and, of course, the Andes. However, geologists have had only a vague, inferred picture of the actual mechanisms and the magnitude of the energy involved. I have been working for many years to create a computer model which would provide us with that understanding."

"And you were close to a breakthrough?"

With a look of chagrin, Singh answered, "I had believed that I was. Although my model accurately predicted the approximate height and mass of several other formations around the Pacific rim, it missed the mark by several orders of magnitude in its prediction of the Andes. The model was grossly inaccurate, to such a degree that I had essentially decided to scrap all of my thousands of hours of work and abandon the project."

Mentally struggling to fit this piece into the puzzle, Judtson, perplexed, said nothing. The silence was filled by Villarreal. "I am curious, Dr. Singh, if the Andes are larger or smaller than your model predicted."

The geologist turned to face him. "Much of the range, particularly the southern section, is roughly as my model predicts, certainly within the acceptable margin for error. And yet, the central portion is larger...much, much larger than it should be." Singh turned red-faced, embarrassed. "How presumptuous of me! I do not mean to say 'should be' as if it were up to me to dictate to nature the size of its mountains."

Villarreal smiled reassuringly. "I did not take your comment that way, sir. So you are saying that the section of the Andes which includes Lake Titicaca, Tiahuanaco, and Puma Punku is taller than your model predicts?"

"Yes, I am. Substantially so. Not only taller, wider as well."

"Fascinating."

"So you were just going to dump the whole project?" Judtson asked.

Singh turned back to the front of the room. "I was. Several of my post-doctoral students, who had worked with me on the model, were urging me to give it one last chance."

"How?"

"They were convinced that our computer model was accurate, but that some additional force had been exerted to create the anomaly, some unknown fault line or even undiscovered volcanic feature which we had not factored into the simulation. They believed that if we could find that cause, a force not accounted for in the model, we would be vindicated."

"Had they convinced you?"

A rueful smile appeared on the geologist's face. "I confess that I have a healthy ego and was not yet ready to accept that I had been so wrong. Yes, they had convinced me and we were in the midst of planning the trip."

"Okay, we have a Puma Punku connection."

"In the interest of accuracy, Mr. Kent, that is misleading."

"Why is that?"

"Although Doctor Villarreal's site lies within the area in question, the anomalous phenomenon involves thousands of square miles of terrain. His site is but a pinpoint upon the area I was planning to explore."

Before Judtson could respond, Kelsey spoke up. "Well, at least it's on the same continent."

As the group laughed at Kelsey's comment, Judtson noticed that Scott was madly tapping the keyboard on his tablet.

"Thank you, Bal."

Once again, several participants in the discussion began talking, some among themselves, others directing questions at the geologist. Judtson allowed the discourse for a few minutes, then lifted his hand for attention. "Let's move on now. Dylan, would you please...?"

The immunologist, a somewhat heavyset man in his mid-forties with a prematurely receding hairline, rose to speak. With a wry grin, he began, "I suppose that I am in the same category as Bal. I have no idea why I would have been selected for conversion. Prior to it happening, I was engaged in a study of universal vaccines."

"Vaccines!" The exclamation came from Kelsey. "The Internet is loaded with all kinds of conspiracy theories on that subject."

His grin broadened. "This is true. And I've heard them all. Every time I'm at a public gathering, you would be amazed at how many people feel free to confront me, even verbally attack me, when they find out what I do for a living."

"Dylan," Judtson interrupted, "was there a specific area of study you were involved in before the conversion?"

"Of course. My primary focus was research. An epidemiologist from the CDC approached me almost a year ago and offered funding for a study."

"Don't they have their own in-house specialists?" Judtson asked. "Why did he or she come to you?"

"I asked her the same question. She told me that she wasn't able to convince her superiors that the direction of the study was worth the budget allocation."

"What was the point of the study?"

"Autism. As Kelsey mentioned a moment ago, there is a sea of ignorance and misinformation on the topic of universal immunizations; however, the epidemiologist suspected that the link between autism and the widespread use of a recent iteration of vaccine was worthy of serious study. She had exhausted all of the avenues within her discipline and, quite honestly, from an epidemiological standpoint, her position was persuasive."

Ricky, as if he were in a classroom, raised his hand. "At the risk of sounding ignorant, would you mind explaining epidemiology?"

Falt turned to face him. "Of course not. Briefly, it is a statistical study within societies which looks for cause-and-effect relationships. The field tends to track, as comprehensively as it can, the available data generated by a culture, correlating the information and searching for patterns. To give you an example on a small scale, if the CDC folks hear that twelve people in a city suddenly die from a rare malady, they will put together all of the data they can on what those twelve did in the days, weeks, sometimes even months leading up to their deaths. An epidemiologist compares all the information and finds one commonality...all twelve had eaten at the same restaurant within a week of demise. At that point, the epidemiologist's work is done. Representatives from other disciplines are sent in to the restaurant: chemists, bacteriologists, et cetera. One of them might find that the cook at the restaurant just returned from some distant country and brought back a nasty bug. He isn't displaying symptoms but is a carrier. Case solved. On a larger scale, epidemiologists will find connections between lead-based paint and brain damage, asbestos and lung cancer, a certain prescription medication and a new affliction."

"I see."

Judtson stepped forward. "What some tend to forget is that a statistical causal link is not necessarily a smoking gun. Statistics, occasionally, can be misleading. I'll give you an example. How many people in this room believe that women are better drivers than men?"

Most of the people raised their hands.

"You believe it since you've been told all your lives that it's the case. And the belief is based upon actuarial statistics. Insurance rates have been lower for women than for men because women do have fewer accidents. It's reasonable to extrapolate from the data that the women are better drivers."

"Well, sure! What else could it mean?" The question came from Kelsey.

"I'll answer your question with a question. For example, if women statistically have thirty-two percent fewer accidents than men but actually drive fifty-three percent fewer miles than men, which of the two genders would be the better drivers?"

Meade, from across the room, answered, "Ha! Men, per mile driven."

"Right."

"Yeah, right!" Kelsey rejoined.

Falt, taking back the floor, said, "Judtson's right. Although I'm not acquainted with the data on male versus female driving, I am familiar with statistics in general. We've been led down several wrong paths due to improperly structured or analyzed data surveys, or conclusions skewed by a bias. That's why, ideally, results are only used as a pointer, an indication that there might be something to consider. To return to my research, I looked at the statistics the CDC epidemiologist provided and was convinced that there was adequate indication for further study. She was able to divert funding to me from the CDC, disguising the nature of the research in order to get it past her bosses. I put together a team."

He stopped talking and glanced around the room as if waiting for questions.

Judtson spoke. "That's it?"

Falt nodded. "I'm afraid so. We hadn't even begun the work when I got my surprise visit from the men in black."

"So they didn't even want you to get started down that avenue."

"I guess not. But I certainly don't have anything tantalizing or even interesting to add to this discussion tonight."

"Dylan," Kelsey asked, "after your conversion, did the substitute Dylan Falt actively drop the vaccine/autism study?"

"Yes. I…he…did. Right off the bat. He called my contact at the CDC and told her he wasn't interested in working on it or with her. In fact, you could say that he burned the bridge with her."

"At least we know the subject they wanted buried."

"Sounds right to me," Judtson concurred. "Chris, would you mind going next?"

The chemist stood. "Not at all. Considering the outlandishness of our experiences and situation and the uncertainty as to who…or even what…our enemies may be, my connection is not exactly inscrutable. We've been batting around the topics of space aliens and ancient civilizations all evening. And, before they strapped the helmet on me and sent me away, I was actively working on the supposed Holy Grail of that whole crowd, monoatomic gold."

Judtson was amused by Ashby's directness. "For the people in the room who aren't up on their reading of David Icke, would you take a moment to describe the lore around it?"

"Monoatomic gold, over the centuries, has been credited with everything from alleviating pain to raising our spiritual vibration to opening the crown chakra."

There was a soft titter from some in the lounge.

"I know," Ashby agreed, glancing around at the faces. "I felt the same way."

"What, exactly, is the stuff?" The question came from Lisa.

"Monoatomic gold is, very simply, a single atom of the element gold."

She continued, "Wouldn't it have the same properties as…you know…regular gold?"

"According to classic chemistry, it should. And that it did was my long-held, scientific belief."

"Then how did you get into researching it?"

"I guess I can blame my sister. She and I have always been as different as night and day. From the time we were growing up, I was the one with his nose in the science books while she was locked in her room playing with a Ouija board. Later, as I went to college, she legally changed her name to Starlight, joined a coven, and opened a crystal-healing shop in Venice Beach. It made for interesting conversations at the table during the holidays."

The levity disappeared from his face. "Then our mother developed Alzheimer's. Fairly rapidly, she descended into a rather severe case, to the point where she did not recognize either my sister or me…or anyone else for that matter. She required continuous, intense care by nurses specifically trained to work with Alzheimer's patients, and was completely disengaged from reality. I had always been very close to my mother. We both had…my sister and I, and we were devastated. I combed the medical literature and knew there was no cure, no treatment for the condition."

"Unfortunately, that's true," Saylor added sympathetically.

Ashby nodded acknowledgment to Saylor. "I can't begin to describe how I felt during those days. It seemed that the remaining time I had left with my mother was being stolen from me. When I had reached the bottom of my emotional pit and was at my most vulnerable, my sister came to me and told me she was certain our mother could be cured by a substance referred to in the metaphysical realm as ORME, or monoatomic gold. I'm afraid my reaction was ugly. All of my repressed feelings from years past about her choice to immerse herself in such a ridiculous, marginal lifestyle came out, and I lashed out at her cruelly. I viciously attacked her for trying to exploit my emotional state to get me to allow snake-oil cures. That brutal tirade directed against my only other family member was the lowest point in my life. She tried to reason with me. She tried to argue. She pleaded with me that even if it didn't do anything, why not give it a try? All of her entreaties I rebuffed in the nastiest of fashions until she ran away, in tears."

The room was silent as everyone tasted the bitterness of his moment.

"Following her departure, I continued to rant for some time, releasing all of the pent-up anger I felt for what was happening to my mother. Once the furor was all spent and I collapsed into a chair, I noticed that my sister had left the vial of white powder. My rage reignited by the sight of it, I picked it up and threw it against the wall, shattering it. The glass shards fell to the floor, but the contents...the powder, which might be lighter than air, I don't know...remained airborne and disseminated. As the minutes passed, I noticed a gradual shift in my thinking. My sister's words resonated with me in a way they had not when she had spoken them. I realized that our mother was already lost to us, and decided that, possibly, we really had nothing to lose by trying the substance."

Kelsey leaned close to Judtson and whispered, "The powder affected him."

"The first thing I did that evening was some research. The claims about monoatomic gold were even wilder and more outlandish than I had imagined. Unbelievable, in fact. But the sources I considered to be reliable could not find any danger to humans if they ingested the substance in reasonable doses. I called Starlight that night and apologized. I then asked her if the monoatomic gold she brought to me was of a higher quality. My brief investigation had found that several sources for the substance were somewhat shady. She insisted that her source was the best. I told her I had broken her vial and she brought another, which I took to my lab and tested a sample for contaminants and impurities. My sister had been right. The monoatomic gold she provided was fairly clean. Even so, I subjected the powder to my own scrubbing protocol to improve the purity. I arranged for Starlight to meet me and together, after sending the nurse away for a break, we gave our mother the maximum dose I felt comfortable giving to her."

The anticipation within the lounge was tangible as he continued. "I had no idea what to expect. My sister later confessed that neither did she. We sat beside the bed and stared at our mother as if she were going to have some dramatic transformation involving screaming, writhing, and even levitating from the bed. Instead, she merely dozed off. Initially, I was afraid that she had died, that we had killed her. After checking her pulse and breathing, we figured out that she was only asleep, a sleep which lasted half an hour while neither of us left her side."

Ashby paused. His recollection of the incident was summoning the emotions he felt at the time. With a shaky, softer voice, he resumed the narrative. "After the thirty minutes my mother opened her eyes, turned her head, and looked directly at the two of us. Then she smiled...she actually smiled at us and" – he hesitated for a moment and swallowed – "she said, 'Hello, Starlight...Hi, Chris. What are you two doing here?'"

"Phenomenal," Saylor murmured under his breath.

Ashby, hearing the comment, nodded at him and continued, "From that moment on she was lucid...she had all of her faculties...her memory was comparable to what it had been prior to onset of the disease. My sister was convinced that our mother's memory was even better than it had been prior to the Alzheimer's. That I can't say. I can tell you that we were able to dismiss the nurses. My mother resumed living on her own and remained functional and independent until she passed, from other causes, two years later."

Gently clearing his throat first, Saylor asked, "It isn't my intention to offend, Chris, but Alzheimer's is still an inferred diagnosis. We don't have a conclusive test for it. I'm not saying it's likely, although there is certainly a possibility that your mother was suffering from a variant of a stroke, an oxygen deprivation which might mimic the symptoms of Alzheimer's. The administering of the monoatomic gold could have been coincident to or possibly even a trigger to the clearing of the obstruction in her brain."

A slight smile crossed the chemist's face. "No offense taken. In the weeks and months following her recovery, I continued my research, which included several consultations with neurologists. The consensus of the medical doctors was just as you said, without exception: she simply could not have been suffering from Alzheimer's. They convinced me. Or perhaps I should say, almost convinced me. Throughout the two years, Starlight never ceased believing that the monoatomic gold had cured our mother of Alzheimer's. Out of respect for my sister I kept that option open in my own mind, despite the opinions from the experts. As you know, Saylor, at that time Alzheimer's could only be truly diagnosed with an autopsy."

"True."

"So when she passed, both my sister and I requested that one be performed. In fact, my mother, while she was alive, had discussed the issue with us and was aware of the contradicting opinions from the doctors. It was also her wish that we determine the answer after her death, for the benefit of others. The autopsy was performed, her brain examined. And the final conclusion was that she had suffered from a severely advanced case of Alzheimer's. The damage, from the plaque and tangles in the brain, was one of the most extreme cases the pathologist had personally seen. He knew nothing about her recovery and the excellent quality of her life during the last years, and expressed profound condolences for the ordeal we must have gone through in the time leading up to her death."

"That's astounding!" Saylor uttered. "But if the monoatomic gold hadn't physically eliminated the deposits, how was she able to return to normal function?"

"That," Ashby answered, "was the question which triggered the direction of my research from that day forward."

The chemist continued, describing how he had at first been able to secure funding for his research by submitting a deliberately vague grant request; and how, once the federal government was informed that he was, in fact, studying a notoriously marginalized and ridiculed substance, the money dried up.

"How did the Feds find out?"

"Someone at the university ratted me out. The grant was withdrawn immediately. However, within days of the cancellation, I received an offer from a private foundation, which presented me with an even greater budget. As I told you during our trip back, we were not able to consummate the arrangement prior to my conversion, and I never found out who or what the foundation was."

Curious, Judtson asked, "Where was your research leading you?"

"I was still in Phase One of my study. We were working with laboratory rats with induced Alzheimer's. At first, we were not able to replicate the recovery experienced by my mother. We were using monoatomic gold right off the shelf from the same supplier my sister had used to obtain the substance we administered to our mother. I was fairly frustrated at that point until I remembered that the dosage we gave to her that day had been scrubbed by me to remove minor contaminants. When I subjected the test substance to the same scrubbing protocol, almost universally the rats went from a condition near vegetative to fully functional. Apparently, there was something in that particular scrubbing process I had developed which made the substance viable. We were working on that question while preparing to proceed into Phase Two, when the funding was pulled."

"What was Phase Two?"

"Human trials."

Chapter 29

Judtson SAT ALONE IN THE LOUNGE, sipping from his mug of coffee and thinking back over the previous evening. After all of the converts had finished describing their experiences, the assemblage splintered into smaller groups and talked for an additional hour, before the day's events and the lateness caught up with them and, one by one, they began excusing themselves and going off to bed.

Judtson's sleep had been fitful as his mind attempted to connect all of the jigsaw pieces acquired in the discussion; he continued the process of matching up the revelations to form a cogent theory, until deciding that lying in the dark was pointless.

"You're up, too, huh?"

He turned to the sound of the voice, a portion of his mind still grateful for the ability, and saw Saylor, bleary-eyed, at the doorway.

"Hey, Popeye. You look like hell."

Saylor plodded to the counter and poured a cup of coffee. "Can't shut my mind off."

"Same here. Come up with anything?"

"Only a headache. You?"

Judtson paused, pulling together his thoughts. "When I did sleep last night, I had a dream."

"The sawmill?"

"No. Different. I was basically Ebenezer Scrooge."

A soft chuckle came from Saylor. "Okay. I have no idea how that fits."

"Oh, it fits. The people we've converted...."

"Romeo insists that we call it 'rescued.' I got the speech from him yesterday."

"All right, rescued. Anyway, the things they told us, the things they were working on...this was all the stuff I shot down like skeet my whole career. Every time someone brought up Roswell, the face on Mars, secret societies, the government using vaccines for some nefarious purpose, ancient aliens...any of it...my first reaction had always been to contact the recognized experts – the legitimate authorities on the subject – build my case, and rip the conjecture to pieces. I systematically savaged all of these topics just as the Dickens character trashed Christmas."

"So were you visited by the ghost of crackpots-past last night?" Expecting a laugh, Saylor was surprised to see a serious intensity color Judtson's features.

"In a way, yes. Remember Crystal Meadows?"

The smile instantly left Saylor's face. "Of course I do. It was almost a year until you got over that."

Judtson's eyes met his. "I still haven't...really."

They were about to continue, when they heard a sound from the hallway and both turned to see Kelsey entering the lounge. She greeted neither of them; her eyes were fixed upon the coffee urn. As she made her way to it, Judtson noticed that her hair was badly disheveled. She was wearing a baggy T-shirt, which was rumpled and extended below her knees. Her feet were covered with what appeared to be men's gunmetal-gray slippers, which made scuffing sounds as she dragged them across the floor.

"You wake up worse than I do," Judtson teased.

"Bite me," she muttered, pulling a large mug down from the cabinet and filling it to the brim. Before taking a single step, she took a long drink from the black brew, seemingly oblivious to the high temperature. The two watched as she swallowed loudly and took another. Returning the mug to the nozzle, she lifted the black plastic lever and topped off her cup, only then joining them at the table.

After sitting and taking one more long drink, she seemed to finally focus on the two of them, who were both staring at her, amused. "What?"

"Nothing."

"Nothing."

They had quickly answered her confrontational tone simultaneously.

"Go ahead and talk. Just pretend I'm not here...'cause I'm not."

Saylor and Judtson exchanged furtive glances, both suppressing smiles, before Judtson said, "All right. Well, as I was saying, Crystal Meadows was in my dream last night. She...."

"That's a bogus name." The murmured snipe came from Kelsey between sips. "Who's she? Some bimbo you know?"

Judtson turned to face her. "I thought you said we're supposed to pretend you aren't here. It's tough to do if you're asking questions."

Over the top of the mug, which she clutched in front of her chin with both hands, she repeated, "*Who* is Crystal Meadows?"

Within a moment Saylor answered, "Meadows was an alien abductee. She was all over the news for a while. She claimed she was taken from her bed during the night and levitated up into a flying saucer, where they stripped her, did all sorts of physical exams, supposedly embedded a chip in her, and finally impregnated her."

Kelsey squeezed her eyes shut for a second. "It all sounds familiar. She was even on Leno."

"Yeah, due to her distinctive name or her personality, which was fairly colorful, or the fact that she was pretty, the media snapped her up. Plus, she gave an entertaining interview. And the lascivious aspect of her story didn't hurt. Anyway, Judtson did one of his cable shows on her...ground her into sausage, found out she was having an affair with a man, and the baby she was carrying was probably his, not some alien hybrid."

Kelsey's eyes widened. "I remember now! Didn't she...?" She suddenly stopped in mid-sentence.

Judtson cleared his throat. When he spoke, his voice was subdued and somber. "Yes. She killed herself. Three days after my show aired. Before she did it, she wrote an email to me."

"Oh! I didn't hear about an email."

"I never released it."

"What did it say?"

Judtson let out a heavy sigh. "She insisted that everything she had told the world was true. She *had* been abducted. They *had* done medical procedures on her. And when she found out she was pregnant after the abduction, she assumed they had inseminated her. She said she didn't really know if the baby was from the abduction or from her lover, but since she had been on the pill, she was fairly convinced it wasn't his."

"Did she say why she was going to kill herself? Was it because of the public humiliation from your show?"

"No. At least that's what she said in the email."

"Then why?"

Judtson's face changed to an expression neither Kelsey nor Saylor recognized. His tone flat, he responded to her question. "In the email, she said she was going to do it to ensure the baby wasn't born."

His comment startled Kelsey. "You're joking? If she felt that way, why didn't she just get an abortion?"

"She was already well into the second trimester and wasn't certain it would be in time. She didn't want to bring it into the world."

"I don't understand. Even at six months, the fetus might not be viable outside the womb."

Leaning back in his chair, Judtson stared up at the ceiling. "Crystal knew it might be the case with a normal...human baby. She was sure what she was carrying wasn't human; as Saylor alluded to earlier, she believed it was some sort of hybrid...a combination of human and...alien."

"Alien! You...she couldn't have been serious!"

"That's what I thought. I was convinced she had gone nuts...she was delusional."

Saylor interrupted Judtson's train of thought. "You're saying that's what you *thought*...past tense. You don't believe...?"

Judtson brought his attention back down to the two people in front of him. "No. I'm not telling you I've changed my mind. It's just that with all we've discovered in the last several days, some beliefs and positions I always chalked off as outlandish don't seem quite so absurd anymore. But what I was saying when you walked in was that she visited me in my dream. She, like the ghost in Dickens, was my guide, taking me through the scenarios we've heard from the others, walking me through my own bizarre experiences, reminding me of other things I've debunked over the past few years, and telling me to open my eyes...to open my mind, or I would risk missing the answer."

"Assuming Patrick Worden is a disciple of Freud, I'm sure he'd tell you that the symbolism in the dream is obvious. You are in the middle of a momentous transition in your philosophical orientation. Beginning with your first meeting with Carlos, followed by all of the events leading up to today, you've been heading from one end of the skeptical spectrum to the other. Crystal Meadows represents everything the side you're moving toward believes in, at least in your mind."

Before Judtson could respond, Luis entered the lounge. Seeing the three seated at the table, his pace faltered and he did a slight double-take. "Kelsey, you're up!"

Her response was accompanied by a wry grin. "I know...I know. You're not used to seeing me conscious this early. What's up?"

"As I was passing the comm room, Scott asked me if I'd seen you."

"Scott's up? He *never* gets up any earlier than noon!"

Luis chuckled. "He didn't. He's been up. All night. He's been huddled with the geologist, Bal

Singh."

"Did he want to see me?"

"Think so."

Kelsey stood up and, addressing Judtson and Saylor, said, "Come on. Let's go see what he has."

▽

When they arrived, Scott was sitting on the only chair in the cramped computer room, intently typing on his keyboard. Singh, teetering on the edge of the work counter, stared at the center monitor over his shoulder.

Kelsey was the first to reach the open doorway. "Morning, guys."

Singh, not hearing their approach, was startled and jumped up. Scott, in his typical unflappable manner, turned to face her. "Morning, boss."

Kelsey took one step into the room, which was as far as she could enter. Saylor and Judtson stood behind her in the doorway. "Luis said you wanted to see me."

He nodded. "Yep. While Bal was talking last night about his computer model for predicting tectonic movement, I got curious and started doing a little searching. There's some strange stuff on the subject, especially down in the Andes. I caught him before he went to bed. We've been working on it ever since."

"What is it?"

"I think I'd better let Bal explain."

The geologist, standing awkwardly in the narrow space behind Scott, began, "It's fascinating. Frankly, an avenue I hadn't considered. Are any of you familiar with microgravimetry?"

The three indicated they were not.

"We've been mapping gravity all over the world for years. Scott, maybe you could show them the globe."

He paused as the tech brought up a graphic of Earth. The image began to rotate.

"Why is it lumpy?" Kelsey asked, leaning forward for a better look.

"This is a gravity map created by the NASA GRACE mission, a space-based sensor which has charted every square foot of the planet. The lumpiness, as you called it, indicates the variations in gravity, as do the enhanced colors. The protruding red areas represent higher gravity than the theoretical idealized level. The sunken blue areas are obviously lower."

Over Kelsey's shoulder, Saylor commented, "I thought that gravity was the same everywhere."

Singh shook his head. "Not at all. There are three categories of fluctuations. The first are normal, calculable variations resulting from elevation. The higher the altitude when you take the measurement, in other words the farther from the center of the Earth, the lower the gravity. These variations are perfectly predictable on a sliding scale. The second factor, which is related to the first, is a result of the fact that the Earth is not a perfect sphere. It bulges at the equator, making the equator farther from the Earth's center than...say, Oslo, Norway...so the gravity is slightly weaker there due to that distance."

"So if I found myself standing on the top of Mount Everest, I'd be lighter than if I were in Death Valley?"

"Not so that you would notice, but yes. The fluctuations in the third category are referred to generically as anomalies. These are slight variations in the surface gravity which vary from the calculated, or expected, level. They are caused by the changes in density of the strata beneath the surface, voids, a wide variety of factors. With the advent of the microgravimeter, a very sensitive measuring device, the resulting data are used in the exploration for oil and natural gas. Now...if you'll notice, as Scott did last night…the global map is showing the central region of the Andes as bright red."

"Wait a minute," Judtson interrupted. "I thought the gravity was supposed to be less at the tops of mountains?"

Singh smiled. "That's what caught our attention. It should be less. However, as you can see, the central region of the Andes has stronger gravity than expected. And this is the same region of the range which was several magnitudes of order different from what my model predicted."

"What's the explanation for this?"

"Well, Judtson, that is where our search became interesting. After noticing this anomaly, both Scott and I began searching the Internet for scientific papers which might explain the phenomenon. It was too obvious, too glaring a discrepancy to not have been spotted and studied by others. Working independently, both of us kept finding references from other scientists to a paper first released at the *Geodesy and Physics of the Earth Symposium* in Potsdam, by one Kevin Berry. From the comments by others, it appeared that Berry specifically addressed the issue. Even so, all we kept finding were oblique references to the paper, not the paper itself. Quite frustrating."

Scott picked up the narrative. "I didn't find anything until I stopped looking at the available links and began clicking on pages cached by the search engines."

"Cached?" Judtson said quizzically. "I've noticed that as an option when I search, and I've never known what it was."

"You need to remember that the sum of the content on the Internet includes not only big-time servers, but also individual PCs. When you do a search on the Internet, the results include a list of everything the engine found on the subject. Most of the time, all of the linked websites displayed on your search results are online. Yet sometimes, especially in the case of the websites maintained by individuals, they aren't. So the search engines regularly take a snapshot of the pages they find and store that picture in a cache."

"All right."

"The net result of this is that occasionally, if something has been deliberately taken off the Internet, it can still be found in cache memory. We couldn't find the paper written by Berry. I did find this, though."

Scott handed a single sheet of paper to Kelsey. Judtson and Saylor immediately peered from behind her to read it.

She made a soft snorting sound of derision as she focused on the host of the site. "NASA, huh?"

"Yep," Scott answered curtly.

Below the NASA logo were three lines:

Fulltext Article not Available
Find Similar Articles
Full record info

Following these lines was the title of the paper written by Berry, *Study of Microgravimetry Anomalies – Central Andes*. Below the author and contributor listings, the date of publication, and the title, date, and location of the conference where the paper was released, there was the single line – Abstract not Available.

"I'll be damned," murmured Judtson.

"Since this is only a cached version of the page, the links near the top regarding similar articles and the full record information are not functional."

Kelsey handed the page back to Scott. "This man's a scientist. Even if NASA took down the paper, he should still have it. It should be on his site. It should be on the website of the university where he teaches. Scientific papers don't just go away."

"That was my first thought, Kelsey," Singh answered. "We've checked. He doesn't maintain a personal website. His department at Columbia lists him on the roster, but has no links to his work."

"It's later back there. Have we tried to contact him?"

"No answer at the listed office number. We left a voice mail. When I tried to send an email, I immediately received an 'out of office' reply." Singh handed another paper to Kelsey.

After reading the terse content, she exclaimed, "He's on a two-year sabbatical!"

She turned around in the tight space and faced Judtson. "I think we just found another candidate for conversion."

He nodded. "You're probably right."

▽

The waves of heat rose from the dry lake bed in the distance, creating a shimmering effect and making it appear that the sandy basin was undulating and rippling. The convertible top was up in deference to the brutality of the sun. Judtson had set the air conditioning to its maximum and was still sweating.

"I can't believe Berry chose to work in the Mojave Desert this time of year," he said loudly, to be heard over the ambient noise from the blower and the intense oscillation of the canvas top, quivering in the slipstream.

Kelsey, sitting in the passenger seat, shrugged. "It took Scott more than two days to track him down here. It should be good info."

"Hope he's right."

Judtson glanced in the rearview mirror and saw that Luis was asleep, his head lolling to the side and his mouth wide open with his tongue hanging out. Occupying the other end of the rear seat was Bal Singh, reading a book and apparently oblivious to both the oppressive heat of the day and the stentorian snoring from his companion.

"I think we turn here." Kelsey pointed to a dirt road on the right. Judtson tapped the brakes and slowed the Olds, turning off the paved highway onto the narrow lane.

"How far?"

She studied the map created by Scott. "Looks like about three miles."

"I think we're fairly close to Fort Irwin, aren't we?"

"Yes, less than a quarter of a mile from the main gate."

"Did you know it's the national training center for the Army?"

Kelsey twisted in her seat to face him. "No, I didn't."

"Yep. They bring groups through on regular rotations, five to seven thousand soldiers at a time, and take them out to an area they call 'the box.' From what I hear, it's a real hellhole."

"How do you know about it?"

"I was invited to do a book signing there. Met a lot of the troops as they were going out to the box. It's their last stop before they get deployed downrange."

"Downrange?"

"Afghanistan, mostly. But anywhere there's some shooting going on."

She flopped back into her seat. "Huh! I still can't believe they do it."

"What do you mean?"

"The way we treat them…I can't believe they'd *want* to go out there and fight for us."

Judtson shrugged. "They're different from us. Better. When I do book signings on military installations, I always thank them for their service. You know what they all say in response?"

"What?"

"That they wouldn't have it any other way."

Kelsey turned her head and stared out the side window, silently.

Neither of them spoke as the Oldsmobile bounced along the rutted road, until Kelsey pointed and exclaimed, "There's his camp!"

▽

Romeo descended the metal stairs to the bottom of the missile well, thinking to himself that having a hostage was not dissimilar to having a pet. No matter what the group did or where the members went, someone had to make certain that Bob received sustenance. The task normally fell to Luis, but since he had insisted upon a break outside the silo and was on the rescue mission to the Mojave Desert, it was Romeo's job for now.

The man was securely bound vertically. The incoherent babbling had stopped after the Devil's Breath wore off, and Bob had been silent for the past three days. On two occasions following that event, Romeo had come down and attempted to interrogate him. Because of his own brief verbal exchange with the man's partner inside the SUV, Romeo believed that Bob was also capable of speaking English, and he was determined to start him talking. Despite these efforts, Bob had remained tight-lipped, displaying an astounding discipline. Not only had the man not spoken, other than the gibberish, he had not once allowed either water or food to pass his lips, in an apparent effort to end his own life by dehydration.

After the hostage's plan had become obvious, Luis hooked up an IV. Even then, Bob took advantage of the slight movements he could perform, repeatedly dragging his arm against the side of his body and knocking out the IV needle. When Romeo and Luis had reinserted the needle, they completely immobilized the man's arm by taping it to the column above and below the insertion.

Positioning himself in front of their hostage at this moment, Romeo observed him carefully. He was already thinner than he had been when they first brought him to the silo. His lips were badly cracked and his skin had taken on a vaguely blue tinge. Romeo expertly replaced the IV bottle with a fresh one and stepped back.

"Sure you don't want a sandwich?"

Not only did the man not answer him, he did not even glance in Romeo's direction.

"Suit yourself. I'd love to hang out here and continue this chat, but I've got to run an errand right now. So, hold your thought. I'll be back."

Still nothing. Taking a final look around, Romeo left.

▽

Detective Garrett was standing in the middle of Judtson Kent's office, staring at the smeared bloodstain that trailed down the wall and trying to visualize what had happened. The forensic team was methodically working the scene, gathering blood samples, lifting fingerprints, collecting spent brass, and bagging the lead paperweight and the guns.

"Hello, Josh."

Garrett turned in response to the voice.

"Ben! Thanks for coming."

Ben Hart, not exactly a departmental colleague whom Garrett considered to be a friend, entered the room stiffly, using a cane for steadiness and support as he walked.

"From what you told me on the phone, I wouldn't have missed it. What do you have?"

Garrett waved his arm in a sweeping panorama of the room. "It looks like a multiple homicide. We have a lead ball which, based on the preliminary physical evidence, was used as a weapon. We have guns, all discharged. Brass on the floor. Two slugs embedded in walls, so far. We have blood all over the place."

Hart took in the scene. "It seems I'm a bit late. I guess the ME has already removed the bodies."

Garrett shook his head. "No. He hasn't. Someone else beat him to it."

"There weren't any bodies when you arrived?"

"No. Just this scene as you see it."

Stepping away from his fellow detective, Hart carefully navigated the room, avoiding the evidence markers, his eyes flitting from one point to another. "Okay, you have what looks like a probable homicide…maybe even a multiple…only without bodies. Homicide is your bailiwick. Interesting, but why did you need to drag me out from behind my desk for it?"

"Ben, why don't we go to the outer office and let these guys do their work."

Hart shrugged. "Lead the way."

As they walked, Garrett began relating to Hart the background, including the brief disappearance of Judtson Kent, the evidence of the paintball incident, and the arrests of Kent and Saylor Costello.

"Judtson Kent, huh?"

"You know him?"

Shaking his head, Hart answered, "No. Not at all. Just hate his books."

"Why's that?"

"He treats everyone who has ever seen a UFO, or…other stuff, like an idiot."

Garrett stared at the man for several seconds, a slight feeling of regret niggling at him for having called Hart in on the case.

"I still don't see why you called me."

"You will. This scene isn't where my day began. I caught a call first thing this morning from a company called RadTech. Apparently, one of their senior engineers, Matthew Wheeler, is missing. Hasn't shown up for work. Doesn't answer his phone. Nothing."

"All right. *That* sounds like a missing-person case."

"It would, normally. But after Wheeler disappeared, they checked their RFID logs…."

"Their what?"

"ID cards with embedded radio transmitters. A lot of companies use them. The employees don't even have to pull them out of their wallets or purses. Every time anyone comes or goes, a sensor picks up the transmission from the card and logs that person in or out."

"So they can tell if their secretaries are taking two-hour lunches."

"I guess. Anyway, Wheeler's log showed that he was at their lab well after midnight on the last day he was seen. Their IT man decided to check the video from the building surveillance cameras for the time just before Wheeler was logged out. I had them copy it onto my tablet. You're not going to believe what he found."

Garrett had an iPad tucked under his arm. He set it down on Ricky's desk and, with a few taps on the screen, opened a video showing the dark parking lot. Setting the silent video in motion, Garrett narrated, "See the black SUV parked out at the edge of the parking lot?"

"I do."

"Okay. If you look closely, you'll see two men dressed in dark outfits come up on the back of the SUV."

Hart watched as Romeo and Luis broke the side windows of the truck. Moments later, he saw

Luis back up and allow the man inside to get out. He saw the brief fight which resulted in the passenger lying on the pavement. He also saw, on the driver's side, the other man fall out, roll over, and take his two shots at Romeo.

"Josh, the one on the passenger side went at the other guy with a knife. The driver got off two shots before the other man fired back. It seems that the guys in the SUV made the first moves."

"You're right. If you don't count sneaking up behind the truck and shattering the windows as the first move."

They kept watching as Romeo checked the driver for a pulse and moved to the other side of the truck.

"Look, the big guy is talking to someone on the phone."

"I know. We've already checked with the cell phone carriers. I thought that with a good time stamp, we'd be able to figure out who it was he called, but the call went to a hotel switchboard, where it was rerouted. That's where we lost the trail. See, here comes Wheeler."

The screen showed Wheeler coming out of the building, carrying a valise and a zippered duffel bag. He walked to where Romeo was standing and the two waited as Luis left, returning in less than a minute with the Hummer. At this point Garrett leaned forward slightly, pointing at the tablet. "Watch this."

Hart saw the two men pull what looked like a body bag from their vehicle and place one of the fallen men in the bag, stopping to tape something over his mouth. When they finished, they loaded the bag in the back, and the three men drove away, leaving the black SUV and the dead man behind.

"Unreadable plate," muttered Hart.

"Yeah, it's obscured somehow. Now I'm going to skip forward an hour and a half." He tapped commands into the tablet, and although the scene appeared identical, Hart could see that the time stamp had advanced. They watched without speaking as another black SUV pulled into the lot and parked beside the first. Three men wearing suits and hats climbed out and efficiently picked up the dead man, putting his body inside the back compartment, then checked the area and bent over a few times to pick things up.

"We're guessing that they policed for brass."

After only a few minutes, two of the men got back into their truck while the third slid behind the wheel of the first SUV, and both vehicles drove away.

"Now both of those plates are readable," Hart exclaimed.

"That's right. They are. But you're not going to like what's next."

Ben turned to face his colleague. "What?"

His lips tight, Garrett spoke softly so as not to be overheard by the others. "Both vehicles are registered to Homeland Security."

"Homeland Sec...?"

"Gets better. When we called their office in Florence, they told us that they did not have two vehicles on their roster with those plates and that they were not missing any personnel."

Hart returned his attention to the screen and stared at the static image of the dark parking lot. "Did they leave any physical evidence?"

"After I caught this call and saw this video, I called in the Crime Scene Unit. We cordoned off the lot. There was blood in both spots. A divot in the pavement where the driver took the slug. Broken glass from the two windows. Enough to corroborate what we just saw."

"How does that tie into this?" Hart asked, indicating with his free arm the bloody mess in Judtson's office.

"Came up in the questioning at Wheeler's office. In the time leading up to his disappearance,

Wheeler had received calls from Saylor Costello, including one on the last day he was seen."

"That's Kent's paintball accomplice?"

"It is. Nothing unusual about the calls. Costello is a neurologist. Wheeler is an engineer for a company that sells medical equipment. I had a uniform make a routine call to Costello to see if he would have any information."

"Straightforward canvass call."

"Exactly. We called his office, and they told us that he had abruptly left town and hadn't told them where he was going. When the uniform told me that, I called Costello's cell phone number, the one we had from the paintball arrest. The phone was turned off. I called his wife's cell. It was turned off."

"This isn't sounding good."

"That's what I thought. Then, we logged in the Wheeler disappearance downtown, and Wheeler's name popped up in the system as a contact on another active missing-person case."

Garrett pulled out his notepad from his shirt pocket and checked it. "A Robyn Reedy. She is a technician at a radiology lab where Wheeler's company sells a lot of equipment. According to the detective on the case, there's a Judtson Kent/Saylor Costello connection with that one."

"Are you joking?"

"Nope. Reedy was the tech on a PET scan done on Judtson Kent during a lightning storm. Lightning struck the building while the test was going on. Supposedly, Kent was acting strangely afterward. Costello was with him during the test and came back to meet with Reedy and Wheeler to discuss it."

Hart reacted to this with equanimity. "Have you talked to Kent yet?"

Garrett chuckled and shook his head. "Not for lack of trying. Same as Costello...his phone was off. I sent out a uniform to check their homes. They live next door to each other. Nobody home at either. Both houses locked up tight. He did a walk-around and peered through the windows. Everything looked normal. And Kent has an assistant, Ricky Ingram. This is his desk. I called him, too."

"His phone was off?"

"Uh-huh."

"With all that's happening, I think you have probable cause to go in those homes. I would think we have a reasonable concern for their safety."

"You're right. We do. But they live in the county. Our dispatcher called the sheriff's office and they sent a deputy. We were going to go in together. In the meantime I called Kristen Kent, Judtson's wife."

"Don't tell me, no answer?"

"No, I actually connected with her."

"Really?"

"Oh, yeah. She's in Albuquerque, staying with her sister."

"Does she know where Kent and Costello are?"

Garrett paused and smiled. "You asked me before why I called you in on this, Ben. Whether you like it or not, ever since the night you took that round in front of the courthouse, you've had a reputation for...thinking outside the box."

Hart laughed. "Some say so far outside it that I can't even look back and see the box anymore."

Garrett shrugged. "Let's just say that after I talked to Kristen Kent, you were the first person I thought of."

Chapter 30

CARLOS VILLARREAL HURRIED DOWN THE CORRIDOR toward Scott's room, his footfalls echoing in syncopation; he was glad for the break in what had become a monotonous regimen underground. The converts had spontaneously established a routine in an effort to ferret out the connections between their various disciplines. Every morning they broke up into groups of two or three for, as the groups referred to the process, brainstorming – or, as Jimmy Meade called the meetings, BS sessions. At midday, the groups would shuffle their members for the afternoon discussions. And a third round, again with different combinations of participants, would happen in the early evening. What Carlos found monotonous was that nothing new was coming from the talking, only endless rehashing of details everyone already knew. He hoped, as he approached the computer room, that Scott had summoned him with a fresh piece for the puzzle.

"You were looking for me?"

Turning away from his seemingly constant position of staring at the monitors, Scott nodded. "I heard from Tevian."

A mild jolt of excitement tickled Villarreal. "Already? That was very rapid."

"He contacted me and wants to do a Skype with you."

"Is that secure? Could someone monitor it?"

"I anticipated that he might want to talk, so I included an encryption program in the flash drive we sent with the audio file. It autoloaded into his computer when he opened the WAV file. As soon as we initiate the Skype, I'll remotely activate the encryption. We should be good."

"You continue to amaze me, my friend."

Scott shrugged off the compliment. "You ready to talk to him? He's waiting."

"I am."

Swiveling back to his keyboard, Scott quickly executed a command. Once the screen for the video conference was open, he continued typing until a man's face appeared. Scott got up from his chair and Villarreal took his place in front of the webcam.

"Shem, how are you?"

After the two exchanged pleasantries, Villarreal asked, "Were you able to make any sense of what we sent?"

The man smiled. "Carlos, you delivered to me quite a package. Where did you come across that audio?"

"To be honest, I cannot speak as to its provenance. It was forwarded to me by a student. Why do you ask?"

The linguist leaned closer to the webcam. "Because it is either an earthshaking discovery or a massively cruel hoax."

Villarreal could feel the precursor of excitement building. Keeping his voice neutral, he asked, "Why do you say that?"

"My original hypothesis when I reviewed the portions of the phonetic transcript you first sent to me was that it was a spoken version of Sumerian. I confess that since your overnight package arrived with the actual audio, I have not slept a moment."

"Please, my friend, end this suspense. Is it Sumerian or not?"

Tevian hesitated momentarily. "Perhaps my sleep deprivation has made me delusional, but I believe that it is. I am fairly certain that you have sent to me the first spoken example of a language which has been dead for thousands of years."

Standing beside Villarreal, Scott grunted in surprise.

"Have you been able to decipher it?"

"That, Carlos, has been the challenge, requiring much educated guesswork and far too many assumptions at this point to be what I consider reliable. The audio you have provided will require months of further study before I can say with any confidence that the final translation is valid, but yes, I have."

"What is he saying? The man on the recording."

"Ahhh, that is also murky for another reason. His words, depending on which theory of the Sumerian culture you subscribe to, could be either a prayer or a sort of pledge of allegiance."

"I am afraid I do not understand."

"He speaks of *EN.LIL* in his monologue. He repeatedly promises to be faithful, loyal and to even die for Enlil."

"That name is familiar, although I cannot place it."

"The conventional wisdom within my discipline is that Enlil was a god to the Sumerians, and later was considered to be a star god."

"It being a prayer makes sense, then."

"Perhaps, Carlos. But there is a fringe theory which has gained considerable popularity within the nonscientific general public."

"You are speaking of Sitchin?"

With a wry, dismissive smirk, Tevian answered, "I am. He has put forth, in his own interpretations of the tablets, that Enlil was an alien from another planet. We, of course, put no stock in this theory whatsoever."

"Then why mention it?"

There was another pause before he responded, "One of the words I was able to translate was *EN.SI*. It was used frequently throughout the monologue and in a way which was somewhat disturbing."

"Shem...."

"I am frustrating you. I am sorry. I'll get to the point. One of the reasons I have not slept since this arrived was that I found it necessary to actually read several portions of Sitchin's books to verify what I suspected. The man in the monologue refers to *himself* as an *ensi*. Mainstream understanding of the language doesn't provide a satisfactory definition of the term. However, Sitchin does. His translation of *ensi* is 'righteous shepherd.' He maintains...and please bear in mind that I am not promoting this as truth...that those referred to by the term *ensi* were humans, or alien-engineered human hybrids, who were basically servants or slaves to the alien master and that it was their role to keep all of the others in line."

"Who were the others supposed to be?"

Even though it was obvious from the digital image of the linguist's face that he was attempting to portray smug dismissiveness, Villarreal could see a hint of something else in his eyes as the man answered, "Why, I suppose we would be the others."

$$\triangledown$$

The brutal afternoon sun penetrated the canvas awning affixed to the side of the modular office, baking Luis and Judtson, who were seated close to the building, attempting to find some shade.

"Man, it's hotter here than in Tucson," Luis complained between gulps of water from a plastic bottle.

"It's higher," was all Judtson said as an explanation.

"So we're closer to the sun."

"That's not the biggest factor. There's less atmosphere between us and it."

Luis seemed to accept the explanation as he fell into silence, his eyes squinting as he scanned the horizon. Despite the oppressive heat, Judtson was grateful for their good fortune upon arriving. Kevin Berry had been alone at the camp, having sent his two interns into Barstow. The scientist had bought the story Bal provided, that the four of them were friends on a road trip to Las Vegas and that he had heard Berry was doing some field work at this site along the route. He wanted to stop and meet Berry, hoping to discuss his work in the Andes. Berry welcomed them into his field office and offered cold drinks. Within minutes, Kelsey was able to slip the roofie into Berry's water. As soon as the man was unconscious, they administered the FDG and were now waiting the mandatory hour until they could convert him.

The screen door on the office swung open, and Kelsey came out and headed toward Judtson.

"I don't know if it's hotter inside or out here!"

"In there, I think. It's a big tin can. Is it time?"

"Yes."

"Let's do it so we can get out of here."

He stood and followed her in. The laptop was open and ready. Bal was seated beside Berry, who remained unconscious. With a final check, Judtson clicked the mouse, starting the procedure, and the three waited. The sequence completed, Kelsey removed the headpiece as Bal crouched in front of his colleague and, taking Berry by the arms, gently shook him, while repeatedly calling his name. In less than a minute, the geophysicist opened his eyes and blinked several times. In a routine now familiar to Judtson, Berry instantly began looking around the room, his eyes darting from one object to the next, convincing himself that he was actually in control.

Judtson leaned forward so that his face was just above Bal's shoulder. "Kevin, yes, it's true. We really did bring you back."

The man went through a series of rapid mouth and lip movements, which under other circumstances would have been comical, finally asking, "How did you do it? How did you know?" His voice was shaky, trembling.

The three explained the incidents and circumstances leading them to him. In the back of Judtson's mind, he was mildly surprised at how quickly they were able to tell their story. He was also amazed by how completely crazy it sounded.

Throughout the narrative, Berry interrupted several times with questions, making them backtrack and provide additional details before he would allow them to proceed. They finished by telling him about his paper which had been taken down by NASA and asking him what had been in it.

"Yes," he answered, his voice still unsteady, "the Andes. It made no sense. I can't imagine why the contents of my study would have resulted in something this drastic."

"What was it?" Bal prompted. "What did you find?"

"Nothing!" With the single-word answer, the geophysicist reared back and laughed.

"I don't understand, Kevin."

"I'm sorry. I'm not fully in control of my emotions yet. I expected, from my gravimetric testing and studies, to find extremely high quantities of sandstone strata, maybe a vast underground reservoir. But I found nothing! Literally!"

Singh stared at the man, wondering if the mental captivity had pushed him into some sort of delusional state. He decided to take a different tack. "Do you still have a copy of your abstract?"

"No! The moron who took me over deleted it, destroyed it, eradicated it, along with all my notes, everything."

"Kevin, I'm sorry if I'm being dense at the moment, but what do you mean when you say that you found nothing?"

Before he could answer, the door was opened by Luis. Peering inside, he saw that Berry was conscious and talking. "Sorry to interrupt. There are two Army guys from Fort Irwin out here. They're saying that we're on a military reservation without proper permission and have to leave."

"That's ridiculous," Berry retorted. "I have all the appropriate documentation for this camp."

"Maybe you should come out and talk to them."

"Of course. Give me a moment to find the papers."

As Berry rummaged through the stacks on his desk, Singh asked, "Kevin, please, what did you discover in the Andes?"

Locating what he was looking for at the bottom of a pile of papers, Berry pulled out a stapled set. "Here they are." He turned to Singh. "Yes. I'm sorry. What I found was a void. Let me go take care of this and then we can talk more."

He hurried out the door to a Humvee parked less than thirty yards from the modular office. Judtson moved to the doorway and stood behind Luis as they watched Berry hand the papers to one of the two men dressed in fatigues. In the bright glare of the sun, it took a moment for Judtson's eyes to adjust. When they did, he grabbed Luis by the arm. "There's something wrong."

Instinctively, Luis shifted the AK-47 slung over his shoulder. "What?"

Speaking softly, Judtson explained, "I've spent a lot of time on Army posts. I notice things…details for my books. The velcroed strips on their ACUs are always oriented the same – U.S. Army on the left, name on the right."

Luis focused on the two men for a second before shouldering his rifle and shouting, "YOU TWO! PUT YOUR HANDS UP!"

His command was the catalyst for an instant rush to action from the two. One of the men pulled his M9 from its holster and shot Berry twice at point-blank range. As the geophysicist fell to the ground, the second imposter reached into the back of the Humvee and whipped out an UZI, swinging it toward Luis and Judtson.

"GET INSIDE!" Luis ordered, pulling the trigger on his weapon and spraying rounds in the direction of the two men, who were both diving to the ground for cover. His shots connected with one of them, wounding him.

As Judtson was ducking back into the doorway, Kelsey, hearing the commotion, was coming out.

"Get back!" yelled Judtson, crashing into her. With a yelp, she twisted and fell to the floor. Judtson moved inside and out of the way, hoping to accommodate Luis, who was backing up and firing off short bursts.

The wounded attacker had managed to roll beneath the truck while his partner had crawled around the back of the vehicle for cover. The man under the truck, still clutching his M9, opened fire on Luis, a slug catching him in the arm just as he was backing through the door. The impact spun him around and he dropped the AK-47 to the floor, only inches from Kelsey. She grabbed the rifle and scrambled forward, angling her body against the wall beside the opening.

"Check Luis!" she barked to Judtson as she pointed the barrel at the bogus soldier under the truck and fired.

His cohort hammered the side of the modular, the bullets not penetrating the metal skin but causing the steel wall to ring clamorously and shattering one of the windows. Judtson scuttled to Luis, who was leaning against a table leg, his hand gripping the wound on his upper arm.

"We need to wrap that," Judtson shouted and looked around. There was a stack of towels on a shelf and he grabbed two of them, returning to Luis.

"You going to be all right?"

Luis, fighting back against the pain, nodded. "I think it went all the way through," he said, removing his grip so that Judtson could wrap the badly hemorrhaging wound. As he applied the second towel higher on the arm to partially work as a tourniquet, Judtson heard Kelsey loose another series of rounds.

"Here," Luis grunted, using his free hand to reach inside his vest pouch. "At the rate she's going, she's going to need these." He handed Judtson three ammo magazines. "Tell her to open the door all the way. If she leaves it cracked like that, she's gonna catch a ricochet."

Judtson instantly glanced at Kelsey and saw that she had pulled the door almost closed, firing through the gap while creating a deflector. "I see what you mean."

He bent low and crossed to Kelsey. "Luis said to open the door all the way. You're creating a perfect ricochet angle for them to hit you." He laid the extra magazines on the floor beside her.

She looked at the door for a second and grasped the situation, immediately shoving the door fully open.

"Judtson, are there any more guns here?"

"I don't know. I'll check."

She triggered her rifle again, spraying dust directly into the face of the man beneath the Humvee, as Judtson ran across the open doorway to check the other side of the office. As he frantically searched, Luis got to his feet and moved to the now glassless window, ducking as the stranger with the UZI peppered the opening. Pulling a pistol from his holster, he waited until the burst ended and he popped up, quickly firing off three rounds toward the truck.

The modular office had only three rooms: the main room where they now were, a private office at one end, and a restroom. As fast as he could, Judtson searched for another weapon and found none. Emerging from the restroom, he shouted to Kelsey, "No other guns!"

"Damn!"

▽

Brad Bledsoe, on a routine patrol with his partner, tapped the brakes on the Tahoe and killed the engine.

"Did you hear that?" he asked PFC Sherman.

Sherman nodded as they both heard another stutter of shots in the distance.

"Probably a live-fire exercise."

Bledsoe shook his head. "Not from that direction. The range and the box are both the other way."

Starting the engine, he slammed the big truck into gear. "Let's go check it out."

▽

Judtson felt useless without a gun as he crouched against the wall between Kelsey and Luis. "What's happening?"

Not looking away from the truck, Kelsey answered, "During that last long volley from the one with the UZI, the wounded guy crawled out from under the truck. They're both using it for cover now."

"So what do we do? Keep shooting at each other until one side runs out of bullets?"

They heard another string of shots from the UZI. The wounded attacker took advantage of the moment to holster his pistol and pull out his own automatic rifle. Charging the weapon, he sent a torrent of slugs through the doorway, burying them in the wall behind.

"I'm guessing," Luis said to answer Judtson's question, "now that they both have UZIs, the wounded guy is going to provide cover while the other makes his move."

"That sounds pretty dicey for the man running at us."

"Don't know if he'll make a frontal assault. He'll probably circle around and start using that window behind us."

Judtson glanced back at the window. "That would be bad. Is there anything I can do?"

Kelsey, again without looking away from her target, barked, "Call Romeo."

"What can he do from Arizona?"

"Nothing. But if we don't make it, he should know what happened."

Up until she spoke the words, the thought that they would not survive this encounter had not yet crossed Judtson's mind. Making no comment back to her, he pulled out his cell phone. Reading the screen, he declared, "No bars. No service." The cellular status, in his mind, suddenly seemed to symbolize their plight.

▽

"We have a situation," Bledsoe shouted into the radio. He and Sherman were standing next to the idling Tahoe on a rise looking down over the dry lake bed. Sherman was silently watching the action through binoculars and listening to both sides of the call, as Bledsoe explained.

"We have a visual on the scientific camp located at the dry lake. They appear to be under fire from two men wearing ACUs and driving a Humvee with painted camo. Are those two men ours?"

"Stand by."

Moving his finger away from the transmit button, he turned to Sherman and remarked caustically, "Yeah, stand by. We've got civilians under fire on a military reservation by unidentified shooters and I'm supposed to just stand...."

"That's negative. There should not be any of ours in that vicinity."

"You're sure? I don't want a blue-on-blue."

"Affirmative."

Bledsoe let out a heavy sigh. "Roger that. We're moving in."

"Backup has been dispatched."

▽

"Oh, hell!" The exclamation came from Kelsey.

"What's wrong?" Judtson asked.

"During that last series, one of them pulled out a cannister launcher."

As Kelsey watched, the non-wounded attacker ducked down to prep the weapon. Despite the high clearance under the Humvee, she did not have a shot at the legs of either of the men, as they both had positioned themselves behind the wheels. In her previous volleys, she had avoided the tires, hoping that one of the men would make a mistake and step into her sights.

"Luis, where's the fuel tank on that thing?"

"Already thought of that. It's on the far side."

"What's going to be coming?" Judtson pressed them.

Luis shrugged. "Probably tear gas."

Kelsey shouted urgently, "Luis, cover me!"

He popped up and emptied his clip in the direction of the truck while Kelsey rolled to her right and grabbed the opened door, slamming it closed just as a fusillade of slugs slammed into it.

With the door closed, she sprang up and moved to the sole window facing in the direction of the assault, squeezing next to Luis. "I thought I'd make it a little harder for them to get one in."

Rising immediately, she let off another rapid burst. As she stopped, Luis, who had replaced his magazine with a fresh one, rose to do the same. He suddenly dropped back down as a salvo came through the opening.

Judtson moved back to the shelves and grabbed the rest of the stack of towels. He then dashed to the bathroom and turned on the sink, jamming the towels into the bowl. The second he returned, Luis shouted, "Here it comes!"

There was a horrendously loud *clank* as something struck the bars on the window.

With momentary elation, Luis yelled, "It bounced off!"

Even though the smoking cannister was on the dirt outside the window, some of the putrid fumes wafted inside, triggering violent coughing from both Luis and Kelsey. Judtson rushed forward, handing them each a saturated towel. Singh, huddled against Berry's desk, took one and covered his face. Luis was able to bunch up his towel to blanket his mouth and nose while leaving his gun hand free. Kelsey, with an AK-47, needed both hands free, so Judtson held the wet cloth on the lower half of her face as she poked the barrel through the window and fired blindly.

They all knew that it was only a matter of seconds before the next cannister arrived. The bad guys were, no doubt, capitalizing on the debilitating effects of the gas to move closer for the next shot. Judtson's mind whirled as he tried to think of a way out of their predicament, coming up with nothing.

The next projectile flew through the opening and slammed into the opposite wall, instantly spewing a white cloud of gas, and the room filled quickly. All three of them dropped to the floor, covering their faces with the towels but convulsively coughing and gagging.

Kelsey knew that the moment she opened the door to escape the gas, she and the others would be cut to pieces. Despite the strength of her will to survive, the tear gas, attacking the mucous membranes of her sinuses and throat, as well as sparking an unbearable burning sensation in her eyes even through the cover from the wet towel, was pushing her inexorably toward the irrational act. Racking coughs shook her and she could hear Luis, Judtson, and Singh suffering the same agony.

Over the hacking and coughing inside the modular, she thought that she could also hear gunfire outside. The still-functioning portion of her brain wondered why the two men would be shooting.

▽

As Bledsoe and Sherman approached at full speed on the powdery lake bed, they both saw the white smoke billowing out of the field office window, and the two counterfeit soldiers standing at the closed door with their guns at the ready.

"What's the play?" Sherman shouted to his sergeant as they barreled toward the scene.

Smiling, Bledsoe answered, "They don't call us the cavalry for nothing. Grab the Mossberg and get ready."

He maneuvered the Tahoe toward the area between the building and the truck, aiming straight for the two men. With their attention fixed on the doorway, the attackers did not notice the approach until the last possible minute. One man dived to the dirt against the side of the modular as the other dodged toward the Humvee. Bledsoe twisted the wheel and slammed on the brakes, pulling the Tahoe into a sideways slide between the two. As the big SUV shuddered to a stop, Sherman, who had already opened his door, was out with the 12 gauge and, using the vehicle as cover, moved swiftly to the hood, laying the Mossberg on the hot metal and pulling the trigger. The man who had run back toward the Humvee had dropped the cannister launcher and was bringing the barrel of his UZI up, when the double-aught pellets from the shotgun ripped into him from a distance of no more than fifteen feet.

Bledsoe, his window facing the man lying on the ground, had no real cover except his own door. Unholstering his M9, he twisted in his seat, fighting the shoulder harness, and stuck the pistol through the open window, bringing it to bear on the second attacker, who had already begun firing wildly on the Tahoe. With steelier nerves than the stranger, Bledsoe waited until his gun sight steadied on the target before he began to pull the trigger, not stopping until the clip was empty. After his third round, the opposing fire had abruptly ceased. By the time he heard the *click* of his pistol firing on an empty chamber, he saw that the man lying on the ground was completely still.

"Sherman," he shouted. "What's your status?"

Through the windshield, he could see his battle buddy bending down where the first assailant had been. "My man's down," came the reply.

Opening his door, Bledsoe climbed out, one-handedly dropping the clip out of the M9 and sliding in a fresh one, keeping his eyes on the body crumpled against the side of the modular. Covering the distance quickly, he crouched and felt for a pulse, finding none.

"Call it in. Let them know we've got it under control."

"Roger that," Sherman answered.

Through the open window, Bledsoe could hear the sound of hacking coughs coming from more than one person. He moved to the opening, standing off to the side to avoid the tear gas as well as any shots fired in panic by those inside.

"Hey! You in there! United States Army Military Police. You can come out now! It's all clear."

▽

Even before she heard the shout from the window, Kelsey, pushed beyond the boundary of her discipline by the effects of the gas, had already grabbed the handle of the door and was about to plunge out, still clutching her weapon. The words from outside were the final catalyst. Twisting the knob, she fell through the doorway to the dirt outside, intending to roll onto her back and wield the AK-47, in case the shouts were a ruse.

Her lungs racked with violent spasms, her vision badly blurred, she was barely able to discern the hazy outline of a figure standing above her as it bent down, seized the rifle by the barrel, and twisted it out of her grip. Once relieved of her weapon, she felt two hands slide under her arms and lift her, moving her away from the doorway. Rubbing her eyes madly in an attempt to clear her vision, Kelsey tried to speak, but her first attempt was thwarted by a horrendous coughing bout.

As the man was moving her, she heard him shout to someone else, "Sherman, open the back gate."

A moment later, Kelsey felt herself placed on the rear deck of the Tahoe. Swallowing repeatedly, she tried to speak again. "Three more…three more inside. One's…one's hurt."

A man's voice, close to her ear, asked, "Are they armed?"

Her throat seizing up again, she nodded first. Finally able to get out a few more words, she croaked, "One. Pistol."

Kelsey heard a voice from slightly farther away. "I'll get them, Sergeant."

The closer voice asked, "Can you sit tight a sec? I'll be right back."

Kelsey nodded, resting the palms of both hands on the deck to steady herself. Less than a minute later, the man returned. "Tilt your head back." She felt a supporting hand behind her neck and leaned back as he poured water over her eyes and face.

"Here you go," he said, and she felt a towel placed into her hand. As she rubbed her face vigorously, she heard another person coughing nearby and assumed it was Judtson. Blinking repetitively, she was able to see somewhat better. The man who had provided the towel was standing about a foot away, smiling at her. "You okay?"

She started to answer, when another round of coughing stopped her. He unhooked a tube from his vest and offered it. "Take *one* sip."

Gratefully, she took the tube and, with her thumb, popped the cap off the end, putting the mouthpiece between her lips. The almost hot water tasted unbelievably wonderful as it rinsed her mouth and trickled down her throat. Heeding his advice, she stopped after the first drink and handed the tube back.

"Thanks," she mumbled, happy to hear her own voice. Reading the name tape and spotting the triple stripes, she added, "Sergeant Bledsoe."

His face crinkled in a deeper grin. "What's your name, ma'am?"

"Kelsey."

He stuck out his right hand. "Good to meet you, Kelsey. I'd better check on the others."

He turned toward the modular, and Kelsey looked to see Judtson sitting on the dirt next to the door with his back against the outside wall. Bal Singh was beside him, coughing furiously into the towel he still held. The other soldier was coming out of the office with Luis, who was bleeding badly from the gunshot wound on his arm.

Kelsey stood unsteadily when it became obvious that the other soldier and Bledsoe were bringing Luis to the Tahoe. She vacated the rear deck just as they arrived, and while the other soldier, whose name she noticed was Sherman, helped Luis sit on the truck, Bledsoe trotted around to the side door and came back with a first-aid kit. As the two busied themselves with bandaging Luis, Kelsey walked to where Judtson was sitting and dropped down to the ground next to him.

"Hey, Squirrel, you all right?" Her voice was hoarse and raspy.

He did not attempt to speak, simply shaking his head.

She took his hand and stood up. "Come on. You too, Bal."

They rose shakily, and she led them around the modular to the side where she had spotted a water tank. Judtson followed obediently as she positioned him under the spigot on the elevated fiberglass reservoir and opened it. The water cascaded onto his head, and she reached up and scrubbed his hair with her fingers, moving down to his face, neck, and then shoulders. Sputtering, he managed to say, "I can do it," and began working the chemical out of his clothing. Judtson stepped from under the stream and allowed Singh access. When he finished, Kelsey stepped in and rinsed herself off completely.

After she was done, Judtson moved forward and turned his face up, filling his mouth with water and spitting it out several times before stepping back and asking her, "How's Luis?"

"They're bandaging him. Let's go check."

He turned off the spigot, and the three walked, dripping wet, to the Tahoe, where the soldier named Sherman was next to Luis, finishing a gauze wrap on his injured arm. Bledsoe was standing several feet away, talking on his telephone.

Addressing Sherman, Kelsey asked, "How does it look?"

"Looks like a through-and-through. Lots of bleeding, but it doesn't appear to have hit the bone."

"I'll be okay," Luis offered. "How's Berry?"

"I...." Kelsey realized that since the shooting began, she had forgotten completely about the man they had come to see. "I'll go...."

Sherman interrupted, "If you're talking about the man over by the Humvee, I'm afraid he's gone."

Bledsoe, who had finished his phone conversation, walked up to the group. "We have a doc on the way. My CO wants to know what happened."

Kelsey began speaking before Judtson or Luis could say a word. "Our traveling companion, Bal Singh, is a geologist. He had heard that Dr. Berry, a geophysicist, was doing some field work here. Dr. Berry's work relates to a subject Bal is studying and he wanted to meet him and compare notes. We had just arrived, when those two men drove up. They claimed to be with the Army and told Dr. Berry that he was on the installation illegally. Berry was showing them his authorization paperwork, and they just shot him for no reason."

Bledsoe stared intently at Kelsey's face, in an obvious attempt to read her. "Ma'am, if you don't mind my asking, why were the three of you traveling with an assault rifle?"

"I can explain," Judtson cut in. "I'm an author, Judtson Kent. Many of my books have irritated some people over the years. I've received threats more than once. Luis is my bodyguard."

A quick smile spread across Bledsoe's face. "You're Judtson Kent? I've read a couple of your books."

Judtson smiled back. "Yes, I am, and I think you've met my friend Kelsey."

The sergeant extended his hand. "I'm Brad Bledsoe."

"Pleasure to meet you, sir."

"The pleasure's all mine. I'm afraid the four of you are going to have to come in with me. You know, there's going to be a sh...boatload of questions."

Chapter 31

Matt Wheeler walked away from the improvised test chamber he and Scott had assembled for the headpiece taken from the assailants at Judtson's office. Stepping around the loom of wires running from the chamber, across the room and hallway, and back to Scott's computer room, he stopped at the doorway.

"Are you sure we're getting nothing?"

Rather than answering, Gumble gestured at the monitor, and Wheeler bent over to see for himself. After a few seconds, he grumbled, "All zeros. I don't get it."

"Maybe it's broken."

Wheeler shrugged. "Could be. It appears to be fine. When we turn it on, it warms up. It consumes electricity. Maybe we don't know how to use it?"

"I don't know. It seems pretty straightforward. On, off, that's it. Not even a laptop in the valise to set duration, strength, anything. Just a power supply. There might be another possibility."

"What's that?"

"Maybe we're not looking for the right thing."

"Explain."

Gumble leaned back in his chair for a moment. "Imagine handing a modern cell phone to an electrical engineer at Bell Labs back in the fifties and telling him that it was a wireless communications device. He'd be looking for an analog signal and only in the lower frequencies. As far as he'd be concerned, the device simply wouldn't work...since it didn't do anything."

"So you're saying that the headpiece in there was built by some advanced civilization and we aren't capable of understanding it?"

This time it was Gumble's turn to shrug. "I don't know about the 'advanced civilization' part. But it certainly could be something you and I have never heard of, some top secret device utilizing a new technology."

▽

Kelsey, Judtson, Luis, and Bal were safely back inside the silo. Exhausted after spending nearly nine hours with the MPs at Fort Irwin, followed by a seven-hour return trip, the four fell into their beds and slept for almost half a day. As they awoke, Luis went off to huddle with Romeo to fully brief him on the details of the attack. Singh sought out Villarreal, hoping to make sense of what Berry had said before he was killed. Kelsey found Judtson once again in the lounge, sitting alone and nursing a large mug of coffee.

"Morning, Squirrel. It is morning, isn't it?"

Her greeting was rewarded with a half smile. "When I'm down here, I have no idea. How are you?"

Kelsey was still wearing the camouflage clothes given to her by the MPs; her clothing had been permanently impregnated with the tear gas. She poured herself a cup and sat down. "I don't know how I am. Nothing but nightmares while I slept."

"About what?"

"The obvious. Trapped in that field office as it filled with gas. Two gunmen standing outside the door waiting to blow us to pieces the second we ran out. The only difference was that the good guys didn't come charging in at the last minute to rescue us."

"Sounds familiar. Have you seen Luis? How is he?"

"I did. He's with Romeo. He'll be okay, I guess. He said the medic at Irwin did a pretty good job patching him up. Yesterday scared me, Judtson."

Judtson was taken slightly aback by the rare appearance of vulnerability on her face, instead of the usual brash confidence she displayed. "Me, too. I'm sorry, by the way."

Her eyebrows rose slightly. "For what?"

"When Luis got hit, I did nothing. If it hadn't been for your quick thinking, immediately grabbing his gun and holding them off, there would have been a very different ending to the story."

She shook her head, dismissing his apology. "That's dumb. I was clumsy enough to get knocked on my butt, so I was already on the floor right by the door. The rifle Luis dropped practically fell into my hands. That was it. I'd probably deserve some credit if I had actually hit either of them. And you did fine. Stopped his bleeding. Thought of the wet towels for us. If you hadn't done that, the gas would've gotten to us a lot sooner. We'd have stumbled outside right into their hands before Bledsoe was able to get there."

Clearly not assuaged, he muttered, "Sure, thanks."

As she took a breath to continue, Singh and Villarreal entered, joining them at the table.

"Did you two come up with something?" Judtson asked hopefully.

"I think Bal might have."

Singh leaned forward, placing his elbows on the tabletop. "I have been thinking about Kevin Berry's last few words."

"I thought he said he didn't find anything."

"Not exactly, Kelsey. What he said was that he found nothing."

"Okay. What's the difference?"

"He also mentioned a void. That might be what he meant by saying he'd found nothing."

"I guess I'm not awake yet," Judtson commented, "but I'm just not getting it, Bal."

"Fluctuations in gravity, when measured in minuscule amounts, can be caused by underground water, sandstone instead of a more dense substance such as granite or andesite, any of several possible variations in the subterranean mass. Obviously, the most dramatic variation would be a void…a cavern…basically an area underground where there is nothing but air."

"I see."

"And that would make sense from my perspective. Remember I told you that the Andes were quite a bit larger than my model predicted."

"Yes."

"If the tectonic forces somehow created a large void, then the model would be…or I guess I should say, could be accurate because the predicted amount of mass would be accurate."

"What you're saying is that when the two plates collided, rather than piling up the rock to make the Andes, they somehow folded over, trapping a huge empty space inside."

"Essentially yes, Judtson."

"So what's our next step?" Kelsey asked.

Villarreal answered her question. "With the nature of my work in Puma Punku causing the other side to convert me, and Bal's work leading him to an investigation into the same region and making him a target, and poor Dr. Berry first being converted and then killed over his paper addressing that location…."

"We need to go to Puma Punku," Kelsey finished his thought.

"But what would we be looking for? I'm all for having something to do, except we can't just go down there and wander around like tourists."

"You're right, Judtson," Singh replied. "My guess is that the void is an extensive cave system and that somewhere near Puma Punku is an entrance. We need to find that entrance."

"Again, how can we do it? All of Berry's papers and field notes are gone."

"That may be. However, you must remember that he would have had help when he was down there, whether it was from students or locals. A study of such magnitude is never completed solo. We need to find a member of his team. Someone should remember what he found and where he found it."

▽

"There it is…Avenida 6 de Marzo," Kelsey shouted. "Turn left."

Judtson followed Kelsey's directions, steering the rental car to the left.

"Now go up the ramp and watch for the Route 1 sign."

Within seconds he spotted the road marker and followed the second ramp onto the highway. Kelsey settled back into her seat. "In about five kilometers, you're going to have to bear to the left. That'll get us headed west."

"Will do."

Even the moderate level of traffic was unnerving as the drivers around him seemed to have a more laissez-faire attitude toward conventional habits of the road, such as signaling ahead of changing lanes. The other difference he noticed, immediately upon departing from El Alto Airport, was the incessant use of horns by the drivers, creating a distracting, cacophonous environment. He checked his rearview mirror and saw that Romeo was close behind in the second van they had rented after arriving on the American Airlines flight from Miami.

Kelsey was rubbernecking from the passenger seat. "Is it just me or are the lanes narrower here than in America?"

Laughing, Judtson said, "It certainly feels like it."

He realized that he was tense, leaning slightly forward and gripping the steering wheel firmly with both hands, and envied Saylor who was already asleep in the backseat.

Seeing him glance back at his friend, Kelsey commented, "I've never seen anyone conk out so quickly."

Judtson nodded. "That's Saylor. He has always been that way."

"He doesn't like airplanes, huh?"

"No. Hates them. That's why he didn't sleep all the way down here."

He consciously forced himself to relax and sit back. Within a few minutes, he successfully maneuvered through the next lane change.

Kelsey took a final look at the directions before setting them aside. "About fifty-four kilometers to Tiahuanaco." She reached out and tapped the fan's speed selector to the highest setting. "I'm freezing! It's weird coming from Arizona to Bolivia this time of year. When we left, it was hotter than hell, and now I feel like my fingers and toes are turning into icicles."

"It *is* the middle of their winter now. Plus, we're at around 13,000 feet. It's going to be cold."

"Is Puma Punku higher?"

"No. La Paz and Tiahuanaco are about the same elevation."

Kelsey dramatically rubbed her hands together to warm them. "I hope Dr. Berry's guy is there."

Finally acclimating to the driving styles of his companions on the highway, Judtson allowed himself furtive peeks to survey the portion of La Paz he was able to see from their route. After several minutes of silence, he commented, "That's unusual."

"What's that?"

"I didn't notice this the last time I was here. The homes down in the valley are beautiful. But look in the distance...the houses on the slope of the mountain aren't as nice. It's usually the other way around. The expensive homes get the view."

The heat from the vents had finally stopped Kelsey's shivering. "When I read all of the stuff Scott printed out about La Paz, there was an explanation of that. It isn't the view they're after. It's comfort. Because La Paz is so high, the lowest part of the valley has the most moderate weather. The higher up the slope you get, the worse it gets."

"Makes sense."

The two again lapsed into silence, taking in the dramatic scenery until they had departed the city and the traffic had subsided considerably. Kelsey was the first to break the reverie. "Judtson, can I ask you a question?"

Detecting a different tone in her voice from their usual banter, he turned to face his companion. She was staring at him intently. "Of course. What is it?"

She did not respond immediately and, alternating his attention between the road and Kelsey, Judtson saw a fleeting uncertainty in her expression.

"Are you and...? Never mind."

She abruptly twisted in her seat to stare out the side window.

Judtson, keeping his voice gentle and encouraging, asked, "What is it, Kelsey?"

Without turning back to him, she shook her head. "Nothing. It was dumb."

"You were going to ask me about Kristen."

Still staring at the countryside, her head moved in an almost imperceptible nod.

He took a moment to marshal his thoughts and feelings. "If you had asked me that question before I was zapped, I would have told you that the two of us hated each other."

Kelsey looked away from the passing vista. "Why would you stay if you hated her?"

"I asked myself that question a hundred times. I don't know. I guess change is hard for me."

"Why did she stay?"

He chuckled. "I have no idea. You'd have to ask her."

Her eyes boring deeply into his during the brief glances away from the road, she pressed him a little further. "You said that was how it was before you got zapped. What about now?"

There was once again a long hesitation until he spoke. "I'm not sure what I feel now. I suppose guilt more than anything."

"And Kristen?"

Smiling ruefully, he answered, "Oh, I think she has changed, too. Before it was only hatred...now it's more like hatred and fury."

Despite herself, Kelsey smiled at Judtson's words. "That's a solid foundation for a relationship!"

"Oh, yeah."

Her voice softer than before, he had to strain to hear her ask, "Then it's over?"

Unable to answer immediately, he took a deep breath and said, "When I went to the house to see her after Saylor brought me back, I asked her for another chance."

"Why would *you* need another chance? It sounds like both of you were a million miles apart in the relationship."

Realizing that he needed to avert his eyes from her intense gaze, Judtson kept his face forward as he responded. "That's just who I am. It probably explains why I was still in the marriage."

"And why do you feel guilty?"

"Because while I was briefly the other Judtson, she swore I was the man she had married. For that short period of time, she was ecstatic. Then Saylor brought me back...and from Kristen's perspective it was a horribly cruel thing to do. I guess I don't see myself as a cruel man. I told her that if she gave me a chance, I'd try to be the other guy when I was with her."

"Sorry for my bluntness, but that sounds stupid."

He allowed himself a brief laugh. "You're right. It is. I know that. I did make the offer, though. She said she'd let me know her decision. And...."

Kelsey interrupted, "And you think that sticking to your offer as long as it's on the table is the honorable thing to do?"

He sighed loudly. "Yeah, that's it."

"Judtson, this isn't some real estate deal where you've made an offer and you're supposed to give the other party a chance to counteroffer before you'll consider any others. This is your *life*."

"I know. But, as I said, it's the way I am. Too many people today feel absolutely no obligation to stick to their word. I guess I'm not one of those people."

He could feel her stare burning into the side of his face, but did not turn his head. After a lengthy pause, he heard her grunt expressively. "Okay. I respect that."

Peripherally, he saw Kelsey turn back to face the side window, seemingly watching the scenery once more. Judtson struggled to identify the fresh emotion which had suddenly sprung up within him, and was surprised to discover that it was disappointment he was feeling when he realized that she had given up.

▽

After their experience in the Mojave with Kevin Berry, Judtson was relieved to see the red Jeep Cherokee parked at the dirt turn-off to Puma Punku, and the young man leaning against its side, waiting. There was no one else in sight. Pulling off the road, he stopped next to the Jeep and killed the engine. As Judtson roused Saylor, Romeo, who had remained on their tail through the entire drive, brought his vehicle to a stop on the dirt approximately fifty yards away.

Everyone in the party had been briefed earlier to allow Romeo to get out first and check the man they were meeting, as well as the area, before they disembarked. Judtson and Kelsey watched as the big man, made to seem even larger by the bulky parka he was wearing, walked over to the stranger and introduced himself. The two talked for a few minutes. Apparently with the stranger's permission, Romeo checked the interior of the Jeep, then did a quick walk-around, his eyes sweeping the perimeter for threats.

"This guy must think we're nuts," Kelsey remarked. "Not exactly conducive to a comfortable working relationship."

"I know. I guess Bal prepared him for it. He told him that I was an eccentric celebrity."

"Well, at least that part's true," Saylor muttered groggily from behind.

Judtson gave him a dirty look in the mirror as Kelsey said, "There's the all clear. Let's go."

The three climbed out of the van and were instantly startled by the intensity of the frigid wind. They followed Bal and Carlos, who had ridden with Romeo, as they walked to the young man. After the two scientists performed shouted introductions, Singh gestured toward Judtson. "Sam, this is Judtson Kent. He is the author I told you about. And this is his physician, Saylor Costello. Judtson, this is Sam Jonassen. He was one of Dr. Berry's assistants on the project down here."

They shook hands and Judtson plunged into his planned cover story. "Pleasure to meet you, Sam. As I believe Dr. Singh has told you, I'm working on a book regarding this area and specifically Dr. Berry's findings. Have you spoken with Dr. Berry recently?"

The man, a lean, tanned, and rugged-looking type who would fit in perfectly on the back of a horse crossing the badlands of New Mexico, shook his head. "I haven't heard from Kevin in weeks. I have tried to reach him on the phone and through email, but he never answered. I was beginning to get worried."

The group had decided earlier to conceal Berry's death, so Judtson proceeded with a partial truth. "We just came from seeing him. He's working on another project in the Mojave and probably won't be returning emails and phone calls in the near future. He spoke quite highly of you and said that you might be able to help."

The stroke of ego had its desired effect, and the young man stood slightly straighter. "I'd be happy to. I just can't imagine anything I could tell you that he couldn't."

Expecting this response, Judtson said, "I don't know if you've read any of my books...."

"I'm sorry, but I haven't."

"Not a problem. My style, or technique, is to tell a story from several perspectives, in the same fashion as Hemingway...."

Saylor snorted, covering the sound hastily with a fake cough.

Ignoring him, Judtson continued, "Except I write in the nonfiction genre. Despite the fact that I deal with truth and reality, it is surprising how many different versions of the same event can be told by various participants. Each person always sees or recalls something from a unique perspective. Since, most of the time, there is no way to ferret out which is the true version, what I try to do is present them all and let the reader decide."

"I understand."

"That's why we're here with you. What I'd like is for you to assume that Dr. Berry has told us nothing at all, and walk us through what you observed while working with him in the field."

"Sure. Happy to."

▽

Matt Wheeler felt like throwing the headpiece against the wall. The device taken from the bad guys had frustrated him at every turn. In his various tests, all he had been able to determine was that it consumed power. He knew it certainly must have an output of some sort, but he was running into a brick wall finding out what it might be. Wheeler wished he were back at his lab, with all of his equipment, as the limited resources available to him in the silo severely hampered his efforts. Hopefully, the additional test equipment he and Scott had ordered would arrive soon.

Standing abruptly, he impatiently crossed the room toward the hallway, planning on a visit to the restroom. As he hurriedly crossed the threshold, he slammed into someone coming down the hallway.

"Excuse…." He stopped in mid-apology, realizing the other was not any of his companions.

▽

Clarkson, Trippiano, Copeland, and Falt were in the lounge. Soon after the four were thrown together in the underground refuge, they had discovered a mutual passion for bridge and were indulging it with gusto while sharing a platter of bread, cheeses, and fruits.

"Hey, Ricky," shouted Trippiano from the table. "Are you sure you don't want to learn how to play?"

Ricky, who was reclined on the sofa reading, looked up from his book and grinned at her. "I'm sure, Lisa."

They were so engaged in the bidding that none of the foursome noticed the two strangers enter the room with guns drawn.

"Down on the floor!" one of them barked.

Startled, Trippiano jumped up from her chair, knocking it over.

"Oh, God, no," murmured Ricky.

"Who are…?" Copeland started to shout, at that moment realizing who the men must be. With his hands above his head, he slowly knelt down, as did Dylan.

Lisa, still standing and panting heavily from the surge of adrenaline coursing through her, took two steps forward, in the direction of the men. "What do you want from us?" she screamed.

Clarkson stood. "Lisa, come back here. Don't…." As he spoke, he took a single step to follow her.

She showed no inclination to heed his warning and took another step forward. "I asked you a ques…."

One of the two men moved swiftly toward her and slammed the butt of his pistol against the side of her head, dropping her suddenly to the floor. Al Clarkson's reaction was instantaneous. Whirling around, he seized the large knife from the breadboard and ran at the man, only covering half the distance before being cut down by two shots from the stranger's pistol.

Scott, at his usual station in front of his computers, heard the reverberations from the two shots, spun in his chair, and sent a message to Romeo, copying it to Kelsey. "Something's wrong here!"

After sending it off, he stood and closed his door, bolting it.

▽

Chris Ashby was sound asleep in his bunk when the door to his room opened.

▽

"Is that the best you can do, Jimmy?" Doni teased, as her legs furiously pumped the pedals on the exercise bicycle in the gym.

"Don't bet against me, little girl," Meade retorted, increasing the pace of his own pedaling on the bicycle beside her.

With all the walls of the room covered with mirrors, the entrance of the two black-clad men was immediately apparent. Seeing the intruders, Meade let go of his grip on one of the handlebars and reached around to his back, when one of the men shouted, "Don't go for it, old man!"

Thinking better of it, he stopped and raised both hands, as did Doni.

▽

Working furiously, Scott captured all of the available recent videos and uploaded them, his fingers flying over the keyboard. Nearly finished, he heard a crashing sound from the door to his small room. Ignoring the attempts by the intruders to gain access, he continued entering commands at lightning speed. A second crash followed the first, and he could hear the screech of one of the hinges beginning to fail. Maintaining his concentration, Scott was relieved to see the progress bar on the monitor hit one hundred percent.

▽

Detective Ben Hart turned to his longtime friend Billy Burke, who was riding in the passenger seat of the unmarked police car. "Thanks for coming along."

The tall, lanky uniformed officer looked cramped in the seat. "You're kidding! From what you said, this sounds like we've fallen into another doozy. A violent crime scene with no bodies, a missing lab tech, a missing medical equipment engineer, a missing doctor and his wife, a video of a mysterious black SUV with a dead guy who is supposed to work for Homeland Security...but no body, and they deny any knowledge of him...and a missing famous author whose wife says that he told her that bad guys dressed in black were controlling his mind. Wouldn't miss it."

Hart laughed as his partner continued, "So why are we heading out to an old Titan missile silo?"

"According to the people I talked to at RadTech, where Wheeler works, there was a big order for some equipment...testing equipment...that came in to one of their suppliers. It wasn't ordered by RadTech. It came from somebody else, somebody they didn't know. But because this stuff isn't exactly retail...I think you need to be licensed to handle it...the supplier won't sell it to just anybody. I guess whoever ordered it gave Matt Wheeler's ID to get the order released. When the supplier heard that Wheeler was missing, they called RadTech. I called the supplier and found out that the delivery address was this missile silo."

"Got it."

As they approached the perimeter fence and call box, Hart noticed something and stopped the car. He gingerly got out, grabbing his cane for support. Burke came around from the other side.

"That looks like blood," Hart murmured, pointing at an extensive stain on the pavement.

Working in a large circle, Burke checked the area and, within a couple of minutes, shouted, "One here, too."

Hart walked over to where Burke was standing and stared down at the hard-packed soil beside the curb. It was saturated with a dark brown stain.

"You'd better call it in, Billy. Have 'em get a van out here."

The two returned to the sedan and climbed in as Burke made the call. Hart pulled forward to the intercom box, noticing that it had suffered damage from an impact, and pressed the button. There was no response. He pressed it a second time. Again, no answer.

"Oh, well. Nobody's home, I guess."

"Hope that's it."

Proceeding slowly to survey the terrain around the vehicle, they drove over the speed hump and followed the serpentine lane until arriving at the steel gate, which stood wide open.

"There's a pretty good ding in that gate," Hart observed as they rolled past, directing Burke's attention to the spot where Romeo had clipped the gate.

Clearing the entrance, they came to the small building with its door standing open.

Ben parked. "That's probably the entrance to the silo."

"You figure? I bet that's why you made detective."

Overlooking the comment, Hart asked, "What do you think, go in or wait for backup?"

Billy surveyed the scene for a moment before answering. "Obviously, the prudent thing to do is wait."

Hart nodded. "You're absolutely right." He grabbed the 12 gauge from its mount between them and handed it to Burke. "It's either carry this or the cane for me. So why don't you take it?"

Taking the shotgun, Burke opened his door and climbed out into the heat, moving toward the open doorway cautiously while giving his limping partner time to catch up.

"Great! Stairs!" Hart muttered as he entered the building.

"We came to an underground missile silo," Burke retorted softly. "What did you expect?"

Tucking his cane under his arm and grasping the steel railing for support, leaving his right hand free to hold his pistol, Hart answered, "An elevator."

"Wuss!"

In the lead, Burke cautiously followed the stairs until he reached the bottom where he stopped and waited. The eerie silence in the underground complex made him feel as if he were entering a crypt. Shaking off the image, he glanced back as he heard Hart come around the final switchback in the stairs, and saw that his friend was red-faced from the pain and exertion of the descent. Completing the last flight, Hart, panting, joined Burke at the massive steel door which also stood fully open.

"You okay?"

"Do I look okay?"

Burke shook his head and spoke in a voice slightly above a whisper. "I'll go ahead. I think we do a quick room-by-room first."

Hart nodded. "I'll cover you."

"I'll go extra slow so you can keep…."

"Billy!"

"All right. I'm going."

The tall cop turned and, holding the 12 gauge at the ready, moved forward, pausing briefly at the security console before continuing. Their car was clearly displayed on one of the small video monitors. His eyes swept the balance of the screens and saw nothing out of the ordinary. Cautiously walking on, he began to methodically check each room he encountered, with Hart following closely behind. Everywhere he looked, he saw signs of recent occupation. When they arrived at the lounge, Burke, who had entered the room, hurriedly stepped back out into the hallway, nearly bumping into Hart.

"We've got one." His voice was flat as he moved aside. The detective proceeded to the doorway and peered in, seeing the body of Al Clarkson facedown on the floor in a pool of blood.

"Probably a waste of time, but you should check him, Billy."

Burke handed the shotgun to Hart, skirted around his partner, and knelt beside the prone figure, careful to avoid the blood. After feeling for a pulse at both the wrist and the neck, he shook his head.

"Well, I guess this case finally has a body," Hart grunted, still positioned in the doorway. "Billy, take a look around. He wasn't the only person here. Seems that a four-handed game of cards was going on at the table. There's a dropped book next to that couch. Can't tell how many, but definitely a group."

Burke stood erect and was slowly turning, taking in the facts Hart pointed out. He then circled the perimeter of the room, searching for any other items not visible from his previous vantage, working his way back to Hart. "We need to keep looking." Taking back the shotgun, he continued at point position, methodically checking the balance of the rooms on the hallway until they reached a badly damaged door, severely canted and hanging on one bent hinge.

"Looks like somebody holed up in here."

"I'd say so," Hart agreed, stepping past his partner into the room. "Can't believe all this stuff."

Burke joined him inside the cramped room and eyed the array of computer equipment. "Quite a setup."

Hart pointed at one of the monitors. "Check it out."

Burke's eyes immediately darted in the direction his partner was gesturing. The screen was displaying an animated image of a donkey face, grinning broadly and shaking its head back and forth. Above the caricature, in large red letters, was the message "KISS MY...."

"I'll bet somebody tried to access the system and didn't get too far."

"Odds are you're right. Billy, I don't get it."

"Get what?"

"You saw what I saw. They had perimeter security, a wall, a steel gate, that vault door at the bottom of the stairs. The desk we passed looked like a security station with camera monitors. Hell, they were ready for World War Three down here."

"But everything was wide open."

"Yep. Whoever came in and killed that man, and apparently took the others, just waltzed right in."

Hart checked his watch. "Backup should be arriving. We've got no radio down here. Phones won't work either. Probably should stop the search and meet them topside."

Nodding his agreement, Burke grinned. "You sure you're ready for the up trip on those stairs?"

Hart smiled back. "Who said anything about me? I'll wait down at that security station."

The two were leaving but heard a muffled noise.

Burke held out his hand to stop his partner. "Did you hear that?"

They waited silently, listening, when from beneath their feet came a muted voice. "Hey!"

Startled, both of them looked down at the floor. Before either could react, one of the two-by-two panels close to where they stood lifted and slid aside, revealing a dark crawl space beneath. Instinctively, Burke shifted the barrel of the shotgun to point at the opening, as a face suddenly swung into view.

"Hello there. Could you help me out of here?"

Chapter 32

THE FREEZING WIND SEEMED TO CLAW AT THEM as the group skirted the edge of the ancient stone platform. They were clustered closely around Jonassen, who seemed impervious to the temperature. "Our base camp was over there." He pointed to a level area a few hundred yards away. "We stayed outside the Puma Punku perimeter."

"There had to be some more accommodating sites closer to Lake Titicaca." The comment came from Singh.

"There were," Jonassen agreed. "But Kevin was fascinated with this place. He wanted to be around it."

Villarreal nodded. "I can understand."

As they walked, Judtson mentally detached from the conversation and immersed himself in the environment. This was not his first visit to the site. He had met Carlos at Puma Punku once, when the archaeologist had shared his revelations with him. He recalled that there had been something about the remnants of the platform or terrace or whatever it actually had been at some distant moment in the past, as well as the amazing precision of the carved stones strewn about the site as if tossed by a tot during playtime, which had affected him in a manner he could not quite describe. He had been curious whether he would feel the same this time and was oddly reassured by the fact that he did. So engrossed in his attempt to absorb the ambiance of the locale, Judtson did not notice Kelsey studying him.

Moving closer and leaning to speak into his ear, she asked, "Are you all right?"

His reverie broken, he smiled at her. "I am. Why?"

"I don't know. You had a funny look on your face."

"What kind of look?"

She thought briefly before responding. "Happy? Serene? Not sure. Almost like you'd look going back to search for your childhood tree house after twenty years and discovering that it was still there."

Her description both surprised and resonated with him. "Really?"

"Is that how you feel here?"

He stopped walking, letting the group move away. She paused to remain with him. "I don't know. That's what I was trying to figure out. I do feel something here. And it isn't a bad feeling. Not at all. But I can't tell you what it is. What about you? Does it affect you?"

She slipped off one of her gloves and gently placed her hand on the stonework, closing her eyes. After less than a minute, she pulled the glove back on. "What I feel here is cold. I think my fingers are going to fall off."

He laughed. "Come on, let's go back with the group. This whole show *is* supposed to be for my benefit."

When they caught up, Singh was asking, "So the microgravimetry readings indicated a large void?"

"Large is an understatement, Dr. Singh. Huge. Mammoth. We must have retested and recalibrated a hundred times. Kevin was certain that the equipment had to be messed up."

"Why is that?"

The young post-doctoral student appeared taken aback by the question. "Because a void that size didn't seem physically possible."

Judtson took the opportunity to join the discussion. "I have a question. With the equipment you had, were you able to determine the depth of the void?"

"I'm not sure I know what you mean by the depth."

"How close it was to the surface."

"Not directly. How technical do you want me to get?"

"Not very. At least not yet."

"All right. There were hints…clues…but any conclusion was mostly inferred. You must understand that whether you are searching for oil deposits, differential sedimentary strata, or voids, the microgravimetry will only point you in certain directions. Mappable data and confirmation are only possible with drilling."

"What I'm specifically curious about is if this gigantic void comes close to or, in fact, reaches the surface anywhere. Did the team come up with any logical or potential sites for this possibility?"

The man nodded. "Two. One site was here. The other was located on an island in the middle of Lake Titicaca."

A surge of excitement welled up inside Judtson. Working to remain outwardly calm, he asked, "Did Dr. Berry's team drill at either of those locations?"

"We did."

Judtson had to stifle his sudden flaring of frustration at the young man's tendency to make him ask questions. "And what did you find?"

"That's what's interesting. At one of the locations, Site Number Two, we ran into an obstacle of some sort, at a depth of eleven meters. We were never able to confirm the existence of the void."

"An obstacle?" Villarreal interrupted. "I do not understand. When you hit a stubborn substrate, is it not the normal protocol to try a different spot? Did you not relocate the drill rig and make repeated attempts?"

"We did. A total of nineteen bores. And each bore yielded the same result."

"I am certain you do not mean the *same* result. An obstinate bedrock stopping your drill would vary somewhat in depth."

"Actually, Dr. Villarreal, no. I do mean the same result. At every location we tried, adjusting for the varying elevation of the surface topography, the obstacle was at precisely the same depth, almost as if it had been a perfectly flat and level layer."

His answer gave Villarreal pause, but Judtson immediately pressed for more information. "And which of the two sites was this?"

"The island."

"So you were not ever able to confirm the presence of the void under the island?"

"That's right."

"Did your group dig down to identify the obstacle?"

"No. An eleven-meter dig for a group of college students with shovels was not practical. Kevin was planning on a return trip with shoring and excavating equipment. That never happened."

"What about here at Puma Punku?"

"Due to the historic significance of this site, the government wouldn't allow us to drill directly upon it."

"I thought your microgravimetry readings indicated that the void was in this general area. Are you telling me it was supposed to be right here…on this specific site?"

"Yes."

"So you weren't able to drill here?"

"Oh, no, we were. We made arrangements for a slant drill which we could position outside the boundary of the site and drill at an angle."

"And? Did you find a void?"

"Yes, sir. We did."

Judtson again felt the frustration building, but before he could say anything else, Kelsey asked, "Where is it, Sam? Exactly?"

Jonassen, who had been leaning against the stone face of the ancient platform, patted it with the palm of his hand. "Right here. As accurately as we could tell, the void comes to, or at least near, the surface directly under this terrace."

▽

After Hart and Burke helped the man out of the crawl space, they were both startled to see a golden retriever follow him through the opening. With the floor panel back in place, the man dropped into the chair and immediately began typing on the keyboard. His initial keystrokes caused the donkey screen to disappear and be replaced by a DOS screen.

"Excuse me, sir," Hart said. "I'm going to have to ask you to stop what you're doing and tell me what happened here. What's your name?"

The man answered him without ceasing his actions. "Scott Gumble. And I'll tell you everything in just a…." He paused for a moment, tapped the enter key, and looked up. "Now. Well, not exactly now, because we need to leave."

Hart, leaning heavily on his cane in the doorway to the computer room, huffed, frustrated at his inability to get control. "There'll be time enough to leave later. Right now I've got a dead body in the other room and I need some answers."

Gumble's brow instantly furrowed at the news. "Someone's dead? You said *a* dead body. Just one?"

"Yes. Just one."

"Thank God. But we really need to go. I mean *really*! Right now."

"Mr. Gumble…."

"Listen to me," Scott interrupted impatiently. "While I was under the floor, I heard them talk."

"Heard who talk?"

"I don't know who they were. I couldn't see them. They came in to get the guy who was trying to break into my system. He wasn't having any luck" – a self-satisfied grin appeared on his face as he said this – "and he wanted to keep trying. They told him they had to leave right away. Before the charges went off."

"Charges!" The exclamation came from Burke, who was standing behind Hart at the doorway. "They set a bomb?"

Scott glanced at his monitor. Satisfied that the routine he had set in motion was finished, he stood up. "Yes. I heard them say this place was going to blow up."

"When?"

Gumble shrugged. "That they didn't say, exactly. They only said they needed to get clear before it did. Could be any minute."

That was all the detective and his partner needed to hear. The two, followed by Gumble and Rocky, turned to leave, hurrying through the passageway with Hart making surprisingly good time. As they reached the security console at the entrance, Gumble hesitated. "Go on. I need to do something."

Hart started to speak and thought better of it, moving across the threshold of the vault door, followed by Burke. After they were through, Scott tapped the red plunger on the panel, hastily moved around the console, and ran through the massive steel door as the hydraulic pistons swung it closed.

"Come on, Rocky!" he shouted, and the golden leapt through behind him with seconds to spare.

Hart was already laboriously navigating the stairs with Burke trailing.

"You want me to carry you?"

The detective answered his partner with a rude rebuff and noticeably quickened his pace, perspiration, triggered by the combination of pain and exertion, saturating his clothes. When he stepped onto one of the landings, approximately halfway up, he moved aside. "You two go ahead. I'm slowing you down."

"Ben," Burke responded, coming to a stop beside his friend. "Keep moving or I'll have to pull my service pistol on you."

Hart saw that neither of the two showed any intention to pass him. Drawing a deep breath, he plunged ahead and the group reached the last landing from the top within minutes. Rounding the turn, they could see the door still standing open above them. Just as they started to climb, Rocky, who was trotting closely behind Scott, barked once, the abrupt sound echoing in the stairwell. A split second later they all heard an intense thump from below, followed immediately by an ominous rumble. They could feel the steel stairs begin to shudder.

"Move it, Ben!" Burke shouted and the detective, completely forgetting about the pain in his hip, scampered up the remaining steps and dashed out the open door to daylight. Burke and Gumble were directly behind him and they all kept moving, putting distance between themselves and the shack.

To the west of them, the retractable reinforced-concrete slab, which covered the missile silo itself, visibly flexed upward, creating booming, cracking sounds as the shock wave impacted the underside of the structure. A mixture of smoke and dust billowed horizontally from the perimeter, and the three men felt the ground under their feet shake violently.

As the tremors subsided, Burke noticed a caravan of squad cars, followed by the Crime Scene Unit van, rounding the bend in the entrance lane.

Sardonically, he commented, "Here's our backup."

▽

Back at headquarters, Scott was seated at Ben Hart's desk, working the detective's computer while talking. "I was in my computer room, where you found me, and I heard the shots. I closed and locked my door, which, thankfully, is reinforced metal, back from the days when it was the room where the launch codes were entered. I normally keep an off-site shadow backup of everything anyway, but I made sure it was up to date. Then I redirected the video feeds from the security cameras to stream to the off-site server in real time."

A window popped up on the monitor, and Hart recognized it as the view of the first perimeter entrance. Scott rapidly advanced the video until the scene changed.

"It appears that they arrived in two SUVs and a large van."

On the screen, Hart saw the three vehicles drive past the first intercom and speed hump.

"That's odd," murmured Gumble.

"What's that?"

"The teeth were down."

Before Hart could ask for clarification, Scott continued, pointing at a spot on the monitor screen. "There is a row of retractable teeth in the roadway…just after the hump, like the tire barriers at parking lot exits, except they are oriented the other way, to keep vehicles out."

"We didn't hit anything like that when we came in."

"That's because they'd been lowered. They were obviously down when these men arrived, too."

With a mouse click, the view changed to the second checkpoint.

His voice so soft that Hart could barely hear him, Gumble commented, "And the gate was already open."

He changed the scene again, this time to the area outside the entrance shack. They watched in silence as the black SUVs stopped and a total of eight men, dressed in black suits, exited the vehicles. All of the men were carrying weapons; two also bore backpacks. Their movements precise, the group filed into the small building. The large van arrived and parked close to the opening. Two more men got out, then moved around to the rear of the van and opened the double doors, where they waited.

"Do you have any interior video?"

"No. Wish we did."

As it became obvious that the two men who were visible in the frame were doing nothing but standing idly, Gumble increased the speed of the playback. He and Hart stared at the jerky movements of the two as the time counter at the upper right corner of the screen ticked off a total of thirty-four minutes from the arrival time of the van. Suddenly, a blurred stream of people burst from the door of the shack. Gumble stopped the video and backed it up until he reached the seconds prior to their appearance, when he began to play it at normal speed.

Hart and Gumble watched as two of the armed men came out, supporting a third man between them.

"Who are they bringing out?"

Scott hesitated for a moment, clicking the mouse to pause the video.

"Mr. Gumble…."

Holding up his hand to stop the detective, Scott answered, "That man was our…guest."

"Guest? Are you telling me that he was…? Oh, I get it. That's the guy I saw zippered into the body bag in front of Wheeler's office."

"Uh-huh."

"You were holding him as a prisoner?"

Scott kept his gaze on the monitor rather than on the detective. "*Prisoner* is such a harsh word."

Tamping down his usual reaction, Hart kept his voice calm and said, "Go ahead and resume the video."

With a click, the images on the screen again sprang into motion, and the two men watched as a total of eight people wearing black hoods over their heads, their hands handcuffed behind their backs, were escorted out. As the group proceeded, Scott narrated, tapping the screen with his fingertip. "That looks like Dean Copeland, the NASA scientist and author. The one they're carrying…that's Lisa Trippiano, a TV producer from *The Jack Bailey Show*. Dylan Falt, an immunologist. Matt Wheeler, the…."

"He's the medical equipment engineer we've been looking for."

"Right. And there's Jimmy Meade."

The name surprised Hart. "The astronaut?"

"Uh-huh. Ricky Ingram."

"Kent's assistant."

"Yeah, and there's Chris Ashby, a chemist. Doni Costello. She's the wife of…."

"Dr. Saylor Costello."

"Yeah. Oh, that's weird."

"What?"

"Where's…oh!"

"What's the matter?"

Gumble clicked the mouse, freezing the frame and turning to face the detective. "I was looking for Luis Tovar."

"Who's that?"

"Our security guy."

Hart leaned forward slightly, staring intently at the still picture. "Didn't he come out? Maybe they killed him."

Gumble shook his head and pointed. "See the man walking with the others, the man whose arm is in a sling?"

"Yes."

"That's Luis."

"He doesn't have the hood over his head. And he isn't handcuffed."

"Nope."

Hart sat back in his chair. "Well, that explains why the tire barrier was retracted and the gate was open."

"And the vault door downstairs," added Gumble.

The eight were taken into the van, accompanied by three of the armed men, and the rear doors were closed. The balance of the contingent climbed into the two SUVs, and the three vehicles departed. Hart had Scott pause the display, zooming in on the license plates, and jotted down the numbers.

After the scene became static, the detective focused on Gumble. "I think now is as good a time as any to tell me what the hell is going on."

He noticed the slight curve of a smile bend up the corner of the technician's mouth.

"Is something funny?"

"Not exactly funny," Gumble remarked, almost wistfully. "I was just enjoying my last few seconds of being considered sane."

▽

"What do you think this all means?" The question came from Saylor, who was in the rear seat of the van, leaning forward between Judtson and Kelsey as they drove back toward La Paz from Puma Punku.

"I have no idea," confessed Judtson, shaking his head slowly.

"I don't either," answered Kelsey, "but everything seems to be leading us here."

As the fringe of the city came into view, Kelsey's phone chimed. She took it out of her pocket and checked it. "We must be back in range. It's a text message from Scott."

As she tapped the screen, she muttered, "That's strange."

Judtson twisted in his seat, concerned by the change in her tone. "What is it?"

"I don't know. The first message just says…'Something's wrong here!'"

"What?"

"And then there's another." She was quickly tapping the pad and scrolling as Judtson noticed movement in his rearview mirror. "Kelsey, I think Romeo wants us to pull over."

She shifted her attention from her phone to the rear window. She could see that Romeo, driving the van behind them, was flashing his headlights and motioning.

▽

Doni woke up slowly, shaking off the residual daze from whatever drug the abductors had used on them, and briefly embraced the alternate reality that the assault in the silo had only been a nightmare, a construct instantly shattered as she focused on the dingy gray ceiling above her, illuminated only by a bare light bulb which was dangling from a wire high above.

She shifted her weight, intending to sit upright. The springs of her cot squeaked loudly in protest to the movement. Unsteadily, using the metal frame of the narrow bed for support, she was able to sit on the edge and look over her surroundings. The room reminded her of a blend of images from old movies in her past. In her mind, it was an amalgam of a dormitory in the dreadful orphanages of England from over a century ago, and a large prison cell, designed to hold multiple inmates. The only difference between this room and what she conjured was that in every movie she had ever seen, there were always windows. They were usually very high on the walls and always cast narrow, dusty beams into the dreariness. This prison/orphanage had none.

Now sitting erect, she was able to discern other bunks in the room. From the minimal lighting it was difficult to tell, but the beds appeared to be occupied. She began to rise shakily, only to fall back onto the thin pad of the mattress. Rallying, she repeated the attempt successfully this time, and wobbled more than walked to the nearest cot, where she found Lisa Trippiano still unconscious. Reaching down, she shook her gently.

"Lisa! Lisa! Wake up."

The producer stirred faintly, her eyelids fluttering for a moment before coming fully open. Doni could follow her fellow prisoner's progress from disorientation through confusion, until finally arriving at recognition.

Trippiano tried to speak, finding that her lips were stubbornly stuck together. Finally able to pry them loose with her tongue, her voice little more than a croak, she uttered, "Where are we?"

Already dizzy from her brief period upright, Doni gingerly lowered herself down and perched on the edge of the cot, the steel frame painfully digging into her thighs. "Wish I knew. I've only been awake for a few minutes."

"Oowww," Lisa groaned, reaching up and gently touching the side of her face, remembering the assailant cold-cocking her with his pistol.

Shifting over to give Doni more room, she rolled onto her side. "Are the others here? Are they okay?"

Doni surveyed the dimly lit room. "Looks like it. You're the first one I woke up."

"We'd better check on them."

With a sigh, Doni stood once again and gave her a hand, steadying Lisa as she rose.

The two remained in place for nearly a minute, Doni firmly gripping Lisa's arm as the producer seemed to stabilize somewhat.

"Ready?"

Lisa nodded and Doni let go. The two women moved from cot to cot until they had roused their six companions. After all of them were awake, they pulled three of the cots together in a circle and sat facing one another, sharing descriptions of their individual abductions.

Her head clearing further, Trippiano suddenly asked, "Where's Al?"

Recalling that Lisa had been unconscious as her friend had been shot, Doni, her voice muted, answered, "He's gone. They killed him."

"NO!" Her hand jerked to her throat and she gasped, staring into Doni's eyes in disbelief before breaking down in quiet sobs.

"Where's Scotty?" Meade asked, an expression of concern on his face.

No one answered, afraid to speak the possibility aloud.

After several seconds, Ricky offered, "I did hear one of the guys complain to the other that they weren't able to get in to our computers."

"But they didn't mention him?"

"No."

"I can't believe they killed Al," Copeland groaned; he appeared crestfallen.

"It was my fault. I should have done what they said. He was trying to help me."

"No, Lisa." The harsh rebuke came from Meade. "It wasn't your fault. That's just what men do when women are in trouble. It's hard-wired."

"But...."

He held up his hand to stop her. "No 'buts.' That's exactly why it was a dumb-ass idea to put women in combat. It's not that they can't handle it. Hell, they can. It's that the men soldiers around them will do the stupidest things if a women gets in a jam...stuff they wouldn't do if it was one of their male battle buddies."

Trippiano's voice was steeped in sadness. "I got to know him when we were preparing to do the show. He was such a sweet and gentle man...verging on timid. One of my assistants teased me at the time that he had a crush on me. I should have known...."

Doni, who was sitting on the cot beside her, reached out and took her hand. "Lisa, this isn't going to do us any good. It happened. We can't change it. What we need to do is figure out where we are and what we're going to do."

"Doni's right," Copeland agreed.

"Before we start," Wheeler added, "there's one thing we need to think about." As he continued, his voice lowered in volume, causing the others to unconsciously edge forward to hear him. "Don't be fooled by the appearance of our cell. Just because it looks as if we're in some dingy warehouse or something doesn't mean this isn't a high-tech operation. We have to assume that we are being watched right now. And listened to. We can't say anything we don't want them to hear."

"Makes sense," Copeland concurred.

"The first thing I think we need to do is assemble a sit/rep."

"What's that, Jimmy?" asked Ricky.

"A representation of our current situation. We need to recon this room. We're all sitting here like a bunch of dolts, just assuming we're locked in."

"You don't think we are?"

"I'm sure we are, Ricky. But we don't *know* we are. Nor do we know what kind of door it is, or whether there are any other openings. We don't know if there's anything in this room that might be useful to us. We don't know squat and that's a dumb way to be."

Meade stood up from the cot. "Who's coming with me?"

Wheeler and Ricky joined him, and the three crossed the dusky room to the nearest wall and began following it around.

As they searched, Doni spoke to the remaining group. "What I can't understand is why they took us. What good are we to them? Why not just kill us?"

"I was wondering that, as well," Falt added.

"There are only two reasons I can think of. Either they want information from us or they want us as bait to draw in the outside group." Copeland, mindful of Wheeler's caution, had kept his answer deliberately vague.

Ashby looked at him. "I think they're going to reconvert us."

"Maybe. That's probably the best-case scenario."

"Why is that?"

His voice adopting a somber tone, Copeland answered, "If I'm right and they need us for information or as bait, then once we've served the purpose...."

Trippiano finished his thought. "We're dead."

▽

"I'm going to personally rip his heart out!"

The outburst erupted from Romeo as he watched the video on Kelsey's laptop and saw the same scene Hart and Gumble had viewed earlier.

The six were in Kelsey's hotel room, clustered around the desk and staring transfixed as they saw the attackers slam the rear doors on the van, enter the SUVs, and drive off.

"I can't believe Luis betrayed us," Kelsey murmured under her breath.

"We need to find them." The anxiety in Saylor's voice was palpable, having seen his wife, handcuffed and blinded with a hood, loaded into the rear of the van.

Judtson put his hand on his friend's shoulder, unable to think of anything reassuring to say to him.

Romeo, still seething, grunted between clenched teeth, "Oh, I'll find them all right."

His face a mask of frustration, anger, and fear, Saylor turned to Judtson. "I never should have talked you into letting me tag along for this trip. I should have stayed at the silo the way you wanted me to. I would have been there with Doni when this happened."

"Saylor," Judtson argued, "then both of you would be prisoners."

"Damn it. At least I'd be there."

"Look at it this way," Romeo offered. "Now you'll be able to help us get her out."

Saylor did not respond.

"How did we get this video?" asked Villarreal, still staring at the laptop.

"Scott uploaded it," Kelsey explained. "He put it on a remote server and sent a text message with a link."

"He did all of that while they were coming for him?"

She nodded.

Judtson cleared his throat, struggling with his own emotions at what he had just witnessed on the video. "I didn't see him come out with the others."

Kelsey's eyes met his. "I know. I didn't see Al, either."

"Look!" Romeo pointed at the laptop screen.

The view of the entrance showed a sedan pull to a stop and two men get out. One, dressed in street clothes, was using a cane. The other, tall and thin, was in a police uniform. Both of them proceeded to enter the shack.

"Cops!"

"Uh-huh," Romeo acknowledged Kelsey's comment.

"Fast-forward it," Judtson suggested. "Maybe we'll see Scott come out with them."

Kelsey clicked the mouse and the static view remained frozen. The only way they could tell that the video was spooling was by the time counter in the corner, until the image abruptly disappeared, replaced by a screen of snow.

"What happened?" The tense question came from Judtson.

"Don't know," Romeo answered. "The cops might have killed the video feeds."

Kelsey felt her phone vibrate. Jumping up from her chair, she pulled the phone out of her pants pocket and shouted, "It's a text from Scott!"

"Thank God," Judtson sighed.

"He says he's with the cops."

"Does he say how they got involved? Did he call them?"

"I don't know, Judtson. He doesn't say. I think he's sneaking this message to us. All it says is that he is with the cops and he's showing them the video. Oh!"

"What?"

"He also says that the silo is blown up."

Working her thumbs rapidly, she typed a message back with her questions, talking as she typed. "I don't know if he's going to get this or if they took his phone by now, but" – she tapped the send button – "there! It's off."

Chapter 33

"OKAY, HERE'S WHAT WE'VE GOT." Meade knelt on one knee, surrounded by the others in the group, with the exception of Ricky, who was thirty feet away, methodically and noisily sliding one of the cots back and forth on the concrete floor. The action of the steel legs on the concrete caused a screeching, grinding ruckus intended to mask their conversation from eavesdroppers.

"This room is big. I have to wonder how many prisoners it would hold. Our cell is approximately two hundred feet long by one hundred and twenty feet wide. The ceiling is, I would guess, about eighteen feet high. I found two ways in and out, a man door at one end and a large roll-up door at the other. Both are locked from the outside. Both are steel."

Copeland asked, "The roll-up door...is it mounted on our side of the wall?"

"Unfortunately, no. Too bad. They're fairly easy to take apart. As we've already noticed, there aren't any windows. As far as potential weapons, notice the piping overhead, which is supported by a bunch of rods and struts. All good stuff for use as clubs or pry bars. The issue is getting to it."

"No ladders?"

"I wish, Dean. They weren't so nice."

"I have a dumb question."

"What is it, Lisa?"

"I saw in a movie once where a woman being held prisoner pulled a fire alarm. I thought maybe...."

"Already thought of that. Nope. No pull station. No sprinkler heads in the room. So we're fairly limited in our options. We should be able to cobble together some of these steel cots and maybe make a ladder. Get at the hardware over our heads and arm ourselves with those nice hefty pipes and Unistruts. Position ourselves by the two openings, and when one of those guys walks in, we bean him, grab his gun, and get the hell out of here."

The members of the group took in what Meade said, some of them nodding in agreement. Wheeler was the first to speak. "You make it sound simple, Jimmy."

Meade shrugged. "Best plans are."

"Think it might work?" Doni asked.

"Don't know, young lady. Worth a try. It's either that or we sit huddled on the cots like good prisoners and wait to see what they have in mind for us."

Chris Ashby, who had been squatting beside Meade, straightened up and said, "Let's go for it."

His words acted as a catalyst for the group, who all rose and went into action. Systematically, they tossed the thin pads off the cots and moved the frames to a wall picked by Meade as the optimum location. As the cots arrived, Wheeler began contriving the most efficient way to utilize them. He stood two of the frames against the wall, lashing them together with his own belt at the midpoint where the long rails abutted. The third frame was laid horizontally across the top of the two with its feet pointed upward. He then positioned the fourth frame so that its narrow end nested inside the frame of the inverted cot. The fit required two tugs on the horizontal frame, spreading the long sides enough to allow the identically sized upper frame to drop in between the L-shaped frames.

He stepped back to examine his structure. Meade came up next to him. "Looks pretty good left to right. But as soon as somebody climbs up the face of that contraption, the extra weight is gonna pull the whole thing away from the wall."

Wheeler nodded. "I know. We can use two cot frames as diagonal braces on the lower section, but once whoever climbs it gets above the joint in the middle, it'll topple."

"Maybe not." The rebuttal came from Ricky, who approached the two carrying a coiled fabric fire hose. Dropping the hose on the floor, he pointed up and explained, "If we can throw the end of this over one of those pipes, I can climb the frames with the hose tied around me. A couple of people can pull on the other end and keep it taut. I've done it a hundred times. You know, like a rock wall with a harness."

"That might just work," snorted Meade.

"Let's give it a try," Wheeler said and picked up one end of the hose. "I need to put more weight on the end." He tied a knot in the stiff material right behind the metal collar and immediately tied another, repeating the process until he had a large, heavy wad of fabric.

With Ricky holding four coiled loops of the hose several feet back, Wheeler swung the weighted end and tossed it upward, aiming for the heavy horizontal pipe suspended from the ceiling, while Ricky quickly payed out the loops he held. The first attempt failed. After nine tries, the pendulous end sailed over the pipe, swinging down the other side. Ricky let out sufficient slack for the end to reach them, and Wheeler hastily unknotted his handiwork. "Let's move it close to the wall."

He and Ricky, tugging on the hose, slid it across the pipe until it was against the wall where the pipe emerged.

"You ready?" he asked Ricky.

"I guess. I do have a question. When I get up there, how do I take apart the pipes and stuff? We don't have any wrenches or anything."

Wheeler looked up at the jumble of metal above him. "All of the Unistruts...those U-shaped, horizontal steel members supporting everything...are held up by threaded rods called all-thread. Lift up a little on the weight they're carrying and you should be able to back off the nuts on the ends by hand. Those rods and the struts are both pretty beefy and should make good clubs."

Ricky squinted upward. "What about the pipes? Would they be better?"

"If you can get them, sure. But unless you can get to the end of a pipe run, I don't see how you can untwist one. And we don't know what's in the pipes. Could be nothing. Of course it might be water or even gas."

Ricky nodded. "Okay then, struts and rods." He took the end of the hose from Wheeler and looped it around his torso, tying it at his chest, and moved to the impromptu climbing structure.

"Matt, do we even need this?"

"Why?"

"Now that I've got this hose tied to me, couldn't two or three of you just pull on the other end and hoist me up?"

"I don't think so. We're not one-hundred-percent sure how secure that pipe is, and it's old, rusted, and rough on top. The hose is flat fabric. We'd be fighting a lot of friction."

Nodding, Ricky flipped the slack hose over his shoulder, turned to the cot frames and, using the metal straps as footholds, began climbing. Wheeler and Meade tugged on the other end of the hose, pulling the slack out of it and creating a slight upward pressure on Ricky.

The slender man was actually quite nimble and easily scaled the bottom section, moving upward to the second. Once he was fully on it, he accidentally allowed his body weight to move too far outward as he climbed, and the top frame began to tilt out away from the wall. Wheeler and Meade increased their pull on the hose as Ricky flattened himself against the frame. The steel frame slapped back to the wall, making more of a banging sound than they would have preferred.

Ricky paused for a moment before proceeding. Careful to keep his center of gravity pressed as firmly against the frame as possible, he resumed his ascent. Soon, he was to the point where he had run out of frame for his hands to grip. Relying upon the upward pull from the hose, he kept the palms of his hands on the face of the wall and climbed the remainder of the upper cot until he was standing on its top edge.

The pipe supporting the hose was directly above him and only inches from the top of his head. Ricky reached up and wrapped both arms around it, swinging his leg up and over.

"Give me a little pull."

The two men below added tension to the hose, helping Ricky swing his body to the top of the pipe until he was straddling it.

"Whoa!" he barked as Wheeler and Meade, unable to see clearly in the darkness, continued to tug and threatened to pull him off the other side. They immediately stopped.

"A little slack." They complied and Ricky was able to sit upright on the large-diameter pipe, his legs wrapped tightly around it. Feeling secure, he untied the hose from his chest and wrapped it three times around the pipe.

"You okay?" Meade asked from below.

"Fine as a frog's hair," Ricky answered, surveying the area around himself.

Meade chuckled. "Haven't heard that in years."

Ricky scooted along the pipe for several feet until he came to the first intersecting assembly of rods and struts, which was supporting an array of conduits. Tucking his shoulder under the horizontal length of strut, he lifted slightly while twisting the large nut on one end of the bottom face.

"Hey, Matt. You were right. It works."

"Good."

Ashby had come over to join the two men below and suggested, "Maybe we should gather up the mattresses and pile them under him. When he drops that steel down, it's going to make one heck of a racket."

"Good idea," Meade agreed, and the three rallied to assemble a pile just in time for Ricky to announce that he was ready to drop the first piece. It landed quietly and was soon followed by another and then the strut.

As Ricky shimmied along the pipe to his next location, Meade hefted a fallen five-foot-long rod. "Not bad. Not bad at all."

▽

Ben Hart shifted uncomfortably in his chair. He and Burke had been listening to Scott Gumble's narration for the past forty-five minutes, and he was filled with incredulity at what he had heard, as well as an overwhelming need to stand up and stretch his tangled and wounded muscles.

"Ben, I recognize that look. You need to stand up for a minute, don't you?"

Hart smiled feebly at his friend. "I wouldn't mind."

He grabbed his cane and, with a great deal of effort, rose from the chair. Gumble was seated in the interview seat at the side of Hart's desk and took advantage of the break in the conversation to pick up his phone, which had been lying on the desk between them, and quickly began typing on the screen.

Enjoying the effects of repositioning his muscles and tendons, Hart stared down at Gumble. "So what you're telling us is that your group – including a wealthy heiress, a famous author, and a neurologist – have been traipsing all around the country kidnapping people?"

Without either looking up or ceasing his typing, Gumble shook his head. "Not kidnapping. Well, maybe the first one…Villarreal. We kind of had to kidnap him to convert him. But after we did it, he was with the program. I don't think he'll be pressing charges. The others were all converted before we brought them back to the silo. They came on their own. Unless you want to call meeting someone at a bar and taking him up to your room to convert him kidna…."

Hart held up his hand. "Never mind. You've already explained all of that. Okay, let's start again. What you're saying is that men in black suits are trying to turn all of you into some sort of zombies, and if you resist them, they'll kill you."

Scott finished the message on his phone and put it back in his pocket. "Yes. That's what happened at Judtson's office. Later they just tried to kill us, in the first attack at the silo by the sniper…that's the one I showed you on the other video…and then in the Mohave Desert."

"And you don't know who they are?"

"No. Wish we did. The two men who showed up at the radiology lab to question Wheeler and the lady who works there…."

"Robyn Reedy?"

"Right. They said they were from Homeland Security. I guess they showed badges, but Wheeler called their office and the people there had never heard of them."

Hart reached into his pocket and pulled out the slip of paper one of the uniformed officers had handed to him when they first arrived at headquarters with Gumble. He slowly turned the folded paper between his fingertips as he hesitated. "Not sure I should be sharing this with you, Mr. Gumble…."

"Please, Scott."

"Okay, Scott. The incident outside Matt Wheeler's office was also captured on video. After your two men did what they did and left with the prisoner…."

"Guest."

"Let's stick with the word *prisoner* for now. Anyhow, another black SUV showed up. They cleaned up the mess, taking their dead agent, or whatever he was, with them. The license plates were visible on the video. Both SUVs were registered to Homeland Security."

"Were…?"

Hart again held up his hand to stop the question. "We called. They don't have those two vehicles on their roster."

Ben could see the man mentally process the information. He unfolded the slip of paper and reread the information on it. "One of the SUVs from your video at the silo was one of the two from that night at Wheeler's. And all of the vehicles, including the van, are registered to HS. And yes, we've already called again and they've told us the same thing."

His face showing some concern, Scott asked, "You don't think they're somehow legit, do you?"

Hart glanced at Burke, who answered the question. "Do we think that Homeland Security agents pranced into a legally owned missile silo, killed one of the occupants, and nabbed the others while setting explosive devices which blew the whole place up? The way things are going in this country these days, sure, I think it's a good possibility."

"But...."

"Wait a sec. You asked if we thought it might be HS. I answered you. Now, if you're asking us if we're on the same side as those guys, the answer is...hell, no!"

Clearly relieved, Scott pressed them, "We need to get my friends back."

Hart put his hand on Gumble's shoulder. "We need to find them first."

"Find them? Oh, I know where they are."

▽

Saylor, Kelsey, and Judtson had moved to Saylor's room at the hotel, leaving Romeo with the two scientists. Since they had viewed the video, Saylor had withdrawn into a state unfamiliar to Judtson. His face was a rigid mask, his eyes focused on some unseen object in the distance. The moment they entered his room, he disappeared into the bedroom, leaving the other two to sit at the small table by the balcony door.

"I had to get out of there," Kelsey confessed. "The tension emanating from Romeo was making me nuts."

"He's mad as hell at Luis."

"I don't blame him. I am, too."

She glanced meaningfully toward the bedroom. "Is he okay?"

Judtson answered softly. "Saylor? I don't know. I've never seen him this way before. He's worried about Doni. So am I."

Kelsey reached across the table and gently placed her hands on his. "You three have known each other a long time, haven't you?"

"Since we were little."

"We'll find her. We'll find all of them."

"How?" he asked, his voice carrying more of an edge than he intended. "We have no idea where to look or even if they're...."

"They're fine," she assured him.

"How can you know that?"

"You saw the video. Why would they go to the trouble of taking them if they were going to kill them? They could have done it there and then blown up the place."

Somewhat mollified by her answer, he nodded. "I suppose."

"My guess is that...." She stopped abruptly, interrupted by her phone vibrating. Grabbing it from her pocket, she exclaimed, "It's a message from Scott!"

"What does he say?"

She scanned the small screen. "This is weird."

"What?"

"Well, it starts out with a line that says, 'The following is a transcription.'" She scrolled down the text. "After that, it's a recap of everything that's happened."

Saylor, having heard her say that a message was coming in, emerged from the bedroom. "What is it?"

As Kelsey was busily reading the incoming message, Judtson replied, "It's a text message from

Scott. We're trying to figure it out now."

"I get it!" she shouted. "It *is* a recap. Lots of questions and answers. Scott must have turned on the voice recognition on his phone and he's streaming it as a text message. We're reading a transcript of his interrogation with the cops."

"Huh!" Judtson grunted, impressed. "Anything new?"

Not taking her eyes from the screen, she shook her head. "Not yet. He's telling them…oh, my God!"

"Kelsey, what?" The impatient question came from Saylor.

"The cops just told Scott that a vehicle showed up at Wheeler's after Romeo and our traitor took care of those two guys. They cleaned up the mess and left. Both…yeah, both SUVs were licensed to Homeland Security."

Judtson let out a low whistle as Saylor commented, "Wheeler told us that the two guys who came to see him and Robyn Reedy showed Homeland Security IDs."

She read on further. "The SUVs and the van at the silo were HS, too. Wait, this is cool! One of the cops, I'm assuming that's who it is, just said that if Homeland Security is doing this kind of stuff, they aren't on the same side."

"That's good news."

Kelsey suddenly gasped and put her hand to her throat.

"Kelsey, what…?"

Her face broke into a wide smile. "One of the cops said something about finding our people and somebody…it has to be Scott…said that he knows where they are."

"He knows?" Saylor blurted excitedly.

"Kelsey, this is streaming to us real-time, right?"

She looked away from the screen for a moment to make eye contact with Judtson. "Yes. Why?"

"It seems that the cops are okay guys. Can't we just call Scott?"

▽

After deciding to split into two groups, Ashby, Wheeler, Doni, and Ricky were stationed at the man door, while the others had positioned themselves at the roll-up. Ricky had obtained enough steel rods and Unistruts for all of them to be armed with makeshift clubs. Chris Ashby was casually leaning against the wall adjacent to the doorknob, as Ricky and Doni sat side by side on a cot they had moved into position directly in front of the door. Wheeler, betrayed by his anxiousness, paced in a track between them.

"Matt, you really should try to calm down a little."

He turned to speak to Doni without breaking his stride. "I can't. They could come through that door any second."

She shrugged. "Or it could be hours. If that's the case, you'll be worn out by then."

With a visible, conscious effort, he stopped walking. "Do you think anyone's looking for us?"

Ashby chuffed softly. "Matt, we've been missing since we all went out to the silo. Sure, our friends, relatives, or coworkers have reported us gone. Sure, the cops have added our names to their missing-persons list. They wouldn't have ever found us at the silo and they certainly aren't going to find us here."

"I don't mean the police. I mean our people."

"I'm positive that Saylor is searching for me…for all of us," answered Doni.

"If they even know we're gone yet," Ashby rebutted. "They were tied up down in Bolivia. They might not know."

"You don't think they've called in?" Although she was trying to keep her voice level and calm, an undercurrent of worry colored Doni's question.

"They might have. Only who would they talk to?"

Ricky chimed in. "Chris is right. Either by Internet or phone, nobody would have answered them. They'd be concerned. I bet that after there was no answer, they'd be hopping on the first flight back to find out what's wrong. Remember, we don't have any idea how long we were knocked out. Romeo, Judtson, and the rest of them are probably still in Bolivia, waiting for a flight at the airport."

Matt began pacing again. "And what's going to happen when they get back? They might be walking into a trap. How do we know that the bad guys aren't waiting for them at the silo? That's what I would do."

Wheeler's words intensified Doni's anxiety. "Matt, maybe Scott made it. He'd let them know."

Stopping squarely in front of her, Wheeler, his voice cheerless, insisted, "How could he have made it? We were all down there, basically rats in a cage. They couldn't have missed him."

Silence fell over the group for a time as the four grappled with their plight. Finally breaking the silence, Ricky said, "I don't think we can just sit here like cattle, waiting for the door to open. We need to get out of here."

"Ricky's right," Wheeler agreed quickly, focusing on the problem.

"Okay, how?" asked Doni gamely.

Wheeler hefted the steel Unistrut in his hand. "I don't know what effect these rods and struts are going to have on this door, or the roll-up on the other side, but I think we should find out."

"If we start pounding on the doors, won't that attract them?"

"It might. So what? It beats sitting and waiting."

Ashby spoke up. "And we might just get out."

Ricky stood resolutely. "Matt, between this door and the roll-up, which do you think we'd have a better shot at getting through?"

Wheeler moved next to the door, examining it carefully. "This is a standard steel-clad door. It's basically a metal skin over an insulated void. The door swings out, so I can't see the hinges. I'm certain they're fairly strong. The frame is steel, also. Depending on how well it was mounted, either it could come out of the wall with some effort on our part or it could withstand a battering ram. Can't tell without trying. I didn't check the roll-up that closely before. It's a sectional door, rather than a true roll-up which withdraws up into a drum, and that makes it a bit more vulnerable. Hard to say, but I'd guess the roll-up."

Doni joined Ricky and Matt standing. "I say, let's go for it."

She checked Ashby, who nodded and said, "You three go talk to the others, and I'll stay by this door in case they decide to come in this way."

"There should be at least two of us here while the rest are at the other end," offered Ricky.

"True."

"I'll stay with you. Doni, you and Matt get with the others. Get us out of here."

Chapter 34

"WHAT DO YOU MEAN, YOU KNOW WHERE THEY ARE?" The surprised question came from Hart.

Rather than answering the detective's question, Scott asked, "Can I use your computer?"

"Sure."

Gumble sprang up from his chair and sat down in Hart's. The two police officers watched him as he accessed the Internet and typed a link which opened a view of a map of the United States. Using the mouse, he zoomed in on the southeastern portion of Arizona. He then dropped down a menu from the top bar and selected one of the items on the list, instantly opening a small prompt box, where he typed in a long string of letters and numbers from memory.

Sitting back in the chair, he stared at the screen as Hart asked, "Do you mind telling us what the hell you're doing?"

Without looking away, Scott explained, "One of the missing people has a tracker on him."

"A tracker! Why didn't you say so right away?"

Scott swiveled in the chair to glance at Hart briefly. "I wasn't confident I could trust you."

"How do you know you can now?" Burke asked, amused at the tech's candor.

"I don't. Not for sure. But I think I can."

The narrow bar across the bottom of the monitor turned a bright red, and Gumble scooted closer, again opening the drop-down menu as he spoke. "It's not picking it up."

"Not picking up! Great. Now what?"

Finishing his selection, Gumble sat back further in the chair and waited. "I'm checking in real time. Right now. Since it isn't picking up the signal, that could mean the kidnappers found the tracker and destroyed it. Or that could mean it's out of range."

"What's the range on this system?"

"All of the continental U.S., the northern part of Mexico, and the southern edge of Canada."

"Your boss spent the money for this kind of system?" Hart asked incredulously.

"Nope. This is a Homeland Security system. I just...you know, borrowed it."

Before the two cops could respond, Scott suddenly leaned forward and pointed at the screen.

"See. There's a trail."

"I thought you couldn't...."

"I switched from real time into history mode. The system stores the locations from the transmitter for thirty days."

They saw a red line on the map which had not been present earlier. It reminded Hart of the route line Google Maps drew when he requested directions. Scott touched the screen on an area south of Tucson. "Here's the silo. That's where the line begins. The system wasn't picking up the signal before that because the transmitter had been underground. Seems they headed north."

Craning to see over Gumble's shoulder, his eyes tracing the line through Tucson and toward Phoenix, Hart muttered, "It's leaving I-10 and following a smaller highway. It ends out in the middle of nowhere. Where is that? Did they find the tracker and toss it out in the middle of the desert?"

Gumble clicked the mouse on an icon in the upper corner and the view changed from a map to a satellite image. "This does not look good," he commented under his breath, as he zoomed in on the location where the line terminated.

Burke had circled around to peer over Scott's other shoulder. "What? What doesn't?"

The view now showed, in excellent resolution, an expansive fenced-in area containing several buildings.

"Do you know where that is?" Hart asked.

Scott nodded. "I do. But I'm not sure you want to know."

His hip muscles aching from bending forward, Hart straightened painfully. "What are you talking about?" His voice sounded testier than he intended.

Reaching out, Scott tapped the monitor in the center of the image, directly on a large building where the red tracking line abruptly ended. "Because that place, that compound, is one of the FEMA camps."

"FEMA...!"

At that moment, Gumble's phone vibrated in his pocket and began playing "Ride of the Valkyries." With a glance at Hart for permission, Scott pulled out the phone. Before he could answer it, the detective instructed, "Put it on speaker."

Setting it down, he touched the screen once and said, "Hello, Kelsey. You're on speaker."

Kelsey's excited voice burst out from the tiny device so loudly it crackled with distortion. "They're in a FEMA camp?"

Confused, Hart asked, "How did she know?"

Scott admitted somewhat sheepishly that he had been transmitting a real-time transcription of their conversation. Glaring at the technician momentarily, Hart cleared his throat and spoke. "Miss Batman, I'm Detective Ben Hart with the Tucson Police Department. Where are you and do you have others with you?"

A harsh sound came from the phone as Kelsey impatiently huffed. "Yes. Yes, I have Judtson Kent, Saylor Costello, Bal Singh, Carlos Villarreal, and...that's it. The five of us. Scott, our people have been taken to a FEMA camp?"

"That's the way it looks, Kelsey."

"Miss Batman...."

"Just a second, Detective. Scott, what happened? We read most of it in the text message. Did Luis screw us over?"

"I think so. How else could they have...?"

"Miss Batman...."

"I said, just a second. Scott, we didn't see Clarkson come out. Is he with you?"

"No."

His answer pushed Kelsey into a brief silence, which Hart capitalized upon. "Miss Batman, where are you?"

"We...we're in Bolivia. La Paz. Detective Hart, how are we going to get our friends out of a FEMA camp?"

Ben stared at the phone for a moment. "I don't know, ma'am."

He could hear Kelsey cover the phone with her hand for a moment before she came back on, only to say, "We're coming back. We'll be there as fast as we can."

The call ended and Hart turned to Scott. "Tell me about Kelsey Batman. Who is she and how did she get involved in this?"

Gumble stared at him without answering. The detective could see that the man was attempting to determine how much he should trust them.

"Listen, Detective Hart, maybe we should wait until she gets here. She can tell you hers...."

Hart cut him off. "First of all, it's Ben. Second, I should probably tell you why Billy and I have been called in on this case. Some people in the department think that the two of us are...."

"Nuts!" Burke finished the sentence for him.

Hart grinned. "That's as good a word as any, I guess. A couple of years ago, Billy and I were involved in a case. Started out as a simple arson but quickly turned into an attempted murder, with quite a cast of characters involved. A man by the name of John Augur was supposed to get married to a woman by the name of Gail Schilling, but he canceled the wedding at the last minute. She didn't take to that too well. So she tried to kill his parents and make it look like an accident. By the time the case was closed, I had a slug in my hip and Schilling had disappeared."

"I heard about that," Scott interrupted. "Wasn't the shoot-out in front of the courthouse?"

"Yes."

Cocking his head quizzically, Scott asked, "Why does that make you two nuts? Sounds fairly straightforward to me."

"Oh, a few minor details," Burke answered. "Like the fact that we were dealing with John Augur, a man in his twenties, and Jack Augur, the same guy except thirty years older."

"Wait. What do you mean, the same guy but older? They were both there?"

"He came back in a time machine to stop John from getting married. That's what got everything started."

"And don't forget Kurt," reminded Hart.

Burke chuckled. "Yes, Kurt Wallace, a man Ben and I both either saw or spoke with more than once during the case, was dead on a slab in the morgue the whole time."

Scott energetically rubbed his face with his hands. "I don't understand."

"You think we do? By the time it was all over, we had seen what we've already told you, plus a flying saucer and a time machine. Let's just say, since that case Ben and I have been a little more opened-minded about things."

"Billy, that's an understatement."

Burke laughed, as Hart turned back to face Gumble. "So whatever it is you tell us, I think we can handle it."

Coming to a decision, Scott began, "When I told you what had happened, I left some things out." He went on to tell the two about the prisoner in the silo speaking a language not heard for thousands of years. He described Chris Ashby's research on monoatomic gold, Meade's photos and personal experience with the flying saucer, Copeland's discoveries at NASA, Singh's anomalies indicating that the Andes were hollow, and Villarreal's work at Puma Punku and Baalbek.

"Is that why Kent and the rest of them are down there?"

"Yes. They went down to try to find a way inside the caves or whatever they are."

"You still haven't told me how your boss got involved in all of this."

"She's my boss now, but I used to work for her father." Scott continued, describing the security software they had developed, the pressure on Kelsey's father to sell the key, and his mysterious death. He then related the attempt on Kelsey's life.

"Let me have my chair back."

Gumble rose and the detective eased himself into the seat. He accessed case archives and found the incident. Scott knelt and rubbed the thick fur behind Rocky's ear, as Hart scanned the digitized file. Within a few minutes, he finished reading. "You're right. This looks fishy as hell. Two men carrying silenced pistols come into her home in the middle of the night, pass by thousands of dollars worth of valuables and head straight to her bedroom, and the investigating officer concludes that it's a burglary gone bad?"

"Who was the IO?" asked Burke.

Hart's mouth twisted in an expression of disdain. "Beaumont."

Before Burke could comment, the phone on Hart's desk beeped and he picked it up. "Hart." After a short pause, he said, "Be right there," and hung up the phone.

"Captain wants to see me."

Burke appeared confused. "The captain?"

Hart's eyes moved from Burke to Scott and back again to his partner. "Uh-huh."

▽

A resounding crash echoed through the huge room as Wheeler slammed the end of the strut against the middle of the roll-up door.

"It's just a thin gauge," he uttered as he bent over to examine the progress he had made. "That last whack broke through."

Meade squeezed next to him and knelt down for a closer look. "Great! Let's see if we can peel it back."

He helped Wheeler jam the narrower rod into the hole that had been created, and the two of them pried the bar, opening the small hole wide enough to insert the strut. Once the strut was through the gap, Wheeler told Meade to steady it while he slid the rod through the tear and against the open side of the U-shaped metal. Then, he left the tip of the rod trapped inside the channel of the strut and lifted, utilizing the leverage to shear the metal skin.

"It's working!" exclaimed Doni.

The two men, employing the strut and the rod, bent the skin around the metal opening, enlarging the hole further. Wheeler dropped the rod. "Jimmy, let me see if I can get my arm through."

Meade stopped prying and withdrew the strut he was using, as Wheeler dropped to one knee and slowly stuck his hand into the tear, careful to avoid the sharp, jagged edges of the mangled steel. His hand through, he continued reaching, while he explained, "The reason I thought we should poke a hole here, in the middle, is that there is a handle right next to the spot we went through. We can't turn it from this side because it's locked."

His explanation was interrupted by grunts as he struggled to bend his elbow, which had now penetrated the opening, and twist his arm around.

"But on the other side, there should be two wire cables which are hooked to the handle. The cables are connected to latches on the outside edges of the door. If I can grab both cables...." He grunted again and barked out in pain as a sharp piece of torn metal sliced into his upper arm. Ignoring the pain and bleeding, he continued, "I have one of them. Now I need to get hold of the other. Okay!"

All of the group who were clustered around him heard a soft creaking, rasping sound of metal against metal.

"Jimmy, slowly, so you don't amputate my arm, lift up on the door."

Meade reached down below the bottom panel and found enough of a gap between the door and the slab for him to insert his fingers. At first gently and then with increasing pressure, he pulled upward. Although resisting initially, the door abruptly lifted.

"Yow!" yelped Wheeler, frantically adjusting his position to move with the sudden thrust. "Hold it. We should be past the latches now. Let me get my arm out before I bleed to death."

"Got it," Meade answered and shifted his body against the roll-up so that it did not move back down and latch again.

"Oh, my God!" Lisa exclaimed as Wheeler slowly extricated his bloody arm from the gash in the door.

Falt started unbuttoning his shirt. "Here, use this." He pulled the shirt off and handed it to Lisa, who took the cloth and wrapped it snugly around the two tears in Wheeler's arm.

Grimacing once, Matt looked over at Meade. "Okay, Jimmy. Pull it up."

With Copeland helping, the two men slowly raised the door. The latches, which had been lifted by Wheeler, now dragged loudly on the outside face of the tracks. The door lifted, and they could see that they were at the end of a long, wide corridor. There were no personnel in sight. Wheeler turned to Doni. "Go get Chris and Ricky. It's time to go."

▽

As Ben Hart approached the captain's office, he saw Tim Sparks, his sergeant, loitering in the hallway.

"Ben, what did you do now?"

Hart smirked at the good-natured tease from the man he had reported to for many years. "Just the usual. Selling confiscated guns on eBay, swiping drugs out of the evidence locker for recreational use, nothing big. Why does the captain want to see me?"

The sergeant shrugged. "Don't know. He called me up here to sit in. Might as well find out."

"Sure. Why not?"

The two men entered the office, and Hart immediately saw something which put him on guard. Sitting in one of the visitor chairs was Davis Ulrigg, from the local office of the FBI. He also noticed Josh Garrett leaning against the wall.

Keeping his voice neutral, Hart greeted the federal agent. "Hello, Davis."

The man stood and shook hands with Hart and Sergeant Sparks.

"Ben, good to see you." Obvious from his inflection, it clearly was not good.

The three men sat and faced Captain Douglas Whitman. The captain wasted no time getting to the point. "Detective Hart, I understand that Garrett called you to give him a hand on investigating the disappearance of several people, including a Matthew Wheeler."

"Yes, sir."

"I have already informed Garrett that he is no longer handling the case, or any of the related incidents arising from it. Since he called you in to assist him, that means you're off it, too."

Hart made eye contact with Garrett for a moment. It was evident that the man was happy to have his caseload lightened by the decision. "Sir, I'm guessing by the presence of the FBI that the case isn't being handed off to another detective in the department."

"That's right, Ben. The FBI has assumed jurisdiction."

The apprehension worsened. "Sir, I'm already hip-deep in this thing. And it seems to be a rapidly evolving situation. I would prefer to keep the case, especially since I don't really see how the Feds can claim jurisdiction on it."

The captain leaned forward, resting his elbows on the top of his desk. "They have reason to believe this is a kidnapping."

"So do I," Hart retorted quickly. "That would still fall under local jurisdiction. There isn't any evidence to indicate that a child has been taken or that anyone has been transported across state lines. I don't see the connection."

Giving Whitman no chance to reply, Ulrigg blurted, "Interstate commerce clause."

"What?" snapped Hart, more harshly than he intended.

The agent gestured in the general direction of Garrett. "According to what your colleague has said, Wheeler, while missing, placed an order for test equipment from a manufacturer in New Jersey."

"That's ridic...."

Hart's rebuttal was cut off by the captain. "Ben, save your breath. You know how it works. If they want the case, they get the case. I'm asking you to blow it off. If asking isn't enough, I'm ordering you."

His mind spinning, Hart looked questioningly at his sergeant, and was met with an expression which made it clear that no help would come from that direction. He changed tactics. "I'm fine with a joint investigation, then. Considering the complexity here, I don't see how that can do anything but help."

In a condescending voice, Ulrigg shot that down. "A joint investigation is not going to happen. I'm certain the Bureau can comprehend the nuances of this case at least as well as you can, Ben."

Resisting the urge to take a swing at the agent, Hart made an outward show of begrudgingly coming to agreement. With a loud exhale to punctuate his resignation, he pulled out his phone and, directing his comment to the captain, said, "I'll message the evidence techs and tell them to box up everything for Ulrigg's people to pick up."

Relieved, the captain sat back in his chair. Before he could make any assuaging remarks to his detective, Ulrigg continued to push. "Ben, I understand you have someone in custody."

Not immediately responding to the special agent's words, Hart finished typing out his text message and sent it. Tucking the phone back into his pocket, he faced Ulrigg. "Custody? No, I wouldn't call it that. He was a victim. Now he's a witness."

"Well, either way, we'll need him for further questioning."

▽

Scott, back in Hart's seat, was rapidly typing something into the detective's computer, when Burke's phone chimed. Reading the text message, he instantly jumped to his feet. He grabbed Scott by the shoulder and, his voice urgent, barked, "Get up. We need to go!"

Scott looked over his shoulder at him. "Just a sec. I need to finish...."

Cutting him off, Burke held his phone in front of Gumble's face. "You don't need to finish anything. We're leaving."

Scott focused his eyes on the screen of the cell phone and read the text. The message was terse: "Get Scott out of here NOW!"

Closing the window of the program he was working on, he stood hastily. "Okay, let's go."

▽

The teenaged boy jumped up, grabbing the printout he had just made, and ran out of the room.

"Mom!" he yelled as he dashed to the kitchen. Finding it unoccupied, he circled back, knocking a pitcher of sun tea from the counter top in his haste. Ignoring the crash of shattered glass and the splattered mess, he hurried toward the master bedroom, repeatedly shouting for his mother.

When he reached the bedroom door, it was locked and he began banging on it loudly. After a few seconds, her voice filtered through from the other side. "What is it, Colton?"

Still panting from the frenzied sprint and his excitement over his news, the youth made three attempts before he could audibly answer. "Mom...Mom...I...I got a message from Dad!"

The door flew open and Colton's mother, soaked from a shower and wrapped in a bath towel, saw the single sheet of paper her son held and took it from his hand, reading it quickly. Her breath caught as she read the short message. He watched as her eyes moved back to the top and she read it a second time, a slight tremor in her hands causing the paper to visibly flutter.

In a voice much calmer than he expected, she said, "Colton, call your Uncle Tommy. Right now. Don't tell him what's in the note. Just tell him to get his butt over here right away."

▽

"Where in the hell is this place?" Meade's voice bounced off the walls of the wide corridor as the group cautiously moved forward. Doni stifled an urge to shush him as the reverberations filled the space.

Muttering quietly, Wheeler answered, "We were blindfolded and then drugged. I don't know if we traveled an hour or a day. We might have even been transferred into a plane. We could be anywhere."

"I suppose it's a dumb question to ask if anyone still has a phone."

No one bothered to respond to Ricky's comment as they reached the first door along the sprawling hallway. Breaking off from the group, Wheeler moved to it and twisted the knob. The door opened with a creak. Copeland and Falt joined him and the trio peered into the space.

Wheeler spoke over his shoulder. "It's another large, empty room."

"Any windows?" asked Meade.

Stepping back out into the corridor, Wheeler shook his head. "No. It's identical to the one we just broke out of, except a little smaller."

"And it's also filled with cots," added Falt.

The three returned and they all continued their progress down the hallway. As they encountered additional doors along the route, all were checked in turn, only to reveal more rooms of a similar nature. Approaching the end of corridor and finding that it terminated in a *T*, they paused.

"I know I asked before where this place was, but now I'm wondering what it is."

Ashby answered, "It's obviously intended to be a holding facility for a huge number of people, Jimmy."

▽

Judtson, Kelsey, Bal, Carlos, and Saylor were in the passenger section of the older Learjet as it followed the western coast of South America, heading northward. Romeo filled the copilot's seat in the front cabin, keeping company during the flight with the hastily hired pilot. The two scientists were occupying facing seats at the front of the cabin, engaged in a muted discussion. Judtson had taken a seat at the rear and, despite Kelsey's attempts at conversation with him, had fallen asleep.

She stood and moved to the seat beside Saylor, who was silently staring out the window of the plane. Surely aware of her arrival next to him, he did not acknowledge her. After a few minutes of mutual silence, she reached out and touched his arm. Her voice soft, she murmured, "We'll get her out."

Without bothering to turn his head, his voice low and intense, he asked, "How? We've got one real soldier and the rest of us are a bunch of sheep. We're going to break into a FEMA camp, take on the government or whoever these people are, and just dance right out again? We don't even know if she's…."

Kelsey cut him off. "Don't go there. She's fine. All of them are. And we'll figure out what we need and we'll get it. Romeo has contacts. He can put together a team."

Finally shifting his gaze away from the view outside, Saylor faced Kelsey and, his voice now bitter, replied, "You mean more men like Luis?"

Quickly shaking her head, she emphasized, "Luis was *not* one of Romeo's. I hired him after I bought the silo. He was my mistake, not his. We need to trust Romeo."

"I don't trust anyone right now."

Chapter 35

BEN HART AND SPECIAL AGENT ULRIGG ENTERED THE BULLPEN.

"Where is he?" the Fed asked.

His voice neutral, Hart answered, "I left him sitting right here, at my desk. I don't know. Maybe he had to use the restroom."

"Check it."

Hart bristled at the agent's attitude. "I'm not one of your men, Ulrigg. Check it yourself."

Glaring at the detective, Ulrigg crossed the floor swiftly and pushed through the door to the men's room on the far wall, slamming into another detective who was exiting, as Hart watched with concealed amusement.

From across the room, he heard Ulrigg say, "Anyone else in there?"

The man leaving, a seasoned veteran who was months from retirement, recognized Ulrigg. "Thanks for the apology, Davey. No, the bathroom is empty enough to accommodate both you and your ego."

Disregarding the snipe, the Fed pushed into the room and checked the stalls himself. When he emerged a moment later, he glowered at Hart, who had reached his desk and was sitting down. Marching across the distance, Ulrigg barked, "Where in the hell is he?"

Taking pride in his level of displayed nonchalance, Ben shrugged. "Have no idea. Guess he took off. As I said, we weren't holding him. He was a victim and a witness. He was free to go."

He could see the jaw muscles working hard on the federal agent's face. Searching the top of his desk, Hart found what he was looking for almost immediately. Copying the information to another slip of paper, he handed it to Ulrigg. "Here's his phone number. Give him a call. He's a very cooperative guy. I'm sure he'll come right in to see you."

▽

"Where are we going?" Scott asked, leaning forward to see around Rocky, who was perched on the bench seat between them, as Burke steered his mud-covered pickup onto the freeway.

"Out to my ranch."

Perking up, Scott twisted in the seat. "You have a ranch?"

"Yep."

"Wow!"

Billy grinned at his passenger. "You sound surprised. You've never seen a black cowboy before?"

"No," Scott blurted defensively. "That's not it. I just…."

"Relax. I'm messin' with you. Nobody meets cowboys anymore."

▽

The Learjet touched down and taxied to the corporate terminal. The hatch was opened and the group tiredly trudged down the steps onto the tarmac. After passing through Customs, they found the rental SUV left there for them and climbed in, with Kelsey behind the wheel.

Judtson, who had taken the passenger side of the front seat, asked her, "Where's Scott now?"

"He's out in the boonies. He sent directions."

She maneuvered the truck out of the lot and turned east.

"I still don't understand how he got there," Romeo commented from behind them.

"I'm a bit fuzzy on it myself," Kelsey answered. "I think he's trying to keep details to a minimum until we're face to face. He even sent the directions broken up into several chunks, and used emails and text messages. It was a bear putting them together. I guess we'll find out when we see him."

▽

Jimmy Meade and Matt Wheeler were leading the group down the quiet corridor, careful to check each room they passed. They arrived at the termination of the hall, finding that there was no intersecting corridor branching out from this end, only a single door. Meade cautiously opened it, wielding a four-foot-long steel strut, and peered inside.

"It's a staircase."

"Going up or down?" asked Wheeler.

"Up." With a single glance back at the group, Meade resolved, "Well, let's go."

Huddled closely, they all followed as he climbed to the first landing. They had not yet encountered anyone else in their search, and their luck held as they turned the switchback and climbed the second flight. The pattern continued through three additional landings and switchbacks, until they reached a more spacious platform and another door.

"I see light coming from under the door," Copeland murmured, as he surveyed the final landing.

"Right," Meade agreed. "I think it's daylight."

"No peephole?"

Meade laughed. "We're not that lucky, Lisa. I can't get over how we've just been able to wander around in this place without running into a single person."

"Maybe they're all outside," offered Ashby.

"Or maybe they're all gone. Might as well take a peek."

"Be careful," admonished Doni, who had moved to stand behind Meade as he reached for the door handle.

"They didn't teach 'careful' at the academy."

He slowly twisted the handle, relieved to find that it was not locked, and edged the door open a few inches. Intense sunlight blazed through, piercing the dimness of the stairwell. It took a minute for his eyes to adjust before Meade reported, "From this angle, I don't see a soul."

Wheeler sidled nearer. "What do you think?"

Meade stared through the narrow gap for another moment, then grunted, "Aw, what the hell," and threw the door fully open.

Momentarily blinded by the acute onslaught of light, they saw a wide sidewalk extending out in front of them, connecting to another building approximately a hundred yards away. No other people were in sight.

"Looks like we're still in the desert," Ricky commented.

"Yeah." Meade grimaced as he spoke. "Feels like it, too." Taking a tentative step out, he checked in both directions and saw other similar buildings spaced out on the dusty grounds.

He stepped back into the shade. "Well, no point in just hanging around here. Let's make a beeline. Maybe there won't be a fence…or guards."

A brief discussion resulted in consensus and the group briskly moved out, again with Meade in point position. They had proceeded no more than twenty yards from the building, when their ears were suddenly filled with the repetitive blaring honks of a siren.

Wheeler, spinning around, was the first to notice the apparent cause. He pointed at the top of the building and shouted to be heard. "Motion sensors!"

The others craned to see, as Meade yelled, "Here comes company!"

They all froze in place as a contingent of men, dressed in khaki uniforms and carrying automatic pistols, converged upon them from two directions.

▽

Kelsey drove into the entrance between two upright creosote-soaked telephone poles, which supported a third. Hanging from the sagging horizontal was a weathered sign which had "Double B Ranch" carved deeply into the wood. It was dark and she slowed the SUV to a crawl on the rutted dirt lane. Nailed to each of the two uprights were three strands of barbed wire, extending in both directions away from the gate. A rusted metal sign tied to the wire warned, "Trespassers will be shot on sight."

"You sure this is the place?" Judtson asked, eyeing the sign nervously.

"Hope so," Kelsey answered. "It's where Scott said to come."

As she rounded a sharp curve, she gasped and slammed on the brakes, causing Judtson to ram his elbow into the dashboard.

"Oow! What the…?"

He stopped himself as he saw the reason she had so abruptly stopped. In the center of the narrow road, a horse with a rider blocked their path. In the headlights they could see that the rider was lean and dark-skinned with legs which seemed impossibly long, his booted feet resting in stirrups well below the belly of the horse. Nestled in the crook of his right arm was a shotgun. Kelsey started to get out of the vehicle, when Judtson cautioned her, "You'd better dim your headlights or put on the parking lights."

She let out a nervous giggle. "That would be the polite thing to do, wouldn't it?"

As she reached for the controls, Romeo, from the backseat, put his hand on her shoulder. "I'll go first. And keep the lights where they are."

Kelsey sighed loudly. "Okay. Go ahead."

The big man climbed out of the SUV and walked forward. Before he could speak, the man on the horse acknowledged him. "I'm guessing you're Romeo Jones."

Jones stopped and looked up at his face. "You have me at a disadvantage, sir."

Shifting the shotgun to the other side, the man leaned down and extended his right hand. "The name's Burke. Billy Burke. This is my ranch."

Jones shook his hand. "We're expected. I believe we have a friend inside."

Burke nodded. "All in good time. Right now let's get the rest of your party out here so I can meet them."

"Okay," Romeo agreed, and headed toward the SUV.

He had taken only two steps, when Burke added, "And one more thing…why don't you just hand me that semi you've got tucked under your shirt in back. I'll keep it warmed up for you."

Jones turned back. "I'd rather not, sir."

Smiling broadly at Romeo's answer, Burke persisted. "Look, we've all got our jobs to do. Your job is to take care of that lady in the truck, and that little piece you carry is your tool to get it done. My job is to make sure nothing happens on my ranch that I can't keep a handle on. You carrying throws a monkey wrench in the works and makes it a little hard for me to do my part."

As he spoke, the door on the truck opened and Kelsey got out.

Burke continued, "But it's no problem for me either way. You don't want to give it up. Just climb back in the truck and head on out of here."

Kelsey reached the two as he finished. Romeo faced her. "Kelsey, I asked you to…."

"What's the matter?" she asked, ignoring his comment.

Before Jones could answer, Burke leaned down again and offered his hand. "Evening, ma'am. I'm Billy Burke."

She shook his hand and repeated, "What's the matter? What's wrong?"

In a calm voice, Burke replied, "No problem, ma'am. I was just explaining to your fellah here that he needed to hand over his pistol if he wanted to enjoy our hospitality this evening."

"You're kidding? That's it?" She whirled toward Romeo. "Give it to him."

"Kelsey…," Romeo began to protest.

Quickly, she stretched her arm around his back and pulled out the 9mm. For a moment it appeared as though Romeo was going to grab her wrist, when he stopped himself. "I…."

"Romeo, it's okay. Scott wouldn't walk us into a trap." She handed the pistol to Burke, who tucked it into his belt.

"Thank you, ma'am. And if you wouldn't mind, please ask the rest of your group to come on over here. I'd like to meet them all before we head on in."

"Sure thing." Kelsey returned to the truck, leaving Romeo, who was glowering up at Burke.

Making eye contact with him, Billy said softly, "Don't blame you, pal. I wouldn't have given it up either," and followed the statement with a wink. Burke's words did nothing to assuage the Ranger.

▽

Judtson, Kelsey, Saylor, Romeo, Singh, and Villarreal were assembled on the large patio, which projected out from the entire length of the sprawling house. Rocky, after the initial enthusiastic greeting of his master, had settled down to his normal position, sitting upright and pressing against the side of Judtson's leg. Burke's wife, Louise, was inside making preparations for dinner, as he stood at a wide barbeque pit tending to a full grill of steaks, a cast-iron pot of beans, and foil-wrapped potatoes. Hart occupied a chair facing both Judtson and Kelsey.

After listening to a lengthy narrative from them, covering most of the events already related by Scott, Hart commented wryly, "This is a lot to swallow."

Judtson chuckled. "You're not exaggerating. I've been living through it, and to this day I have a problem wrapping my mind around it all. Honestly, I'm a little surprised you bought into it this so soon."

The detective took a swig from a longneck and then responded, "Sometimes you just have to go with what feels right. I don't think I was all that ready to dive into your story headfirst, but when the FBI showed up as quickly as they did, it pushed me into a choice. Hope I made the right one."

"You did," Kelsey assured him. "Now we need to get our people out of that FEMA camp. Do you have any ideas?"

Holding up both hands defensively, Hart stopped her. "Whoa! Billy and I slipped Scott out of headquarters before the Feds could grab him. I was happy to do that, but I'm not so sure about strapping on the bandoliers and attacking a federal facility. Besides, with this gimpy hip, I'm also not sure I'd be much help."

The disappointment was obvious on Kelsey's face, as Judtson responded, "I understand. And, believe me, we appreciate you and Billy, both for getting Scott away from there and for giving us a place to hide out tonight."

"Yeah, we're kind of running out of hiding places," concurred Kelsey.

"Our pleasure. Besides, after dinner, Louise is going to want to hear your whole story, from beginning to end. She eats this stuff up." Hart directed his gaze toward Saylor, who was alone on the fringe of the lighted area and staring out into the desert. He tipped the neck of his beer in that direction. "Your friend okay?"

Judtson shrugged. "Would you be if your wife was being held in that camp?"

The comment silenced the detective. Before any of them could think of something to say, the patio door slid open and Scott came out. He walked straight to the three and pulled up a chair. "I think I might have a little good news."

Saylor, noticing Scott's arrival, joined them. "What? What is it?"

Romeo, who had been standing with Burke, also moved to the gathering.

"I've regained the signal from the tracker."

"That's great, Scott!" gushed Kelsey. "That means they're still all right, doesn't it?"

Shrugging, Scott answered, "It could. I followed the tracking signal. It popped up earlier today in the middle of the FEMA camp and then moved slightly…about two hundred yards…and stabilized again. At least that tells us that they're still there and still moving around a little."

Judtson asked, "You told us that the tracker is on Ricky, right?"

Scott nodded.

"So all we really know is that Ricky is there. They might have split up the group."

With a meaningful glance at Saylor, Scott replied, "Yes. That's true. Except why would they split them up?"

Catching the glance, Judtson backed off. "You're right. I'm sure they're all together."

"Anyway," Kelsey interrupted, "we need to figure out a way to get them free."

Saylor burst in angrily, "Figure out a way? We need to go there! We need to go there and do something!"

"We will," Judtson responded, attempting to calm his friend.

Romeo, who had been quiet since their arrival at the ranch, finally spoke. "Maybe he's right. Maybe we just need to get there and figure it out as we go."

Kelsey's head jerked in his direction. "You're not serious? Shouldn't we have a plan? Something?"

"Sometimes you can't," Jones explained. "Yes, it's a good idea to have the intel, to know what you're walking into and prepare for it. But if a part of your team is captured, there isn't always time for that. There are situations when you just need to go in, figure it out on the fly, and hope for the best."

"Right!" Saylor agreed forcefully.

▽

Since their recapture, the eight were now being held in a different location within the compound – not the dim, dusty holding area of earlier, but a brightly lit, well-secured space approximately the size of a large conference room. Their captors had been remarkably mute as they intercepted the group and escorted them at gunpoint to their new cell. The lights in the room had been dimmed overnight; however, few slept and what sleep occurred had been fitful. Copeland, Falt, Trippiano, Wheeler, and Ashby were now seated. Ricky was pacing. Meade moved from one part of the room to another, carefully examining every component and looking for weaknesses, while Doni stood off to the side, watching her fellow prisoners and thinking. Since being placed into this second area, they had all been relatively silent. No one had anything new to say.

The door to the room suddenly swung open, catching them all by surprise, and two men entered, carrying TEC-9 automatics. Before anyone could react, one of the men pointed his weapon at Ashby and barked, "You! Come with us."

Meade, the closest to the two men, took a step forward and began to speak, when the second guard brought the barrel of his gun to bear on him, stopping Meade in mid-stride. Ashby slowly rose from his chair and walked out of the room, giving a final glance back at his friends as he left.

The guards followed him out into the hallway, and one moved around him to take the lead position.

"Where are you taking me?" Ashby asked, his voice weaker than he had hoped it would sound.

"Keep walking," was the only response he received. Yet his answer came quickly as they soon stopped at a doorway. The guard in front opened the door and motioned for Ashby to enter. Stepping into the room, he immediately saw something which chilled his blood. The room was bare, save for a single chair and a small table – and a man he recognized. It was the same man who had converted him weeks ago, again dressed in black. On the small table beside the chair was the familiar headset and open valise.

Dread filled him, and his mind desperately spun in an effort to come up with a way to avoid what was to come next. But no plan of action emerged. Not realizing that he had stopped moving upon catching sight of the man and the device, he felt the prodding from a gun barrel jammed harshly in his back, and trepidatiously stepped forward, sitting down in the chair. There were no words from the man in black as he efficiently placed the headset on Ashby and pressed a button.

Having gone through the process once before, Ashby knew what to expect. Essentially, there was no sensation of a transition. His mind, his thoughts, his consciousness would seem to be intact and unaffected after the procedure was completed. It was only when he attempted to influence his body that the change would become obvious.

Oh, God, please not again! he thought to himself.

His ears heard the soft *beep* from the device, indicating that the process was complete. He felt the man's hands grip the headset and remove it. Through the eyes, still fixed forward, he saw the two guards relax their vigilance and lower their weapons, since he was no longer a possible threat.

"Take him to his quarters," the man in black instructed the guards.

One of the two came to Ashby and gently gripped his arm, guiding him from the chair. He docilely rose and walked beside the man, out of the room and along the corridor until they reached another door. The guard released the grip on his arm and opened the door. Ashby stepped into what appeared to be a residence dormitory with several bunk beds and heard the door close behind him.

Chapter 36

As ROMEO DROVE NORTH FROM TUCSON, Judtson thought back to their early-morning departure from Billy Burke's ranch. It had been decided that Bal and Carlos should stay behind. Billy, and particularly Louise, had been insistent that they remain at the ranch, along with Scott, who could do them all much more good from a secure location with an Internet connection.

Romeo had been relieved to have his pistol returned to him, not to mention surprised when Burke took him into an anteroom off his master bedroom, where he opened a large cabinet filled with an impressive assortment of rifles, shotguns, semi-automatic and fully automatic weapons, and told him, "Take what you need."

Alternating his gaze between the arsenal and the cop, Romeo grunted, "This is great, Billy. Thanks."

Burke grinned in response. "Don't thank me – just bring 'em back. Personally. And if you mess them up, I'm gonna kick your butt into next Tuesday."

After making three trips to the rental SUV and filling the rear compartment with hardware, the two men had parted company with a long handshake, followed by an apology from Burke that he could not join them, and a rather intense wish for good luck.

Twice during the ride, Judtson attempted to engage Romeo in a conversation about what his plans would be after they arrived at the camp. Both times, Romeo was noncommittal, stating only that he would figure it out when they arrived. Even Kelsey was considerably more subdued than normal, content to stare out the passenger window from the front seat and watch the desert scenery. Saylor, occupying the opposite end of the rear seat from Judtson, also fell into an impenetrable silence which Judtson wanted to break through; and yet, he had no clue as to what he could say to his friend. Finally settling back in the seat, Judtson turned his face toward his own window and stared, unfocused, in the general direction of the now receding Pusch Ridge.

The driving was interrupted twice. The first stop was in Florence where the four ate lunch at a hamburger chain and topped off the fuel tank. The second stop was miles from anything. Romeo picked a location where he could steer them several hundred yards off the highway. After parking the truck, he got out and told the others to do the same. They met him at the rear hatch, where he was pulling out four M4 rifles he had taken from Burke's stash and giving them the once-over. When he finished, he slapped in fully loaded magazines and handed them out to his companions.

"I don't want to go into that compound without firing my weapon. And I definitely don't want to go in without all three of you firing yours."

He gave them a quick course on charging the rifle, changing out the magazine, and clearing a jam. Then he turned to a stand of prickly pears approximately fifty yards away and emptied his clip in four brief bursts, the rounds shredding the broad cactus sections and sending a spray of pulp into the air behind. Finished, he turned to the three. "What you have in your hands is the M4A1. The only real difference between this carbine and the M4 is that with the M4, you choose between single-shot semi-automatic mode and three-shot bursts, and with the M4A1, you get either single-shot or full automatic. The magazine holds thirty rounds and in fully automatic mode at 700 rounds per minute, or about 12 rounds per second, you will empty your magazine in no time. Kelsey, I already know your capabilities on a range. Judtson and Saylor, unless either one of you is a marksman, I would prefer that you use the fully automatic mode and try to keep each use to as short a burst as you can. Now, on the side you'll see a selector. Your choices are S or 1 or F. The S is safety mode. The 1 means you are in single-shot mode. The F is for fully automatic. Set your weapons to F and practice. Work on keeping your bursts short."

He stepped back and Kelsey raised her rifle. Aiming at the same patch of cacti, she managed eight bursts, burying all of the slugs in the soft flesh of the plant.

After she fired, Judtson smiled at Saylor. "This looks like my paintball M4."

"Probably a bit more of a kick," his friend answered.

Judtson did not have quite the control Kelsey had displayed, emptying the magazine after only five bursts.

"Not bad," commented Romeo.

Saylor stepped up and shouldered his rifle. Picking off different sections of the cluster with each burst, he was able to accomplish nine before running out.

"Excellent. All right. Let's go. And watch the barrels. They tend to get a little warm."

The Ranger stowed his rifle, watched the others do the same, then closed the hatch and climbed back into the driver's seat. They completed the final leg of the drive in silence. It was not until they neared their destination that Kelsey began informing Romeo on their proximity to the camp and the location of the area where Scott had suggested he park the vehicle. Off the highway, they took what began as a two-lane blacktop road, soon turning into a dirt lane. Her finger tracing their path on the tablet which showed an aerial view, Kelsey almost shouted, "There! That arroyo. Turn right."

The SUV had all-wheel drive and Romeo steered onto the flat, sandy bottom of a wash which, during monsoon season, would fill to the top of its banks, but was now bone dry.

"Okay. Now north. About half a mile."

Romeo checked the odometer and, keeping the truck centered in the wash, drove at a slow and deliberate speed until they reached the desired number on the digital readout.

"Now what?"

She checked the aerial one more time before answering. "You can park it wherever you'd like. Scott is suggesting that we use that hill over there for reconnaissance."

With a cursory glance at the hill, Romeo drove the SUV up the gradually angled bank of the wash and parked it under a large mesquite. The sharp thorns on its branches made a scratching sound against the metal, which reminded Judtson of nails on a chalkboard. Romeo dropped the shifter into park and opened his door, leaving the engine and air conditioning running. The other three climbed out and joined him at the rear of the truck.

"Right now, you three stay here," Romeo instructed, keeping his voice only loud enough for them to barely hear him. "I'm going to move to the hill and see what I can see."

"Romeo...," Kelsey began, but was immediately cut off.

"Kelsey, this time, no arguments. I'm going up there alone."

A halfhearted grin spread across her face. "I wasn't going to argue. I was about to say that I think I should contact Scott and see if there has been any change in the status of the tracker."

He shook his head. "No. Not a good idea. As close as we are to their complex, we have no idea what kind of ELINT they might have. I don't want a signal from us to be picked up."

"Got it."

As Romeo opened the rear gate, Judtson asked Kelsey, "What's ELINT?"

"Electronic intelligence."

Rummaging through the gear, Romeo added, "Technically, it is the detection of any electromagnetic radiation. Step one is to pick up a new signal, any signal. After that, they can try to determine what it might be saying and where it's coming from."

As he explained, he dragged a tan ACU coat, a hot weather balaclava, a boonie hat, and a set of binoculars out of a duffel bag. In practiced motions, Romeo pulled the balaclava over his head and straightened it on his face. Next came the boonie, then the coat, both with the latest digital camouflage patterns for the desert. Last, he looped the binocular strap around his neck and buttoned the coat, covering the optics.

After a final quick check, he cautioned Kelsey, "Stay put and stay quiet. I'll be back soon."

She gave him a mock salute. "Yes, sir."

Judtson, Kelsey, and Saylor watched as Romeo turned away and began trotting rapidly toward the small hill.

"Kelsey," Judtson chided, "sometimes I'm surprised he doesn't deck you."

▽

By the time Romeo returned, his three companions had reentered the cool SUV. The sudden opening of the driver's side door caused Kelsey to jump. Romeo climbed onto the seat and pulled off the boonie and balaclava, his head glistening with perspiration.

Kelsey was the first to speak. "Well?"

"It's as we expected. There is a perimeter fence with concertina wire at the top. I counted a total of ten large buildings and four smaller ones."

"What about guards? Or people inside?"

"Essentially none. No guards that I could see. No guard towers, either. I'm guessing they are doing it all electronically, with motion sensors. I did see a group of three men in uniform crossing the grounds from one building to another. They were carrying small automatic weapons. Looked like TEC-9s."

From the backseat, Saylor asked, "Did you see anyone else? Any of our people?"

"No. The one trio was all I saw."

"What do you think?"

Romeo twisted around in his seat to face Saylor, a slight wisp of sympathy in his eyes. "The use of motion sensors and the conspicuous absence of guards and personnel in general could work in our favor. They may be so dependent upon the gizmos that they have a fairly light force to deal with. Of course, we have no way of knowing how fast they can muster a backup team and deliver them to the site, so whatever we do, we're going to have to move quickly."

"Do you have a plan?" Kelsey asked.

"I think so. The inherent problem with motion sensors is that there are blind spots. Rather than attempting to blanket every inch of the grounds, installations that utilize the sensors rely upon the tendency of intruders to pass through or across key areas. So I think we can get inside the fence."

"How? Over the top?"

"No. I wouldn't want to try that, Kelsey. Too risky. Too vulnerable. The site is laced with washes. They've got chain link extending down into them, but there are always gaps and weak spots. Leave it to the javelinas to force their way inside and create those. I think we follow one of the washes to the fence and try to get in that way. If the first wash we pick is buttoned down tight, we fall back and move to another until we find our wide-open entrance."

"And then what?"

"Once we're inside, we execute a basic extraction raid."

"I hate to sound dumb," Judtson interjected, "but what exactly is a basic extraction raid, and how does it work?"

Romeo grinned at him. "From Scott's tracking, we know which building our people are probably being held in. That's great intel, better than we would usually get. When we're inside the fence, we move fast and we move hard to that building. By the way, the first arroyo we try should be the one closest to our target building, because once we clear the fence and begin an open-field run, lights and sirens will be going off all around us."

"And bad guys with machine guns will be shooting at us," Judtson added.

"Exactly!"

"No, Romeo, I meant that as a question. What do we do when the bad guys with machine guns start shooting at us?"

"We shoot them first."

"I'm not trying to be a wet blanket, but that plan sounds a little dicey. What if about a hundred of them come pouring out of the buildings? We can't shoot them all."

Romeo made eye contact with Judtson for a moment before answering. "You're right. We can't. If that happens, we drop our pieces on the ground and we raise our hands and hope they don't take us out on the spot."

Kelsey cleared her throat. "Is there another way to do this? Remember, Romeo, you're the only one trained to do this stuff."

"Believe me, I know that. Sure, there are other ways. But they take time. We set up camp. We take shifts. We watch the place day and night for two...three days. We count bodies and memorize routines. We do all of that in hopes of putting together a pretty good count of how many men we're up against and when they are at their weakest."

"Two or three days!" Saylor exclaimed. "We can't...."

Judtson interrupted him. "We need to go in right away."

"I agree," Kelsey said.

"Okay, let's suit up."

Surprised, Judtson barked at the Ranger, "Whoa! Right now? Shouldn't we wait till dark?"

Shrugging, Romeo explained, "Night would only work in our favor if we had NVGs...sorry, night vision goggles...and some flash-bang grenades. No, I think a daylight run with clear terrain works in our favor. Besides, if we go crawling through the washes after dark, I'd probably lose one of you to a rattlesnake bite."

Kelsey shifted her gaze to Judtson. As their eyes connected, she saw a subtle change in his before he said, "All right. Let's do it."

▽

The four lay side by side in the coarse sand of an arroyo a few feet from the perimeter fence of the compound. Keeping his voice muted, Romeo briefed them. "Remember, once we get inside and go as far as we can on our bellies, we have to make a run for it the rest of the way to our target building. The men inside, who are supposed to be the guards, are sitting on their butts, watching television and playing video games. They've been at this for months and nothing has ever happened. They're dull. They don't have their weapons in hand. And, it's likely that wild animals have breached the fence in the past, so there have probably been a lot of false alarms. All this works in our favor. It's going to slow down the guards' response time and it's going to just slightly reduce their readiness attitude when they come out the door. There's a good chance that once we break into a run, we'll make it all the way to our target before a door even opens."

Kelsey sighed. "I hope you're right."

"So do I, boss. But remember one thing, all of you. When those doors do open, when those men do come out, whichever one of us has the shot…we need to take it. The *only* thing we need to make sure of is that it isn't one of ours. Once we figure that out, we pull the trigger. If you wait, if you hesitate for any reason because you want to be certain before you kill somebody that he's really a threat, you're going to be the one on the ground bleeding. And you'll probably cost the rest of us our lives. Not to mention our friends inside. Everybody clear on this?"

The first to answer was Saylor. "Absolutely."

"Yes, sir," Judtson replied.

"Got it," came from Kelsey.

"All right, let's go. And please, let's not get excited and shoot each other."

"That would be good," Judtson muttered, and began to follow Romeo as he shimmied forward in the sand.

▽

Jimmy Meade walked apace with the two men, his mind spinning.

I could take these two guys if I hadn't been zapped, he thought to himself. *Their guard is down. They're not even paying any attention to me.*

The three reached the door, and the first escort opened it, stepping aside for Meade to enter. Inside, the astronaut could see Chris waiting, sitting on the edge of a bunk. Pausing outside the doorway, Meade again entertained the idea of taking the gun from the man, frustrated at the fact that he had been once again mentally exiled. To his surprise, his right hand began to move toward the guard who was holding the door open.

"Jimmy!" Ashby suddenly shouted, jumping up from the bunk. "How are you?"

Meade stopped his motion and focused on the chemist, who was hurrying to greet him. As soon as their eyes met, he saw a slight shake of Ashby's head. Confused, he dropped his hand back down to his side, both motions not sufficient to catch the attention of the khaki-clad guard, and stepped inside the room. The moment he did, the door closed behind him.

"Chris, what the…?"

Ashby instantly held a single finger up in front of his lips, and Meade stopped talking. Placing his arm on the older man's shoulder, he led him away from the door. As they walked, he leaned close to Meade's ear and whispered, "The conversion didn't work this time."

Meade came to a halt. His eyes darted around the room. He looked down at his hands and performed a series of movements, wiggling and flexing his fingers. Finishing his self-examination, he murmured, "I'll be damned. What's the deal?"

"I don't know. All I know is that I'm still out. I'm still the one running my body."

Meade was befuddled. "How could that happen? The guy zapped me, just like last time."

Ashby shrugged. "Don't know. The only thing that seems probable is that Matt's device must have actually trashed whatever mechanism we have inside which made it work before."

"Makes sense. But they're going to catch on soon enough. One of the others will react wrong after the conversion and spill the beans. I almost did. God knows what they'll do to us then."

"You're right, Jimmy. That's why we need to act now. Even if all of the former converts end up in here with none of them revealing the fact that the machine doesn't work on us, what are they going to do with the others?"

"I hadn't thought about that."

"I think we need to make a move fast. I was waiting for one more to come in to help me, and I'm glad it was you."

Meade smiled. "Well, you know I'm in."

▽

Romeo arrived at the fence and was relieved to see that he had been correct. The chain link, when the fence was installed, had been extended down to follow the terrain. Past monsoons, turning the arroyo into a raging flow, had battered the obstruction, piling branches and tumbleweeds against it. He saw that the force of the water, pushing against the blockage, had broken the heavy-gauge wire links securing the fence to the buried spikes in the ground.

Kelsey crawled forward beside him. "Can we get through?"

Romeo pointed at the loosely hanging bottom. "Not a problem. It's been torn free."

He started to reach forward, but Kelsey grabbed his arm. "It's not electrified, is it?"

With a soft chuckle, he took hold of the chain link. "Nope." She gasped as he did this.

"You've seen too many movies," he told her. "Even with these screwballs, in the middle of the Arizona desert you're not going to see an electrified fence without a zillion warning signs and flashing red beacons. Anyhow, if it had been, there'd be carcasses by the fence – coyotes, javelinas, rabbits. Did you notice any?"

She allowed herself a smile, the motion causing the mixture of dirt and sweat to crack along the crease lines on her face. "Okay. What's...? Aaahhhh!"

Romeo snapped a glance in the direction Kelsey was staring, and saw a movement in the dead brush.

"Back off! It's a rattler."

The snake was uncoiled at this point, but was quickly pulling its body into the circular position needed to strike. As Kelsey scooted backward, Romeo's hand shot out into the dried tumbleweed, grabbing the diamondback behind its head and pulling. The muscular body thrashed and wrapped around his forearm, the rattle itself slapping against his face and slightly lacerating his cheek. The inch or two of body between the head and the top of Romeo's grasp arched frantically in an effort to bring the exposed fangs to bear on his wrist. Using his free hand, Romeo reached down to his belt and brought out a hunting knife, and with a smooth motion, cut off the snake's head, careful to keep himself clear of it as it spasmodically snapped its jaw.

The headless body continued to writhe in his grip. Rolling onto his side, Romeo tossed the snake over the bank of the arroyo. He then broke a stiff branch from a tangle of mesquite trapped against the fence, and skewered the still-moving head. After throwing the branch away from them, he turned to speak to Kelsey, who was huddled against Judtson, wide-eyed. "Glad you saw him. That would have been a nasty surprise."

For once she was speechless. Judtson gave Romeo a lopsided grin. "Any more of them in there?"

"Don't know. I'll check."

Working from the outside edge, he removed the debris piece by piece, keeping a lookout for any other creatures. Within minutes, the organic jumble was cleared and the base of the fence fully exposed. With a single nod at his team, giving them the all clear, he pulled up on the chain link and crawled under, moving several feet past it before he turned around to watch the three come through. Judtson was second, allowing Kelsey to hold back. She followed him and Saylor entered last.

As they gathered on the inside of the fence, Judtson, his eyes automatically checking out the piles of brush, asked, "Now what?"

Romeo pointed over his shoulder with his thumb. "We follow the wash for about fifty yards. That brings us closest to the target building and keeps us below the motion sensors. That's where we make our run."

Kelsey finally found her voice. "What if they have cameras?"

"Oh, they have them. I saw them earlier."

"Well, what about…?"

He cut her off. "Have you ever tried to sit and stare at unchanging scenes on a screen for hours at a time? Believe me, you quit watching. No. They rely on the motions. When one of those is tripped, then they'll look at the cameras to tell them where the action is."

"Oh."

Romeo turned and moved off, using his elbows to drag himself forward in the sand. The others followed him. Judtson, now crawling in the wash behind Kelsey, was miserable. Without the benefit of gloves, the coarse sand and the sharp rocks had badly abraded his palms, fingers, and forearms. His shirt and pants were filled with grit. His neck was already sunburned, and his knees felt as if they were about to begin bleeding from the constant grinding they were receiving. He envied Romeo, who had donned knee pads, in addition to the long-sleeved camouflage jacket. They had not been prepared for a commando raid and had not brought that type of gear for all of them. Ignoring the pain and discomfort, he stretched around to see Saylor, who was behind him. His friend showed no indication of irritation, discomfort, or pain, even though his clothes were comparable to Judtson's, if not flimsier. Rather, his face portrayed only intense determination. They made eye contact and, yet again, Judtson drew a blank as to what comment to make. He faced forward and continued to crawl, doing his best to disregard the distractions.

▽

As Lisa approached the door the two guards were leading her toward, she was engulfed in a flood of emotion. The mental prison was a place she had never wanted to experience again. Yet here she was, once more trapped. As the man in front reached out to open the door, she suddenly became aware of the cascade of tears down her cheeks.

Confusion filled her mind. *Wait a minute*, she thought. *I wouldn't be crying. I mean, that witch I turn into wouldn't be crying.*

She started to speak, when a flurry of actions happened almost at once. The guard turned the knob and swung the door inward, but had not yet released his grip, as someone grabbed the man's wrist and pulled him violently inside. The unexpected tug caused him to lose his balance and he fell. Through the open doorway, Lisa saw Jimmy leap onto the man and punch him as Chris grabbed his weapon.

The second guard, seeing what was happening, was lifting his gun and pointing it past her into the room. She could see that he was going to succeed in getting off a shot before Chris could bring his weapon around. Her first thought was to knock the gun out of the guard's hand. Even as a part of her consciousness became furious that she could no longer act, the rest of her mind performed flawlessly while she gripped her hands together as if she were praying, raised them high above her head, and brought them down as hard as she could on the top of the gun, knocking it from the man's grip.

He swore at her and bent to retrieve his weapon, but Jimmy was already coming out the door and slammed into the man, both of them crashing against the opposite wall of the hallway.

As they fought, Lisa snatched up the dropped gun, and with three steps stood beside them. "FREEZE, JERKBALL!"

The fight immediately went out of the guard. Jimmy stepped back and ordered him into the room, where Ashby was already using handcuffs from the first guard's belt to lash him to a thick fire riser in the corner. They did the same with the second man, gagging both to keep them quiet and finding the handcuff keys in the men's leather snap pouches.

Pocketing both sets of keys, Meade put his arm on Lisa's shoulder and felt that she was trembling. "You were great."

"I…I can't believe…why are we still…ourselves?"

"Don't know," Ashby answered her, breathing heavily. "I'm not about to look a gift horse in the mouth."

"We'd best get moving," Meade grunted. "I don't know how long we have until these two are missed. We've got to get the others out now."

Nodding, Lisa offered the TEC-9 to Ashby, who did not take it.

"You're probably better with that thing than I am. Keep it."

She sucked in a deep breath, let it out loudly, and pulled back on the bolt, charging the weapon. "Okay. Let's go."

▽

The four huddled in the wash, soaked with sweat and covered with dirt and grime, leaning their backs against the bank as Romeo laid out their next move.

"We're as close as we're going to get. There are buildings to both sides of our direction of assault, as well as our target building. I'll take point. Kelsey, you're second. Then Judtson. Saylor, you're last. This is crucial, so listen carefully. The entire front hemisphere is mine. Somebody pops out, I take him. Kelsey, you have the left. Judtson, the right. If you see a threat and you aren't certain the person responsible for that zone sees him, shout out. If it gets crazy and men start running across our field, don't fall victim to tunnel vision and follow them with your weapon as they cross over, or you'll shoot the team member in front of you."

"What about me?" Saylor asked.

"You can take shots of opportunity. Just be careful. Mainly, your job is to make sure they don't flank us and come around behind. Not as important during our run, but once we get in the building, we need you to cover our six."

Saylor nodded.

Romeo looked carefully at each of the three. "If any of you might be thinking that I'd rather have somebody else with me on this, you're wrong. Those are your friends…and your wife…in there. You are all going to do what it takes. I couldn't ask for three better battle buddies."

He paused to let his words sink in, and could see that they had the desired effect as all of his companions' faces lost any trace of uncertainty, the emotion now replaced by resolve.

"Let's go!"

▽

As the three passed the closed door where the man in black was waiting with his equipment, Meade stopped and reached for the door handle. Ashby whispered, "Jimmy, do we need to mess with him? We just want to get out of here."

Thinking about it for a moment, Meade nodded and withdrew his hand. They continued down the hallway, encountering no other personnel. When they found the room where their group was being held, they discovered that the door was locked with a keypad entry system.

"How do we get in without a code?" asked Lisa, when Meade kicked the door right beside the handle. It did not budge. Rearing back, he kicked it again, this time even harder, and the latch snapped, flinging the door wide and crashing it against the wall.

As Lisa and Chris ran into the room, Meade leaned against the doorjamb for a moment and muttered, "Man, that hurt!" before he limped in behind them.

The group, startled by the dramatic entrance, all spoke at once, excitedly swamping them with questions. Ashby held up his hand to get their attention. "Look, we don't what happened or why. When they took us away, they tried to reconvert us, but it didn't take. They thought it did. Because of that, we were able to get the drop on two of the guards and get their guns. We don't have much time now. They're going to miss those two. Something's going to happen to sound the alarm, so grab whatever you can for a weapon and let's get the hell out of here."

Chapter 37

$\mathbf{A}$S PREARRANGED, ROMEO, KELSEY, JUDTSON, AND SAYLOR had inched their way up the bank of the arroyo, the four staying flat and hugging the ground to delay detection from the motion sensors. Romeo had wanted all of them out of the wash, not slipping and scrambling up the bank, before they began their assault. He conspicuously flipped the selector on his M4 to fully automatic and watched as the others did the same. Satisfied they were ready, he nodded and sprang up, instantly breaking into a full run toward the target building two hundred yards distant.

Glancing back as he ran, Romeo saw that the others were up and running, as well. He crossed no more than twenty yards, when the Klaxons erupted in sound. Gripping the stock of his gun tightly, he bowed forward and pushed himself faster, hoping to make it to the entrance before the first man appeared. In his mind, he visualized the guards setting down their cups of coffee, jumping up from their chairs and sofas, grabbing their weapons, and trotting to the nearest exits, unsure whether this was another false alarm, while keying their communication devices and looking for guidance from whoever was manning the closed-circuit surveillance cameras.

Another forty yards rushed beneath him and still no one had appeared. In between the harsh blasts from the alarm horns, he could hear the footfalls of his teammates right behind. Reaching the halfway point of the sprint, Romeo thanked the Archangel Michael for their good fortune thus far and prayed that it held. No sooner had he finished the short prayer than the door directly in front of him flew open. Forcing himself to focus in the intense sunlight, Romeo saw that the five men running from the building were all clad in khaki uniforms and, more important, that none of them were members of his group.

With the M4 already aimed straight ahead, he triggered the weapon and sent a short spray of slugs into the zone occupied by the enemy combatants. Two men went down, hard and fast. Even at approximately seventy yards, Romeo could see the red splatter on the wall behind the targets. The remaining three dived to the ground and rolled. Romeo sent another short volley at two of them who were close together. From the scream, he guessed that his bullets had connected with one; the man dropped his weapon and was clutching his upper arm.

The part of Romeo's mind trained to think tactically determined that the enemy were carrying

TEC-9s, not extremely effective at longer ranges. As he saw one of the men roll into a shooter's position, he began swerving as he ran, making a harder target. As he changed his pattern, he yelled, "EVASIVE!" over his shoulder for the others to do the same, not glimpsing back to see if they had.

The man on the ground began firing, his rounds kicking up small clouds of dust twenty feet from Romeo. Using the trails in the sand as tracers, the man guided his weapon nearer, and Romeo could see the pattern zeroing in on him. Cutting hard to the left, the big man dodged in the direction the rounds had been going and, while at a full sprint, lifted his rifle and, keeping his elbows bent, pulled the trigger, holding it down. Even from a run, his first slugs smacked into the dirt only a few feet from the target. He compensated slightly and watched as the 5.56mm slugs ripped into the prone shooter.

That left one man, who was also shifting into position for a shot. Romeo knew his magazine was empty. He was reaching to his vest for another as he prepared to dive, but suddenly heard a long burst from behind. Twisting, he saw that Saylor had separated from the others and come to a full stop, his M4 shouldered steadily, and was emptying his entire magazine toward the last shooter. One look back toward the building told Romeo that Saylor had hit his mark, and then some, as the body on the ground continued to jump and shudder from the impact of the slugs.

Breaking his stride, he shouted to Saylor, "Reload!" while he did the same. He saw that Kelsey and Judtson were still running toward the building, each watching the assigned flank. Taking a final peek to make sure that Saylor was indeed slapping a new magazine into his gun, Romeo turned back and resumed his run. The three of them were now within twenty yards of the building, when Romeo saw something. "DOWN!" he shouted and dived to the dirt, seeing that Kelsey and Judtson, who were slightly in front of him and off to the side, did the same. Two more men had appeared at the doorway and, obviously having heard the shooting, wisely remained inside, using the frame as cover. The two guards, one on each side of the opening, extended their TEC-9s and began firing. Romeo instantly returned fire and brushed them back. They popped out a moment later and each got off a few rounds. One of the slugs caught Kelsey, who was the closest to the doorway, in her leg. She only let out a brief yelp of pain before blasting the opening with her M4.

Saylor, who had hit the dirt only seconds after reloading, checked to his right and saw more men coming out of the adjacent building. Wriggling around so that he faced the new assault, he fired off a short series, dropping one of the men. Judtson became aware of the second group and turned to assist Saylor, firing and hitting no one. The grounds were flat and open between the buildings, providing no cover for anyone, and the flanking party dived down to minimize their profile.

Romeo knew they were in an untenable position. They were out in the open with absolutely zero protection. Two men were inside the target building, only twenty yards away, with another group coming from the right. One of the two men in the near building swung his machine pistol out and fired wildly. Romeo did not even bother to return fire.

The group to the right were taking selective shots, keeping them down, and Romeo guessed that reinforcements must be on the way. Almost to answer his suspicions, a string of bullets kicked up the dirt forty yards to his side, a ricochet slicing through the shoulder of his vest, tearing the tough fabric but missing his skin. Turning, he saw another group running toward them from the left building. The men were still quite far away, and he laid down suppression fire across the advancing party, causing them to dive to the ground, as well.

"We need to get in that building!" shouted Judtson from his position.

"I know. Wish I had a grenade. Or a bazooka," Kelsey barked, firing to her right.

"How's your leg?"

"I'll live."

Romeo began crawling forward toward the open door.

Judtson noticed the movement. "Romeo, what in the hell are you doing?"

"Cover me. Keep them back."

"I'll do it, Judtson. You watch our right."

As Romeo edged forward, the two men inside continued to take turns firing blindly out the door. Unless dumb luck was on their side, their shots would not hit anyone. That would change, Romeo thought, when they saw that he was moving closer. At that moment, one of the two chanced a fast peek out and saw him, just as Kelsey sent a short volley toward the door frame. It looked as though the man had jumped back in the nick of time, but Romeo saw him suddenly fall forward, his body collapsing outside the threshold. For a moment, despite the fact that neither he nor Kelsey fired a shot, both of them heard a confusing jumble of rounds discharged, all coming from inside the building. In a few seconds, the second man took two staggering steps outside and fell, almost farcically embracing his dead comrade on the stoop.

Romeo shouted to Kelsey, "Hold off!" and a moment later he saw Jimmy Meade stick his head out into view.

"Get in here!" Meade yelled.

Romeo reacted instantly. "Judtson, Kelsey, lay down fire at the group to the right. I'll hold down the left. Saylor, get in there."

Before he could finish his commands, Kelsey fired off a slightly longer series of rounds to the east. He triggered his weapon toward the more distant group on their opposite flank, and peripherally saw Saylor dash from behind them at a full run. The attackers saw him also and tried to take him down, but the long-range weakness of their weapons caused none of the rounds to connect.

Meade stepped aside, making room for Saylor, who barreled through the open doorway at a sprint, cradling the M4 against his chest. As he came to a staggering stop, he heard Doni.

"Saylor! Oh, my God! You're here!" His eyes darting around in the dimmer surroundings, he saw her just as she ran to him.

He held her awkwardly with one arm, his rifle sandwiched between them, and found he was unable to speak. From behind, Meade shouted, "Saylor, we need to get the rest inside."

Tilting his head back, he kissed Doni passionately and released her, murmuring, "I love you."

Lisa, emerging from a room to the side, yelled, "This room has windows!"

Still taking command, Meade ordered, "Saylor, you and Lisa bust out a couple of windows on that side and hold off the group to the east."

Saylor nodded, tripped the release on the magazine of his gun, and slapped in a full one as he followed Lisa. She was already across the room and breaking out a window with the butt of the TEC-9. He joined her and did the same with another pane. Without delay, they began firing at the closer of the two attacking parties.

Romeo, seeing the attackers to his right being held down with fire from the building, barked to Judtson, "Get Kelsey inside!"

Judtson stood to a crouch and scrambled to Kelsey, glancing down at her thigh and seeing the pant leg saturated with blood. "Come on, let's go."

She slung the rifle around her neck and put her arm over his, standing painfully, as Saylor and Lisa maintained an almost constant barrage. Not waiting for Kelsey to become fully upright, Judtson rushed forward, ignoring her sudden scream of pain as she put her weight on the injured leg. Half-dragging her, he reached the doorway, where Matt Wheeler was waiting. Out of the line of fire, she managed a weak grin at Judtson and urged, "Go! Cover Romeo," as she transferred her arm from his neck to Wheeler's.

Judtson spun around and saw Meade holding open a door to a room on the opposite side from where Saylor and Lisa were hunkered down. Hurrying, he followed the astronaut into the room and dashed to the far wall, breaking out a window and opening fire on the enemy to the west.

The moment Romeo saw the suppressing fire directed at the group he had been holding at bay, he stood and charged forward, covering the short distance to the open door in seconds. He had no more than cleared the entrance, entering like a rampaging bull, when Ashby slammed the door behind him. Kelsey was propped against the wall with Ricky bent over her tearing open the bloody pant leg to expose the wound. Ashby, before closing the door, had relieved the two dead guards of their guns and was handing one of them to Copeland.

"We need to cover the hallway!" Romeo bellowed above the din of automatic gunfire. "There may be more coming at us that way. Is there any furniture in these rooms we can use as a barrier?"

"Yes," Doni shouted.

"Get some help, pull it out into the hall, and pile it up just past these doors."

Wheeler, Copeland, and Doni went into the room where Saylor and Lisa were maintaining intermittent fire from their positions at the windows. Keeping low, the three began pulling chairs and tables out into the hall.

Romeo ducked into the opposite room and checked on Judtson and Meade, then returned to the hall and knelt beside Kelsey, who was biting her lower lip and staring down at the wound Ricky was cleaning with his shirt. Romeo reached into one of his vest pockets and pulled out a roll of gauze, still wrapped in plastic. Tearing it open, he handed it to Ricky. "Here, use this." Ricky nodded and began circling her lifted and exposed thigh with the white bandage.

"Hey, boss. How are you holding up?"

Kelsey's eyes rose to meet Romeo's. "Hurts like the devil, but it only sliced me open. The bullet never went in."

He put his hand on her shoulder. "You lost quite a bit of blood. You're gonna be weak. Don't try jumping up for a while, okay?"

Chuffing once, she smiled feebly. "Not a chance. Right now I don't think I'll ever be jumping up again."

Through the nearer doorway, Romeo heard a cacophony of shattering glass. He quickly moved to the opening. Saylor and Lisa were crouched below the window sills, and Romeo saw that the entire bank of windows along the length of the room had been shot out. In the distance, he could see that reinforcements had arrived for the group to the east. There were at least eight more men joining the fray and they had held back, keeping close to the building. Romeo saw the glint of sunlight bouncing off the optics of a scope attached to a tripod-mounted rifle brought into the fray by one of the new arrivals.

Lisa started to rise to return fire. "STOP!" Romeo shouted. "They have a sniper! Keep your head down." Just as he finished the order, he heard the whizzing sound of a bullet passing his head and pounding into the wall behind. He jumped back and around the corner, making his way carefully to the opposing room where he warned the others of the new development.

From a bullhorn outside, they all heard, "We have you surrounded. There is another unit inside the building, moving toward your position. You are trapped and have no way out. I demand that all of you put down your weapons and exit the building immediately with your hands on your heads."

The random firing from the guards outside, as well as the return fire from Romeo's people, had all stopped and the silence was eerie. Romeo was back in the hallway with Kelsey. "What now?" she asked quietly.

Taking a minute to think through the options before he answered, Romeo muttered angrily, "We don't have a lot of choices. They've probably got...."

Abruptly, the amplified voice continued, "Within minutes we will begin sending in tear gas and flash-bang grenades. We have a team suiting up to follow those in. They'll be wearing Kevlar suits and carrying shields. You know what will happen if they have to come in, don't you? This is your last chance. Three minutes from now is all you have."

The man on the bullhorn fell silent. Lisa, Saylor, Judtson, and Jimmy came out of the side rooms, keeping low, and joined the rest of their group in the wide corridor. Judtson was the first to speak. "Romeo, do we have any options?"

Hesitantly, the big man shook his head. "Not without a lot more equipment and weapons."

Almost nonchalantly, Judtson shrugged and said, "Well, it's fairly clear. We either die in here or turn ourselves over to them and hope for the best."

Chris added, "They obviously want us alive."

Romeo shifted his gaze, connecting with each of them one at a time. None of the rest spoke. He felt a brief upwelling of admiration as he saw a gamut of emotions on their faces, but not one of them displayed a trace of fear.

He moved to the edge of the open doorway, cupped his hands around his mouth, and shouted, "WE'RE COMING OUT!"

The man on the bullhorn answered, "Excellent choice! Single file! Hands on your heads!"

Facing the group, Romeo ordered, "Pile up everything we have...all the guns, magazines, everything...right next to that door."

Reluctantly, they all began to move around, except for Kelsey, who remained propped against the wall. "Romeo, maybe they don't know how many of us there are. Maybe a couple of us stay in here and hide. We might be able to rescue the rest later."

Romeo shrugged. "Worth a try. But you aren't one of the two to stay. You won't be doing any rescuing with that wound."

She eyed him defiantly. "Well, you can't stay either. I'm pretty sure they'll be specifically watching for the giant-sized black guy to come out."

Frustrated with the accuracy of her assessment, Romeo looked around. "Judtson, you and Meade! Grab some of the guns and find a hidey-hole, now!"

Taking two M4s and two of the TEC-9s, the two men hustled past the partially assembled blockade in the hallway. Waiting until they were out of sight, Romeo crouched beside Kelsey and she put her arm around his neck. Together, they stood, and as he walked toward the door, he spoke to the remaining members of the group. "About a five-second gap between each of you coming out."

Saylor, who was standing nearby and holding Doni close, nodded; and the Army Ranger, with Kelsey clinging to his side and limping, opened the door and stepped out into the brilliant sunlight. They immediately saw a man dressed in black standing approximately thirty yards away from them, and holding the bullhorn with his left hand and a TEC-9 with his right. He was flanked by six men in khaki, three to a side, all pointing their guns directly at Romeo's chest. The apparent balance of the security forces had assembled several yards away, their stance more casual. As the two hobbled forward, Romeo was able to make out a smug grin on the man's face. They continued until they were within a few feet of him.

"Hello, Miss Batman. We've been hoping to see you."

Taking a moment to swallow first so that her voice would not crack, Kelsey responded, "I was hoping to make your acquaintance, as well."

The man's smile broadened. "I'm sure under slightly different circumstances."

She shrugged. "We take what we can get."

One by one, the others arrived, spreading out to form a rough line to each side of Kelsey and Romeo. When it was obvious no one else was leaving the building, the man slowly surveyed the group twice. "Is this everyone?"

"This is it," Romeo answered.

The man, who was the evident leader, shook his head and *tsk*ed. "We *can* count, you know. There were eight of you inside before this began. My men clearly saw four more arrive to carry out this foolish rescue attempt. That would be twelve. There are only ten standing in front of me."

"We lost two inside," came Romeo's terse reply.

The insincere smile remained fixed. "Did you? Then, of course, there will be two bodies inside for my men to find. It's such a hot day and I'm already tired of all this running around. I know my men are, as well. So, before we do that, let me give you a choice. Abandon your position that you have lost two of your friends in the firefight and tell me where they are, and all of you will live. Maintain that position and I will send someone to check. If the bodies are not found, I will execute one of you on the spot."

The stranger paused, rivulets of sweat trailing down his cheeks as he waited for an answer. Giving them a full thirty seconds, he turned to two of the guards and nodded. They promptly trotted into the building.

Kelsey, not even feeling the pain in her leg, tensed, waiting for their return. As she was still holding onto Romeo for support, she could feel the muscles in his body tighten. She dared not glance at the other members of her group, lined up on both sides of her, not wanting to portray any nervousness or apprehension to the man in black. The time the two guards were absent seemed like an eternity in the blistering sunlight. Twice, Kelsey had to fight off a vague combination of nausea and dizziness triggered by her loss of blood. Her eyes straight ahead, she saw the man look past her, as she simultaneously heard the crunching footfalls of the two guards exiting the building.

Obviously, the men had not found anyone and were conveying that to him. With what appeared to Kelsey as a genuine sigh of disappointment, the man stepped forward, hastily accompanied by two of the four remaining guards, and walked straight to her and Romeo.

"Pity," he stated dispassionately, and slowly raised the TEC-9 toward Romeo. "Most of this group we either have sought or have a need for. You, Mr. Jones, we do not."

Kelsey's mind whirled as she tried to think of something she could do, anything which would protect her loyal friend. She owed the world to Romeo, the man who had saved her life in the past. Her free arm started to move, when she heard her comrade spit out, "Kelsey, don't!"

There was only a flicker of movement in the other man's eyes as he briefly acknowledged her, then shifted his focus back to Romeo. The pistol was inches from the big man's forehead and Kelsey felt as though she would explode, wanting to break away from his steely grip and tear into the stranger. Yet prior to her execution of a desperate plan, right before her eyes, the side of the stranger's head exploded outward, splattering her with his blood and brains.

Time and space seemed to suddenly slip into slow motion. She watched, transfixed, as the man's arm was still extended, his body illogically upright, as if the bulk of the organism had not yet received the word that its control center was now pulp. Even though the shocking turn of events had frozen her in place, Romeo reacted swiftly. His free hand, the one not being used to support Kelsey, snaked upward and snatched the TEC-9 out of the dead man's mindless grip. Turning it around quickly, he fired upon the two nearest guards flanking the dead man, dropping them both instantly.

He released Kelsey who, rather than collapsing, was driven by a surge of strength catalyzed by the unexpected stimulation and dived forward, leaping to one of the just-fallen guards. She snatched his machine pistol and, using his body as a firing rest and partial cover, opened up on the two security men in front of her. They were caught off-guard, remaining stunned by the suddenness of their leader's violent demise.

Romeo bent and took the gun from the other dead guard. Turning, he tossed it back to Saylor, who was the nearest of the group, and shouted, "Behind you!"

Saylor spun and dropped, shouting for the others to get down. He was about to bring his weapon onto the two targets who were returning from searching the building, when he saw one them suddenly slammed backward as if jerked by a rope. The other was raising his pistol to fire, as a second high-powered slug impacted him in mid-chest, reversing his impetus and tossing him to the ground.

Romeo, seeing that Kelsey had taken out the two nearby guards, turned his attention to the larger unit assembled several yards farther away, who were frantically attempting to free up their holstered weapons and bring them into use. He picked off one of the pack as Kelsey clipped another, wounding the man badly and sending him sprawling. But the remaining force had now cleared their pistols and were beginning to return fire, their first shots wild as they dialed in their emotions. Romeo dived down as a volley passed over him. He grabbed additional clips for his weapon off the closest dead guard's vest and, taking a fast look, saw that the rest of his group were hugging the dirt. As he was about to turn back, there came a horrendous screeching, rumbling sound from his right.

Risking another look and fearing the worst, he saw a 4x4 monster pickup, jacked up ridiculously high and outfitted with massive off-road tires and multiple roll bars, crashing through the chain-link fence. The front end of the vehicle was protected by a makeshift welded steel plate, vaguely resembling the blade on a snowplow, which shielded much of the undercarriage, the front grill, and the lower portion of the windshield. Standing in the bed of the truck, leaning forward against the back of the cab, were three men, tenaciously clinging to the headache rack to avoid being tossed out. Once the 4x4 was through the fence and the tires bit into the flat dirt, the men laid what appeared to be AK-47s on the roof in between the mounted floodlights, and opened fire on the cluster of guards as the driver accelerated straight at them.

The men on the ground, still oriented toward the threat from Romeo's group, madly flailed around, attempting to take out the driver of the truck, their rounds ricocheting harmlessly off the plate. Romeo, seizing upon the distraction, stood and ran directly toward the guards at full speed, unaware that he was screaming at the top of his lungs as he sprinted. Slapping in a fresh clip, he indiscriminately sprayed the group with slugs, his shots intermingling with the rounds from the three men on the 4x4, and at the back of his mind was amused as he visualized the arguments for kill credits later.

From a tactical perspective, the twenty or so guards were bunched too closely together to begin with, and consequently suffered massive casualties from the two-pronged assault. Romeo skidded to a halt as he approached the bloodied jumble of men and was about to slam his last clip into his empty weapon to finish off the two remaining guards, who were tangled in the midst of the mayhem and trying to get their shots off at the truck. At that moment he heard the approaching mammoth rev even higher, its engine screaming. The four-wheeled monster simply continued on its path, rolling and bucking over the heap of living, dead, and wounded guards.

The enormous truck bounced free of the pack and locked its brakes, making a tight, sliding turn and kicking up a billowing cloud of dust before coming to a stop. Romeo felt a hand on his shoulder and jerked around to see Saylor standing behind him.

"Friends of yours?"

Romeo shook his head. "I have no idea who they are, but they are most definitely my friends now."

The rest of his group straggled up to form a semicircle around Romeo. Kelsey was again clinging to one of them for support, this time Copeland.

The three men in the bed of the pickup had hopped out, still toting their weapons, and the driver's side door opened. An older man, wearing a white cowboy hat, twisted in the seat and slid off, dropping nimbly to the ground. Once down, he removed his hat and waved it broadly while squinting toward a hill outside the fence. Romeo saw a lone figure on the hilltop stand and wave back. Someone on the passenger side of the truck, a younger male, exited from the far door.

Shoving the hat firmly back on his head, the driver walked slowly toward them, and Romeo, handing his gun to Saylor, stepped forward to meet him.

As he reached the man, he stuck out his right hand, introducing himself. "It is a pleasure to meet you, sir. I'm Romeo Jones."

"Tommy Coburn." The man pointed his thumb over his shoulder at the younger man who could not have been more than eighteen. "This is my nephew, Colton."

The three men from the back of the truck remained alongside the vehicle, watching.

Romeo shook the hand of the older man and then the younger. "I don't know who you fellows are or why you did what you did, but thank you."

The young one, his face flushed from their dramatic entrance, spoke first. "We're here to get my dad."

Saylor stepped forward. "Your dad?"

"Yeah, Nelson Coburn. We got a message from him that he was being held here."

"I know who that is," exclaimed Kelsey. "He's the head of a militia group in Kingman. He disappeared recently."

"That's right," the youth answered expectantly. "Have you seen him?"

Romeo shook his head. "I'm afraid not. All these folks here are with me. I came to get them out."

"By the look of things I saw," the older Coburn drawled, "it didn't seem like you were doing too good a job of that."

His nerves on edge, Romeo began to snap back, "I...."

Kelsey interrupted, "I'm sorry we don't know anything about your brother, Mr. Coburn, but I just can't thank you enough for coming in like the cavalry. You saved all of our lives."

"Can't say that it wasn't a bit on the amusing side. I sure wish I knew who sent that message and got us all excited."

"COLTON!" Everyone, reacting to the shout, turned to see the source. Emerging from the building were Judtson, Jimmy, and a third man, who had broken into a run in the direction of the Coburns.

"Dad!" the youth yelled and took off in a sprint toward the stranger. When they met, the two wrapped arms around each other and held on tightly, as Judtson and Meade passed them.

Judtson moved close to Kelsey. "Are you okay?"

Her eyes still on the emotional reunion, she nodded. "I'm fine. Who...where...?"

"As Jimmy and I were searching for a good spot to hide, we found him handcuffed in one of the rooms. Jimmy just happened to have a key."

Chapter 38

"SO THEIR HEADSET DIDN'T WORK?" Kelsey asked Ashby, as she hungrily took a large bite from a cheeseburger. The entire group, not having any alternatives at the moment, had crammed into the single SUV and returned to Billy Burke's ranch. Louise Burke had removed the hastily applied bandage on Kelsey's leg, cleaned the wound, covered it with antiseptic, and bandaged it again, as Billy once more stood at the sprawling grill and cooked. Brightly glowing flecks, intermingling with the smoke like fireflies, rose into the night air from the burning combination of charcoal and cured mesquite.

"No," Chris answered. "It didn't. On me, Jimmy, or Lisa."

"I wonder why?"

She directed her question at Matt, who shrugged. "The only thing I can think of is that whatever type of implant they've put in their heads...an implant the headset was supposed to activate...was fried by what we did when we turned them back into themselves."

"There's something else I'm curious about," interjected Doni, directing her question to Scott. "How did you know where we were?"

Circumspectly, he explained, "As we were getting ready to go to New York with Romeo, I kinda talked Ricky into getting rid of the slip-on shoes he was wearing."

His attention captured, Ricky, who had skipped the hamburgers but had a tablespoon full of ranch beans halfway up to his mouth, sat forward at the table, listening.

"I told him he needed something a little better suited for the field and gave him a pair of combat boots. One of the boots, actually both of them, had a tracking device installed."

"What? You put a tracker on me?"

"That is awesome!" gushed Wheeler, impressed. "How is it powered?"

To Ricky, Scott said, "Yes, I did. Since you were a little bit of a novice in the field, I thought it might be a good idea." He then addressed Matt. "Are you familiar with the athletic shoes that link to a smartphone?"

"Yes. I've seen them."

"Well, I borrowed from that technology and from those tennis shoes for little kids, the sneakers that flash red LED lights as they walk. The power for the lights actually comes from…."

"The pressure of each step," Matt finished the sentence.

"I installed the tiny generator in each boot, put in a capacitor to store up the voltage until there was enough to send out a short, strong signal, and added the transmitter. The GPS network does all the hard work."

"Slick!"

"Hey, why didn't you tell me I was a walking beacon?"

Scott seemed genuinely apologetic. "I don't know. I guess I should have."

"Either way, it worked out," Kelsey jumped in. "The real lifesaver, literally, was the militia showing up when they did. I can't believe our luck. What's driving me nuts, though, is how the father was able to get off a message while he was handcuffed in that room."

"He didn't."

All eyes returned to Scott as they heard his sotto voce comment. "I sent the message."

"You sent it?" Kelsey's question was nearly a squeal. "How did you know he was being held there?"

As he averted his gaze downward, his mumbled answer was all but impossible to hear. "I didn't."

"What? I don't understand."

"I felt I needed to do something. Anything. I didn't know how soon you would get back from Bolivia and I didn't know what you'd be able to do when you did. Colton's email address wasn't that hard to find, and I thought pointing the militia in the direction of the FEMA camp couldn't hurt."

Several people in the group began talking at once. Kelsey finished her sandwich and rose unsteadily, hobbling out to the penumbra cast from the light of the porch, and found Judtson, a statue in the semidarkness, with Rocky at his side, both studying the surrounding desert.

Judtson heard her shuffling arrival and turned around. "You shouldn't be up on the leg."

"You weren't there, so I thought I'd come here."

Searching, he saw a boulder a few feet away. "Come on, let's get you seated."

Taking her arm and putting it around his neck, he walked her to the large piece of granite. After she was situated, with her weight off the injured leg, he slid beside her onto the rock. The two remained silent for some time, each lost in thought, the quiescence broken by a single abrupt bark from Rocky, who turned rigid and was staring out into the darkness.

"What do you think he saw?"

"Saw? Probably nothing. Of his senses, sight is nowhere near as powerful as his hearing and especially his ability to smell. I'm guessing he caught a whiff of a javelina, maybe a pack of them."

She pressed harder against him. "I confess I'm not that much of a desert girl. Do I need to be worried that a herd of wild boars are going to attack us?"

Judtson chuckled. "Us? No. Rocky, maybe. They don't bother people, but a dog…oh, yeah. That's why he's hanging back here with us instead of charging out there."

They both stopped speaking again, this time focusing their feeble human senses in the direction Rocky was so intently staring. It was Kelsey who first broke the silence. "Judtson, what are we going to do next?"

She reached down and rubbed the golden behind his ear. "I feel like I'm the dog, out in the middle of nowhere and they – the bad guys – are the herd or pack, or whatever it's called, of javelinas, circling me in the darkness and picking the time for their next attack."

"It's called a pack and I know what you mean," he replied. "That's all I've been thinking about."

"We don't have a lot of choices."

"No. We don't. We can't just keep scurrying around the world finding people they've turned into brain-dead stooges and converting them back. It's not really getting us anywhere. We've lost your fortress of a home as a base. And now we've lost the silo. Thank God for Billy and this ranch. At least we have a place to hide tonight."

"But what about tomorrow? What's our move?"

He turned to face her. "First, I think we need to find a new base for our operations."

"Okay."

"Our next step is to find out who's behind this, who the top person is."

"That's easier said than done."

"Not necessarily. Maybe we can flush him out…make him come to us."

"How?"

"It might not be as difficult as it would seem. They evidently don't know how much we know. They're also obviously afraid that whatever we might know will get out. I think we can use those two things to our favor. We can put out the word that we're onto their scheme, and all of us, with our collective credentials, prominence, and credibility, are going to go public with it unless he meets with us."

"Except we haven't figured it out."

"No. But they don't know that."

"Sounds pretty chancy."

In the near darkness, she could just barely discern the sour smirk on his face. "Got a better idea?"

Kelsey's eyes drifted away from him, and she focused her attention once more on the surrounding darkness. Judtson kept his thoughts to himself, allowing her to mull over whatever avenues she was considering, without interruption. After a long silence, she twisted on the rock to face him again. "No. I don't."

▽

Billy Burke slid the long-handled spatula under the last sizzling patty on the grill, moving it to the platter. Delivering the mound of burgers to the extra-long concrete picnic table he had formed and poured himself, he placed the utensil next to them and looked around. Most of his and Louise's guests were lined up on the two benches at the table, engaged in the animated chatter of people who had only recently escaped a serious situation. He had observed Kelsey hobble away from the group to talk with Judtson. Saylor and Doni were also separated from the party, snuggled together on a porch swing and talking. Nowhere among the assemblage was the person he sought.

Untying his apron and dropping it on a vacant chair, he encountered Louise as she was exiting the patio door, carrying a pie. Intercepting her, he bent and kissed her on the cheek. "Thank you, Lou," he murmured into her ear.

His wife of many years smiled up at him. "Just racking up the points, Big Billy. After I get my house back, you're going to owe me. Truth be told, I like them. And they have some interesting stories to tell."

He chuckled. "Have you seen Romeo? Is he inside?"

She shook her head. "No. Haven't seen him."

He glanced down at the pie. "Cherry?"

"Uh-huh."

"Save me a piece."

"There's another one in the oven."

Leaving her with another peck on the cheek, he grabbed the 12-gauge shotgun propped against the wall and crossed the lighted patio area, pausing at the table long enough to assemble two hamburgers on a plate before proceeding into the desert, slowing his pace slightly to give his eyes a minute to adjust. He walked as confidently as he would if he were navigating his own bedroom in darkness. With a minimum of meandering, he found a lone man crouched under the boughs of a large palo verde. Approaching from behind, Billy saw Romeo start at the sound of the cowboy's boot crunching on the gravelly surface.

"Brought you dinner."

The Army Ranger stepped out from under the dense shadows of the tree and took the plate. "Thanks," he uttered, his voice flat.

In the moonlight, Burke could see an expression of irritation on the other's face. "What? You're pissed off 'cause I walked right up to your hiding place?"

He could tell that his comment hit the mark. "This is my ranch, Romeo...my home. I know it like I know the back of my hand. And if it was *my* job to protect somebody inside, this spot is where I'd be. I figured you were smart enough to pick it, too."

Romeo took a bite from one of the burgers and nodded. Burke stood and watched him chew for a minute, before continuing. "Look, you need to quit beating yourself up. You made it. They made it. Everybody is okay."

"In spite of me."

"That's a load of bull."

Setting the half-eaten sandwich back on the plate, Romeo shook his head. "No, it's not. I should have spotted Luis as a turncoat. That was bad enough. Then I led a group of amateurs into a guarded FEMA camp without the slightest clue as to what we were facing. If it hadn't been for Scott and those militia guys, we'd all be toast."

"It's called teamwork. You did what you did. Scott did what he did. And everything came out all right."

"But it almost didn't."

"So? You know damn well that you didn't have a choice. When the bad guys have your people hostage, you act and you act fast. Sometimes you save them, and sometimes you don't...what you don't do is sit on your butt and wait for better circumstances. And you already know all this. So what if you *almost* didn't make it? We don't count the 'almosts.' We count the wins and we count the losses. Today was a close game, but the other side ended up in the dirt and you walked away. That's a win."

"But...."

"But nothing. You want to feed yourself into a meat grinder over it, fine. It's good for you. That's how to be sure that we don't make the same mistakes again. Just be careful that what you're thinking doesn't turn into a loss of confidence. Because you start second-guessing yourself, and you *will* get somebody killed."

Romeo absorbed the man's words, turning them around in his head, looking for the flaws. Finally, he allowed a weak grin onto his face. "Thanks for the burgers."

"Not too many things a man needs in life – a good woman, a good friend, a good meal, and a good night's sleep. I can't help you with number one on the list. That's up to you. I think you've got a good friend or two back there on the patio. Number three and number four are a different story. Finish up those burgers and get back to the house. Lou will tell you where you're going to bunk tonight."

"I'd better…."

Burke cut him off. "I told you before, this is my ranch. Ain't nobody coming in to mess with my guests. You head on inside and get some sleep. I'll keep watch."

▽

Kelsey entered Billy Burke's den, where she found Scott using their host's computer. "Did you find what you wanted?"

He nodded. "I got lucky. There's a cool site with everything we need."

She tossed a credit card on the desk, along with a sheet of paper. "Judtson and I both wiped out most of our cash picking this up."

"Using a prepaid card is the only way to get this stuff without popping up on their system."

"I know. That's the address Judtson gave me. Have it all shipped there. Do they do overnight?"

"Yep."

▽

"This place is cool!" Ricky exclaimed. "You said it originally served as the nurses' quarters for the old company hospital?"

Judtson smiled at his exuberant friend. "Yes. Early in the last century, when Phelps Dodge was in high gear, they built this to house the nurses and staff for the small hospital that took care of the miners and their families."

The balance of the group was wandering from room to room, exploring and picking out where they would sleep.

Meade approached Judtson. "How did you know about this place?"

"I stayed here once. Did a cable show on ghosts. This building and several of the other old ones in Bisbee are supposedly haunted. They rent rooms here now. During the winter, forget it. The place is packed. This time of year, I was able to rent the whole place."

"I remember that show," Ricky said. "You never did see any ghosts."

"Nope. Maybe you will while you're here."

Ricky's eyes widened. He was about to respond, when Judtson caught sight of Romeo, who was nearing them after his circuit of the perimeter.

"So, what do you think?" Judtson asked Romeo, as the big man walked toward them.

"Not bad. Only one exterior set of steps up to the front door. Even the lowest-level windows require a ladder to reach from the outside. Tall iron fence around the edge of the lot. Solid brick walls. Not perfect but not too hard to defend."

"Good. Once we get everyone settled in, we should be going."

Romeo acknowledged him with a single nod and walked away. Judtson left to find Kelsey, who had stayed outside. She was sitting on one of the many metal benches placed around the grounds. As she saw him approach, a bright smile filled her face. "This is great. I wouldn't mind hanging out here after this is all over."

He sat down next to her on the bench. "I love Bisbee. I have since I did that show. Even thought about moving here."

Her eyes darted from the original Phelps Dodge headquarters, now converted into a mining museum, to the former company store across the boulevard, now a collection of gift shops, a restaurant, and a coffee shop. She twisted around in her seat and looked behind at the facade of the Copper Queen Hotel. "The whole time I've lived in Tucson, I never once realized all this was here."

"I hate to pull you back from tourist mode, Kelsey. We should get moving."

Her eyes swung back to focus on his. "You're right. Do you think they'll be okay here?"

Judtson shrugged. "I think so. I have a feeling that being in this small town is better than being out in the middle of nowhere, in your house or the silo. I could be wrong, but I don't believe that the bad guys are ready to be overt…public…when they make their move. And the cool thing about Bisbee is…this time of year, the town is mostly filled with only the residents. They know each other. If our men in black show up, they will stick out like sore thumbs. I told the few friends I've made here to alert Jimmy if anyone of that ilk pops up."

She put her hand on Judtson's arm. "Too bad we don't have time to wander through those antique shops on Main Street. I'll bet I'd find some more pretties to add to my collection."

He placed his hand on hers. "I promise you, when this is all done, we'll come back and do just that."

"Deal!"

"How's the leg?"

"Still hurts, but it'll be okay."

"Sure you don't want to stay here with the others and take it easy?"

The lightness left her voice. "Not a chance."

▽

The hour-and-a-half drive back to Tucson was uneventful, the three of them lost in their own thoughts. Romeo had insisted upon his usual role of driver, and as he continued straight rather than turning into the driveway of Judtson's office, Kelsey, who had taken the back so that she could sit sideways and extend her injured leg across the bench seat, squawked, "Hey, you just passed it."

"Uh-huh. It's being watched." He gestured, and his two passengers noticed the unmarked white van parked across the street.

Judtson turned in his seat and stared at the apparently empty vehicle. "How can you tell?"

"Under it…beneath the engine is a large puddle of water. That's condensation from the AC. In this heat, they'd keep it running. Otherwise, the back of that van would be about a hundred and eighty degrees."

"They might have arrived a few minutes ago and parked. Wouldn't the AC drip for a while?"

He shook his head. "If they just parked, the asphalt would be hot. The water would evaporate almost immediately. For there to be that big a puddle, the shade from the van would have to cool off the pavement some, and the dripping from the unit would need to go on for a long time until it saturated the pavement. No, a couple of men are in the back and they've been there all day."

"FBI?"

"That would be my guess. Okay. Your office is out. I'll bet they're watching your house, Saylor's, and yours, Kelsey."

"That's a lot of manpower to devote to us," Kelsey commented, shaking her head.

"I think we're fairly high on their priority list. Where to? Any suggestions?"

After a pause, Judtson answered, "All we actually need is the Internet. Any place with a little bit of privacy and Wi-Fi should do it."

"Everyone has Wi-Fi," offered Kelsey. "Fast food, coffee shops, bookstores…."

"We don't have a laptop now, and we'll need one."

"If you're thinking about buying one," Romeo interjected, "we have to be careful."

"I know. We need cash, and Scott cleaned us out." Judtson thought for a moment. "Turn right at the light. I have an idea."

▽

The teller smiled brightly. "Hello, Mr. Kent. How are you today?"

"I'm well, Pat."

"What can I do for you?"

"I need to cash a check, but I don't have my checkbook with me."

Her smile remained. "You can use your card."

"I don't think so. I'm sure the amount I need is well above the limit for a transaction."

"Oh, I see. Well, of course you can use a counter check."

She pulled a single sheet from the small vertical file on the counter and, after a few keystrokes on her computer, handwrote his account number on the check before turning the paper around and sliding it to him. "On the pay-to line, you can write 'cash.' Then fill in how much you need and sign it."

He followed her instructions and handed it back. If she had been surprised by the sum, Pat did not show it. "I don't have this much in my drawer, Mr. Kent, so please give me a minute."

"No problem."

As she left, he glanced at Kelsey, who was sitting in one of the lobby chairs pretending to peruse a magazine. They exchanged smiles and he turned back to the teller window as Pat arrived, holding three wrapped bundles of bills. "I assumed that you wouldn't want all of it in hundreds. Is a thousand in fifties all right?"

"Perfect. And if you wouldn't mind, two or three hundred in twenties would be great."

"Not a problem."

She efficiently slipped the wrappers off the bills and verbally counted the money, keeping her voice soft. When she finished, Pat bent each pile lengthwise and slid the wrapper back on, finally handing all of the cash to Judtson. "Would you like a bank bag or an envelope?"

"No thanks, Pat."

"Let me get someone to walk you out to your car."

He smiled reassuringly at her. "That won't be necessary. Thanks again."

"My pleasure, Mr. Kent. Have a wonderful day."

Tucking the cash into his pants pockets, Judtson stepped away from the window, wishing her a good day as well, and nodded at Kelsey. The two walked out of the bank and climbed briskly into the idling SUV. Romeo slipped the truck into gear and they sped away.

Their next stop was only a few blocks away, an office supply superstore where Judtson purchased two laptops and paid cash.

▽

Since it was summer and the fall semester had not yet begun, the mall and patio of the Student Union at the university were not heavily crowded when Kelsey and Judtson arrived. The two had no trouble finding an outside table with shade and a nearby electrical outlet. They quickly unpacked the new laptops, plugged them in, and switched them on. As Judtson waited for his to boot up, he surveyed the mall, looking for Romeo, and spotted him approximately a hundred and fifty yards away, sitting on a retaining wall in the shade of a large tree.

As the welcoming screens appeared on their laptops, they configured and registered the machines using fictitious names. That step completed, Kelsey logged on to the Internet and created a new email address. As she typed, she giggled, catching Judtson's attention. "What?"

"The name I picked for my email is *inanna@gmx.us.*"

"What's 'inanna'?"

"Not what, who. Inanna was one of the ancient reptilian goddesses. Kind of a troublemaker. She darted all over the place, raising hell wherever she went."

"That fits."

She grinned at him puckishly. "Got one for you."

"What is it?"

"Use *sciuridae@outlook.com*."

"What does it mean?"

"Oh, it's just a heroic character from an old French novel I read."

He eyed her suspiciously. "Are you sure?"

"Yes!" she answered with mock hurt. "If you don't like it, that's fine. I thought it fit you."

He stared at her for a moment. "How is it spelled?"

She gave him the spelling and he set up the account.

"While you're doing that, I'll contact Scott and see if he's been able to find anything."

She composed a vaguely worded email to Scott and sent it. His response arrived within two minutes.

"He sent an email with an attachment."

"What is it?"

"Looks like an executable. I'll run it."

The install routine completed, she read the pop-up message.

"He thinks of everything. It's an add-on for Outlook Express. It automatically turns an outgoing email into an image file and sends it as an attachment."

"I don't understand. What does that do?"

"If the bad guys are scanning emails for key words, they're looking at text, not pictures. Scott's add-on sends what is basically a photograph of the message, not words."

"That's cool."

"Yeah, it is. There's another message from him." She opened the attachment and an image of a page popped up on her screen.

"He found the email address we wanted."

"Good. Anything else? Is everyone there okay?"

Chuckling, Kelsey told him, "Yes, they're fine. Ricky thinks he saw a ghost. He's changed rooms three times."

Judtson laughed.

"Do you know what you're going to say?"

He nodded. "I've been rewriting it in my head over and over. I think so."

"Well, get to it."

As he typed, Kelsey went inside and bought lunch for them, bringing it out to the patio. She left him alone as he worked, his head bowed down toward the screen, his fingers working the keys. Just as she was about to take the last bite of her sandwich, he stopped typing.

Rotating the laptop so she could read, he picked up his sandwich. "Tell me what you think."

As she read, he hungrily took a sizable bite.

Taking her time reading the text, she finally sat back. "It should work."

"You like it?"

Kelsey found the earnestness in his voice endearing. "Yes, I do. If this doesn't make the man want to meet us, nothing will. I hope we're starting with the right possible target."

"If he takes the bait, we'll know. Should I send it?"

"Yes, Judtson. Send it. Why? Are you nervous about this?"

"No. Not really. It's only...."

She suddenly realized the issue. "I can't believe this! You're self-conscious about your writing!"

His uncertain, almost timid expression betrayed him.

"You're kidding. You're a writer. I just can't…."

"I want to be sure it's right."

Confounded by his sudden vulnerability, Kelsey leaned to him and placed her hands on his shoulders. "Judtson, it's perfect. I can't imagine how it could be any better. Send it!"

After a moment's hesitation, he shrugged. "All right." Turning the laptop back toward himself, he asked for the recipient's email address. Kelsey read it off Scott's message and he typed it in, reading it back to her before clicking the mouse once to send the message.

"Okay. It's on its way."

The two gathered up the laptops and the remnants of their lunch, and stood. With a casual look around to ensure that no one other than Romeo was watching them, Judtson dropped his computer into a nearby trash can, and they crossed the wide grassy area to the spot where their guardian angel was waiting. Kelsey tossed a white paper sack to Romeo and handed over a drink cup. "Here's lunch."

He opened the bag. "Thanks."

Joining him on the low wall, they waited in the shadows. The vigil was not a long one; within forty minutes they saw three black SUVs converge on the Student Union building, tires tearing ruts in the grass as the trucks came to haphazard halts and men spilled out from the vehicles.

The agents fanned out. Some entered the building, while others circled around it.

"That was fast," observed Judtson.

"Doesn't take long to backtrack the ISP to see where your email came from," answered Kelsey.

"I think this proves we're right about him." Judtson pointed at the trash can. "Look, they found the laptop."

Two Feds were standing at the receptacle, one of them pulling out the brand-new computer as the other spoke into his radio. Romeo observed, as the others arrived and congregated on the patio, "We'd better get out of here before they spread the search."

They rose and surreptitiously cut between two buildings to the lot where their rental was parked.

▽

Several miles from the campus, they pulled into a McDonald's parking lot. Staying within the vehicle, Kelsey opened her laptop, the charger still plugged into the dashboard, and turned it on. As Judtson waited for the boot-up sequence to complete, he stared out at the people entering and leaving the busy restaurant, his mind drifting back to only a few days ago when his life was as normal as theirs appeared. He was surprised to discover that the mundane did not appeal to him.

"Got it!" Kelsey exclaimed.

"What does it say?"

"Let's roll first. I downloaded it. I have no idea if the act of checking emails will lead them to us."

"I thought you said that Scott had that figured out."

She shrugged. "He used a remote server to retrieve it…turned it into an image file and re-sent it to my new email instead of yours…but better safe than sorry."

She had already switched off the Wi-Fi transponder, shut down the laptop, and closed the lid as Romeo sped out of the lot. After three traffic signals were between them and their last stop, she restarted the device. After once again waiting through the process, she broke into a broad grin, "He wants to meet. He agreed to our terms."

Chapter 39

T HE BIG ENGINE WHINED IN PROTEST as the rental truck climbed the steep incline. Romeo followed Judtson's directions through the narrow, winding residential streets until he found the address. As they approached the Victorian-style house, which appeared as if it had been carved into the side of the hill, Kelsey spotted Scott standing on the wide front porch, waiting. These old homes, built before the widespread popularity of automobiles, offered no driveways or garages, so Romeo parked as far off the lane as possible, and the three exited the SUV.

Kelsey, despite her limp, was the first to reach the steps. "Did you get them?"

As an answer, Scott dangled the key ring, the realtor's yellow paper tag still attached.

Judtson joined them on the porch. "Have you looked around yet?"

"Yeah. This place is great. How old did you say it was?"

"As I recall from the time I stayed here, almost a hundred years."

The quartet walked inside, led by Judtson. "Back when the Copper Queen Mine was at its peak, Bisbee was a bustling place. At one point, it was the largest town in the Arizona Territory. In fact, it was the biggest city between St. Louis and San Francisco and was on the tour routes for all of the famous stars of the day. There was a distinct duality here. The mine owners and their managers, as well as the merchants, bankers, and others of their class, lived in these houses. In the evenings, they went to the opera house or the theater. All of their homes and businesses were modeled after European styles."

Kelsey followed Judtson closely, her eyes darting from the architectural features to the ornate furniture and decor provided with the rental of the home. "This is amazing."

"At the other end of this canyon were the residences for the miners. Not nearly as grand. Quite basic, in fact. And the workers spent their evenings in the saloons and brothels of Brewery Gulch. Back in the day, it was a quite rowdy part of town, an area to be avoided by the upper crust."

Romeo broke in, "I hate to interrupt the tour, but why did you pick this place for the meeting?"

Judtson stopped walking. "This was one of the buildings I actually stayed in when I did the cable show on ghosts. I know it well. Plus, I think that since it is so hard to get to, it might pose some difficulties for the other side."

"There are pluses and minuses," conceded Romeo. "That street we came up is barely wide enough for two cars to pass. The terrain all around us is steep. The other homes are far enough away."

"And that road up is the only way here. It dead-ends about five hundred yards past this place."

"That helps. On the other hand," Romeo continued, "because of the topo and the trees, there are about a hundred places a man could hide himself. It all allows opportunity to sneak up and get fairly close. Ideal for two or three snipers, working as a team, to set up."

"To do that, they would need enough advance time, wouldn't they?"

"Yes."

Judtson nodded. A slight smile playing across his face, he remarked, "I'm not the expert, you are. However, there is one other amenity this place offers which might just make the difference."

▽

The antique train shuddered and wobbled its way out through the portal of the Queen Mine, coming to a slow stop at the loading platform. Wilbur Deel, the tour guide, eased himself from the driver's platform and turned to face the group of tourists as they disembarked from the cars.

"Please leave your helmets, lamps, and slickers on the table. Make sure you turn off the lights before you do. Just because *your* work shift is over doesn't mean the next crew won't be needing them. You leave 'em on, I'll have to tell the foreman and he'll dock your pay."

The tourists chuckled at his comment.

"I want to thank all of you for joining me today on this little ride through the place where I worked my entire adult life. I hope you had a good time and you'll come back to see us again. And tell your friends."

He watched as the twenty-eight guests unhooked the rechargeable battery packs from their waists, switched off the attached flashlights, and removed the bright yellow raincoats provided at the beginning of the tour. Deel moved along the table, making certain all of the lights were extinguished. Four of his passengers approached, thanking him for the tour, and as he spoke to the last of them, he noticed a man in his thirties, hanging back and waiting.

When the two of them were alone on the platform, the stranger approached, extending his hand. "Hello, Mr. Deel. I'm Saylor Costello."

They shook hands. "What can I do for you, Mr. Costello?"

Saylor grinned, hoping to put the guide at ease. "I was hoping you had a few minutes to talk."

Deel laughed. "Young man, I retired from this mine years ago. Other than the two tours a day I do here, I've got all the time in the world."

"Is there somewhere we can go for a little privacy?"

The old-timer swung his head back and forth, surveying the platform and the adjacent steel building containing the ticket booth, mining exhibits, and a rock shop. "The next tour isn't for a couple hours. It looks like you and me are the only folks here at the moment. Talk away."

"Good enough. I hope you'll forgive my prying, but while I was nosing around earlier, I found out that your wife is having some health problems."

Deel's eyes narrowed suspiciously. "I hope you aren't here to talk about selling me a burial plot or cremation or something. Her medical bills have already wiped us out. If that's your purpose, this little chat just ended."

"No! Not at all. I'm here because I might be able to help."

The retired miner was still leery. "How so?"

Relieved at the slight opening, Saylor plunged forward. "Two ways, actually. First of all, I'm a physician. Anything I can personally do to treat her, I would be happy to, at no charge. And second, I have a friend who is quite wealthy. You might have heard of him. Judtson Kent."

Deel nodded. "Sure have. He was here in Bisbee a while back. Didn't meet him, but Laura over at the Bisbee Grille did. She said he was a pretty nice man."

"That he is. Judtson's my best friend."

"And I suppose you're telling me that he heard about my plight, felt sorry, and now wants to give me a hand, like he's Oprah or something."

"No. That isn't it, sir. Actually, we need a favor in return."

The old guide's eyes narrowed again. "This favor...it wouldn't be illegal, would it?"

Saylor allowed himself a short laugh. "Not strictly speaking, Wilbur."

"Not strictly speaking? That sounds a little hedgy. Does anyone get hurt?"

"No. As a matter of fact, the reason we need your help is to make sure no one does get hurt. Or worse."

The man paused and Saylor was about to embellish his sales pitch, when he was cut off. "How much is your pal thinking about giving me?"

Saylor told him. Hearing the sum, Deel's eyes widened.

▽

The sun had set behind the Mule Mountains more than an hour earlier and, despite the fact that it was late summer, the temperature had already dropped to a comfortable coolness on the porch where Judtson sat alone, his boots propped atop the ornate wood railing. The silence of the evening was pierced by the soft squeak of the springs on the screen door. Turning, he saw Kelsey emerging from the house, using her back to hold the door open as she carried two tall iced teas. He jumped up and relieved her of the drinks, and the two sat down side by side, facing the streetlight-speckled vista of Tombstone Canyon.

She took a sip from her glass, then asked quietly, "Worried about tomorrow?"

"Of course I am. Aren't you?"

"Uh-huh. Probably not as worried as Romeo. But it's his job to worry."

He chuckled. "Kelsey, anything could happen tomorrow. Are you sure you're going to be able to handle it? You know, with your injured leg."

Her voice was overly firm. "Don't worry about me. Besides, is there anyone else in the group who could pull off my part?" Judtson saw a twinkle in her eyes as she answered him. "Are we ready?"

"As ready as we can be," he grunted expressively.

She sank deeper into the padded chair and guardedly propped her leg onto the lower rung of the porch railing. Neither spoke. Both wanted to become imbued with as much of the peacefulness as they could from the surroundings. The lushness of the mountaintop canyon bred a menagerie quite unlike the desert denizens to which Judtson was so acclimated. Immersed in his reverie, he could not help but jump at the sudden sound of an animal scurrying through the brush.

Kelsey chuffed. "Squirrel."

"What?"

She broke into laughter. "No, I wasn't calling you 'Squirrel.' That's what you just heard...a squirrel."

Her childlike giggle, as well as her comment, tickled him and he, too, began to laugh.

Kelsey caught her breath. "Are you ever going to tell me about that nickname?"

"No."

"Why?"

"Because."

"It's something embarrassing, isn't it?"

"Not going to say."

"I bet I can find out."

He turned and faced her. "Don't."

Instantly regretting the abruptness of his comment, he added, "Please?"

She stared at him in the darkness before releasing a soft sigh. "Okay. I guess."

Another brief silence passed until Kelsey changed the subject. "I'm still not sure how tomorrow is going to fix things."

"What do you mean?"

"Well, everything that was being discovered, by Carlos and Chris and Bal and...everyone, was pointing toward something a lot different from the government. Something much bigger and spookier. What good is confronting Samuel Beckleman going to do?"

"Kelsey, that's who we keep bumping into. According to Ben, the men at Wheeler's...and at the silo...were from Homeland Security, driving SUVs, not flying saucers. If we were up against some space aliens with advanced powers, then why have we been thwarted every step of the way by run-of-the-mill men dressed in clichéd black suits?"

"Simple. They're slaves, puppets, zombies, I don't know. Something like that."

"That doesn't make sense."

She huffed at his retort. "After all of this, you still don't believe, do you?"

Judtson shrugged in the darkness. Taking a long drink from his tea first, he answered, "I'm not certain what to believe." Before she could tear into him verbally, he continued, "Look, I'm not saying that Carlos didn't discover something amazing. He did. And, remember, I was the one about to go public with it. I'm not saying all of the others weren't onto some kind of revelation or truth, either. I *have* changed my mind. About a lot things. I do believe that there are some aspects to our past which the so-called mainstream experts have been dead wrong about, and that they've even been guilty of covering up the truth. But as far as what's happening now...what has been happening to all of us...it has all been pretty damn explainable. And I think that we're going to get to the bottom of it tomorrow, one way or another."

"What about the mind control they did to you and the others?" Kelsey protested. "That isn't off-the-shelf technology."

"Simply because we haven't heard of it is not proof that it doesn't exist. Our scientists could have cooked up anything secretly. Didn't you ever read about the MKUltra program?"

"Well, yes, but...."

"No 'buts.' For three decades our government researched methods for mind control. Plain and simple. That was the object of their work. And even though it was *officially* shut down in the seventies, that doesn't guarantee that it wasn't continued as some sort of a 'black ops' program. The idea never completely went away. The Administration recently poured a hundred million into the study of how the mind works. Who knows what they've come up with? We have no clue as to what they have. No, I think that if all goes according to plan tomorrow, we'll be face to face with the real enemy...the actual nemesis we've been battling. And he isn't going to be grey with gigantic eyes."

He waited for her emotional response. When none came, Judtson asked, "Are you disappointed?"

"What do you mean?"

"Just what I said. If we find out that everything is some mundane, ugly government program, you're going to be sad that it isn't actually an intergalactic conspiracy, aren't you?"

She thought for a moment. "A little, I guess."

▽

Assembled in the former dining room of the nurses' quarters were Judtson, Kelsey, Saylor, Scott, Jimmy, Lisa, Romeo, Matt, and Ricky. The early morning sun, having just broken over the peaks of the ridge to the east, cast a dramatic beam through the partially open blinds of the window, providing a lattice of light in the room.

Sitting at the head of the table, Judtson read over his notes one final time before looking up. "Saylor, are you ready?"

His friend nodded. "I've got the old truck and trailer from Wilbur."

"Ricky?"

"Ready!"

"Matt?"

"Oh, yeah."

"Jimmy?"

"Damn right."

"Lisa?"

"Sure. My part's easy."

He smiled at Romeo. "I know I don't need to ask you."

His face an unreadable mask, he answered, "I'm ready."

Judtson surveyed the group. "Unless anyone has any last-minute thoughts about this, I guess we're set."

No one spoke.

He then directed his attention to Scott, who had his laptop open. "Send the invitation."

▽

Jimmy Meade was crouched uncomfortably beside a tree as he watched Highway 80 at the junction to Sierra Vista. From his vantage point, he was able to see the approach of vehicles from either route. The time, he noted, was 8:09. Squinting in the bright daylight, he saw a black SUV as it came around the bend, followed by a second and then a third and finally a fourth. He seized the high-powered binoculars dangling on his chest and quickly focused on the front windshield of the lead vehicle. As it drew closer, he pulled the walkie-talkie from his shirt pocket and keyed the microphone.

"Beckleman is in the lead. Repeat. Target is in the front SUV."

Ricky, sitting in the rental pickup and positioned less than half a mile down the road, acknowledged Meade's message. The engine already running, he waited, easing the truck forward to the edge of the road.

Within seconds, the lead SUV came around the curve and Ricky pressed the button on his radio, alerting, "They're coming," and heard Saylor's voice in return, acknowledging his warning.

He stepped down hard on the accelerator, the rear tires of his truck churning in the dirt and spitting a plume of pebbles and sand behind. The black SUV had to swerve slightly to avoid him as he merged into the narrow lane and fell in line behind it. A single glance at the rearview mirror showed that the other three vehicles were tight on his tail, the driver of the nearest showing frustration at the unwelcome intrusion into their caravan. He would have certainly wanted to pass Ricky, but they had reached a serpentine portion of the mountain highway with essentially no shoulders along the edges of the pavement.

Easing off on the gas, Ricky widened the gap between his truck and the first SUV, adding an additional two or three car lengths. Before the driver in front could respond and slow down to close the gap, he rounded a turn and passed a road maintenance shack on the right, situated less than fifty yards outside the entrance of Mule Pass Tunnel. Pulling out of the parking area in front of the shack was a bright red heavy-duty pickup truck hauling a long flatbed trailer, loaded high with cords of firewood. The driver of the front SUV blared his horn at the interloper, while veering to his left until the wheels on the driver's side bit into the narrow dirt strip alongside the asphalt, barely avoiding impact. Jerking the steering wheel back to the right, he was able to get all four tires on the pavement mere feet ahead of the tunnel entrance.

Ricky, feeling a flash of uncertainty as to whether he had buckled his shoulder harness in his haste earlier, hit the brakes and wrenched the steering wheel, putting the rental into a sideways slide as it slammed into the red truck. There was a deafening crash and the screech of tearing metal. The flatbed flopped onto its side, scattering the entire load of wood over the narrow highway. The two trucks came to a shuddering halt, and Ricky was aware of the closest of the trailing black SUVs stopping only inches from his door. His hand steadier than he expected, Ricky pulled out his cell phone and called 9-1-1.

The driver of the black SUV trapped behind the accident, jumped out and, ignoring Ricky and the occupant of the red truck, dashed around the end of the flatbed trailer and peered into the tunnel. Seeing the red brake lights flare on the SUV carrying his boss, he trotted into the dimness as the driver dropped the vehicle into reverse and backed up. As they met, Beckleman, sitting in the front seat, powered down his window.

The agent, winded from his sprint, was still panting. "We're...we're blocked."

Beckleman glanced at his watch and saw that it was 8:17. "Is there another way into town?"

His driver tapped the dashboard screen and, after a minute, answered, "Yes. They'll have to backtrack, circle around, and come in on the Douglas Highway."

"How long will that take?"

"Looks like about an hour."

At that, Beckleman turned back to the agent standing outside his door. "Get rolling."

"Sir, this was a set-up to separate us from you."

"Probably."

"Why don't you let me ram my way through? We might lose one vehicle in the process, but at least we'll be with you."

"Not a bad ide...."

As he was speaking, their ears were suddenly pierced with the scream of a siren from the far end of the tunnel.

Beckleman shouted over the din. "THAT'S OUT! BACKTRACK AND CIRCLE AROUND! HURRY!"

The sheriff's car shot past them, braking abruptly before reaching the tangle of vehicles and wood at the tunnel's mouth. The agent turned and ran back to his vehicle, climbing in and jockeying it around to avoid being detained by the officer, the two accompanying vehicles following directly behind.

▽

Ricky watched the three black SUVs depart, and opened his door, calmly climbing out and keying his radio. "Number one is on his way. The others are taking the scenic route."

He heard Romeo's voice come back to him. "Roger that."

Saylor, unable to open the driver's side door of the red truck, slid over and exited on the passenger side. As he neared Ricky, he asked, "You all right?"

Ricky seemed to take a moment to check on the individual elements of his body before answering. "Yes. I'm good. You?"

Saylor nodded. "Neither one of us was going that fast. I'm okay other than my back. Hurts like hell. Wonder why the air bag didn't deploy."

"Only works if you hit something with the front of the vehicle. We slammed into each other's side."

Eyeing the sheriff's deputy as he approached, Ricky muttered, "We're going to be here for a while."

▽

The lone SUV climbed the steep street and stopped in front of the house. The vehicle's doors opened and five men, including Beckleman, emerged. The four others were dressed in the mandatory black suits. One of the four was carrying a large zippered bag. The remaining three pulled out their pistols and began surveying the surroundings, when they heard the unmistakable sound of an automatic weapon's bolt being pulled back. Reacting, they saw Romeo as he stepped out from behind the trunk of a massive tree. He had the muzzle of his weapon trained upon Beckleman's chest.

"I'm not asking you gents to drop your weapons. That won't be necessary. But you do need to holster them."

Since they did not immediately comply, he loudly barked, "NOW!"

Receiving a nod of permission from their boss, the men put their guns away.

"Mr. Jones, I presume."

Romeo nodded. "And you must be Beckleman."

"Quite a clever plan this morning. I'm impressed. You instruct us yesterday to wait in Tucson for your word. This morning, you give us less than two hours to make an hour-and-a-half trip to Bisbee, not transmitting the final address until we're through the tunnel. And as we are driving here, you stage that accident at the tunnel, cutting off the rest of my men."

"Just attempting to even up the odds a bit – which is exactly what we're going to do before you go inside that house."

There was a moment of concern in the Homeland Security chief's eyes as he heard Romeo's words.

"I'm not going to shoot any of you, if that's what you're thinking, Beckleman. That's more your style. There are less drastic ways to level the field."

The Army Ranger reached around behind his back with his free hand and unhooked a pouch from his belt, tossing it to the closest agent. "Inside that are some handcuffs. Beckleman, pick out which one of your men will come inside with you. The other three get to play 'Ring Around the Rosy.'"

Beckleman turned and nodded at one of the men, who stepped forward two paces.

"He's your choice? Okay. You…the one going in with us…take the pouch. You other three, step over here."

As Romeo spoke, he carefully moved away from the tree where he had been hiding. When the agents neared, he explained, "The three of you get to hold hands, spread out around that trunk, and hug it like you love it, like you're trying to pull it out of the ground. You with that zipper bag, put it down." He momentarily shifted the barrel toward the fourth agent. "Cuff them together in a daisy chain."

The man with the pouch began speak to his boss. "Sir, I don't think...."

"DO IT!" boomed Romeo, his voice echoing in the canyon.

Seeing another curt nod from his supervisor, the man circled around the tree, handcuffing each of his cohorts to the next. After they were lashed together in a closed ring, Romeo ordered, "Now, reach back in that pouch and pull out three sets of leg irons. Hook your pals together at the ankles."

The agent followed the orders.

"Drop the pouch and move back. Matt!"

Wheeler stepped out from around the corner of the house. "Matt, check that our friend here didn't leave those cuffs too loose. I'm sure he wouldn't do it on purpose, but we should check anyway."

Moving forward wordlessly, Matt went around the tree and, at every connection, squeezed the handcuffs hard, coaxing an additional two or three *clacks* from each one.

"Now the legs, Matt."

He repeated the circuit and made certain the fetters were all as snug as they should be, before he faced Romeo. "Anything else?"

"One more thing. Check the contents of their zipper bag."

Wheeler opened the nylon valise and pulled out two objects. "These are both used to sweep a room for bugs."

"Is that all that's in there?"

"That's it. Do you need me any longer?"

"No. We're good. Thanks."

Wheeler pivoted on his heel and walked away, briskly heading down the lane on foot.

Romeo addressed the lone unshackled agent. "Take the sweeping gear and go inside. Check the place, but leave your gun out here."

The man again looked at his boss and, receiving silent permission, snatched up the bag, placed his pistol on the ground, and trotted into the house.

Romeo and Beckleman stood silently, waiting several minutes until the agent returned. "It's clean."

"Pick up your gun and holster it," Romeo instructed.

Surprised, Beckleman said, "I thought you'd want him unarmed when we went in."

With a single shake of his head, Romeo answered, "Not at all. He keeps his. I keep mine. Only difference is, mine stays out. Now, if *you're* carrying, we can't have that."

The Cabinet member slowly reached inside his jacket and pulled out a Glock, holding the butt with his thumb and forefinger.

Romeo smiled. "Nicely done. Lay it down. Right there is fine."

The man bent and gently placed the pistol on the mat of pine needles at his feet.

With the barrel of his rifle, Romeo gestured toward the porch steps. "Okay, let's go in. Your hosts are waiting."

Chapter 40

JUDTSON WAS SEATED BESIDE KELSEY at the dining room table as the three men came in, with Beckleman first, his agent second, and Romeo trailing. Taking a moment to size up the bureaucrat, Judtson was surprised at how unctuous a presence he projected. Perhaps five-seven or five-eight, the Cabinet member was slight of build, his blue pin-striped suit fitting him loosely. With angular features and gray eyes, he broke from the conservative customs of high-ranking government officials by having long achromatic hair, pulled back into a ponytail.

Rising, Judtson gestured toward a chair at the table and with false cordiality said, "Mr. Secretary, glad you could make it. Please have a seat."

Beckleman sat and nodded to each of them. "Mr. Kent, Miss Batman."

Romeo moved to stand next to the front door so that he could cover both the agent and the secretary.

With an expression of wry amusement at the circumstances, Beckleman began to speak as Judtson sat. "The two of you requested this meeting. I presume that you have an agenda."

Kelsey snorted. "If anybody has an agenda, Beckleman, it's you." She spat out his name as if it were coated with bile.

"Miss Batman," their guest sneered dismissively, "I haven't the foggiest idea what you are talking about."

"Really?" she exclaimed.

Before she could continue, Judtson gently placed his hand on her arm in an ostensibly calming gesture, and spoke. "Sir, over the last several days I myself and several others have received visits from men in attire identical to that of your agent here. In those visits, frequently at gunpoint, we've had a headset forcibly placed upon us...a device which actually altered the way our minds functioned. After we were able to find a way to reverse the effects of the device and were unlucky enough to encounter your men again, they attempted to kill us."

With mocking incredulity, Beckleman laughed. "Honestly? Helmets used for mind control. That's absurd!"

Ignoring the interruption, Judtson resumed, "In fact, when we traveled to the Mojave Desert, your men, posing as Army soldiers, killed Kevin Berry, an unarmed scientist, at point-blank range and attempted to kill both of us, as well as Bal Singh. During a raid your men committed at Miss Batman's missile silo, they killed Al Clarkson in cold blood. He, too, was unarmed. They then planted explosive devices and destroyed the facility. In that same raid at the silo, your men took my friends hostage and later confined them at a FEMA camp."

"Mr. Kent, first off, I have no knowledge of these things."

"You're lying!" shouted Kelsey. "You're the one who sent hit men to my home to kill me in my sleep!"

Patiently waiting for Kelsey to finish, Judtson asked the man, "Then why are you here?"

"Quite simply because I was invited. And because the three of you are wanted in connection with several…issues."

Kelsey again jumped in. "That's beyond ridiculous! Since when does the Secretary of Homeland Security go out to make a bust?"

"Sir," Judtson continued calmly, "we both know that you are here because, in our email to you, we threatened to go public with everything we have uncovered."

His smugness unrelenting, Beckleman responded imperiously, "And what might that be?"

Allowing a momentary glint of frustration to contort his face, Judtson looked at Kelsey. "Maybe you were right. Maybe this is a waste of time."

Disregarding their invitee as though he were not there, she heatedly responded, "I told you! This isn't going to get us anywhere and his goons are going to arrive soon."

Making a visible show of mulling it over, Judtson sighed resignedly and nodded at her. A maniacal grin instantly sprang across her face and she exclaimed, "Yes! Let me do it. Can I do it?"

Judtson studied Kelsey, impressed by her performance.

"What are you two talking…?"

Before Beckleman could finish his sentence, Kelsey swung around and backhanded him across the face. "SHUT UP!"

She returned her attention to Judtson, who shook his head. "I don't think it should be you. We'd better have Romeo do it."

"No! Dammit, this is probably the sonofabitch who killed my father." Her voice rose in pitch. "I want to do it! Judtson, please. I *need* to do it."

Feigning reluctance, he reached under the table and pulled out a 9mm Beretta, sliding it toward her on the polished tabletop. "All right."

"Hey!" Beckleman yelped.

Acting as if she were a child receiving her yearned-for toy at Christmas, Kelsey snatched up the Beretta and, in a fluid, practiced motion, cocked it and snapped off the safety. Just as she aimed it at the man, two things happened at once. The bureaucrat leapt to his feet, sending his chair skittering backward, and the lone agent behind him shouted, "Stop!" and grabbed for his pistol. His hand never even clutched the grip before the butt of Romeo's rifle slammed into the back of his head, knocking him cold.

Kelsey jumped up from her chair, holding the Beretta forward with both hands, and glanced over Beckleman's shoulder. "Romeo, move. I don't want you to get hit with a bullet coming out of the back of this bastard."

The secretary was frozen in place. His hands, held out from his sides, were shaking. "Don't. Please," he uttered, his voice quavering badly with the two words.

Kelsey smiled scornfully at him. "Why shouldn't I? If anyone's ever deserved it, it's you!"

"What do you want? What is it? Whatever it is…."

"WHAT DO I WANT?" Her voice almost a shriek, she stepped closer. "I want to shoot you. And you know what? I want to shoot you a *lot*. And I mean, a lot of times. Over and over and over again. Until *this* clip is empty. And then I'll put in another clip and I'll shoot you some more. And I'm going to do my absolute best to make sure you stay alive long enough for each and every one of them!"

Her speech climaxing in a crescendo, he could feel her breath on his face.

Judtson moved to where the two were standing. "Kelsey…."

Hearing the sound of his voice, she spun around, pointing the gun at his chest. "WHAT?"

Judtson, his eyes widening, took a small step back. "Whoa! Kelsey, maybe…."

"MAYBE NOTHING!"

Beckleman, seizing upon a glimmer of hope, once again sputtered, "What is it? What do you want? I'll do it."

"Kelsey," Judtson urged soothingly, "what's the harm in giving him a minute or two? Maybe he'll tell us the truth."

"He's not going to! He can't. He's a pathological liar," she railed, wild-eyed.

Truly unnerved by her intensity, Judtson stammered, "Just… just a few minutes. What difference does it make?"

Her face was a bright red, her breathing so rapid she appeared to be on the verge of hyperventilating. Both men watched as she exerted her will and slowly reined in the rampant emotions. After several successive long, deep breaths, she muttered, "All right. Just a few minutes," and lowered the pistol.

Beckleman, his face and scalp saturated with sweat, appeared bewildered at the sudden reprieve, and blurted, "What do you want to know?"

Judtson shifted into the spot directly in front of the man, causing Kelsey to begrudgingly move slightly to the side. "All of it. Why you mind-controlled us. Why you killed Berry. Why you took my friends to the camp. Everything."

"And why you killed my father!"

"Killed your father? Why would I do that? He was of no consequence!"

Kelsey jumped toward him. "No conseque…?"

Judtson stepped between the two. "Kelsey! Let him talk. Let him talk."

His eyes darting from one to the other, the secretary licked his lips and began. "You were getting too close. We had to stop you. If your transformation had worked, hadn't been undone, none of the…other things would have been necessary."

Kelsey stood rigidly silent as Judtson conducted the interrogation. "Close to what?"

"The truth."

"Stop playing verbal games, Beckleman! What truth? That there has been some kind of a massive government cover-up about a visit from aliens?"

"No. It's the opposite. That there hasn't."

His answer stopped Judtson cold for a moment. "What do you mean? That there hasn't been a cover-up?"

"Exactly. There has been no cover-up, because there has never been anything to cover up."

The loud crack of a shot from the Beretta, immediately followed by a horrible shriek of pain from the bureaucrat, hammered Judtson's ears. Confused, he looked at Kelsey, who was staring straight at the man now collapsed on the floor, gripping his leg.

His eyes wide with disbelief and fright, his smug and imperious demeanor shattered, Beckleman howled, "YOU SHOT ME! MY GOD, YOU SHOT ME!"

Her face was cold and fixed as she stepped forward and knelt, leaning close to him. "Beckleman, you're lying."

Confusion, shock, and terror held him in their grasp as the secretary stared up at her incredulously. "No. I'm not. Kent, Villarreal, Ashby, all of you were about to collapse a program we've been maintaining for decades."

Judtson, stunned by his words, moved down to the man's side. "What program? Tell us."

Squeezing his eyes shut in an attempt to block out the neuronal impulses pushing him past his threshold, Beckleman began talking. "Ever since the forties...since Roswell...we've been keeping this whole UFO, 'ancient alien' thing going. It never took much. Most of time it had a life of its own. A whole...a whole lot of people want to believe it. All we had to do was nudge it...feed it occasional morsels! That's the beauty of it."

Kelsey jammed the muzzle of the Beretta against the side of his head. "Explain."

He whimpered pathetically. "It was so easy. Set up a quick flyover. Jettison some unusual debris. Drop flares. Set fires and scorch the earth. And people would be certain they saw a flying saucer crash, or land, or just fly over them. Recently, we started using disguised drones."

"I don't believe you," accused Judtson.

"It's true. We'd stage the incidents. Then we'd swoop in, in the most heavy-handed way possible, and gather up all of the evidence and whisk it away, take it back to Nevada for another day...another show. Please...I need a doctor!"

"No, you don't," snapped Kelsey. "Nevada? Area 51?"

"Yes. Yes. That's where we keep the fake flying saucers and all of the other props for the ruses. Later, we'd release some official explanation which was deliberately full of holes. If the people wouldn't buy our contrived story, then we'd stonewall. Nothing works better...to stir up the conspiracy theory crowd. We would also intentionally lose evidence. Force the public to use the Freedom of Information Act to compel us to reluctantly turn over worthless, dummied-up internal memos with two-thirds of the contents redacted. And all of the crackpots took care of the rest...cooking up an endless stream of theories. It was surprising how well it worked. Hell, we even staged abductions."

"What?"

He nodded jerkily. "We would select people when they were home alone or out in the middle of nowhere. Sometimes even when they *were* with a group but separated from them, on a camping trip or whatever. They would be knocked out with an odorless gas and taken to one of the sets we had created. Actors in alien suits would be standing over them when they awoke, when they were still groggy and dazed from the drug. The role players would perform meaningless medical procedures on them...even implant tiny pieces of metal, stamped to look like chips, somewhere in their bodies. And then return them to where they had been picked up."

"What about the silent flying saucers that supposedly whisked them up?"

"Stealth helicopters with mounted light arrays. They can fly right by you and you can't hear anything. We didn't beam them, just knocked them out."

Judtson shook his head, struggling to make sense of what they were being told. "This is crazy. Why on Earth would the government be doing this?"

Beckleman hesitated. "I...can't."

The barrel of the gun in Kelsey's hand dug deeper into the man's temple. "Talk or die right now, Beckleman. Pick!"

His abject fear burgeoning, the secretary continued, "At first, back in the forties and fifties, it began as a Cold War thing. The Soviets knew there weren't any aliens coming to Earth. So they assumed that the sightings from our hysterical public, plastered all over the newspapers, were reliable eyewitness reports of new technology we had. It forced them to waste billions of rubles on wild-goose chases trying to engineer hardware to match things we didn't even have. Our leaders at the time also realized that it was an excellent way to keep the people distracted from how bad things were, how close we were to a nuclear war with the Russians. And they figured out fairly soon that it had the benefit of actually allowing us to test certain hardware...certain technologies. As long as we mixed in the real tests with the bogus ones, the Soviets were always off-balance."

"What kinds of tests?" she pressed.

"Some of the applications were military...planes and other aerial platforms."

"And the rest?"

"Before long, somebody came up with the idea to use it for medical and...human testing."

"You said the abduction procedures were staged hoaxes."

"They were, at first. But we already had other programs going. There were people who saw the whole UFO program as an opportunity to field-test what they were working on."

"Like MKULTRA?"

Beckleman nodded.

"Good God," muttered Judtson, taking over the questioning. "Exactly what kind of field testing did they do on the public?"

"Mind-control drugs. Actual implants. Various other drugs to produce infertility and other side effects. Whatever the university researchers or defense contractors dreamed up that they thought would be useful against our enemies."

"And this has been going on for more than seventy years?"

"No. Gerald Ford somehow got wind of it during his term and killed the program."

"What do you mean, 'somehow got wind of it'? Weren't Presidents briefed on what was being done under their Administrations?"

A harsh laugh burst from the official's lips. "Not a chance! With the revolving door of seat warmers in the Oval Office, there's no way. You'd be surprised how many long-term projects are kept from the so-called leader of our country. Ford's order to shut it down is an example of why. For God's sake, he wasn't even an elected President and he terminated a three-decade program which was producing amazing results."

"So if it has been shut down since the seventies, why did you come after all of us now?"

It was evident from the look on the man's face that he did not want to continue, so Judtson gave a subtle nod to Kelsey, who took the lead once more. She moved the pistol to Beckleman's leg and jammed the tip of the barrel into the wound, triggering an infantile scream of pain. Moving the now bloody muzzle to his face, she pressed it against his cheek and leaned even closer. "Talk, you bastard."

Panting rapidly, their prisoner brought himself back from the emotional brink. "I reactivated it."

"*You* restarted the program. Why?"

Clenching his teeth briefly, he answered, "As a diversion. As an excuse."

"An excuse for what?"

"I *wanted* the people to believe." He paused as tears streamed down his cheeks. Then, he gulped several successive breaths before resuming. "I wanted them to think that the aliens were real. Not only that they were real, but that they were coming."

Kelsey, her voice so soft Beckleman had to strain to hear it, whispered intensely, "What did you have to gain by that?"

The secretary paused again and Kelsey was about to provide him with another nudge of motivation, when he blurted, "In Phase One someone was going to reveal that the government had always known we were being visited, and had been aggressively, unscrupulously concealing the truth about aliens and UFOs from the American public for decades. Blow the lid off the whole thing."

"And that someone was going to be you?"

"Y…yes."

"You would be considered a crusader…a hero of the people."

Despite his untenable position, a prideful expression passed fleetingly across Beckleman's face, soon returning to a grimace. "Exactly."

"And Phase Two?"

"We were going to escalate. After the…after the initial disclosure that the aliens were real…once that fact had been thoroughly propagated by the complicit media and assimilated by the masses…then with the use of some cutting-edge technology and a few special effects, we were going to convince people that extraterrestrials were returning and that their intentions were not peaceful. Our only option, if we were to survive as a country…to defend ourselves…would be to institute martial law."

The man's words hit Judtson like a sledgehammer, his mind reeling with the ramifications. "All of the bullets stockpiled, the trained and armed non-military corps, the FEMA camps scattered all over the country, gun control, cuts in the military, the armored vehicles purchased by Homeland Security…it was all to prepare for a *permanent* martial law. You were going to nullify the few remaining vestiges of our rights, shred our Constitution, and turn our government into an autocracy, the President into a dictator."

"The President? That buffoon? No. He knew nothing about any of this. I doubt he could understand it if I explained it to him using one-syllable words."

"So…" – Judtson struggled to put all the pieces into the correct order – "it was for you! You were planning a coup where *you* became the new leader."

Beckleman nodded wordlessly.

Judtson's mind whirled as the puzzle took shape in his mind's eye. "I have to hand it to you. The Secret Service, Border Patrol, Coast Guard, as well as TSA, ICE, and FEMA have already been placed under you. The Patriot Act and a slew of executive orders continue to heap more and more unchecked power directly into your lap. Add to that your new popularity with the populace and…."

"That moron in the White House would no longer be the most powerful man on Earth. I would."

There was a soft, shuffling sound from the front of the house, and Judtson looked up to see that Romeo, who had been listening to everything, had taken a step forward, his face contorted by fury. Shifting his glance from Romeo to Kelsey, he saw, as her eyes blazed at the Homeland Security chief, a palpable hatred. And he also noticed that her finger, poised on the trigger of the Beretta, was taut. He worried whether she was even aware of how much pressure she was pulling as she pointed the barrel at the man's cheek.

In a soft voice, he murmured, "Kelsey."

It took a moment for her eyes to pull away from Beckleman and connect with Judtson's. When they met, his gaze flitted down to the gun in her hand, meaningfully. She followed the movement and, thankfully, her index finger relaxed and slowly lifted off the trigger, to rest on the outside guard. Breathing a sign of relief, he returned his attention to the secretary.

"I still don't understand why you came after all of us…why you killed Berry and Clarkson."

"Simple, Mr. Kent. Baalbek, Puma Punku, NASA, monoatomic gold, inoculations used for implants…all were fictions created by us, made from whole cloth and promulgated and nurtured by us, with the intention of using them as part of the upcoming plan. The last thing we needed was to have a credible, authoritative group announcing that it was all fake…a con, just as we were about to tell the world it was real."

"But how…?"

Beckleman interrupted Judtson's question, his words coming rapid-fire. "The mysterious Baalbek stones Villarreal discovered, and the Puma Punku connection, were all planted by us. The saucer Meade and the others saw at Edwards was built by us. Eisenhower did come and did go inside the tent, emerging hours later and telling an airman about the meeting. Good God, Kent, did you really believe that could happen? That, in a million years, he would have told his *Jeep driver* something which would shake up the whole world? And the epidemiological data about immunizations that Falt was shown by our person at the CDC were all distorted by us to feed the conspiracy theory machine. And the photos Copeland found and presented to his boss, who immediately and clumsily destroyed the evidence and created the appearance of a cover-up? Those photos, the *first* ones he showed to his supervisor…they were the altered photos. The real pictures were the ones later substituted.

"It was all a house of cards and we knew it. As long as fringe nutcases poked around ineffectually, it served our purposes. But when you and the others began investigating, I knew it was only a matter of time until you found the first clue as to the truth. Then the rest would fall, hard and fast. We couldn't have you debunking it all before, or during, Phase One."

Romeo pressed his earpiece deeper for a moment, listening. "Judtson."

Not wanting to be interrupted at this point, Judtson looked up impatiently. He saw concern on Romeo's face as the man tilted his head in the direction of the front porch. Standing abruptly, he followed the Ranger outside. The moment they were no longer in earshot, Romeo told him, "Meade just called in. There are three military helicopters on the way, no doubt carrying strike teams."

"How much time do we have?"

"Not more than a minute or two."

Judtson reentered the house and knelt beside the injured detainee. He saw that Kelsey was watching him inquisitively and he subtly tilted his eyes upward, hoping to convey what was coming.

She must have understood, and urgently resumed the questioning. "What about my father? Why did you kill him?"

"We didn't. We had nothing to do with that."

So quickly that her hand was a blur, she swung the pistol away and brought it back hard, whipping him across the face. "Don't lie to me. I know you did it. Why?"

Blood streaming into his mouth from a cut across the side of his nose, Beckleman sputtered and spit, trying to clear his throat. Turning his head to the side, he finally answered, "I swear I don't know anything about it. Maybe…maybe one of my people acted alone."

Before she could manage a retort, she heard the distinctive sound of the approaching helicopters. Romeo stepped inside from the porch and announced unnecessarily, "They're almost here."

Turning back to their captive, Judtson could see that the man heard them, too. A slight smile modified the previous tortured expression on the secretary's face. Coughing out more blood, he uttered defiantly, "Looks like your time is up. Private contractors with Special Forces training will be dropping out of the sky and onto your heads in moments. And the rest of my team shouldn't be far behind."

The thundering sounds of the blades were getting closer. Judtson stood, grabbing Kelsey's arm.

"Come on. We need to go to the basement. We can hold them off there."

She jerked her head up fiercely. "No! I want an answer!"

Romeo slammed the front door and bolted it, then trotted to her side and roughly seized her other arm. "Kelsey, now."

With a final hateful glare at Beckleman, she allowed herself to be raised to her feet, and the three dashed across the room and opened a door off the kitchen, shutting and locking it behind them. Their former hostage rolled over until he was facedown, and forced himself up, supported by both of his arms and one good leg. Awkwardly, he crawled the short distance to the spot where his man lay unconscious, as the whumping sounds from directly above shook the old house. Turning the agent over, he slapped his face repeatedly, shouting for him to wake up. Just as the lieutenant's eyes began to flutter open, one of the side windows exploded inward, the barrage of shattered glass followed by a man clad in a black assault uniform. A second later, another man came crashing through the front door.

"THEY'RE IN THE BASEMENT! THROUGH THE KITCHEN!" shouted Beckleman, pointing in the direction of the door where the three had disappeared.

As the two team members swiftly crossed the room, two more entered from the rear of the house, and they all converged at the basement entrance. The team leader, before ordering his men to batter the antique door, turned back to face the Homeland Security chief, who was still near the front of the house. "Sir, what are the ROE?"

Beckleman, holding the bleeding gunshot wound in his leg, looked up and screamed, "KILL EVERY ONE OF THEM! I WANT THEM ALL DEAD!"

Nodding acknowledgment of his orders, the leader turned to the two who were holding the ram at the ready. "Let's go."

The duo slammed the weighted ram into the aged wood, splintering it instantly. The moment the opening was clear, a third man pulled the pin on a flash-bang grenade and tossed it down the steps into the darkness below. Another threw a second. They pulled back and protected their ears as the two devices exploded below. The moment the second grenade detonated, the team leader, holding his AK-47 at the ready, dashed down the stairs, followed seconds later by the rest of the team.

Chapter 41

===

JENKINS, THE LEAD MAN ON THE ASSAULT TEAM, returned from the basement to find the medic in the kitchen, having finished with Beckleman. "How is he?"

Out of earshot of their superior, the PA rolled his eyes in disgust and grunted, "Just a graze. I could've patched him up with a butterfly Band-Aid."

Before he could say anything else, their boss shouted, "I didn't hear any gunfire. Did you get them?"

"No, sir. No one was down there," Jenkins replied, moving toward the dining room. "Are you sure that's where...?"

"Yes, I'm certain! What do you mean, no one was there?"

"It's a fairly small basement, more of a root cellar with a bedrock floor. No place for them to hide and no other way out."

"Help me up."

Chancing a quick smirk back at the PA, Jenkins assisted the secretary, and the two hobbled to the kitchen and down the stairs to the basement. It was just as his man had described...no more than a ten-by-ten room with a raw stone floor and a steel manhole cover, set into a collar and cemented in place. "You fool. They went down that manhole. It must be a sewer or something."

"I already thought of that, sir. It hasn't been opened in years. The cover can't be budged."

Bewildered, Beckleman thought for a moment. "Idiot. They had this planned. That cover must have been off before I arrived. When the three of them ran down here, they hightailed it into that sewer, slid the cover back on, and somehow secured it from below."

Jenkins was staring at the lid, not saying anything, until his boss barked, "Get something, whatever you need to break that open. Follow them!"

▽

The absolute silence was broken by a vague scratching, shuffling jumble of sounds, echoed and multiplied by the surrounding rock. The pure and utter darkness was pierced by the jittering, swinging shafts of yellowish light from five wildly swaying lamps. The shadowy figures, formed into a rough single file, walked while hunched forward, neither dallying nor hurrying in their progress.

Kelsey, who had not spoken a single word since their escape, was second in the procession. She took each step forward as if dazed...in a trance. Judtson came up from behind. "Kelsey, are you all right?"

The old man leading the way peeked over his shoulder. "Claustrophobic, miss?"

She did not answer either of them, continuing her plodding pace and staring down at the dusty floor.

Worriedly, Judtson asked, "Wilbur, how far do we have to go?"

He answered without turning back. "When you're in the mine, distance is a strange thing. You can be a hundred feet from the portal, but it's a mile walk to get to it." As he spoke, he arrived at a split, the third they had encountered since beginning their trek, and, without pausing, veered to the left. The others followed. "Are we still dragging the tanglebush behind us?"

From the rear of the line, Lisa's voice called out, "You bet, Wilbur."

"Good. Don't want to leave any trail. All those years I worked this mine, that was the trick I used every time I wanted to slip away for a little sip. There are so many old drifts and crosscuts down here. It's a real maze." The old-timer chuckled at the recollection. "The foreman never found me, not once."

Judtson edged past Kelsey, turning sideways to get around her in the narrow passage. As he moved ahead, he noticed that she did not even glance at him. "Wilbur, where does that other tunnel go, the one we just passed?"

"It's not a tunnel. It's a drift. And that last one followed a vein that inclined down to a lower level. If those fellows behind us make it this far and take that one, they'd better bring their scuba gear."

"Scuba gear?"

"Yep. It's flooded. Back when we still worked this mine, we ran pumps twenty-four hours a day to keep out the groundwater. Now that all we do is give tours, those pumps are turned off. All of the levels below this one are filled right up."

"Why is it called a 'drift'? I thought it was a tunnel."

"Beats me. Probably because the direction of it follows a vein of ore instead of going in a straight line. It drifts. There's not a tunnel in this mine."

"I don't understand. I thought...."

"A tunnel is only a tunnel if it goes through and through. Comes out to daylight on the other side. If it's a dead end, it's called an 'adit.'"

"Ouch!" The exclamation came from Romeo. "Why does this ceiling have to be so low?"

Deel chuckled. "Sorry about that. Didn't think to bring helmets. You're a tall fellow. This is the older section of the mine. Dug before machinery. It was all hand cut. Backbreaking, slow work. It was so difficult they didn't go an inch higher than they had to. Just high enough for the mules pulling the ore wagons. And by the way, it's not called a ceiling. It's called the 'back.'"

"I don't give a damn what it's called," Romeo muttered, his deep voice carrying easily to the front of the line. "By the time we get out of here, I'm not going to have any skin left on my head."

▽

Working with hastily assembled tools, the assault team hammered and pried at the steel cover. Quickly discovering they were not going to loosen it from the steel ring, they focused on the decades-old concrete which was securing the collar to the stone floor. With three men combining their weight on the long pry bar, the ring and cover flipped free of the opening, crashing loudly onto the bedrock beside the hole.

Jenkins lay on his stomach, his head suspended over the opening, and shined his high-intensity halogen flashlight downward. After only a moment, he rolled onto his back and sat up, addressing Beckleman, who was resting on the steps.

"Sir, that isn't a sewer."

"What is it, then?"

"I don't know. Some kind of shaft. Could be a mine shaft."

"You think? This *is* a mining town. Get down there with some men, and follow them. I'll send another team to that mine tour entrance I saw right as we got to this godforsaken town. That might be where they are going to come out."

▽

The tow truck was pulling the rental pickup off the highway, clearing both lanes. Ricky and Saylor had only moments earlier finished with the deputy, when Meade, who had been stuck in the backed-up line of cars waiting to get through, arrived and they climbed inside his van.

▽

"You can stop brushing out our trail now. We're to the part of the mine where our tours come through every day. There'll be more footprints than they can count. If they do make it this far."

Lisa tossed the makeshift bundle into a corner of the huge room, and hugged herself, shivering. "I can't believe how cold it is in here."

"Forty-seven degrees, year-round. That's why I brought coats for y'all."

"Got an extra?"

Wilbur smiled at her. "No, ma'am. But we'll be back out in the heat real soon now. And you, big guy," he remarked, turning to face Romeo, who was groaning as he stretched his back muscles, "it's all clear from here on out. More headroom than even you need."

Lisa repeated Judtson's question of earlier. "How much farther a walk is it?"

"We're done walking, young lady." With that, he turned and led them down a long set of wooden steps to the mine train he used for the tours. "Hop on. The rest of the way is on the rails."

▽

Jenkins dropped a rope ladder into the hole and started down, followed by three of his team. When he reached the bottom, the first thing he saw was another rope ladder, tossed against the side of the drift. Beside it was a portable welder, its long leads tangled in a heap.

"That's how they secured the manhole cover. They welded it."

He and the others carried AK-47s with barrel-mounted flashlights, and swiftly surveyed their surroundings.

"Carrillo, you take point. I'm pretty sure they made a run for it, so I don't think we need to proceed slowly."

The man peered down the dark passageway, extending in both directions from where he stood. "Which way?"

Jenkins pulled out his GPS. "They probably headed toward the highway. That's where the mine entrance is." He looked down at the screen and uttered a single expletive.

"What's wrong?"

Jenkins tucked the GPS back into his pocket. "No signal down here. You and Norton take one direction. Carver and I will go the other. Come on, let's move. Double time!"

The team split up and trotted into the darkness.

▽

Rattling and clanging, the old mine train emerged from the portal, the bright sunlight momentarily blinding the group after their time underground. A van was parked idling in the open area which bordered the rails, and Chris was standing next to the open doors. Glad to be above ground, they shed their coats and stacked the lamps on the seat of the train, disembarked, and climbed in. Judtson held back, standing with Deel. "Wilbur, I can't tell you how much I appreciate what you've done for us."

The old man looked him in the eye. "Mr. Kent, you're probably going to save my wife's life with the help you're giving me. What I've done ain't one-hundredth of what I would do to repay you. Now you'd best get moving. From what your friends told me, those folks won't be taking too long to make it here searching for you."

They shook hands, and Judtson slipped into the seat beside Kelsey, who still had a distant expression on her face. He reached to hold her hand, but she did not reciprocate. Ashby had the van rolling before Romeo was able to slide the side door shut.

▽

After five minutes of a steady trotting gait, Carrillo came upon the first Y in his path. Stopping, he keyed the microphone on his headset. "Beaver One, this is Beaver Three."

Hearing no reply, he repeated his call to Jenkins, as his partner, Norton, walked a few yards down each of the routes, shining his light forward in an attempt to spot any tracks in the powdery dust. Giving up, he returned.

"I can't get an answer."

"Not down here you won't. Which way?"

"Hell, I don't know. Got a coin?"

▽

Jenkins, fully aware that it was a wild guess anyway, did not bother to hesitate at each junction, proceeding through the intersections in an alternating pattern, first left and then right. Sensing that his most recent choice was taking him gradually downward, he was about to double back, when his light bounced off the black surface of water in the path ahead, casting a reflection upward.

He came to an abrupt halt, Carver sliding to a stop behind him.

"Dead end," he grumbled and turned around.

▽

Wilbur Deel was just finishing the process of connecting the five lamps to the chargers, while two black SUVs pulled into the parking lot, spraying the loose gravel before they came to an abrupt stop. He casually occupied himself by hanging up the coats as the government agents burst in loudly.

"You gentlemen are a couple hours early for the tour."

One of the men approached him. "How long have you been here?"

Deel took his time answering. "Generally, in the course of a civil discussion, it's customary to introduce yourself, youngster."

Impatiently, revealing a holstered Glock in the process, the man pulled out his wallet and flipped it open for Deel to see. "Department of Homeland Security. We're looking for three fugitives. We think they might have come out of the mine. Have you seen anyone?"

"Today?"

"Yes!" the man snapped back. "Today."

"Nope. I sure haven't. Especially coming out of the mine. Why do you boys think they'd be in there?"

The agent, obviously frustrated with Deel, tersely replied, "That's not important. We have reason to believe they are."

Slowly shaking his head, Deel drawled, "Well, if some folks you're lookin' for found their way into the Queen, I *have reason to believe* there's a better than fifty-fifty chance you won't ever see 'em again."

"Why is that?"

"There's several miles of drifts, crosscuts, shafts, and stopes under this whole canyon. You can't go more than a hundred yards in any one of them until you come to a fork in the path. A map of the Queen reads like a plate of spaghetti. And don't forget, we're not just talking about lefts and rights. We're talking about ups and downs, too. A fellow could go wandering around down there for months, if he had the food and water, and might not even walk the same drift twice."

"Is this the only way out?"

Deel laughed. "Oh Lord, no. Must be at least a couple hundred stopes where the miners got a little carried away tracking some rich vein in the rock, and followed it right on up into somebody's living room. That was before the days of fancy surveying and GPS and such."

The Fed peered over his shoulder at the other men for a moment, then turned his attention back to the old miner. "We need to go in and look around. From what you've described, we'll need you to guide us."

The smile left Deel's face. "Well, you're right about needing a guide. No doubt about that. But as to whether it's me, that's a different story."

"What are you saying? Don't you know your way around down there?"

"Absolutely. Like the back of my hand. But that don't mean I'll be taking you youngsters."

"Sir, this is official government business. I'm afraid we can require you to assist us."

The old man's eyes turned a steely gray as he responded. "First of all, youngster, nowhere in everything I heard you say did I here a *please*."

The agent started to speak; however, Wilbur raised a wrinkled hand to stop him. "Getting a common courtesy after it's asked for don't count for a thing.

"Secondly, I've got a very sick wife at home. Ain't nothing wrong with her that can't be fixed. The problem is…that government you're talking about told her that what she needed would be a waste of resources. That she wasn't young enough to 'justify the expenditure.' So *require* away. Go ahead. What are you gonna do if I say *no*? Arrest me? Pull that little plastic gun on me? I'm retired. I do the tours here. Like I told you when you walked up, the next one is in a couple hours. You can buy your tickets and take the tour with me. Till then, I'm not going into the mine."

Fighting to control his frustration, the agent said, "Very well. My men and I will go in without you."

The grin returned. "Oh, that's fine. After all, you're with *the government*. Can't stop you."

▽

As they parked in front of the nurses' quarters, Judtson leaned close to Kelsey. "That was quite a performance with Beckleman. Remind me to never get you mad at me."

His compliment, intended to produce a smile, elicited no reaction from her.

"That was a performance, wasn't it?"

"I...I don't know." Her cryptic comment was so muted that he was unsure he had heard it accurately.

Staring at her, he did not know what direction to take. Before he could say anything, she unbuckled her seat belt and climbed out of the van. When Judtson entered the building, the rest of the group were already there, clustered around the desk where Scott was sitting.

"Scott, did we get it?"

Glancing away from his computer screen, he looked back at Judtson and beamed proudly. "Oh, yes. We got it all. Check it out."

Working his way closer to the monitor, Judtson saw a clear video of Beckleman screaming to his men, "KILL EVERY ONE OF THEM! I WANT THEM ALL DEAD!"

Chapter 42

In THE FIRST TWENTY-FOUR HOURS after the incident in Bisbee, what initially began as a curious collection of videos grew and spread across the Internet, much as a small atmospheric disturbance in the Atlantic would grow and swell into a Category 5 hurricane. The raw footage, shot from multiple angles within the house, captured and conveyed every second of the meeting with Beckleman. The moment Scott had received the feeds from his equipment, he had redistributed the files in all available formats, embedding them within hundreds of servers around the world.

The first to seize upon the images and sound were the conspiracy theorists, posting links to them on their blogs and social media pages, and typing what would soon become an avalanche of tweets. The network and cable news organizations, bombarded with inquiries, provided heavily edited versions of the videos, emphasizing the segments where Kelsey had shot and later pistol-whipped the unarmed Secretary of Homeland Security.

One enterprising photojournalist successfully captured Beckleman on camera as the bureaucrat hobbled, with the aid of crutches, down the steps from an airplane, his leg immobilized with a splint, his face bandaged. Even though deluged with persistent requests, the Cabinet member remained unavailable for comment.

The White House Press Secretary called a hasty news conference, announcing that the Administration was investigating the issues raised by the videos, but was certain that it was all a hoax and would be easily explainable. He went on to warn the reporters, and the American public, how critical it was not to overreact.

Despite the best efforts of the media to put a spin on the startling revelations and to divert the focus to Kelsey and Judtson, villainizing them and bringing out a procession of experts who decried their behavior as reckless and pathologically violent, the momentum grew. An Air Force MP at Area 51, after seeing the admissions from the Homeland Security chief, managed to covertly gain access to a hangar which had been restricted to an extremely limited roster of personnel for the two years he had been stationed on the base. While inside, using his phone, he videoed two sections of the facility: a large room where a lightweight replica of a flying saucer was stored; and a smaller area, constructed to resemble the high-tech interior of the craft. The second space was eerily similar to the environment several abductees had described in vivid detail. In a modular storage pod adjacent to the saucer mock-up, he found a large closet filled with several costumes and headpieces which could only be described as the infamous greys of UFO lore. The military's initial reaction, after the MP posted his video on the Internet, was to arrest him. He was later released.

The first person within the Administration to crack under the barrage of inquiries was the NASA manager Copeland had met with after finding the anomalous photographs. The man, months from retirement, admitted to a reporter that he had been instructed by his superior to deliberately plant the faked pictures for Copeland to discover.

Later, Dylan Falt's contact at the Center for Disease Control admitted that she had modified the numbers in the epidemiological study she sent to him.

One by one, either voluntarily or under pressure, more and more participants in the plot described by Beckleman stepped forward, corroborating the facts, hoping their admissions would ameliorate their inevitable punishment. By the end of the first day, leaders from the House of Representatives were calling for Beckleman's arrest for the crime of treason, and announced the empaneling of a special committee to investigate the allegations.

The colorful Arizona lawman the media labeled "Sheriff Sam," leading a handful of volunteers he referred to as his posse, raided the FEMA camp north of Florence. After detaining the Homeland Security personnel in one of the buildings, a room-by-room search was performed. With his typical flamboyance, Sheriff Sam held a press conference on the grounds of the camp, the dead bodies of the HS agents, killed during the earlier rescue, lined up on the ground behind him in body bags, and Robyn Reedy, dazed and emaciated, standing at his side.

The White House, both bowing to the tidal wave of public outrage and attempting to distance itself from the offenses of its appointee, ordered Samuel Beckleman to be placed under house arrest. Also, during the twenty-four-hour period, Kelsey Batman, Judtson Kent, Romeo Jones, and the remainder of their group went from the status of most wanted by federal authorities, to persons of interest, to material witnesses, to invitees of the White House as special guests of the President. Through it all, none of them had been located.

Shortly after the initial release of the video, a large contingent of FBI agents, led by Special Agent Davis Ulrigg, descended upon the small town of Bisbee, searching for the group. Ulrigg's first discovery was that the residents of the town were not overly impressed with his credentials, his imperious and heavy-handed demeanor, or the federal government in general. Not only was cooperation difficult to find, outright misdirection was the rule, sending his men and women on several wild-goose chases throughout the area.

In the course of the search, Ulrigg was eventually successful in obtaining a cooperative guide to take some of his team into the mine, where they found the unit of men from Homeland Security who had failed in persuading Wilbur Deel to help. The men were cold, hungry, filthy, and dehydrated. After evacuating this group, they resumed the search, eventually locating Jenkins and Carver, collapsed upon the stone floor of a crosscut. Reviving the two and hearing their story, Ulrigg organized a more comprehensive search and, after twenty hours, the agents came upon Carrillo and Norton, huddled and shivering in the pitch darkness, their flashlights long ago dead, both men in substantially worse condition than their team members.

After half a day of frustrating efforts above ground, Ulrigg and three agents broke down the front door of the nurses' quarters. There they found indications that the subjects of their search had been in residence, but were now gone. Taped to a wall in the main dining area was a single sheet of paper. Someone had drawn a large smiley face on it, captioned with a handwritten note: "Hello, FBI. We're not here. Have a great day!"

Ulrigg, ready to burst with anger, smashed his fist into the smiley face and the wall behind it, unaware that in this old building, rather than encountering half an inch of wallboard, his knuckles would connect with a thick layer of Imperial plaster applied over a solid brick wall. His scream of pain could be heard by the tourists on the front porch of the saloon at the Copper Queen Hotel.

▽

Billy Burke ran into the detective's bullpen. Seeing Ben at his desk, he shouted, "Turn on the TV! You aren't going to believe what's going on."

The two cops, soon joined by others in the department, huddled around the set, mesmerized by the unfolding drama. After numerous revelations were detailed, Ben moved closer to his friend and muttered, "Seems that we picked the right side."

▽

The ragtag band had scattered throughout the cabin of the chartered plane, all of them exhilarated from the prior hours and days, none able to sleep. When they first boarded, Judtson had attempted to speak with Kelsey. She told him that she wanted to have some time to think, so he left her alone in her seat in the front of the plane. Worried about her, he was not able to focus on the animated conversations of the others, who were all on a mutual adrenaline high from their mission.

After an hour passed and she had not budged from her seat, Judtson moved up the aisle and stood next to her. "Ready for some company yet?"

She turned her face away from the window, and he saw a haunted, distraught specter in her eyes as she shook her head. Ignoring her wishes, he dropped into the empty seat beside her. "Kelsey, don't shut me out. Talk to me."

She replied to him flatly, "I'm surprised you'd want to."

Confused, Judtson stammered, "What...why?"

"That glimpse of me you saw back in Bisbee...back with Beckleman...I wouldn't want to be around me. Hell, I *don't* want to be around me. That person was crazy. A psychopath."

He took both of her hands in his, holding them tightly. "Kelsey, that wasn't you. It was an act."

She snorted, disgusted. "Might have started that way. But I saw your eyes...you were afraid...afraid of me. And I don't blame you. I was out of control."

"Okay, you're right. At a couple of points I was a little unnerved. I admit that. In any case, the plan worked. It had to be real or Beckleman would not have believed it."

The intensity of her stare as she listened to his words, trying to read the thoughts behind them, was disconcerting. After a moment of silence, she spoke. "I didn't mean to shoot him."

He started to say something.

"Please, Judtson, let me finish. Yes, I was going to shoot. I knew I needed to scare him. I knew I had to make him believe that his life was in danger. But I was just going to shoot close to him. Freak him out, you know."

Judtson listened, meeting her eyes with his, as she talked.

"When I pulled the trigger and he screamed...that horrible scream...and I looked down and saw his leg bleeding...I don't know. I actually checked around for a second. I was sure someone else had done that. Not me."

He thought back to the paintball episode which had started everything, and the conversations he and Saylor had about how the mind worked. "Sometimes we do things that aren't really who we are. Sometimes our minds play tricks on us."

She shook her head hard. "I figured out pretty quickly that I screwed up. Meant to fire off the gun right next to him, but hit him instead. My mind covered all that. Whether it was a mistake or some subconscious desire to hurt him, I'll probably never know. But, Judtson…a moment later…just a few seconds after those first thoughts, I found out that I was happy! I was enjoying his pain! Like some monster."

Her ugly truth out, Kelsey began to cry. Judtson immediately pulled her close, holding her, speaking softly into her ear. "Kelsey, you were facing the man who killed your father, and the same man who tried to kill you. I can't say whether what you did or how you felt was right or wrong. The point is, you didn't kill him. You didn't sink to his level. All I can tell you is that if I were in your shoes, and holding a gun on someone who had killed a loved one, I have no idea how I'd react…what I'd do. I am sure as hell about one thing…I can't judge *you* harshly."

After the long flight, the group of fifteen traveled across La Paz until reaching Villarreal's home, a sprawling, colonial-style building with a red clay tile roof, and a covered patio spanning the full front of the stucco structure. Wearily, the ensemble trudged inside, substantially oblivious to the clean lines and stylish features of the foyer and living room.

"Come, I will show you to your rooms," exclaimed Carlos, seemingly immune to the exhaustion felt by the others. Kelsey separated from the rest and walked across the expansive living room to the wall-to-wall array of French doors leading out to the courtyard. She opened one and stepped out. With Rocky at heel, Judson followed her to a bench, obviously positioned for Carlos and his guests to appreciate a tall five-tiered fountain, nestled in the midst of a lush jungle of plants and trees, the sparkling water cascading noisily over the layers of carved stone to the bottom pond.

He sat beside her and waited, deciding to let her begin the conversation. After several minutes, she murmured, "It's hard to believe there is still some beauty in the world."

"It's gorgeous. I love the parrots."

"The parrots?" She looked in the direction of his gaze and saw the two vividly colored birds, roosting on the branch of an exotic tree she could not identify. Without turning away, Kelsey asked, "Do you think we solved anything?"

"I don't know. We missed quite a bit of the news on the flight here. From what I heard at the airport and what Scott was able to find on the Internet, it sounds as if Beckleman's house of cards is coming down fast."

"Maybe I missed the memo," she commented, her voice sounding more normal than it had for hours, "but there's one thing I wanted to ask."

Judtson chuckled. "Just one?"

"Well, after I get about twelve hours of sleep, I'm sure I'll have lots more. But when that guy came inside the house in Bisbee and swept the place for bugs, how could he miss all of the gizmos Scott planted?"

"New technology. Each bug has a sensor to detect a scan. The instant it senses one, it shuts off the device and times out. After a minute, it comes on again, only for a millisecond, to see if the scanner is gone. As soon as it senses an all clear, it turns the bug back on again."

"Huh!"

Returning her attention to the lavish jungle foliage, Kelsey leaned against Judtson; without hesitation, he put his arm around her shoulder. The two of them sat together silently, listening to the relaxing splashes and gurgles from the fountain. Feeling a progressive slackness in Kelsey's body, he was not surprised to see that her head had dipped down, her chin was resting on her chest, and her eyes were closed. To his four-legged buddy, who was staring unwaveringly at the duo of parrots, he whispered, "Hey, pal, I think we should get her to bed."

Moving slowly to not wake her, Judtson stood and lifted Kelsey in his arms, carrying her back into the house.

▽

When Judtson awoke, he had no clue as to the time, except that daylight was sifting through the tight slats covering his bedroom window. Taking a moment to recall where he was in the world, he crawled out of bed, noticing he still wore yesterday's clothes. Gradually, as he slipped on his shoes and left the room, the details of the previous day returned and his curiosity grew. Quickening his step, he found the dining room and saw that everyone else was awake and assembled around the massive, heavy oak table.

Someone, apparently Scott, had rounded up three flat screens from the other rooms and had arranged them on the table in a circle facing outward. All of the sets were tuned to the same cable news channel. As the others noticed him, he responded groggily to the morning greetings and walked past the table to a sideboard with a coffee urn. Pouring a cup for himself, he returned and found an empty chair next to Saylor. Sliding onto it carefully to avoid spilling any of his coffee, he leaned close to his friend and whispered, "What's happening?"

Saylor, appearing happier than he had in some time, whispered back, "Beckleman's in custody. So are at least nine of his top lieutenants. His civilian armed forces are going to be disbanded. Area 51 and Wright-Patterson have both been thrown open for a full inspection by the press. You wouldn't believe the things they are finding. Congress is already talking about revisiting the Patriot Act, and there are some rumors from unnamed sources that the Department of Homeland Security is going to be dismantled so that no one person ever holds that much power again."

"What about all of us?"

"Charges are dropped. Hell, some of the senators and representatives are even calling us heroes, talking about giving us medals."

Judtson laughed. "I think I'll pass."

He quieted and concentrated on the television, watching the seemingly endless parade of politicians, pundits, military officers, and experts as they all droned on with their opinions on the events. Occasionally, Judtson took his eyes off the screen and glanced to his side, at Saylor and Doni. To say they were glued together would be an understatement, and he knew, as he watched them, that it would be a long time, if ever, before he and his friend ventured out for any escapades together. He then shifted his attention to Kelsey, and was glad to see the haunted sunken-eyed expression gone from her face.

A lull in the flow of new input became obvious as the news channel began rehashing what they had covered earlier. Judtson cleared his throat and suggested, "Maybe we could turn off the sound. I think we all have a lot to talk about."

There were several assenting nods from the group, and Scott, tapping the remotes, muted the sets.

Judtson looked around at his friends. "I guess it's over. It seems as though we can all go home and get on with our lives."

"Thank God!" exclaimed Ricky from across the table. "I can't wait."

"That's true. You have quite a mess to straighten out at the office. And with all the damage we've done in the past few days…you have quite a few checks to write."

"Thanks a lot, boss," he commented sardonically. "After all of this excitement, I hate to admit this, but I am actually eager to settle back into the old routine."

Lisa chimed in. "No kidding. I've already received a text from my network. They want to promote me to full producer."

Judtson grinned. "That's great, Lisa."

"We're definitely ready," Doni declared, and Saylor nodded his agreement.

The person apparently least happy at the moment was Meade. "I can't wrap my mind around what a fool I was."

"You weren't a fool, Jimmy," Judtson assured him. "Why would you have suspected that your own government was pulling a hoax on you?"

"You think *you* were a fool?" asked Copeland, clearly disgusted with himself. "I trashed my personal life, my reputation, my career, everything over a bunch of dummied-up pictures deliberately fed to me. They used me like a pawn."

Lisa, sitting beside him, touched his arm. "You couldn't be blamed for what you did. It didn't turn out the way you thought it would, but your actions and your book contributed to bringing them all down today."

He snorted derisively. "Tell that to Al."

She fell silent. As did the rest.

After a minute or two, Judtson focused on Ashby. "Chris, you've been quiet. What is it?"

The chemist shrugged. "I know you ran out of time when the helicopters arrived, but I wish we could have found out more about my research. I don't understand why I was stopped."

Kelsey, who had been quiet to this point, added, "I've been wondering about that, too. I really can't believe they somehow faked your mother's recovery. And that makes no sense, anyway."

"Exactly. And what was I going to discover which would have caused them to convert *me*?"

"And what about my work down here in the Andes?" Bal asked. "And Kevin Berry's? Were his findings real or weren't they?"

"I don't know," Judtson responded, having mulled over the same questions. "Hopefully, we'll get some answers in the next few days and weeks."

Matt joined the discussion. "I still want to figure out how they converted all of you."

"I don't see how you can, now. We lost their device during the silo raid, and it didn't turn up at the FEMA camp."

Judtson noticed that Romeo, sitting at the far end of the table, was disengaged from the discussion, staring out the window. "Romeo, what are you thinking about?"

The big man turned in his chair, his voice even deeper than usual as he replied, "Luis."

"Has there been anything about him on the news?"

Romeo answered with only a slight shake of his head.

Once again, the conversation lagged until Kelsey changed the topic. "Since we're no longer on the most wanted list, my pilot is on the way here with the Gulfstream. Carlos, as wonderful and gracious a host as you are, and as breathtakingly beautiful as your home is, I think we're all ready to go back to our lives."

Chapter 43

THE TUCSON-BASED MEMBERS OF THE GROUP stood on the hot tarmac outside the Gulfstream, feeling the late afternoon sun on their backs. All of the good-byes and promises to stay in touch behind them, they watched as Kelsey's pilot taxied back out to the runway, carrying Jimmy, Chris, Dean, Lisa, Bal, and Dylan.

As the high-pitched whine of the engines faded, Judtson turned to Kelsey. "Your pilot has quite a trip ahead, taking them all home."

"He'll be making plenty of overtime."

After the jet disappeared from view, they walked to the first in the line of rental cars awaiting them. Ricky opened the door, reached in, started the engine, and turned on the air conditioning. Straightening back up, he saw Judtson waiting, a pensive expression on his face.

"Ricky, you got a lot more than you bargained for when you came to work for me."

The younger man smiled. "Boss, if I've told you once, I've told you a thousand times...I don't work *for* you. I work...."

"*With me.*"

"Right. And I don't know if you remember or not, but during the interview you did promise me that if I got the job, I would never be bored. You certainly weren't kidding."

Judtson laughed. "I do remember that promise. I just never envisioned a situation like this. You're probably going to want a raise now."

"You have no idea."

Both were out of anything light to say. First to break the awkward silence, Ricky, the timbre of his voice deeper, said, "I wouldn't have missed it, boss."

Judtson was at a loss for a comeback. The two simply shook hands. Waving a good-bye at the others, Ricky asked Matt, "Ready?"

"I am." Grinning at Judtson, Wheeler shook his hand. "Well, it was interesting."

"That it was. Thanks, Matt."

The engineer dropped into the passenger seat and closed the door.

Noticing that Scott and Romeo were also sharing a car, Judtson walked over to them and extended his hand. "You two are amazing. Without either one of you, God knows how this would have turned out." Scott reacted to the compliment in his usual fashion, casting his eyes downward and uttering something unhearable.

Romeo firmly took Judtson's hand and shook it, looking him straight in the eye. "It was a pleasure to meet you, sir."

"You, as well, Romeo."

As they departed, Judtson joined Kelsey, who was standing with Saylor and Doni. "I see a car for them. And only one more, Kelsey. Which one of us is walking home?"

She laughed. "I chased down your Olds. It's in the impound lot of the police department. I'll give you a ride."

"That's great."

"Judtson...Doni and I are going to get going."

As he turned to face his two oldest friends, Kelsey casually moved away, giving them some privacy. There was a glistening of incipient tears in Doni's eyes. "Hey, Squirrel, looks like a wrap. I think we did it."

Judtson hugged her. She squeezed him fiercely for a moment, then stepped back. Holding Doni firmly by her arms, he said, "I'm sorry."

"For what?"

"Everything. From the very beginning...I dragged both of you into this and I shouldn't have. You or Saylor could have been...."

She touched her finger to his lips, stopping him in mid-sentence. "We're fine. Both of us. And so are you."

From the side, Saylor added, "But the next little adventure you cook up, I think we might just sit out and watch it on the news."

Judtson was relieved to see his friend smiling broadly at him. "You two get home. I'll be in touch with you soon."

He watched until their car headed around the corner of the hangar. Kelsey came up and stood beside him, quietly waiting until his friends were out of sight.

"You want to drive?"

She nodded and climbed behind the wheel, while he opened the back door for Rocky before sliding into the front passenger seat himself. As they pulled away from the parking lot, Judtson suddenly said, "I just thought of something. Are they going to release my car? I have those charges against me for the paintball thing."

She shook her head. "You forget, we're heroes right now. I guess the City thought that dragging you into court for that, at the same time the White House is talking about a dinner in your honor, would be a bit much."

They arrived at the impound lot, and Kelsey kept Rocky company as Judtson took care of the paperwork to get his vehicle released. After the attendant brought the bright red convertible to the front where they waited, Kelsey stepped around Judtson so that she was standing directly in front of him. Their eyes met and held for several seconds. She finally spoke, her voice softer, gentler than usual. "Judtson, am I going to see you again?"

Her question surprised him. "Of course. You don't still think that what you did back there scared me off?"

"No...well, maybe a little. Except I was talking about...."

His mind made the connection. "Kristen?"

Not trusting her voice, she answered with a clipped nod of her head.

"Hey...you and I are friends. I don't know what's going to happen next. But no matter what, we're still friends."

As she heard his words, Kelsey's lips pursed tightly together for a moment, her eyes riveted to his. Swallowing hard, she opened her mouth and tried to say, "Okay," yet the lone word escaped soundlessly.

Her unconcealed vulnerability touched and saddened him, and he leaned the few inches forward, kissing her on the forehead. The instant his lips touched her, Kelsey threw her arms around him and pulled him close. He held her and the two stood for a time, bound together silently.

When they finally released each other, she pulled back and quickly turned away, hurrying to the rental car without another word, her black hair tossing as she almost ran across the asphalt. Judtson watched Kelsey drive away, feeling a pain in his gut as she raced, with a loud squeal of tires, out of the lot.

He heard a muted whimper come from Rocky who stared in the direction of her departed car, the plaintive sound echoing Judtson's own sentiments.

Reaching down, he scratched his friend's ear. With a heavy sigh, he said, "Come on, boy. Let's go home."

▽

As Judtson pulled the Olds into his driveway, he had the unshakable feeling that it had been months, instead of days, since he was last there. So much had happened. So much had changed. Grabbing the garage door opener from the console tray between the seats, he pressed the button. The door did not begin its rise, and he looked down at the plastic device. It was cracked. Confused for only a moment, he suddenly remembered Kelsey's playful attempt to hop into his car and her haphazard landing across the two seats and the console. Realizing she must have broken the opener in her exuberance, he chuckled aloud as his mind replayed the event, this momentary amusement instantly pushed aside by an undefinable melancholy.

Carefully setting the device back where it had been, he killed the engine. Circling around to the front of his home, he pulled out his keys as Rocky loped behind him. On automatic pilot, he opened the door and stepped inside the foyer, sensing unmistakably that someone else was there.

"Hello!"

From across the house came Kristen's startled voice. "Judtson!"

Following the sound into the living room, he encountered her, running to greet him.

Embracing him, her words tumbled out in an emotional jumble. "Oh, Judtson! Sweetheart! I've been watching the news and trying to call your phone over and over, but you never answered. I've been going crazy. Are you all right?"

His hands holding her shoulders, he told her he was fine.

After a moment, she leaned back and studied his face, her hand rising to gently rest on his cheek. "Judtson, I am so sorry. You tried to tell me that something was going on...something was horribly wrong. I just wouldn't listen. I'm sorry."

"It's okay, Kristen. No one would have believed it."

"I'm your wife. I should have. Please forgive me."

She again drew him near and, his face against the side of her head, he murmured, "There isn't anything to forgive, Kristen. Honestly."

"Judtson?" she began, her voice wavering.

"Yes?"

"I'm back...if you'll have me. I never should have left you. I do love you."

As he responded…as he told her that he loved her, too…Judtson was unable to ignore a blankness inside, a flatness, rather than the emotions he knew he should be feeling.

▽

Kelsey parked under the porte cochere at her home, left the car door open, and ran, limping, to the entrance. Fumbling with keys and dropping them twice, she finally managed to unlock the door. No sooner had she stumbled inside than she threw herself onto the sofa, burying her face in the velvet cushion. Her tenuous resolve to complete the trip satisfied, Kelsey allowed herself to break down, and the large, vacant room reverberated with the sounds of her sobs.

Twenty minutes passed before she rose from the sofa, unsteadily walked into the kitchen, filled a glass with water, and took a long drink, followed by another. Feeling faint as she stood in front of the refrigerator, one hand on the counter top for support, she tried to analyze her feelings. Certainly, she knew, she had become attached to Judtson. More than attached. There was no doubt of that. Yet, a portion of her mind was telling her that those feelings alone could not justify the intensity of her ragged emotions. The frantic pace and the rush of the past few days had worn her nerves…frayed them…made them raw. There was also the injury to her leg. And the inevitable letdown of it all being over was surely going to take some adjustment.

Slipping off her shoes, Kelsey padded across the house to her office and, out of habit, switched on her computer, staring blankly at the screen as it booted up. After the sequence completed, she checked her email and was mildly surprised by the number of messages waiting for her.

Idly, her thoughts drifting elsewhere, she began scrolling down the list, scanning the subject lines for anything important, and suddenly heard a soft, single *beep* from the speakers. For a moment, the tone confused her. She could not recall any software she had installed which was configured to give audible alerts. Then, remembering, she checked the bar across the bottom of the screen and saw the button for the instant-messaging account she had established to connect with Alchemist. It was flashing.

Curious, she clicked on it. As the box opened, a query from the unknown acquaintance appeared, requesting a chat. Tersely, she muttered to herself, "I'm not in the mood for that right now."

Her hand moved to close the box; however, she paused, recalling that it had been Alchemist who had put her on the right track when she was so frantic and needed help. Using the mouse, she logged in to the account, acknowledged the query, and waited. Within less than a minute, a dialogue box opened on the screen with a single line.

"Hello! Are you there?"

She typed, "I am. Hello."

"I've been watching the news. Please tell me that you're unharmed."

"I'm fine. Not really. Got shot in the leg, but it'll be okay."

"My God. Are you sure?"

"Yes, I am. Thanks for asking."

"I wanted to reach you so many times during the last few days. I've been worried."

"I'm good. I am. Besides, plenty of time to give it a rest…now that it's all over."

Alchemist's previous responses had been immediate; this time he paused. Kelsey watched the box on the screen…waiting. Finally, she began to type a message asking if he was still there, when his next message arrived.

"No, it's not."

The words captured her attention, breaking through her mental fog. "What do you mean?"

"I mean, it isn't over."

"Of course it is. Beckleman's in jail, and so are his people. It looks like they're going to dismantle Homeland Security. And the public all know how they've been scammed for decades. It's over."

As she typed her definitive retort, her mind wandered back to her own earlier thoughts, her own doubts. She also remembered the unanswered questions from Chris and Bal. Before he could reply, she added, "Why do you think it isn't over?"

"Because this is how they work."

"Who? How *who* work?"

"The forces truly behind what has been happening."

"Are you actually saying that they would throw Beckleman and all of the rest of those people to the wolves just to keep us off the track?"

"Yes. I am. And much, much more."

"I'm asking again…who?"

There was another pause; then his message appeared. "I can't say. I'm not positive about exactly who they are."

"So how do you know?"

"I've been watching them for a long time. Secretly tracking their progress. I know."

Something in her snapped. She could feel her temper rising quickly as she typed. "Here's the deal. I'm real tired and I'm in no mood for this mumbo-jumbo crap right now. I'm going to log off. Maybe we'll talk later."

"Wait."

"Nope. Sorry. Bye."

She shifted the mouse to close the window on the program, not even waiting for a response, when she saw in the IM box, "Kelsey, wait."

Her hand froze. Taking a minute, she thought back through all of the online conversations she had with Alchemist in the past. She was certain that never once had she used anything but her screen name with him, or with any of the other people who had participated in her blog. Now, more alert, Kelsey also recalled that their conversation had begun with Alchemist telling her that he had followed the story on the news, and asking if she was all right. There should have been no way for him to make that connection. As Kelsey processed the thoughts, a corner of her mind tickled at her consciousness, hinting that she was overlooking a detail, a detail too elusive to bring to the fore.

Slowly, her hands moved back to the keyboard. "Who are you?"

After a few seconds, the reply came. "A friend."

"Don't lie to me!!! How do you know my name? How do you know it was me involved in what's been happening? And you'd better tell me the truth or I will never connect with you again…ever!"

This time the pause was even longer than the last, enduring for well over a minute, stretching to the point where she was beginning to suspect that he was not going to answer.

As she was about to disconnect, three words appeared, their meaning palpable, triggering a delusional sensation of two hands gripping her throat.

"I'm your father."

Kelsey was hammered with a gamut of emotions: the first fleeting elation at the possibility that it might somehow be true; the pain and anguish, as her feelings for her lost father overwhelmed her an instant later; and the inevitable anger, flashing to a blaze of nearly blind fury. Slamming the keys so hard the act hurt her fingers, she typed, "You are despicable! How dare you say that! My father is dead."

Mere moments after she transmitted her message, the harsh text of her tirade shifted upward in the box, accommodating his response. "I'm not dead, Kelsey."

"Stop it. Stop saying that."

"Why? It's true."

Every muscle in her body taut, her breathing rapid and shallow, Kelsey forced herself to rein in her feelings. Taking her time, waiting until her hands were no longer trembling, she typed, "Prove it."

Her stare at the screen intense, she could not have blinked if she wanted, for fear of missing a split second of Alchemist's reply. Moments ticked by. She waited without breathing until, finally, the line of text exploded into view.

"I love you, Frasier."

Coming soon...Part Two

From the author –

To all of my loyal friends and readers…I hope you enjoyed this particular outing. *The Mutatus Procedure (Part One)* has been quite a departure for me in several ways, not the least of which is that it marks the first time I have created a multi-book story. Albeit not my original intent, I quickly discovered that all I wanted to say could not possibly be confined between two covers. Judtson, Kelsey, Saylor, and all of the others will be returning in Part Two.

This was also the first time I brought in characters from one of my other novels. For those of you who have already read *Time Cursor*, I'm sure you recognized two of my favorites from that story – Detective Ben Hart and Officer Billy Burke.

Although fiction, to be compelling, often has roots in fact, there are a few things I should mention to avoid any confusion. Chris Ashby's work on monoatomic gold is pure fabrication. The substance has no curative powers for Alzheimer's. Also, Bal Singh's work in the Andes was another literary liberty taken. (There are some unexplained gravitational anomalies in the area; however, if that mountain range is hollow, it has yet to be discovered.) Villarreal's discovery that the stone blocks at Baalbek were indeed quarried from the area around Lake Titicaca was sheer fancy. There were other minor embellishments along the way to feed the story.

On the other hand, many facts cited have their origins in reality. For further reading on unusual objects and formations on the Moon and Mars, you can read *Dark Mission: The Secret History of NASA*, by Richard C. Hoagland and Mike Bara. For a cornucopia of fascinating facts, discoveries, and interpretations, I direct you to all of the books by Zecharia Sitchin and, of course, Erich von Däniken.

The tale of the UFO landing in the 1950s on the dry lake bed at Edwards Air Force Base in California was related to me by no less than three retired Air Force men, now late in years, who insisted that they saw it, that the tent was built, that Eisenhower did, in fact, come to meet with those inside, and that he told his driver the tale on the way back to his plane.

I would also like to share one of the spooky synchronicities which happened during the writing of *Mutatus*. I had already created the passage in the story where Scott and Bal attempt to chase down the paper written by Kevin Berry, only to find that it had been removed from the Internet. After writing the chapter, I decided it would be best to do some research. I found multiple articles written by scientists who all referenced a symposium presentation, titled *Evaluation of Microgravimetry for Southern Central Andes Recent Crustal Movement Determination*, by Becker, M. et al. Yet, when I attempted to find it, I failed repeatedly. Eventually, as Scott did in the story, I clicked on a link to the cached page of the paper, and found on The Smithsonian/NASA Astrophysics Data System that not only was the fulltext article not available, neither was the abstract. The formatting of this notice is reflected on the page found by Scott. No doubt there is a perfectly mundane explanation for the removal of the paper. Still, the eeriness of the coincidence was chilling.

Even though Wilbur Deel is a fictional character, the Bisbee mine tour is quite real and quite fascinating. If you make it there, get a room at the Copper Queen Hotel and have the "B" Hill Burger at the Bisbee Grille. And while you're there, say hello to my friends Dan and Connie at the Copper Queen and Laura at the Grille.

On a final note, I want to thank all of you for your diligence and enthusiasm spreading the word about my novels. In these difficult economic times and with the demise of bookstores around the country, nothing is more valuable to me than word of mouth. Whether you post a comment about one of my books on your Facebook page…Tweet about them…blog about them…or put up a comment on Amazon, the impact is amazing and, I want you to know, deeply appreciated.

Until the next one, thank you for your constant support, encouragement, and the occasional pester about each next book.

All the best,
John David Krygelski

If you enjoyed reading *The Mutatus Procedure (Part One)* by John David Krygelski, you will be truly enthralled by his previous novels. You can order a personalized and autographed copy of any of his books in either the softcover or the hardcover edition by going to ***www.krygelski.com***.

The Aegis Solution

In this, John David Krygelski's third and perhaps most powerful novel yet, he creates a spine-tingling story of suspense, drama, and intrigue. After the only child of the President – his teenaged daughter, Neve – commits suicide in a violent and senseless act, President Walker proposes an institution where people who have lost all hope may enter.

Impelled by his grief and compassion, Aegis, intended to be a civilized alternative to suicide, is built and opened. There are only two rules in Aegis: no communication is allowed between the outside world and those who enter, and once individuals go in…they can never leave.

Twelve years pass and what began as a noble social experiment has turned into a hideous nightmare, fraught with controversy and public outrage. In response, Elias Charon is selected by the new President to be the first to enter Aegis and be allowed to leave. Ostensibly he is sent in to investigate the claims of abuse, but a darker and heinous personal motive arises.

With pulse-pounding suspense, *The Aegis Solution* takes the reader through a twisting, turning plot to an explosive and electrifying climax.

Praise for – *The Aegis Solution*

"When I am 90, one of my only regrets in life will be waiting until I was done reading my other books before I started reading yours. I did not see the ending coming at all – how a small isolated problem affected the whole world! It had me on the edge of my seat."

"All I can say is…Damn! That was a great story!!!!! It kept me on edge the whole time and it was hard to put it down. It kept me wanting to know what would happen next. Again, thanks for the great book."

"*The Aegis Solution*, I have to say, was an amazing book. Every time I picked it up, the action kept me on the edge of my seat. The character development, as well as the plot twists, made for an awesome read."

"I wondered what the alternative to suicide was going to be for these folks. Would they be in suspended sleep? Would they go through intensive therapy? Alternate universes?

Parallel timelines? One way in, no way out. I was really painting many pictures in my head. Nice layering of who was the baddest bad guy. When I thought I was close to one decision, you would spin me another way. Again, a fantastic read! Cover to cover, I was trying to decide where you were going, and I had many roads open, yet you led me down one I hadn't seen. Thanks for another fun ride."

Time Cursor

Jack Augur comes back from thirty years in the future to stop his own wedding. Although warned of the dire consequences if he tampered with any other events, within minutes of meeting his younger self, he is responsible for the accidental death of the man who is to eventually invent the time machine. As the older and younger versions of the same man join forces to undo the damage they've done and get the world back on track, mysterious beings thwart their every attempt. *Time Cursor* is a roller-coaster ride of suspense, action, and intrigue with an ending that will not disappoint.

Praise for – *Time Cursor*

"It is amazingly brilliant, right there with some of the best I've read. In terms of science fiction, it's up there with greats like Heinlein; definitely a book I'm going to make sure stays in my possession."

"I couldn't put it down! I really enjoyed it. I truly hope that they make a movie out of it!!! Seriously…it was amazing!!! The ending freaked me out!!! :) I actually was sad when I finished it!!!!"

"The only thing I can say is **WHAT A RIDE!!!!!!!!!!!!!!!!!!!!** Far exceeded my expectations. I've been reading SF since Asimov & Bradbury started, and this was a treat and a blast. Thanks again for a great run."

"Finished the book yesterday…WOW! Great story – super plot. Really twisted my mind on the intricacies of time travel, or time segment repositioning, if you prefer."

"I finished it over the weekend…LOVED it!!! Never saw the ending coming."

"Just finished *Time Cursor*, and I loved it! So enjoyable to read a book that wasn't dumbed down!"

"What an incredible read!!! Quite the twist at the end that I wasn't expecting."

The Harvest

John David Krygelski's suspenseful debut novel – *The Harvest* – is a stunning tour de force! Whether tackling the epic battle between good and evil, or answering the subtle and persistent questions which haunt us all, Krygelski writes a compelling and startling story centered around the mysterious arrival of a man who claims to be The Creator.

Clearly not a mortal, Elohim – as the stranger prefers to be known – astounds those he meets with unexplainable miracles and reality-altering answers. All of this is but a prelude to his announcement that he has come to do something…something which will affect every person on Earth…something which will occur in five days.

Against the backdrop of a world reacting to the announcement that God has arrived, a hastily assembled group of interviewers question and test Elohim…while hidden forces emerge to thwart his plans.

The Harvest is a gripping page-turner – a book which will change your view of the world.

Praise for John David Krygelski's debut novel – *The Harvest*

"It is, in one word, a masterpiece! The best book I've ever read, and I've read thousands."

"*The Harvest* is amazingly written, intriguing, very different and fascinating, deep…highly recommended reading."

"I have been reading nearly all of my 60 years. This is the most profound book I have ever read. I can't believe that this is the first novel of Mr. Krygelski."

"…this book was one of the most extraordinary books I have ever read. It touched me and made me examine my entire life. It is hard to believe that this is anyone's first book. Thank you for writing it."

"*The Harvest* had me completely enthralled from beginning to end. I never wanted to put the book down, being one of the most interesting reads I have ever had the pleasure to experience. I have difficulty expressing in words how much I truly loved this book."

"This dense and carefully plotted story involves a thoughtful look at religion. Reese Johnson, a professor at the University of Arizona, is teaching 'Religion Under Assault' when he suddenly finds himself investigating a man who calls himself 'the Creator.' For hopefuls everywhere looking for a second chance to create a better world, this is an intriguing novel." – J. C. Martin, *Arizona Daily Star*

www.ingramcontent.com/pod-product-compliance
Lightning Source LLC
Chambersburg PA
CBHW032141010726
47494CB00002B/309

Coming in 2013:
Grabbing the Brass Ring
Michael Earl Nolan

This epic saga of the life of Richard Mansan, a front-line fighter and adventurer who recognizes early in life that he is destined to "grab the brass ring," is masterfully written with uncanny insights into human character. During Mansan's far-flung iliadic exploits, he forms lifelong friendships with the great leaders of his day: General O'Riley, his courageous battlefield commander whose own nation eventually turns its back on him; Tyron Jrcy, a young foreign soldier whom Mansan sends safely on his way and who later becomes his nation's Chief Council; and Nele Martel Moran, the feisty youngster who serves under Mansan on her parents' fishing fleet and who later becomes the visionary President of her nation.

All three are profoundly and irrevocably influenced by this extraordinary, unconventional man. When the world crises worsen to the breaking point, Mansan himself receives the ultimate mantle of power, the daunting responsibility for humanity's survival. This futuristic novel grapples with the frailties and strengths of humankind, the nature of true leadership, and the possible destiny of planet Earth; it is as prophetic as it is exciting.

Included with the novel is the fascinating biography of the author – a legendary real-life hero. Truly a "Renaissance man," Nolan distinguished himself on the field of battle, in athletics, in engineering, and in the heart and mind of everyone he met.